Praise for *Look Aga...*

"A pulse-racing novel."   —*USA Today*

"In *Look Again,* Scottoline resembles a figure skater who . . . exe-cutes a fine sequence of laybacks, sit spins, and double lutzes."
                                        —*The Washington Post*

"Scottoline is a star!"   —*Time* magazine

"Honest and hugely emotional, with very real characters you care about, and will remember long after you finish this terrific book."
                                        —James Patterson

"Lisa Scottoline scores another bull's-eye with this terrifying thriller."
                              —*Publishers Weekly* (starred review)

"*Look Again* will have faithful fans and new readers singing her praises."   —*Library Journal* (starred review)

"A surefire winner."   —*Booklist*

"In *Look Again* Scottoline has created a tension that draws the reader in from the first page."   —*Deseret Morning News*

"Scottoline has set up a plot that will suck readers in—and make them shiver a bit the next time they get a 'Have You Seen This Child?' card in the mail."   —*San Antonio Express-News*

"Scottoline's edgy and emotional thriller proves once again why she's such an accomplished writer. . . . A great read!"
                                        —*RT Book Reviews*

"Scottoline is one of my favorite authors, and here she blends a fasci-nating premise with tense action."   —*Record-Courier*

"The great Scottoline gives us a terrific woman at the center of a tangled and terrifying story. . . . As usual, a terrific novel."
—*Sullivan County Democrat*

"Scottoline moves the story with terrific pace and drama . . . for any crime fiction reader looking to the bestseller list, the clear choice is Scottoline over Clark and Grisham."
—*Toronto Star*

"Scottoline keeps the suspense high with short, fast-paced chapters and escalating tension . . . readers will applaud her strong, appealing heroine. They will also be astonished by the unexpected conclusion."
—*Mystery Scene*

Praise for *Think Twice*

"A thriller that feels like an instant classic."
—*Connecticut Post*

"So engaging [you] can't help but read it in one sitting."
—*Seattle Post-Intelligencer*

"A pulse-pounding thriller."
—*Booklist*

"The intricate plot will keep thriller fans turning those pages."
—*Library Journal*

"Scottoline unfolds her story in breathlessly quick cuts . . . you won't put it down."
—*Kirkus Reviews*

Praise for *Save Me*

"Each staccato chapter adds new and unexpected turns, so many you could get whiplash just turning a page. Scottoline knows how to keep readers in her grip." —*The New York Times Book Review*

"The Scottoline we love as a virtuoso of suspense, fast action, and intricate plot is back in top form in *Save Me*."
—*The Washington Post Book World*

LOOK AGAIN
&
SAVE ME

Also by Lisa Scottoline

Rosato & DiNunzio Novels
Damaged
Corrupted
Betrayed
Accused

Rosato & Associates Novels
Think Twice
Lady Killer
Killer Smile
Dead Ringer
Courting Trouble
The Vendetta Defense
Moment of Truth
Mistaken Identity
Rough Justice
Legal Tender
Everywhere That Mary Went

Other Novels
Most Wanted
Every Fifteen Minutes
Keep Quiet
Don't Go
Come Home
Daddy's Girl
Dirty Blonde
Devil's Corner
Running from the Law
Final Appeal

Nonfiction (with Francesca Serritella)
I've Got Sand in All the Wrong Places
Does This Beach Make Me Look Fat?
Have a Nice Guilt Trip
Meet Me at Emotional Baggage Claim
Best Friends, Occasional Enemies
My Nest Isn't Empty, It Just Has More Closet Space
Why My Third Husband Will Be a Dog

LOOK AGAIN
&
SAVE ME

Lisa Scottoline

ST. MARTIN'S GRIFFIN ⚜ NEW YORK

LOOK AGAIN. Copyright © 2009 by Lisa Scottoline. SAVE ME. Copyright © 2011 by Lisa Scottoline. All rights reserved. Printed in the United States of America. For information, address St. Martin's Press, 175 Fifth Avenue, New York, N.Y. 10010.

www.stmartins.com

The Library of Congress Cataloging-in-Publication Data is available upon request.

ISBN 978-1-250-14054-8 (trade paperback)

Our books may be purchased in bulk for promotional, educational, or business use. Please contact your local bookseller or the Macmillan Corporate and Premium Sales Department at 1-800-221-7945, extension 5442, or by email at MacmillanSpecial Markets@macmillan.com.

First Edition: June 2017

10 9 8 7 6 5 4 3 2 1

LOOK AGAIN

For my beloved daughter

Where did you come from, baby dear?
Out of the everywhere into the here.
Where did you get your eyes so blue?
Out of the skies as I came through.
  —George MacDonald
  At the Back of the North Wind

Where have you been, my blue-eyed son?
  —Bob Dylan
  "A Hard Rain's A-Gonna Fall"

Chapter One

Ellen Gleeson was unlocking her front door when something in the mail caught her attention. It was a white card with photos of missing children, and one of the little boys looked oddly like her son. She eyed the photo as she twisted her key in the lock, but the mechanism was jammed, probably because of the cold. Snow encrusted SUVs and swing sets, and the night sky was the color of frozen blueberries.

Ellen couldn't stop looking at the white card, which read HAVE YOU SEEN THIS CHILD? The resemblance between the boy in the photo and her son was uncanny. They had the same wide-set eyes, smallish nose, and lopsided grin. Maybe it was the lighting on the porch. Her fixture had one of those bulbs that was supposed to repel bugs but only colored them yellow. She held the photo closer but came to the same conclusion. The boys could have been twins.

Weird, Ellen thought. Her son didn't have a twin. She had adopted him as an only child.

She jiggled the key in the lock, suddenly impatient. It had been a long day at work, and she was losing her grip on her purse, briefcase, the mail, and a bag of Chinese takeout. The aroma of barbecued spareribs wafted from the top, setting her stomach growling, and she twisted the key harder.

The lock finally gave way, the door swung open, and she dumped her stuff onto the side table and shed her coat, shivering happily in the warmth of her cozy living room. Lace curtains framed the windows behind a red-and-white-checked couch, and the walls were stenciled with cows and hearts, a cutesy touch she liked more than any reporter should. A plastic toy chest overflowed with plush animals, Spot board books, and Happy Meal figurines, decorating never seen in *House & Garden*.

"Mommy, look!" Will called out, running toward her with a paper in his hand. His bangs blew off his face, and Ellen flashed on the missing boy from the white card in the mail. The likeness startled her before it dissolved in a wave of love, powerful as blood.

"Hi, honey!" Ellen opened her arms as Will reached her knees, and she scooped him up, nuzzling him and breathing in the oaty smell of dry Cheerios and the faint almond scent of the Play-Doh sticking to his overalls.

"Eww, your nose is cold, Mommy."

"I know. It needs love."

Will giggled, squirming and waving the drawing. "Look what I made! It's for you!"

"Let's see." Ellen set him down and looked at his drawing, of a horse grazing under a tree. It was done in pencil and too good to be freehand. Will was no Picasso, and his go-to subject was trucks. "Wow, this is great! Thank you so much."

"Hey, Ellen," said the babysitter, Connie Mitchell, coming in from the kitchen with a welcoming smile. Connie was short and sweet, soft as a marshmallow in a white sweatshirt that read PENN STATE, which she wore with wide-leg jeans and slouchy Uggs. Her brown eyes were bracketed by crow's-feet and her chestnut ponytail was shot through with gray, but Connie had the enthusiasm, if not always the energy, of a teenager. She asked, "How was your day?"

"Crazy busy. How about you?"

"Just fine," Connie answered, which was only one of the reasons that Ellen counted her as a blessing. She'd had her share of babysitter drama, and there was no feeling worse than leaving your child with a sitter who wasn't speaking to you.

Will was waving his picture, still excited. "I drew it! All by myself!"

"He traced it from a coloring book," Connie said under her breath. She crossed to the coat closet and retrieved her parka.

"I *drew* it!" Will's forehead buckled into a frown.

"I know, and you did a great job." Ellen stroked his silky head. "How was swimming, Con?"

"Fine. Great." Connie put on her coat and flicked her ponytail out of the collar with a deft backhand. "He was a little fish." She got her brown purse and packed tote bag from the windowseat. "Will, tell Mommy how great you did without the kickboard."

Will pouted, a mood swing typical of toddlers and manic-depressives.

Connie zipped up her coat. "Then we drew pictures, right? You told me Mommy liked horses."

"I *drew* it," Will said, cranky.

"I love my picture, sweetie." Ellen was hoping to stave off a kiddie meltdown, and she didn't blame him for it. He was plainly tired, and a lot was asked of three-year-olds these days. She asked Connie, "He didn't nap, did he?"

"I put him down, but he didn't sleep."

"Too bad." Ellen hid her disappointment. If Will didn't nap, she wouldn't get any time with him before bed.

Connie bent down to him. "See ya later . . ."

Will was supposed to say "alligator," but he didn't. His lower lip was already puckering.

"You wanna say good-bye?" Connie asked.

Will shook his head, his eyes averted and his arms loose at his sides. He wouldn't make it through a book tonight, and Ellen loved to read to him. Her mother would turn over in her grave if she knew Will was going to bed without a book.

"All right then, bye-bye," Connie said, but Will didn't respond, his head downcast. The babysitter touched his arm. "I love you, Will."

Ellen felt a twinge of jealousy, however unreasonable. "Thanks again," she said, and Connie left, letting in an icy blast of air. Then she closed and locked the door.

"I DREW IT!" Will dissolved into tears, and the drawing fluttered to the hardwood floor.

"Aw, baby. Let's have some dinner."

"All by myself!"

"Come here, sweetie." Ellen reached for him but her hand hit the bag of Chinese food, knocking it to the floor and scattering the mail. She righted it before the food spilled, and her gaze fell on the white card with the photo of the missing boy.

Uncanny.

She picked up the bag of Chinese food and left the mail on the floor.

For the time being.

Chapter Two

Ellen put Will to bed, did a load of laundry, then grabbed a fork, napkin, and a cardboard container of leftover Chinese. She took a seat at the dining-room table, and the cat sat at the other end, his amber eyes trained on her food and his tail tucked around his chubby body. He was all black except for a white stripe down the center of his face and white paws like cartoon gloves, and Will had picked him because he looked so much like Figaro from the *Pinocchio* DVD. They couldn't decide whether to name him Figaro or Oreo, so they'd gone with Oreo Figaro.

Ellen opened the container, forked chicken curry onto her plate, then dumped out the leftover rice, which came out in a solid rectangle, like sand packed in a toy pail. She broke it up with her fork and caught sight of the Coffmans, her neighbors across the shared driveway, doing their homework at their dining-room table. The Coffman boys were tall and strong, both lacrosse players at Lower Merion, and Ellen wondered if Will would play a sport in high school. There had been a time when she couldn't imagine him healthy, much less wielding a lacrosse stick.

She ate a piece of chicken, gooey with bright yellow curry, which was still warmish. It hit the spot, and she pulled over the mail, sorted out the bills, and set them aside. It wasn't the end of the month, so she didn't have to deal with them yet. She ate another bite and was about to daydream her way through the Tiffany catalog when her gaze fell on the white card. She paused in midbite and picked it up. HAVE YOU SEEN THIS CHILD? At the bottom it read, American Center for Missing and Abducted Children (ACMAC).

Ellen set her fork down and eyed the photo of the missing boy again. There was no blaming the lighting this time. Her dining room had a colonial brass candelabra that hung from the ceiling, and in its bright light, the boy in the photo looked even more like Will. It was a black-and-white photo, so she couldn't tell if they had the same eye color. She read the caption under the photo:

Name:	Timothy Braverman
Resides:	Miami, Florida
DOB:	1/19/05
Eyes:	Blue
Hair:	Blond
Stranger Abduction:	1/24/06 *

She blinked. They both had blue eyes and blond hair. They were even about the same age, three years old. Will had just turned three on January 30. She examined the photo, parsing the features of the missing boy. The similarity started with his eyes, which were a generous distance apart, and the shape, which was roundish. They both had small noses and shared a grin that was identically lopsided, turning down on the right side. Most of all, there was a likeness in their aspect, the steady, level way that they looked at the world.

Very weird, Ellen thought.

She reread the caption, noticed the asterisk, and checked the bottom of the card. It read "Timothy Braverman, Shown Age-Progressed to Three Years Old." She stumbled over the meaning of "age-progressed," then it registered. The picture of Timothy Braverman wasn't a current photo, though it looked like one. It was an approximation of how the boy would look right now, a projection done by computer or artist. The thought eased her, unaccountably, and she remembered the day she'd met Will.

She'd been doing a story on nurses in the pediatric cardiac intensive care unit at Dupont Hospital in Wilmington, and Will was in the CICU being treated for a ventricular septal defect, a hole in his septum. He lay at the end of the sunny unit, a tiny boy in a diaper, in an institutional crib with high white bars. He was undersized, failing to thrive, and it made his head a bobblehead doll's on a bony frame. His large blue eyes were his most prominent feature, and he took in everything around him, except people. He never made or held eye contact with anyone, which Ellen later learned could be a sign of neglect, and his was the only crib with no plush toys or colorful mobiles attached to the bars.

He was between heart operations when she first saw him—the first procedure was to patch the hole with a Dacron graft, and the second to repair the graft when one of the stitches came loose—and he lay silently, never crying or whimpering, surrounded by monitors that relayed his vital signs to the nurses in glowing red, green, and blue numbers. So many tubes led to him that he appeared to be tethered; an oxygen tube was taped in place under his nose, a feeding tube disappeared into a nostril, and a clear tube popped grotesquely from the center of his naked chest, emptying fluids into a plastic canister. His IV snaked to his hand, where it ended, adhesive-taped to a board and topped by half of a plastic cup, jury-rigged to make sure he didn't pull it free. Unlike the other babies, Will never tried.

Ellen kept doing research for the story and found herself visiting Will more frequently than necessary. The story became a series, and the angle changed from the nurses to the babies, among them, Will. But amid the cooing, gurgling, and crying babies, it was the silent one who held her attention. She wasn't allowed to approach his crib because of CICU regulations, but she would watch him from a short distance, though he always looked away at the blank white wall. Then one morning, his eyes found her, locking in and latching on, their blue as deep as the sea. They shifted away, but after that stayed on her longer and longer, connecting with her in a way she began to sense was heart to heart. Later, when everyone asked why she'd wanted to adopt him, she would answer:

It was the way he looked at me.

Will never had any visitors, and one of the mothers, who had a baby girl awaiting a heart transplant, told Ellen that his mother was a young girl, unwed, who hadn't even seen him after his first operation. Ellen followed up with his caseworker, who investigated and told her that adoption was a possibility, and she'd gone home that night, elated and unable to sleep. She'd been elated ever since, and in the past two years had come to realize that even though Will wasn't born to her, she was born to be his mother.

Her gaze fell again on the white card, and she set it aside, feeling a pang of sympathy for the Braverman family. She couldn't imagine how any parent lived through such an ordeal, or how she would cope if someone kidnapped Will. A few years ago, she'd done a piece in which a father had kidnapped his children after a custody dispute, and she toyed with the idea of calling the mother, Susan Sulaman, and doing a follow-up. She had to keep the story ideas coming if she wanted to keep her job, and it would give her an excuse to meet with her new editor, Marcelo Cardoso, a sexy Brazilian who'd come to the paper a year ago, having left behind the *L.A. Times* and a model girlfriend. Maybe a single mother would make a nice change, and if he'd seen enough of the fast lane, she could show him the checkout lane.

Ellen felt a smile spread across her face, which was embarrassing even though the only witness was a cat. She used to think she was too smart to crush on her boss, but Marcelo was Antonio Banderas with a journalism degree. And it had been too long since the man in her life was older than three. Her old boyfriend had told her she was a "handful," but Marcelo could handle a handful. And a handful was the only woman worth handling.

She scraped curry from a few chicken pieces and slid her plate over to Oreo Figaro, who ate with a loud purr, his tail bent at the tip like a crochet needle. She waited for him to finish, then cleaned up the table, put the bills in a wicker basket, and threw away the junk mail, including the white card with the missing children. It slid into the plastic kitchen bag, and the picture of Timothy Braverman stared at her with that preternatural gaze.

"*You're a dweller,*" she heard her mother say, as surely as if she'd been standing there. But Ellen believed that all women were dwellers. It came with the ovaries.

She closed the cabinet door and put the white card out of her mind. She loaded the dishwasher, pushed the Start button, and counted her blessings again. Butcher-block counters, white cabinets with glass fronts, and a hand-painted backsplash with painted wildflowers, matching walls of pinkish white. It was a girl kitchen, down to the name of the wall color—Cinderella. Though there was no Prince Charming in sight.

She performed her final chores, locking the back door and retrieving the used coffee filter from the coffeemaker. She opened the base cabinet and started to throw the grinds away, but Timothy Braverman looked back at her, unsettling her all over again.

On impulse, she rescued the white card from the trash and slipped it into her jeans pocket.

Chapter Three

The alarm went off at six fifteen, and Ellen got out of bed in the dark, staggered in bare feet onto the cold tiles of the bathroom, and hit the shower, letting the hot water wake her. Even people who counted their blessings never counted them in the morning. For one thing, there wasn't time.

She finished dressing by seven so she could get Will up and dressed before preschool, which started at eight thirty. Connie would arrive at seven thirty to feed and take him, and Ellen would hand Will to her on the fly, like a domestic relay. Mothers ran this race every morning, and they deserved the gold medal in the most important event of all—life.

"Honey?" Ellen switched on the Babar lamp, but Will was sleeping soundly, his mouth partway open. His breathing sounded congested, and when she stroked his forehead, it felt hot to the touch. She told herself not to worry, but once you've had a sick kid, you hold your breath forever.

"Will?" she whispered, but was already wondering if she should send him to preschool. A crust had formed around his nostrils, and his cheek looked pale in the soft light from the lamp. His nose was a ski slope that was the beginner version of hers, and people often mistook him for her biological child, which she liked more than she should. She found herself wondering if Timothy Braverman looked like his mother, too.

She touched Will's arm, and when he didn't move, decided not to send him to school. Perspective was in order, and construction-paper snowflakes could wait another day. She didn't kiss him because she didn't want to wake him and instead patted Oreo Figaro, sleeping at the foot of the bed, curled into a Mallomar. She switched off the lamp, tiptoed from the bedroom, and went back to her room, to use the extra fifteen minutes.

"Don't you look nice!" Connie said with a smile, coming out of the dining room, and Ellen grinned as she tiptoed down the stairs. She had used the time to change into a tan corduroy jacket, nipped at the waist, and brown suede boots worn on top of her jeans. She had even done a better than usual job on her makeup, blown her hair dry, and put her liquid eyeliner back in rotation. She was going to see Marcelo this morning and wasn't sure if she wanted to look hot, employable, or both.

"Will's running a low fever, so I figured he'd stay home today."

"Good decision." Connie nodded. "It's twenty degrees out."

"Yikes." Ellen crossed to the closet and grabbed her black down jacket. "So stay inside, take it easy. Maybe you can read to him?"

"Will do." Connie set down her tote bag and slid out her newspaper, folded in half. "I loved your story today, about the old man who trains pigeons."

"Thanks." Ellen tugged her coat on and fought to get into her sleeves. Maybe the cropped jacket had been a bad idea.

"The other sitters all read your articles, you know. I'm like a celebrity."

"Sell autographs," Ellen said, with a smile. She knew that the sitters were curious about her, the single reporter with the adopted kid. Like that song on *Sesame Street,* she was the thing not like the others.

"You'll be home regular time?"

"Yes. Thanks for everything." Ellen felt a familiar tug inside her chest. "I hate when I don't get to say good-bye to him. Give him a kiss for me, will you?"

"You know I will." Connie reached for the doorknob.

"Tell him I love him."

"Gotcha." Connie opened the door, and Ellen stepped reluctantly outside. A frigid wind bit her cheek, and the sky was a dull pewter. She wished she could run back inside, send Connie home, and take care of her own child, especially when he was sick. But the front door was already closing behind her, leaving her outside.

She didn't remember about Timothy Braverman until she got into work.

Chapter Four

Ellen entered the building with a lunch-truck coffee and flashed her laminated ID at the security guard. She wanted to hit the ground running on that follow-up story, but her thoughts kept returning to Timothy Braverman. She made her way through the dim hallways of the old building and finally popped out into the newsroom, an immense, bright rectangle that ran the length of a city block, its ceiling three stories high.

Sunlight filtered in from tall windows covered with old-fashioned blinds, and blue banners that read CITY, NATIONAL, BUSINESS, NEWS DESK, ONLINE, and COPY DESK hung over the various sections. She started down the aisle to her desk, but everyone was collecting in front of the glass-walled editorial offices that ringed the newsroom, gathering around Marcelo.

This can't be good.

She caught the eye of her friend Courtney Stedt, who detoured to meet her midway up the aisle. Courtney was her usual outdoorsy self in a forest green fleece with jeans, but her expression looked uncharacteristically grim. The office earth mother, Courtney was the one who got sheet cakes for everybody's birthdays. If she was worried, something was wrong.

"Please tell me this is a surprise party," Ellen said, and they fell into step.

"I can't. I have a journalist's respect for the truth."

They reached the back of the crowd, and staffers filled the aisles between the desks and borrowed one another's chairs. The crowd was collectively restless, with low talk and nervous laughter. Ellen leaned back against one of the desks next to Courtney, and thoughts of Timothy Braverman flew from her head. Unemployment had a way of focusing the brain, because of its direct connection to the mortgage lobe.

Marcelo motioned for order, and everyone quieted, a sea of heads turning to him. He was tall enough to be seen over everyone, with a lean frame, and his thick, dark hair curled unprofessionally over his collar, in a raggedy line. Strain showed in his dark brown eyes, and a fork creased his forehead. His eyebrows sloped down unhappily, and his pursed lips spoke volumes.

"First, good morning, friends," Marcelo said, his voice deep and soft, with a pronounced Portuguese inflection. "I'm sorry to surprise you first thing, but I have bad news. I'm sorry, but we have another round of layoffs to make."

Somebody cursed under his breath, and the crowd stiffened. Ellen and Courtney exchanged glances, but neither said anything. They didn't have to, which was the friends part.

"I have to make two cuts today and one more by the end of the month."

"Two, *today*?" someone repeated, echoing Ellen's thoughts. Her chest tightened. She needed this job. Someone else called out, "No chance of a buyout?"

"Not this time, sorry." Marcelo began rolling up his sleeves in a black shirt, European-cut, which he wore without a tie. "You know the reasons for the cuts. No newspaper has the readers it used to.

We're doing everything we can here, with blogs and podcasts, and I know you guys are working very hard. None of this is your fault, or management's fault. We can't dance any faster than we are."

"True, that," someone murmured.

"So we have to deal with the reality of more cuts, and it's terrible, because I know you have families. You'll have to find another job. Relocate. Take kids out of schools, spouses from jobs. I know all that." Marcelo paused, his somber gaze moving from one stricken face to the next. "You know, when my mother used to spank me, she would always say, 'This hurts me more than it does you.' But, *sabia que nao era verdade.* Translated? I knew it was bullshit."

The staff laughed, and so did Ellen. She loved it when Marcelo spoke Portuguese. If he could fire her in Portuguese, she would be happy.

"So I'm not going to tell you it hurts me more than it hurts you. But I *will* tell you that I know how you feel, and I do." Marcelo's smile reappeared. "You all know, I've been laid off by some of the best papers in the world. Even by the *Folha de São Paulo,* my hometown paper."

"Way to go, boss," a page designer called out, and there was more laughter.

"But still I survived. I'll survive even if this paper lets me go, and I'll never quit the newspaper business, because I love it. I love this business. I love the feel of the paper." Marcelo rubbed his fingerpads together, with a defiant grin. "I love the smell of a good lead. I love finding out something nobody else knows and telling them. That's what we do, every day, on every page, and I know you love it, too."

"Hear, hear!" somebody called out, and even Ellen took heart. She loved the business, too. She'd grown up with the newspaper on the kitchen table, folded into fourths for the crossword, next to her mother's coffee cup, and she still got a charge when she saw her own byline. She had never felt so right for any job in her life, except motherhood, where the pay was even worse.

"But this business doesn't love us back, all the time, and especially not lately." Marcelo shook his glistening head. "After all we do for her, after how much we love her, she's a faithless lover." He flashed a killer smile. "She goes home with other men. She's always looking around. She strays from us."

Everybody laughed, more relaxed now, including Ellen, who almost forgot she could lose her job.

"But we love her still, so we'll stay with her, as long as she'll have us. There will always be a place for the newspaper, and those of us, the crazy-in-love ones, we will put up with her."

"Speak for yourself!" cracked one of the business reporters, and everybody laughed, relaxing as Marcelo's expression changed, his forehead creasing again, so that he looked older than his forty-odd years.

"So I will make the hard decisions, and I have to cut two of you today, and another one at the end of the month. To those of you I have to let go, please know I won't hand you off to human resources and forget about you."

Somebody in front nodded, because they all had heard that he had helped place one of their laid-off business reporters at the *Seattle Times.*

"I think you're all terrific journalists, and I'll do everything in my power to help you find another job. I have friends all over, and you have my word."

"Thank you," a reporter said, and then another, and there was even a smattering of applause, led by Courtney. Ellen found herself clapping, too, because Marcelo reached her at a level she couldn't explain merely by good looks, though it helped. Maybe it was his openness, his honesty, his emotionality. No other editor would have talked about loving the business or taken the reporters' side. Marcelo's eyes swept the crowd, meeting hers for a brief moment, and Ellen got so flustered she barely felt the nudge in her side.

"Down, girl," Courtney whispered, with a sly smile.

Chapter Five

A ladies' room is a girl headquarters, so it was only natural that Ellen, Courtney, and another reporter, Sarah Liu, would end up talking about the layoffs by the sinks. A photographer had been let go after the meeting, so they were waiting for the other shoe to drop. Courtney and Sarah were in News, but Ellen was in Features, traditionally the most dispensable of reporters. She washed her hands, and the water felt hot, though it could have been her imagination.

"Marcelo won't fire anybody in Sports," Sarah said, and anxiety speeded up even her normally fast speech. She was slim and petite, with pretty eyes and a small, lipsticked mouth that never stopped moving. "I think it's going to be a reporter, either News or Features."

"One more to go today," Courtney said, and her Boston accent made it, *One ma ta go taday.* "I think it'll be News."

"No, it can't be. They need us." Sarah raked a hand through her glossy black hair, layered around her ears. Diamond studs twinkled from her earlobes, and she looked typically chic, in a tailored white shirt with black slacks and a skinny, ribbed black sweater. "They can't get it all off AP."

"That's why God invented Reuters." Courtney chuckled, without mirth.

Ellen reached for a paper towel and caught sight of herself in the mirror. Her lips flattened to a grim line, and she'd swear she had more crow's-feet than when she got up. Her extra makeup emphasized the hazel green of her eyes, but she felt like she'd dolled up for her own firing.

"You're just wrong, Courtney," Sarah was saying, and it reminded Ellen of why she'd always disliked her. Aggressiveness was an occupational hazard in journalism, and Sarah never knew when to turn it off. She said, "They need news reporters, with Iraq and the new administration."

"Why? It's not like we have somebody in the White House pressroom." Courtney shook her head. "And it's our turn, because they already cut in Features. Remember Suzanne?"

"She deserved it," Sarah said, and Ellen tossed away a paper towel, her stomach a clenched fist.

"Suzanne didn't deserve it. None of us deserves it."

"If it's News, it won't be me, it can't be." Sarah folded her arms. "I'm too well sourced in City Hall, and they know it."

"It'll be me," Courtney said, and Ellen turned to her, hating the sound of it.

"No, Court, they can't let you go."

"Yes, they can, and they will. Bet me." Courtney's gaze, devoid of eye makeup, looked resigned. "Look, it is what it is. My uncle used to set hot type with Linotype machines, and he and his friends lost their jobs when computers came in, in the seventies. The cuts that everybody went through in production have come to editorial, that's all." She shrugged. "I need a vacation, anyway."

"It won't be you." Ellen managed a smile, but she knew the truth. "It'll be me, and we all know it. Marcelo thinks Features is kitten-up-a-tree, so I'm outta here. At least I'll get canned by somebody hot."

"There's the upside." Courtney smiled. "I heard he made *Philadelphia* magazine's list of the most eligible bachelors."

Ellen rolled her eyes. "I can't believe they do those stupid lists."

"I can't believe they use the word 'bachelor.' "

Courtney and Ellen laughed, but Sarah was deep in thought, then she looked up.

"It's gonna be you, Courtney."

"Sarah!" Ellen frowned. "Don't sugarcoat it or anything."

"She said it herself," Sarah shot back.

"That's not the point." Ellen turned away, ashamed of her next thought. Courtney's husband owned three summer camps in Maine, and Sarah's was a thoracic surgeon. She was the only one who didn't have a husband, like a salaried safety net.

"El, you look kinda sick." Courtney eyed her. "You gonna barf?"

"No, Boston, I'm not gonna *bahf.*" Ellen shook her head. She was going to lose her job today, and that damn white card gnawed at the edge of her thoughts. "Look, let's calm down, okay? We'll know any minute which one of us is getting let go. It doesn't help to obsess."

Sarah turned to her. "Oh, get real. You know Marcelo will never let you go. He's hot for you."

"He is not." Ellen felt her face flush.

"He looks at you from his office, like you're the one behind glass, like a fish in a bowl." Sarah's eyes flickered. "Like a little blond fishie."

"That's ridiculous," Ellen said, but Courtney placed a hand on her shoulder.

"El, here are my famous last words. You're single, he's single, and life is short. I say, go for it."

Suddenly there was a knock at the bathroom door.

And the three women looked over.

Chapter Six

Filling the newsroom were fifty-odd L-shaped desks furnished with computers, multiline phones, and atmospheric clutter, but only a few were occupied. Ellen had been at the paper long enough to remember when all the desks were full and the newsroom had the self-important hustle-bustle depicted on TV and the movies. There had been an electricity in the air then, from working at the epicenter of breaking news. Now the epicenter of breaking news had moved to the Internet, leaving too many of the desks vacant, now one more. Courtney's.

The room felt so much emptier to Ellen, even though she knew it wasn't possible. Mostly everybody had gone out on assignment, fleeing the scene of the crime. Sharon Potts in Business and Joey Stampone in Sports were at their desks, writing away and avoiding each other's eyes, stricken with survivor's guilt. Only Sarah chatted happily on her cell phone, the sound incongruous as laughter at a funeral.

Ellen set down her cold coffee and sat at the computer, checked her email, and opened her address book. She was supposed to be starting her follow-up story and looking for Susan Sulaman's phone number, but she felt shaken. Courtney hadn't shed a tear when she'd packed her desk, which only made it harder, but they'd hugged and promised to stay in touch, even as they both knew they'd get too busy.

You're single, he's single, and life is short. I say, go for it.

Her thoughts circled back to Timothy Braverman, and she reached into her purse, slid out the white card, and looked at the photo in the middle. The likeness between Will and Timothy struck her again as unmistakable, even for an age-progressed depiction. The bottom of the card read ACMAC, and she Googled it, then clicked through. American Center for Missing and Abducted Children, read the screen, and Ellen skimmed "About Us." ACMAC was a national organization to recover abducted children and runaways, and the page listed Amber Alerts.

She found the search button, typed in Timothy Braverman, and pressed Enter. The screen changed.

And Ellen almost gasped.

Chapter Seven

On the screen was a color photo of Timothy Braverman as a baby, and his features were identical to Will's, especially the eyes. Timothy had blue eyes, a shade she had never seen in anyone's eyes but Will's.

My God.

She read the webpage. The top said, **Timothy Braverman,** and underneath were two photos, side by side. On the right was the black-and-white thumbnail, the age-progressed picture from the white card, but on the left was the color baby photo of Timothy that had made Ellen gasp.

Timothy at one year old, read its caption. The photo had been cropped, a close-up of the baby's face in excellent focus, and it was taken outdoors in front of a lush green hedge. Timothy's blond hair caught the light, his highlights ablaze in the sun, and he grinned broadly, with his mouth turned down on the right, showing only two front teeth. Ellen had seen that very same grin on Will, after he'd finally got healthy.

She studied the screen, wondering what Will looked like when he was that little. She hadn't met him until he was a year and a half old, and the shape of his face then had been more elongated than Timothy's, due to his illness. He had been paler, his skin thin and curiously aged. Timothy had the exact same face, only healthier, his cheeks a rosy hue under a cheery layer of baby fat.

Ellen read on, avoiding a creeping sense of unease. The page said, **For further information, please see www.HelpUsFindTimothy Braverman.com.** She clicked on the link. The screen changed, and the top of the page read: Help Us Find Our Beloved Son, Timothy Braverman. It was a homemade website with Thomas the Tank Engine chugging around the perimeter. Her heart fluttered, then she dismissed it. It didn't mean anything that Will loved Thomas the Tank Engine, too. All little boys did, probably.

She scanned the webpage. It showed the same baby picture as the ACMAC site, but the photo hadn't been cropped, and she could see the whole picture. Timothy was dressed in a blue Lacoste shirt and jeans, and his legs stuck out straight in front of him, his feet in new white Nikes, their bottoms clean. His pudgy fingers grasped an oversized set of Fisher-Price plastic keys, and he was sitting very straight in his navy blue stroller. Will used to sit that way too, remarkably erect, as if he didn't want to miss anything.

Ellen reached for her coffee, then set it down without taking a sip. It was so damn eerie, like seeing Will's double. Was it possible that he had a twin somewhere? A brother she hadn't been told about? Those things happened, at least according to Oprah.

She clicked the link for the next page. There were more photos of Timothy as a baby; nine in all, a chronological progression from birth to his first birthday. She scanned the photos of Timothy as an infant, swaddled in a white receiving blanket, then flopped on his tummy, next propping himself up on soft arms, and finally ensconced in a bucket car seat. She had never seen Will as an infant, so she had no idea how he'd looked, but at about ten months old, Timothy began to look exactly like Will. She read the text below the photos:

We, Carol and Bill Braverman, will be eternally grateful to anyone who can help us find our son, Timothy Alan Braverman. Timothy was kidnapped by a Caucasian male, about thirty years old,
approximately five-foot-ten and 170 pounds. The man stopped the
Mercedes driven by Carol, pretending to be a motorist in distress.
He pulled a gun on Carol, carjacked the Mercedes, and shot and
killed Timothy's nanny, Cora Elizondo, when she began screaming.
He drove away, with Timothy still in the car seat. The suspect
called with a ransom demand, which we paid in full, but Timothy
was never returned. For a composite drawing of the suspect, see
below.

Ellen shuddered. The wrong place at the wrong time; a car driven
away with a baby inside. It was every parent's nightmare. Guns,
screaming, murder, and in the end, a kidnapped child. She looked at
the composite drawing, sketched with simple pencil lines and only
slight shading. The suspect had a thin face with narrow eyes, a long
nose, and high cheekbones, like your average scary guy. She continued reading:

Carol Braverman says: "In the year God shared Timothy with us,
we came to know him as a loving, happy, joyful little boy who adores
Thomas the Tank Engine, his cocker spaniel Pete, and lime Jell-O.
As his mother, I will never stop looking for him and won't rest until he
is back home."

Ellen would have felt exactly the same way, if it had happened to
her. She never would have given up on finding Will. She returned to
the webpage:

The kidnapper is currently wanted by federal and state authorities. The Braverman family has posted a reward of $1,000,000, pay-
able to anyone who has information that leads to finding Timothy.

Please do not call with false leads or pranks, or you will be prosecuted to the fullest extent.

Ellen's heart went out to the Bravermans, maybe because of the similarity between the boys. A million bucks was a huge amount for a reward, so the family must have been wealthy, but all the money in the world hadn't kept them safe from harm. She clicked back to the first page of the website and looked again at the baby photo of Timothy. On impulse, she scrolled over the picture and hit the Print button.

"Hey, girlfriend," said a voice at her shoulder, and Ellen reflexively clicked the mouse, so her screensaver of Will popped back onto the monitor. Standing next to the desk was Sarah Liu, who shot her a quick smile. "How you doing?"

"Fine."

"What's up?"

"Nothing, why?"

"You don't look good. Courtney was right. You sick or something?"

"Nah." Ellen felt unaccountably nervous. The photo of Timothy edged in noisy increments from the printer on her desk. "I just feel bad about Courtney."

"She'll be fine. She knew it was coming."

"No, she didn't." Ellen frowned.

"She said as much in the bathroom."

"But she didn't mean it. And still, it's a shock when it happens."

Sarah lifted an eyebrow. "She was the obvious choice. She wasn't sourced that well, and her writing wasn't as good as yours or mine."

"That's not true," Ellen shot back, hurt for Courtney, even in absentia. Meanwhile, the photo of Timothy slid from the printer tray, showing a rectangle of clear blue sky.

"What are you working on, anyway?"

"Research." Ellen was a bad liar, so she asked, "How about you?"

"An embezzlement piece, if Marcelo okays it." Sarah wiggled some papers in her hand. "The police commissioner just agreed to meet with me. An exclusive, which he never gives. So, what are you researching?"

"A follow-up on an old abduction story." Ellen wondered why she kept lying. She could have just told the truth. *Funny, I just saw a picture of a kid who looks exactly like Will.* But something told her to keep it to herself.

"What abduction story?"

"Sulaman, a family abduction I did a while ago."

"Oh, right, I remember. It was so *you*." Sarah snorted, and Ellen hid her annoyance.

"What do you mean?"

"It was heartfelt. Unlike me, you can pull it off."

"You can do heartfelt," Ellen said, though she wasn't so sure. The photo of Timothy had almost finished printing, and suddenly she wanted Sarah gone. "Sorry, but I have to get back to work."

"Me, too." Sarah's gaze fell on the printer just as the photo shot out, and she plucked it from the tray. "Aha! You're not working."

Ellen's mouth went dry as Sarah scanned the photo of Timothy.

"You took more baby pictures than anybody I know."

"Guilty." Ellen didn't know what else to say. Obviously, Sarah had mistaken Timothy for Will.

"See you later." Sarah handed her the photo and took off, and Ellen bent down and slid it into her purse.

Then she picked up the phone to call Susan Sulaman.

Chapter Eight

Fifteen minutes later, Ellen had hung up the phone, and Marcelo was motioning to her from his office doorway.

"May I see you for a minute?" he called out, and she nodded, seeing through his glass wall that Sarah was still sitting in one of the chairs across from his desk.

"Sure." She rose and walked to his office, which was lined with colorful photographs that he had taken in his native São Paulo. One was a series of exotic stone arches in warm gold and tan hues, and another of weathered doors painted germanium red, vivid orange, and chrome yellow, with a pot of magenta petunias on one threshold. Ellen realized she had a crush on Marcelo's office, too.

"Please, take a seat." He gestured her into a chair, and Sarah smiled quickly at her. He took his seat behind his desk, uncluttered except for stacked screen shots beside his laptop and a pencils-and-pens mug with a soccer ball on it that read *Palmeiras*. He sighed. "First let me say, I know it's hard on you both, losing Courtney. If I could have avoided it, I would have. Now, Sarah just told me a great story idea." Marcelo brightened, nodding at Sarah. "You wish to explain or shall I?"

"You can."

"Fine." Marcelo faced Ellen directly. "We all know that Philly's homicide rate is among the highest in the country, we cover some angle of it every day. Sarah's idea is that we do a major think piece on the issue, not treat it as episodic news. Sarah, this is where your editor steals your idea." Marcelo flashed Sarah a grin, and she laughed.

Ellen, confused, couldn't even fake a smile. Sarah had told her she was going to Marcelo with an embezzlement piece, but that wasn't true. She had gone to him with a think piece, which was a much bigger deal. With one layoff to go at the end of the month, Sarah was making damn sure it wasn't her.

Marcelo continued, "We need to explain why this is happening here, as opposed to other big cities in the States. What's more important? It's life or death."

"Exactly," Sarah said, and Ellen felt a half step behind, like a middle schooler during a pop quiz.

Marcelo nodded. "I see this as a cause-and-effects story. A thoughtful, in-depth examination. I will assign Larry and Sal to analyze the causes. Talk to social scientists and historians."

Ellen blinked. Larry Goodman and Sal Natane were the A-team, finalists for the Pulitzer for their investigative series on municipal bonds. All of a sudden, she was playing in the hard-news bigs.

"I'd like to get you two started on the effects, and it has to be good, new work. Sarah, I want you to look at the effects from the perspective of costs. How much does violent crime cost the city in law enforcement, cop and court time, lawyer time? How about in tourism, lost business, and prestige, if you can quantify that. Crunch the numbers, as they say, but make it understandable."

"Will do." Sarah took notes, her glossy head down.

"Ellen." Marcelo turned to her again, and she guessed that if he had a crush on her, either he hid it well or the murder rate had killed the mood. "I want you to put a human face on it. The homicide rate has to be more than a number. Don't be politically correct about it. We can't fix it if we don't tell the truth."

Sarah interjected, "I have good stats on the race issue, and that's the part I already wrote. Maybe I should take that angle, too."

Marcelo dismissed her with a wave. "No, please give your notes to Ellen. As far as deadlines, today is Tuesday. Let's talk on Friday, before the weekend. Can you both do that?"

"No problem," Sarah answered, then rose, papers in hand.

"Okay by me." Ellen may not have studied for the quiz, but she was a fast learner. "By the way, can I ask you about another story?"

"Sure. Go ahead." Marcelo leaned back in his chair, and Ellen became aware that Sarah was lingering behind her in the threshold. Marcelo seemed to read her mind because he raised his gaze. "Thank you very much, Sarah. You don't have to stay around."

"Thanks," Sarah said, and left.

"Okay, what is it?" Marcelo asked, his voice almost imperceptibly gentler, and Ellen wondered if he really did like her.

"I did a story once on the Sulaman family, a wife whose kids were taken by her ex-husband. I just got off the phone with Susan and I'd like to do a follow-up."

"Why? Did she get the children back?"

"No, not yet."

"Then what happened?"

"They're still gone, and I thought it would be interesting to let Susan tell us how it feels, as a mother."

Marcelo frowned, with sympathy. "It feels horrible, I assume."

"Right."

"Well." Marcelo opened his palms on the desk. "A mother who grieves the loss of her children, still. It's terrible for her, but there's no story there."

"It's more than that." Ellen couldn't explain the pull of the story, but then again, she never could with any of her stories. She sensed that the idea was connected to the Braverman baby, but she wasn't about to tell that to Marcelo. "Why don't I go see Susan, then write it up and see what you think? It might pay off."

"I don't understand you." Marcelo shifted forward on his chair, an incredulous smile playing around his lips. "I just asked you to make our readers feel the tragedy of murder. Isn't that enough to keep you busy, Ellen?"

She laughed. Humor was as strong an aphrodisiac as power, and the man had both. Also that accent, with the soft esses like a whisper in her ear.

Marcelo leaned further forward. "I know you're feeling unhappy about me today."

"What do you mean, unhappy?"

"Sarah told me you were no longer a fan of mine, because I let Courtney go. I made the best decision I could." Marcelo's expression darkened. "Please, try to understand that."

"I do understand." Ellen didn't get it. Why would Sarah tell him such a thing? Time to change the subject. "So what do you say, about the Sulamans? Gimme a chance?"

"No. Sorry."

"Okay." Ellen rose, hiding her disappointment. It wouldn't do to give him a hard time. She had to get out of the office before she got herself fired.

"Good luck with the homicide piece."

"Thanks," Ellen said, leaving to talk to Sarah.

She felt a catfight coming on.

Chapter Nine

Sarah's desk was empty, and her coat wasn't on the hook, so Ellen went to the desk nearest hers, where Meredith Snader was on her computer, her short gray hair barely visible above the monitor.

"Meredith, excuse me, have you seen Sarah?"

Meredith looked up over her tortoiseshell glasses, though her eyes remained vague, her thoughts with whatever she'd been writing. "She left."

"Where to, did she say?"

"No, sorry." Meredith focused on Ellen belatedly, her gaze sharpening like a camera lens. "So how are you, now that Courtney is no longer?"

"Sad. How about you?"

"Terrible." Meredith *tsk-tsk*ed like everybody's favorite aunt. "You know, they say war is hell, but I've been in a war and I've been in a newsroom. To me, you pick your poison."

Ellen smiled, grimly. Meredith had been a nurse in Vietnam, but she rarely mentioned it. "You have nothing to worry about. You're an institution around here."

"I hate it when people call me that. Institutions close at three o'clock." Meredith mock-shuddered.

"They'll never cut you, ever."

"Brings me no joy. I feel like you do, that cutting one of us cuts us all. Courtney was a real sweetheart and a helluva reporter." Meredith shook her head. "I heard how upset you are."

"What do you mean?"

"Sarah said you took it hard."

Ellen could barely hide her pique, and Meredith leaned over her keyboard, lowering her voice.

"She also mentioned that you blame Arthur. By the way, so do I. It's corporate greed of the highest order."

Ellen stiffened. Arthur Jaggisoon and his family owned the newspaper, and it was career suicide to bad-mouth him. In truth, she didn't blame him for the layoffs at all. "She said that?"

"Yes." Meredith's phone rang, and she turned away. "Pardon me, I've been waiting for this call."

"Sure." Ellen went back to her desk, glancing around the newsroom. Sharon and Joey, on the phone, looked pointedly away, and she wondered if Sarah had been talking to them, too.

Ellen's face burned as she sat down in her chair. Marcelo's back was to her, so there were no more eye games, and she wasn't in the mood anyway. On top of her computer keyboard sat a messy stack of printed notes with Sarah's name at the top.

Ellen picked up the pages and thumbed through them, and they included a draft, research, and stats. She wanted to confront Sarah, but didn't know her cell phone number. She reached for her coffee and took a cold sip. Her distracted gaze met Will's on her screensaver, but his face morphed into Timothy Braverman's.

She had to get her head back in the game. She rose, grabbed her purse, and got her coat.

Chapter Ten

Ellen sat in a lovely family room that had everything but the family. Susan Sulaman sipped water from a tumbler, curled up in a matching chintz couch opposite her, in jeans, a pink crew neck, and bare feet, a remarkably down-to-earth woman who looked oddly out of place in her own home. An Oriental rug covered a floor of resawn oak, and the couches faced each other in front of a colonial-era fireplace that had authentic cast-iron hooks and a swinging iron bracket inside. A perfect circle of cherrywood table held the latest magazines, a stack of oversized art books, and a tape recorder, running, now that the small talk was over.

"So you've heard nothing about the children at all?" Ellen asked.

"Nothing," Susan answered quietly, raking fingers through thick brown hair that curved softly to her chin. Her pretty eyes were brown, but her crow's-feet went deeper than they should for her age. Two lines had been etched in her forehead, over the bridge of a perfect nose. Susan Thoma Sulaman had been Miss Allegheny County when she became the trophy wife of her worst nightmare, multimillionaire builder Sam Sulaman.

"What have you done to find them?" Ellen asked.

"What haven't I done?" Susan smiled weakly, a fleeting glimpse of a dazzling grin. "I hound the police and the FBI. I hired three private investigators. I posted on the missing kids sites on the web."

"Like the ACMAC site?" Ellen was thinking of the white card.

"Of course, that's the main one. Nobody's turned up anything, scam artists, but no leads. I offered a fifty-thousand-dollar reward. Real money."

"Sure is." Ellen thought of the Bravermans and the million-dollar reward.

"I'll never forget the day he took them. It was October, a week before Halloween. Lynnie was going as a fish." Susan's smile reappeared. "We glued glitter to a piece of blue oak tag, and she was going to wear it like a sandwich board. It was from *The Rainbow Fish*."

"I know the book."

Susan's eyes lit up. "Oh, right, you have a son now. How old is he?"

"Three."

"Goodness, already?"

"I know, right?" Ellen didn't have to say, *time flies,* though it was her favorite mommy conversation. Some things never got old.

"I read that. I loved the articles you wrote about his sickness."

"Thank you. Anyway, you were saying."

"Yes, well, Sam Junior was going as a turtle. He had this chicken-wire shell we made"—Susan stopped herself—"well, never mind about the costume. My ex picked the kids up, loaded them in the car, and I never saw them again."

"I'm so sorry." Ellen lost her bearings, momentarily. Now that she'd become a mother, it was even harder to imagine. Maybe her mind simply refused to go there. "Does it get easier with time?"

"No, it gets harder."

"How so?"

"I think about all that I'm missing with them. All that time, with each of them. Then I start to think that, even when I get them back, I'll never be able to catch up." Susan paused, a stillness coming over her. "I worry they won't remember me. That I'll be a stranger to them."

"Of course they'll remember you," Ellen rushed to say, then switched tacks. "Is it easier because at least you know they're with their father? That they're not abducted by some stranger, who could be doing them harm?" She was thinking of the Bravermans again.

"Honestly, no." Susan frowned. "Sam was a terrible father. He lost the custody battle and he didn't like the settlement, so this is the way he got me back. At the end of the day, they need me. I'm their mother."

"So you're hopeful."

"I am, I have to be. The FBI thinks like you do, that it's less of a priority because it's family. Not all victims are alike." Susan pursed her lips. "Anyway, the theory is that he took them out of the country. His money is all offshore, and they think he told the kids I died."

"Would he do that?" Ellen asked, aghast.

"Of course, he's an egomaniac, a narcissist." Susan sipped her soda, and ice rattled in the tumbler. "I don't agree with the FBI, and if I tell you what I think, it'll sound crazy."

"No, it won't, and honestly, I don't even know if this will run. It depends on my editor."

Susan frowned. "Any press at all could help find them. You never know."

"I'll try my best. Please, go on."

Susan shifted forward on the cushion. "I believe my kids are in the country, nearby even. Maybe not in Philly, but in Jersey or Delaware. Near here. I think it because I feel them, inside. I feel my children, close to me." Certainty strengthened Susan's voice. "When they were babies, if someone took them out of my sight, I felt nervous. When we were in the same room, I knew it. I *feel* them here, still." Susan put a hand to her heart. "I carried them, they were *inside* me. I think it's a mother's instinct."

Ellen reddened. Was there such a thing? Could she have it if she had never been pregnant? Evidently, not everything came with the ovaries.

"I've posted their photos everywhere. I had somebody design a website and made sure it comes up first if they ever search their own name. I go on the Internet all the time, checking out all the sites where they might go, even the gamers' sites, because Sammy loved Nintendo."

Ellen watched Susan, who slumped in the soft couch as she continued.

"I drive around the neighborhoods, the schools. I check out the Gymboree for Lynnie and the T-ball leagues for Sammy. In summer, I troll the beaches in Holgate and Rehoboth. Sooner or later, I'll spot one of them, I just know it." Susan needed no encouragement to keep speaking, her words flowing from a pain, deep inside. "There's not a minivan that goes by that I don't look in the backseat, not a ball field I don't look on the bench and the bases. I stop by pet stores because Lynnie liked kittens. If a school bus passes, I look in the windows. I drive around and call the kids' names at night. Last week I was in Caldwell, in New Jersey, calling them, and a woman asked me what kind of dog Lynnie was."

Susan stopped talking abruptly, and a sudden silence fell.

And Ellen understood firsthand that after the loss of a child, a mother would be haunted for the rest of her life.

Chapter Eleven

Back in her car, Ellen stopped at a traffic light, dwelling. She'd had a glimpse of Susan Sulaman's world, and it made her want to drive home and hug Will. Her BlackBerry rang in her purse, and she rooted in her bag until she found it, then hit the green button.

"Elly Belly?" said the familiar voice.

"Dad. How are you?"

"Fine."

"What's the matter?" Ellen could tell he was upset by the way he said he was fine.

"Nothing. I'm about to have lunch. You free? I just got back from the doctor's."

"Are you sick?"

"Nah."

"Then why'd you go to the doctor?"

"A checkup, is all."

"You had a checkup in September, didn't you?" Ellen remembered because it was near her birthday.

"This was just a thing, a routine thing."

Ellen glanced at the car's clock, then did a quick calculation. Her father lived in West Chester, forty-five minutes from the city. Being closer to her parents was the reason she had come here from the *San Jose Mercury*. "Are you home today?"

"Yeah, doing email and expenses."

"Why don't I drop by? I'm actually in Ardmore."

"Great. The door's open. Love you."

"Love you, too." Ellen hung up, then slid the phone back in her purse. She cruised to the corner in light traffic, turned around, and headed back down Lancaster Avenue. She felt a pang of guilt, realizing she hadn't been to visit her father in almost a month. She just hadn't had the time, between work and Will. Every week, she mentally shifted the hours of her days, as if her life were a handheld puzzle with tiles that slid around to make a picture. The tiles fit differently every week, and no matter how hard she tried, the picture didn't come together. The lines connected to nothing.

She accelerated.

Chapter Twelve

"Hi, Dad." Ellen entered her father's kitchen, which overlooked the golf course at Green Manor, which billed itself as a Community for Active Adults. Her father had moved here after her mother died, which was when he got Active, especially in the Adult Department.

"Hi, sweetheart," he said, standing at the counter, absorbed in slicing a tomato onto a plate. His wrinkled forehead knit over his brown eyes, set close together and hooded now, and his nose had a telltale bulb at the tip from the drinking he'd given up, years ago. Even at sixty-eight, her father had enough black in his thinning hair to make people wonder if he colored it, and Ellen was pretty sure he didn't.

"Dad, are you gonna die?" she asked, only half-joking.

"No, never." Her father turned with a broad smile that served him well on the back nine and the road, where he drove a thousand miles a week as a sales rep for an auto-parts company.

"Good." Ellen slid out of her coat and purse, dumped them on a kitchen chair, and kissed him on the cheek, catching a whiff of strong aftershave. None of her perfume lasted as long as her father's aftershave. She fleetingly considered picking up a bottle of Aramis.

"You look nice, honey. Dressed up."

"I'm trying not to get fired."

"Succeeding?" Her father sliced another pink-red tomato. Already on the table sat a plastic tub of Whole Foods tuna fish, a loaf of multigrain bread, and a pitcher of green tea, permanent fixtures in Don Gleeson's Antioxidant Heaven.

"So far." Ellen crossed to the counter, plucked a floppy tomato slice from the plate, and plopped it into her mouth. It tasted like nothing, a winter tomato.

"Don't let the bastards get you down. How's my grandson?"

"He has a cold."

"I miss him. When am I gonna see him?"

Ellen felt a guilty twinge. "Soon as I can. So, what's up with the doctor? You're scaring me."

"I waited lunch for you."

"I see that, thanks. You're avoiding the question."

"Sit down like a civilized person." Her father carried the tomato plate to the table and set it down, then eased into the chair with a theatrical groan. He always moaned for comic effect, though he kept in great shape, fit and trim in his pale yellow polo shirt, Dockers, and loafers.

"Dad, tell me." Ellen sat next to him, worried. Cancer was the worst sort of coward, sneaking up on people, and her mother had died from lymphoma, having lived only three months after her diagnosis.

"I'm not sick, not at all." He untwisted the tie on the plastic bag of bread, extracted two slices from the center of the loaf, and set them on his plate, open-faced.

"Then why did you go to the doctor?"

"Make yourself a sandwich, then we'll talk."

"Dad, please."

"Suit yourself, but I'm hungry." Her father popped the plastic lid of the tuna, then picked up the serving fork, speared himself a small mound, and patted it onto his bread with the tines of the fork, making crosshatches.

"You're stalling, Dad. It's tuna fish, not rocket science."

"Okay, here it is. I'm getting married."

"What?" Ellen was dumbfounded. "To who?" She had no idea. He was dating four women here. He was Romeo, with an enlarged prostate.

"Barbara Levin."

Ellen didn't know what to say. She didn't even know the woman. Her parents had been married forty-five years, and her mother had passed a little over two years ago. Somehow this meant her mother was really gone. As if someone had put a period on the sentence that was her life.

"El? I'm not dying, I'm getting married."

"Why, is she pregnant?"

"Ha!" Her father laughed, then stabbed the tuna with the serving fork. "I'll tell her you said that."

Ellen hid her ambivalence. "This is kind of a surprise."

"A good one, right?"

"Well, yes. Sure." Ellen tried to get a grip, but a hard knot in her chest told her she wasn't doing such a great job. "I guess I just wasn't sure who the lucky lady was."

"Barbara's the one that matters." He picked up a tomato slice with the serving fork. "You gonna congratulate me?"

"Congratulations."

"I needed a cholesterol check. That's why I went to the doctor's."

"Oh. Thank God you're not sick."

"You got that right." Her father placed his tomato on top of the tuna, added a piece of bread, then lined up the two pieces, leaning over as if he were sizing up a putt. He pressed his sandwich closed, lowering his hand, then eyed her. "You don't look happy, El."

"I am." Ellen managed a smile. She loved her father, but he had spent her childhood on the road. The truth was, everybody had a go-to parent, and with him away from home so much, Ellen's had become her mother.

"El, I'm entitled to be happy."

"I didn't say you weren't."

"You're acting it."

"Dad, please."

"I don't like to be alone and I'm not getting any younger."

Silence fell between them, and Ellen made no move to fill it. The ugliest of thoughts popped into her head—the wrong one had died. She felt ashamed of the very notion, and confused. She loved her father.

"I guess I knew you'd get upset. You and your mother were two of a kind. Peas in a pod."

Ellen couldn't speak for a moment. Her mother had been her best friend in the world. That said it all.

"Life goes on."

Ellen felt the knot again, then flipped her thinking. "So when's the wedding? I need to get a dress and all."

"Uh, it's in Italy."

"Italy? Why?"

"Barbara likes it there, near Positano." Her father cut his sandwich and took a bite, leaving Ellen to fill in the blanks.

"Am I going? Is Will?"

"Sorry, but no." Her father looked back at her over his sandwich. "It's not a big deal, not at our age. We're just doing it, no muss, no fuss. We're getting on a plane end of the week."

"Wow, that soon?"

"I told her you'd be fine with it. Her kid's fine with it."

"I understand." Ellen tried to shrug it off. "I'm officially fine with it."

"She has a daughter, too. Year older than you. Abigail."

"I thought she had a boy in the Peace Corps."

"That was Janet."

"Oh." Ellen smiled. It *was* kind of funny. "Well, good. I always wanted a sister. Can I have a pony, too?"

At that, he smiled, chewing.

"What does she do, my new sister?"

"Lawyer in D.C."

"I always wanted a lawyer, too." Ellen laughed, and so did he, setting down his sandwich.

"Ha! That's enough, wise guy."

"I think it's good, I really do." Ellen felt better saying it, and her chest knot loosened just a bit. "Be happy, Dad."

"I love you, kitten."

"I love you, too." Ellen managed a smile.

"You gonna eat or what?"

"No, I'm waiting for the wedding cake."

He rolled his eyes.

"So tell me what she looks like."

"Here, I'll show you." Her father leaned over, slid a brown wallet from his back pocket, and opened it up. He flipped past the second plastic envelope, which had an old photo of Will, and the third, he turned sideways and set down on the table. "That's Barbara."

Ellen eyed the woman, who was attractive, with her hair in a short, classy cut. "Mommy!"

"Gimme that." Her father smiled and took the wallet back.

"She looks nice. Is she nice?"

"Of course she's nice." He leaned over to put the wallet into his back pocket. "What do you think? She's a jerk, that's why I'm marrying her?"

"Are you going to move in with her, or is she moving in here?"

"I'm selling the house and moving in with her. She's got a corner unit with a deck."

"You gold digger, you."

He smiled again, then leaned back in his chair, regarding her for a moment. "You know, you gotta move on, kid."

Ellen felt the knot again. Time to change the subject. "I interviewed this woman whose husband kidnapped her children. Susan Sulaman, if you remember the story I did."

He shook his head, no, and Ellen let it go. Her mother would have remembered the story. She'd kept scrapbooks of Ellen's clippings, starting with the college newspaper and ending three weeks before she died.

"Anyway, Susan thinks there's an instinct that mothers have about their children."

"Your mother had that in spades." Her father beamed. "Look how good you turned out, all because of her."

"Hold on, let me show you something." Ellen got up, opened her purse, and extracted the photo of Timothy Braverman as a baby, then handed it to her father. "How cute is this baby?"

"Cute."

"Do you know who he is?"

"What am I, stupid? It's Will."

Ellen stood over him as if suspended, not knowing whether to tell him. He and Sarah had both mistaken Timothy for Will. She felt funny about it, and not good funny. It made her uncomfortable. She realized now why she was missing her mother so much. She could have told her mother about Timothy Braverman. Her mother would have known what to do.

"He's grown up a lot since then, hasn't he?" her father asked, holding up the photo with unmistakable pride.

"How so? I mean, what differences do you see?"

"The forehead." He circled the area with an index finger knotted from arthritis. "His forehead got a lot bigger, and his cheeks, they're full now." He handed her back the photo. "He just grew into his face."

"He sure did." Ellen lied more easily than she thought, for a bad liar. She folded the paper, put it back inside her purse, and sat down, but her father was looking reflective, pouring them a glass of tea.

"You were like that, too, just like that. When you were little, your face was so wide. I used to say you looked like a salad plate. Will's the same way. He gets it from you."

"Dad, he's adopted, remember?"

"Oh, right." Her father laughed. "You're such a good mother, I always think you're his real mother."

Ellen let that go, too. She usually felt like Will's real mother, until someone told her she wasn't. But she knew what he meant.

"You got that mother instinct from your mother. You're every inch her daughter. That he's adopted, it doesn't matter. That's why we keep forgetting. It's like proof."

"Maybe you're right." Ellen nodded, oddly grateful.

But then again, Don Gleeson could sell anybody anything.

Chapter Thirteen

Ellen finally got home and closed the front door behind her. "How is he?" she asked Connie, keeping her voice low.

"Hanging in. I gave him Tylenol at two." Connie checked her watch. "He's been asleep since four."

"Did he eat?" Ellen shed her coat and hung it in the closet as Connie reached for hers, the domestic changing of the guard.

"Chicken soup and crackers. Flat ginger ale. We took it easy today. All he wanted to do was stay in bed." Connie slipped into her coat. "I read to him after lunch until he got sleepy."

"Thanks so much."

"Don't know how much he heard of it, though. He was just lying there." Connie zipped up her coat and picked up her tote bag, which was already packed.

"Poor thing."

"Give him a kiss for me." Connie got her purse, and Ellen opened the door, said her good-byes, then shut the door and locked it, preoccupied. If Will had just gone to sleep, she had a window of time to do something that had been bugging her on the ride home. She kicked off her boots and hurried upstairs.

Half an hour later, she was sitting cross-legged on her bed, bent over her task. A blown-glass lamp cast an ellipse of light on two photos of Timothy Braverman, the age-progressed picture from the white card and the computer printout of his baby photo from ACMAC. com. Next to those were a pile of ten photos of Will, chosen because they showed his features the best. Oreo Figaro sat beside her like the Sphinx, keeping his own counsel.

Ellen arranged Will's photos in two rows of five, in chronological order. The top row was a younger Will, the first year she had him, at age one-and-a-half to two-and-a-half. The bottom row was the second year she'd had him, ages two-and-a-half to present. She looked at them all, examining his face over time, from its thinnest and least healthy to a beaming little boy. It was like watching a sunflower open and thrive, turning to the sun.

She returned to the top row of photos and picked the youngest one that was the most representative of Will's features. It showed him at about one-and-a-half years old, in a flannel shirt and overalls, sitting next to an oversized pumpkin at Halloween. Suddenly, Susan Sulaman broke through Ellen's consciousness.

It was October, a week before Halloween. Lynnie was going as a fish.

She shook it off, staying the course. She picked up the Halloween photo of Will and held it next to the photo of Timothy, taken at about a year old. He was also sitting, but in his stroller, and when Ellen put the photos side by side, she felt an undeniable jolt.

Their faces looked so much alike as babies that they could have been identical twins. Their blue eyes were the same shape, size, and hue, their noses carbon copies, and their mouths plastered with the same goofy smile, in which the right corner turned down. Both boys were sitting in the exact same way; oddly upright for such young children. No wonder Sarah and her father had mistaken them. She held the photos closer to the lamp, and it spooked her. She shook her head in disbelief, yet couldn't deny what she was seeing.

She set the photos down and went to the second row, of older photos of Will. She picked one of the most recent, in which Will was sitting on their front porch on the first day of preschool, wearing a new green T-shirt, green shorts, and green socks. It was an unfortunate choice for a favorite color, unless you were a leprechaun.

She picked up the age-progressed photo of Timothy and held it next to the photo of Will. They were almost dead ringers, even though the photo of Timothy was only black-and-white. Their eyes were the same shape, round and wide set. The smiles were similar, though she couldn't see all of Timothy's teeth and she knew Will's were perfect. The only slight difference was their hair, because Timothy's was described as blond, and Will's was dark blond. There was a likeness, too, in the configuration of their features, and again, their very aspect.

Ellen set the photos down, but she had one more thing she wanted to try. She picked up the baby photo of Timothy and held it next to the older photo of Will, starting preschool. She eyeballed them, and it was almost as if Timothy got older and turned into Will. Eyes, nose, mouth; all were the same, but bigger, older, more mature. Ellen felt her stomach tense.

Then she got another idea. She set down the photos, then picked up the older photo of Will going to preschool and the baby photo of Timothy in the stroller. She compared them, and before her eyes, Will regressed back into Timothy as a baby. Ellen's mouth went dry.

"Connie!" Will called out from his bedroom.

"Coming, honey!" she called back, leaping from the bed so quickly she almost tripped on the duvet. Oreo Figaro jumped out of the way, objecting with a loud meow.

The photos scattered, unwanted, to the floor.

Chapter Fourteen

"It's Mommy, honey." Ellen went over to Will's bed, and his sobs intensified, cranky wails in the dark room.

"I'm hot."

"I know, baby." Ellen scooped him up and hugged him close, and he flopped onto her, resting his head sideways on her shoulder and clinging to her like a baby koala. His face was damp against her neck, and she rocked him as she stood. "My poor baby."

"Why am I hot?"

"Let's get you out of these clothes, okay?" Ellen lowered him back into the bed, and he was too listless to squirm. He had fallen asleep in his turtleneck and overalls. "I'm gonna turn the light on, so be ready. Cover your eyes. Ready?"

Will slapped two small hands over his eyes.

"Good boy." Ellen leaned over to the night table and switched on the Babar lamp. "Okay, move your hands away from your eyes, nice and slow, so they can get used to the light."

Will moved his hands away, then came up blinking. "I'm getting used."

"Right, good." Ellen retrieved the board books that had gotten wedged inside the bed frame and set them on the night table. She unhooked the fasteners at the top of his straps, then shimmied him out of his overalls. "You had a big, long nap."

"Mommy." Will smiled shakily at her. "You're home."

"I sure am," Ellen said, with a twinge. "I'm so glad you got such a good rest. That's going to help you feel better. Reach for the moon, partner." She pulled off his damp shirt as Will raised his arms, and she could barely see the thin white line that divided his little-boy chest down the center, though he felt embarrassed enough to wear a T-shirt when he swam. Once it had been a knotted zipper of flesh, in days she would never forget. "You hungry?"

"No."

"How about soup?" Ellen placed her palm on his forehead. She couldn't remember the last time she'd used a thermometer, as if it proved her motherhood bona fides.

"No soup, Mommy."

"Well, then, how about bugs and worms?"

"No!" Will giggled.

"Why, did you have that for lunch? Are you sick of bugs and worms?"

"No!" Will giggled again. Oreo Figaro appeared in the threshold and sat silhouetted in the hall light, a fat cat with a back hump like Quasimodo.

"I know, how about you eat some cat food? I bet Oreo Figaro would share with you." Ellen turned to the cat. "Oreo Figaro, would you share your dinner?" Then she turned back to Will. "Oreo Figaro said, 'No, get your own food.' "

Gales of laughter, making Mommy feel like a comic genius. "He *has* to share."

"Oreo Figaro, you have to share. Will says so." Ellen turned to

Will. "Oreo Figaro says, 'I make my own rules. I'm a cat, and that's how cats roll.'"

"Oreo Figaro, you're gonna get a time-out."

"Right." Ellen got the liquid Tylenol from the night table, un-screwed the lid of the small bottle, and sucked some into the drop-per. "Here's medicine. Open up, please, baby bird."

"Where's Oreo Figaro?" Will opened his mouth, then clamped down on the dropper.

"In the doorway. Did you swallow?"

"Yes. Get him, Mommy."

"Okay, hold on." Ellen put the sticky dropper back in the bottle, closed the cap, and went over and picked up the cat, who permitted himself to be carried to the bed and placed at its foot, curling his tail into a shepherd's crook.

"Oreo Figaro, you gotta share!" Will wagged a finger at him, and Ellen rooted around on the night table for a bottle of water.

"Drink this for me, please, sweetie." She helped him up to sip from the bottle, then laid him back down. A slight, pale figure in his white undies, he took up barely the top half of the bed, and she covered him lightly.

"No books, Mommy."

"Okay, how about we cuddle up, instead? Scoot over, please." Ellen turned off the light, eased herself over the side of the guardrail, and gentled Will up and onto her chest, where she wrapped her arms around him. "How's that feel, baby?"

"Scratchy."

Ellen smiled. "It's my sweater. Now, tell me how you are. Does your throat hurt?"

"A little."

Ellen wasn't overly worried, she hadn't smelled strep on his breath. You didn't have to be a good mother to smell strep. Even a drunk could smell strep. "How about your head? Does it hurt?"

"A little."

"Tummy?"

"A little."

Ellen hugged him. "Did you have fun with Connie today?"

"Tell me a story, Mommy."

"Okay. An old or a new one?"

"An old one."

Ellen knew the one he wanted to hear. She would tell it and try not to think about the photos in her bedroom. "Once upon a time there was a little boy who was very, very sick. He was in a hospital, all by himself. And one day, a mommy went to the hospital and saw him."

"What did she say?" Will asked, though he knew. This wasn't a bedtime story, it was a bedtime prayer.

"She said, 'My goodness, this is the cutest little boy I have ever seen. I'm a mommy who needs a baby, and he's a baby who needs a mommy. I wish that little boy could be mine.'"

"Oreo Figaro's biting my foot."

"Oreo Figaro, no, stop it." Ellen gave the cat a nudge, and he went after her foot instead. "Now he's got me. Ouch."

"He's sharing, Mommy."

Ellen laughed. "That's right." She moved her foot away, and the cat gave up. "Anyway, back to the story. So the mommy asked the nurse, and she said, 'Yes, you can take that little boy home if you really, really love him a lot.' So the mommy said to the nurse, 'Well, that's funny, I just happen to love this baby a whole lot.'"

"Tell it right, Mommy."

Ellen got back on track. She'd been distracted, thinking about Timothy Braverman. "So the mommy said to the nurse, 'I really love this baby a whole lot and I want to take him home,' and they said okay, and the mommy adopted the little boy, and they lived happily ever after." Ellen hugged him close. "And I do. I love you very much."

"I love you, too."

"That makes it perfect. And oh, yeah, they got a cat."

"Oreo Figaro's head is on my foot."

"He's telling you he loves you. Also that he's sorry about before."

"He's a good cat."

"A very good cat," Ellen said, giving Will another squeeze. He fell silent, and in time she could feel his skin cool and his limbs relax.

She remained in the dark bedroom, listening to the occasional hiss of the radiator and looking at a ceiling covered with phosphorescent stars that glowed WILL. Her gaze fell to shelves full of toys and games, and a window with the white plastic shade pulled down. On the walls, cartoon elephants lumbered along in a line, knockoff Babars holding onto each other's tails and balancing one-legged on bandbox stands. She had put the wallpaper up herself, with the radio blasting hip-hop. It was the child's room she'd always dreamed of, ready just in time to bring Will home from the hospital.

Her gaze returned to the WILL constellation, and she tried to count her blessings, but failed. Until that damn white card had come in the mail, she'd been happier than she'd imagined she ever could be. She hugged Will gently, but her thoughts wandered back down the hall. Then she got another idea, one that wouldn't wait.

She eased Will from her chest and shifted out of bed, clumsily because of the stupid guardrail. She got up, covered him with his thermal blanket, and padded out of the room on fleece socks.

Oreo Figaro raised his head and watched her sneak off.

Chapter Fifteen

Ellen went into her home office, flicked on the overhead light, and sat down at her fake-wood workstation, a floor sample from Staples that held an old Gateway computer and monitor. The room was tiny enough that the Realtor had called it a "sewing room," and it barely accommodated the workstation, an underused stationary bicycle, and mismatched file cabinets containing household files, research, appliance manuals, and old clippings Ellen kept in case she had to get a new job.

I'll have to cut one more by the end of the month.

Ellen sat down, opened her email, and wrote Courtney an email telling her she loved her, then logged on to Google and typed in Timothy Braverman. The search yielded 129 results. She raised an eyebrow; it was more than she'd expected. She clicked on the first relevant link, and it was a newspaper story from last year. The head-line read, CORAL BRIDGE MOM KEEPS HOPE ALIVE, and Ellen skimmed the lead:

> Carol Braverman is waiting for a miracle, her son Timothy to come home. Timothy, who would now be two-and-a-half years old, was kidnapped during a carjacking and is still missing.
>
> "I know I'll see my son again," she told this reporter. "I just feel it inside."

It sounded like what Susan Sulaman had said. Ellen read on, and another paragraph caught her eye.

> Asked to describe Timothy in one word, Carol's eyes misted over, then she said that her son was "strong." "He could get through anything, even as a baby. He was smaller than most one-year-olds, but he never acted it. At his first birthday party, all of the other babies were bigger, but nobody got the best of him."

She printed the interview, then went back to the Google search and read the line of links, scanning each piece on the Braverman kidnapping. There was a lot of press, and she contrasted it with Susan Sulaman, who had to go begging to keep the police interested. She learned from the articles that Timothy's father, Bill Braverman, was an investment manager, and his mother had been a teacher until her marriage, when she stopped to devote herself to being a mother and doing good works, including fund-raising for the American Heart Association.

The Heart Association?

Ellen saved the articles, logged on to Google Images, searched under Carol and Bill Braverman, then clicked the first link. A picture appeared on the screen, showing three couples in elegant formal wear, and her eye went immediately to the woman in the middle of the photo.

My God.

Ellen checked the caption. The woman was Carol Braverman.

Carol looked so much like Will, she could easily have been his mother. The photo was dark and the focus imperfect, but Carol had blue eyes the shape and color of Will's. Her hair was wavy and dark blond, almost his color, and she wore it long, curling to her tanned shoulders in a slinky black dress. Ellen scanned Bill Braverman's face, and he was conventionally handsome, with brown eyes and a nose that was straight and on the small side, a lot like Will's. His smile was broad, easy, and confident, the grin of a successful man.

Her stomach clenched. She closed the photo, went back to Google, and clicked the second link, which retrieved another group picture in shorts and T-shirts at a poolside party. The photo was dark, too, taken at night, but Carol's hair had been cut around her ears in a boyish style that made her look even more like Will. And Bill's body looked lean but cut, with muscular arms and legs that showed the same wiry build that Will had.

"This is crazy," Ellen said aloud. She shoved the computer mouse away, got up from her chair, and went to the first file cabinet. She slid open the top drawer, moved the green Pendaflex files aside, skipping folders hand-labeled Bank Statements, Car Payments, Deed, until she found the Will file. She slid the file out, took it back to her chair, and opened it on her lap.

On top were folded clippings of the series she'd done on the CICU nurses, then the one she did on adopting Will. She leafed through them, pausing at an early photo of Will in his crib. The paper had run it on the first page, and Will looked nothing like himself then, so thin and sick. She moved it aside, shooing away the memories. Finally she found Will's adoption papers and slid out the packet.

At the top of the final adoption decree, it read, "The Court of Common Pleas of Montgomery County, Pennsylvania, Orphans' Court Division," and the order was in bold: **"The Court hereby orders and decrees that the request for adoption is hereby approved and that the above-captioned adoptee is hereby adopted by Ellen Gleeson."**

She felt satisfied, in an official sort of way. Will's adoption was all sewn up, legal, certified, and irrevocable. The court proceedings had been routine, and she had appeared on the second floor of the courthouse in Norristown, for the first time in public with Will. The judge had pounded the gavel, then issued the decree from the bench with a broad smile. She would never forget his words:

I have the only happy courtroom in the entire courthouse.

It gladdened her to remember that day, holding baby Will in her arms, her first day as a mother. She read the decree again. **"The needs and welfare of ADOPTEE will be promoted by approval of this adoption and all requirements of the Adoption Act have been met."** So her adoption was a done deal, and it was closed, meaning that she didn't know the identity of the birth mother and father. They had consented to relinquish their parental rights, and their written consent forms had been submitted to the court by Ellen's lawyer, as part of the adoption papers. The lawyer's name and address were at the bottom of the page:

Karen Batz, Esq.

Ellen remembered Karen well. Her office was in Ardmore, fifteen minutes away, and she had been a smart, competent family lawyer who had guided her through the adoption process without overcharging her, the thirty-thousand-dollar fee in line with a standard private adoption. Karen had told her that the birth mother was thrilled to find someone with the desire and the means to care for such a sick child, and that taking a sick baby would be her best chance to adopt as a single mother. Even the judge had commented on the unusual facts of the case:

It was a stroke of luck, for all concerned.

The paperwork had been completed without a hitch, and Ellen became responsible for Will's medical expenses to the tune of $28,000 and change, but the hospital permitted her to pay in installments. She had just paid off the last penny, and in the end, she got Will, safe and sound, and they became a family.

She sighed happily, closed the file, and put it away behind the others. She shut the file drawer, but stood there, lost in thought for a minute. On the wall over the cabinets hung a Gauguin poster she'd had framed, and she found herself staring at it, the tropical blues and greens blurring her thoughts. The house was quiet. The wind whistled outside. The radiator knocked faintly. The cat was probably purring. Everything was fine.

Still, she was thinking about her lawyer.

Chapter Sixteen

The next morning, Ellen's wardrobe was back on autopilot, and she slipped a down coat over her jeans-sweater-clogs trifecta. Her hair was still wet from the shower, her eye makeup only perfunctory. She felt raw and tired, gone sleepless after a night of quality dwelling.

"You're leaving early?" Connie asked, shedding her coat by the closet. Bright sunlight shone through the window in the door, warming the living room.

"Yes, I have tons of work," Ellen lied, then wondered why. "He didn't have a fever this morning but he slept badly. I still wouldn't send him to school."

"We'll take it easy."

"Good, thanks." Ellen kept her back turned, grabbed her bag and the manila envelope, then opened the door. "I told him good-bye. He's playing in bed with his Legos."

"Ouch."

"I know, right?"

"Looks like the snow's holding off," Connie said, cheery.

"See you, thanks." Ellen went to the door and left, catching a glimpse of the babysitter's puzzled expression through the window, then she pulled her coat tighter and hit the cold air, hustling across the porch and toward the car.

Ten minutes later, she reached the two-story brick building behind Suburban Square and pulled up at the curb in front of the sign that read PROFESSIONAL BUILDING. She'd called Karen Batz's office from her cell phone this morning, but no voice mail had picked up, so she'd decided to drop in. It was on the way to the city, and she was hoping Karen would see her. Even a feature reporter knows when to be pushy.

Ellen grabbed her bag and the envelope and got out of the car. She walked down the walkway and went inside the blue door, which they kept unlocked. There was a colonial-style entrance hall with a hunting-scene umbrella stand, and she opened the door on the right, which read, LAW OFFICES, and went inside. She stood, disoriented, for a minute.

Karen's office was completely different. There was a navy carpet and a paisley couch and chairs she didn't remember from before. The huge bulletin boards blanketed with baby photos had been replaced by beach-and-surf scenes and a mirror framed with fake seashells.

"May I help you?" a receptionist asked, coming out of the back room. She was about sixty-five, with red reading glasses and her brown hair cut short. In her hand she held an empty Bunn coffeepot, and she had on a cardigan embroidered with stick-figure skiers and a long corduroy skirt.

"I was looking for Karen Batz," Ellen answered.

"Her office isn't here anymore. This is Carl Geiger's office now. We do real estate."

"Sorry. I called Karen's old number, but they didn't pick up."

"They should disconnect the line. I keep telling them to, but they don't. You're not the first one to make this mistake."

"I'm a client of hers. Do you know where she moved to?"

The receptionist's eyes fluttered briefly. "I'm sorry to have to tell you this, but Ms. Batz passed away."

"Really?" Ellen asked, surprised. "When? She was only in her forties."

"About two years, maybe a year and a half ago. That's how long we've been here."

Ellen frowned. "That would be right around the time I knew her."

"I'm so sorry. Would you like to sit down? Maybe have some water?"

"No, thanks. What did she die of?"

The receptionist hesitated, then leaned closer. "Frankly, it was a suicide."

Ellen felt stunned. "She *killed* herself?" Memories came back to her. Karen's desk had photos of her three sons. "But she was married, with kids."

"I know, such a shame." The receptionist turned toward a noise from the back room. "If you'll excuse me, I should get ready. We have a closing this morning."

Ellen was nonplussed. "I wanted to talk to her about my son's adoption."

"Maybe her husband can help you. I've directed her other clients to him." The receptionist went to the computer and hit a few keys, the bright monitor screen reflected in her glasses. She pulled a pen from a mug, then scribbled on a piece of paper. "His name's Rick Musko. Here's his office phone."

"Thanks," Ellen said, accepting the sheet, which had a 610 phone number, the Philly suburbs. "Do you have the address?"

"I'm not authorized to give that out."

"Okay, thanks."

Back in her car, Ellen was on the cell phone to Karen's husband before she pulled away from the office. It was only 8:10, but a man answered the phone.

"Musko here."

"Mr. Musko?" Ellen introduced herself and said, "I'm sorry to bother you, but I'm, er, was, a client of Karen's. I'm very sorry for your loss."

"Thank you," Musko said, his tone cooler.

"She helped me adopt my son, and I had wanted to speak with her. I have a question or two about—"

"Another lawyer took over her practice. You should have gotten a letter. I can give you his information."

"I just wanted my file. Does he have the files, too?"

"How old is the case?"

"It was about two years ago." Ellen winced at the coincidence of timing, but if Musko noticed it, he didn't miss a beat.

"I have the dead files in my garage, at the house. You can come by and look for your file. That's the best I can do."

"Wonderful. When could I come by?"

"I'm busy this month, we have a project at work."

"Please, could it be sooner? This is important." Ellen heard anxiety thin her voice, surprising even herself. "If I could just come over this week? Tonight, even? I know it's short notice but I won't make any trouble for you, I'll just go out to the garage and find it myself."

"*Tonight?*"

"Please?"

"I suppose the housekeeper can let you into the garage. Her name's Wendy. I'll call her."

"Thanks so much. I'll be there by six." Ellen prayed Connie could stay late.

"Make it seven, then the kids will have eaten. Look for the U-Haul boxes in the garage. Wendy will show you. You can't miss them." Musko gave Ellen an address, and she thanked him and hung up, then typed it into her BlackBerry.

As if she would forget it.

Chapter Seventeen

"Ellen, come on in!" It was Marcelo, calling from his office as she hustled into the newsroom.

"Sure." She waved to him, masking her dismay as she spotted Sarah sitting inside his office. She slipped off her coat and stuffed it under her arm with her bag and envelope.

"Good morning." Marcelo stood smiling behind his desk, in dark pants and a matte black shirt that fitted close to his body, showing broad shoulders tapering to a trim waist. Either he'd been working out, or Ellen was in lust.

"Hi." Sarah nodded at her, and Ellen took a seat, barely managing a smile.

Marcelo sat down. "Sarah was just telling me she spent the afternoon with the new police commissioner. Great, no?"

Grrrr. "Great."

"He was willing to talk on the record about the homicide rate. Wait until you see her draft, it's terrific." Marcelo turned to Sarah.

"Make sure you copy Ellen. I want you two to keep each other up to speed."

"You got it." Sarah made a note on her pad, but Marcelo was already turning to Ellen.

"How's the story going?" His dark eyes flashed expectantly.

"Nothing significant yet." Ellen had to think fast. "I have a lead but nothing to get excited about."

"Fair enough." Marcelo nodded, and if he was disappointed, it didn't show. "Let me know and copy Sarah whenever you get something drafted."

Sarah asked, "Ellen, did you see those leads I listed on page three? The top one, Julia Guest, said she'd love to talk to us. You might want to start with her."

"Maybe I will." Ellen hid her annoyance, and Marcelo clapped his hands together like a soccer coach.

"Okay, ladies," he said, but his gaze focused on Ellen, and not in a come-hither way. More in a you're-gonna-get-fired way.

"Thanks." She left the office behind Sarah, who slid a sleek Black-Berry from her waist holster and started hitting the buttons. Ellen dumped her stuff on an empty desk on the fly and caught up with Sarah before she started the call. "Hold on, wait a sec."

"What?" Sarah turned, her cell to her ear.

"We need to talk, don't you think?"

"Maybe later," Sarah answered, but Ellen wasn't about to let it go. She snatched the phone from Sarah's hand and pressed the End button, then turned on her heel.

"Meet me in the ladies' room if you want your toy back."

Chapter Eighteen

"Give me back my phone!" Sarah held out her palm, her dark eyes flashing. "What's your problem?"

"What's *my* problem?" Ellen raised her voice, and the sound reverberated off the hard tiles of the ladies' room. "Why are you talking to everyone about me?"

"What do you mean?"

"You told Marcelo I was upset about Courtney, and you told Meredith that I was bad-mouthing Marcelo and Arthur."

"I did no such thing and I want my phone back." Sarah wiggled her hand impatiently, and Ellen slapped the BlackBerry into her palm.

"Meredith told me, and so did Marcelo. *Marcelo*, Sarah. Our *editor*. You can get me fired, talking me down to him."

"Oh please." Sarah scoffed. "Meredith misunderstood. I didn't say you said anything bad about them, specifically."

"I didn't say *anything* about them."

"You called them bastards!" Sarah shot back, leaving Ellen incredulous.

"What? When?"

"In here, before they came for Courtney. You said, 'Don't let the bastards get you down.'"

"Gimme a break, Sarah. It's an expression. My father says it all the time."

"Whatever, you said it." Sarah snorted. "I only told one person in the newsroom."

"One is enough. That's why they call it a newsroom."

"Meredith never talks."

"Everybody talks, these days."

Sarah rolled her eyes. "You're overreacting."

"And what about Marcelo? You told him, too. You said I wasn't a fan of his."

"He asked me how was morale in the newsroom after Courtney got fired. I told him it was bad and that you felt the same way. That's all." Sarah put her hands on her hips. "Are you telling me you didn't feel that way? That you're happy Courtney got fired?"

"Of course not."

"Then what are you whining about?"

"Don't talk to the boss about me, got it?"

Sarah waved her off. "Whatever I said, it's not gonna hurt you. Marcelo wants you around, and you know why."

Ellen reddened, angry. "You know, that's insulting."

"Whatever. We need to talk about the think piece." Sarah straightened up at the sink. "Do us both a favor and use my lead. Call Julia Guest. My job's riding on this, and I'm not about to let you screw me up."

"Don't worry about it. I'll do my part, you do yours."

"You'd better." Sarah brushed past her for the door, and Ellen heard her mutter under her breath.

Ironically, they were saying the exact same thing:

Bitch.

Chapter Nineteen

Ellen worked on the homicide piece through lunch, reading Sarah's notes and doing her own research before she made any contacts, but she found it almost impossible to concentrate, distracted by thoughts of Karen Batz. Tonight she'd find the file on Will's adoption, and it had to help fill in some of the blanks. She'd already called Connie, who'd agreed to stay late.

Her gaze returned to the notes on her desk, and she told herself to focus on the task at hand. She had to look busy, too, aware that Marcelo was in his office, holding meetings. She glanced up, and at the exact same moment, Marcelo was looking at her through the glass.

Ellen smiled, flushing, and Marcelo broke their eye contact, returning to his meeting, gesturing with his hands, his shirtsleeves folded carelessly over his forearms. She put her head down and tried to focus. She had only a few hours of daylight left.

She picked up the phone.

Chapter Twenty

Night came early to this neighborhood, the sun fleeing the sky, leaving heaven black and blue, and Ellen circled the block, scribbling notes as she drove. Trash blew in the gutters, swept along by unseen currents, stopping when it flattened against older cars. Sooty brick rowhouses lined broken sidewalks; some houses had graffitied plywood where windows used to be, and others had only black holes, unsightly as missing teeth. Porch roofs sagged, peeling shutters hung crooked, and every home had bars covering its doors. One house had encased its entrance in bars, curved inward at the top like a lion's cage.

A boy had been shot to death on this block of Eisner Street, only two weeks ago. Lateef Williams, age eight.

Ellen turned right onto Eisner, where only one streetlight worked, and it threw a halo over a pile of trash, rubble, and car tires dumped on the corner. She stopped at number 5252, Lateef's house, and his memorial out front was bathed in darkness, the shadows hiding a purple bunny rabbit that sat lopsided against Spider-Man figurines, crayoned drawings, a king-size box of Skittles, sympathy cards, and a mound of spray-painted daisies and sweetheart roses, still in plastic wrap. A sign handwritten in Magic Marker read WE LOVE YOU, TEEF, and a few candles sat around it, unlit in the cold and wind. Lateef Williams was denied the smallest measure of warmth and light, even in death.

Ellen felt a wrench in her chest. She didn't know how many children had been killed in the city last year, but she could never get used to the idea. She never wanted to get to the point at which a child's murder was old news. She fed the car some gas and pulled into a parking space, then gathered her things to meet Lateef's mother.

Laticia Williams was twenty-six, with a slim, pretty face, narrow brown eyes, high cheekbones, and a prominent mouth, devoid of lipstick. Long earrings with wooden beads dangled from her earlobes, showing just under chin-length hair colored reddish. With her jeans, she wore an oversized black T-shirt that bore her son's photo and the caption, R.I.P. LATEEF.

"I appreciate you coming," Laticia said, setting a mug of coffee in front of Ellen as they sat at her round table. The kitchen was small and neat, the cabinets refaced with dark wood and the Formica counters covered with Pyrex oblongs of cakes, cookie tins, and two pies covered with tinfoil, which Laticia had said were "too ugly" to serve.

"Not at all, I appreciate your talking to me at a time like this," Ellen said, having already expressed her condolences. "The only thing I hate about my job is barging into people's houses at the worst time of their lives. Again, I'm so sorry for your loss."

"Thank you." Laticia sat down with a weary smile, showing the gold rim of her front tooth. "I want it to be in the paper, so everybody know what's happenin'. So they know kids are gettin' killed every day. So it's not just a number, like Powerball."

"That's the point. That's what I'm here to do. Make them see it and understand what it's like to lose Lateef this way."

"I cried all I can cry, we all have. But you know what they don't understand? What they're never gonna understand?"

"Tell me."

"That with me, and with Dianne down the block, who lost her child, it's different. We're mad, too. Mad as all hell. Sick to *death* of all this *dyin'*." Laticia's voice rose and fell, with a cadence almost like a prayer. "All the mothers are *sick* our kids are bein' shot at, like it's a damn shootin' gallery, and it makes no never mind. Ain't nothin' gonna change here, and this is *America*."

Ellen absorbed her words, and her emotion. She wondered if she could convey all that feeling in the piece.

"It's like *Katrina,* we're livin' in a different country. We got two sets of rules, two sets of laws, two things you can get outta life, whether you're white or black, rich or poor. That's the thing in a nutshell." Laticia pointed a stiff index finger at Ellen. "You live in America, but I don't. You live in Philadelphia, but I don't."

Ellen didn't know how to respond, so she didn't.

"Where I live, my kid can get shot on the street, and nobody sees nothin'. You wanna blame them, tell people to snitch, I know, but you can't blame people. I *can't* and I *don't*. If they snitch, they're *dead*. Their family's *dead*. Their kids are *dead*."

Ellen didn't want to interrupt Laticia with a question. Nothing could be as valuable as what she was saying and she deserved at least that much.

"So I could sit here and tell you all about Teef and how cute he was, 'cause he was." Laticia smiled briefly, light returning to her angry eyes, softening them for just an instant. "He was a funny child, a *goofball*. He cracked us *up*. At the last reunion, he was freestylin', he tore it *up*. I miss him every minute."

Ellen thought of Susan Sulaman, talking about her son. And Carol Braverman, praying for a miracle on her website.

"But even though Teef was mine, what matters is he isn't the only one killed here." Laticia put her hand to her chest, resting on the painted photo of her son's face. "Three other kids were killed in this neighborhood, all of them shot to death. Lemme aks you, that happen where you live?"

"No."

"And that jus' this year. You figure in the year before that and the one before that, we got eight kids killed. You can make a big pile outta those bodies."

Ellen tried to make sense of the number. Everybody counted bodies, to quantify the cost. But whether it cost nine kids or twelve, it was no worse than one. One child was enough. One body was one too many. One was the only number.

"We don't have kids walkin' around here, we got *ghosts*. This neighborhood's full a ghosts. Pretty soon they'll be nobody left to kill. Philly's gonna be a ghost town, like in the wild wild west. A *ghost* town."

Ellen heard the bitterness in her words, and she realized that Laticia Williams and Susan Sulaman, two very different women from two very different cities in the same city, had that much in common. Both of them were haunted, and they always would be. She wondered if Carol Braverman felt the same way, and it nagged at her. She thought of the files, waiting for her in the garage. Answers would be inside.

"You got a child?" Laticia asked, abruptly.

"Yes," Ellen answered. "A boy."

"That's good." Laticia smiled, the gold winking again. "You hold that baby close, you hear? Hold him close. You never know when you gonna lose him."

Ellen nodded, because for a minute, she couldn't speak.

Chapter Twenty-one

Ellen surveyed the garage, her breath chalky in the cold. Kids' bicycles stood propped up in front of metal shelves that held Nerf footballs, a black plastic mountain of Rollerblades and kneepads, and a spare jug of sea-blue antifreeze. There were greasy jars of Turtle Wax and Bug-B-Gone, and an exercise bicycle had been relegated to a corner, wedged behind a workbench. Fluorescent panels overhead cast light on the left well of the garage, where Rick Musko must park, because there were a few grease spots on the concrete floor. In the other well, where Karen Batz's car would have been, sat cardboard boxes piled like a Rubik's Cube. An old green tennis ball hung uselessly from the ceiling, resting on the top of the boxes, its string slack.

Dead files.

Ellen fastened her down coat, went over to the boxes, and started moving them aside. They were piled alphabetically, and she searched for the G's. Ten minutes later, boxes lay all around the garage floor, and she wasn't cold anymore. She wedged off the lid of a box labeled Ga–Go and looked inside. It held manila folders packed tight, and she took out a batch at the front, allowing them to move freely. Each file had a white label with the client's name, last name first. Ellen started at the beginning, and predictably, most of them were couples: Galletta, Bill and Kalpanna; Gardner, David, and Melissa McKane; Gentry, Robert and Xinwei; and Gibbs, Michael, and Penny Carbone. Her heart was pounding by the time she got to Gilbert, Dylan and Angela, but the next file wasn't Gleeson, Ellen. It was Goel, John, and Lucy Redd.

She thumbed past Gold, Howard and Mojdeh; and Gold, Steven and Calina, and even onto Goldberger, Darja. No Gleeson. Not even misfiled. She skipped ahead to Golden, Golen, Gorman, then to Grant and Green. Still no Gleeson. Puzzled, she looked up at the pile of boxes, then eyed the ones she'd left lying around the floor. There had been other G boxes, and Gleeson could be misfiled anywhere. She took a deep breath and got busy. She was finished two hours later, but still hadn't found her file.

What gives?

She was putting the Rubik's Cube back together when she heard the loud rumbling of a car engine, and the garage door slid up noisily, leaving her in the blinding glare of the high beams from an SUV. The driver stepped out, walked toward her, and introduced himself as Rick Musko.

"You're still here?" he asked, stepping into the fluorescent lights. He was tall and bald, in his fifties, older than Karen.

"Sorry, but I can't find my file. I'm almost finished putting all the boxes back."

"Wait a minute." Musko blinked. "I know you. Aren't you the reporter who did the story on the baby you adopted?"

"Yes, right." Ellen introduced herself again.

"Your name didn't register, when we spoke. I was in the middle of something." Musko extended his hand, and they shook. "I was pretty rude to you, I wish I had known who you were. That story you wrote made Karen so happy."

"She was a great lawyer. I'm so sorry about your loss."

"Thank you."

"Do you know where my file could be?" Ellen picked up a box and heaved it on top of another. "Could it be with the lawyer who bought her practice? I figured I'd call him tomorrow morning."

"No, he won't have it." Musko picked up a box. "He went through all of Karen's files with a fine-tooth comb and took only her active files, mostly divorces and custody fights. Said he didn't have the space for the dead files. That, I believe." Musko straightened the tower of boxes and gave them a pat. "These have been sitting here all this time. I'm too cheap to put them in a storage space. I wonder where yours could be."

"No idea?" Ellen shelved another box, pressing the lid on tight. "It seems strange that it's missing."

"It should have been here." Musko's tone turned thoughtful as he reached for another box. "I have some of Karen's personal papers inside, from her desk drawers. Maybe your file is in there."

"Why would it be?"

"Because of the article?" Musko grabbed the last box. "She bought thirty copies."

Ellen felt touched. It was a secret pleasure of being a reporter. You never knew where your words landed.

"Maybe she saved the file. I haven't even looked in those boxes yet."

Ellen felt a twinge of guilt. "I hate to put you to this, if it's difficult."

"No, let's get it done. I'll set you up in my study. You can look through them there."

"That would be great," Ellen said, her hope surging. She grabbed her coat, and Musko parked the car.

Then they turned out the lights and went into the house together.

Chapter Twenty-two

Musko left Ellen in a home office that put hers to shame. His desk was a lustrous walnut, and he had a maroon leather chair with brass bolts around the edges. Built-in bookcases ringed the room, holding technical manuals and bound newsletters about structural engineering. The walls were lined with golf scenes and framed photographs of three towheaded boys. There were no photos of Karen.

Ellen turned her attention to the three boxes on the desk. She'd been running out of steam but the sight revitalized her, and she took off the first lid, which read Top Drawer. She felt nosy to be going through Karen's desk, but she wasn't about to hesitate. She started digging, and inside were a slew of Bic pens, pencils, Post-it pads, a ruler, loose change, a pink leather Filofax, and a stray lipstick. She found a few legal pads with notes and recognized the neat handwriting, with its detached capitals, as Karen's. She flashed on the lawyer, who had joked that her penmanship was so parochial school.

Odd.

Ellen was a lapsed Catholic, but even she knew that suicide was one of the bigger no-no's. She wondered fleetingly what would have driven Karen to such an act, and she dug further in the first box. She reached the bottom, but there were no files inside. She closed the lid and moved to the second box, whose lid read Second Drawer. She dug through more legal pads, then checkbooks, piles of bills from Comcast, PECO, a web hosting site, old Filofax sheets with rubber bands, and dues invoices for various bar associations. Still no client files, and Ellen started to worry. She closed the lid and moved to the last box, which reminded her of a joke her father used to tell:

Why is the thing you're looking for always in the last place you look? Because after you find it, you stop looking.

She opened the box and looked inside. It was a hodgepodge of bills, stray invoices, reminders for continuing legal-education courses, and more legal pads. She started rummaging, then all of a sudden, spotted a letter from Karen to her, notifying her about Will's adoption hearing.

Bingo!

She felt her heart start to pound and kept searching, shuffling papers aside until she came across a printed email from her to Karen, asking questions about adoption procedures. She rummaged further, spotted some newsprint, and pulled it out excitedly. It was the front page of the Features section, and on the bottom right was Ellen's piece on Will's adoption. The headline read, HAPPY ENDING, and on the right was the photo of Will, looking so sick. She dug back into the box, and at the very bottom lay a manila folder. She grabbed it and read the label.

Gleeson, Ellen.

"Yay!" She tore it open, but it was empty, which is when she realized that the contents of her file folder were mixed up with the other papers.

"Did you get lucky?" asked a voice from the door, and she looked up to see Musko in the threshold. His jacket was off, his tie gone, and he'd pushed up his shirtsleeves. He entered the study and sat down tiredly in the leather chair across from his desk.

"Sort of." Ellen held up the empty folder. "This is my file, but the papers are scattered all over the box."

"That's Karen. She wasn't the most organized person in the world. In fact, she was messy."

Don't speak ill. "The files in the garage were neat."

"That was her secretary's doing. They were made for each other." Musko leaned over and plucked Ellen's article from her hand, eyeing it. "You know, it wasn't too long after this article appeared that she was dead."

"When was it that she died, if I can ask?"

"July 13." Musko's smile vanished, and his crow's-feet deepened. He handed the article back. "Her secretary found her at her desk when she came in that morning."

"That was about a month after Will's adoption was final, on June 15. The article ran about two weeks after that." Ellen paused, puzzled. "I'm surprised I didn't hear. I paid my final bill, and the office didn't send me a letter that she was dead. I didn't even see an obit."

"I didn't run one. I kept it quiet, for the kids' sake. The funeral was just family. The neighbors know from the gossip mill, but I never told them." Musko gestured down the hall. "I still haven't told the boys how she really died, just that she got sick."

"Didn't they ask questions?" Ellen asked, surprised. She was thinking of Will, the question machine.

"Yes, but I just said she was sick and we didn't know it, then she died."

Ellen kept her own counsel. She'd made it a policy always to be honest with Will. She even felt bad lying to him about Santa Claus, but no child should have to live in a world without magic.

"I know, it was probably wrong, but what do you say—hey, guys, Mommy went to work today and put a gun in her mouth?"

Suddenly Ellen wished she could leave. The conversation was turning creepy, and she'd liked Musko better in the garage.

"Didn't mean to spring that on you." He laughed, but it sounded bitter. " 'How did she do it?' That's the thing everybody wants to know. Gas, gun, pills? The cops told me it was unusual for a woman to use a gun. I told them, 'But this woman is a lawyer.' "

Ellen stiffened. "I'm sure it's hard to deal with."

"You're damn right it is. They say suicide is selfish, and for once, they're right." Musko jerked a thumb behind him. "I got three kids who pray for her every night. What kind of mother abandons her kids like that? They were babies then. Rory was *two*."

"We can never really understand why people do the things they do." Ellen was trying to say something comforting but knew she sounded like a Hallmark card, or Yoda.

"Oh, I *know* why she did it. She did it because I caught her having an affair."

"Really?" Ellen said, shocked.

"He called her at the house one night, and I picked up. Then she went out and didn't get back until after midnight. She said she was at the gym, but it was the same night they had an electrical fire." Musko snorted. "She was getting her workout from her boyfriend."

Ellen didn't like the cruel twist to Musko's lips. She rose to go, but it didn't stop him from continuing.

"I confronted her, and she admitted it. She had to, I knew there was something going on. She'd been acting funny, moody. Anyway, she said she would stop seeing him, but I told her I wanted a divorce, that I'd fight her over the kids, too." Musko stopped abruptly, as if he'd just heard himself. "The next morning was, you know, when she did it." He leaned over, resting his head on his elbow, and began rubbing his eyes. "I quit therapy, but I better get back in, huh?"

"I'm sure it would help."

"So they say." Musko looked at her, then rose slowly. "You found the papers you needed?"

"Well, they're in the box somewhere but I didn't get a chance to go through and see which papers are mine."

"Then take the whole box. Take all three, for all I care. Take them with you."

"What if there's things in there you want?"

Musko waved her off. "I don't need anything in those boxes. I should get rid of the ones in the garage, too. I should just burn the damn things."

Ellen realized then why the dead files were still in the garage. It wasn't that he didn't want to spend the money on a storage space. It was that he wanted to keep them and he wanted to burn them, both at once.

"Thanks," she said. "I'll send you back what's not mine." She put a lid on the third box, shutting its secrets inside.

At least until she got home.

Chapter Twenty-three

The night was starless and black, and the windows dark mirrors that reflected Ellen at her dining-room table, sifting through the contents of the third box, sitting next to a glass of emergency merlot. Oreo Figaro sat in his spot at the far end of the table, watching with a disapproving eye.

She set aside bills and legal pads, then pulled out the papers that should have been in her file and read each one as she put them in chronological order, oldest to most recent, re-creating Will's adoption file. There was printed email correspondence to Karen and from the home-study people, who had come to see the house and interview Ellen before the adoption was finalized. She went back to the box, shoved aside pencils and a half pack of gum, and unearthed another typed letter to Karen, this one printed in a larger font, on thin paper. She read it with a start:

Amy Martin
393 Corinth Lane
Stoatesville, PA

Dear Karen,

Here are the papers you asked me to get signed. They are from the baby's father and he says he will give up his rights to the baby. Please make sure the woman who wants to adopt him takes good care of him. He's a good baby, and it's not his fault he's fussy and sick. I love him but I know this is what is the best thing for him and I will remember him always and keep him in my prayers.

Sincerely,
Amy

Ellen's heart thundered in her chest, and she read the letter again, feeling a tingle just holding it in her hands. It was from Will's birth mother, who had held this paper, had written this note, and had printed it out. So her name was Amy Martin. She sounded so sweet, and her pain in putting Will up for adoption came through even her simple lines. It was all Ellen could do not to pick up the phone and call her, but instead, she reached for her wine and raised her glass in a silent toast.

Thank you, Amy, for the gift of your child.

Oreo Figaro looked over, blinking, and she set down the wine, returned to the box, and kept digging, finally reaching more court papers, with her caption at the top. **Consent of Birth Parent**, read the heading, and the form showed Amy's name and the Stoatesville address, and her birth date, which was July 7, 1983, and marital status, which read **single**. The paper was signed by Amy Martin under the sentence, **I hereby voluntarily and unconditionally consent to the adoption of the above-named child.** The paper had also been witnessed by Gerry Martin and Cheryl Martin, from the same address.

Ellen skipped to the next form, which was the consent of the birth father, and she learned his name and address with her heart in her throat:

Charles Cartmell
71 Grant Ave
Philadelphia, Pennsylvania

She eyed his signature, a messy scrawl with barely comprehensible loops. So Charles Cartmell had been Will's father, and she couldn't help but wonder what he had been like. What he looked like. What he did for a living. How did he and Amy meet, and why did they never marry?

She returned to digging in the box but found nothing else relating to Will except his medical information sheet, which she already had in her file, stating that both birth parents had a history of high blood pressure. There was no mention of any heart problems, which was consistent with what she'd been told by the hospital, that Will's heart defect could have originated with him. The state had a voluntary medical registry online, but Will's birth parents had never registered. Still, the consent papers were a tangible answer to a question Ellen hadn't been able to articulate, even to herself.

"Well, that settles that," Ellen said aloud, startling Oreo Figaro. Her gaze fell on the papers on the table, and her thoughts strayed to poor Karen. She remembered that Karen had called to congratulate her on the day Will's adoption papers were processed. It was so hard to believe that she would be dead a little over a month later, by her own hand. Ellen shuddered and took a sip of wine. It was so awful to think of Karen doing that, with three little kids at home. Musko had been right about that much.

Where was a mother's instinct then?

She couldn't think about it now. It was late and she had to get to bed. She'd done enough for one day, except on her homicide story. She'd normally have drafted something after her interview with Laticia Williams, but tonight she was too beat. She set the wineglass down next to the box, but a bright pink splotch amid the clutter caught her eye. She moved the papers aside. It was the hot pink of Karen's leather Filofax.

She picked it out and opened it, idly. It was a standard date book, a week on two opposing pages, and each page bore Karen's neat script, noting her appointments and meetings by client name. Ellen felt a pang, looking at the record of a woman's life, her time on earth divided into billable increments. What the diary couldn't show was that, in those increments, this woman had changed lives.

She flipped back in time through the Filofax, slowing when she reached the week of July 13, the day on which Karen had committed suicide. That week began on Monday, July 10, and the Filofax showed a neat lineup of appointments. The eleventh showed Karen had a client meeting in the morning and a Women's Way luncheon.

Ellen scanned the rest of the week, including the day Karen died. The lawyer had had appointments scheduled all day long, which made sense. Karen couldn't have known that the night before, her husband would find out about her affair. Ellen was about to close the book when she noticed that one of the appointments, on Wednesday, didn't have a name, but only an initial:

A, written next to the time: 7:15 P.M.

Ellen was intrigued. A nighttime meeting? Maybe A was Karen's lover? She skipped back to the week before that, but there was no A, and then the week before that. There, in the middle of the week, on Wednesday, June 28.

A, also at 7:15.

She flipped pages to the week before, and then the week before that, which brought her to Wednesday, June 14.

A, this time at 9:30 P.M.

She mulled it over. That was the day before Will's adoption was final, on June 15. She flipped back to earlier weeks, checking each one, but there were no other meetings with A. She sat back, thinking, and her gaze shifted to the letter on the table, from Amy Martin. The date on the letter was June 15.

Ellen thought a minute. There had been a meeting with A, and then the next day, a letter from Amy Martin. She put two and two together. "A" wasn't Karen's boyfriend. "A" could stand for Amy.

She sank into a chair at the table, her good mood evaporating. She looked again at the letter. It even said "in our meeting." So Karen had had a meeting with Amy. But Ellen didn't remember seeing Amy's name in the Filofax, anywhere. She paged through it again, around June, and double-checked. There was no notation of a meeting with Amy Martin or Charles Cartmell, though all the other client meetings had been noted.

Ellen set down the Filofax and reached for her wine. She took a sip, but it tasted warm and bitter. She knew what she had to do, first thing tomorrow morning. Finish this thing once and for all. Put an end to her dwelling. She was driving herself nuts.

"Why can't I leave well enough alone?" she asked, aloud.

But Oreo Figaro merely blinked in response.

Chapter Twenty-four

The next morning as Ellen put on her coat, she was already wondering how soon she could call Amy Martin. Will's fever had broken, and he was running around the living room with a new Penn State football that Connie had just brought for him. Ellen withheld the lecture on not introducing new toys before school. Working mothers had no time for spontaneity unless it was scheduled.

"He knows just what to do!" Connie said, delighted. "My Mark was like that, too."

"Look at me!" Will circled the coffee table with the blue football tucked under his arm. "Look, Mommy!"

"Watch where you're going, buddy," Ellen called back, and Oreo Figaro jumped out of the way as Will hurtled past him, turned left into the dining room, and ran into the kitchen. He ran through the kitchen, up and over the stairway, and ended up back in the living room, a circular floor plan designed for little boys and NASCAR drivers.

Connie said, "You know, he looks like a natural athlete."

"You think?" Ellen picked up her purse and briefcase, listening to the pounding of Will's feet through the kitchen. Whoever coined the expression pitter-patter-of-little-feet had a kitten, not a child.

"I should get Mark over here to throw the ball with him sometime."

Will came running back into the living room and looked up grinning, his cheeks flushed. "I did it! I made a yesdown!"

"You mean a touchdown?" Connie corrected him, and Ellen laughed and held out her arms.

"Gimme a hug. I gotta go to work and you gotta go to school."

"Mommy!" Will ran to her, and Ellen hugged and kissed him, brushing his bangs from his eyes.

"Love you. Have fun at school."

"Can I bring my football?" Will's eyes widened with hope.

"No," Ellen answered.

"Yes," Connie said, at the same minute.

"I WANT TO!" Will hollered, jiggered up.

"Hey, quiet down, pal." Ellen held his arm, trying to settle him. "No shouting in the house."

"I want to bring my ball, Mommy!"

"Fine, okay." Ellen didn't want to leave on a bad note, another axiom of Working Mother Guilt.

"Goody!" Will rewarded her with another hug, dropping the football and throwing his arms around her neck.

Ellen felt a twinge of separation anxiety, worse than usual.

Maybe because she knew what she was about to do, after she left.

Chapter Twenty-five

Ellen eyed the cars stacked ahead, their red taillights a glowing line, their exhaust trailing white plumes. The day was overcast and cold, and freezing rain had left an icy sleeve on the tree branches and a black veneer on the roads. The traffic stayed bad on the two-lane roads to Stoatesville, and in time, she found Corinth Street among the warren of rowhouses in a working-class neighborhood around an abandoned steel mill. She traveled down the street, reading the house numbers. Suddenly her cell phone started ringing in her purse, and she fumbled for it. The display showed a number she didn't recognize, and she hit Ignore when she realized that the house coming up was number 393.

Amy Martin's house.

A woman was standing in its driveway, scraping ice off the windshield of an old black Cherokee. Her back was turned, and she wore an Eagles knit cap, a thick black parka, jeans, and black rubber boots.

Amy?

Ellen pulled up in front of the house, grabbed her bag and file, got out, walked up the driveway. "Excuse me, Ms. Martin?" she asked, her heart thumping like crazy.

She turned, startled, and Ellen saw instantly that the woman was too old to be Amy Martin. She looked to be in her late sixties, and her hooded eyes widened under the Eagles hat. She said, "Jeez, you scared me!"

"Sorry." Ellen introduced herself. "I'm looking for Amy Martin."

"Amy's my daughter, and she don't live here anymore. I'm Gerry."

Ellen tried to keep her bearings. Gerry Martin had been one of the witnesses on the consent form. She was looking into the eyes of Will's grandmother, the first blood relative of his she had ever seen. "She gave this address as hers, two years ago."

"She always does, but she don't live here. I get all her mail, all those damn bills, I throw 'em all away."

"Where does Amy live?"

"Hell if I know." Gerry returned to scraping the windshield, shaving fragile curls of ice, making a *krrp krrp* sound. She pursed her lips with the effort, sending deep wrinkles radiating from her mouth. Her black glove was oversized, dwarfing the red plastic scraper.

"You don't know where she is?"

"No. *Krrp krrp.* "Amy's over eighteen. It ain't my business no more."

"How about where she works?"

"Who said she works?"

"I'm just trying to find her."

"I can't help you."

For some reason, Ellen hadn't imagined there'd be an estrangement. "When was the last time you saw her?"

"A while."

"A year or two?"

"Try five."

Ellen knew it couldn't be true. Gerry had signed the consent form two years ago. Why was she lying? "Are you sure?"

Gerry looked over, eyes narrowed under the fuzzy hat, scraper stalled on the windshield. "She owes you money, right? You're a bill collector or a lawyer or somethin'?"

"No." Ellen paused. If she wanted the truth, she'd have to tell the truth. "Actually, I'm the woman who adopted her baby."

Gerry burst into laughter, showing yellowed teeth and bracing herself against the Jeep, scraper in hand.

"Why is that funny?" Ellen asked, and after Gerry stopped laughing, she wiped her eyes with the back of her big glove.

"You better come in, honey."

"Why?"

"We got some talkin' to do," Gerry answered, placing her gloved hand on Ellen's shoulder.

Chapter Twenty-six

Gerry went into the kitchen to make coffee, leaving Ellen in the living room, which was barely illuminated by two retro floor lamps, their low-wattage bulbs in ball-shaped fixtures on a stalk. Beige curtains covered the windows, and the air was thick with stale cigarette smoke. Flowered metal trays served as end tables flanking a worn couch of blue velveteen, and three mismatched chairs clustered around a large-screen TV.

Ellen crossed the room, drawn to photographs that ran the length of the wall. There were oversized school pictures of boys and girls in front of screensaver blue skies, photo montages cut to fit the various circles and squares, and a wedding photo of a young man and a woman in an elaborate bridal headdress. She shook her head in wonderment. They were Will's blood, but complete strangers, and she was his mother, known and loved by him, but having none of his blood. She went from one photo to the next, trying to put together the puzzle that was her son.

Which girl is Amy?

The photos showed girls and boys at all different ages, and Ellen tried to follow each child as he or she grew up, picking blue eyes from brown and matching young smiles to older smiles, age-progressing all of them in her mind's eye, searching for Amy. One of the girls had blondish hair and blue eyes, plus Will's fair skin, with just the hint of freckles dotting a small, pert nose.

"Here we go." Gerry came into the room with a skinny brown cigarette and two heavy glass mugs of murky coffee, one of which she handed to Ellen.

"Thanks."

"Siddown, will ya?" Gerry gestured at the couch, her cigarette trailing an acrid snake of smoke, but Ellen stayed with the photos.

"Can I ask, is this one Amy, with the blue eyes and freckles?"

"No, that's Cheryl, her sister. The girl with her is my oldest. I had three girls, one boy."

Ellen remembered the name Cheryl Martin as the other signature on the consent form.

"This one's Amy, the baby of the family in more ways than one." Gerry tapped a smaller photo in the corner, and Ellen walked over, feeling a frisson of discovery.

"So this is Amy, huh?" She leaned close to the photo of a young girl, maybe thirteen years old, leaning on a red Firebird. Her dark blond hair was in cornrows, and her blue eyes were sly. She had a crooked grin that telegraphed too-cool-for-school, and Ellen scrutinized her features. Amy and Will had the same coloring, but their features weren't alike. Still, one picture wasn't a fair sample. "Which of the other photos are Amy?"

"Uh, lemme see." Gerry eyed the photos with a short laugh. "None! I tell you, by the time you get to your fourth, you're a little sick of it, you know what I mean?"

Arg. "I only have the one."

"Oh, after the first, you stop springing for the forty-five-dollar pictures, the refrigerator magnet, the keychain, all that happy horse-shit." Gerry motioned to the couch again. "Come on, sit."

"Thanks." Ellen walked over, sank into the couch, and sipped the coffee, which was surprisingly good. "Wow."

"I put in real cream. That's my secret." Gerry sat down heavily, catty-corner to the couch, pulling an ancient beanbag ashtray onto the chair arm. Her expression looked softer, her hard lines smoothed by the low light. Her hair was a tinted brown with gray roots, the ends frayed, and she wore it tucked behind her ears. Her nose was stubby on a wide face, but she had a motherly smile.

"Why did you laugh outside?" Ellen asked, her fingers tight around her glass mug.

"First, tell me about Amy and this baby." Gerry took a drag on the brown cigarette.

"He was sick, in the hospital. I did a story on it, a series." Ellen reached into her purse, pulled out the clipping from her file, and showed it to Gerry, who barely glanced at it, so she put it back. "You may have seen them in the paper."

"We don't get the paper."

"Okay. Will, the baby I adopted, was in cardiac intensive care when I met him. He had a heart defect."

"And you think he was Amy's baby?"

"I know so."

"How?" Gerry sucked on her cigarette, then blew out a cone of smoke from the side of her mouth, meaning to be polite. "I mean, where'd you get your information?"

"From a lawyer, who died. My lawyer, mine and Amy's. It was a private adoption, and she brokered the deal between us."

"Amy brokered it?"

"No, the lawyer did. Karen Batz."

"It's a lady lawyer?"

"Yes. Does the name mean anything to you?"

Gerry shook her head. "You *sure* it's Amy? My Amy?"

"Yes." Ellen set the coffee down on the metal tray, reached into her envelope, and rifled through the papers. She found Amy's consent to the adoption and the letter with the Corinth Avenue return address and handed them to Gerry, who took them and didn't say anything for a minute, reading to herself and dragging on her cigarette. The smoke hit the court papers and billowed back on itself, like a wave crashing against a seawall.

"This is nuts," Gerry said, half to herself, and Ellen's chest tightened.

"Is that Amy's signature, on the consent?"

"It looks like it."

"How about on the letter?"

"There, too."

"Good. Now we're getting somewhere. So it's your Amy." Ellen reached over and turned the page to the consent form, pointing. "Is that your signature?"

"No way. I never signed this." Gerry's lips flattened to a grim line, again bringing out the wrinkles around her mouth. "And this other signature, it's not Cheryl's, either."

Ellen's heart sank. "Maybe Amy forged the signatures. Maybe she wanted to put her baby up for adoption and didn't want her family to know."

"That can't be it."

"Why not?" Ellen asked, and Gerry shook her head, the papers reflecting white on her face.

"Amy couldn't have kids."

Ellen's mouth went dry.

"She had an operation, when she was seventeen. She had a problem with her ovaries. What was it called?" Gerry paused a minute. "One day she woke up in cramps real bad, so I knew she wasn't fakin' to get outta school. We took her to the emergency and they said she had a twisted ovary, it was called. The ovary got all full of blood, and they had to take it out right away. They said she had almost no chance of getting pregnant."

Ellen tried to process it. "But not no chance. She still had one ovary left, right?"

"Yeah, but they said it was very—what did they say—*unlikely* she could have kids."

"But she had a child."

"I think if you take out an ovary, it affects the hormones, at least that's what they said, something like that, is all I remember." Gerry looked confused. "Whatever, if she had a kid, it's news to me."

"She didn't tell you?"

"No, like I said, we haven't talked. She didn't tell me nothin' anyway. I don't even know where she is. I was tellin' you the truth, outside."

Ellen couldn't accept that it was a dead end. "What about any of her sisters, or her brother? You never heard from any of them about her having a baby?"

"I don't think she talks to anybody but Cheryl, and she lives down in Delaware. I can call her and ask. I will, later." Gerry snorted, her nostrils emitting puffs of smoke. "Nice to know if I had another grandchild."

Ellen tried another tack. "Or maybe when the baby got really sick, that's the kind of thing you might tell someone."

"If Amy had a baby that got really sick, she couldn't handle it. She'd be lookin' for an easy out."

Ellen cringed at the harsh words. "That's the sort of thing that would overwhelm anyone, especially a young girl."

"It didn't take much to *overwhelm* Amy. If I asked her to take out the trash, that *overwhelmed* her."

Ellen let it go. She needed more information. "Can you just tell me a little more about her? What is she like?"

"She was always my wild child. I never could get a handle on that girl."

Ellen found it hard to hear. She had imagined Amy so differently. She wondered if all adoptive mothers had fantasy birth mothers.

"Smart girl, but got lousy grades. Didn't give a shit. I always thought she had, like, ADD, but the teachers said no." Gerry took another puff. "She did her share of drinkin' and drugs. I had no control with her. She was outta here after graduation."

"She ran away?"

"Not like that, just left."

"No college?"

"No way." Gerry smiled crookedly, and Ellen caught a trace of Amy's wisecracking grin.

"Why did she go, may I ask?"

"Didn't like my boyfriend, Tom. They used to get into it all the time. Now she's gone and so's he." Gerry emitted another puff. "I made her stay and graduate high school, but after that, she went off on her own."

"Hold on a sec." Ellen rifled through the papers and handed Gerry the father's consent form. "Look at this. My son's birth father is Charles Cartmell, from Philly. Do you know him?"

"No."

"The name isn't familiar at all? He lives on Grant Avenue in the Northeast." Ellen had checked online last night but couldn't get a phone number or find a listing of the address.

"I don't know the name."

"If Amy is twenty-five now and gave birth to Will three years ago, it means she had him when she was twenty-two. So maybe the father was someone from high school, or the area?"

"She didn't go steady in high school." Gerry shook her head. "She saw a lot of different guys. I didn't ask no questions, believe me."

"Do you have her high school yearbook? Maybe we could look at it?"

"She didn't buy the yearbook. She wasn't the type." Gerry waved her off. "She was my baby, and I spoiled her, yes I did."

"Could I see her bedroom? There might be something in there that would help me."

"I cleared it out a long time ago. I use it for my son's girlfriend now."

Ellen began thinking out loud. "She must have stayed in the Philadelphia area, because she chose a lawyer in Ardmore. She even had meetings with the lawyer."

Gerry shrugged. "Cheryl might know."

"Can I have her number?"

Gerry hesitated. "Why exactly are you tryin' to find Amy?"

"It's a medical thing, about the baby," Ellen lied, having prepared for the question.

"Does she have to give it a kidney or something?"

"No, not at all. At most it's a blood test. His heart is acting up again, and I need to know more about her medical history."

"She didn't have no heart problems. None of us have heart problems. We got cancer, runs in the family."

"I'm sure, but the blood test will show more than that." Ellen was freewheeling. "If you'd prefer it, maybe you could give Cheryl my number and ask her to call me?"

"Okay, I'll do that." Gerry reached out and patted her hand. "Don't worry. I'm sure the baby will be okay."

"I don't want to lose him," Ellen added, unaccountably.

Chapter Twenty-seven

Ellen got into the cold car, turned the heat up, and took off down the street under a cloudy sky. Her BlackBerry started ringing as soon as she left the block, and she steered the car with one hand and dug in her purse with the other, finding the device by its smooth feel. She pulled it out, and the screen showed the same unknown number as before, so she answered the call.

"Ellen, where are you?" It was Sarah Liu, sounding panicky. "I've been calling you. You missed the projects meeting. Marcelo asked about the think piece."

"Damn." The Thursday projects meeting. She'd completely forgotten about it, preoccupied with finding Amy.

"Where are you?"

"I wasn't feeling well this morning." Ellen was fast becoming an accomplished liar. "Was Marcelo pissed?"

"What do you think? When are you coming in?"

"I'm not sure, why?" Ellen checked the dashboard clock—10:37.

"We should meet about the think piece. I want to see your draft."

Ellen tensed. The week had flown. She hadn't even transcribed her notes from Laticia Williams. "We don't need to meet and my draft isn't ready—"

"When will it be? Our deadline's tomorrow."

"Sarah, we're grown-ups. I don't have time to give you a draft, and I don't need yours. Don't tell Daddy."

"What the hell are you doing? You didn't call Julia Guest, and I greased it for you."

Ellen switched lanes to pass a VW Beetle, fighting annoyance. "Thanks, but I have my own leads. I won't need to talk to her."

"She's connected in the community, and she wants to talk to us."

"People who want to talk are never good leads. I don't need the community spokesperson."

"Why not call her, even for background?"

"I know what I'm doing." Ellen braked, checking the car on the way downhill. "Let me handle my end. You handle yours."

"Have it your way, but make that deadline."

"I will."

"Good-bye." Sarah hung up, and Ellen hit the gas. She had to make the deadline, or she was out of a job. She pressed the button for information, then took the ramp to the expressway.

Heading east under a threatening sky.

Chapter Twenty-eight

Ellen got ahold of Lateef's teacher, Vanessa James, while her class was down the hall at the library. Tall and rail-thin, the teacher munched on a green apple as she moved quickly around the classroom, picking up stray books and crayons, straightening undersized chairs, and restoring a knit hat to its cubbyhole.

Vanessa asked, "It's all right with Laticia if we talk, right?"

"Yes, I called her on the way over. Sorry it's such short notice."

"No problem." Vanessa wore a long red sweater with black slacks and low heels. She had large eyes, a smile slick with lip gloss, and her hair straightened into a stiff bob, which showed off tiny diamond earrings winking in her earlobes. "We have fifteen minutes until they get back. What do you want to know?"

"Just a few things." Ellen slid her notebook from her purse and flipped over the cover, pen at the ready. "What kind of kid was Lateef?"

"Right to it, huh?" Vanessa paused in midbite, the apple at her mouth, her gaze suddenly pained. "Teef was like a light. You could say he was a class clown, but that wouldn't do him justice. He was the one who made everybody laugh. But he was a leader."

"Is there any example you can recall?"

"It hurts my heart to think about it." Vanessa tossed the apple into a scuffed brown wastebasket, where it made a loud *clunk*. "Okay, here's one. On picture day, he combed his hair flat as he could, which wasn't much, and he said he was Donald Trump. The photographer told him to cut it out, and he said, 'You're fired.'" Her pretty face relaxed into a smile, which vanished as quickly as it had appeared. "All the kids looked up to him. We just finished our unit on African-American history. It's part of the new core curriculum in social studies the SRC set up."

"SRC?"

"School Reform Commission. For Dr. King's birthday, Lateef was voted to be Dr. King. He memorized a few lines of 'I Have a Dream,' and he did a great job. He liked to be in front of the class." Vanessa paused at the memory. "He was quick as a whip. We do basic addition and subtraction, but he could have moved on to the third-grade curriculum, fractions and geometry. He was good on sentence structure, too; we have to get them ready for the PSSA's."

"What's that?"

"State tests. On our report cards, I have to pick from a lot of categories, like 'eager to try new things.'" Vanessa chuckled softly. "Lateef was my category buster. He was his own little category."

Ellen made rapid notes. "So how did the class deal with his murder?"

Vanessa shook her head, with a sigh. For a second, she seemed to focus on the large bulletin board on the wall, which was covered with red construction-paper hearts, each with a fold down the center. At the top of the board, gold glitter read, Get Ready For Valentine's Day In 2B!

Ellen waited for the teacher to respond. Experience had taught her that silence could be the hardest question to answer.

"These kids, they're used to death. We lost two kids already this school year, and it's only February." Vanessa kept her face to the bulletin board. "But Lateef, everybody knew him. Everybody *felt* him. The District sent us grief counselors. That child was too full of life not to be missed."

"Do the kids talk about it?"

"Some of them, and some of them cry. They'll never be the same. They're not innocent, like children are supposed to be." Vanessa turned to her, her lips forming a tight line. "What I see is a real deep sadness, and it goes all the way inside. These kids, they're *heartsick*. And those are the lucky ones."

Ellen didn't get it. "What you mean?"

"The unlucky ones, they don't even know what's bothering them. They can't express their feelings. They have an underlying grief and fear, but instead of expressing it in words, they act out. They fight. Bite. Kick. Bully each other. Their world isn't safe, and they know it." Vanessa pointed to one of the desks by the window, in the second row. "That was Teef's seat. It's there, empty, every day. I think about moving it, but that only makes it worse."

Ellen felt a pang. She thought instantly of Will's cubbyhole in his preschool, with his name card and a picture of Thomas the Tank Engine. What if one day that were empty, never to be filled again? "What will you do?"

"I'll leave it there. I have no choice. The first week, we made a little memorial and the kids brought flowers. Here, come look at this." Vanessa crossed to the desk with Ellen following her, and she lifted up the desk lid. Inside the well sat a huge pile of cards and dried red roses, their petals shriveling to black. "These are his Valentine's Day cards. Every day somebody comes by with another one. It kills me."

Ellen looked at the cards, thinking. *It kills all of us.*

"You know who you should talk to, if you really want to understand the effects of the murders in this city?"

"Who?" Ellen asked her, intrigued. The best leads always came from other leads.

"My uncle. He'll see you, if you can handle it."

Chapter Twenty-nine

Ellen was standing in the Glade-scented entrance hall of the funeral home with its proprietor, Ralston Rilkey. He was a slight man with a compact frame, in his early sixties, and he wore his hair cut short and natural, with steel gray coils tangled at the temples. He had a short forehead, and his eyes were worried above a wide nose and neatly groomed mustache, also going gray.

"And what is it you want to know again?" Ralston asked. "I'm fairly busy. We have two viewings tonight."

"I'd like to know how you've been affected by the murders in the neighborhood. There's been so many lately, especially of children like Lateef Williams. Your niece told me you might help, and Laticia gave her permission to talk to me."

"I'll speak with you, but the interview must be respectful. Here at Ralston-Hughes, we practice dignity in death."

"I understand."

"Then follow me." Ralston left, and Ellen followed him across a red-carpeted hallway, through a paneled door that read EMPLOYEES

ONLY, and downstairs into the basement of the converted rowhouse. The carpeting morphed into institutional gray tile, the temperature dipped slightly, and the fake-floral scents were eradicated by a starkly medicinal odor.

"Is that formaldehyde?" Ellen asked, making a note.

Ralston nodded, his bald spot bobbing as he walked ahead, and they reached a set of white double doors, which he opened. The odor grew stronger, and on the wall hung white smocks and plastic face shields. Stainless-steel shelves held boxes of cotton, jars, and bottles with labels that read Kelco Gold Series Arterial Embalming Fluid and Aron Alpha Instant Adhesive. Ellen made notes, trying not to shudder.

Ralston opened another door, and she found herself in a larger room with a glistening white table at its center, tilted at an angle. He stood behind the table in his suit of dark green, gesturing with evident pride. "This is our preparation room, one of them. You'll notice the table is porcelain. Porcelain doesn't react with the embalming chemicals."

"Would you fill me in on the procedure, generally?"

"The first step is washing and disinfecting the body. Embalming is simply the process of displacing blood with fluid, usually of formaldehyde preservative with a red dye, to give the flesh a lifelike appearance. Even African-American skin takes on a pallor once the blood is removed."

Ellen made a note.

"Then we inject the fluid, and this machine does its work, replacing the blood with fluid." Ralston rested his small hand on a yellowish pump at the head of the table. "We insert a trocar, which punctures the viscera and removes fluid. We disinfect the cavities as well, then inject preservative and we pack the orifices."

Ellen wasn't about to ask.

"We wash the body again and apply lotion, to protect against dehydration. After death, the eyes begin to sink into the skull, and we pack cotton into the eye socket, place a plastic eyecap under the eyelid, then pull back the eyelid to apply adhesive and keep the eye closed."

Ellen's stomach turned over.

"Death also causes the facial muscles to relax, and the jaw drops open. We make the eyes and mouth as lifelike as possible. As we say, we set the features."

Ellen tried to remain professional. "Now, how was the procedure in Lateef's case?"

"With Lateef, there were so many gunshot wounds on one side of his face that we had to use his school photo as a guide and build from that foundation."

Ellen tried to visualize it. That little face, smiling from his memorial T-shirt. "Couldn't you use the other side of his face?"

"No. With as many gunshots as he had, there was significant facial swelling, which distorted even the good side of his face. The trauma, you understand. We use chemicals to reduce the swelling."

"How did you cover the bullet wounds?"

"On his face?" Ralston frowned. "You misunderstand me. There was no covering. There was nothing there. So in his case, we reconstructed. We snipped away the excess tissue around the wounds and glued the skin that was left to his cheekbone and eye socket."

Ellen didn't want to know more. Nobody should know this stuff. It was unthinkable. She couldn't help but think of losing Will this way. Of him being the child on the table. Of his beautiful face being the one glued together.

"We poured wax into the bullet holes to fill the gap and used cosmetics to match the shade of the wax to his skin, which was lighter than his mother. Some mortuaries have airbrushes, but we don't need that. I'm forty-two years in this business, and my father had it before me. We don't airbrush."

Ellen rallied at the businesslike note in his tone.

"The result wasn't perfect, but it was acceptable to Laticia and the family, and it gave them comfort, to see him as they knew him in life. Even my niece gave us a good grade."

"That's wonderful," Ellen said, with an admiration she didn't try to hide, but Ralston shrugged it off.

"Even for a single gunshot wound, we wouldn't cover it, that would never work. The putty would simply sink into the wound." He held up an index finger. "That's one thing I've had to order more of, wax and putty. We've already used four times the amount that we did last year, and the manufacturer can't keep it in stock. I have a friend in Newark, he's in the same bind."

Ellen scribbled away. These would be the effects of murder that would flesh out the story, from a tragic perspective.

"And all the eyecaps I have are too big for children. For Lateef and the others, we have to resize the eyecaps. Cut them down with scissors."

Ellen wrote that down, too. "I hope the day never comes when they make eyecaps for kids."

"I hear that." Ralston nodded. "In addition, with Lateef, we didn't use a wire in his mouth. We sutured the muscle and used adhesive, and it worked very well. He had so much bruising, but luckily, the displacement during the injection cleared a lot of that. That's what we'd hoped for."

"You use the word 'we' a lot. Did you have help with Lateef?"

"My son John. We worked together." Ralston's tone softened. "We started at eight o'clock and we finished at dawn. My grandson, he's Lateef's age, and well, it wasn't easy for either John or me." He coughed slightly, and Ellen was about to ask a question, but held her tongue when she saw his head bow slightly and a stillness sweep over his slight frame. "Lateef, he's the one I'll never forget. I knew that boy. When he came in, looking the way he did, at first I didn't know what to do." Ralston shook his head, still downcast. "I didn't know what to do. I had to go outside. I stood in the back, by receiving. I asked the Lord to help me, to give me strength."

Ellen nodded. She didn't take a note. It would be off the record. It was too personal. Suddenly her cell phone rang, destroying the quiet and jarring them both. Embarrassed, she reached for her purse. "I'm so sorry," she said, digging. "I should have turned it off."

"Feel free to take the call." Ralston checked his watch, the moment having passed. "I should get back to work."

Ellen found the phone and switched it off, but not before she saw the area code. 302. Delaware.

Cheryl Martin.

Chapter Thirty

Ellen tore south toward Wilmington, racing the rush hour. The sky had turned black, and snow flurries had begun to fall, flecks of white lace frozen in her headlights. The radio news was predicting a storm, and she felt as if she were outrunning that, too. She was in an uneasy state, hyperexcited, even after the long, sad afternoon. She couldn't remember the last time she'd eaten, but it didn't matter. She found herself accelerating, going to seventy miles an hour, then eighty. She wondered if she was speeding toward something. Or away.

Ellen found the house, parked at the curb, and looked out her car window. Cheryl's home was a lovely Tudor with a white stucco façade and dark brown trim, set among plenty of open space. A white sedan sat in a circular driveway, and the evergreens and hedges landscaping the property were dusted by new flurries, so that the scene looked like a suburban snow globe. She grabbed her bag and her file and got out of the car.

They were sitting in a beautiful living room, on an L-shaped sectional couch in an oatmeal fabric that coordinated perfectly with a nubby sisal rug. The lighting was recessed and the walls were eggshell white, adorned with horsy landscapes that would undoubtedly echo the view from the picture window.

Cheryl was saying, "I have to admit, part of the reason I wanted to meet you is because I read your articles."

"Thank you." Ellen remembered the photos of Cheryl Villiers, née Martin, from her mother Gerry's house. Cheryl had been the pretty sister with large blue eyes and the sprinkling of freckles on a perfect nose, and in person, she resembled Will, despite the crow's-feet and the laugh lines bracketing her wide mouth.

"I even remembered the articles you wrote about adopting your baby, or Amy's baby. I reread them online after my mom called. I thought they were really good."

"Thanks."

"They had a photo of the baby in the paper. It's so strange to think that that little baby is Amy's. My new nephew. I just can't deal." Cheryl smiled uncomfortably, showing lightened teeth. "My mother said you showed her some court documents. Could I see them?"

"Yes, of course." Ellen dug in her purse and produced the adoption papers. "I really need to find Amy. I guess your mom told you, it's just to get some medical history. If you remember from the article, Will had a serious heart problem when I adopted him."

Cheryl read the papers, her head inclined at an inquisitive angle, so that her dark blond hair fell into her face. She had on a tan V-neck knit sweater, tight-fitting beige pants, and black leather flats.

"Do you think that's Amy's signature?"

"Yes, I do. It's absolutely her signature."

"How about on the consent form. Is that your signature?"

"No, I never signed this." Cheryl looked up, her eyes frank in light makeup. "She forged it."

"So what do you think's going on here?"

"Amy didn't want us to know about the baby, obviously."

Bingo. "What about this twisted ovary business?"

"Look, my mom thinks that Amy couldn't have had a baby, but I don't agree. All the doctor said was that she probably couldn't have a baby, and Amy made a big deal of that. Even my husband said she could conceive." Cheryl's tone resonated with resentment. "She's a major drama queen. She just used the twisted ovary to get attention."

"So do you think she had a baby?"

"Of course, it's certainly possible. We all stopped seeing her about the same time. If she had a baby three years ago, I have no way of knowing it for sure. I was married by then, and we don't see as much of my family." Something flickered behind Cheryl's eyes, but she guarded that emotion. "They all smoke, for one thing. We don't tolerate smoking around the house."

"Your husband's a doctor, you say?"

"Yes, a physician. He just left to take the kids to pizza for dinner. We have twin girls. We thought it wouldn't be a good idea if they were around while you were here."

"Right." Ellen considered it. Twins. They'd be Will's cousins. But back to business. "So do you have any idea where Amy could be? Your mom thinks she stays in touch with you."

"Amy does email, but hardly ever. When she needs money."

"Do you send her any?" Ellen wanted the address.

"No. My husband didn't think I should, so I stopped, and she stopped asking."

"May I have her email address? It really is important that I get in touch with her."

Cheryl frowned. "I should email Amy first and make sure that she wants to hear from you. After all, if she gave up her baby for adoption, she had a choice about whether she wanted to hear from you, didn't she?"

Damn. "Yes, but as your mom probably told you, the lawyer who brokered the adoption has passed away, and I have no other way to get this information."

Cheryl handed her back the papers. "My husband said that they can disclose medical information in an adoption, even if they keep the identity of the parent secret."

"That's true, but I find that I need to ask one or two more questions." Ellen tried another tack. "Tell you what. Would you give Amy my email address and have her contact me?"

"Okay."

"Thanks." Ellen hadn't come this far to be turned away. "What if she doesn't email me back? Will you give me her email?"

"Cross your fingers."

Ellen thought of her earlier request, which she'd made by phone. "I was wondering, too, if you were able to find any photos of her."

"Sure, I found two I had in the computer, one young and one more recent. I suppose it's okay if you have them." Cheryl turned to the end table, picked up two papers, and handed one to Ellen, pointing with a manicured index finger. "That's Amy, when she was little."

Ellen looked down at a photo of a cute girl holding an American flag and wearing an Uncle Sam hat. "How old is she in this picture, do you know?"

"She'd just turned five. Before she turned into a freak." Cheryl chuckled softly. "Does your son look like her?"

"Not that much." Ellen had to admit it. Amy's nose was wider than Will's and her lips fuller. "Frankly, he looks more like you."

"It must run in our family. I look nothing like my kids, either. Can you imagine that, carrying twins for nine months and they don't look like you?"

"It doesn't seem fair." Ellen was too preoccupied to smile. "Will must look more like his father, but I don't know what his father looks like. Does the name Charles Cartmell mean anything to you?"

"No."

"According to the adoption papers, he's the father."

"Never heard of him. Amy dated tons of guys. She was never in a committed relationship."

"If she got pregnant, would she tell the father? I mean, would she feel as if she should?"

Cheryl scoffed. "Are you kidding? If I know my little sister, she probably didn't know who the father was. She could have made up the name on the form, couldn't she?"

Ellen leaned forward. "But why would she make up his name and not her own, or yours?"

"I don't know." Cheryl shrugged, but Ellen considered it for a minute.

"Wait, I bet I do. She couldn't make up her name because she had to produce ID at the hospital when Will got sick. But if she never married Charles, or Will's father, he never appeared. She could make up his name." Ellen's thoughts clicked ahead. "Tell me, did she have a boyfriend back then, three years ago, that you remember?"

"Oh, she had plenty. Is that the same thing?" Cheryl laughed, but Ellen didn't.

"No name you can recall?"

"No. Maybe this photo will help. It has a guy in it, and they look pretty chummy." Cheryl handed over the second photo. "This is the most recent picture I have of Amy. She emailed it to me, and you can see the date. June 5, 2004."

"That would be shortly before she had Will," Ellen said, cheering inwardly. It was a picture of Amy, grinning on the beach, in a black bikini, with a brown beer bottle in her hand. Her arm was looped around a shirtless man who raised his bottle to the camera. If Will was born on January 30, 2005, she would have been about two months pregnant when the photo was taken, assuming it was taken when it was sent. But she had no baby bump, though maybe she wasn't showing yet, and there was that beer bottle.

"What are you thinking?" Cheryl asked.

"That if Amy was seeing this man around then, he could be Will's father."

"He's so her type. Amy went for bad boys."

Ellen eyed the man, who wasn't bad-looking for a bad boy, with narrow eyes and a long brown ponytail. Something about him looked almost familiar, but maybe it was that he looked a little like Will. He had the smile, a little tilted down, but it looked like a smirk on him. The photo was too blurry to see more detail and it had been taken from a distance. "In the email, did Amy say who he was, or where they were?"

"No."

Ellen mulled it over. "It could be anywhere it's warm, which could be anywhere, in June. What did she say in the email, if I can ask?"

"Nothing. She just sent the photo. Nice, huh?" Cheryl scoffed again, but Ellen's gaze remained on the photo. She could be looking at Will's birth parents. Charles Cartmell, if it was him, had a sleeve of multicolored tattoos she couldn't read and he looked a little drunk, even in the fuzzy resolution.

"The focus is so bad on this."

"It could be my printer. Keep that copy and I'll email you another, if you want."

"Please, do." Ellen told Cheryl her email address. "Did Amy have any girlfriends?"

"She never got along with other girls. She hung with the guys."

Ellen made a mental note. "You said Amy emails you. Did she ever mention any men in her emails?"

"Not that I remember."

"Would you mind looking back at the emails, so we can check?"

"I can't, I deleted them." Cheryl checked her watch. "Well, it's getting kind of late."

"Sure, I should go." Ellen rose with her papers, hiding her frustration. "Thanks so much for meeting with me. Think she'll email me?"

"God knows."

Ellen said her good-byes and left, wondering if it was really Charles Cartmell in the photo. She hit the cold air outside and looked up at the sky, dark and starless.

Maybe it wasn't too late to take a drive.

Chapter Thirty-one

Ellen sat in her car with the engine off, watching the snow fall in the dark, holding the court papers. She was parked outside of an elementary school, a three-story redbrick edifice that had been there since 1979, according to its keystone. The school was at Charles Cartmell's address, but obviously, he didn't live here. He had never lived here. Amy must have pulled the address out of thin air and made up the name, too. She might as well have picked Count Chocula.

Ellen wasn't completely surprised. She had known that Grant Avenue was one of the busiest streets in the Northeast, in a commercial area, but she had been hoping that there would be an apartment house or maybe a converted rowhouse.

Cars rushed past her, their windshield wipers pumping and their red brake lights burning holes into the night. She looked again at the photo of Amy and the man on the beach. The streetlight cast an oblong of purplish light across his face, but his eyes remained in shadow.

"Who is my son?" she asked the silence.

Chapter Thirty-two

"Thanks so much for staying, Con." Ellen closed the front door behind her, feeling a wave of guilt. It was after eleven o'clock, and on TV, a bow-tied weatherman was sticking a yardstick into three inches of snow. "I really do appreciate it."

"S'okay." Connie rose tiredly from the couch, her Sudoku book in hand. "Everything go okay at your meeting?"

"Yes, thanks." Ellen got Connie's coat from the closet and handed it to her. "How's my baby boy?"

"Fine." Connie slipped into her coat. "But it was Crazy Shirt Day at school, and you forgot his shirt. I reminded you, last week. I thought it was in his backpack and just went."

"Oh no." Ellen felt another wave of guilt, which made two in two minutes, a record even for her. "Was he upset?"

"He's three, El."

"I should have remembered."

"No, I should've checked. I will, next time."

"Poor kid." Ellen kicked herself. Will hated to be the one who was different. The one who was adopted. The one with no dad. Neither she nor Will was like the other. "You even reminded me."

"Don't beat yourself up. It's easy to lose track. Crazy Hat Day, Snack Mom, Pajama Day, whatever. I didn't have to deal with that when Mark was little." Connie slid her puzzle book into her tote bag, picked up her things, then straightened up. "They're working you too hard."

"And I'm working *you* too hard." Ellen squeezed her shoulder. "Please tell Chuck I'm sorry for keeping you."

"He can get his own meal for a change. It won't kill him." Connie opened the door, letting in a blast of cold, wet air. "Snow's already stopping, isn't it?"

"Yes, but drive safe. Thanks again." Ellen held the door, then closed and locked it behind her. She took off her coat and hung it up, dwelling. She was screwing up left and right lately. Forgetting the crazy shirt. Missing the projects meeting. It had all started with the white card in the mail. She hoped Amy emailed her soon and she could put it all behind her.

Ellen went into the kitchen and brewed herself a fresh mug of coffee, pushing Amy to the back of her mind. She had a story to write and she was starved. She scarfed a bowl of Frosted Mini-Wheats over the sink, leaving her leftover milk to Oreo Figaro, who leapt onto the counter, purring deeply as he lapped it up. When he was finished, he looked up from the bowl, blinking his yellow-green eyes in a silent request for more. The tiniest droplet of milk clung to his chin.

"We have to get to work," Ellen said, taking back the bowl.

Up in her home office, she began as she did with any story. There were no shortcuts, at least none that worked. She built her stories from the bottom up, and her first step was always transcribing her notes. If she needed to quote directly, she'd go to the tapes. Then, usually, if she'd had enough caffeine, her brain would lurch into action and an angle for the story would suggest itself. She took a sip of hot coffee, glanced at the notes beside her, and started with the interview of Lateef's mother, typing:

Pies "too ugly" to serve. She wants it in the paper, so kids are not a number "like it's Powerball."

Ellen kept going, trying to remember the mood of the interview and how she felt sitting in Laticia's kitchen, but her thoughts strayed back to Cheryl's house and the picture of Amy and the man on the beach.

"Ain't nothin' gonna change here, and this is *America*."

Ellen flipped the page of her notebook and kept transcribing, but it was only mechanical. She'd learned a lot about Will in one day. She'd met his mother, grandmother, and aunt. She might have seen what his father looked like. She tried to keep typing but her fingers slowed and thoughts of the Martin family intruded. She found herself wondering if Cheryl had emailed her a copy of the photo of Amy and the man on the beach.

She minimized her Word file and opened up Outlook Express. Incoming emails piled onto the screen, and she ignored the one from Sarah with the attachment and subject line: FYI, I EMAILED MARCELO MY PIECE. Suddenly an email came on the screen from twinzmom373@gmail.com.

Ellen clicked it open. It was Cheryl's. The message read, **Nice meeting you,** and there was an attachment. She opened the attachment, and the photo of Amy and the man on the beach popped onto the screen. Though she'd seen it before, she couldn't wrap her mind around the fact that Amy was Will's mother and the man on the beach his father, glowing on her computer screen. She looked over her shoulder in case Will had gotten out of bed, but there was nothing behind her except Oreo Figaro, his front legs stretched on the rug like Superman in flight.

She squinted at the picture. It was brighter online, but still blurry and the images too distant. She knew how to rectify that. She saved the photo to My Pictures and opened Photoshop, then uploaded the photo, drew a box around Amy's face, and clicked Zoom. The image exploded into pixels, so she telescoped it down a little, then examined Amy's features with care. The shape of her eyes didn't look much like Will's, though they were blue, but her nose was longer than Will's and too wide.

Not everybody looks like their mom.

Ellen zoomed out to the original photo, outlined the man's face with the mouse, then clicked. Her heart beat a little faster. The man did look a little familiar, and his smile was like Will's, with that downturn on the right. She sipped some coffee and clicked Zoom again, enlarging his face to fill the screen. She'd hoped the blur would let her sense the general configuration of his face, but it didn't. She set down her coffee, almost spilling it on her notes, so she moved the notebook out of the way. Sticking out from underneath was the white card with the photo of Timothy Braverman.

Hmmm.

She slid out the white card and looked at the age-progressed version of Timothy, then set the card down, went back into My Pictures, and found Will's last school picture. She enlarged it and set it up on the screen next to the photo of the man on the beach. Then she compared the two photos—the most recent of Will with the man on the beach—taking a mental inventory:

Will, eyes blue and wide-set; Beach Man, eyes close together and blue
Will, nose, little and turned up; Beach Man, long and skinny
Will, blond hair; Beach Man, light brown hair
Will, round face; Beach Man, long, oval face
Will, normal chin; Beach Man, pointed chin
Similarities—blue eyes, lopsided smile

Ellen reviewed the list, then leaned back and eyeballed the photos from a distance. She wasn't able to reach a conclusion, as much as she wanted to. Beach Man could be Will's father, or maybe he was someone Amy was dating around the same time, or a random guy with a beer. Or maybe Will didn't look that much like either of his parents. He looked like Cheryl, and that counted for something.

Ellen went back online. She clicked through to the Braverman family's website, then captured the age-progressed photo of Timothy and saved a copy to My Pictures. She was going to put it on the screen next to Will's and Beach Man's, then compare all three of them when something else on the Braverman family website caught her eye.

The composite drawing of the carjacker.

On impulse, Ellen captured the composite and saved a copy to My Pictures, then uploaded it and placed it next to recent Will, age-progressed Timothy, and Beach Man—all four images in a line. She blinked, and her heart beat a little faster. She captured the composite drawing and the photo of Beach Man, then placed them side by side on their own page. The photos were different sizes, so she outlined the composite drawing and clicked Zoom to enlarge it to the approximate size of Beach Man, and clicked.

She froze. The composite drawing of the carjacker looked like Beach Man. She double-checked, and there was no doubt that they looked alike.

"Oh my God," she said aloud, and Oreo Figaro raised his chin, his eyes angled slits disappearing into the blackness of his fur.

Ellen looked back at the screen, getting a grip. It was impossible to compare a black-and-white pencil drawing with a color photo of a flesh-and-blood man. She flashed on Will's tracing of a horse from the other day, and it gave her an idea. She clicked Print, and her cheap plastic printer chugged to life. Then she got up and hurried downstairs, rummaged through the toy box, and ran back up with a roll of tracing paper.

The printer had spit out a copy of the composite drawing, and she took a black Sharpie and went over the lines of the carjacker's features, blackening them so they'd be darker and thicker. Then she took the piece of tracing paper and placed it on top of the composite drawing, tracing the image onto the crinkly transparent paper, ignoring the thumping in her chest. She set the traced composite aside, slid the copy of the Beach Man photo from the printer tray, then moved her computer keyboard to the side and set the printed photo on the desk.

Then she stopped.

She wanted to know and she didn't want to know, both at once.

"Get over it," she said under her breath, and she took the traced composite of the carjacker and placed it over Beach Man's face.

It was an exact match.

Ellen felt her gorge rising, and she jumped up and bolted for the bathroom.

Chapter Thirty-three

Ellen lingered on the threshold to Will's room, lost in her thoughts. She couldn't work any longer, not after what she'd learned, or what she thought she'd learned. She could barely give it voice inside her own head, but she couldn't ignore it, either.

Is Will really Timothy?

She tasted bile and Colgate on her teeth and sagged against the doorjamb, willing her brain to function. Tried to reason it out and spot any failures of logic.

Begin at the beginning. Remain calm.

Ellen thought a minute, trying to articulate the scenario she feared. If the composite matched the photo of the man on the beach, then Beach Man was the carjacker. He had shot Carol Braverman's nanny. Kidnapped Will. Taken the ransom money but kept the child. He had a girlfriend who pretended to be the baby's mother. Amy Martin.

Why not kill the baby right after the kidnapping?

Ellen shuddered, but she could guess at some answers. Amy wanted a baby and couldn't have one. Or they thought they could sell the baby on the black market. She folded her arms against her chest, hugging herself, and picked up the narrative in her mind, detecting another fallacy.

Why give him up for adoption?

That answer, Ellen knew for sure. Because he got sick. Will had a heart problem no one knew about. At least she assumed as much, because the Braverman site didn't mention that Timothy had any heart problems. The doctors at Dupont Hospital had told her that his murmur had gone undetected, which wasn't unusual. Will would have failed to thrive. He wouldn't eat well and he'd have been sickly. That would have overwhelmed Amy, even her mother said so, and it would have made it too risky to keep him. Too many blood tests, forms, and questions that could show Amy wasn't the mother and the boyfriend the father.

So what do they do next?

Ellen composed it like a nightmare news story. They'd take the baby to a hospital far from Miami, back to where Amy had grown up. They'd essentially abandon the baby in the hospital, and then a solution would come, in the form of a nice lady reporter, who falls in love with the baby. She adopts the baby and takes him home, where he sleeps under a sky of ersatz stars.

My God.

Ellen let her gaze wander around Will's bedroom, over the shadows of Tonka trucks and Legos, over shelves of skinny books and Candy Land and plush bears and bunnies, their soft pastels reduced to shades of gray. The window shade was up, and outside the sky was oddly bright, the world aglow with a new snowfall that insulated the house like a sheet of practical cotton, keeping her and Will safe inside.

"Mommy?" he asked sleepily, from the bed.

Ellen wiped her eyes, padded over to the bed, and leaned over Will, brushing his bangs from his forehead in the light from the doorway. "Sorry I woke you."

"Are you home?"

"Yes, it's night and I'm home."

"Connie says you have to work hard."

"I do, but I'm home now." Ellen swallowed the knot in her throat, but she had a feeling it would only travel down to her chest and cause a heart attack, or maybe she'd just spontaneously combust. She eased onto the guardrail and tried to regain her composure. "Sorry I forgot your crazy shirt."

"It's okay, Mommy."

Ellen's eyes welled up. She reached down and stroked his cheek. "You're the best kid in the world, do you know that?"

"You brushed your teeth."

"I did." Ellen was uncomfortable, sitting on the guardrail. "I hate this guardrail. I'm taking it off." She stood up and began to slide the wooden rail from the bed, jiggling the frame.

"I won't fall out, Mommy."

"I know that. You're too smart to fall out of your own bed." Ellen jiggled one last time and finally wrenched the guardrail from the bed. "Sorry."

Will giggled.

"Stupid guardrail."

"*Stupid* guardrail!"

"See ya, guardrail." Ellen took the guardrail to the other side of the room and set it on the floor. "Wouldn't wanna be ya."

Will giggled again.

Ellen came back to the bed, where she could see Will wriggling in his bed. "Are you being a wiggle worm?"

"I am!"

"I'm coming in. We're having a slumber party."

"What's that?" Will scissored his legs.

"It's people having a party when they should be sleeping." Ellen eased onto the skinny bed, on her side. "Scoot over, wigglehead."

"Okay." Will edged backwards, and Ellen reached for him and

wrapped him up in her arms. She didn't want to think about Amy Martin and the Bravermans anymore. She wanted to be where she was, right this moment, holding her son close.

"How's that feel? Good?"

Will hugged her back. "I made a snowball."

"You did? Cool."

"It's on the porch, did you see?"

"No." Ellen gave him a squeeze. "It'll be there tomorrow. I'll look at it in the morning, first thing."

"Do you have to go to work tomorrow?"

"Yes." Ellen didn't know what would happen at work tomorrow, with her story unfinished. Right now, she didn't care.

"I hate work."

"I know, sweetie. I'm sorry I have to work."

"Why do you?"

Ellen had answered this more times than she could count, but she knew it wasn't a real question. "I work so we have all the things we need."

Will yawned.

"Maybe we should settle down and go to sleep. Party's over, and slumber is beginning."

"I won't fall out," Will said again, and Ellen hugged him close.

"Don't worry. You won't fall out. I'm here to catch you."

"Good night."

"I love you, sweetie. Good night." Ellen cuddled him, and in the next minute, she could feel his body drifting back to sleep. She caught herself beginning to cry and willed herself to stop. If she went that way, she'd never come back, and this wasn't the time or the place anyway.

Flip it.

She really couldn't be sure that Beach Man was the carjacker. A tracing couldn't tell anything with accuracy, and composites were based only on a verbal description. Lots of men had narrow eyes and long noses. If the composite was too unreliable to prove that the car-jacker was Beach Man, then there was no link between Will and Timothy.

Ellen smiled in the dark, feeling a tiny bit better. Maybe Amy would email her, tell her the story of Will's birth, and explain why she'd put him up for adoption.

Will shifted in his sleep, and she snuggled him. She couldn't resolve tonight whether her fears were founded or completely insane. But behind them lurked an unspoken question, one that she couldn't begin to acknowledge, much less articulate to herself. It had been lurking in the back of her mind from the moment she'd seen the infernal white card in the mail.

She hugged Will closer, there in the still, dark room, and the question hung in the air above the bed, suspended somewhere between mother, child, and the false stars.

If Will is really Timothy, what will I do?

Chapter Thirty-four

Ellen entered the newsroom the next morning, exhausted after only two hours of sleep. She hadn't been able to stop her brain from thinking about Will and Timothy, and she felt raw, achy, and pre-occupied. She had on the same jeans and shirt she'd worn yesterday, but with a different sweater, and she hadn't had time to shower. She'd checked her email too many times on the way in, but there'd been no email from Amy Martin.

Get a grip.

"Good morning, dear," Meredith Snader said, passing her with an empty mug on the way to the coffee room, and Ellen managed a smile.

"Hey, Mer." She tried to put the Braverman business behind her, but her head was pounding. The newsroom was mostly empty, and she hustled down the aisle, trying to get her thoughts together for the meeting about the homicide piece. Through the glass wall of his office, she could see Marcelo at his desk and Sarah sitting across from him, laughing about something.

Great.

Ellen figured the laughter would stop when she told them she'd be late with her end of the story. She dropped her handbag on her desk, shed her jacket, and hung it on the coatrack, seeing that Sal and Larry were entering Marcelo's office, holding styrofoam cups of coffee and looking like the journalists Ellen had grown up idolizing. She hated that she was about to crash and burn in front of the local Woodward and Bernstein. She girded herself and headed to Marcelo's office, where he looked up expectantly from behind his desk.

"Come in, Ellen." Marcelo smiled, his eyes flashing darkly. "I didn't get your draft. Did you email it?"

Ellen arranged her face into a professional mask. "Marcelo, I don't have the piece done. I'm sorry."

Sarah looked over. Larry and Sal turned around. Marcelo blinked. "You don't have it?" he asked, lifting an eyebrow.

"No, sorry." Ellen's temples thundered. "I got a little bogged down and I need a few extra days."

"Maybe I can help. That's what they pay me for."

"No, you can't," Ellen blurted out, but Marcelo was still smiling, his head cocked and his eyes sympathetic.

"Let me see what you have so far. I'm not looking for perfection. I can't be, with these two slackers on the story." Marcelo gestured at Larry and Sal. "Their draft needed the usual overhaul."

"Kiss my ass," Sal said, and they all laughed except Ellen, who had to come clean.

"Marcelo, to be honest, there is no draft. Not yet." She felt vaguely sick, unmasked and vulnerable. They were all looking at her in surprise, Marcelo most of all.

"Nothing?" Marcelo frowned, confused.

"No worries," Sarah chirped up. "I've got it covered."

"Please wait." Marcelo held up a large palm, but Ellen was looking over at Sarah, too angry to let it go.

"What do you mean, you have it covered?" she asked.

Sarah ignored the question. "Marcelo, Ellen refused to talk with my source, Julia Guest, so I did and wrote it up. I think it puts a human face on the issue quite nicely." She handed him some sheets from a stack she cradled against her chest. "Check it out."

Ellen felt stunned. Sarah had just stuck a knife in her back. The girl wanted her job and was taking no prisoners.

"Who's this source again?" Marcelo was asking, eyeing the pages.

"She's been active in the efforts to stop the violence and has organized the community on the issue. She knows all the players and she feeds to the Mayor's Office."

"What's her stake in this?"

"She organized last month's demonstrations and one of the vigils."

"Is she in local politics?"

"Not officially."

"Thanks, but that's not what I had in mind." Marcelo, troubled, handed her back the pages. "It sounds to me as if she has no stake. If she doesn't have a stake, she's not the story."

Ellen cleared her throat. "I interviewed one of the mothers who lost a son, a second-grader who was murdered. I also spoke with the boy's teacher and the funeral director who prepared his body."

Sal whistled. "Grieving mothers are a homerun."

Larry nodded. "I like the funeral angle, too. It's different. Original."

Marcelo looked relieved. "Okay, Ellen. Good. So you just don't have the draft yet. When can you finish it?"

"Next Friday?"

"She's been working on that Sulaman follow-up," Sarah interrupted, and Ellen turned on her, not bothering to hide her feelings.

"What are you talking about?"

"You've been working on Sulaman, right?" Sarah asked calmly, lifting an eyebrow. "That's the real reason you blew this deadline, isn't it?"

"That's not true!" Ellen shot back, but she could see that Sarah had gotten Marcelo's attention.

"Yes, it is," Sarah continued, her tone measured. "I know because Susan Sulaman called yesterday. She said she'd been calling you and couldn't reach you, so the switchboard sent the call to the newsroom, and I picked up. She said you'd interviewed her and wanted to know if you'd talked your editor into running the story."

Marcelo's eyes flared, and Ellen's face burned.

"You have no idea what I've been doing, so stay out of my business!"

"I knew you wouldn't make the deadline." Sarah remained calm, but Ellen raised her voice.

"Your story is separate from mine!" She couldn't stop herself from shouting even though everyone had fallen into shocked silence. Her head was about to explode. "It's not your concern whether I make my deadline or not!"

"Beg to differ." Sarah sniffed. "I pitched the piece in the first place and you're screwing it up. We're all ready, why aren't you?"

"Ladies, hold on." Marcelo stood up behind his desk, raising his hands. "Everyone, please, give Ellen and me a minute."

"Good luck," Sal said with a smile, plucking his coffee from the edge of the desk, and Larry followed suit, both of them edging past Ellen, who turned her head away when Sarah brushed by her, trailing perfume and adrenaline. After they had left, Marcelo put his hands firmly on his hips.

"Close the door, please," he said quietly.

Ellen did, then faced him.

"What's going on? You never miss a deadline." Marcelo looked mystified, and his tone sounded more disappointed than angry. "Is she right? Was it the Sulaman follow-up that delayed you?"

"No."

"Did you interview the mother?"

"Yes. Only once."

"When?"

Ellen could hardly remember. She rubbed her face. Everything before the white card was a blur, as if a line had been drawn down the middle of her life, dividing it into Before and After. HAVE YOU SEEN THIS CHILD? Her head hurt so much she felt dizzy. "Tuesday?"

"But I asked you not to." Marcelo's tone wasn't disappointed, Ellen realized, but hurt.

"I'm so sorry. I just had to."

"Why?"

"I was just curious, I had to see her again." Ellen knew it sounded lame, and Marcelo looked grave, his eyebrows sloping down.

"Ellen, let's be honest with each other. Ever since I let Courtney go, I feel you've been distant. You've acted differently toward me. It's as if we're on different sides."

"No, we're not, I swear."

"Please, don't work against me. We have too much work for anybody to be doing that. We're doing more with less, and every day it gets worse."

"I'm not working against you."

"But all this fussing with Sarah, it's not needed."

"It won't happen again."

Marcelo finger-raked his hair from his forehead and fell silent a moment, eyeing her. "I can tell something's wrong. You're not yourself. Is it Will? I know he was sick when he was little. Is he sick again?"

"No." Ellen couldn't tell him anything, as much as she would have loved a sounding board. "I'll have the story to you early next week. I said Friday because I wanted to be realistic."

"Tell me what's wrong," Marcelo said again, his voice even softer. "You look tired."

"I don't feel that great." Ellen winced inwardly. *You look tired* was code for *you look ugly.*

"Are you sick?"

"I threw up last night," Ellen blurted out, then watched Marcelo's eyes flare in brief surprise. Throwing up was definitely not hot, and suddenly she felt like a frigging mess. Doing and saying the wrong things, exhausted and undone. "I should just go home. I really don't feel well at all."

"Okay, that's fine, of course." Marcelo nodded, walking around his desk toward her. "If you're sick, you must go home. Take care of yourself."

"Right, thanks." Ellen moved to the door, feeling oddly dizzy. She broke out into a sweat. Her head was light. She hadn't had time for breakfast. Even Connie had looked at her funny.

And in the next second, the office went black.

Chapter Thirty-five

"Surprise, I'm home!" Ellen called out from the doorway, slipping out of her coat. The living room was bright and peaceful, with a winter sun streaming through the windows, and the sight brought her back to reality, after having fainted in Marcelo's office. She'd blamed it on her mystery illness when she regained consciousness in his arms, their faces close enough to kiss. Or maybe she had imagined that part.

"Mommy!" Will zoomed from the dining room, his rubbery sneakers thundering on the soft pine floors.

"Honey!" Ellen let her coat fall to scoop him up and give him a big hug, and Connie came out of the kitchen, looking pleased. She was dressed to go to Happy Valley for the weekend in her Penn State wear, gray stretch slacks and a blue Nittany Lions sweatshirt.

"Hi, El. Is there much ice on the road?"

"No, and thanks for shoveling the walk."

"That's all right. Will helped."

"Good for you, sweetie." Ellen set Will down, and he hit the ground moving. She had called Connie on the way home, telling her she was taking the day off, though she'd edited out the fainting. "No school today, huh?"

"No, Mommy. We read four books!" Will held up four fingers, and Ellen grinned.

"Good for you!"

Connie said, "I don't know why they closed. It's a gyp, for what you pay."

"It's all right." Ellen smiled at Will, cupping his warm head. "I wanna have some fun, don't you, honey?"

"Fun!" Will started jumping up and down, and Ellen laughed.

"How about sledding? Is that fun?"

"YES!" Will shouted, jumping like crazy.

"Good idea." Connie reached for her coat, purse, and tote. "TGIF, hey?"

"Exactly." Ellen smiled, glad to give her the time off after she'd been working so hard. "Who are we playing this weekend?"

"Nobody as good as we are."

"So we're winning?"

"Of course. Mark might even start." Connie grinned.

"Go Lions!" Ellen raised a fist, and Will did, too, still jumping. She stroked his silky hair, beginning to feel better. "Will, say good-bye and thank you to Connie."

"Good-bye, Mommy!" Will shouted, throwing his arms around Connie's legs, and Ellen cringed.

"See ya later," Connie said, bending over and hugging Will back.

"Alligator," he replied, his face buried in her coat, and Ellen opened the door while Connie left, waving happily.

Ellen closed the door behind her with a grin for Will. "Hey, pal, did you eat lunch yet?"

"No."

"Me neither. How about we eat and then go sledding?"

"Sledding!"

"Not yet." Ellen glanced at the dining-room table, covered with crayons and coloring books. "Go pick up those crayons, please, and I'll get lunch ready. Okay, buddy?"

"Okay, Mommy!" Will ran into the dining room and thundered into the kitchen, where she could hear the scrape of the footstool as he pulled it up to the counter. Oreo Figaro jumped down from the couch with his characteristic chirp, and she bent over to pet him hello, then felt her BlackBerry vibrating on her waistband. She took the BlackBerry from its holster, and the screen showed a red asterisk next to the email.

She hit the button. The email was from twinzmom373, Cheryl Martin. Ellen felt her chest tighten. She opened the email and read:

> Ellen,
> I sent Amy an email about you and told her your email address. I'll let you know if I hear from her, but don't hold your breath. Hope your son gets better. Sorry I couldn't help more.
> Best,
> Cheryl

Ellen bit her lip, her gaze lingering on the tiny screen. At least Cheryl had gotten through to Amy. If the email hadn't bounced back, it was still a good email address. She'd have to hope for the best, but in the meantime, she was back to Before and After. Either the carjacker was Beach Man or he wasn't. Two choices. Do or die.

"Mommy, I'm done!" Will called from the dining room. He was kneeling on a chair, trying to hold a logjam of crayons. They were dropping everywhere, and Oreo Figaro was chewing Burnt Sienna.

"Let me help, honey." Ellen got up, putting the BlackBerry away.

During lunch, she tried to tuck her anxiety away in the back of her brain, but it kept coming to the fore, even as she got Will dressed in his snowsuit and retrieved the orange plastic saucer from the basement. She slid into her coat and took him in one hand and the saucer in the other, then went outside in the cold sun, inhaling a deep lung-ful of fresh air.

"Freezing, Mommy!" Will said, his breath making tiny puffs in the frigid air.

"Look, your breath looks like a little train. You're Thomas the Tank Engine."

Will giggled. "Choo-choo!"

"Here we go!" Ellen scanned the street, which was covered with a soft snow that blanketed the rooftops, filled the rain gutters, and lined the porch steps. The houses, mostly stone or clapboard, sat close together, and many of them shared driveways, like freshly shov-eled Ys. Narberth was a stop-time neighborhood, where everybody looked out for one another.

They were making their way down the porch steps when Ellen realized something. Her neighbors must have gotten the white card in the mail, showing the photo of Timothy Braverman. They could have noticed how much he looked like Will, and everyone on the street knew that Will was adopted. They had all read her series, and she had even thrown a welcoming party for him when he was well enough. She used to be glad that Narberth was so chummy, but that was Before. After, it terrified her. She squeezed Will's hand.

"Ow, too tight, Mommy." He looked up in surprise, stiff in his puffy blue coat and snow pants, his arms sticking out like a ginger-bread man.

"Sorry." Ellen eased her grip, shaken. She looked up and down her block, worried about running into her neighbors.

Two doors away, Mrs. Knox, an older woman, was brushing snow from her sidewalk, and on the far side of the street, stay-at-home moms Elena Goldblum and Barbara Capozzi were talking while their kids played in the snow. All of them could have seen the white card, espe-cially the moms. Ellen stood frozen on the sidewalk.

"Mommy?" Will asked. "Are we going?"

"I'm just looking at the street. It's so pretty with the snow, isn't it?"

"Go!" Will tugged her hand, but Ellen's thoughts raced ahead. They always went sledding a few blocks away at Shortridge Park, and the place would be packed with Will's friends, their mothers, and the occasional stay-at-home dad, probably Domenico Vargas, who usually brought an old-fashioned plaid thermos of Ecuadorian coffee. All of them would have gotten the white card.

"Will, guess what?" Ellen knelt to see him at eye level and held him by the shoulder. His face was a circle of adorable features—those blue eyes under a pale fringe of feathery bangs, upturned nose, broad smile—framed by the drawstring of his hood. "Today, how about we go to a new place to sled?"

"Where?" Will frowned.

"Valley Forge. I used to sled there when I was growing up. Did I ever tell you about that? I loved it there."

"What about Brett?" Will's lower lip puckered. "Is he there?"

"No, but we can tell him how great it is. It's good for a change. Why don't we give it a try?"

"I don't want to."

"Let's try it. We'll have fun." Ellen straightened up, took him by the hand, and walked him over to the car before he could object. She got her keys from her pocket, chirped the back door unlocked, hoisted him into his car seat, and locked him in, kissing his cold nose. "This will be an adventure."

Will nodded, uncertain. "We didn't say good-bye to Oreo Figaro."

"He'll forgive us." Ellen closed the car door, stuck the saucer in the trunk, and was going to the driver's side when Mrs. Knox appeared from nowhere in her black down coat, cackling.

"I know what you're up to!" she said, pointing with a red leather glove. "You're playin' hooky!"

"You got that right." Ellen opened the car door and got in. "It's a snow day for grown-ups, too. Gotta go!"

"Why're you drivin' to Shortridge? It's only around the corner."

"See you!" Ellen shut the door, started the engine, and backed out of the driveway, giving a disappointed Mrs. Knox a last wave.

"Mommy?" Will said from the backseat.

"What?"

"Connie doesn't like Mrs. Knox."

"Really?" Ellen backed out of the driveway and adjusted the rearview mirror to see him. He looked stuffed into the car seat, immobilized. "Why not?"

"Connie says Mrs. Knox is a busy-busy."

"A what?" Ellen steered the car down the street. "You mean a busybody?"

"Yes!" Will giggled.

Ellen hit the gas, hard.

Chapter Thirty-six

An hour later Ellen was still driving through Valley Forge Park, trying to find the sledding hill she remembered. She'd checked her BlackBerry at a few traffic lights on the way, but Amy Martin hadn't emailed yet. The road wound through snow-covered log cabins and lines of black cannons, passing George Washington's encampment from the Revolutionary War, but she had stopped pointing out the historical sites to an increasingly cranky three-year-old, kicking in his car seat.

"I'm hot. My coat is hot." Will pulled at his zipper, and Ellen steered right, then left, and finally spotted a packed parking lot.

"We're here!"

"Yay!"

"This is gonna be great!" Ellen turned into the lot and found a space next to a station wagon that disgorged a slew of teenage boys. The tallest one undid the bright bungee cords that fastened a wooden toboggan to the roof rack.

"He's a big boy!" Will craned his neck.

"He sure is." Ellen shut off the ignition, and the teenager slid the toboggan onto his head, where he struggled to balance it. The other teenagers hooted when it dipped like a seesaw.

"He's gonna drop it! Watch out!" Will squealed with delight. "Mommy, what is that thing on him?"

"It's called a toboggan. It's like our saucer." Ellen put on her sunglasses and gloves. "It goes down the hill."

"Why doesn't he have a saucer?"

"He must like a toboggan better."

"Why don't we have it?"

"Someday we will, if you want one. Now, let's rock." Ellen got out of the car, went around to his side, and freed Will from his car seat. He reached for her with his fingers outstretched, then wrapped his arms around her neck when she held him.

"I love you, Mommy."

"I love you, too, sweetie." Ellen set him down and took his hand, then went to the trunk and got the saucer. Laughter and shouting came from the hill on the other side of the road, the sound echoing in the cold, crisp air, and she and Will walked through the plowed parking lot, rock salt crunching under their boots. The teenage boys crossed the street ahead of them, but there was such a crowd on the other side that Ellen couldn't see the hill.

"Isn't this fun, Will?" Ellen held Will's hand as they crossed.

"So many people!"

"That's because they know it's a good place to sled." Ellen surveyed the view beyond the crowd, a gorgeous vista of snowy evergreens, stone houses, and horse farms surrounding the park. The sky was a cloudless blue, and the sun pale gold, and distant. "Isn't this pretty?"

"Very pretty," he answered agreeably, but Ellen realized he couldn't see anything for the kids in front of him, so she picked him up.

"How's that? Better?"

"Oooh! Pretty!"

"Here we go!" Ellen dragged the saucer by its rope and threaded her way through the crowd, noticing that they were older than she'd expected, high school and even college kids in Villanova hoodies. She and Will reached the front of the crowd and looked out over the hill, and Ellen hid her dismay. The hill was much steeper than she remembered it, if it was even the same hill. It dropped off as steeply as an intermediate ski slope, and the snow had been packed hard by the sledding, so its surface glistened, icy-hard.

"Mom, whoa!" Will shouted, blinking. "This is so BIG!"

"I'll say." Ellen watched with concern as the teenagers shot down the hill on sleds, toboggans, and inflatable rafts, laughing and screaming. Two rafts collided on a mogul, and boys popped out and went skidding downhill. It looked dangerous. "This is kind of big for us, honey."

"No, Mom, we can do it!" Will wiggled in her arms.

"I'm not so sure." Ellen was jostled by a snowboarder, who shouted an apology before he launched himself down the hill. She scanned the slope for younger children, but didn't see a one. She wanted to kick herself. They could have been having fun at Shortridge, but she had dragged him to Mount Everest.

"Now, Mom, put me down!"

"Okay, but hold my hand and let's move over, out of the way." Ellen set him down, and they moved aside. The hill didn't get less steep at the edge, but the crowd lessened. A brutal wind bit her cheeks, and her toes were already freezing. She looked ahead to a tree line of evergreens and scrub pines, and beyond them was a slope that was gentler, with only a few teenagers. "Wait, I think I see a better place for us."

"Why can't we sled here?"

"Because it's better there. Hold on to my hand."

Will ignored her and bolted ahead, along the icy crest.

"No, Will!" Ellen shouted, lunging forward and catching him by the snowsuit. "Don't do that! It's dangerous!"

"Mommy, I can do it! You said! I can do it!"

"No, we're going down the hill over there, so please be patient."

"I am PATIENT!" he yelled, and a group of teenagers burst into laughter. Will looked over, wounded, and Ellen felt terrible for him.

"Come here, sweetie." She took his hand and they walked with effort, dragging the saucer to the other hill, where they stood at the top, both of them sizing it up in silence. It was less of an incline, but no baby hill, like Shortridge.

"Let's go, Mommy!"

"Okay, we'll go together."

"No! I wanna do it by myself!"

"Not here, pal."

"Why can't I go by myself?"

"It's better if I go with you." Ellen placed the saucer on the ground and plopped into it cross-legged, yanking her coat under her butt. Wind whipped across the hill, and she pushed up her sunglasses as Will climbed onto the saucer and stuffed himself into her lap. She wrapped her arms around him like a seat belt, steeling herself. "We can do this."

"Go, Mommy, go! Like him!" Will was looking at another snowboarder in a red fleece dragon hat, about to go down the hill.

"Hold on to my arms, tight as you can. Keep your legs inside." Ellen gritted her teeth and paddled to give them a running start, setting the saucer sliding down the hill. "Ready, set, go!"

"Whooooo!" Will shouted, then Ellen started shouting too, holding him as tightly as she could until the saucer started spinning. All she could do was yell and hang on to him, watching the world fly by in a blur of snow, sky, trees, and people, completely out of control. Ellen prayed for the ride to be over and clung to Will as he screamed, and finally the saucer slowed toward the bottom of the hill, where they and the snowboarder hit a hard bump that jarred them all loose and sent them sliding downhill.

"NO!" Ellen shouted, as Will pinwheeled past her on his back, and when she finally stopped herself, she jumped to her feet and straggled down the hill after him.

"WILL!" she screamed, on the run. She reached him and fell to the ground beside him, but he was laughing so hard that he couldn't catch his breath, his smile as broad as his face, his arms and legs flat against the snow, like a starfish on the sea floor.

"Way to go, dude!" The snowboarder clapped his gloves together, and Will squealed.

"I wanna do it again, Mommy!"

Ellen almost cried with relief, and the snowboarder eyed her warily from under his dragon hat.

"Lady," he said. "You need to calm down. Seriously."

Chapter Thirty-seven

Ellen trudged along the top of the hill carrying Will, who was crying and hollering in a full-blown tantrum. Teenagers hid their smiles as they passed, one young girl covered her ears with her mittens, and another looked over in annoyance. Ellen had long ago stopped being embarrassed by temper tantrums. She flipped it and wore it like a badge of honor. A temper tantrum was a sign that a mom said no when it counted.

"I want to . . . go again!" Will sobbed, tears staining his cheeks, snot running freely from his nose. "Again!"

"Will, try to calm down, honey." Ellen's head pounded at his screaming, and teenagers packed the hill, shouting and laughing, adding to the din. She sidestepped to avoid two older boys shoving each other, and she accidentally dropped the rope to the saucer.

"Mommy! Please! I want . . . to!"

"Oh no!" Ellen yelped, turning around, but before she could catch the saucer, it went spinning down the icy slope. She had no choice but to let it go. She needed to get both of them home and down for naps.

"I can . . . do it myself!" Will wailed.

"Please, honey, settle down. Everything's going to be all right." She finally reached the car, where she stuffed Will into his car seat, jumped behind the steering wheel, and pulled out of the parking lot with his crying reverberating in her ears.

"I . . . can, Mommy! I wanna go again!"

"It's too dangerous, honey. We can't."

"Again! Again!"

Ellen left Valley Forge Park, looking for the route back into the city. Traffic was congested because the Friday rush hour was beginning early, due to the snow. She slowed through the intersection, trying to read the route signs, which were confusing. Routes 202 and 411 were so close to each other, and horns honked behind her.

"I want to do it . . . again!" Will cried. "We only went one time!"

"We'll go home, and I'll make some hot chocolate. How about that? You love hot chocolate."

"Please . . . Mommy, please, again!"

"When you're older," Ellen said, but she knew it was the wrong thing to say the moment the words escaped her lips.

"I'M A BIG BOY!" Will howled, and Ellen didn't rebuke him, knowing it was disappointment and fatigue, a kiddie Molotov cocktail. She took a left turn, looking for the highway entrance when suddenly she heard the loud blare of a siren.

"Is it a fire truck, Mommy?" Will's sobbing slowed at the prospect, and Ellen checked the rearview mirror.

A state police cruiser was right behind her, flashing its high beams. She blinked, startled. She hadn't even known he was there. She said, "Perfect."

"What, Mommy?"

"It's a police car." Ellen didn't know what she had done. She'd been driving slow enough. Her headache returned, full blast. She waited for traffic to part and pulled over to the shoulder, with the police cruiser following.

"Why, Mom?" Will sniffled.

"I'm not sure, but everything's okay."

"Why do they make that sound?"

"So you know they're there."

"Why are they there?"

Ellen sighed inwardly. "Maybe I went too fast. We'll find out in a minute."

"Why did you?"

"Just rest, sweetie, don't worry." Ellen waited as the cruiser door opened and a tall cop emerged and walked along the side of her car, holding a small clipboard. She pressed the button to lower the window, letting in a blast of cold air. "Yes, Officer?"

"License and registration, please."

"Oh no." Ellen realized that she had neither, because she hadn't taken her purse. She had been going to Shortridge before she changed the plan. She took off her sunglasses and rubbed her eyes. "This isn't my day. I left the house without them."

The cop frowned. He was young, with light eyes under the wide brim of his brown hat, worn pitched forward. "You don't have any ID on you?"

"Sorry, no. It's at home, I swear it. What did I do?"

"You ran a stop."

"I'm sorry, I didn't see it. I was looking for the sign into Philly."

"What did you do, Mommy?" Will called out, and the cop bent from the waist and eyed Will through the open window.

Ellen felt a bolt of panic, out of nowhere. What if the state police had a registry of kidnapped kids? What if there was an Amber Alert out for Timothy Braverman? What if the cops got those white cards? What if the cop somehow recognized Will as Timothy? Ellen didn't know if the questions were paranoid or not, but couldn't stop them from coming.

"Cute kid," the cop said, unsmiling.

"Thanks." Ellen gripped the steering wheel, her heart beginning to thump.

"He looks unhappy," the cop said, his breath foggy in the frigid air. His gaze remained on Will, and Ellen told herself to stay calm. She was acting like a criminal and she hadn't done anything wrong.

"He's just tired."

"I'M NOT TIRED, MOMMEEEE!" Will screamed.

"I got a nephew hollers like that." The cop finally cracked a smile. "All right, Miss, this is your lucky day. I'll let you slide on the license but don't make a habit of it, we clear?"

"Yes, thank you, Officer," Ellen said, hearing the tremor in her own voice.

"Eyes front when you're driving, and no cell phones."

"I will, I swear. Thanks."

"Good-bye now, and be careful pulling out." The cop backed away from the car, and Ellen pressed the button to raise the window. She exhaled with relief as the cop rejoined the line of traffic, then she checked the rearview mirror. Will was falling asleep, his head listing to the side and his cheeks glistening with tear tracks, like tiny snail trails.

She looked for an opening in traffic, then pulled back onto the highway. Her forehead felt damp but her heartbeat was returning to normal. She fought the impulse to check her BlackBerry, but part of her knew that Amy Martin wouldn't be emailing her anytime soon.

Her head hurt, and she wished for the umpteenth time that her mother were still alive. She needed to talk to someone about Timothy Braverman, and her mother would have known what to do and what to think.

Ellen felt like she was losing her grip. Fainting in the office. Blowing her deadline. She could lose her job to Sarah if she didn't get her act together. She needed a saner head to prevail.

The traffic started to move, and she accelerated.

She had a new destination in mind.

Chapter Thirty-eight

"Hey, Dad," Ellen said, closing the front door behind them.

"Pops!" Will raised his arms to her father, revitalized after his long nap in the car. Given the traffic, it had taken over an hour to get to West Chester.

"My little buddy!!" Her father's face lit up, his hooded eyes alive with animation. "What a nice surprise! Come here, you!" He reached for Will, who jumped into his arms, wrapping his legs around him like a little monkey.

"Dad, careful of your back," Ellen said, though her father looked fine, his face only slightly red.

"Are you kiddin'? This makes my day! I missed my grandson!"

Will hung on tight. "Pops, I went down the big hill!"

"Tell me all about it," her father said, carrying Will into the living room. Ellen took off her hat and coat, set them on the chair, and looked around. The rug was rolled up, leaving a dull yellow square on the hardwood floor, and cardboard boxes sat stacked all over.

"We only went down the hill one time, and Mommy wouldn't let us go down again." Will held up an index finger while her father set him down, then unzipped his coat, tugged it off, and tossed it aside, leaving the sleeves inside out.

"Why wouldn't she, Willy Billy?"

"She said it was too big."

"She's so mean!" Her father stuck his tongue out at Ellen, which sent Will into gales of laughter.

"Hope this isn't a bad time." She gestured at the boxes. "Did we catch you in the middle of packing?"

"Nah." Her father carried Will over to the couch and sat with him in his lap. "Barbara did all that. She's finished for today."

"You didn't put the house up yet, did you? I didn't see a sign."

"Nah, but it'll go fast. Frank Ferro was asking me about it already." Her father gestured to a small cardboard box on top of the TV. "That one has some things from your mother, pictures and whatnot. You might want to take it home."

"Sure, thanks," Ellen said, caught off-balance at the notion of Barbara, packing her mother into a box.

"Where's my Thomas the Tank Engine?" Will asked, looking around in bewilderment. The toy box that had been tucked in the corner was gone.

"I got the horse right here," her father answered. He got up, took Will by the hand, and crossed him to a large cardboard box, with the top flaps open. "Look inside, cowpoke. The gang's all here."

"My truck!" Will dug in the box, pulled out a red truck, and knelt and zoomed it back and forth on the floor, where its hard plastic tires made a satisfyingly rumbling sound.

Ellen said, "Will, I'm going to talk to Pop in the kitchen."

"Be right back, pal," her father said, straightening up, and they went into the kitchen, where her father leaned against the counter and faced her. He crossed his arms in a pale yellow golf sweater and khakis, with a smile. "God love that kid."

"I know."

"He got so big! He grows like a weed."

"He sure does."

"You gotta bring him over more, El. Barbara's dyin' to meet him."

"I will."

"He's so much smarter than her grandkids. They hardly talk, and him, you can't shut up!"

Ellen laughed, marveling at the emotion Will always brought out in her father. He became a different man when Will was around, and she loved it. Just not now. She had called him for a reason. "Dad, I need to talk to you."

"Sure. Right. What's on your mind, kiddo?"

"This is going to sound strange, so prepare yourself." Ellen lowered her voice, though Will was out of earshot. "What if I told you that Will might really be a boy named Timothy Braverman, who was kidnapped from a family in Florida, two years ago?"

"*What?*" Her father's eyes widened, and Ellen filled him in quickly, starting with the white card, going through to the composite drawing, and ending with the visits to Gerry and Cheryl. They were interrupted twice by Will, and Ellen sent him back to the toy box with a foil bag of potato chips, always a handy bribe.

"So, what do you think?" she asked, when she was finished.

"What do I think?" Her father looked mystified. "Are you serious?"

"Yes."

"I think you're just like your mother."

"What does that mean?" Ellen felt resentment flicker like an ember in her chest.

"It means you're a worrywart. You worry too much!"

"How am I worrying too much?"

He shrugged. "You dreamed this up. It's crazy."

"I'm not crazy, Dad."

"But you don't have any facts. You only have assumptions." Her father frowned, making deep wrinkles in his forehead. "You're assuming lots of things that may or may not be true. I'm surprised at you, a newspaperwoman."

Ellen hadn't heard that term in years. "What are the assumptions?"

"You can't tell anything from those stupid cards about the missing kids. I get them, too."

"Did you see the last one, with Timothy Braverman?"

"Who the hell knows? They're junk mail. I toss them out."

"Why? They're real people, real kids."

"They have nothing to do with me, or you. Or my grandson."

Ellen tried another tack. "Okay, remember that photo I showed you, last time I was here?"

"No."

"You said it was Will. You thought it was Will. Remember?"

He frowned. "Okay, whatever."

"It wasn't Will, it was Timothy Braverman. You thought it was Will."

"What was that, a trick, then?"

"No, Dad. Keep an open mind. I need you to take this seriously."

"But I can't. It's just silly."

"Dad." Ellen touched his arm, the cashmere soft under her fingertips, and the tight line of his mouth softened just a little. "It wasn't a trick, but the photo wasn't Will. It was Timothy. They look that much alike, exactly alike."

"So the kid looks like Will, so what?" He shrugged.

"They could be the same kid."

"No, they can't." Her father almost laughed. "You can't tell anything from those police drawings. I know, they're on TV news all the time." He pointed to the doorway. "They look like one of Will's coloring books, in that damn chest out there."

"They have an artist who does them. They're real tools the police use."

"There's no way in the world you can tell who a composite is by tracing a picture over his face." Her father looked at Ellen with a smile reserved for the delusional, and for a minute, she almost saw it his way. "You adopted that little boy in there—my only grandchild—legally. You had a lawyer."

"Who killed herself."

"So what? What are you saying?"

Ellen didn't even know. "It just seems strange. Coincidental."

"Bah!" Her father waved her off, chuckling. "Forget about it, it's crazy talk. You adopted that boy, and he loves you. He was half-dead. Nobody wanted him but you. Nobody was there for him but you."

Ellen felt touched, but that wasn't the point. "What matters now is whether he's Timothy."

"He is *not* Timothy. He's just a kid who looks like Timothy. He's not the same kid. He's Will. He's *ours*." Her father paused, then looked at her with a half smile. "El, listen to me. Barbara's grandkids, Joshie and Jakie, you could swap 'em out and nobody would know the difference."

"Are they twins?"

"No, but they look alike, and they look like Will, too. They're all little boys, and they all look alike."

Ellen burst into laughter, and it felt good.

"Well, it's the truth." Her father warmed to the topic, moving closer. "Didn't anybody ever say to you, 'Hey, you look just like somebody I know?' That ever happen to you, Elly Belly?"

"Sure."

"Of course. It happens to me all the time. I look like people, who knows? Handsome men. George Clooney, maybe." Her father grinned. "That's all you got goin' on here. Don't worry about it."

Ellen's heart eased a little. "You think?"

"I know. They look alike but they're not the same kid. Will is ours, forever. He's *ours*." Her father gave her an aromatic, if awkward, hug, and Ellen knew he believed he had closed the deal.

"You sold me, Dad."

"I'm always selling somebody, kiddo." Her father grinned again. "But it's easy when you believe what you sell, and I believe this. Relax, honey. You're getting all worked up over nothing. Forget all this nonsense."

Ellen wanted to believe him. If Will wasn't really Timothy, then it all went away and they could be happy again.

"You seein' anybody?"

"Huh?" Ellen didn't know when the topic changed. "You mean, like a date?"

"Yes, exactly like a date." Her father smiled.

"No."

"Not since what's-his-name?"

"No."

"Not interested in anybody?"

Ellen thought of Marcelo. "Not really."

"Why not?" Her father puckered his lower lip, comically, and she knew he was trying to cheer her up. "A knockout like you? Why put yourself up on the shelf? You should go out more, you know? Live a little. Go dancing."

"I have Will."

"We'll sit for him." Her father took her hand in his, encircled her with his other hand, and started humming. "Let me lead, you follow."

"Okay, okay." Ellen laughed, finding the box step of the fox trot, letting herself be danced around the kitchen to her father's singing "Steppin' Out with My Baby" as he steered her from the small of her back, his firm hand a perfect rudder.

"Will, come see your ol' Pops!" he called over his shoulder, and in the next minute, Will came thundering into the kitchen.

"Ha, Mommy!" He ran to them, and they took his hands and the three of them shuffled around in a ring-around-the-rosy circle, with her father singing and Will looking up from one to the other, his blue eyes shining.

Ellen couldn't sing because of the sharp ache she felt inside, a sudden pain so palpable that she almost burst into tears, and she wished that her mother were still alive to take Will's hand and dance with them in a circle, all four of them happy and whole, a family again.

But it was an impossible wish, and Ellen sent it packing. She looked down at her child with tears in her eyes and all the love in her broken heart.

He's ours.

Chapter Thirty-nine

It was late by the time Ellen got Will home, having had dinner at the clubhouse with her father. Will and his repertoire of napkin antics had been the focus of attention during the meal, which had helped her forget about Timothy Braverman, at least temporarily. She wondered if God had intended children to provide such a service for alleged adults. We were supposed to be taking care of them, not the other way around.

She read Will a few books before bed and tucked him in, then went downstairs to close up the kitchen. The cardboard box of her mother's things sat on the butcher-block counter, and Oreo Figaro crouched next to it, sniffling it in his tentative way, his black nose bobbing to and from the box.

Ellen stroked his back, feeling the bumpiness of his skinny spine, regarding the box with a stab of sadness. It was so small, not even a two-foot square. Could a mother be so easily disposed of? Could one mother be so quickly traded for another?

You could swap 'em out, and nobody would know the difference.

Ellen opened the lid of the box, and Oreo Figaro jumped from the counter in needless alarm. Stacked inside the box was a set of photographs in various frames, and the top one was an eight-by-ten color photo of her parents at their wedding. She picked it up, setting aside her emotions. In the picture, her parents stood together under a tree, her father wearing a tux and his I-made-my-quota smile. Her mother's smile was sweet and shy, making barely a quarter moon on a delicate face, which was framed by short brown hair stiffened with Aqua Net. She had roundish eyes and a small, thin nose, like the tiny beak of a dime-store finch, and at only five-foot-one, Mary Gleeson seemed to recede in size, personality, and importance next to her larger-than-life husband.

Ellen set the photo aside and looked through the others, which only made it tougher not to feel sad. There was a picture of her parents in a canoe, with her father standing up in the boat and her mother laughing, but gripping the sides in fear. And there was another of them at a wedding, with her father spinning her mother on the end of his arm, like a puppeteer.

Ellen set the photo down. She remembered seeing it and the others at their house, and now they were all being exiled, along with that part of his life. She resolved to find a place for them here. No mother deserved to be forgotten, and certainly not hers.

She went to the cabinet under the sink, got a spray bottle of Windex and a paper towel, and wiped the dust from the top photo. She cleaned all of them, working her way to the end of the stack until she noticed that between two of the photos was a packet of greeting cards, bound by a rubber band. The top one was a fortieth wedding anniversary card, and she took out the packet and rolled off the rubber band. She opened the card, and it was from her father to her mother, the signature simply, *Love, Don.*

She smiled. That would be her father. He was never big in the elaboration department, and her mother would have been happy just to have the card, on time. Ellen went through the other cards, all saved by her mother, but the last envelope wasn't a greeting card. It was an envelope of her mother's stationery, the pale blue of the forget-me-nots that grew by their sugar maple in the backyard.

Ellen knew what it was, instantly. She had gotten a note like that from her mother, too, written right before she died. The front of the envelope read, *To Don*. The envelope was still sealed, and she ran her fingertip along the back of the flap, double-checking. Her father had never opened the note.

Ellen didn't get it. Had he really not opened the note? Didn't he want to hear the last words of his wife, written after she knew she was going to die? She wasn't completely surprised, but she slid a nail under the envelope flap, and tugged the note out, its paper thick and heavy. The top flap bore her mother's embossed monogram, MEG, in a tangle of curlicues, and she opened the note, welling up at the sight of her mother's handwriting.

Dear Don,

I know that you have always loved me, even if you have forgotten it from time to time. Please know that I understand you, I accept you, and I forgive you.

Love always, Mary

Ellen took the note and went to sit down in the dining room. The house was still and quiet. Oreo Figaro was nowhere in sight. The windows were inky mirrors, the dark sky moonless. For an odd moment she felt as if she were suspended in blackness, connected to nothing in this world, not even Will, asleep upstairs. She held the note in her hand and closed her eyes, feeling its heavy paper beneath her fingers, letting it connect her to her mother through space and time. And at that moment, she knew what her mother would say about Will and Timothy, in that soft voice of hers. It was what she had written to Ellen in her final note.

Follow your heart.

And so there in the quiet room, Ellen finally let herself listen to her heart, which had been trying to tell her something from the moment she first got the card in the mail. Maybe her father thought it was crazy to worry, but inside, she knew better. She couldn't pretend any longer and she couldn't live the rest of her life looking over her shoulder. She couldn't feel like a criminal when a cop pulled her over. She couldn't hide Will from his friends and neighbors.

So she vowed to follow her heart.

Starting now.

Chapter Forty

Ellen entered the lawyer's office and took a seat, surrounded by bronze, glass, and crystal awards, like so many blunt instruments. She had met Ron Halpren when she did the series on Will's adoption, having interviewed him for his expertise on family law, and she counted herself lucky she could call on him on such short notice.

"Thanks for meeting me on a Saturday," she said, and Ron walked around his cluttered desk and eased into his creaky chair.

"That's okay, I'm in most Saturday mornings." Ron had light eyes behind tortoiseshell glasses, a halo of fuzzy gray hair, and a shaggy graying beard to match. His frame was short and pudgy, and he looked like Paddington Bear in his yellow fleece pullover and thick jeans. "Sorry we're out of coffee. I was supposed to bring it in, but I forgot."

"No problem, and thanks for accommodating Will." Ellen gestured to the secretary's desk outside, where Will was eating vending-machine Fig Newtons and watching a *Wizard of Oz* DVD on the computer.

"It's great to see him so healthy. What a difference, eh?"

"Really." Ellen shifted forward on the chair. "So, as I said on the phone, I'm seeing you in your official capacity, and I want to pay for your time today."

"Forget it." Ron smiled. "You made me look like Clarence Darrow in the paper. I got tons of clients from that press. I owe *you*."

"I want to pay."

"Get to the point." Ron gestured toward the door. "I hear the scarecrow singing. We don't have much time."

"Wait, let me ask you something first. Is what we say absolutely confidential?"

"Yes, of course." Ron nodded. "How can I help you?"

Ellen hesitated. "What if a crime is involved? I didn't commit it, but I know, or I suspect, that a crime has been committed by someone else. Can you still keep this confidential?"

"Yes."

"So if I tell you about this crime, you wouldn't have to report it to the police?"

"I'd be barred from so doing."

Ellen loved the authoritative note in his voice. "Here goes. I think that Will could be a kid named Timothy Braverman, who was kidnapped in Florida two years ago."

"Will? *Your* son Will?"

"Yes."

Ron lifted a graying eyebrow. "So the crime in question is the kidnapping?"

"Yes, it was a carjacking gone wrong, and the kidnapper murdered the boy's nanny."

"Those are past crimes, unless we consider the fact that you retain custody of a kidnapped child as a continuing crime, which I don't think it is. You did legally adopt him."

"Here's what I need to know. If Will is really Timothy, what are my legal rights? Could the Bravermans, his birth parents, take him from me? Would I have to give him up if they found out or if they came and found us? Wouldn't it matter to the court that he lived with me for two years?" Ellen had so many questions that they ran into each other on the way out of her mouth. "That I'm the only mother he's ever really known? Would that—"

"Please, slow down." Ron held up his hands. "Tell me how you found this out, about Will."

So Ellen told him the story from the beginning, showing him her adoption file, the composite drawing, and her computer printouts of Timothy and Will at their various ages. "By the way, my father thinks I'm crazy. He's the only other person I've told."

Ron studied the photographs on his desk, even placing the composite tracing over the photo enlargement of Beach Man. Finally, he looked up at her, his expression grave behind his glasses.

"What do you think?"

"You're not crazy, but you are speculating." Ron's gaze remained steady. "The composite drawing is the linchpin, and you can't support your belief that Will is Timothy Braverman by comparing the composite with a photograph. It just isn't reliable enough. I see some similarity, but I can't be sure it's the same person."

Ellen tried to process what he was saying, but her emotions kept getting in the way.

"I'm not an expert, and neither are you. Composites, as a legal matter, cannot stand alone. Any one of my first-year law students can tell you that a composite is merely an aid to the identification and apprehension of a suspect. They're not a positive identification." Ron shook his head. "You don't have enough information on which to base any conclusion that Will is the kidnapped child."

It was the same thing her father had said, only in lawyerspeak.

Ron continued, "Now, the first question you should have is whether you have an obligation to go to the authorities with your suspicion. Answer? No, you don't."

Ellen hadn't even thought of that.

"The law doesn't impose responsibility on the citizenry to report crimes that are so speculative in nature."

"Good."

"That's not to say that you couldn't voluntarily report your suspicion to the authorities, if you wished. I'm sure there are fingerprints of Timothy Braverman on file, or blood tests that could be done, or DNA analysis that would determine if Will is Timothy." Ron tented his fingers in front of his beard and looked at her directly. "Obviously, you're concerned that if you tell the authorities and you're right, you would lose Will."

Ellen couldn't even speak, and Ron didn't wait for an answer.

"You're also concerned that if you're not right, you'd cause the Bravermans more pain and upset."

Ellen hadn't thought of them, but okay.

"Let's take a hypothetical. Assume for a moment that you're right. Will is Timothy."

Ellen hated the very sound of the sentence. "Could that even happen?"

"Hypothetically, it's easy, now that I give it some thought. All that is required for a valid adoption is a birth mother to produce a birth certificate, which is easy enough to fake. Unlike a driver's license or a passport, it doesn't even have a photo." Ron stroked his beard. "And she has to supply a signed waiver of her parental rights, from the birth father, too, which is also easy to forge, and she could make up the father's name. There are plenty of cases from mothers who put a child up for adoption without the father's consent. They're very common."

Ellen was remembering the elementary school, where Charles Cartmell's house was supposed to have been. The Charles Cartmell that nobody had heard of and who didn't exist.

"The second question is what are your parental rights, if any? And what are the Bravermans' parental rights, if any? That's the question that's worrying you, isn't it?" Ron paused. "If you're right, who gets Will?"

Ellen felt her eyes well up, but kept it together.

"You raise an interesting question under Pennsylvania law, and one not well understood by laymen. It involves the difference between adoption cases and custody cases."

Ellen couldn't take the suspense. "Just tell me, would I get to keep Will or would I have to give him back to the Bravermans?"

"You'd have to give him back to the Bravermans. No question."

Ellen felt stricken. She struggled to maintain control, teetering on the fine line between crying and screaming. But Will was in the next room, lost in a world somewhere over the rainbow.

"The Bravermans, as the child's birth parents, have an undisputed legal right to their child. They're alive, and they didn't give him up for adoption. If he was kidnapped, your adoption is simply invalid. Therefore, as a legal matter, the court would return Will to them."

"And he would go live in Florida?"

"That's where they live, so yes."

"Would I have the right to visit him?"

"No." Ron shook his head. "You would have no rights at all. The Bravermans may permit you to, perhaps to wean him from you, so to speak. But no court would order them to permit you to visit."

"But I adopted him lawfully," Ellen almost wailed.

"True, but in the hypothetical, no one gave him up for adoption." Ron cocked his head, tenting his fingers again. "As you remember from when you adopted him, you presented the court with signed waivers, consents to adoption from his mother and his father. That's a prerequisite to any adoption. If the consents were false, forged, or otherwise fraudulent, the adoption is invalid, whether you knew it or not."

Ellen forced herself to think back to her online research, done last night in anticipation of this meeting. "I read online about the Kimberley Mays case, in Florida, do you remember that? She was the baby who was switched at birth in the hospital, with another baby. In that case, the court let her stay with her psychological parent instead of her biological parent."

"I know the case. It got national attention."

"Doesn't that help me here? Can't we do it that way?"

"No, it doesn't help you at all." Ron opened his hands, palms up. "That's what I started to tell you. There's a fundamental difference between adoption and custody. The Florida court in the Mays case was applying a custody analysis, which involves an inquiry into the best interests of the child. The court decided that it was in the child's best interests for her to stay with her psychological father." Ron made a chopping motion with his hand. "But we have an adoption case here. It has nothing to do with what's in Will's best interests. It's simply a matter of power. Your case is like those in which the father's consent to the adoption was forged by the mother."

"What happens in those cases?"

"The child goes to the biological father. It's his child, and he didn't validly waive his right to him."

Ellen tried a different argument. "What if Will were ten or older, you think he'd get sent back?"

"Yes. As a legal matter, time won't cure the fact that he was kidnapped, even though you were unwitting."

"So it doesn't matter that I'm the only mother he's ever known?" Ellen found it impossible to accept. "My house is the only house he's ever known. The school, the classmates, the neighborhood, the babysitter. We're his world, and they're strangers."

"They happen to be his natural parents. It's a very interesting dilemma."

"No, it's not," Ellen shot back, miserably.

"Aw, wait." Ron's voice softened, transitioning from professor to friend. "We were speaking hypothetically. Come back to reality with me for a minute. I was there, when you were considering adopting him. Remember when we met, back then?"

"Yes."

"There was, and there still is, no reason in the world to think there was anything wrong with his adoption."

"But what about the mom with the twisted ovary? The lawyer's suicide?"

"People who can't get pregnant get pregnant, every day. My daughter-in-law, for one. And sadly, lawyers commit suicide. Life happens. So does death."

"I'm not crazy, Ron."

"I didn't say you're crazy. I don't think you're crazy. I think you got a bee in your bonnet, like my mother used to say. It's what makes you a good reporter. By the way, it's what made you adopt Will in the first place." Ron wagged a finger. "You couldn't get him out of your head, you told me."

"I remember." Ellen nodded sadly. Her gaze found a heavy crystal award, its beveled facets capturing a ray of sun, like an illustration of refraction in a physics book.

"You want my advice?"

"Yes."

"Good. Then listen to me."

Ellen felt as if it were a moment of truth. She hardly breathed.

"Take these papers and put them away, at the bottom of the drawer." Ron slid the file, the photographs, and the composite drawing across his messy desk. "Your adoption was valid. Will is your child. Enjoy him, and invite Louisa and me to his wedding."

Ellen packed up her papers, wishing she could take his advice. "I can't do that. I want to know what's true."

"I told you what's true. You've elevated suspicion to fact."

"But it doesn't feel right." Ellen fought her emotions to think clearly, and it was clarifying to talk about it out loud. "You know what I really feel? I feel that my kid is sick, but the doctors keep telling me he's fine. Not just you, my father, too."

Ron fell silent.

"But *I'm* his mother. I'm Dr. Mom." Ellen heard a new conviction in her voice, which surprised even her. "Call it a mother's instinct, or intuition, but I have it inside, and I know better."

"I hear you. You believe what you believe."

"Yes."

"Nobody can tell you different."

"Right!"

"You feel certainty. You are certain."

"Bingo!" Ellen said, but a slow smile eased across Ron's face, spreading his beard almost like a stage curtain.

"But you have to have a valid proof to support your certainty, and you have none. Do you understand?"

"Yes," Ellen answered, and she did. She gathered up the photographs and papers, and rose with them. "If proof is what I need, then proof is what I'll get. Thanks so much for your help."

"You're very welcome." Ron rose, too, his expression darkening. "But be careful what you wish. If you find proof that Will is Timothy Braverman, you'll feel a lot worse than you do already. You'll have to make a choice I wouldn't wish on my worst enemy."

Ellen had thought of nothing else, when she was trying to sleep last night. "What would you do, if it were your kid?"

"Wild horses couldn't make me give him back."

"No doubt?"

"Not a one."

"Then let me ask you this, counselor. How do you keep something that doesn't belong to you?" Ellen heard herself say it out loud, though she hadn't thought of it that way until this moment.

"Och. My." Ron cringed. "Excellent question."

"And how do I explain that to Will, when he grows up? What if he found out? What do I say? That I loved you, so I kept you, even though I knew the truth? Is that love, or just selfishness?" Ellen heard the questions pouring out, her heart speaking of its own accord. "This is the thing, Ron. When I adopted him, I felt like he belonged to me because another mother gave him up. But if she didn't, if she had had him taken from her by force, then he doesn't belong to me. Not truly."

Ron looked away, hitching up his jeans by his thumbs.

"So what do you say to that?" Ellen felt her eyes well up, then blinked them clear. "What would you do then?"

Ron sighed. "Fair points, all, but I have an easy out. In that case, saner minds would prevail. Louisa would kill me."

"Well, I don't have a Louisa. There's no saner head around. It's the me show. I just can't forget about it. Put it back in the bottle."

"Did you try?" Ron smiled, weakly.

"I've been trying since the minute I saw the card."

"Give it time, then. You might feel differently, next month, or next year."

Ellen shook her head. She hadn't gotten this far in life without knowing herself. It was other people she had trouble with. "I'm not built that way. When I see a thread hanging from someone's clothes, I have to pull it. If I see trash on the floor, I pick it up. I can't step over it. I can't pretend it's not there."

Ron laughed.

"This is almost like that, only ten times more. A million times more. It'll be in the back of my mind for the rest of my life, if I don't resolve it."

"Then I feel for you," Ron said softly, meeting her eye.

"Thanks." Ellen managed a smile, picked up her papers and coat, and moved to the door, where the *Wizard of Oz* soundtrack grew louder. "I'd better go. Will hates the flying monkeys."

"Everybody hates the flying monkeys," Ron said, with a final smile.

Chapter Forty-one

Ellen spent the afternoon in Quality Time Frenzy with Will, building a multicolored castle from Legos, stamping Play-Doh with cookie cutters, and making Boca burgers for dinner together. Will set the table, running back and forth with a squeeze bottle of ketchup and sliced tomatoes, and Ellen felt as if the kitchen were their domestic cocoon, with its soft lighting, warm stove, and chubby housecat curled up on the floor, in his tuxedo.

"I have a surprise dessert for you," Ellen said, but Will flashed her his picky-eater frown, as dubious a look as a three-year-old can muster.

"What is it?"

"I can't tell you, or it wouldn't be a surprise."

"Don't we have ice cream?"

"It's better than ice cream. Wait right here." Ellen got up, collected the dinner plates, and took them into the kitchen, where she set them in the sink. She fetched the dessert from the refrigerator, carried it to the dining room, and placed it on the table.

"Eeew, Mommy!" Will scrunched up his nose, the only reasonable response to what looked like a bowl of green plastic.

"Give it a chance. It's Jell-O, in your favorite color." Ellen had spent last night rereading the Braverman website and had seen the detail that Timothy loved lime Jell-O. Will had never eaten it before, as far as she knew, and she wanted to see if he liked it. Her test wasn't scientific, but that would come later.

Will wrinkled his nose. "Is it spinach?"

"No, it's lime."

"What's lime?"

"Like lemon, but better."

"What's lemon?"

"You know lemon. It's yellow, like the water ice we get at the pool. Or like lemon sticks." Ellen let it go. "Did you ever have lime Jell-O before?"

Will shook his head, eyeing the bowl warily. "I had red. That was good."

"Red is cherry."

"Do we have red?"

"No. I made green."

"Can't you make red?" Will looked at her with plaintive baby blues, and Ellen managed a smile.

"Not this time. Today, let's try green Jell-O."

Will scrambled to a kneeling position in his chair and leaned farther over the table on his elbows, sniffing the bowl. "Why doesn't it smell?"

"Give it a try and tell me if you like the taste."

"Do you like it?"

"I don't know, I never had it either." Ellen hated lime Jell-O, but didn't want to prejudice him. "I like to try new foods." She couldn't resist propagandizing, but Will ignored her.

"Why is it all flat on top?"

"That's how it comes out. Grab the bowl and give it a little shake."

Will did, giggling. "It wiggles! Just like on TV!"

"Fun, huh? Food you can play with." Ellen scooped some Jell-O into his dessert bowl and held her breath as he picked up his teaspoon, dipped the tip into the shiny green mound, then touched the tip of his tongue to the spoon. She said, "Give it a real taste."

"Do I have to?"

"Please."·

Will put the Jell-O in his mouth, and for a minute, didn't react.

"Well, do you like it?"

"It's good!" Will answered, his mouth full.

Chapter Forty-two

Ellen spent the evening in her home office, figuring out where and how to find the proof that Will was or wasn't Timothy. It was nutty to try to prove something she didn't want to be true, but she didn't have to decide now what to do after she learned the facts. She could find out, then decide whether to keep Will or, inconceivably, to give him up. It was a process, and she could take it in stages. At stage one, all she wanted was the truth. And, happily, if it turned out that Will wasn't Timothy, she could stop driving herself crazy and put the whole thing behind her. She took her BlackBerry from the holster and pressed speed dial C, and Connie picked up.

"Hey, El, how are you?"

"Fine, thanks. I have a huge favor to ask you, Connie. Something big came up at work, and I have to leave town for a few days." Ellen hated lying, but she couldn't risk telling even Connie the truth. "Is there any way you can cover for me?"

"Sure. Where you goin'?"

"Couple of different places, I'm not sure yet. It's a big story, and

I'm sorry, but it can't be helped." Ellen rarely went out of town on business, but she was praying she could sell Connie. She wasn't Don Gleeson's daughter for nothing. "I'll pay you overtime, whatever it takes. It's that important."

Connie hushed her. "I never worry about that. I can do it, but we're having people over tomorrow. Can it wait until Monday?"

"Yes, I really appreciate it."

"I'll pack my toothbrush. See you Monday, regular time. How many days will it be?"

God knows. "Just a few, the situation is fluid. Can you live with that?"

"Yep. See ya then."

Ellen hung up, with one more thing to do. She logged onto Outlook, skimmed her incoming email, and found one sender that surprised her. Marcelo. She clicked Open.

> **Dear Ellen,**
> **I'm concerned about you. I hope you're feeling better. Please do call a doctor. We lack a human face without you! Best, Marcelo**

Ellen felt a little thrill. He was such a great guy. It was worth fainting to get him to hold her. She smiled at the memory of being cradled against his chest, but it faded when she thought of what she had to do next. She hit Reply and started typing, then stopped. It was the point of no return, and the stakes were the job she loved and needed. Still, she typed on:

> **Marcelo,**
> **Thanks for your nice note, but unfortunately, I need to take this week off. I have plenty of vacation time coming, and I'll take the time out of that.**

Ellen paused, not knowing whether to mention the think piece, which was still due Friday. She continued, typing:

I'm not sure if I'll get my piece finished by deadline, but I'll stay in touch with you about this. I'm sorry, and hope this doesn't cause too much of a problem. Thanks and best, Ellen

She clicked Send and swallowed hard. Taking a vacation with a layoff pending could be career suicide, but she had no choice. The situation with Will and Timothy put everything into perspective, and her job would always be second to her child.

"So be it," Ellen said aloud.

Oreo Figaro looked up at the sound, lifting his chin from his front paws, regarding her with disapproval.

Chapter Forty-three

Ellen awoke to the ringing of her BlackBerry, which she kept on the night table as an alarm clock. She grabbed it before it woke Will. "Hello?" she asked, muzzy.

"It's Marcelo." His voice always sounded so soft on the phone, his accent more pronounced, and Ellen blinked herself awake, checking the digital clock. Sunday, 8:02 A.M.

"Oh, jeez, hi."

"Did I wake you?"

Yes. "No."

"Sorry to bother you, but I got your vacation request and I wanted to discuss it with you. It's a problem for us, right now."

"It's just that—"

"I'm going to be in your area tonight. I can stop by, if you like, and we can talk about it."

Marcelo, here? I'll have to vacuum. And put on makeup. Not in that order.

"Ellen? I don't mean to intrude—"

"No, it's fine, a great idea."

"What time is good?"

"Will goes to bed around seven thirty, so any time after eight o'clock."

"I'm free at nine. See you then."

"Great. Thanks." Ellen pressed End. Marcelo was coming here? Her boss, her crush? Was this a date or a firing? It was exciting and unnerving, both at once. At best, she'd have to lie to his face about where she was going on Monday, which wouldn't be easy. Especially if he wore that aftershave, eau d'eligible bachelor.

"Mommy?" Will called out, waking up in his bedroom.

"Coming, sweetie," Ellen called back, becoming a mom again.

Chapter Forty-four

"Marcelo, hi, come in," Ellen said, opening her front door onto a living room that looked as if no one lived there. Will's toys, books, and DVDs had been put away, and the rugs had been vacuumed. Cat hair had been lint-rolled from the sofa cushions, and paw prints wiped from the coffee table. The house was so clean, it should be for sale.

"Thanks." Marcelo stepped inside, and Ellen edged back, suddenly awkward. She had fantasized about him walking through her door, though the fantasy didn't include vacuuming.

"Let me take your coat," Ellen said, but Marcelo was already sliding out of his black leather jacket, and she caught a whiff of spicy aftershave, a scent that spoke directly to her I'm-Very-Single cortex, bypassing the saner He's-Your-Boss lobe.

"What a nice house," he said, looking around. He had on a black ribbed turtleneck with nice brown slacks, and Ellen found herself wondering if he'd been on a date. He asked, "How long have you lived here?"

"Six years or so." Ellen brushed a stray hair from her eyes, surprised that even a single strand had escaped her product-heavy blow-dry. She had changed her outfit three times, only to end up in her trademark loose blue sweater, white tank underneath, jeans, and Danskos. She didn't want to signal that she considered this anything but a meeting between colleagues. "Would you like a Diet Coke or something?"

"Sure, great."

"Hang on a sec. You can sit down." Ellen gestured at the sofa cushion without hesitation.

"Let me help you. I'd love a house tour."

"Okay, but, it's a short one." Ellen waved awkwardly at the dining room. It was odd, having him in her house, standing so close to her when she wasn't even unconscious. "Speaks for itself, huh? And over here's the teeny tiny kitchen."

"Very nice." Marcelo followed her, looking around with his hands linked loosely behind his back. "It's warm and friendly."

"And clean."

Marcelo nodded, with a smile. "I was going to say it was clean. Very clean."

"Thank you." Ellen went into the cabinet, found a decent tumbler, then went in the fridge and got him ice and a soda. Oreo Figaro sat on the counter, watching the goings-on with interest.

"I like cats. What's his name?"

"Oreo Figaro."

Marcelo lifted an eyebrow. "Back home, many people have two names, like my brother, Carlos Alberto. But I didn't think that was so common in the States."

"It's not. He's Brazilian."

Marcelo laughed. He popped the soda and poured it fizzling into the glass. "I live in town."

I know. We all know. You're the hot, single Latin boss, and therefore the most-talked-about person in the newsroom, if not the Western Hemisphere.

"I think about moving out here, but I wonder how you meet women in the suburbs."

"At the sandbox, mostly."

Marcelo smiled.

"The men are short, but they're single."

Marcelo laughed again. "I was out here on a blind date. Can you imagine that?"

"Unfortunately, yes." Ellen liked the way his accent made it *e-magine*. "How was it?"

"Excruciating."

"Been there. Excruciating conversation, excruciating restaurant, excruciating kiss good night. It's excruciating."

Marcelo laughed again. "Glad to see you're feeling better."

I always make jokes when I'm nervous.

"It was very strange to have you faint, so suddenly." Marcelo frowned slightly, and Ellen recognized a flicker of concern behind his eyes, which made her warm all over.

"Thank you for being so kind about it."

"Give me no credit. I wanted to leave, but you were lying in my way."

Ellen laughed, and Marcelo sipped his soda and set it down.

"So, to your email."

"Yes."

"Please explain."

"I'm not sure where to begin."

"Let's be honest with each other. You're reliable. You make deadlines. You didn't take a vacation last year, I checked. All of a sudden, you're fainting and you need time off for a mysterious reason." Marcelo glanced away, then back again. "I will tell you, I usually keep my private life to myself, but my mother was recently diagnosed with breast cancer. She's at home, in Pinheiros, getting treatments, and she tells me they make her very tired."

Ellen felt for him, having been there herself, and the pain on his face was visible. "I'm sorry."

"Thank you. If that is what's going on with you, or if you have some other illness, you can be sure I'll keep it confidential."

Ellen felt touched. "I don't have cancer, but thank you for asking."

"Is it another illness? Is that it?"

Ellen didn't know what to say. His tone was so calm and the excuse so handy that she almost considered making up a short-lived disease. She could keep her job, if she lied.

"Do you have a drug problem, or alcohol? We have counseling for that, you know."

"No, that's not it, at all."

"Well, what then? Am I being too intrusive? I feel like I'm doing that a lot lately, with you, though I'm trying to help you. It's a difficult situation, having to make these layoff decisions, and I'm doing everything I can to save your job." Marcelo stood straighter, shaking his head. "But a vacation request, at a time like this, how do you justify that?"

"All I can tell you is that I need to take these few days off to settle something personal."

Marcelo looked at her, his regret plain. "That's it?"

Ellen was so tempted to tell him, but she couldn't. "Sorry," she answered. "That's it."

"Are you going somewhere or staying here?"

"I'd rather not say. I'm taking vacation time, is all."

Marcelo's lips pursed. "Will you get the homicide piece written on time?"

"Honestly, I don't know."

"How does your draft look?"

"I haven't started drafting yet."

"May I have your notes?"

"I haven't transcribed them yet." Ellen felt a wave of guilt at his dismayed expression.

"How am I supposed to give you an extension and no one else? How can I justify treating you specially?"

"If you have to fire me, I understand. But I need this time for myself."

"Would you rather get fired than tell me what's going on?" Marcelo asked, his eyes disbelieving. "Can that be what you truly want?"

"Yes," Ellen answered, though she hadn't thought of it that way.

"It matters *that* much to you, whatever you're doing?"

"It matters more to me than anything in the world."

Marcelo blinked.

Ellen blinked back. For a minute, they played eye chicken.

Marcelo sighed, and his expression softened. "Okay, you win. Take the time you need this week, but that's it. I'll tell everyone you're not feeling well. It'll make sense, after you fainted dead away."

"You're saying yes?" Ellen was dumbfounded. "Why?"

"I'm trying to show you that I'm not a jerk."

"I know that. I never thought you were."

Marcelo lifted an eyebrow, dubious, but Ellen knew she'd never convince him otherwise, after what Sarah had told him.

"What about the homicide piece?"

"It can wait a week. The fire in the Yerkes Building is the new story."

"What fire?" Ellen had been in the love cocoon with Will and hadn't heard. The Yerkes was one of the biggest buildings in town.

"Three people killed, cleaning personnel, so sad. The building burned to the ground. Police suspect arson."

"Wait a minute," Ellen said, as the truth dawned on her. "Does that mean you didn't really need my draft, just now?"

"Uh, yes." Marcelo looked sheepish. "Oh well."

"You rat!"

"You don't think I'm a rat. You like me."

Ellen was mortified. "How do you know?"

"I run the newsroom. You think I don't know the news?"

Ellen laughed, embarrassed. "Oh yeah, so what else do you know?"

"Is it true?" Marcelo's dark eyes glittered in a teasing way.

"You answer me. Then I'll answer you."

"I know everybody believes that I'm attracted to you, and that's why you're not getting laid off."

Ellen flushed.

"And I have to say, they're half-right," Marcelo answered, his voice suddenly serious. His eyes met hers across the counter, with a very adult honesty. "I would love to take you out, I admit it."

Ellen felt a smile spread across her face.

"But that's not the reason you're keeping your job. You're keeping your job because you're a great reporter."

"Thank you. And what if this crush is mutual?"

"So is it?" Marcelo was grinning, but she couldn't believe they were having this conversation. Oreo Figaro listened, in shock.

"Yes."

"That's very nice to hear, but it's too bad. Nothing will happen between us. It compromises you. It compromises me. This is romance in the time of sexual harassment, and that means nothing good happens, never ever. Except maybe this." In the next second, Marcelo leaned over and planted the softest, sweetest kiss on her unsuspecting lips, and when it was over, he pulled away. "Never ever again."

"Excruciating," Ellen said, meaning it.

Chapter Forty-five

"Mommy, don't go!" Will wailed, grabbing Ellen around the knees and holding on for dear life. She was dressed for the early flight, her purse on her shoulder, her roller bag packed and ready, but she wasn't going anywhere, blocked by the Wall of Guilt.

"Honey, I have to." Ellen rubbed his little back. "Remember, we talked about this? I have to go away for work but I'll be back very soon, in four or five days, probably."

"FOUR DAYS!" Will burst into new tears, and Connie intervened, putting a hand on his shoulder.

"Will, you and me will have a great time. I brought ice cream, and we can make sundaes after school today. Won't that be fun?"

"Mommy, no!"

"Will, it's all right." Ellen had learned from experience that he would never calm down, so she gave him a last hug and kiss on the head while she pried his fingers off one by one, like the dewclaws of a kitten. "I have to go, honey. I'll call you tonight. You'll see, I'll be back soon."

"Say good-bye, Will." Connie had him in hand. "Bye, Mommy, see you soon!"

"Love you, Will," Ellen said, opening the door the second she was freed and running out into the cold with her bag.

Wondering if every mother felt like a fleeing felon, at times.

Chapter Forty-six

The sky was a supersaturated teal, and kelly green fronds on the palm trees fluttered in the breeze. Lush olive green hedges lined the curbs, and thick lawns, edged to perfection, bordered dense reds of climbing bougainvillea, the orange and yellow of tiny lantana flowers, and dark purple jacaranda. And that was just the Miami airport.

Ellen slipped on a pair of sunglasses, driving a rental car, leaving the window open until the air-conditioning kicked in. She sweltered in her navy sweater and took it off when the traffic slowed to a stop. According to the dashboard, the temperature hovered at ninety-nine degrees, and the humidity mixed ocean salt, heavy perfume, and cigarette smoke like a beachside cocktail. In less than an hour, she'd be at Carol and Bill Braverman's.

She dug in her purse and found the paper with the home address, which she'd gotten online and MapQuested last night. The exit wasn't far up the highway. She leaned over the steering wheel, craning her neck like a sea turtle, not wanting to miss it. The traffic was stop-and-go, in impossibly heavy congestion that took up four lanes, wider than any expressway back home.

Traffic stopped again, and Ellen reflected on her mission. She'd have to wait for an opening to get the proof she needed and she couldn't predict when that would happen. She'd have to keep on her toes, and the hard part would be staying undercover. Nobody could know why she was here, least of all the Bravermans.

She left the highway, got off at the exit, and in time found herself cruising along a smooth concrete causeway over a choppy turquoise bay lined with mansions, many with glistening white boats parked along private slips. She reached the other side, where the traffic was lighter than it had been and the cars costlier. She took a right and a left, then saw the street sign outlined in bright green. Surfside Lane. She took a right onto the Bravermans' street.

Did Will start his life here? Was this his street?

She passed a modern gray house, its front a huge expanse of glass, then a Spanish stucco mansion with a red-tiled roof, and finally an ornate French chateau. Each house was different from the next, but she noticed right away that they all had one thing in common. Every home had a yellow ribbon tied out front, whether it was to a palm tree, a front fence, or a gate.

She slowed the car to a stop, puzzled. The ribbons were pale and tattered, like the one her neighbors, the Shermans, had back home, for their daughter serving in Iraq. But all these people couldn't have family serving in the war. She sensed the explanation before she saw it, cruising ahead to 826, then closing in on 830, which confirmed her theory.

HELP US FIND OUR SON, read a large white sign, festooned with yellow ribbons, and it stood planted in an otherwise picture-perfect front lawn. The sign showed the age-progressed photo of Timothy Braverman from the white card, and tiger lilies and sunny marigolds grew around its base, a living memorial to a son the Bravermans prayed wasn't gone forever.

Ellen's throat caught. She felt a pang of sympathy, and conscience. She had known from the Braverman website that they were missing Timothy, but seeing the sign with her own eyes made it real. The boy on the sign, Will or Timothy, looked back at her with a gaze at once familiar and unknown.

Please, no.

She set her emotions aside and looked past the sign. The Bravermans' house was like something out of *Architectural Digest,* a large contemporary with a crushed-shell driveway that held a glistening white Jaguar. Suddenly two women in tank tops and running shorts walked past the car, pumping red-handled weights, and Ellen hit the gas, not to arouse suspicion.

She circled the block, composing herself and cooling down as she eyed the homes, one more lovely than the next. She had expected that the neighborhood would be wealthy; any family who could afford that reward would live in a nice place, and her online research had told her that she was driving through a neighborhood of three-million-dollar houses. In fact, according to zoom.com, the Bravermans' house cost $3.87 million, which she tried not to compare with her three-bedroom, one-bath back home.

It's warm and friendly.

Ellen pushed that thought away. She took a left and another left, going down the next block, getting the lay of the land. No one was out except a gardener using a noisy leaf blower and a laborer edging a lawn. The sun beat down on the shiny foreign cars, dappling the lawns through the palm fronds, and she turned around and headed back to the main drag, Coral Ridge Way, the two-lane road that led back to the causeway. It was busy, and when the light changed, she parked across the street from the entrance to Surfside Lane. She didn't park on the Bravermans' block for fear of being noticed.

She cracked open a bottle of warm water and checked the clock—1:45. She turned away when an older man strolled past with a chubby Chihuahua, and she watched the traffic to the causeway. By

1:47, her sunglasses were sliding down her nose, and the car had grown impossibly hot, proving that she was a stakeout rookie. She turned on the ignition and slid down the window.

She had barely taken a second sip of water when she saw the chrome grille of a white Jaguar nose out of Surfside Lane, pause at the stop sign, and pull a left. It had to be the Bravermans' car because theirs was the only Jaguar on the block. In the driver's seat was the outline of a woman, alone. She had to be Carol Braverman, herself.

Yikes!

Ellen turned on the ignition, hit the gas, and found a place in the brisk line of traffic to the causeway. Her heartbeat stepped up. Carol was two cars ahead as they picked up speed and soared over the causeway, the wind off the water blowing her hair around. She kept an eye on the white car as they wound through the streets, which grew increasingly congested, but she stayed on Carol as she turned into a strip mall and pulled into a parking spot.

Ellen parked several rows away and cut the ignition, then held her breath waiting for Carol Braverman to emerge. She remembered the photos of her online but was dying to see her in person, to see if she looked like Will, or vice versa.

The next moment, the driver's door opened.

Chapter Forty-seven

Ellen couldn't see Carol Braverman's face because she had on large black sunglasses and a hot pink visor, but she still felt a tingle of excitement at the sight of her. Carol got out of the car, tall and shapely in a white cotton tank top and an old-school tennis skirt. Pink pom-poms wiggled from the backs of her sneakers, and a bouncy dark blond ponytail popped out of her visor. She slipped a white quilted bag over her shoulder and hurried to the gourmet grocery, where she picked a shopping cart and rolled it inside the tinted glass doors of the store.

Ellen grabbed her keys and purse, got out of the car, and hustled through the parking lot to the grocery, snagging a shopping cart for show. The entrance doors slid aside, and the air-conditioning hit like January, but two women shoppers stood bottlenecking the entrance, looking at the green stand for cut flowers. She kept an eye on Carol but didn't want to draw attention to herself, especially when she realized how out of place she looked. Nobody else had on a thick white turtleneck, Mom jeans, and brown clogs accessorized with Pennsylvania mud.

She ducked into the back row of the flower department, going around the shoppers, and fake-lingered at the bird-of-paradise plants, then glanced over her shoulder. In the next minute, the women moved, leaving Carol right behind her, using the ATM machine, and so close that Ellen could almost hear her humming. She couldn't risk Carol seeing her and maybe recognizing her later, so she kept her head down and her sunglasses on her nose. The ATM beeped, and the humming grew fainter, so she knew that Carol had moved on.

Time to get stalking.

Ellen never knew when she'd get another opportunity and she had to see Carol's face, close up. She drifted sideways past a wall of nuts in plastic scoop-it-yourself canisters and fake-browsed the roasted unsalted almonds, raw salted almonds, and raw unsalted almonds. For a minute, she couldn't even fake-decide. Out of the corner of her eye, she could see Carol looking at the peppers, her back turned.

Ellen pulled a plastic bag from a perforated roll, picked up a plastic scoop, and dug out some raw almonds, then spotted Carol moving around the perimeter of the produce department, bagging a head of romaine and putting it in her cart, her back still turned. Ellen got a twist tie for her almond bag and crossed nearer to Carol, keeping her head down in the apple aisle, where rosy galas, fat Macintoshes, and Golden Delicious sat mounded like Egyptian pyramids. She positioned herself midway down the aisle, so that she could get a good look at Carol's face if she turned around.

Ellen picked up a Granny Smith and examined it with ersatz absorption, and in the split second she bent over to put it back, Carol spun around with her cart.

No!

The rest happened even before Ellen could process it. Carol's cart crashed squarely into Ellen's hip, startling her so that she backed into the apple pyramid, and before she could stop them, Gala and Fuji apples were rolling toward her in a pesticide-free avalanche.

"Oh no!" Ellen yelped, punching up her glasses.

"I'm so sorry!" Carol tried to catch the apples, but they hit the lacquered floor and shot off in all directions, like billiard balls.

"Oh, jeez!" Ellen bent over to hide her face, fake-collecting apples, just as Carol straightened up, her cheeks slightly flushed, her hands full of apples.

"I can't believe I did that! I'm so sorry!"

"It's okay," Ellen said, but she glanced up and almost gasped.

Carol had taken off her sunglasses, and in person, the resemblance between her and Will was obvious. She had Will's sea-blue eyes and creamy coloring. Her lips were on the thin side, like his, and her chin slightly pointed, too. Carol struck her instantly as being *of* Will, as if Ellen could smell the blood they shared. Stricken, she put her head down, but Carol knelt next to her, gathering apples in her tennis skirt.

"It was my fault. That's what I get for rushing."

"No, it was me. I knocked them over." Ellen collected the escaping apples, flushed with emotion, keeping her face to the floor.

"I was doing too much. I always think I can squeeze in one little errand. You ever do that?"

"Sure."

"Of course that's when things go wrong."

"Mrs. Braverman, let me help you," a stockboy said, hurrying over in a pepper green smock and checkered Vans. He bent down and corralled some of the apples, his fuzzy dreadlocks falling into his young face.

"Thanks, Henrique." Carol rose, brushing off a pair of tan, finely muscled legs. "I'm such a klutz today. I hit this woman with my cart."

"Really, I'm fine." Ellen rose, looking for the exit, but suddenly, Carol placed a manicured hand on her arm.

"Again, I'm so sorry."

"It's nothing, thanks." Ellen shed Carol's hand, turned away as calmly as possible, and walked through the produce department and out of the store. She hit the humid air and made a beeline for the rental car. Her eyes welled up behind her sunglasses, and her throat thickened. She fumbled in her purse for the car keys, let herself inside, then slumped low in the driver's seat.

She sat in the car, staring out the windshield. Cars broiled in the Miami sun, and pink flowers ringed the parking lot. She gazed at them without really seeing them, wiping her eyes and trying to process what she'd seen. Carol Braverman, a grieving mother. She seemed like a nice woman, she seemed like Will. She could be missing the child who was at her home right now, up north.

Ellen thought of Susan Sulaman, haunted by the loss of her children, and then Laticia Williams, bereft. She knew how they felt, and she could guess how Carol Braverman felt. A wave of conscience engulfed her, and she felt awful that she might be causing another woman that sort of pain. Another mother.

His real mother.

She reached for the bottle of water and took a sip, but it was hot and burned her throat. She couldn't help but feel it was a penance, of sorts.

A swinging white bag drew her attention, and Ellen looked out the window. Carol was leaving the grocery store and hurrying to her car, carrying a brown paper bag, then she chirped the car unlocked, got in the driver's seat, and reversed out of the space.

Ellen started the ignition, shaken.

Chapter Forty-eight

Carol drove faster than before, and Ellen had to concentrate not to lose her in the heavy traffic. The task checked her emotions and focused her thoughts. Her subjective sense that Carol was Will's mother wasn't scientific. She still had to get the proof she needed, despite what her heart was telling her.

The two cars threaded their way through the congested downtown, and Ellen stayed within three cars of Carol, not risking falling farther behind. The sidewalks were packed with tourists in bathing suits and cover-ups, and loud music *thumpa-thump*ed from a convertible. A sleek black Mercedes pulled up in the next lane, and its cigar-puffing driver grinned at her.

Ring! The sound jarred Ellen from her thoughts. It was her BlackBerry, and she kept an eye on Carol as she hunted for the device with her hand, fumbling around in her purse until she located it and checked the display. She recognized the number. It was Sarah Liu's cell number.

Ellen pressed Ignore and tossed the phone aside. She followed

Carol through a fork in the road, then over a causeway, which was less busy. They drove out over a spit of land, where condos and high-rises gave way to suburban houses, with flowerbeds and manicured hedges. People strolled with small dogs, a young man pedaled a collapsible bicycle with tiny tires, and women power-walked, carrying water bottles.

Carol took a right and a left, with only one car between them, and Ellen spotted a sign painted melon, which read BRIDGES, and beyond it lay a small building with a red-tiled roof. A tall hedge concealed the building, but she guessed it was a spa or salon, and two women drove in ahead of her. She stayed behind Carol as they snaked through the tall hedge.

Ellen was last in the line of cars that trailed up the lovely winding drive, and the sight on the other side caught her by surprise. A large group of children toting backpacks clustered around several women, obviously teachers, under the shaded entrance to the building. The children couldn't have been more than five years old, so it had to be a preschool.

Will could have a brother? Or a sister? Instead of just a cat?

She watched the scene with a sinking sensation. The teachers brought each child to the waiting car, waving a cheery good-bye, and she kept an eye on Carol to see which child was hers. Ellen hadn't thought about whether the Bravermans would have another child, or Timothy a sibling. The Braverman website hadn't mentioned another child. Maybe they hadn't wanted to risk his security, given what had happened.

Carol reached near the head of the line, but instead of going to the entrance, she peeled to the left and found a space in the parking lot. Ellen hung back, idling the car, and the next minute, Carol got out with her quilted purse and a black Adidas bag and hurried toward the entrance. The teachers waved to her as she jogged up to them, greeting her with smiles and chatter, but Ellen couldn't hear what they were saying.

She had to get out of the line for pickups. She took a quick right and parked at the far end of the lot, reversing into the space so she could have a clear view of the entrance, to see when Carol left with her child.

She lowered the car windows before she switched off the ignition, having learned her lesson, and waited. The dashboard clock read 2:55. It was a late dismissal for preschool, but if this school was like Will's, the parents could pick up at any time of the day.

But this preschool isn't like Will's. It's a lot nicer.

By three fifteen, she was sweltering in the parked car. The thermometer on the dash read one hundred degrees. Her shirt clung to her neck, and her legs were so hot that she wanted to tear her pants off. By three thirty, she'd rolled them up to capri length and wrapped up her hair in a messy topknot, having found a stray barrette in her purse. She waited, watching the entrance, but it seemed as if all of the kids had been picked up. By three forty-five, her sunglasses were melting onto the bridge of her nose, and she decided to take a risk.

She grabbed her bag, got out of the car, and walked through the parking lot to the entrance under a tall breezeway. There were no more teachers or children out front, and she walked to the front door and tried it, but it was locked. A VISITORS MUST REPORT TO THE OFFICE sign was taped to the glass, and she peered through. She could see the barest outline of a large entrance hall with a glistening tile floor, and colorful bulletin boards hung on the left wall, across from a glass-walled office on the right. Carol was nowhere in sight.

Ellen pressed a buzzer beside the door, and almost immediately a mechanical voice asked, "Can I help you?"

"I'm new to the area and I'd like to see the school."

"Come right in. The office is on your right." A loud buzz sounded, and she yanked on the door and let herself inside. A slim, attractive woman with dark, curly hair emerged from the office and strode toward her with a smile, extending a hand.

"Welcome to Bridges, I'm Janice Davis, the assistant director." She looked pretty in a pink cotton top, white pants, and light blue flats.

Ellen shook her hand. "I'm Karen Volpe, and I thought I'd stop in to see your school."

"Of course. Did you have an appointment?"

"No, I'm sorry." Ellen was wondering if Carol was in one of the classrooms. "My husband and I haven't moved down yet, and I wanted to see the preschools in the area."

"I see." Janice checked her watch, a slim gold one. "I don't have time now for the meeting we like to give with the tour. Let's make an appointment and you can return."

"I'm not sure when I can get back. Can you give me the quick version of the tour? We can chat as we walk."

"Sure, okay." Janice smiled. "You must be from New York."

Works for me. "How did you know?"

"Everything's quicker. You'll live here a week and your pace will slow down." The softness of her tone took the sting from her words, as did a hostess wave toward the hallway. "I'll show you our classrooms and our media center."

"You have your own library, in a preschool?"

"We all know how important reading and libraries are, and modesty aside, Bridges is the best preschool in south Florida, if not the entire state. We draw from three different counties." Janice went into lecture mode. "Now, when are you moving down?"

"We're not sure." Ellen scanned the hallway ahead, which was empty, with classrooms off to the side, five in all, their doors closed. She wondered which one contained Carol. "My son is three, and we like to be prepared, to do things in advance."

"You'd need to, for us." Janice stopped at the first door. "This is our classroom for two-year-olds, the ones who stay later, that is. We like to mix them with the older children, too, so they get the socialization that's so vital, especially for our onlies."

"Onlies?"

"Only children."

"Of course." Ellen looked through the window in the door, and inside was a sunny classroom with two teachers, finger-painting with toddlers in coral smocks. Carol wasn't inside.

"Admissions are very restrictive."

"My son is very bright." *He can trace all by himself.*

Janice led her to the next door. "The three-year-olds," she said, and inside sat a circle of children shaking tambourines, with two teachers standing in front of the room. Still no Carol. Janice showed her to the next door, where they paused. "And this is our classroom of four-year-olds. They're learning French right now."

"Really." Ellen peered through the window, where the kids and their teachers looked *très contents.* But there was no Carol.

"We believe that language skills should be taught early, and they take to it like ducks to water. I'll give you our literature on our postgraduate placement rates. We're a feeder for all the best private schools."

"Let's see the five-year-olds."

"What is it you do, did you say?" Janice asked, but Ellen walked ahead and peeked into the classroom full of five-year-olds in little chairs, books open in their laps. No Carol.

"Which language are they learning?" she asked, to avoid the question.

"Reading skills. We drill and drill."

Sir, yes, sir. "Good for you." Ellen straightened up. "And the media center?"

"This way." Janice led her down the hall to a double door. "This is one of the special enrichment events we have each day, for after-care. Monday is story time and on Tuesday we do science . . ."

Ellen tuned her out when she saw what was going on inside. A group of children sat in a semicircle, laughing and pointing while a teacher in a Mother Goose costume read to them. But a telltale pink pom-pom stuck from beneath the hem of her hoop skirt. It wasn't a teacher in the Mother Goose getup. It was Carol Braverman.

Janice said, "Here, you see story time, where we perform stories for the children."

"And the teachers do this?"

"No, she's not a teacher. She's one of our moms, who used to be an actress."

"An actress?"

"Yes. Her name is Carol Braverman, and she worked at Disney World. She was Snow White."

Of course she was. "Is her child in the class?"

"No, Carol just comes to read to the children." Janice paused. "She doesn't have a child in the class."

Ellen couldn't ask a follow-up without blowing her cover. "That's very nice of her, to do that. I guess you pay her very well."

"Oh, she won't take a dime for it. Carol does it because she loves children. Come with me." Janice took Ellen by the elbow and led her back up the hall. "It's actually a terrible tragedy. Carol's little boy, Timothy, was kidnapped a couple of years ago and they never got him back. That first year, she was a mess. Depressed, in hell. But she pulled herself together and decided that it actually helps her healing process to be around children."

Ellen felt a wave of guilt. "How can she do that? I would find that so painful."

"I agree with you, but do you want to know what she said to me, when I asked her that very question?"

No. "Yes."

"She said, 'If I'm around children, at least I get to experience what it would be like if Timothy were still with me. I don't miss out on everything this way, and when I get him back, I'll be right up to speed.'"

Ellen felt like crying. She didn't want to know this, any of it. She couldn't believe she was doing this to another woman. She wished she'd never come.

"I know, right? It's so sad."

"Think she'll get him back?"

"I'm sure the chances are low, but we're all pulling for her. If anybody deserves it, Carol does." They reached the office, and Janice brightened. "If you'll come in with me, I'll give you that literature I mentioned."

Ellen followed her inside the office, but her thoughts had skipped ahead.

She didn't know if she had the heart to stalk Carol to her next stop.

Much less to get the proof she didn't want in the first place.

Chapter Forty-nine

The late-day sun was even hotter, and Ellen was trailing Carol back through the luxurious suburbs when her BlackBerry started ringing. She plucked it from her purse and glanced at the display, which showed the newspaper's main telephone number.

Marcelo!

"Hello?" she said, picking up, but it wasn't him, it was Sarah.

"Marcelo told us you're taking a few days off. Listen, I won't keep you, but I wanted to apologize."

"That's okay," Ellen said, surprised. Sarah sounded genuinely contrite.

"I'm sorry I got so hyper about the story. When you fainted, I felt awful."

"Thanks. It's just this bug, I feel dizzy."

"Okay, so, we cool?"

"Sure." Ellen took a right turn, keeping up with Carol in rush-hour traffic. They were driving back through the congested part of the city, but she switched lanes, staying with Carol.

"I assume you heard, we got bumped for the Yerkes fire." Sarah snorted. "One man's ceiling is another man's floor."

"Listen, I gotta go back to bed."

"Feel better. Take care."

"Thanks. See you." Ellen hung up and accelerated to make a green light as they wound left and right through traffic and finally traveled over the causeway to Surfside Lane.

Carol turned right onto Surfside, and Ellen drove down the main drag and took a U-turn, coming back to park in her position across the street, so that she could see if Carol went out again. She lowered the windows and twisted off the ignition, craning her neck to see down Surfside. If she tilted her head, she had a partial view of the Bravermans' house and driveway. More people were walking on Coral Ridge than before, but no one seemed to notice her. A man who looked like a model jogged past, and behind him, two Rollerbladers skated toward the causeway, their thighs pumping away.

Ring Ring! Ellen reached for her BlackBerry, checking the screen. HOME. It had to be Connie. "Hey, Con, how's it going?"

"Another day, another macaroni picture."

"Art you can eat, right?" Ellen smiled. Her thoughts traveled back to her snug little house though her gaze remained on the Bravermans'.

"I don't know if this matters, but I wanted to give you a heads-up. I think somebody just called here. Her name was Sarah. Is that someone from the newspaper or a story?"

"The paper." Ellen tensed. "When was this?"

"About half an hour ago. Will answered the phone and told her that you weren't home."

"*What?*"

"I'm sorry. He got to the phone before I did. He thought it might be you. He talked to her and hung up. I heard him say Sarah. I didn't even get to talk to her."

"Will said I wasn't there?" Ellen couldn't process it fast enough. "Tell me exactly what he said."

"He told her you went on the airplane for work."

"Oh no!" It was exactly what Ellen had told him yesterday. She rubbed her forehead and came away with flop sweat. "This isn't good, Connie."

"Why doesn't she know what you're doing for work, anyway?"

The proverbial tangled web. "My editor wanted to keep it on the QT. We generally share our assignments, but Sarah is getting a little competitive lately, between you and me."

"Oh. Oops."

Ellen was trying to figure what to do. Sarah had caught her in a lie, then called her to confirm it. It was great journalistic technique, and it would get her fired for sure.

"Will wants to talk to you, okay?"

"Of course." Ellen could hear Will calling for her, so close he was probably reaching for the phone.

"Mommy, Mommy! When are you coming home?"

"Soon, sweetie." Ellen felt a pang at the sound of his voice, even as she slumped in the driver's seat, keeping an eye on the Bravermans' house. "Tell me about your macaroni picture."

"Come home soon. I have to go."

"Love you," Ellen called after him, and Connie got back on the line.

"We're about to have dinner. So how bad is it?"

"Don't worry. Just don't let him tell any more state secrets, okay?"

"Gotcha. Sorry."

"See you soon." Ellen hung up and called Marcelo for damage control, waiting nervously for the call to connect. Another runner darted by on the sidewalk, glancing back at her. His shoulder cap bore a MOM tattoo, but she was pretty sure it was a coincidence.

"How are you?" Marcelo asked, his voice unusually cool, which took Ellen aback.

"Long story short, Sarah called my house and Will told her that I went away on business."

"I know. She just left my office. She came in to tell me that you lied to me."

Oh no. "What did you say?"

"What could I say? I couldn't admit that we confessed our mutual admiration in your kitchen, before we fabricated a story."

Ellen reddened. "I'm so sorry, Marcelo."

"I shouldn't have told them you were sick. So, in theory, you lied to me, and I lied to the staff, and Sarah came in to let me know. If I had just said that it wasn't their business, we'd be fine."

Ellen had undermined Marcelo's authority. A reporter couldn't lie to an editor without consequences. The entire newsroom would be talking about it and waiting to see what he would do. "So what did you say to her?"

"I told her I'd talk to you about it when you got back." Marcelo shook his head. "For an intelligent man, I act so stupid sometimes."

"No, you don't," Ellen rushed to say, hearing the subtext: *I never should have crossed the line with you.*

"I can't show you any favoritism, and I don't want to have to let you go." Regret freighted his tone, but Ellen straightened up, determined.

"There's no reason to do that, not yet. I'm still away, and that buys us a few days. I have to get clear of this situation."

"What situation?" Marcelo asked, a new urgency in his voice, but all of a sudden the white Jaguar was pulling out of the Bravermans' driveway and turning left toward the main drag.

"Uh, hold on." Ellen tucked the BlackBerry in her neck, twisted on the car's ignition, and hit the gas. She launched herself into rush-hour traffic, an overheated lineup of blaring music, cigarette smoke, and cell-phone conversations. She couldn't afford to let too much space get between her and Carol.

"Ellen? Are you there?"

"Marcelo, hang on a sec."

"Please tell me what is going on. I can help you."

"Sorry, but this isn't the best time for me and—" She lost her train of thought because Carol took an unexpected right turn before the causeway. Ellen steered her car into the right lane but the movement dislodged her BlackBerry, which slid off her lap and fell near the gas pedal.

"Good-bye, Marcelo!" she called out, then she hit the gas and swerved around the corner, in pursuit. She had to stay on track. She couldn't worry about her job now, or even Marcelo's. Sooner or later she had to catch a break. She ran the light, staying on Carol's tail.

Chapter Fifty

Ellen followed Carol through the carnation-and-canary-hued buildings of South Beach, where traffic on Collins Avenue was a sizzling stop-and-go. Between them was a white Hummer, like a giant bar of Ivory on wheels. Ahead, the Jag turned left, followed by the Hummer and Ellen. They traveled up a skinny back street lined with delivery entrances to a cigar store, boutiques, and restaurants. Dumpsters alternated with flashy cars parked so haphazardly that they looked strewn there. Carol pulled up behind a parked convertible, and the Hummer powered ahead, leaving Ellen no choice but to keep going or risk being recognized from the grocery store.

She cruised slowly ahead and watched Carol in her rearview mirror. The driver-side door opened, and Carol emerged, stepping out in a tight-fitting tomato red dress, her long dark blond hair loose to her shoulders. She chirped the car locked and walked around to its back fender, heading for the cross street on the far side.

Go, go, go!

Ellen parked illegally, turned off the ignition, grabbed her purse, jumped out of the car, and hustled down the street. Her clogs clopped along, and she made a mental note not to wear Danskos the next time she stalked somebody, unless it was a Clydesdale.

Carol took a left at the cross street, with Ellen tailing her on foot at a safe distance. They reached a street that was closed to traffic, Lincoln Road, and Carol plunged into the crowd of gorgeous models, crazies with face paint, gay men with matching mustaches, and European tourists speaking an array of languages. Pomeranians shared the packed sidewalk with a boa constrictor worn around the neck of a woman who had forgotten the feather part of her feather boa. Kiehl's, Banana Republic, and Victoria's Secret stores were interspersed with boutiques and gift shops, and Ellen walked along, marveling. It looked like a street party, with merchandise.

She never lost sight of Carol, helped by the bright red dress. They threaded their way past Cuban, Chinese, and Italian restaurants, their tables spilling out onto large café areas for outdoor dining. Carol paused at a sushi restaurant and talked with a camera-ready maitre d', so Ellen slowed her step, watching them. In the next minute, a tall, dark-haired man slipped from the crowd and stopped beside Carol, kissing her on the cheek and encircling her slim waist in a proprietary way.

Bill Braverman.

She recognized him instantly from the online photos. He was slim, in a light gray sport jacket with jeans, but was too covered up to show the wiriness she'd seen online. Nor could she see his features clearly at this distance. She fake-read a menu posted in front of one of the restaurants, letting the crowd flow around her and waiting to see what the Bravermans would do. The crowd chattered away, and the sun vanished behind the palm trees, their spiked fronds waving. She glanced back at the Bravermans, and hidden by the crowd, edged closer to their table.

They were seated in the center of the outdoor dining area, and she got a good look at Bill's face. He was handsome, with his spray of black bangs over dark round eyes and a nose that looked like an older version of Will's. From time to time, he leaned back in his bistro chair, his cigarette smoldering between his fingers, and he spoke animatedly, laughing frequently.

Time to rock.

Ellen slipped her purse onto her shoulder, walked toward the maitre d' of their restaurant, and asked, "Is there a ladies' room inside?"

"In the back, to the right."

"Thanks." Ellen went inside the restaurant, and it smelled like Thai curry, reminding her that she hadn't eaten in ages. She found the ladies' room, went inside, and slipped off her sunglasses. She headed into one of the stalls, closed the door, and went into her purse. On the bottom was a white plastic bag, her DNA kit.

She took it out and checked the contents. Directions she'd downloaded, two pairs of blue plastic gloves she'd had under the sink, and two brown paper bags, which she used to pack Will's snack for school. She opened the directions and read them again, because she didn't want to screw up:

Our paternity test is the most accurate in the country! We analyze your samples at our state-of-the-art laboratory, using a 16-marker DNA test! Be thorough and collect all samples possible! Results are ready in 3 business days, but can be expedited for a small RUSH charge!

Ellen skipped the blah blah blah, which she'd read online. There had been plenty of DNA-testing companies on the web, including the one she was using. Her research had taught her that there were two testing options: the first was a standard paternity kit, which was admissible in court and required collection of the DNA by a cheek, or bucal, swab. She didn't need that one, and she doubted the Bravermans would offer up a sample. The second test was the one she was using, a nonstandard DNA test for paternity. Her gaze returned to the form:

> **For times when the bucal swab method just isn't possible, simply obtain one of the following items, place it in a brown paper bag, store it at room temperature, and send it to us. Follow precautions below!**

Ellen read the precautions:

> **Must wear gloves so as not to get your DNA on the sample. Store at room temperature and do not get the sample wet. Must be put in a paper bag, not plastic.**

She scanned the list of permissible collection items, just to make sure she remembered it correctly:

> **No need for silly collection kits! You can get DNA from a licked envelope, chewed gum, a soda can or any kind of can, including beer, glass, toothbrush, semen, dried blood stains (including menstrual blood), a strand of hair with the follicle attached, or a cigarette butt!**

Ellen folded the papers up and put them in her purse, then slipped the plastic gloves into her jeans pocket. She used the bathroom and left the stall, washing her face and freshening her makeup, which made her feel almost civilized, then took a last look at herself in the mirror, letting her eyes meet their reflection. She had her mother's eyes, a fact that secretly made them both happy, as if it were confirmation of their closeness. Even now, looking at herself, she could still see her mother, within.

Follow your heart.

It was showtime.

Chapter Fifty-one

Ellen got a table in the outdoor dining area of the restaurant next door to the one with the Bravermans, with a clear view of their table. While the couple ate dinner, she checked her email on the Black-Berry, but there was nothing from Amy Martin. Then she'd called home and said good night to Will while she'd devoured a delicious seviche appetizer, a red-lacquered model boat of sushi, and a frothy cappuccino with almond biscotti.

She watched the Bravermans finish their coffee and share a tiramisu. Bill smoked a final cigarette, his third of the evening, but Carol didn't smoke, so Ellen would have to take her glass to get a DNA sample from her. The couple had laughed and talked throughout the entire dinner, cementing their qualifications as a happily married couple.

Which doesn't mean they're better parents than me.

Bill signaled for the check, so Ellen did the same, catching her waiter's eye. They paid at about the same time, and she rose right after the Bravermans, ready to swoop down on their table.

Now!

They left and threaded their way to the aisle, and Ellen made a beeline for their table. Suddenly a group of tourists shoved in front of her, blocking her way, and she didn't reach the table until after the busboy had gathered the glasses.

Damn!

"Table no is clean," the busboy said in an indeterminate accent, picking up the plates and setting them with a clatter in a large brown tub.

"I'll just sit a minute." Ellen plopped into Bill Braverman's chair. "I only want dessert."

"No is clean." The busboy reached for the full ashtray, but Ellen grabbed it from his hands.

"Thanks." She checked it for gum, in case Carol had chewed some, but it only contained three cigarette butts, all Bill's. "I'll need this. I smoke."

The busboy walked away, but the maitre d' was craning his neck and peering at the table, along with a foursome of hungry patrons. She had to act fast. Her heart pounded. She slid the gloves from her pocket and shoved her right hand in one. The maitre d' was making his way over, with the foursome. She gathered the three cigarette butts from the ashtray, opened the paper bag under the table, tossed the butts inside, then closed it up and shoved it back into her purse.

"Miss, do you have a reservation?" the maitre d' asked, reaching the table just as Ellen rose, shaking her head.

"Sorry, I was just resting a minute, thanks." She headed out of the dining area to the sidewalk, crowded with dogs, skateboarders, Rollerbladers, and a tattooed man on a silver unicycle.

She melted into the crowd, exhilarated. Bill's DNA sample was safe in her purse. She wondered if she could get Carol's tonight, too.

One down, two to go.

Chapter Fifty-two

Ellen cruised around the block after Carol had pulled into her drive-way, followed by Bill driving a gray Maserati. The sky was a rich marine blue, and the street silent, the fancy cars cooling for the night. Lights were on inside the houses, and high-def TVs flickered from behind the curtains.

She had a second wind, energized by her success with the ciga-rette butts, and was thinking of the other ways you could get DNA samples. Cans, glasses, licked envelopes.

Licked envelopes?

Ellen rounded the corner onto Surfside and eyed the Bravermans' green cast-iron mailbox. It was at the end of their driveway, but the red flag wasn't up, so there was no letter inside.

Rats.

She drove slowly past the house, reconnoitering. All the lights in the house were off, its modern oblong windows gone dark, and the only movement was the gentle whirring of its automatic sprinklers, watering the thick grass like so many mechanical whirligigs. Flowers bloomed at the foot of the HELP US FIND OUR SON sign, and the larger-than-life face of Timothy, or Will, floated ghostly in the dark.

Maybe not tonight.

Ellen was about to leave for the hotel when a light from the Bravermans' first floor went on from on the far right. She slowed to a stop, just past the house. The window had no curtains, and she could see Bill walk through the room and seat himself at a desk, inclining forward. In the next minute, his profile came to life, illuminated by the light of a computer laptop.

Ellen pulled the car over and parked on the opposite side of the street, then lowered the window, turned off the ignition, and watched Bill. She could see bookshelves and cabinets in the room, so she gathered that it was a home office. Bill spent a few more minutes on the computer, then got up and moved around the room, doing something she couldn't see. In the next minute, the front door opened and he emerged, carrying a black trash bag.

Yikes!

She ducked in the front seat and watched in the outside mirror. Bill put the trash bag in a tall green trashcan and rolled it to the end of the driveway, then went back toward the house. She stayed low until she heard the front door slam, then she eased up in the seat, looking behind her. The light in the home office switched off, and the house went dark again.

Trash could contain DNA.

She scanned the street, front and back, but there was no one in sight. She slid off her clogs, opened the car door as quietly as possible, and jumped out, her heart pounding. She bolted for the trash-can, tore off the lid, plucked out two bags at warp speed, and dashed back to the car like a crazed Santa Claus.

She jumped in the car, threw the bags in the passenger seat, and hit the gas, then went around the block and ended up on the main drag, speeding to the causeway with her booty. She pulled over and cut the ignition, turned on the interior light, and grabbed one trash bag. She undid the drawstring and peeked inside, but it was too dark to see the contents. It didn't smell like garbage, so she dumped it out onto the passenger seat, dismayed at the sight.

The trash was shredded, and it tumbled out like a ball of paper spaghetti. She pawed through it anyway to see if there was any item that could contain Carol's DNA, but no dice. It was Bill's home-office trash, strips of numbers, portfolio statements, and account statements. She remembered that Bill was an investor, so it made sense that he'd shred his trash. She never shredded anything, but her home office trash consisted of Toys"R"Us circulars.

She gathered up the trash, stuffed it back into the bag, and tossed it into the backseat. Then she reached over and grabbed the other bag, which was heavier. She yanked on the drawstring and opened the bag, releasing the yucky smell of fresh garbage. She held the open bag directly under the interior light and peeked inside. On top of the trash sat a heap of gray-blue shrimp shells that stank to high heaven, and she pushed them aside, going through wet coffee grounds, the chopped bottom of a head of Romaine, a Horchow catalog, and underneath that, a mother lode of mail. None of this would yield a DNA sample for Carol.

Bummer.

She pulled out the mail on the off-chance there was a sealed envelope. She flipped through it, but no luck. It was all unopened junk mail from Neiman Marcus, Versace, and Gucci, plus a glossy copy of *Departures* magazine. Stuck inside the magazine was a pink card from the dentist, a reminder that somebody had to get her teeth cleaned next month. She flipped the card over. The front read, Carol Charbonneau Braverman.

Ellen blinked. Charbonneau sounded familiar. She couldn't place if she'd heard it or if she was imagining it, her exhaustion finally catching up with her. She rooted through the rest of the trash, but there was nothing yucky enough to contain Carol's DNA. She tied the drawstring tightly, so it wouldn't stink up the car, and hoisted the bag into the backseat with the other. She took off for the hotel and threw the trash in a Dumpster on the way.

But when she finally reached her hotel room, she checked her email.

Amy Martin hadn't written yet, but her sister Cheryl had.

And her email brought the worst news imaginable.

Chapter Fifty-three

Ellen felt as if she had been punched in the stomach. She sank slowly onto the quilted bedspread, staring at her glowing BlackBerry screen. The email from Cheryl had no subject line, and it read:

> Dear Ellen,
>
> I'm sorry to tell you that yesterday, we found out that Amy passed away. She died of a heroin overdose in her apartment in Brigantine on Saturday. Her wake will be Tuesday night, but there will be a private one for the family before her burial, on Wednesday at ten o'clock in Stoatesville, at the Cruzane Funeral Home. My mother says you can come to either time, and she would like to see you.
>
> Sincerely, Cheryl

The thought overwhelmed her with sadness. Amy was too young to die, and so horribly, and Ellen thought of how Cheryl must be feeling, then Amy's mother, Gerry, who had been so kind to her. Her thoughts came eventually to herself and Will. She had just lost her chance to learn anything from Amy.

Her gaze wandered over the blue-and-gold bedspread, the photographs on the wall, of nautilus and generic conch shells, and the balcony sliders. The glass looked out onto a bottomless Miami night, the same night that was falling at home. The sky was dark and black, no way to separate earth from heaven, and she felt undone, again. Loosed, untethered. She had a nagging fear, gnawing at the edges of her mind.

Quite a coincidence.

It seemed odd that Amy would turn up dead now, just when Ellen had begun asking questions about her. It seemed stranger still, considering the suicide of Karen Batz. Now, both women with knowledge of Will's adoption were dead. The only one left alive was Amy's boyfriend, and he was the one who looked like the kidnapper in the composite.

Not just a kidnapper. A murderer.

Ellen started to make connections, but even she knew she was entering the wild-speculation realm. There were innocent explanations for everything, and she flipped it. Amy had lived a fast life. Heroin addicts overdosed all the time. Lawyers committed suicide. Not everything was suspicious.

God help me.

Ellen willed herself to stop thinking, because she was making herself crazy. This had been the longest day in her life. She had one DNA sample, which was one more than she thought she'd get the first day. Her job was in jeopardy, as was her love life, but that was back home, which seemed suddenly very far away. Another world, even. She flopped backwards on the bed, and exhaustion swept over her, mooting even her darkest fears.

In the next minute, she fell into a terrible sleep.

Chapter Fifty-four

The next morning, Ellen parked her car in the same spot on the main drag, perpendicular to Surfside Lane. It was another hot, tropical day, but she was dressed for it today. She'd stopped at the hotel's overpriced gift shop and bought a pink visor, a pair of silver Oakley knockoffs, and a chrome yellow T-shirt that read SOUTH BEACH, which she'd paired with white shorts from home. Inside her pockets were a plastic glove and a folded brown paper bag.

She took a slug from a bottle of orange juice, still cold from the minibar. She felt weighed down by the news of Amy Martin's death and couldn't shake the fear that the overdose wasn't accidental. She put aside her dark thoughts to tend to the task at hand, especially because she wanted to get back home in time for the funeral.

She set the bottle in the cup holder and scoped out the scene, which was quiet except for people exercising. Two older women power-walked around the block, carrying water bottles and yammering away, and a younger woman was running in a sports bra with a black bathing suit bottom. Yet a fourth woman walked her white toy poodle, her cell phone and pedometer clipped to her waist like so much suburban ammunition.

Ellen was trying a new tack, so she got out of the car, pocketed her keys, and started walking. She strolled ahead with purpose, scanning the houses on either side of the street. No one had any red flags up on their mailboxes, and she wondered what time the mail would be picked up. She hoped Carol would mail a letter, so she could get DNA from the envelope.

She picked up the pace, gaining on the two older women who motored ahead in their sneakers. They wore Bermuda shorts in pastel colors and patterned tank tops, and even at seventysomething, looked in terrific shape. Each had short silver hair, but the woman on the left wore a yellow terry-cloth visor, and the one on the right had a white baseball cap. Ellen fell into stride with them before the Bravermans' house.

"Excuse me, ladies," she began, and they both turned around. "Do you know what time the mail pickup is in this neighborhood? I'm house-sitting on Brightside Lane for my cousins, and I forgot to ask them before they left this morning."

"Oh, who are your cousins?" Yellow Visor asked pleasantly.

"The Vaughns," Ellen answered without hesitation. Earlier this morning, she had driven down Brightside, about eight blocks away, and picked a name from one of the mailboxes. "June and Tom Vaughn, do you know them?"

"No, sorry. Brightside's a little too far over." Yellow Visor cocked her head, eyeing Ellen with confusion. "So why are you walking here and not there?"

Uh. "There's a big dog on that street, and I'm afraid of dogs."

"I agree with you. We're cat people." Yellow Visor nodded. "Mail gets picked up around eleven o'clock in the morning. I'm Phyllis, and you're welcome to walk with us, if you're all alone."

"Thanks, I appreciate that." Ellen hoped to pump them for information until Carol mailed a letter or her DNA otherwise fell out of the sky.

"Good, we like new faces. We've been walking every day, two miles for the past six years, and we're sick of each other." Phyllis laughed, and her friend in the baseball cap nudged her.

"Speak for yourself, Phyl. You're not sick of me, I'm sick of you." She looked at Ellen with a warm smile. "I'm Linda DiMarco. And you?"

"Sandy Claus," Ellen answered, off the top of her head. They approached the Bravermans, where Carol's car was in the driveway, but Bill's was gone. She gestured casually to the memorial on the lawn. "What's that sign all about, do you know? And all these yellow ribbons?"

"Oh my, yes," Phyllis answered. A petite woman, she had bright eyes, a hawkish nose, and deep laugh lines that bracketed thin lips. "Their baby was kidnapped several years ago and they never got him back. Can you imagine, losing a child like that?"

Ellen didn't want to go there. "Do you know the family?"

"Sure, Carol's a doll, and so is Bill. And that little baby, Timothy, he was adorable."

"Adorable," Linda repeated, without breaking stride. "That baby was so cute you could eat him."

Ellen hid her emotions. The brown bag crinkled in her pocket when she walked.

"What a shame." Linda shook her head, her rich brown eyes tilting down at the corners. She had an oval face with a largish nose, and a thick gold chain with a coral horn bounced on her bosom as they turned the corner, passing a large brick Georgian mansion, more Monticello than Miami.

"It's so sad." Phyllis made a clucking sound. "They shot the babysitter, too. It doesn't seem fair. It's like when people rob a store and shoot the clerk. Why do they have to shoot somebody? I don't know what gets into people nowadays."

Ellen didn't say anything. Phyllis and Linda didn't need the encouragement to keep talking, and she was running out of breath anyway. A fireball sun climbed a cloudless sky, and the humidity was 120,000 percent. They passed a woman walking a black poodle, and Phyllis waved to her.

"Carol and Bill were in terrible shape, after it happened. It just about killed them. There were reporters camped out on the street day and night, bothering them all the time. Cops and the FBI, always coming and going."

Ellen let her talk, to see what she could learn. They reached the next corner, turned around the block, and walked past a house intended to look like a Roman temple.

"Bill was a great father, too." Phyllis sipped from her water bottle. "You know, he has his own investment company, very successful. He makes a lot of money for people in the neighborhood, and he doted on his son. Bought him golf bibs and a golf hat, too. Remember we saw him, Lin?"

Linda nodded. "Carol had such a hard time getting pregnant. I'm not telling stories out of school here. She talked about it all the time, right, Phyl?"

"Yes, she had a *very* hard time." Phyllis's lips flattened to a lipsticked line. "They tried for a long time. She really wanted that baby, they both did. Now look what happened."

Ellen felt a stab of guilt, flashing on Carol as Mother Goose.

"The poor woman." Linda wiped her upper lip. "Isn't that just the worst luck? They finally had their miracle baby, then they never see him again. End of story."

"There's no justice," Phyllis said, puffing slightly.

"It's a sin," Linda added.

Ellen didn't know it was possible to feel more guilty than she felt already. She had always thought of Will as her miracle baby. But he could have been Carol's miracle baby. Only DNA would tell for sure. She needed that sample.

The moment passed, and Linda said, "You know, if you live long enough, you realize there's nothing you can't handle. I lost my husband and I lost my kid sister. If you asked me, I never would've thought that I'd be standing here afterwards. Life makes you strong, and death makes you strong, too."

Ellen was thinking of her mother.

Phyllis shook her head, which jiggled slightly as they rounded the block. "She always says that, but I think she's full of baloney."

"Ha!" Linda waved her off. "Go ahead, tell her about the waves."

"Okay." Phyllis looked over at Ellen and her lined face grew serious, even as she pumped her arms like a pro. "I lived in Brooklyn all my life. We couldn't believe it when we retired down here, everywhere with the water, the intercoastal, and the ocean. We loved it. My Richard used to fish, I went out with him on the boat. On the boat is where I get my best ideas."

"It's boring, take it from me," Linda stage-whispered behind her hand. "She makes me go. I wanna drown myself."

"Are you going to let me talk to our guest?" Phyllis asked, mock indignant.

"Go ahead, just don't take the long way." Linda turned to Ellen. "I'm Italian, so I love to talk, and she's Jewish, so she loves to talk."

Phyllis smiled. "That's why we're best friends. No one else can put up with us."

They all laughed, passing Ellen's car on the main drag, then taking a left onto Surfside Lane again, lapping the block.

"Here's my theory about waves." Phyllis extended her arms, palms up. "Bad things are like waves. They're going to happen to you, and there's nothing you can do about it. They're part of life, like waves are a part of the ocean. If you're standing on the shoreline, you don't know when the waves are coming. But they'll come. You gotta make sure you get back to the surface, after every wave. That's all."

Ellen smiled, considering it. "That makes a lot of sense."

Suddenly Phyllis and Linda fell silent, their gaze on the open door of a wooden contemporary on the left side of the street, catty-corner to the Bravermans'. A pretty redhead was emerging in a crisp black dress, with a black bag on her arm. She locked the door, then clacked in stylish black pumps down a concrete path to her driveway and a silver Mercedes.

"Who's that?" Ellen caught the mischievous look Phyllis and Linda exchanged. "Someone we don't like, evidently."

Phyllis burst into laughter. "I forgot my poker face."

Linda looked over at her. "You don't have a poker face. I know, I play poker with you."

"Fill me in, ladies." Ellen smiled. "I love to dish."

"She's a big snob," Phyllis answered, with the trace of a smile. "Her name is Kelly Scott and her family has more money than God. She's from Palm Beach."

"Pink and green country," Linda added with a naughty giggle, and Phyllis nodded.

"I've met her at least four times, and she acts like she never met me before. I hate that."

"Me, too," Linda said.

"Me, three," Ellen said, and they all laughed again. But she was watching the Braverman house as they walked by, looking past the yellow ribbons and the Timothy memorial and the curtains. Inside was Carol Braverman.

And Ellen needed her DNA.

Today.

Chapter Fifty-five

The sky began to cloud over, cutting the temperature, and Ellen sat low in the driver's seat of the car with the window open, watching the Braverman house. It was 10:36 A.M., but there'd been no sign of Carol, and the red flag on her mailbox was still down.

Ellen was still hoping that she'd mail a letter. She checked her BlackBerry, and Marcelo hadn't emailed or called. She wondered if she still had a job to go back to, or a crush.

Please tell me what is going on. I can help you.

She kept an eye on the house and straightened up as a mail truck appeared on the main drag and began stopping at the houses, delivering packets of mail. No sign of Carol with an envelope to be mailed, and now it was too late. The mail truck turned onto Surfside, traveled up the street on the right side, and delivered the mail to the Braverman house.

Damn.

Ellen felt on edge. Hot and testy. She sipped warm juice, then dug in her purse for the notes from the DNA test, reminding herself of the sample possibilities. Gum, soda can, cigarette butt, blah blah blah. She tossed the list aside and glanced back at the Bravermans' house, where there was finally some activity. Carol was stepping out the front door.

Ellen's senses sprang to alert. She couldn't keep waiting for something to happen. She had to make something happen. She got out of the car in her sunglasses and visor and went into her I'm-just-a-walker routine, strolling across the main drag and entering Surfside. She walked slowly, staying on the opposite side of the street as Carol walked from the front door and disappeared into the garage.

Ellen cut her pace, taking smaller steps, and the next minute, Carol came out of the garage with a green plastic gardener's tote. She had on a cute sundress and another visor, with her dark blond hair in its ponytail again.

Ellen kept her eyes straight ahead, but watched Carol cross the lawn to the memorial to Timothy, then she knelt down, setting the gardener's tote next to her. She slid on a pair of flowery cotton gloves and began to weed in front of the memorial.

It's as if she's tending a grave.

Ellen felt a twinge of conscience as she turned the corner, and as soon as she was out of sight, she broke into a light jog. She didn't know how long Carol would be out front and she couldn't blow this chance. It was almost too humid to breathe, and she was panting by the time she lapped the block and reached the intersection of Surfside Lane and the main drag, where she knelt next to a tall hedge, pretending to tie her sneaker.

Carol gardened at a leisurely pace, pulling the weeds and putting them in a neat pile on the left. A small plastic bag of peat moss and a large flat of yellow marigolds were sitting on the lawn next to the memorial, and a full sun bathed the front lawn. Ellen's breathing returned to normal, but she was sweating behind her sunglasses, and Carol must have been feeling the same way, because in the next second, she took off her sunglasses and visor and set them down. Ellen flashed on the DNA list:

Hair with the follicle still attached.

She couldn't be sure there would be a hair on the sunglasses or visor, and she wouldn't get another chance, so she rejected the idea. She shifted her feet and fake-tied the other sneaker, watching as Carol moved to the marigold flat and twisted off a small packet of flowers. Ellen watched her from her crouching position, and Carol gentled the plant from the flat and set it on the ground. She reached into the gardener's tote and pulled out a can of soda, then popped the tab, and took a sip.

Bingo!

Ellen scanned the block, and there was no one in sight. She slid the plastic glove from her other pocket, put it on her hand, and rose slowly. Then she slid her BlackBerry from her pocket and pressed the number for information in Miami. She asked for the Bravermans' phone number, and while the call connected, she walked toward Carol, who was bent over her flowers, making a hole for the new marigolds with her fingers. The phone rang once in Ellen's ear, then again, and in the next second, Carol looked up at her house.

Get the phone, Carol.

Ellen slid the paper bag from her pocket and started walking down Surfside Lane, keeping her gloved hand at her side, out of view. In the meantime, Carol was rising, taking off her gardening gloves on the fly, and hurrying toward the house.

Yes!

Ellen crossed to the Bravermans' side of the street, her heart pounding. She hustled up the sidewalk, getting a bead on the soda can. There was nobody exercising or walking dogs, and she wouldn't get another chance. She broke into a light run, the ringing cell phone to her ear. Ten feet away, then five, then right in front of the Braverman house. Carol's soda was a Diet Sprite, sitting next to the tote.

Now, now, now!

She ran straight up the Bravermans' lawn, swooped down with her gloved hand, grabbed the Diet Sprite and took off like a shot, running down the block. She turned the can upside down so the soda poured out, and she ran like she'd never run in her life. She tore around the block, bolted all the way to the main drag, then darted across the street.

HONK HONK! went a truck, skidding to a stop behind her.

Ellen tore open her car door, jumped in, and dumped the can in the brown paper bag. She twisted on the ignition, floored the gas pedal, and headed straight for the causeway. She felt like cheering. Wind off the causeway whipped her hair around, and she hit a red light, taking off the glove and leaving it on the seat, its purpose served. She took off her visor and sunglasses, relieved to finally shed her disguise. She caught a glimpse of the street sign and did a double take.

Charbonneau Drive?

The traffic light turned green, but instead of going straight over the causeway, she turned right onto the street.

Chapter Fifty-six

CHARBONNEAU DRIVE, read the street sign, and Ellen flashed on the dentist's reminder from the Bravermans' trash bag. She had known that Charbonneau sounded familiar, though she couldn't remember how. She'd passed the street every time she'd driven back and forth to the causeway. Charbonneau Drive had to be connected to Carol Braverman. It was too distinctive a name not to be.

Curious, she drove along Charbonneau Drive, which was winding and pleasant. She passed a white stucco rancher, a fake French château, and a brick McMansion; the houses had the same variety as on Surfside Lane, but all of them were the same, more recent, vintage. Palm trees lined the road, throwing dappled shade on the street, but they weren't as established as the palms on Surfside, and the vegetation, white oleander and bougainvillea, looked newer. A woman in a running singlet and shorts jogged by, and two men walked matching dachshunds.

She followed the street, and at the end of a cul-de-sac stood an immense mansion of pink stucco with a clay tile roof. It was three stories tall, with at least thirty arched Spanish windows and a covered walk-way that sheltered a grand main entrance. A sign on the lawn read, CHARBONNEAU HOUSE, and underneath that, OPEN TO THE PUBLIC.

I'm the public.

Ellen pulled into a parking lot of crushed shells and turned off the ignition. She'd make it quick, but she put her DNA samples under the seat anyway, then got out of the car and walked to the house. The stucco had been repainted and the tiles on the roof meticulously maintained, but the mansion was much older than the houses surrounding it on the drive. The lot was at least three acres of lush lawn, the breeze was fragrant, and the place a reminder of a slower, older Florida. She walked up the breezeway, climbed stairs of red Mexican tile, and went inside the door, looking around.

The entrance hall had a black-and-white tile floor and was dominated by a huge staircase, covered with an Oriental carpet. There were three large rooms off the hall, furnished as meeting rooms, and she entered the center room, which overlooked an expanse of green lawn and a small circular fountain.

"May I help you?" a voice asked, and she turned around. It was a woman with a dark brown bob, light eyes with friendly crow's-feet, and a warm smile. "Were you looking for something?"

"I was driving past the sign, and I'm not from around here. I thought the building was so pretty, I wanted to see it."

"Why, thank you. We're very proud of Charbonneau House and the work we do here."

"What is that, may I ask?"

"We promote theater arts and other cultural events to children in the community." The woman, professional in a crisp white blouse and a khaki cotton skirt, with red espadrilles, gestured to the main hall-way. "In addition to the conference rooms and classrooms, we have a full theater in the back, which seats seventy-five people. We have a large backstage and several dressing rooms. We stage three productions a year and we just finished our run of *Once Upon a Mattress*."

"How nice," Ellen said, meaning it. "And I see there's Charbonneau House and Charbonneau Drive. I assume it's related to the Charbonneau family?"

"Yes, exactly. The Charbonneaus are one of the oldest families in the area, and they've donated the house for the community's use." The woman gestured to an oil portrait in an ornate golden frame, one of two flanking the windows. "That's our benefactor, Bertrand Charbonneau, who unfortunately passed away about five years ago, at the age of ninety-one."

"How interesting." Ellen looked at the painting, of a reedy, silver-haired man in glasses and a light green business suit, leaning against a wall of bookshelves. She tried not to stare at the picture, to see if there was any resemblance to Will. Her head was already swimming, and the bag in the car would eliminate any guesswork.

"Bertrand was a wonderful man, a friend of my father's. He was one of the community's first residents and developed much of the real estate here. This house, his childhood home, was only one of his many gifts to our community."

Ellen was trying to piece together where, if anywhere, Carol Charbonneau Braverman fit in, but didn't want to show her hand, especially since this woman knew the family. "I gather Bertrand Charbonneau had an interest in theater?"

"His wife Rhoda had a brief career as an actress before she retired to raise their children. Even then, she remained very active in children's theater." The woman strolled over to the other oil portrait, and Ellen followed her. The painting showed another man, this one in a casual brown sweater, by a pool. The plaque read Richard Charbonneau.

"So this must be Bertrand's son?" Ellen asked, scanning the man's features. He had the same blue eyes she'd seen on Carol, and Will. It was the tour of Will's bloodlines, maybe, but she'd know soon enough.

"Yes, Richard was my father's contemporary. He and his wife Selma continued their father's efforts. Unfortunately, they both passed away many years ago, in a car accident."

"That's too bad. Do you think the family will carry on this tradition? It really seems like a wonderful idea."

"No worries there." The woman smiled pleasantly. "Richard and his wife had a daughter, Carol, and she works with the children every Wednesday and Friday morning. She understands all aspects of children's theater and even directs a play a year."

"Well, that's wonderful." Ellen's chest tightened, and she looked away from the portrait, hiding her emotion. If Will was really Timothy, then Bertrand Charbonneau would be his great-grandfather and Richard Charbonneau his grandfather. Will would be part of a wonderful family, born to extraordinary wealth. She thought ahead, to the day she'd get the DNA results, when she'd have to make a decision, or not.

You'll have to make a choice I wouldn't wish on my worst enemy.

"Will that be all?" the woman asked, cocking her head.

"Yes, thanks," Ellen answered, turning away.

She said another good-bye, walked from the room, and hurried out the entrance hall to the door. By the time she hit the walkway, her pace picked up from a light jog to a full-out run, and her footfalls crunched the seashells. She wanted to forget Charbonneau House, Charbonneau Drive, and her DNA samples, which would answer a question she never wanted to ask. Her chest heaved and panted, and she reached the car out of breath, then she flung open the door, grabbed the paper bag from under the seat, and raised her arm to throw it across the gorgeous lawn.

Her hand halted in midair. She thought of Will, and stopped herself. It was his birthright, not hers. His truth, not hers. She'd come here to learn whether he belonged to her or to the Bravermans, but neither was true. He belonged to himself.

She lowered her arm. She walked back to the car, sat in the driver's seat, and stowed the bag on the passenger seat.

It was time to go home.

Chapter Fifty-seven

The ticketing line wound back and forth, and Ellen assessed it, worriedly. She didn't want to miss the flight and she'd been lucky to get a seat. She couldn't wait to see Will, and she felt almost herself again, having changed back into her sweater and jeans, which she needed in the air-conditioned terminal anyway.

She checked her watch. She'd scarfed down a turkey sandwich in the first fifteen minutes of her wait in line, and now she had nothing to do but look at the other travelers who had nothing else to do. The girl in front of her bobbed to music playing on her iPod, and the man in front of her was a middle manager, his thumbs flying over his BlackBerry keyboard at the speed of carpal tunnel syndrome. A man before him talked on a cell phone in rapid Spanish, which reminded her of Marcelo. She'd called him this morning but he hadn't answered, so she'd left a message saying she'd be back to work tomorrow.

"Excuse me, is our line even moving?" asked an older man behind her, and Ellen stood on tiptoe to see the ticket counter. Only one agent was manning the counter, and two of the self-service kiosks bore Out of Order signs.

"Honestly, no." Ellen smiled, but the man grumbled.

"I can walk to Denver faster."

"You got that right." Ellen looked away, and her gaze fell to the first-class line, only four people deep. "I wonder how much first class costs."

"Highway robbery," the old man shot back, and the line shifted forward an inch.

Her gaze drifted back to the first-class line, where a pretty redhead had just arrived, rolling a Louis Vuitton bag behind her, her head held high. She looked vaguely familiar and when she dug in a black purse, Ellen remembered where she had seen her before. It was the young woman who lived across the street from Carol Braverman.

Her name is Kelly Scott and her family has more money than God.

Ellen watched the redhead fan herself with some papers, looking sexy in black stilettos and a cobalt blue dress, whose bold color stood out among the Miami pastels. Businessmen passing by gave her more than a second glance, running their eyes over her body and shapely legs.

The line shifted, and Ellen moved up. Another businessman strode past her, carrying a lightweight bag and moving so quickly that his tailored sport jacket blew open. He joined the end of the first-class line, and Ellen looked over.

She recognized him instantly, stunned.

Chapter Fifty-eight

The businessman was Bill Braverman, and Ellen marveled at the odds that he would show up at the airport at the exact same time as his neighbor. She got a closer look at him than she had before, and he was an attractive man with a tall, wiry build, dark hair, and a nose that looked like Will's, even in profile. She tried not to stare as he took out his wallet and cleared his throat, and at about the same time, the redhead turned around and glanced behind her. She looked right at Bill, who stood behind her, but strangely, she didn't say hello. Instead, she turned away and faced the ticket counters.

Ellen didn't get it. The redhead had to have seen Bill. He was right behind her and the tallest man in the line, not to mention her neighbor.

"We're moving," the old man said, and Ellen shifted forward, glued to the goings-on. Something was fishy between Bill and the redhead, but she wasn't jumping to conclusions. She stayed tuned as Bill took out his wallet and faced the front of the line, showing no sign that he recognized his neighbor, who was standing in front of him, with bright red hair and a killer dress. Men all over the terminal were looking at her, yet Bill was pointedly looking away.

Ellen considered it. These two people had to know each other, and they clearly had seen each other, but they were acting as if they were strangers. There was one possible explanation, but she resisted it.

"You can move up again," said the older man behind her, and Ellen filled in the gap. She kept watching, hoping that she was wrong. The redhead walked to the ticket counter, and the balding ticket agent brightened immediately. Bill looked in her direction, and the redhead got her ticket, bunny-dipped for her Vuitton bag, and rolled it away. Bill seemed not to notice her as she sashayed off, and Ellen lost sight of the redhead as she walked toward security.

The coach line shifted forward, and one of the ticket agents walked to the front of the line, made a megaphone of her hands, and called out, "Anyone for Philly? Philly, come on up!"

"Here!" Ellen ducked the tape to get out of line and hurried to the front, maneuvering to stand next to Bill, standing so close she could smell the residual cigarette smoke wreathing him. As casually as possible, she said, "Hard to go back to Philly in the cold."

"I bet."

"Where are you headed?"

"Vegas."

"Wow. I've never been. Have fun."

"You, too. Safe trip." Bill flashed her a grin, then went to the front desk, got his ticket, and walked off toward security, his jacket flying open.

Three people later, Ellen got her ticket and hurried ahead to security, but lost sight of Bill and the redhead. She found herself again at the back of the line and in time made it through security, then took a quick look at the lighted departure signs for Las Vegas. The Vegas gate was two down from hers. She hurried toward the gate, scanned the passengers waiting for the flight, and spotted them in no time.

Bill sat reading a *Wall Street Journal* in one of the wide gray seats, and directly across from him was the redhead, flipping through a thick copy of *Vogue* and crossing and uncrossing her legs. It was a game they were playing, frequent-flier foreplay.

Ellen lingered behind a round pillar and watched Bill and the redhead until it was time for first class to board. They joined the line, leaving a few travelers between them. The redhead got her boarding pass swiped, and just as she entered the jet way, she turned behind her, ostensibly for her bag, and flashed Bill the briefest of smiles.

He's cheating on Snow White?

Ellen went ahead to her gate, disgusted and sad. She boarded, and her heart went out to Carol, planting marigolds on Timothy's memorial on the front lawn. Being nice to the grocery stockboy. Playing Mother Goose to toddlers. Teaching children's theater at Charbonneau House. Ellen was so preoccupied that she barely heard the ticket agent asking for her boarding pass.

She boarded, found her seat, and stowed her roller bag in the overhead, then sat down, suddenly exhausted. Outside on the tarmac, a baggage train chugged past, but Ellen closed her eyes. She didn't want to see anything anymore. Not Miami or its heat. Not Bill Braverman or his mistress. Not Charbonneau Road. Not the marigolds.

She felt awful inside, raw and depressed. She didn't want to think about letting Will go to the Bravermans. She didn't want to think about letting Will go at all. Will was her son and he belonged with her. And her father, and Connie. And Oreo Figaro.

Ellen stopped herself in mid-dwell. There was no point to making herself crazy until she had the DNA results.

She vowed to keep the melodrama to a minimum until then.

Chapter Fifty-nine

"Mommy!" Will shouted, leaving his Legos and running to meet Ellen just as she closed the front door against the cold.

"Honey!" she called back, hoisting him up and hugging him close, ambushed by a fierce rush of emotion. She kissed him on the cheek and tried to pretend this was a homecoming like any other.

"I'm making a castle! A big castle!" Will kicked to be let down.

"Good for you." Ellen set him on the ground with his feet still kicking, and he hit the hardwood floor like a windup toy. He ran back to his Legos, hit the rug, and sprawled on his tummy in his overalls. Ellen wished she could take a mental snapshot and keep it forever.

"Welcome home!" Connie smiled, wiping her hands on a dishcloth as she came into the living room. "You made it early, huh?"

"Got it all done early." Ellen slid out of her coat, shaking off the unaccustomed cold, and felt happier than ever to be home. Oreo Figaro looked up from the back of the sofa, where he sat with his front paws neatly underneath him. The living room smelled deliciously of hot coffee and chicken with rosemary. "Connie, am I dreaming or is that dinner?"

"It'll be ready in ten minutes, and Will took a good nap, so he's up and at 'em." Connie met her eye meaningfully, and Ellen impulsively grabbed her and gave her a huge hug.

"Will you marry me?"

"Anytime," Connie answered, releasing her with a grin, then she went to the closet, got her coat, and put it on. Her overnight bag, purse, and tote sat packed on the windowseat. "You got a sunburn, eh?"

"I know." Ellen's hand went to the tip of her nose. It would be hard to explain at work tomorrow. Then again, everything would be hard to explain at work tomorrow.

"One last thing." Connie picked up her bags, and her smile vanished. "I'm sorry about the phone business. Hope I didn't get you in too much trouble."

"Don't worry, I can deal with it," Ellen said, though she didn't know how. "You took great care of him, and that's what matters."

"Thanks." Connie turned to Will. "See you later, alligator!"

"In a while, crocodile," Will called over his shoulder, playing happily on the floor, his world order restored.

"See you!" Connie let herself out, and Ellen went over and touched Will's hair. The dark blond filaments felt soft under her fingertips, and she tried not to notice his hair color was almost the same as Carol's.

"Please say thank you to Connie."

"Thank you, Connie!" Will scrambled to a standing position, then ran over and hugged his babysitter, and Ellen could see how happy it made her. She didn't want to think about how Connie would react if Will turned out to be Timothy. She put it out of her mind as she let Connie out the door, then kicked off her clogs and got down on the rug to play with Will.

She still had one DNA sample to collect, but she could do that after the Lego castle.

Chapter Sixty

Ellen scanned the directions for the DNA sample while Will stood at the kitchen sink and rinsed his mouth with warm water, his small fingers wrapped like a gecko's around the glass tumbler. Though she had to use the nonstandard test for Carol and Bill, she was collecting Will's sample by the conventional method, and she had to get it tonight because all the samples had to be sent to the laboratory together.

"Spit, Mommy?" Will asked, his eyes trustful over the rim of the glass.

"Two more times, pal."

Will took a second gulp of water and spit it into the sink. "Is this good?"

"Yes, and we have to do one more thing."

"Okay." Will took his third gulp, letting the water dribble out of his mouth and down his chin for fun.

"Good, thanks." Ellen wiped his wet grin with a napkin, then took the glass from his hand, set it on the counter, and turned to face him, placing a hand on his little shoulder. "Now open up, sweetie, just like you do for the doctor."

"Is it gonna hurt?"

"No, not at all." Ellen took the Q-tip in hand. "I'm going to rub the inside of your cheek with a Q-tip, that's all. It's the same kind of Q-tip we use to clean your ears."

"Are you cleaning my mouth?"

"Yes." *Sort of.*

"Why is my mouth dirty? I brushed my teeth this morning."

"Ready to open up?"

Will opened his mouth like a baby bird, and Ellen rolled the swab on the insides of both of his cheeks for about a minute, making sure to cover most of his inner cheek. Then she withdrew the swab and set it on a folded piece of paper to dry, according to the instructions.

"Good job, sweetie."

Will began jumping up and down.

"We just need one more, okay?"

"Why?" Will opened his mouth again, and Ellen picked up another Q-tip and swabbed the inside of his cheek.

"Just to be sure. All finished. Great job."

"Now can we have dessert?"

"We sure can."

Anything but lime Jell-O.

Chapter Sixty-one

Ellen had just stepped out of the shower when her cell phone started ringing. She ran into her bedroom, picked up her BlackBerry, and checked the display screen. It was a 215 area code, a Philly phone number she didn't know. She pressed Answer.

"Hello?" It was Marcelo, and Ellen warmed to the sound, sinking onto her bed and drawing her pink chenille robe closer around her.

"Hey, hi."

"I got your message. Sorry I couldn't get back to you until now. Are you at home?"

"Yes, I'll be back to work tomorrow, like I said. If you're free, we can meet in the morning and talk over this thing with Sarah."

"I don't think it can wait. I'd like to come over tonight, if I may."

Wow. Ellen checked her watch—9:08. Will was in bed, fast asleep. "Sure."

"It's not a social call," Marcelo added, and she felt herself flush.

"Understood . . ."

"I'm on my way. I'll be there in half an hour."

"Great," Ellen said, and as soon as they hung up, she bolted to the closet. She changed her clothes four times, ending up with a light blue V-neck and jeans, but instead of a tank top underneath, she went with a lace-topped ivory camisole.

Though her underwear was the last thing on her mind.

Chapter Sixty-two

By the time Marcelo knocked on the door, Ellen's hair had dried loose and curly to her shoulders and she had doused herself with perfume, made up her eyes, and patted concealer on her telltale sunburn.

"Hello," Marcelo said, unsmiling as he came inside.

"Good to see you." Ellen knew she couldn't kiss him hello, but she didn't want to shake his hand, so she settled for closing the door behind him. "Can I take your coat?"

"That's okay, I won't be staying long."

Ouch. "Would you like a drink or something?"

"No, thanks."

"Do you want to sit down?"

"Thanks." Marcelo crossed to the couch and sat stiffly down, and Ellen took the chair catty-corner to him. He said, "I thought it would be better to talk here than in the office, since we're conspiring."

"I'm really sorry about what happened."

"I know." Marcelo looked tense, a new tightness around his mouth. "I've been struggling with what to do, how to handle the situation." He linked his fingers between his legs, leaning forward slightly. "To start with, I shouldn't have done what I did . . . started anything romantic with you. It was wrong, and I'm sorry."

Ellen swallowed, hurt. "You don't have to say you're sorry, and it wasn't so terrible."

"It was, especially considering how it turned out."

"But we can set it right."

"No, we can't."

Ellen felt like they were having a lovers' quarrel, and they weren't even lovers.

"I'm your editor, and there's no way we can be together, in the end."

"But we just started." Ellen was surprised at the emotion in her voice. "Other couples at the paper date."

"Not editor and staffer. Not a direct report." Marcelo shook his head, downcast. "Anyway, to the point. I lied to my staff. I've never lied to my staff, ever. I showed you a favoritism I wouldn't have shown anyone else, and I did it because I care for you." His voice softened, but his gaze remained firm. "But now I know what to do."

"I do, too." Ellen had thought about it on the plane, but Marcelo held up his hand.

"Let me, please. That's why I came here tonight. I don't want you to come in to work tomorrow morning."

No. "Why not?"

"I'm going to hold a meeting of the staff and I don't think you should be there. I'm going to tell them what happened. Not about my . . . feelings, I'm not that crazy." Marcelo smiled. "I'm going to tell them that I lied about your whereabouts because you had a personal matter that you didn't want me or them to know about, and I thought it was the best way to handle the situation."

"You're going to tell the truth?"

Marcelo chuckled. "It's not that crazy. We're a newspaper. We care for truth."

"But not now, not this way." Ellen couldn't let him do it. It was career suicide.

"I'm going to apologize and say that I realize, in retrospect, that it was poor judgment on my part."

"You can't do that, Marcelo." Ellen didn't know where to begin. "It undermines your credibility forever. They're already talking about you, and this will only add fuel to the fire. You'll never live it down."

"Reporters are intelligent and verbal people. They talk, they speculate, and they gossip. There's nothing to be done about it."

Ellen leaned forward, urgent. "That's not the way to handle this. One of us has to admit that they were lying, and that person can't be you."

"If I tell the truth, it will pass."

"No, it will follow you forever. I can't let you do it."

"You have no say," Marcelo said with a sad smile, and Ellen realized that if he wouldn't do it for him, maybe he'd do it for her.

"You'd hurt me more if you did that. They'll think we're sleeping together, and I'll be branded forever. It's better for me if you suspend me for lying to you."

"You *want* that?" Marcelo frowned.

"It's the only way. If you suspend me, I look like just another employee who lied to the boss. Everybody lies to the boss."

"They do?" Marcelo looked horrified, which Ellen thought was adorable.

"If we tell them I lied to you, then I'm just somebody who played hooky."

"Hooky?"

"Ditched work for the day. I even have a tan. But, on the other hand, if you tell them you lied for me, it makes it a bigger deal and it never goes away."

Marcelo pursed his lips, searching her face, and Ellen could see she was making headway.

"You're a journalist, so you should know. Employee lies to boss. That's no story. Boss lies *for* employee? A headline."

"I don't know." Marcelo ran his fingers through his hair, muttering. "*Que roubada.* What a mess."

"Marcelo, if you care about me, you'll suspend me without pay."

"Is that what you want?"

"Yes. For a week."

Marcelo's lips flattened to a sour line. "Three days."

"Done."

Marcelo eyed her, his regret plain. "It's a disciplinary action against you. It jeopardizes your job."

Ellen knew that, but this wasn't the time to cry about it. She'd gotten them into this mess and she was going to get them out. "Look on the bright side. If you fire me, you have to take me out. I could lose a job, but gain a boyfriend."

"You're killing me." Marcelo winced, rising, and Ellen stood up, too. They were standing about three feet apart, so close they could embrace, but nobody was touching anybody.

"I'm joking," she said, but Marcelo turned away and walked to the door, where he stopped and flashed her a final, sad smile.

"Then why aren't we laughing?" he asked.

For that, Ellen had no answer.

Chapter Sixty-three

Ellen set her DNA instructions on her bedspread and unpacked the two paper bags from her suitcase, the one containing Bill's cigarette butts and the other Carol's soda can. She set them next to the white business envelope that contained the Q-tips with Will's sample. From the corner of the bed, Oreo Figaro watched all of her movements with concern.

Ellen sat down beside the cat, petting his spiny back idly and picking up the Paternity Testing Form she had downloaded. She scanned the first few paragraphs that contained legal terms and conditions, then the form authorizing how to send the results.

The form contained various lines to fill out to identify the sample; name, sample date, race, and relationship, Suspected Mother, Suspected Father, Suspected Grandfather (paternal or maternal), Suspected Grandmother (paternal or maternal), and Other. She filled in Suspected Mother for Carol's sample, Suspected Father for Bill's, and Child for Will's. Then she made matching labels that the form requested, cut them out with scissors, and taped them on the two brown paper bags and Will's envelope, like the arts-and-crafts project from hell.

She gathered the brown bags, the envelope, and the forms, and placed them in a padded FedEx Pak. She filled in the address slip, sealed the FedEx envelope, and set it on the nightstand. She would mail the FedEx Pak after she dropped Will at school, not that she wanted to think about the juxtaposition of those two events.

She sat back down on the bed and petted Oreo Figaro, but he declined to purr. In three days, she could find out that Will didn't belong to the Bravermans and she could keep him happily for the rest of their life together. Three days seemed forever to wait, and at the same time not nearly long enough. Because in three days she could also find out that Will did belong to the Bravermans, then . . .

That was where Ellen stopped her thinking. She had promised herself on the plane.

And Oreo Figaro withheld his purr.

Chapter Sixty-four

The next morning was freezing, the sky an opaque gray and the air holding a wet chill in its clenched fist, and Ellen was sitting in her car in the parking lot of a local strip mall. Traffic rushed back and forth on a busy Lancaster Avenue, the car tires stained white with road salt and their back windshields still deicing. She watched idly, and her car grew cold, the last heat dissipating. She had dropped Will off at school only half an hour ago, but it seemed longer. The FedEx Pak containing the DNA samples sat next to her like an unwanted hitchhiker.

Ellen was stalling, and though she knew it, she couldn't stop herself. All she had to do was slide down her car window, pull up the metal handle on the FedEx mailbox, and toss the package inside. As soon as she did that, it was out of her hands. The deed would be done. The lab would charge her credit card, process the samples, and email her the results. Yes or no. Hers or theirs.

Ellen couldn't believe she was still hesitating, not after she'd stalked the Bravermans and placed her professional career in jeopardy, in addition to losing a man she was profoundly attracted to, before she'd even had him. She reminded herself that she didn't have to do anything with the test results once she had them. Even if it turned out in the Bravermans' favor, she didn't have to tell a soul. It could stay her secret forever. Why should she stall, given all she had gone through?

Her gaze shifted to the FedEx mailbox, and she reread its pickup sticker for the umpteenth time. The stores in the strip mall hadn't opened yet, and the glass front of a Subway remained dark, the display counters and cash registers shapeless shadows. She took a sip of coffee but couldn't taste it, and set it into the cup holder. Hot steam curled from her travel mug, which had no lid. She'd been too distracted to find it this morning, dreading the task at hand.

I can forget the whole thing.

Ellen turned on the ignition, and the car turned over, throaty. Her coffee vibrated in the cup holder, a tiny ripple appearing on its surface. She didn't have to mail the samples. She could just drive away and let them decompose or whatever they did. She could stop this insanity right now. Her lawyer, Ron, would approve, and so would her father. He'd kill her if he knew what she doing. The car idled, and the heat vent blew cold air. Still she didn't hit the gas.

I can't forget the whole thing.

She pressed the button and lowered the car window, struck by the frigid blast, then she yanked the handle on the mailbox and tossed the FedEx Pak inside. The drawer closed with a final *ca-thunk.*

So be it.

Ellen hit the gas, knowing the day was about to get even worse.

Chapter Sixty-five

Ellen pressed thoughts of the DNA samples to the back of her mind, trying to ignore the irony as she drove to Amy Martin's funeral. She steered through the run-down neighborhood outside Stoatesville, its residential blocks struggling to survive after all the manufacturing had gone, leaving behind corner bars and empty storefronts. She took a left and a right among the streets, finally spotting the converted rowhouse that stood out because of its freshly painted façade of ivory stucco, the only well-maintained place on the block. She knew it must be the funeral home, because they were always the prettiest buildings, even in a terrible neighborhood. The thought depressed her. You shouldn't have to die to be in a nice place.

She found a space on the street, parked, and got out of the car. Cold air blew hard, and she drew her black dress coat closer as she walked down the street. Her boots clacked against the gritty pavement, and she reached the funeral home, with a fake gold sign beside the door. The glass door was smudged, and she yanked on the handle and went inside, warming up momentarily and getting her bearings. An entrance hall contained a few oak chairs and a fake walnut credenza, on which rested a maroon vase of faded silk flowers and an open guest book with a vinyl cover. The place looked empty, and the air smelled dusty, only vaguely perfumed with flowers. A burgundy rug covered the floor and a long corridor to the left, leading to two louvered doors. Only the second door was open, and light spilled from the room. No sign indicated it was Amy's viewing, but it was a safe assumption.

Ellen crossed to the guest book and looked at the open page, scanning the list of names: Gerry Martin, Dr. Robert Villiers and Cheryl Martin Villiers, Tiffany Lebov, William Martin. It gave her pause. Amy had been so disconnected from these people in life, but they had gathered here to mourn her, death having mooted the estrangements and differences, the angry words or hurt feelings. Ellen felt moved to be among them, connected in the most tenuous of ways, if at all. She picked up the long white pen next to the book and signed her name.

She walked down the hall toward the open door, lingering for a moment on the threshold. The room was rectangular and large, but only two rows of brown folding chairs had been set up toward the front, where a group of women huddled together. The casket was closed, and she felt macabre admitting to herself she was almost disappointed. She wouldn't get a chance to see what Amy Martin looked like, even in death, to compare her features to Will's. But it didn't matter now anyway. The DNA samples would solve the mystery that was Amy Martin.

Ellen walked toward the group at the front and when she got closer, saw that Gerry was being comforted by Cheryl, who caught her eye and smiled.

"Ellen, how nice of you to come," she said softly, and Gerry turned in her embrace and looked up. Grief deepened the folds bracketing her mouth, which tilted down, and she looked like she was sinking in an oversized black pantsuit.

"I'm so sorry about your loss." Ellen approached, extending her hand.

"Real nice of you to come." Gerry's voice sounded hoarse, and she blinked tears from her eyes. "I know Amy woulda wanted to meet you. Someday maybe you can bring your little boy over to the house."

Behind her, Cheryl nodded. "I'd like to meet him, too, when he's feeling better."

"I'd be happy to do that," Ellen said, with a twinge. She'd forgotten that she had lied to them about needing Will's medical history.

Cheryl said, "Too bad you missed my husband and my brother. They were here last night and earlier, but they had to go." She gestured next to her at another mourner, a young woman. "This is a friend of Amy's."

"Melanie Rotucci," the girl said, extending her hand. She looked to be in her twenties, and on another day, would have been pretty, if a little hard-looking. Her gray eyes were red and puffy from crying, and her fair skin pale and wan. She had a cupid's-bow mouth, and her best feature was long, dark hair that spilled over the shoulders of her black leather jacket.

Ellen introduced herself, surprised to meet her. Cheryl and Gerry had told her that Amy didn't have girlfriends.

Cheryl must have been reading her mind. "Melanie met Amy in rehab, and they were really good friends."

"Amy was in rehab?" Ellen asked, confused. It was all news to her.

"We didn't know until we met Melanie. It turns out Amy was really trying to turn her life around. She went to rehab twice, for heroin. She was almost better, right, Melanie?"

"I really thought she was going to make it." Melanie's mouth made a resigned line, in dark lipstick. "She was clean for thirty-five days the second time. At ninety days, she was going to tell everybody, all of you."

"My poor, poor baby," Gerry whispered, collapsing into new sobs, and Cheryl hugged her closer.

Strain etched Melanie's young face. "I need a cigarette," she muttered, rising.

"I'll keep you company," Ellen said, intrigued.

Chapter Sixty-six

"This must be hard on you," Ellen said as they stepped outside the funeral home and shared a grimy top step, its small size forcing them close together. Melanie cupped her cigarette against the cold wind, firing it with a thumb flicked on a yellow plastic Bic lighter.

"It's the worst."

"Were you good friends?"

"I mean, we didn't know each other that long, but when you meet people in rehab, you get tighter a lot faster. Amy said that rehab was like dog years, one is like seven." Melanie dragged on the cigarette, and smoke leaked from her sad smile.

"Where is the rehab center?"

"Eagleville, in Pennsylvania." Melanie leaned back against an iron rail and crossed long legs, in skinny jeans and black boots.

Ellen had heard of the place. "Can I ask, how old are you?"

"Twenty-two."

"A lot younger than Amy."

"I know. She took care of me like a big sister, or a mom or something."

It struck a chord. "Did Amy ever mention to you having had a child?"

"No way!" Melanie looked at her like she was crazy. "Amy didn't have a kid."

"I think she did and she put it up for adoption." Ellen almost didn't believe it herself, after Miami. "She had a baby, but I guess she didn't mention it to you."

"It's possible, I guess."

"It was a very sick baby, with a heart problem."

"I didn't know *everything* about her." Melanie's eyes narrowed behind a curtain of cigarette smoke. "Amy was her own girl, that's for sure, but we went through group together, the seminars they make us take, the lectures, rec activities all day long. We even spent our smoke breaks together. She never mentioned a sick baby."

Ellen set her emotions aside. "She ever mention a boyfriend? His name could've been Charles Cartmell."

"No. She used to date a lot, but she was changing that, too. She said in group that she was sick of hooking up with abusive guys. She wasn't going there, anymore."

"Did any of them visit her at rehab?"

"No. We're allowed visitors on weekends but she never got any. Neither did I, which was fine with me. If my mom came, I'd a kicked her ass."

Ellen let it go. "I'm wondering about one guy in particular, someone Amy was dating about three or four years ago. He wasn't a bad-looking guy, on the short side, white, with longish brown hair. They might've gone on a trip together, to someplace warm. Did she ever mention a vacation with a guy, at a beach?"

Melanie paused a minute, frowning. "No, but I know that a while ago, she used to see a guy named Rob. Rob Moore."

Ellen felt her heartbeat quicken. "What did she say about him?"

"Just that he was a jerk."

"How long ago was this, that she saw him?"

"I don't know, but it was old news."

"Three or four years ago?"

"Yeah. Really in her past."

Ellen gathered that if you were in your twenties, three years ago was history. "Did she mention where he was from?"

"Not that I remember."

"Did she tell you anything else about him, like where he lived or what he did for a living?"

"No, nothing like that." Melanie blew out an acrid cone of smoke.

"How about his age? Or what kind of car he drove or where he was from? Anything like that?"

"No, just that he was a bad dude. Used to smack her around, and she dumped him. She wouldn't take that, forever. That was the thing about Amy. She was the one we all thought would make it." Tears glistened in Melanie's bloodshot eyes. "Two of the counselors came by earlier this morning, they woulda told you the same thing."

Ellen's thoughts raced ahead. "I hate to ask you, but I feel like I need to know. What was it that happened to her? How did they find her?"

"I was the one who found her," Melanie answered flatly.

"That must have been awful for you."

Melanie didn't reply.

"So she overdosed on heroin? How do you know something like that? Was there a needle in her arm?"

"No. She didn't shoot it, neither of us did. She snorted it. There was junk on the table and the credit card she used, a Visa." Melanie tossed her hair over her shoulder. "Anyway, we were supposed to go out that night, but she never met me, so I went over around nine the next morning. She was on the couch, dressed to go out."

"How did you get in?"

"I have a key. She was all stiff. The family thinks she overdosed, but I wonder if it was bad junk." Melanie faltered, then took a drag. "The cops said that she died the night before."

Ellen processed the information. "Why do you think it was bad junk and not just an overdose?"

"You never know with street junk."

"She lived in Brigantine?"

"Yeah."

"By herself?"

"Yeah. She got a room in a nice house and a new job, waitressing at this restaurant. She was going to meetings, too, every day. She never missed." Melanie shook her head sadly. "She's the one who told me to carry Subutex."

"What's that?"

"A pill. If you take it and you do H, you don't get high. Amy always carried two pills with her."

Ellen had heard of drugs like that. She'd done a story once involving Antabuse, a drug that made alcoholics sick if they drank.

"But that night, she didn't take a pill. The bottle was right on her nightstand with the two still in it."

Ellen thought it sounded strange. "So why did she take heroin instead of Subutex?"

"She musta missed it so much. Heroin's like that. You love it and you hate it, so much. She shoulda known better than to buy off the street, even in a nice neighborhood."

"Wouldn't she have mentioned to you that she was thinking of using again? How often did you speak to her, generally?"

Melanie tossed her cigarette butt to the sidewalk. "We talked on the phone, like, every day, and she was queen of texting. She texted all the time."

"Did you look at her texts from before she died?"

"Whoa, weird. I didn't. I totally forgot." Melanie was already reaching into her purse and extracting a silvery phone with a fake-jeweled face, which she flipped open. She pressed several buttons to retrieve the texts, then started scrolling backwards. Ellen edged close to her, and they read the text together:

scored new 7 jeans on sale. wait till u see them! xoxo

Ellen glanced at the top of the screen, which showed the time the text had come in—9:15 P.M. "She sounds happy."

"Yeah, mos def." Melanie pressed a few more buttons. "Here's another one, from earlier that day, around five o'clock."

Ellen and Melanie put their heads together, and read the previous text, which said:

$228 in tips, my best day ever! going to the mall 2 celebrate! see u soon! xoxo

"That's so random." Melanie shook her head. "It doesn't sound like she was thinking about using."

"It sure doesn't." Ellen thought about it. "Recovering addicts get sponsors, right? Did Amy have a sponsor?"

"Sure, Dot Hatten. She was here this morning. I don't know if she got a call from her that night. I was too much of a wreck to ask her, and she might not say anyway. They keep everything confidential, like lawyers or something."

"You don't think she'd talk to me?"

"I know she wouldn't."

"Do you have her phone number, anyway?"

"No."

"Where does she live?" Ellen could get the number online.

"Jersey, but if you want to know more about Amy, you should ask Rose. She was here before. She's another friend of ours. She's older." Melanie wrinkled her nose. "She was in rehab with me and Amy."

"Great, can I have her phone?"

"I have her cell number right here." Melanie pressed a few keys on the phone, found a number, and rattled it off.

"Hold on, I have to get a pen." Ellen rooted around in her purse, but Melanie dismissed her with a wave.

"You don't need one. Give me your cell number, and I'll text it to you."

"Of course," Ellen said, a reminder of her age, as she stood on the front step of mortality.

Chapter Sixty-seven

Rose Bock turned out to be a middle-aged African-American woman with oversized aviator glasses and a sweet smile. She wore her hair cut natural and had on a blue-checked Oxford shirt underneath a navy suit, looking every inch the accountant. Ellen had reached her on her cell phone, and she was in Philly, so they'd met at a burger joint full of noisy students near the Penn campus.

"Thanks so much for meeting me." Ellen took a quick sip of a Diet Coke. "My condolences about Amy. Melanie told me that you two were close."

"We were." Rose's smile faded quickly. "So how did you know her? You didn't say on the phone."

"Long story short, I adopted a baby that I think was hers. At least that's what the court papers say."

"Amy had a baby?" Rose's eyebrows rose, and Ellen grew officially tired of the reaction.

"Hi, ladies." The waitress arrived with a cheeseburger in a blue plastic basket, set it down on the table, then went off. Rose picked up the burger and smiled sheepishly.

"I can't resist the double cheeseburger here. I traded one addiction for another."

"Enjoy yourself." Ellen managed a smile. "If you don't mind my saying so, you don't look like the typical drug addict."

"Yes, I do," Rose said, without rancor. "I was addicted to prescription drugs, Vicodin and Percocet, for almost nine years. I started with a back injury and never stopped."

"I think of Vicodin as in a different category from heroin."

"You shouldn't. They're both opiates and they work the same way. I might have been in a different income bracket from Amy, but we're both junkies. It could just as easily have been me, lying there today in a box." Rose picked up her heavy burger and took a bite in a way that looked almost angry to Ellen, but she wanted to stay on point.

"I'm trying to learn about Amy's death. The family told me she overdosed accidentally, or that it was bad heroin, street heroin."

"She didn't overdose." Rose shook her head, and laughter burst from a nearby table, a group of caffeinated undergraduates. "More likely, the junk was bad. Street junk gets cut with strychnine."

Ellen shuddered. "Poison."

"Yes."

"Melanie told me that Amy still had her Subutex on her, which she didn't take, and we both read her last texts, which were upbeat. Amy didn't mention to Melanie that she was looking to start doing drugs again. Had she mentioned anything like that to you?"

"No, not all." Rose finished chewing, then reached for her coffee and took a sip.

"I wonder why she didn't call you or Melanie, if she felt tempted to do drugs again."

"*You* wonder?" Rose winced, between bites. "I'm not her sponsor, but I am, I was, her friend. I would think she'd call me if she wanted to use. I'll never get over this, until I go to my own grave."

"I'm sorry. You can't blame yourself."

"That's what my husband says, and thanks for it, but it doesn't help." Rose set the sandwich down. "I would have bet a thousand bucks on Amy. She had relapsed twice, but that's part of the process, for some of us. She was finally able to get clean."

"So she never called you, to say she was tempted?"

"No, never." Rose's face fell into pained lines. "We talked on the phone every couple days, and all the talk was easy. She got a new job and she was getting ready to reconcile with her family. So that she started using again, two days after we spoke, well, it was a real blow." Rose shook her head.

"Melanie told me about a guy named Rob Moore, who Amy dated three or four years ago. He was abusive and she got away from him. You know anything about him?"

"Not really. Amy told me that she had a toxic relationship once, that much I know. I never knew his name. She talked about him in group. The therapists might know more, but they won't tell you, that's confidential."

Ellen tried another tack. "Did Amy say where he was from or where he lived? Anything that he might have done for a living? I ask because there's an outside chance that he's the father of my son."

"I wish I could help you, but I can't."

"Wait, maybe this will help." Ellen picked up her purse and pulled out a flurry of papers, one of which was the photo of Amy and the man on the beach, then handed the picture to Rose. Luckily, she hadn't cleaned out her purse after the Miami trip. She pointed at Beach Man. "I think this man might be Rob Moore. Did you ever see him?"

"No."

"She ever show you a photo?"

"No, just told me that he was a jerk." Rose handed back the picture, then paused, her eyes narrowing. "Hold the phone. Last week, she called me on my cell. I wasn't there to take the call, but she left a message, saying something about a 'blast from the past.'" Rose looked away, her lips parting slightly as she reached for a thought. "What was it she said? She had a visit from a blast from the past."

Ellen met her eye, and her blood ran cold.

"Do you think she meant Rob Moore?"

"Maybe." Ellen's thoughts came fast and furious, but it was risky to tell her much more. "What did she say when you called her back?"

"She said she was fine. I forgot about the message, and we started talking about other things." Rose's mouth tilted down, and the realization dawned on her. "You think that this guy came back in her life, but she didn't want to let on? Or she thought better of it?"

"I don't know what I think. I'm trying to figure out what happened. What day was it that she called you?"

"Friday. I missed the call because I was at my son's piano recital."

Ellen thought back quickly. She had met with Cheryl on Thursday night, after which Cheryl sent Amy the email telling her that Ellen was looking for her. Friday would be the night after Amy got the email, assuming she checked her email with any frequency. Ellen felt an ominous tightening in her chest, trying to put two and two together on the spot.

"Why does any of this matter? Do you think Rob Moore had something to do with Amy's using again?"

"I don't know," Ellen answered, feeling an odd momentum building within her. She wished she could tell Rose that she intended to find out, but she was too stricken to speak. Too many things weren't making sense, or maybe they were. She sensed it wasn't speculation. That Amy's death was connected to her visit to Cheryl. That she had set it all in motion. And that Rob Moore had everything to do with Amy's death.

"You there?"

"Sorry." Ellen fake-checked her watch, then rose. "Jeez, I'm late, I should probably get going, thanks so much."

"Now?" Rose blinked in confusion. "We're in the middle of a conversation."

"I know, but I have to go." Ellen grabbed her coat and purse from the seat. "I'll follow up and let you know if I learn anything new. Thanks again."

"You think we should call the police?"

"No," Ellen said, too quickly. "I'm sure it's speculation, but I'll give it some thought. Have to go now. Thanks again."

She turned and fled the restaurant.

Chapter Sixty-eight

Ellen hurried from the restaurant, her head swimming. She broke into a light jog, pulling her coat around her with a shaky hand. Her heels clacked along the frozen concrete, and she almost ran into two students who came suddenly out of a bookstore. She hurried ahead, ignoring their laughter. Her breath came in short, ragged bursts, fogging from her mouth. Her eyes stung, and she blinked the wetness away, telling herself it was the cold. She reached her car, fumbled for her keys, jumped in and turned on the engine, then lurched into the lane of traffic.

HONK! HONK! A van driver blared his horn, but Ellen didn't look back. It was late afternoon and a premature night was falling, frigid as black ice. Cars clogged the street in both directions, their headlights aglow. She drove on autopilot, through a world that had gone topsy-turvy around her.

She had thought that Will was hers and would be forever. She thought that he had a young mother somewhere and a wandering father. She thought that they were gone for good, a young couple who made a mistake. But it had been a fantasy, created by a writer's imagination. All of it was fiction. And now Ellen was deathly afraid of what was true.

Her hands gripped the wheel. Her heart thundered. She skidded to a stop at a traffic light, the burning red circle searing into her consciousness like a hot poker. She was too emotional to think straight. She didn't know where to go or what to do. She couldn't go to the police because she'd lose Will. She had been going it alone for so long, she couldn't do it for another minute. She picked up her cell phone and pressed in a phone number.

"Please be there," Ellen was saying, when the call connected.

Chapter Sixty-nine

"Come in, what's the matter?" Marcelo swung open his front door, and Ellen hurried past the threshold, compelled by a force she didn't understand completely, whether pulled or pushed inside she didn't know. It had taken her an hour to get to his house in Queens Village, but the ride over hadn't calmed her down. It had been all she could do to hide her panic when she'd called Connie and asked her to stay late.

"There's a problem but . . . I don't know where to begin." Ellen raked a hand through her hair and found herself pacing back and forth in his neat living room, a blur of exposed-brick walls, glass tables, and black leather furniture. Marcelo closed the front door behind her, and she spun on her heels to face him. "I don't even know where to begin."

"It's all right," Marcelo said softly, his dark eyes steady. "Try the beginning."

"No, I . . . can't." Ellen didn't know why she'd come here. She wasn't sure it was the right thing. She knew only that she needed to talk to someone. "I think I'm in the middle of something . . . I don't know what."

"Did you do something illegal?"

"Yes, and no." Ellen didn't know how to answer. She didn't know what to think. Her hands flew to her face, and she felt her fingerpads burrow into the flesh of her cheeks. "No, but . . . I think I stumbled onto something . . . I wish I never started. It's the worst . . . the worst thing that could happen."

"What could be so bad?" Marcelo asked, disbelieving, stepping closer to her and taking her by the shoulders. "What is it?"

"It's too awful, it's just . . ." Ellen couldn't continue, afraid to give it voice, as if she'd fall into an abyss, a darkness that would follow as inexorably as nightfall. She felt something tear loose in her chest, as if her heart were actually ripped from its moorings, untethered from everything that held it in place, everything that kept her alive, and she heard herself erupt in a sob that came from deep within and burst free. The next thing she knew, she was crying and Marcelo had put his arms around her, wrapping her in a strong embrace, and she could feel herself sagging against his soft shirt, hiccuping in the civilized office smells clinging to him, the remnants of her life before.

Marcelo was saying, "Whatever it is, we can figure it out. Everything is going to be all right, you'll see." He held her tight, rocking her slightly, and she heard him saying again that everything was going to be all right, and she listened to his words as if she were a small child, permitting herself to be told a fairy tale.

"I made a . . . a mistake, a terrible mistake." Ellen looked up at him through her tears and she could see in his expression that he had let his guard slip away, and all that was left was a naked pain that must have mirrored her own. He stroked her cheek gently, brushing away her tears, and Ellen felt his other arm behind her back and leaned against it fully, letting him support her. His eyes met hers, so full of feeling that she felt a kind of wonderment, and she couldn't remember anyone ever looking at her that way, and in the next instant he lowered his face and kissed her softly on the lips, once, and then again.

"Everything's going to be all right," he murmured. "You're here now, and we'll make it right."

"Really?" Ellen asked, still wondering, and when Marcelo leaned down to kiss her again, more deeply and with urgency, she had her answer. In that moment she gave herself over to him and her own emotions, kissing him back deeply, drawing from him comfort and strength, escaping into the delusion of his embrace, just for now, for the few moments before he learned the truth and understood that everything was most decidedly not going to be all right, but that all of her worst fears were about to happen and there was nothing and nobody who could stop them.

And in the next minute Ellen felt her own hands reaching up Marcelo's back, her fingers rough against the thin fabric of his shirt, pulling him as close as she possibly could, and he responded, holding her tighter, kissing her with more urgency, his breath quickening as they sank, fumbled, and stumbled together onto the couch.

Ellen felt him press her backwards against the leather, or maybe she pulled him up and onto her, almost embarrassingly eager to lose herself in him and forget about everything else. About Amy. About Carol. Even about Will. For a moment she wasn't a mother anymore but simply a woman, and the heat of Marcelo's kiss and the weight of his body chased every thought from her head and obliterated every worry. In the soft light, she saw him smile with pleasure as he helped her wriggle out of her coat and they shoved it slip-sliding off the couch and onto the rug.

"Here, allow me," Marcelo whispered, and Ellen eased partway up and put her arms in the air, letting him pull her sweater over her head, and when her head popped out of the black neckline, she saw the softest expression cross his face, and he stopped for a second, halting the urgency of before, and his gaze traveled from her face, lingering at her neck and finally coming to rest on the black lace of her bra.

"*Meu deus, voce tao linda,*" Marcelo said softly, and though she didn't know the translation, the way he said it communicated so much desire that it slowed her down and stopped her teenaged clawing. She eased backwards against the cool leather and lay with her head back and throat open, her chest rising and falling with need, her heart pounding in her ears, looking at him through tears that had stopped flowing, taking him in with her eyes.

"You are so beautiful," Marcelo said, and for a second, they were both suspended in place and time, letting the frank lust of their first kisses cool and ebb away, and they regarded each other as two mature adults, each sensing that they were starting something real by whatever came next. Marcelo looked down at her with a grave smile, then he cocked his head in what could only be a question, silently asked.

"Yes," Ellen whispered, raising her arms.

Marcelo lowered himself onto her in reply, and they kissed deeply and slowly, wrapping their arms and legs around each other, their tongues flickering and teasing, and in time, their clothes peeled off layer by layer until skin met skin, warmth met warmth, and heart met heart.

Until there was nothing between them at all.

Chapter Seventy

Ellen woke up naked, her limbs intertwined with Marcelo's and her head resting on a musky patch of his chest. She wondered what time it was, disentangling herself. Marcelo had turned out the lamp at some point, leaving the room dim except for the glow of a streetlight, bleeding through the slats in the window shutters. She propped herself up on an elbow and squinted at her watch. Nine o'clock. Her life rushed back at her like a freight train, full of noise, power, and something else. Fear. Suddenly she knew what had happened, all at once, as if she had seen it in a nightmare.

Amy was murdered. So was Karen Batz. Rob Moore is killing everyone who knows that Will is really Timothy.

Ellen sprang from the couch, looking for her clothes. She wiggled into her skirt, slid into her sweater, jumped into her boots. Marcelo slept on, his snoring soft and regular, and she didn't wake him to explain. She didn't have a minute to lose. She grabbed her coat, found her purse, and fumbled for her car keys, her heart beginning to beat fast. She crossed to the front door, and something was telling her that she had to hurry home.

Right now.

Chapter Seventy-one

Ellen shut Marcelo's front door behind her, clutched her coat closed, and hurried down the stoop into a snowstorm, keeping her head down. Flakes fell like hail, driven by an angry wind, biting the flesh of her cheeks as she hustled down the sidewalk. Snow covered the sidewalk, and she almost slipped on the way to the car.

She chirped the door open, jumped inside, and turned on the ignition and windshield wipers. Ice clung to the windshield in patches, but she wasn't waiting for it to thaw. She cranked the defrost, backed out of the space, and reached into her purse for her BlackBerry. She pulled it from her purse and pressed speed dial for Connie as she pounded the gas. The car zoomed down the dark street, and the call connected.

"Connie? You hanging in?" Ellen asked, trying to keep the nervousness from her tone. She didn't even know what she was nervous about. She just knew she had to get home.

"Sure. I'm watching TV. You said you might be late."

"Not this late." Ellen felt a twinge of guilt, but tried to pay attention to her driving. She switched lanes to pass a truck, took a right, then a left in slow traffic, everybody cautious in the snowstorm. Her windshield wipers flapped madly, a frantic beating that reminded her of her own heart.

"Take your time, El. Chuck had to work late, too."

"How's my boy?"

"He's out like a light."

"Good." Ellen waited for the familiar easing in her chest when she heard that everything was fine, but there was no easing tonight. She steered around a sluggish Toyota and switched lanes, heading for the cross street to the expressway.

"Oh yeah, the cat's throwing up, so I had to put him out back for a while."

"Okay. I'll be home in less than an hour."

"Drive safe. It's really coming down out here. We already have six inches."

"I hear you, 'bye." Ellen pressed End, tossed the BlackBerry aside, and flew around a pickup truck pulling into a parking space. She fed the car gas to the intersection, where the traffic light was turning red, then blasted through the intersection, heading home.

By the time she reached the highway, she knew exactly what she was going to do.

Chapter Seventy-two

Ellen hurried to her front porch in a full-fledged snowstorm, keeping her head down and barreling into the wind, her heels punching footfalls into the freezing, wet snow. She'd thought about calling the cops but didn't want to blow her cover. She was on her own.

She ran up the snowy porch steps and willed herself to get calm, arranging her face into a mask of normalcy. She plunged her key into the lock and twisted, opening the door onto a comforting scene that brought her no comfort.

Connie greeted her from the couch, with a big grin. "It's Nanook of the North!"

"Cold out there." Ellen fake-smiled and slid out of her coat. The lamps lent the living room a homey glow, the toys had been put away, and the TV played on mute, a plastic-surgery show. She grabbed Connie's coat and handed it to her, barely able to hide her urgency. "You'll be safe going home, right? You have four-wheel drive?"

"Sure, it's no problem." Connie put on her coat, flipping her ponytail over her collar, then got her tote and purse from the windowseat. "No way he's having school tomorrow."

"Then it's good I'm home, huh?" Ellen opened the door to let Connie out. "We'll just hibernate and make some cookies."

"I vote for chocolate chip."

"You got it." Ellen managed another smile as Connie picked up her stuff and crossed to the door. "Seriously, be careful out there."

"No worries, I'm invincible." Connie flashed her a final smile and headed outside, and Ellen shut the door, locked it, and threw the deadbolt.

Go go go.

Ellen didn't know how or why, but she knew what she felt inside. If Rob Moore was killing people who knew about Timothy, then she and Will had to get out of there immediately, tonight. She hurried up the stairs, hustled into Will's room, and hurried to the bed.

"Will, wake up, honey." Will slept on his back, his arms open and askew, stirring. Oreo Figaro didn't move, a black-and-white ball at the foot of the bed. She lifted Will up, hoisted him to her shoulder in his Elmo thermal pajamas, and he made a snuffling noise.

"Mommy?"

"Hi, honey." Ellen rubbed his back. "You can just stay asleep, I want to put you into something warmer."

Will put his arms around her neck, and Ellen moved quickly to the bureau, dipped sideways to yank open the bottom drawer, and grabbed one of his snowsuits. She crossed back to the bed, unfolded the snowsuit with a quick snap, and fumbled to stuff Will's feet into the legs. "Mommy, what?"

"Everything's fine, sweetie. We're just going out for a little bit." Ellen pulled the snowsuit up and unwrapped his arms from her neck, then stuck on his sneakers. "Hold on around my neck. We're going for a ride."

"Okay," Will said sleepily, holding tighter as she picked him up again, left the room, and hurried down the stairs, keeping a steadying hand on his back. She reached the bottom and glanced at the clock on the entertainment center—10:15. She had to get going. She grabbed her purse from the windowseat, then remembered she needed cash. She kept two hundred bucks in the kitchen drawer for emergencies and she was pretty sure this qualified.

She hurried through the living room, noting that the Coffmans' station wagon wasn't in the driveway and their windows were dark. It was a lucky break that they weren't home, because if they spotted her going out this late in a snowstorm, they might have a question or two. She hurried with Will through the dining room and turned the corner into the dark kitchen.

She went to flick on the light switch, but all of a sudden there was a shadowy blur and the back of her head exploded in pain.

Her arms released their grip. Will slipped through her fingers. Everything went dark, and the last thing she heard was Will's scream.

"Mommy!"

Chapter Seventy-three

Ellen regained consciousness, lying on her side on the kitchen floor. Her head thundered and she tried to scream. Tape covered her lips. She tried to move her hands but they were wrenched behind her back, stuck together. Pain arced through her shoulder joints. Her ankles were bound. She was facing the dining room, her back to the kitchen.

Will.

Ellen felt a bolt of terror rattle through her very bones. Her Black-Berry rang in the living room, the sound of another place and time. She heard a noise behind her, a harsh ripping sound. She rolled herself over on the floor, in horror at the sight.

Will lay on his side facing her, a strip of duct tape over his mouth. He was crying hard, his small body shaking with sobs. A man bent over him, wrapping duct tape around his ankles in his blue snow-suit.

"Good morning," the man said, looking up with a sly grin.

It was the man from the beach. Rob Moore. He had a droopy

brown mustache and he looked older and craggier than he had in the photo with Amy, but it was the same man. Shaggy brown hair curled over the collar of an old black coat he had on with jeans and snowy Timberlands. A red plastic jug with a long spout sat next to him on the floor. It had to be gasoline. The kitchen reeked of it. Ellen screamed in her throat, a mother's howl of outrage and dread.

"I second that emotion," Moore said, chuckling again as he tore off the duct tape with the side of a crooked incisor.

Tears poured from Will's eyes, and they widened in fear. Ellen shimmied closer to him, making noises.

Moore straightened, a smile twisting his lips. Suddenly he lifted his foot in the heavy boot and put it down hard on Will's head. "Move and I'll squash him like a bug."

Ellen felt paralyzed by fear. Will burst into new tears, his cheeks turning a violent red. Moore leaned forward and stepped harder on his head.

Will squeezed his eyes shut, his small forehead buckling with pain. Dirt and snow from the boots dumped onto his little face. Moore was crushing his skull.

Ellen screamed and screamed, shaking her head frantically.

"Lady, get back and shut the hell up."

Ellen scrambled backwards, writhing this way and that, finally bumping the back of her head on the stove. She looked up at Moore, begging him to stop.

"Is that the look of love you're givin' me?" Moore kept his boot on Will's head but eased backwards slightly. The redness ebbed from Will's cheeks. He was choking under the duct tape.

Ellen prayed to God he could breathe. That his skull wasn't injured. That his heart could withstand the pressure.

Moore said, "I woulda thought you got your fill with your boyfriend."

Ellen struggled to think through her panic. Moore must have been following her. Had he been to the funeral? What was he going to do with the gasoline? She refused to go to the obvious answer. Her throat emitted primal noises.

"Oh, shut up." Moore took his foot from Will's head, leaving him crying hysterically, his tears mixing with the mud on his face.

Ellen silenced herself, making eye contact with Will, trying to tell him that everything would be all right. She had to figure out what to do. Her thoughts raced. Nobody was coming for help. The Coffmans weren't home. Her neighbors on the other side were never home. Everyone else was hunkered in their beds for the snowstorm.

Moore picked up the plastic jug and twisted off the lid, releasing the unmistakable odor. He tipped the container over on top of Will, and gasoline spewed from the spout, splashing onto Will's legs in the snowsuit, the solvent darkening the material from blue to black.

Stark cold horror paralyzed Ellen's thoughts. Moore was going to set them on fire. He was going to kill them both. She started screaming behind the duct tape.

Bing Bong!

Suddenly, the doorbell rang in the living room.

Ellen screamed louder behind the tape, even though she knew it was useless.

"Shut up!" Moore set down the gasoline jug and stepped hard on Will's head.

Ellen shook her head back and forth like a madwoman. She prayed frantically that Moore would stop hurting Will. She didn't know who was at the door. It was too late at night for a visitor, unless it was Martha Coffman. Maybe they'd come home in the meantime and needed to borrow something. Maybe one of her boys was sick.

Bing Bong!

Moore grimaced, angry. Will's face turned blue-red before her eyes. A silent scream contorted his features. Tears poured from his eyes. Snot streamed from his nose over the duct tape.

Bing Bong!

"Give it up!" Moore whirled around, finally taking his foot off Will.

Ellen willed herself to think. If it was Martha Coffman, maybe she had seen something from her kitchen. She would call 911 if Ellen didn't answer the door.

Bing Bong!

"Shit!" Moore flew into a rage, his eyes wild and out of control. He plunged his hand into his coat pocket, and when he withdrew it, he was holding a large revolver with a steel barrel.

Ellen froze.

Chapter Seventy-four

"You see your kid?" Moore bent down and drilled the barrel of the gun into Will's temple. "I'll blow his head clean off."

Ellen was too terrified to cry, her emotion strangling the sounds in her throat.

"I'm gonna cut you loose, only because they're not goin' away. You answer the door and tell whoever's there to go. Do one thing wrong, just one, and I blow this kid's head offa his shoulders."

Ellen nodded frantically. This could be her only chance. She had to make something happen. Could she risk it? Could she not?

"I'll kill him. You understand?"

Ellen pumped her head, yesyesyes.

Bing Bong!

"All right then." Moore raised the revolver, sprang over to Ellen, and reached behind her back. He yanked her into the air by her wrists, hissing into her ear. "Up to you, bitch. One word and I shoot the kid."

Ellen shook her head, desperate to reassure him. In the next second, her hands were cut free and she fell like a broken doll to the hardwood floor.

Moore cut loose her ankles, flipped her over, and tore the duct tape from her mouth. It stung until he drilled the gun between her eyes.

"Don't hurt him, don't hurt him," Ellen heard herself whisper over and over, like a prayer.

"No tricks." Moore's face was six inches from hers, a close-up of bloodshot eyes, greasy mustache, and breath foul with beer.

Ellen scrambled to get her feet under her, her knees jelly. Her thoughts clicked ahead, running the possibilities. "What if it's my neighbor? What if she won't go?"

"Make her." Moore shoved her from the kitchen, and she half walked, half stumbled through the dining room, glancing quickly out the windows. The lights still were off at the Coffmans'. Connie would have let herself in. So who was ringing the bell?

Marcelo!

He was the only possibility. He would help her. Together they'd get Will out of this. She hurried through the dining room. Her heart thundered, and she crossed the living room toward the door.

Bing Bong!

Ellen couldn't see the face at the door, but a shadow stood silhouetted in the yellowish porch light. She opened the door and stood stricken against a blast of frigid wind.

At her front door was the last person in the world she ever expected to see.

Chapter Seventy-five

It was Carol Braverman, standing in a long black coat, a quilted purse slung over an arm. Her hair was slicked back in a chignon, her eyes glittered with emotion, and her mouth made a glossy line. She asked, "Ellen Gleeson?"

Ellen nodded, stunned as Carol entered the house and began looking around the living room.

"I'm Carol Braverman, but you knew that already." Carol turned on her heel, the coat making a chic swish. She looked at Ellen with determined blue eyes. "You adopted my son."

"What? I'm sorry?" Ellen struggled to react. A million thoughts flooded her head. She couldn't process any of them fast enough.

"I came as soon as I had it verified. He's my son Timothy. He was kidnapped in Miami right after his first birthday."

"I don't know what you mean," Ellen said, beginning to think clearly. Will was in the kitchen under a gun. Moore could hear every word through the other entrance to the kitchen, over the landing.

She had to get Carol out of here. One distraught mother was enough. Carol was a variable she couldn't predict right now.

"Sorry, but I think you do." Carol's eyes softened slightly. "I can only imagine what you must be going through, and I feel sorry for you, I really do. But we both know the truth. You have my baby, and I want him back."

"No, I don't." Ellen stepped toward her, leaving the front door open, filling the room with frigid air. "Please, leave my house."

"You have my son, don't pretend you don't know. You were in Miami two days ago."

"No, you're wrong." Ellen's mouth went dry. How did Carol know? No matter, a plan was coming together in her mind. She wasn't tied up anymore. As soon as she got Carol out of the house, she'd be free to move. She said, "I don't know what you're talking about. Leave my house, right now."

"Let me explain." Carol put up a hand. "A reporter who works with you called me at home and told me everything. Sarah Liu is her name. She told me about you and the boy you call Will."

Ellen felt it like an electric shock. Sarah had called the Bravermans? How? Why?

"She caught you on our website, printing out my son's picture. She called your house and verified that you were out of town. She figured out you'd come to Miami." Carol paused, cocking her head. "Why did you? Did you want to check us out?"

Ellen's mind reeled, then she fought to recover. She had to save Will. Moore would be waiting, the gun to her son's head.

"Sarah claimed the reward, of course." Carol smiled in gentle triumph, her diamond earrings flashing. "It's a million dollars, life-changing money. That's why we set it so high. We knew that sooner or later it would bring somebody out of the woodwork, and it did."

"This is insane. Get out."

"I Googled you online, I found the articles you wrote about him.

I know you didn't know he was kidnapped, but that's not my problem. He's mine, and I want him." Carol's tone turned indignant. "My husband's on the way. His plane was delayed in the snow, and I didn't want to wait."

Ellen almost spiraled into an emotional stall. She used to think this was her worst nightmare, but now she knew better. Her worst nightmare was in her own kitchen. She had to get Carol out of here. Suddenly a noise came from the stairwell, and they both turned. Oreo Figaro appeared on the stair landing, where he stopped and sat down with a yawn, curling his inky tail around him.

"Where is Timothy?" Carol demanded. "I demand to see him."

"He's not Timothy, he's my son, and he's at a sleepover."

"A three-year-old, at a sleepover?" Carol moved toward the stairway, but Ellen shifted over and blocked her way.

"Stop right there. You have no right to walk around my house." She raised her voice to regain some authority. If Carol took one step closer to the stairway, she'd be able to see the kitchen from its other entrance. She'd smell the gasoline, and they'd all end up dead. Ellen put a firm hand on Carol's coat sleeve. "Get out, right now!"

"I thought we could do this without the police, but maybe not. You have my son, and I won't leave here without him." Carol tried to wrench her arm free, but Ellen held on to it with all her might. She was trying to save Carol's life, but the woman was endangering the son they both loved.

"I don't know who you are. I don't know what you're talking about."

"You know he's mine, and I'm appealing to you, mother to mother." Carol's eyes filled with sudden wetness. "I held out hope, all this time, I *knew* he'd turn up. I knew he was alive. I could *feel* him."

"Get the hell out!" Ellen fought a rising panic. She could imagine Moore listening. They were running out of time. She could stand losing Will to Carol, but she couldn't stand Will leaving this earth, not while she drew breath.

"We hired a detective, and he confirmed everything Sarah said, including your plane ticket down and back."

"Go!" Ellen shoved her to the threshold, but Carol shoved back, her expression fierce.

"I'm not going!" She braced herself in the threshold, rooted as a tree. "I've waited two years to see him and that's long enough. I'll stand on your porch all night if I have to. I want my *son!*"

"He's not here!" Ellen shouted, loud enough for Moore to hear. "Go! NOW!"

"Call the police then." Carol folded her arms. "But you won't do that, will you? Because you know that you're keeping my child."

"Get OUT!" Ellen shouted louder, fighting a wild impulse to run to the kitchen, grab Will, and go like hell, but Carol's eyes narrowed with a new suspicion.

"Your eyes just moved. You just looked somewhere in back, behind you. He's back there, isn't he?"

"No, I didn't. Now—"

"I know he's here!" Suddenly Carol hit Ellen in the face, and she reeled backwards, off-balance, recovering too late.

"No, stop!"

"Timothy!" Carol broke free and bolted for the dining room.

"NO! STOP! WAIT!" Ellen chased her, took a desperate flying leap, and caught Carol by the hem of her long coat. The two women fell to the dining room floor, sliding on the hardwood and knocking into the dining room chairs like bowling pins.

"I want my son!" Carol screamed, as the two mothers wrestled on the dining room floor, bumping the chairs aside.

"NO!" Ellen struggled with all her might to pin Carol to the floor and had almost succeeded when they both heard the sound of raucous laughter.

"What was *that?*" Carol asked, her back on the floor.

Ellen felt her heart stop with fear, and she twisted behind her.

Rob Moore stood over them, his legs spread like a commando. He aimed his gun down at them. "Girl-on-girl action," he said.

"*You!*" Carol said, hushed, and Moore smiled slyly.

"Carol? Long time, no see."

Chapter Seventy-six

"Let's get this party started." Moore gestured toward the kitchen with the muzzle of his revolver. "In the kitchen, ladies."

"I could kill you!" Carol shot back, scrambling to prop herself up on an elbow. "You kidnapped my baby!"

"Boo hoo, princess." Moore snorted.

"I got you the money, and you were supposed to give the baby back! That was the deal. You were never supposed to keep the baby. Never!"

"The deal changed."

Ellen looked from Moore to Carol, dumbfounded. They had a deal? She straightened into a sitting position, incredulous. Meanwhile she wracked her brain for a way to save Will. She had to get him out of this alive.

"Why did you do it, why?" Carol cried. "All you had to do was give him back to me. You got your money."

"My girlfriend wanted him. She was always sayin' she couldn't have a baby, and when I tol' her no, she split with him."

Ellen needed to stall, to give herself time to think. "Was that Amy? Was Amy Martin your girlfriend?"

"Yeah. The dumb bitch."

"You killed Amy?"

"Duh," Moore answered.

"And the lawyer, too? Karen Batz?"

"Sure."

"But why? Did she know?"

"I wasn't leavin' a loose end. If she figured it out, she woulda squawked. Carol woulda had the best lawyers money could buy, and I woulda gone to the joint."

"You bastard!" Carol's gaze bored into him. "That was my baby! I thought about him every minute! You ruined my life!"

"You ruined your own life, you brat. You went through your money like water."

"This isn't about me, it's about you. You told me you'd give the baby back. You lied! You took him!"

Ellen kept thinking about how to save Will. Sooner or later, she'd get an opening.

"Do you know what you did?" Carol scrambled to stand up, and Oreo Figaro walked into the dining room. "You almost *killed* my husband. You *ruined* my marriage."

"You shoulda told him the truth, then. You shoulda said to him, 'Honey, wifey-poo isn't the good girl you think.' 'I used our kid to pay for my little hobby.'"

"She used her kid?" Ellen said, stalling. "*She* did it?"

"Yeah, it was all her idea." Moore sneered. "You didn't think that, did you? You didn't figure that out. Little Miss Goody-Goody here, she gambled up all her money, so she needed to tap her kid's."

"Shut up!" Carol shouted, but Moore ignored her.

"She knew me from the casino, Miccosukee. I was parkin' cars for rich bitches, and she hired me to kidnap her kid. She got the ransom from the kid's trust fund. She told me the nanny would be there and—"

"Stop it, stop it!" Carol shouted louder, startling Oreo Figaro, who ran under the dining room table. "You weren't supposed to kill her. You weren't supposed to keep the baby!"

"Enough!" Moore gestured with the gun, his gaze shifting toward the kitchen. "You wanna see your son? He's in there."

"He is?" Carol's face flooded with happiness. She rushed to the kitchen, and the sudden movement sent Oreo Figaro scooting to Ellen.

Just then a lethal glimmer flickered through Moore's eyes. Ellen didn't have time to think, only to act.

And everything happened at once.

Chapter Seventy-seven

Carol reached the kitchen threshold and saw Will, lying on the floor. "My baby!" she cried.

Moore raised the gun and aimed it at the back of Carol's head.

Ellen scooped Oreo Figaro off the floor and threw him right at Moore's face.

"Reowwh!" The fat cat screeched in protest, his thick body twisting this way and that, and the surprise knocked Moore off-balance. He raised his hands and fell backwards. The gun fired into the ceiling. Oreo Figaro fell to the floor, righting himself and scampering off.

Ellen launched herself like a missile, aiming for Moore's gun. She barreled into him, and he staggered backwards into the kitchen. She grabbed the gun with all her might and struggled to wrest it from his grip.

"Get offa me!" Moore howled. He held on to the gun, whipped Ellen around, and slammed her into the doorway. Her head banged against the wood but she hung on to his wrist, fighting for the gun even as he pointed its muzzle at Carol, who had picked up Will and was taking him out the other doorway.

"RUN!" Ellen screamed.

"Shut up!" Moore threw her against the stove, shaking her hand loose and training the gun on Carol.

Carol looked over her shoulder, and in one motion, put Will on the landing behind her, blocked him with her body, and raised her arms protectively, facing Moore. She shouted, "Don't you dare hurt my son!"

Moore squeezed the trigger, firing point-blank, and Ellen screamed in horror.

Carol's chest exploded in wool tatters. Her mouth dropped open. Her head snapped forward. She dropped onto the kitchen floor, crumpling at the knees, her legs grotesquely askew.

"NO!" Ellen hurled herself at Moore, but this time, in her hand was the cast-iron burner from her stovetop. She swung the burner as hard as she could into Moore's face. The spiked end speared his forehead, and a gaping hole appeared. In the next second, it spurted a gruesome freshet of bright red blood. Moore's eyes flew open, and he slumped against the wall, then slid down, insensate.

Ellen heard herself shouting something, but even she didn't know what she said. The gun fell to the floor, and she picked it up and aimed it at Moore as he landed in a sitting position. She pointed the gun at him, not knowing whether to shoot him or save him. A crooked grin crossed his face before his eyes cut away and his gaze fixed.

Ellen hurried over to Carol, picking her up with care and feeling under her chin for a pulse. There was none. Blood soaked her coat from the hole in her chest, right over her heart.

Ellen leaned Carol back down on the floor, bent over her, and listened for breath. No sound. She opened Carol's mouth and began to breathe air into her, but it was too late for CPR. She tried anyway, but it was no use. Carol's head fell back, too loose on her neck, her mouth hanging open, and Ellen heard herself moan, stricken. She set her down on the floor carefully, saying a silent prayer.

Will.

Ellen half crawled, half stumbled to the landing, where Will lay bundled, sobbing. His terrified eyes met hers, so much like Carol's that for a minute, it gave her a start. She picked him up and hurried out of the kitchen with him, shielding him from the grisly scene and telling him everything was going to be all right. She hurried him into the living room and sat with him on the couch, putting him on her lap and comforting him as she unpeeled the duct tape from his mouth. She started slowly, but he cried even harder, his nose bubbling.

"Hold on, sweetie, it'll only hurt for a second." She yanked off the duct tape, letting it fall, and he erupted in the full-blown wail of a newborn.

"Mommy! Mommy! It hurts!"

"It's all over now, it's all over." Ellen kept talking to him, grabbing a Kleenex from the coffee table and wiping his nose. The tape had pulled some of the skin around his mouth off, leaving it irritated and sticky, and the adhesive made an ugly pattern around his lips.

"It hurts!"

"Here we go, it'll stop soon." Ellen dried his eyes with a new tissue, then tried to comfort him as she untaped his hands and feet, the stench of gasoline filling her nostrils. She was sliding him out of his wet snowsuit when she caught a glimpse of blood dripping behind his right ear.

God, no.

"It's okay now, honey," she said, but his tears kept flowing. She pulled a Kleenex from the box, held it to the wound, and flashed on Moore's big boot crushing Will's face in the same spot. She felt stricken, but masked her emotions. She didn't know if Will was bleeding internally, inside his ear or even behind his eye. He needed an ambulance. She pressed the tissue to his wound, hurried with him to the living room phone, and called 911 with Will crying in her arms.

"What is your emergency?" the dispatcher asked, and Ellen collected herself, composing a lead paragraph on the spot.

"An armed intruder broke into my house tonight. He tried to kill me and my son, and I killed him in self-defense." Ellen felt her throat catch. She couldn't believe her own words. She had never harmed another human being, much less killed one. "He shot and killed a woman named Carol Braverman. He also injured my son, who's three, and he's bleeding from behind his ear. I need an ambulance right away, and the police."

"You say there were *two* people killed?"

"Yes. Listen, I need an ambulance for my son. His head was . . . stepped on and it's bleeding. He's crying, and I'm worried."

"Mommy!" Will cried harder, and Ellen struggled to hear the dispatcher.

"Keep him awake, and the ambulance will be there right away. You can stay on the line until they get there."

"Mommy! Mommy!" Will cried, louder.

"No, that's okay. I'd rather take care of him. Just hurry, please, hurry!" Ellen hung up, hugged Will close, and rocked him a little like the old days until his tears finally slowed. She grabbed a few more Kleenex and cleaned him up, then got a fresh one for the wound behind his ear. "What hurts, honey? Tell me."

"My head!"

Please, God, no. "That's why we're going to the doctor, so he can fix it."

"Dr. Chodoff?"

"No, a special doctor."

"I want Dr. Chodoff!" Will sobbed.

"Let's get your coat," Ellen said, narrating her actions to calm them both as she walked to the closet, took his corduroy hoodie from a hook, and sat back down on the couch with him, slipping his arms into the puffy sleeves, getting him ready. His sneakers reeked of gasoline, so she took them off.

"Stinky shoes, huh?" Ellen asked, as part of the narration, and Will nodded, his small chest shuddering from his final sobs. She touched lightly behind his ear, and in the lamplight she could see a large cut on his scalp, bleeding. She prayed there wasn't a skull fracture and reached for another tissue, pressing it over the wound.

"Mommy, what?"

"You have a boo-boo behind your ear. We're going to take a ride to the doctor. We have to get you looked at."

"Who was that man?"

"In the kitchen? A very bad man. A terrible man, but he's not going to hurt you anymore."

"Did he hurt you, Mommy?"

"No, I'm okay. So are you. You're going to be fine after we see the doctor." Ellen cuddled him, and Will rubbed his eye with a balled-up fist.

"My head hurts."

"Stay awake, okay, honey?" Ellen jiggled him a little and talked to him about nothing, even as the bright red blood from his cut soaked Kleenex after Kleenex until they looked like the tissue-paper poppies he made in school. She hid them from his view until the bleeding finally slowed, which only worried her more. Oreo Figaro wandered in, sat down in front of the couch, and tucked his legs underneath him.

Will sniffled. "You hurt Oreo Figaro, Mommy."

"No, I didn't. I knew he'd be okay."

"You throwed him."

"I know." Ellen didn't correct his English. He could make all the grammar mistakes he wanted, from here on out.

"That wasn't nice."

"You're right." Ellen turned to Oreo Figaro. "I'm sorry, Oreo Figaro."

The cat signified his forgiveness by looking up and blinking, and he kept watch over them both until the police cruisers arrived, their red lights slashing the cozy living room with bloodred splotches, spattering the stenciled cows and country hearts.

"What is that, Mommy?" Will asked, twisting to see.

"It's the police, here to help us, buddy." Ellen rose and looked out the windows to the street, which had been transformed to a staging area. Police cruisers were parking out front, their exhausts billowing into the snowy air and their high beams slicing the dotted darkness. Uniformed cops sprang from the cars, black figures against the whiteness, running up her front walk to the porch.

"Here they come, Mommy."

"Right, here they come." Ellen crossed to the door as the cops hustled onto the porch, their shoes heavy as soldiers as they reached the front door.

They were coming to save Will.

And to destroy the only life he knew.

Chapter Seventy-eight

Ellen opened the door, and police filled the living room and immediately began looking around, hurrying into the dining room and
toward the stairs, their shoes heavy on the hardwood. Outside the
window, she saw flashlights flickering as cops searched her front and
side yards. Will quieted in her arms, gazing wide-eyed at an older
cop with wire-rimmed glasses who took her aside, his hand on her
elbow.

"I'm Officer Patrick Halbert," he said. Snowflakes dusted the
shoulders of his nylon jacket. "You're the homeowner who called
911?"

"Yes." Ellen introduced herself. "Where is the ambulance?"

"On its way. Are you injured, ma'am?" Officer Halbert looked at
her coat, and she realized that there was blood all over her.

"No, this isn't my blood. It's my son who's hurt. When will the
ambulance get here?"

"Five minutes, tops." Officer Halbert's tone sounded official, but
under the wet patent bill of his cap, his eyes looked concerned and

they scanned Will, up and down. He asked, "Now, you told our dispatcher it was a home invasion?"

"Yes, it was."

"Is there anyone else in the house?"

"Pat!" one of the cops called from the kitchen. "We got two in here!"

Ellen said, "We need to get going, he's bleeding from the head. Can't you take us to the hospital?"

"It's best to wait, so they can treat your boy on the way." Officer Halbert chucked Will's stocking foot. "No shoes, fella?"

Will recoiled, and the cop plucked a Bic from inside his jacket, slid a notepad from his back pocket, and flipped open the pad. "Ms. Gleeson, why don't you fill me in on what happened?"

"Can't we talk about this after my son is treated? That's my priority, and it's not good to talk in front of him, anyway."

"This won't be your formal statement, we'll talk later at the station house. I know who you are, my wife reads you in the paper." Officer Halbert smiled, more warmly. "We'll talk until the ambulance arrives."

"It's a long story, but there was an intruder in my house. He had a gun. He broke in and tried to kill me and my son. He poured gasoline on him." Ellen glanced at Will, whose gaze remained on the cop, though she knew he was listening. "Then a woman named Carol Braverman came in and interrupted him, and he shot her when she tried to save Will. I tried CPR on her but it was too late." Ellen felt a stab of guilt but stayed in control. It wasn't the time to break down. "They're in the kitchen."

"They're the bodies?"

"Yes." Ellen caught a glimpse of bright red lights in the street. It was the ambulance pulling up, spraying snow from its back tires. "They're here."

"Let's go." Officer Halbert quickly put away his pen and pad. "We'll escort you to the hospital, Ms. Gleeson."

Ellen was already out the door, cuddling Will against the storm, and he held her tight as Halbert and some other cops fell in beside them, and they descended the porch stairs into the snowy night. A paramedic jumped out of the cab and flung open the ambulance's back doors, spilling harsh fluorescent light onto the snow.

Ellen hurried down the walk with Will, plowing through wet snow in her boots. "Lots of snow, huh?"

"So much!" Will answered agreeably.

"Already eight inches," Officer Halbert added, steadying Ellen by the arm as the paramedic rushed to meet them.

"This the boy?" the paramedic shouted over the idling engines. He held out his arms for Will, and Ellen handed him over.

"Yes, he's three, bleeding from behind his ear. His head was . . . pressed from the side."

"You ride in back, Mom." The paramedic hustled Will to the back of the ambulance and climbed inside, and Ellen followed, stepping up onto the corrugated metal floor.

"Here we go, Will," she said, putting a hand on his stocking foot. She must have been crazy not to get him another pair of shoes. "We're riding in an ambulance. Cool, huh?"

"Wait, wait!" came a shout, and they all looked back. A black sedan had pulled up behind the police cruisers, and a man was running toward them in the snowstorm, waving his arms, his sport jacket flapping in the whirling snow. Cops surged toward him, blocking him, but in the light from the open ambulance, Ellen recognized his agonized features.

It was Bill Braverman.

"Stop, wait!" He fought the cops to get to the ambulance, but they held him back, the melee silhouetted in the high beams of the cruisers. A bitter wind picked up, and the snow swirled as Bill struggled free of them and reached the ambulance doors, shouting, "Wait, stop, let me see!"

"Mister, get outta here! We gotta go!" the paramedic shouted back, pushing him away, but Bill took one look at Will and his expression filled with joy.

"Timothy, it's *you*! Thank God, it's you!" Bill held out his arms, and Will burst into terrified tears.

"Mommy!" he screamed, and Ellen jumped up, blocking the way.

"Bill, we'll sort this out later. I have to get him to the hospital. He has a head injury."

"*You!*" Bill went wild with outrage. "*You're* the one! You're the woman who adopted our son!" He started to climb into the ambulance, hoisting himself up by the open door, but the cops pulled him back and the paramedic held him off. He shouted, "That's *my boy*! That's Timothy! Where's my wife? What did you do to my wife?" He turned angrily to the cops flanking him. "I'm Bill Braverman! Where's my wife, is she here? Is she all right?"

"She's right here," the paramedic answered, gesturing in confusion at Ellen, who had turned to calm Will.

"Mommy! Mommy!" Tears spilled from his eyes, his lower lip shuddering.

Officer Halbert put a hand on Bill's arm. "Sir, is your wife Carol Braverman?"

"Yes, where is she? Is she all right?"

"Sir, please come with me," Officer Halbert said. "I need to speak with you." The other cops crowded around, clearing the ambulance as snow whirlpooled around them all.

"But that's my son! My son! Is he hurt? Where's my wife? That's our *son!*"

"Mommeeee!" Will screamed, confused, and Ellen smoothed the hair back from his head. Blood leaked down the back of his neck, and bright red drops stained his hoodie.

"It's all right, baby, it's all right."

"We gotta go!" the paramedic shouted, buckling Will onto the gurney, then he shifted over to shut the back doors and twisted the handles closed. He climbed around Ellen and leaned toward the driver in the cab. "Locked and loaded, Jimmy!"

"It's all right," Ellen kept saying, holding Will's hand. She looked back through the windows, and just before the ambulance pulled away, she heard an anguished cry through the howling storm. Bill Braverman had lost his wife on the very night he'd found his son.

"Okay, little man, this won't hurt a bit," the paramedic said to Will, wrapping a child-size pressure cuff around his arm.

"It's all right, honey," Ellen said, holding his hand, but Will cried harder. "It's all right, everything's going to be all right."

Through the back window, the cops became stick figures against the whirling white, and Ellen felt a wrench of deep sadness. For Bill, for Carol, and for herself.

And especially, for Will.

Chapter Seventy-nine

Ellen slumped in the cloth-covered chairs of the waiting room of the emergency department, ignoring the back issues of *People* and *Sports Illustrated*. The place was empty except for two young cops, who watched TV on low volume. The doctor had sent her out to the waiting room while Will was taken up to MRI and X-ray.

She closed her eyes, tilting her head back on the hard edge of the chair, trying to block out the images. Will, with gasoline on his snowsuit. Rob Moore, looking excited as he aimed his gun at Carol. Carol, raising her arms to protect Will. Bill, screaming against the snowstorm. The blood on her shirt.

Ellen looked down numbly, and the blood had dried to a stiff, oddly shiny patch of red-black. For some reason, it bothered her that she didn't know whether the blood was Moore's or Carol's.

She sank deeper into her chair. She had set out to find the truth, and she had her truth. She'd have to give Will up, when the time came. She understood it on an intellectual level, but couldn't begin to let herself feel it. That would come later, after she finally handed him over. Then she could lose it, after she knew he was alive and well. Healthy, again. She heard a noise and looked up.

The doors of the emergency room whooshed open, and through the glass she could see Bill Braverman, his sport coat bloodied, entering with Officer Halbert and another cop. She felt a sinking feeling in the pit of her stomach as they spotted her, then came into the waiting room.

"Ms. Gleeson?" Officer Halbert's smile was wearier than earlier. "How's your son?"

"Not sure yet."

"The docs here are great, you'll see." Officer Halbert pulled up a chair opposite her, while the other cop took a seat to the side. Bill Braverman sat with them, glaring at her. His eyes flashed with hostility, and his mouth became a straight line. He had probably gotten the blood on his coat holding Carol, and Ellen couldn't help meeting his eye.

"I'm so sorry about your wife," she said to him.

"Thank you," Bill answered, hoarsely, but his dark eyes, puffy and red, didn't soften. "I'd like an explanation from you."

Officer Halbert raised a hand. "Mr. Braverman, we'll get her statement later, as I told you."

"I'd like to know now," Bill shot back. "She's sitting here, my son is in the hospital, and my wife is dead. I want to know what happened."

"That's not our procedure, Mr. Braverman."

"Ask me if I care about your procedure."

Officer Halbert was about to reply when Ellen raised a hand.

"It's okay," she said. "He has a right to know and there's no reason to stand on formality."

Halbert pursed his lips. "We'll still need your statement. Later."

"Fine." Ellen took a deep breath and shifted in her chair to face Bill. "It all started with a white card I got in the mail, about a kidnapped boy." She filled them in on what she'd figured out about Amy Martin and Rob Moore while Officer Halbert took notes, and she brought them up to date, telling them how she'd rushed home tonight. "I was worried that Moore might come after Will and me, and I was trying to get us out when he showed up."

Officer Halbert broke in, "We were wondering, how did Rob Moore get into your house? There was no sign of forced entry."

"I think the back door was left open. The cat goes in and out a lot, and we leave it unlocked sometimes. It's Narberth, after all."

"I hear that." Officer Halbert smiled. "We've never had a murder in the borough."

"Now you have two," Bill interjected, but Officer Halbert continued:

"If I may get a few things out of the way, did Moore attempt to rob you?"

"No, he was there to kill me and Will. He had us taped up and was pouring gasoline over my son."

"We saw the plastic jug." Halbert checked his pad. "Now, can you tell us what happened earlier, when Carol Braverman came over?"

Bill said, "Yes, do tell."

Ellen nodded, suddenly shaky. She hated him to find out this way, but it couldn't be helped. "Well, evidently, they had planned to kidnap the baby together. Carol paid Moore to do it."

Bill reddened. "*What?*"

"It's true."

"The hell it is!"

"I swear it—"

"How do you know?"

"Carol said so. She said Moore was supposed to give the baby back but he didn't. That she had gambling debts and had to use her son's trust fund to pay them off."

"That's not possible!" Bill shot back, and Officer Halbert looked over at him, but didn't say anything.

Ellen said, "I was surprised, too, but she did. Moore said it was all her idea."

"How would she even know Moore? There's no way she knew such trash."

Ellen thought a minute, remembering the ugly scene, her stomach tense. "She said they met at a casino. Miccosukee, I think they said. Does that name mean anything to you?"

Bill blinked.

"What is Miccosukee?" Halbert interjected.

"It's a casino, on an Indian reservation outside of Miami," Bill answered, and Ellen breathed a relieved sigh.

"Moore said he was a parking valet there."

Bill asked, "He said she had gambling debts?"

"Yes." Ellen could see he didn't believe her, but something she said had hit home, she just didn't know what. She continued and told them every detail of what had happened, from Carol's entering the house to when Moore pulled the gun on them in the dining room. "He said that Carol had used up her trust fund money to pay her gambling debts and that she wanted to use Will's, er, Timothy's money."

Bill's eyes narrowed. "Who said that?"

"Moore did, and she didn't deny it. How else would I have known it?"

Bill had no reply, and Officer Halbert remained silent, watching the two of them.

Ellen continued, "She said you didn't know anything about the plan. She said you were so upset when he kept the baby that it almost killed you, and that it ruined your marriage."

Bill scoffed. "We have a wonderful marriage."

Ellen hesitated. "I saw you catch a plane a few days ago, from Miami to Vegas."

Bill's eyelids fluttered when he got her meaning, and he raked a hand through his hair. "Okay, well, we did have problems. We tried so hard to have Timothy, and after we did, it was like Carol didn't want anything to do with him. She had postpartum depression, I guess that's what it was. She'd always gambled, poker on the computer, but then it got worse. I confronted her, and she told me she was going to casinos. She told me she would stop. I thought she had." Bill's eyes glistened, and he hung his head. "I told her if she kept gambling, I'd leave her and take Timothy."

"Maybe that's why she kept it from you."

"I'm sure," Bill said, suddenly subdued, and Ellen saw a change in him, as if together, they were solving a puzzle, each providing some of the pieces.

She asked, "I'm curious, how would she pay the debts off with the ransom? How did that work?"

Officer Halbert and the other cops seemed to wait for his answer, and Bill rubbed his face.

"Lemme think. The kidnapper, when he phoned—this Moore— said that no FBI or police could be involved, and we went along with it. He also said the mother had to deliver the money. I said no, I was worried about her safety. I didn't want to send my wife out there to meet a killer." Bill's lips flattened. "But Carol said she wanted to do it by herself. She said she felt responsible because she didn't get Timothy out of the car in time, and I believed her."

Ellen could see why he'd believed her. She looked like the perfect wife and mother. The Mother Goose outfit; the children's theater at Charbonneau House. After her scheme had gone awry, Carol must have been expiating the guilt of a lifetime.

Bill shook his head. "We got the money from Timothy's trust, which was set up by my in-laws. They were very wealthy. The executor is a lawyer in town and he approved it, and before Carol made the delivery, she must have taken some cash off the top. God knows how much or where she hid it. That must be what she used to pay off her debts."

Ellen considered it, and it made sense. "She skimmed the money before she turned it over, and Moore must have agreed. How did she deliver it?"

"In a gym bag, he specified that."

"Did you check the bag?"

"No, why would I?" Bill kept shaking his head. "We packed it, she took it, and she left with it."

Ellen had no answer. It was an ingenious scheme, until it wasn't.

"If Moore had given Timothy back, the plan would have worked. It would have been fine. But he killed our babysitter and he kept Timothy. God knows why."

Ellen told him that Amy wanted the baby because she couldn't have one herself, and Bill's eyes widened in disbelief.

"So why not keep him then?"

"He got sick, as you know. Carol said she'd read my articles about him."

"I read them, too."

"So when I wanted to adopt him from the hospital, Timothy Braverman became Will Gleeson."

Bill's upper lip curled in disgust. "Someone can put a baby that isn't theirs up for adoption and get away with it? You'd think that somebody, the state or some agency, would catch that. You think they'd do background checks or something so this doesn't happen."

Ellen agreed. "They do background checks on the adopting parent, like me, but they don't do them on the women putting their baby up for adoption. Funny, huh?"

Bill sighed, his shoulders slumping. "I just cannot believe that Carol did this to me and Timothy. For money."

"Desperate people do desperate things." Ellen paused, feeling an odd sort of peace that came either from perspective or exhaustion. "She's beyond judgment now. She came up with a terrible solution to a terrible problem, one that resulted in a murder, and eventually, even her own."

Officer Halbert interjected, "I'm looking at two parents, and both of you love the same boy. Neither of you did anything wrong. It's a lose-lose situation, and I'm sorry for you both."

"Thanks," Ellen said, having nothing better to say, and Bill sighed again, looking at her with new eyes. He had learned the truth, and his truth was as terrible as hers.

"I'm sorry," he said after a moment, and Ellen nodded, trying not to cry.

"Me, too." Then she added, because it needed saying, "It sounds awful now, but I want to tell you how Carol died, because she redeemed herself. She gave her life, for Will. For Timothy. She saved his life."

"What happened?" Bill's lip trembled, and Ellen told him the story, after which he heaved a great sob, then collapsed into hoarse, choking sounds that hunched his broad shoulders, collapsing his frame and driving his face into his hands, in his own private hell.

There was a soft knock at the doorway, and the emergency-room nurse appeared, leaning into the room. "Ellen, your son is back from X-ray."

"How is he?" she asked, rising.

"The doctor will give you a full report," she answered, and Ellen went to the door.

"No, wait." Bill looked up from his hands, his eyes red and his cheeks tear-stained. He gave a mighty sniffle. "I'm his father. Can I go in, too?"

Ellen turned to him. "If you don't mind, Bill, would you not? It might upset him. I'll be sure to come out and tell you."

"He's all I have, now. For God's sake, I just lost my wife."

"This isn't about you or me. It's about Will."

"Timothy," Bill corrected, rising. He wiped his face with the back of his hand.

"Whatever his name, he needs comfort now. He needs me." Ellen watched as Bill's eyes hardened, even wet. "Please, be realistic. He doesn't know who you are yet. You're a stranger to him."

Officer Halbert stood up, too. "Mr. Braverman, she adopted him, and she's still his mother."

"She was never his real mother," Bill shot back, and Ellen swallowed hard, but the ER nurse raised an authoritative hand in Bill's direction.

"Sir, are you listed as next of kin on the intake form?"

"No."

"Well, Ms. Gleeson is. She's on the form as his mother, and only she can be admitted to the unit, per this hospital's regulations. You are not permitted back with us."

Ellen turned to go. "Bill, I'll ask someone to come out and tell you how he is," she said, following the nurse, who led her to the emergency-unit door, pressing in the code to unlock the door.

"What was that all about?" the nurse asked.

"It's a long story." Ellen only shook her head. "I just want to see if my son is all right."

Chapter Eighty

They reached Will's examining room, and Ellen felt a wave of déjà vu. Will lay under the covers, wearing a print hospital gown, looking tiny in the adult-size hospital bed. His head was bandaged with gauze, and he lay on the pillow with his eyes closed. Another nurse was putting up the guardrails of his bed, next to the ER doctor, a young man with rumpled hair who stopped writing on his clipboard to flash Ellen a reassuring grin.

"Don't worry, he's fine," the doctor said quickly, and she almost cheered with relief.

"What did the X-ray show?" Ellen went to the bed and held Will's hand, which felt oddly cool to the touch. His eyelids looked bluish, and she assumed that was okay, if scary.

"There's no fracture. Children's bones have a lot more give than adults, and it served your son well. The cut behind his ear is all stitched up."

"Thank God. How about his heart?"

"All good." The doctor looked sympathetic. "You've gotta get over that, Mom. He's fine now. Don't worry so much."

I'll get right on that.

"I'd like to admit him and keep an eye on him overnight."

"Sure, better to be on the safe side. I can stay, right?"

"Yes. We'll get him a room and put in a cot for you."

"Great." Ellen looked down at Will. "He's sleeping so soundly."

"I gave him a light sedative, and he'll rest until morning."

"Good, thanks." Ellen pulled up a chair. "You know, he saw terrible things tonight, people getting shot right in front of him, and in the next few weeks, there will be a major disruption in his life. Can you give me the name of some counselors that can help him?" Her throat went tight. "With the transition?"

"I'll have the social worker make some recommendations." The doctor moved away, touching her lightly on the shoulder. "Take care."

The nurse left with him, saying, "We'll let you know when we have a room for him."

"Good, thanks." Ellen turned to the other nurse. "Would you tell the man in the waiting room that he's okay?"

"All right, but only as favor to you. Don't like him, myself." She scuffed off, and Ellen took Will's hand.

His breathing was slightly congested, and his crusty nose bubbled away.

Ellen closed her eyes, to listen better.

The sound of him breathing.

It was the sweetest thing she had ever heard.

Chapter Eighty-one

Two hours later, Ellen cuddled Will in a private room, holding him close in the darkness while he slept and the TV played on mute, showing photos of Ellen's own house. DOUBLE HOMICIDE IN BABY DRAMA, said the red banner on the screen, and she read the closed captioning, its spelling occasionally funky:

> Police report that Narberf resident Ellen Gleeson was attacked
> in her home in an attempt to kill her and her baby, who she adopted
> but who was really Timothy Braverman, a child kidnapped from
> wealthy Miami socialites . . .

Ellen looked away to the snow swirling outside the window. The hospital was quiet, and the only sound was the faint talking of the nurses down the hall. The door was partway closed, and she felt the world at bay. Snow inched up the panes, making a drift with an icy edge, thin as a knife. Steam heat fogged the glass, blurring the lights outside. She and Will had come full circle together, ending up in a hospital. She wondered how they could ever be separated, if that were even physically possible, but she'd insulate herself from thinking about that as long as she could, surely as the snow insulated the room, the hospital, and the world entire.

Somewhere out there was Marcelo, who had been trying to call her, but she couldn't take the call and had switched off the cell phone. Hospital signs read that cell phones interfered with the equipment, and she wanted to spend the time alone with Will.

She thought fleetingly of her father, still off in Italy, but she'd call him tomorrow when they got home. She wasn't sure when he was coming back. She had no idea how she'd tell him the news, which would crush him. She'd have him over to say good-bye to Will and she couldn't imagine that scene.

He's Will. He's ours.

She thought of Connie, too, and how upset she'd be. The babysitter loved Will and would feel his loss almost as acutely as Ellen would. There would be no see-ya-later-alligator, this time. She worried most of all about how Will would cope. He loved Connie, as surely as he loved her, and he would need help to deal with the trauma and the transition. The child had known, and lost, three mothers in three years. She would get one of those therapists that the doctor recommended as soon as she got him home.

Will stirred in her arms, breathing deeply, and Ellen gazed down at him, his bandaged head on her chest. Multicolored lights from the TV flashed across his face, mottling his features like a kaleidoscope, but she could make out the gentle hillock of his cheek, his cheekbone still buried under baby fat, the contours of his face yet to be formed by time. She tried not to think that she wouldn't know what Will would grow up to look like. Or how he'd do in school. Who his friends would be, or his wife. Or the minutiae, like if he'd always love cats or would dogs count, too? How would he dance at a party? What about later, when SATs came, and shaving, and college? What would he be when he grew up? All the stuff of a boy's life. Her boy's. Not her boy. Her boy no longer.

She held on to Will while a Bowflex commercial came on, and in time she drifted into an anguished sleep, wondering about the thousand other questions to which she would never know the answer.

And someday, wouldn't permit herself even to ask.

Chapter Eighty-two

Dawn came late, the sky dark until well after six, when the winter gloom lifted like a black velvet curtain, revealing yet another curtain, one of dark pewter. Ellen woke up slowly, still cuddling Will, and waited, lying in bed, listening to the hospital come slowly to life, with the nurses talking in low tones about the snowstorm, the skeleton crew, and the mom with the kidnapped baby in Room 302. Today, the reporter was the news.

"Mommy, when we get home, can we make a snowman?" Will asked, after the doctor had cleared them for discharge.

"We sure can." Ellen zipped his hoodie, and he was dressed to go, except for being shoeless. All he had on was a pair of blue cotton socks, stretched out of shape. "What was I thinking last night? I forgot your feet!"

Will giggled, looking down, so that their heads almost touched. "My feet are in my socks!"

"They are? Show me, just to make sure. Wiggle them for me."

"Look." Will's tiny toes popped around in their socks. "See, there they are. Under."

"What a relief. Whew. You know what that reminds me of?"

"What?"

"Of Oreo Figaro, when he's under the sheets. Remember how every time I make the bed, he gets under the new sheets and runs around?"

"He gets lost."

Ellen popped on his hood. "Right, he doesn't know how to get out, and we have to get him out."

Just then the nurse came in with the discharge papers on a clipboard. "Can you give me your John Hancock?" she asked, handing the clipboard to Ellen and smiling at Will. "How you doing?"

"I have my feet."

"Good." The nurse smiled. "You need your feet."

Ellen stuffed her purse under her arm, took the pen the nurse was offering, and scribbled her name. "Thanks."

"Just to give you a heads-up, there are reporters out front."

"Great." Ellen managed a smile for Will's sake, then turned to him. "Hear that, pal? You know what a reporter is, don't you?"

"*You're* a reporter!" Will pointed at her, smiling, and Ellen grabbed his finger and gave it a quick kiss.

"Right, and there'll be lots of people like me out front, only they might shout your name and take your picture. You ready for that?"

"Ready!"

"Good. Let's go home."

"I want to make a snowman!" Will shouted, and Ellen hushed him. The nurse asked her, "Do you have a ride home?"

"I called a cab. I used my cell phone, so please don't throw me in hospital jail."

"Don't worry." The nurse waved her off. "If I were you, I'd call the cab back and tell him to go to the emergency exit, not the main entrance. The security guard can give you the heads-up. His name is Mel."

"Good idea," Ellen said, grateful. "I'll stall in the gift shop."

"Gift shop!" Will cheered, and both women smiled.

"You know what that is?" the nurse asked him.

"Toys!"

Ellen picked Will up. "Thanks."

"Good luck," said the nurse, her eyes compassionate.

Ellen knew the nurses were feeling terrible for her, but she wasn't feeling terrible because she was still insulated. And she realized then that it wasn't the snow or the hospital that insulated her. It was Will himself. As long as she had him with her, she would keep it together, because she had to, for him. That was what it meant to be a mother.

"Let's go home, Mommy!" Will kicked his feet.

"First, say thank you to the nurse."

"Thank you," Will shouted, waving.

"You're very welcome," the nurse said, leaving.

"Thanks," Ellen said briefly, then carted Will out of the room and down the hall, where he waved and thanked the nurses, all of whom waved back with brave smiles.

"Bye, Willie!" the last one said, sitting at the desk nearest the elevator.

Will scowled. "That's *not* my name."

Ellen hit the button to go down. "Let's forgive her and go to the gift shop."

"Yay!" Will said, and the elevator came, the doors opening. "I want to push the button!"

"What do you say?" Ellen stepped inside, and Will twisted himself to lean down toward the button panel.

"Please!" he said, and the doors slid closed. When they opened again, Ellen stepped out of the cab and looked for a sign to the gift shop.

"There she is!" a man said, and she looked over, startled. People were rushing toward her, and she raised a hand.

"I have no comment, boys. Not now, not ever."

"We're not the press, Ms. Gleeson," the man said. "I'm Special Agent Manning from the FBI and this is Special Agent Orr."

Chapter Eighty-three

"Oh," Ellen said, surprised. She noticed for the first time that a few uniformed cops stood behind them, one of whom she recognized from last night. The young one. Something was wrong. Her mouth went dry.

"Mommy, where's the gift shop?"

"In a minute, sweetie." Ellen asked the first FBI agent, "What are you doing here?"

"Is this boy Will Gleeson?"

"Yes."

"We're here to take him into protective custody."

"What? Why?" Ellen was dumbfounded. "He doesn't need protecting. He's with me."

"As you know, he's Timothy Braverman, a child of Carol and William Braverman, kidnapped in Miami, and we're here to facilitate his return."

"What? Here? *Now?*" Ellen's arms tightened on Will. Her thoughts tumbled one over the other in confusion. She hadn't expected this, not yet. "He hasn't even eaten. He has no shoes. We have to go home."

"Ms. Gleeson, we are authorized to take the child. Here are the papers, you can take a look." Special Agent Manning extended a packet of blue-backed paper folded in thirds, and Ellen glanced at the caption. The letters WARRANT and SEIZURE swam before her eyes. She found herself looking for an exit, but the only one lay ahead. The press clustered outside. Reporters watched them through the glass doors. Camera flashes fired like explosions. Ellen started to panic.

"Wait, listen, I know Bill Braverman. I was going to get his number from the police and set up a timetable that's best for Will."

"Ma'am, we're here at the request of Mr. Braverman. I'm sorry but, by law, you can't keep the child. We have to make certain that you don't abscond with him."

"We're going to the gift shop, Mommy!" Will said loudly, his voice trembling with new anxiety.

"I won't abscond with him, I promise. I know I have to make a transfer, but just not yet. Not this way. I wanted to explain it to him, and he hasn't even had breakfast, and my father—"

"Ms. Gleeson, we have to take him now. Please don't make this harder on the child than it already is." Special Agent Manning held out his hands, but Ellen stepped back with Will.

"I'm not giving him up this way. I'm still his mother. I have a lawyer. I would have called him last night, but I wanted to make sure Will wasn't hurt."

"I told you we'd have a problem," said a voice from behind the FBI agents, and Bill Braverman emerged from the back of the group, flanked by an older man in a suit. "I told you she'd try to run."

"I'm not trying to run!" Ellen shouted, shocked. "I just didn't think we'd be doing it this morning, right now. He just got out of the hospital. I need to talk to him, to prepare him—"

"Mommy, who are they?" Will asked, clutching her shoulder.

Bill pushed next to the FBI agents, his dark eyes cool and his expression hardened. He had on different clothes from last night, and he was all business. "I'm his father, and I have a legal right to him. Right now."

"We have to talk about it. The timing, I mean."

"No, we don't."

"Mommy, what?" Will started to cry.

"Bill, look at him, think of *him,*" Ellen said, desperate. She couldn't believe this was happening. It was her against all of them. "This is the craziest way to do this. This is the worst possible thing for him."

"You mean for you," Bill shot back, and Ellen's heart pounded.

"He doesn't know what's going on. I have to explain it to him. I was going to call a therapist when we got home."

"I'll call a therapist. We have them in Miami, too. I'll take good care of him. He's mine." Bill advanced a step, but the man in the suit restrained him and turned to Ellen.

"Ms. Gleeson, I'm Mike Cusack and I'm representing Bill. You have no right to the child by law, and we have reason to believe you will leave the jurisdiction with him."

"I won't, I swear. I wasn't going anywhere but home."

"You tried to flee last night, didn't you? That's what you told the police."

"That was different." Ellen tried to think through the panic. "That was when I thought he was in danger, but not now."

"You didn't return him to the Bravermans after you knew he was Timothy. You intended to keep him."

Ellen felt accused and convicted, both at once. Everyone watched. The photographers outside fired away. "I wasn't sure what to do, I wasn't sure he was theirs and—"

"My client wants his child back, and the police are here to enforce his legal right. Please, don't be selfish. Do the right thing."

"Mommy?" Will sobbed. "Mommy!"

"Honey, it's all right." Ellen patted his leg, frantic inside. She turned to the FBI agents. "I'll turn him over, I promise, just not this minute. Come to my house. Follow me home. You'll see, I'm not going anywhere."

"We can't do that, Ms. Gleeson. We're here to take him, whether you cooperate or not. If you have a complaint, you can call—"

"Call who?" Ellen exploded, losing control. "I don't need to call! I'm going to give him up, later! I just want to make this orderly! He's a boy, a little boy!"

"Mommy, no!"

"I'm sorry, Ms. Gleeson." Special Agent Manning reached for Will, and the cops advanced behind the agents as if on cue.

Ellen shouted, "We're not doing it this way! Not this way!"

"Ms. Gleeson, please." Special Agent Manning grabbed Will by the shoulders and he screamed.

"Mommeeee!!"

"Don't touch him!" Ellen stepped back with him, but the elevator door was closed behind her. Will cried louder, and she whirled around holding him tight, looking for the emergency exit, but one of the FBI agents grabbed her elbow, and Special Agent Manning wrenched Will from her arms. "He's my son!" she screamed, suddenly empty-handed.

Will wailed louder. "MOMMEE!"

"We're moving, people!" Special Agent Manning called out, carrying a hysterical Will out toward the exit.

"No!" Ellen screamed, trying to grab Will's foot but coming away with his blue sock. "Will! It's all right!"

"MOMMEEEE!" Will's eyes widened with fright, and he reached for her over the FBI agent's shoulder, his bandaged head bobbing as they swept him through the entrance hall in a moving phalanx.

"WILL!" Ellen lunged after them, but two cops held her back as she torqued this way and that, then another cop joined them, and she fought them all while Officer Halbert tried to get her attention, his eyes sympathetic.

"Ms. Gleeson, please stay here. Please, stop. Don't make us arrest you."

"MOMMEE, COME!" Will screamed, before the hospital doors slid closed behind him and a thousand lightbulbs went off.

"Let me go, you bastards!" Ellen screamed, out of control. Will was gone, just like that, and it hit her. She couldn't stop screaming. She couldn't breathe. The room spun around, a blur of polished floors, shocked faces, camera flashes. She felt as if she were going crazy. She flailed out with the court papers, then her open hand. "They just can't take him, just like that! Just like that!"

"Ellen, no!" a man called out, and the next thing she knew, Marcelo appeared next to the cops, and she reached for him.

"Marcelo! They took Will! Call Ron Halpren! Call Ron!"

"Let her go!" Marcelo shoved the cops aside. "Are you guys insane? You're hurting her! I have her, I've got her now."

"She has to let the kid go!" one of the cops shouted.

"She did! What, are you trying to kill her?" Marcelo circled an arm around Ellen, and in one sure motion, ran her away from the cops and the entrance. She half stumbled and half sagged against him, her brain finally giving up and her heart taking over. There were too many tears to see anything clearly. There was no air to breathe.

"WILL!" She heard herself howl at the top of her lungs, a sound she'd never heard come out of her; it didn't even sound human, and she was going insane, she could tell by the stunned expression on the nurses walking by and an old man carrying a stack of morning newspapers and another woman so upset her hand flew to her mouth.

Ellen screamed again but Marcelo kept her from falling, and suddenly security guards in dark blue uniforms were running beside them and Marcelo said something to them, and they all ran down one shiny hallway then another until they hit doors and freezing air and a parking lot and a red-lighted sign that read EMERGENCY, and there was a maroon car with the engine running and another security guard sitting in the driver's seat.

Marcelo shoved her into the backseat and she landed screaming with her wet face and snotty nose against the cold leather seat and Marcelo threw himself in after her, holding her from behind as she fought and howled and choked and cried, and the car lurched finally off.

Chapter Eighty-four

When Ellen woke up, she was lying in her clothes in a bedroom she didn't recognize, and Marcelo was sitting at the end of the bed, holding on to her hand. Her head felt fuzzy and strange, her thoughts blank. The room was very dark. The wood blinds were closed, the walls covered with black-and-white photographs, and the dresser a lacquered black, under a mirror of onyx.

Marcelo focused on her, a tiny buckle creasing his forehead. His expression looked strained, the corners of his lips turned down. He had on an open white shirt, and the edges of his body blurred in the darkness.

"You awake?" he asked softly.

"What time is it?"

Marcelo's gaze shifted to his left, then back again, presumably to check a bedside clock. "Seven thirty at night. You've been asleep since this morning."

Ellen tried to understand. "I slept the whole day?"

"You needed to."

"Where am I? I feel funny."

"You're at my house, and you took a Valium."

"I did?" Ellen didn't remember.

"Yes, you were so . . . upset. I offered one to you, and you said yes. I drug my women only with their consent."

"Why do you have Valium?"

"An old girlfriend. The relationship expired, but the pills didn't." Marcelo smiled, and Ellen sensed from under her pharmaceutical cloud that he was trying to cheer her up. She didn't dare rewind the day's events to remember why she was here. She knew, but she didn't want to know. She had traded in one insulation for another.

"Why did you bring me here and not home?"

"Your house was a crime scene."

Of course.

"Though it's since been released. Also, there was press out front."

"Who did we send?"

"Sal."

Ellen lifted an eyebrow.

"Who better?"

"Make him tell it right, Marcelo. Tell it true, all of it. I'm fine with it."

"Good."

"Just so it's not Sarah." Ellen felt bitterness even through her drug haze. "She's the one who called the Bravermans, you know, for the reward."

"I heard from the police." Marcelo's smile vanished. "Which would probably explain why she quit the other day."

"She did?"

"Walked in and quit, packed up her desk, and left. No notice, nothing."

"Did she say she didn't need it, because she's rich now? She won the lottery."

"No, she said I was the worst editor in the country and I was just"—Marcelo paused a minute, smiling—"a pretty boy."

"She said that?"

"It's not that funny. I am pretty." Marcelo stroked Ellen's cheek, and she started to feel something, which worried her. She didn't welcome any emotions right now, even good ones.

"Do you have another pill?"

"Yes, but I don't think you should take it yet. Your lawyer's here."

"Lawyer?"

"Ron. You asked me to call him, and he came over at the end of the day."

"He's here?" Ellen started to get up, but Marcelo gentled her back down.

"Stay put. I'll have him come up." He rose and left the room, and Ellen lay still, trying to maintain an equilibrium. It wasn't time for emotion, but action. Maybe there was still something that could be done. In the next minute, footsteps scuffed on the stair and Marcelo came back into the room, followed by Ron Halpren, in a dark suit and tie.

"Hi, Ron," Ellen said, to show that she was a functioning human being. "Please don't say anything nice or I'll lose it."

"Fair enough." Ron sat down on the bed, his beard grizzled and his crinkly eyes soft.

"Also don't look at me like that."

Ron chuckled, sadly. "Okay, I'll be the lawyer, not the friend. I heard what happened, I read the papers."

"Papers?"

"The court papers they gave you at the hospital," Marcelo said, standing behind Ron, his arms folded.

Ellen thought back. Whatever. "So is there anything I can do?"

Ron hesitated. "Nothing."

Ellen tried to stay in control. "I mean, just about the timing."

"What about it?"

"It's so . . . soon. Abrupt. He has clothes at home, and toys, and books, and DVDs, and a cat." Ellen stopped herself. Will would miss Oreo Figaro. Maybe she could get the cat to him. "Why can't we ease the transition? And for his benefit, not mine." She was remembering what they'd said at the hospital.

"It doesn't work that way, at least not with Braverman. I spoke with Mike Cusack, a big gun at Morgan, Lewis. I gather Mr. Braverman has some dough."

"Yes."

"Well, he got out the heavy artillery, and as a legal matter, you can make a transition, as you say, only if they agree, and they're not agreeing. They don't trust you or the situation."

"It's not about me."

"I know that, and you should hold on to that thought. It's not personal." Ron patted her hand. "Braverman has to go home and bury his wife, and his lawyer says that he wants to start over. Pick up the pieces."

Ellen's heart sank. "I can see that, but what if that's not what's best for Will? Sending Will into a funeral, his father a grieving widower, right off the bat? He'll freak."

"You're talking best interests again, and remember, that's not the law. It's a power notion. Braverman has absolute power and he's wielding it." Ron's gaze rested on hers. "I think you need to pick up the pieces, too. You need to understand that Will will be loved and very well cared for. They already contacted a pediatrician and a therapist specializing in young children."

Ellen felt tears fighting to surface, but held them back. Will would have medical experts, but no mother. She couldn't even say the words.

"In time, he'll be fine."

"He's not property, to be delivered. He's a child, with feelings."

"Kids are resilient."

"I hate when people say that," Ellen shot back, more harshly than she intended. "It's like we'll all pretend that the kid's feelings don't matter, because they get in the way. But you know what happens,

Ron? Kids swallow the hurt, and sooner or later, it comes out. One way or the other, the hurt comes out. And you know who gets hurt then? Not the adults. The kid. *Will.* Someday he'll be hurting and he won't even know why." Ellen gave a little hiccup and covered her mouth, holding back a sob. "He lost a mother at a year old. Now he's losing another. Can't we be a little sensitive? Is it so much to ask?"

"We have no choice, and he will be fine, in the end." Ron patted her hand, then squeezed it, as Marcelo left the bedroom for a minute, then came back with a glass of water.

"Have another pill," he said, offering her the tablet in his open palm, and Ellen raised herself, popped the Valium, and drank the water like she lived on the Sahara.

"Ron, can I call Will? Can I talk to him at least?"

"No."

"You're kidding."

"No." Ron shook his head. "They think a clean break is best."

"For who? Them or him? They accused me of being selfish, but they're the ones who're selfish."

"I hear you, but there's nothing we can do."

Ellen hoped the pill worked fast. "Where is he now, do you think?"

"Will? In the city, still. They'll be in town until the coroner releases Carol Braverman's body."

Ellen felt a pang. "When will that be?"

"A couple of days."

"So knowing Bill, they're at the Ritz or the Four Seasons. I say the Ritz."

"I say the Four Seasons," Marcelo said, but Ron frowned.

"Don't even think about it, either of you. Cusack told me if you try to see Will, they'll take out a restraining order."

Marcelo frowned. "These people, they're cruel beyond belief."

"There it is." Ron shrugged. "Cusack said, and I believe him, that this guy is just trying to protect his kid."

"From me?"

"Yes."

Ellen tried to process it. "I really can't call Will?"

"No. Their child therapist said it would be confusing for him and prevent his bonding with his father again."

"An expert said that?"

"You can find an expert to say anything."

"Then we should find our own expert."

Ron shook his head. "No, there's no trial here, and no judge. They won. They win. On the good-news front, I asked if they'd give you an update on his condition, physical and emotional, next week, and they agreed."

"Big of them." Ellen felt anger flare up, muted by the drug.

"We'll take what we can get and go from there."

"They need to know his medical history. They didn't even know that. I have his records."

"I'm sure we can send it to them or his pediatrician."

Ellen slumped back into the pillow, trying not to hit somebody. Or cry. Or scream. Or turn back time, to the day she read that awful white card in the mail.

"Try to rest, Ellen. You know what Shakespeare says. 'Sleep knits up the ravell'd sleave of care.' "

"Shakespeare was never a mother."

Ron rose. "Call me if you have any questions. Hang in there. I'll be thinking of you. So will Louisa."

"Thanks." Ellen watched Ron go to the door, followed by Marcelo, and she called out after them, "Ron, thanks for not saying, I told you so."

Ron didn't answer and they walked down the steps, the footsteps scuffling again, and in time, Marcelo came back upstairs with another drink.

"Please tell me that's whiskey."

"Coke."

"Or not." Ellen raised herself and took a sip, tasting the sweetness.

"Are you hungry?"

"No." Ellen gave him the glass and lay back down, her head mercifully fuzzy again. Thoughts of Connie and her father popped through the oncoming clouds. "I have to tell the babysitter what happened."

"She probably knows. It's all over the TV."

"She'll be so upset." Ellen felt a deep twinge. "She shouldn't have to find out that way."

"I'll take care of everything." Marcelo put the glass on the night table. "I don't want you to worry about it. What's her phone number?"

"It's in my phone, in my purse. Her name is Connie. Also my father needs to know. He's in Italy. Getting married."

Marcelo frowned. "When does he get home?"

"I forget."

"It'll wait, then."

"I need to feed the cat."

"Let it go. Time to rest." Marcelo squeezed her arm.

"Thank you for being so nice."

"Ron's right, you have to pick up the pieces. I'll help."

"You don't have to."

"I want to. I'm privileged to." Marcelo stroked her arm, and Ellen felt her body relax.

"Am I staying here tonight?"

"Yes."

"Where are you sleeping?"

"You tell me. I do have a spare room, but I'd like to stay here with you."

Ellen's head started to fog. "Is this a date?"

"We're beyond dates."

Ellen closed her eyes. She liked Marcelo's voice, nice and deep, and the accent that made his words sibilant, his speech more like a purr than words. "But what about work? I mean, you're my editor."

"We'll figure it out."

"You were so worried about that, before."

"Let's just say that since then, I've gotten a better perspective."

And whether Marcelo kissed Ellen on the cheek or she just dreamed it, she couldn't tell.

Chapter Eighty-five

Ellen woke up, and the bedroom was still dark. She was lying on top of the comforter in her clothes, and Marcelo was spooning her, fully clothed, his arm hooked over her waist. The bedside clock glowed 3:46 A.M., and she waited for sleep to return, but it was as if a switch had been thrown in her brain. A light seared through the dark room of her mind, illuminating every corner, flooding every crack in the plaster, filling the grain in the floorboards, setting even the dust motes ablaze.

Will is gone.

Ellen imagined him in a hotel. He'd be wondering where she was, what had happened, why he wasn't home, why he wasn't with his cat, why he wasn't going to school. Bill would be calling him Timothy and smiling in his face, and there would be lawyers and pediatricians and shrinks, but there would be no mother. His world had been turned upside down and stood on its head. He'd gone from life with a single mother and no father, to a life with a single father and no mother, like the negative to his positive, his existence in obverse.

He's just a little boy.

Ellen knew what she had to do next, or tears would flow and engulf her. She plucked Marcelo's hand from her hip, edged toward the side of the bed, and rolled out as quietly as she could. She padded downstairs in the dark, running her fingertips along the rough brick wall to guide her way. Her feet hit the floor, and she crossed the room to the glass coffee table, where a black laptop sat with its lid open. She hit a key, and the screensaver appeared, a color photograph of an old wood fishing boat at ebb tide, its orange paint weathered and peeling, with a tangle of worn netting mounded from its bow, in a twilight sun.

She opened Microsoft Word and pressed a key, so that a bright white page popped onto the screen, then slid the laptop around and sat down on the couch, pausing a second before she began. The title came easily.

Losing Will

She stopped a minute, looking at it in black and white, the faux newsprint making it real. She swallowed hard, then set her feelings aside. She had to do this for her job. And for Marcelo. And mostly, for herself. Writing had always helped her, before. It always clarified her feelings and her thoughts, and she never felt like she could understand something fully until the very minute that she'd written about it, as if each story was one she told herself and her readers, at the same time. In fact, it was writing that began her relationship to Will, and she found herself coming full circle again, so she began:

Last week, I was asked to write a story about what it feels like to lose a child. We were concerned that, among all of the statistics and bar graphs attending an article about the city's escalating homicide rate, the value of a child's life would be lost. So I set out to interview women who had lost children.

I spoke with Laticia Williams, whose eight-year-old son La-teef was killed by stray bullets, a victim of violence between two gangs. I also spoke with Susan Sulaman, a Bryn Mawr mother whose two children were abducted by their father several years ago.

And now, to their examples, I can add my own.

As you may know, I lost my son this week when I learned that, unbeknownst to me, my adoption of him was illegal. My son is, in fact, a child by the name of Timothy Braverman, who was kidnapped from a Florida couple two years ago.

I hope you don't think I'm being presumptuous in insert-ing my own experience into this account. I know that my child is alive, unlike Laticia Williams. But forgive me if I sug-gest that how you lose a child doesn't alter the fact that, in the end, he is lost to you. Whether you lose him by murder, abduction, or a simple twist of fate, you end up in the same place.

Your child is gone.

What does it feel like?

To Laticia Williams, it feels like anger. A rage like a fire that consumes everything in its path. She feels angry every minute she spends without her child. Angry every night she doesn't put him to bed. Angry every morning that she doesn't pack him his favorite peanut-butter-and-banana sandwich and walk him to school. In her neighborhood, all the mothers walk their kids to school, to make sure they get there alive.

Of course, that the children remain alive after they get home is not guaranteed.

Her son "Teef" was shot in his own living room, while he was watching TV, by bullets that flew in through a window to find their lethal marks in his young cheek. The funeral director who prepared Lateef's body for burial took all night to restore the child's face. His teacher said he was the class clown, a leader among his classmates, who stuffed his desk with post-humous Valentines.

To Susan Sulaman, losing a child feels like emptiness. A profound vacancy in her heart and her life. Because her children are alive with their father, or so she assumes, she looks for them everywhere she goes. At night, she drives around neighborhoods where they might live, hoping for a chance sighting. In the daytime, she scans the small faces on school buses that speed past.

Susan Sulaman is haunted by her loss.

I asked her if she felt better knowing that at least the children were in their father's hands. Her answer?

"No. I'm their mother. They need me."

I know just how she feels, and Laticia, too. I'm angry, I feel haunted, and it's still fresh. It's so new, a wound still bleeding, the flesh torn apart, the gash swollen and puffy, yet to be sewn together or grafted, years from scar tissue, bumpy and hard.

Losing Will feels like a death.

My mother died recently, and it feels a lot like that. Suddenly, someone who was at the center of your life is gone, excised as quickly as an apple is cored, a sharp spike driven down the center of your world, then a cruel flick of the wrist and the almost surgical extraction of your very heart.

And like a death, it does not end the relationship.

I am still the daughter of my mother, though she is gone. And I am still the mother of Will Gleeson, though he is gone, too.

I have learned that the love a mother has for her child is unique among human emotions. Every mother knows this instinctively, but that doesn't mean it doesn't need articulating.

And it remains true, whether the child is adopted or not. That, I didn't know before, but I've learned it now. Just as it doesn't matter how you lose your child, it doesn't matter how you find him, either. There's a certain symmetry in that, but it's no comfort now.

I didn't give birth to Will, but I am tied to him as surely as if we shared blood. I am his real mother.

It's the love, that binds.

I fell in love with Will the moment I saw him in a hospital ward, with tubes taped under his nose to hold them in place, fighting for his life. From that day forward, he was mine.

And though, as his mother, I certainly felt tired at times, I never tired of looking at him. I never tired of watching him eat. I never tired of hearing the sound of his voice or the words he made up, like the name of our cat. I never tired of seeing him play with Legos.

I *did* tire of stepping on them in bare feet.

It's hard to compare loves, and it may be silly to try, but I have learned something from my experience in losing Will. Because I have loved before, certainly. I have loved men before, and I might even be falling in love with a man now.

Here is how a mother's love is different:

You may fall out of love with a man.

But you will never fall out of love with your child.

Even after he is gone.

Ellen sat back and read the last line again, but it began to blur, and she knew why.

"Ellen?" Marcelo asked softly, coming down the stairs.

"I finished my piece." She wiped her eyes with her hand, but Marcelo crossed to her through the darkness, his mouth a concerned shadow in the glow of the screen. He reached for her hand.

"Let's go lie down," he whispered, pulling her gently to her feet.

Chapter Eighty-six

The next morning dawned clear, and Ellen rode in the passenger seat of Marcelo's car, looking out the window, squinting against the brightness of the sun on the newfallen snow. Its top layer had hardened in the cold, and the crust took on a smooth sheen. The streets on the way to her house had been plowed, leaving waist-high wedges beside the parked cars.

They turned a corner, and a trio of kids in snowsuits and scarves played on the mounds. One child, a girl named Jenny Waters, was from Will's class, and Ellen looked away, pained. They left Montgomery Avenue, and she noticed how the landscape had changed with the snow. It made unrecognizable blobs of shrubs, lay like a mattress on the roofs of parked cars, and lined the length of barren tree branches, doubling their thickness. Everything familiar had changed, and she tried not to see it as a bad metaphor.

Last night after she'd finished her piece, she'd fallen back to only a restless sleep and felt raw and nervous inside. A morning shower had helped, and she'd changed her top, slipping into an old gray sweater of Marcelo's. Her hair was still wet, falling loose to her shoulders, and she didn't bother with any makeup. She took it as a measure of confidence in her new relationship, and she didn't want to see her own face in the mirror, anyway.

"I should call my father," Ellen said, mentally switching topics.

"Your phone's in your purse. I charged it for you."

"Thanks. I feel bad that I didn't call Connie, either. She's probably at a football game today. She loves Penn State."

"She called you, and I spoke to her. She's meeting us at your house. I hope that's okay with you. She thought it would be."

"It is, sure." Ellen felt her heart gladden. "How is she? Is she okay?"

"She's very upset, but I think it will do you good to see her." Marcelo swung the car onto her street, and Ellen swallowed hard as she looked at her house. Newsvans parked in every available space, with microwave towers that pierced the blue sky. Reporters with videocameras mobbed her sidewalk.

Ellen said, "I hate the press."

"Me, too." Marcelo's gaze shifted to her, worried. "Would you like me to go around the block, one time?"

"No, let's do it." Ellen pulled her coat closer around her.

"Looks like national, too, and TV." Marcelo craned his neck, slowing the car as they neared the house. "I'll let you read Sal's piece before we file."

"You filing this afternoon, by two?"

"It can wait. I'll email it to you."

"Thanks." Ellen knew he was pushing the deadline for her. "Are you coming in?"

"If you would like. I'm happy to meet Connie."

"Come in and meet her, then I think I'll be okay." They approached the house, and to Ellen's surprise, her neighbor Mrs. Knox was out front, ignoring the reporters and shoveling her walk for her. The sight gave her a sudden pang, of guilt and gratitude. Maybe she wasn't such a busybody, after all.

"Here we go." Marcelo pulled up, double-parked, and hit the emergency lights. "We'll have to do this fast."

"Okay." Ellen grabbed her purse, and they both opened the doors and jumped out. She hustled around the front of the car, almost slipping on the snow, and Marcelo took her arm and they hurried together to her front walk. The reporters surged toward them almost as one, brandishing microphones, aiming videocameras, and shouting questions.

"Ellen, when did you know he was Timothy Braverman?" "Ellen, were you gonna give him back?" "Marcelo!" "Hey, El, how did the FBI find out who your son was?" "Ellen, aren't you gonna make a statement? Marcelo, give us a break! You're one of us!"

Ellen hurried up her walk with Marcelo right behind her, keeping the press at bay. She hustled to the porch steps, spraying snow, and crossed to the front door, which Connie opened for her.

"Connie!" she cried, more in anguish than in greeting, and the women fell into each other's arms.

Chapter Eighty-seven

After Marcelo had gone home, Ellen sat with Connie in the living room, telling her everything while they shared a box of tissues, and they cried all over again when they came to the same awful conclusion, that Will was gone from both their lives.

"I can't believe this happened." Connie mopped up her eyes with a Kleenex, her voice raspy. "It's unreal."

"I know." Ellen kept stroking Oreo Figaro, who sat in a silky ball on her lap.

"I hope you don't mind, but I got here early and I went up to his room. I looked around at all the stuff, all his toys, all his books." Connie sighed, her chest heaving in her sweatshirt. "I put his books away, force of habit, and I closed his door. I didn't think you'd want to go in. Is that okay?"

"It's all okay. Anything you do is okay."

Connie smiled sadly, her ponytail on her shoulder. "I should've read to him more. I didn't read to him enough."

"You read to him plenty."

"You thought I should read to him more." Connie looked at her directly, cocking her head, her eyes glistening. "You used to think that, didn't you?"

"You were the best babysitter I could have ever asked for."

"Really?" Connie asked, her voice breaking, and she dabbed at fresh tears.

"Really. You can't imagine how grateful I am to you. I could never have done my job without you, and I needed to do my job. For Will and for me."

"Thanks for saying that."

"I should have said it before, a thousand times. It's true." Ellen scratched behind Oreo Figaro's ear, and he began to purr happily, his chest thrumming against the palm of her hand. "You know, I used to be a little jealous."

"Of what?"

"Of you, of your time with Will. Of how close you were. I used to not like it that you loved him, and he loved you. It threatened me."

Connie remained silent, inclining her head, listening. The sun coming through the living room windows was too bright to bear, and Ellen didn't really understand what was powering her confession. But it didn't matter why she said it, only that it needed saying, so she continued.

"I'm sorry about that, because now I know better. The more people who loved that boy, the better. We loved him up, really, between the two of us." Ellen felt her eyes fill again, but blinked them clear. "I used to think that kids were like a glass or something, that they'd break if you poured too much love into them. But they're like the ocean. You can fill them up with love, and just when you think you've reached the brim, you can keep on pouring."

Connie sniffled. "Agree, but here's the thing. Will may have loved me, but he always knew who his mother was. He knew the difference between you and me, and he never forgot it."

"You think?" Ellen asked, though the words only hurt more now that he was gone.

"I know. I've sat for kids all my life, and take it from me, the kids always know who Mom is. Always."

"Thanks." Ellen set the cat aside on the couch and rose slowly, on joints that seemed suddenly stiff. "Well, I guess I have to go see what the kitchen looks like."

"No, you don't." Connie wiped her eyes with finality. "I went in there. It made me sick to see it, and it'll make you even sicker."

"I have to live here. I thought about moving, but no way." Ellen walked into the dining room, which was still in disarray. She flashed on Carol on the floor next to her, the two of them looking up at Rob Moore, standing behind the muzzle of his gun.

"I know it's not a crime scene anymore. But I didn't know whether to put the chairs in order or not."

"I will." Ellen picked up a chair from the floor and slid it noisily into place under the table, then did the same to the other, feeling the beginning of an odd sort of satisfaction. Maybe this was what everybody meant by picking up the pieces. She took a deep breath, braced herself, and headed for the kitchen threshold. "Let's see how bad it is."

"Right behind you," Connie said, and they both stood together, eyeing the kitchen.

My God.

Ellen supported herself against the doorjamb, scanning the scene. A large, shiny pool of black-red blood had dried into the floorboards, filling the grain and knots in the hardwood, making a macabre drawing etched in ink. It must have been where Carol had died.

"Disgusting, huh?" Connie asked, and Ellen nodded, her chest tight. She flashed on poor Carol, her arms raised protectively, then chased that thought away.

Across the room, near the back door, lay another island of blood, smaller but just as nauseating, where Moore must have fallen. The stink of gasoline hung in the air, and a dozen yellow spots stained the floor where the solvent had splattered. She squeezed her eyes shut against an instant replay of Will's mouth taped shut, his snowsuit drenched with gasoline.

"I told you it was bad."

"It's worse than bad." Ellen bit her lip, thinking. "Do you think I can scrub the blood out?"

"No, and I swear I smell it."

"There's only one solution."

"Cover it with a rug?"

"No." Ellen crossed to the window and opened it, then fumbled around for the metal slides and threw open the storm windows, letting in a blast of fresh, snowy air that somehow felt cleansing. "I'm going to rip up the whole damn floor."

"You mean do it yourself?" Connie smiled, surprised.

"Sure. How hard can it be? It's just destruction. Any idiot can destroy something." Ellen went to the base cabinet, found her orange plastic toolbox, and set it out on top of the stove, trying not to notice that one burner was missing. She opened the toolbox and took out her hammer. "I'm no contractor, but the sharp end looks like it could do the trick. If I start now, I can get it done by tonight."

"You want to do it *now*?"

"Why not? One way or the other, this floor is getting thrown away. I don't want it in my house another minute." Ellen took a gulp of fresh air, wielded the hammer, and bent down over one of the gasoline stains. She raised the hammer high over her head and brought its sharp end down with all her might.

Crack! The edge of the hammer splintered the wood, but unfortunately embedded itself there.

"Oops." Ellen yanked on the handle of the hammer, and its head came free, splintering the wood. "Looks like it works, but at this rate, I'll be finished by next year."

"I have a better idea." Connie stepped around her, opened the door to the basement, and went downstairs, and by the time she returned, Ellen had destroyed only part of a single floorboard. She looked up to see Connie hoisting a crowbar like the Statue of Liberty on *This Old House.*

"Way to go!" Ellen said. "I didn't even know I had one of those. Thanks." She rose, delighted, and reached for the crowbar, but Connie held it tight.

"I'll use this. You use the hammer. We'll get this done together. It'll go twice as fast, and besides, I wanna destroy something, too."

"Isn't there a football game?" Ellen asked, touched.

"No matter." Connie got down on her hands and knees, then wedged the end of the crowbar underneath the splintered floor. "Mark will have to win without me this time."

Tears came to Ellen's eyes, and she didn't know what to say. For once, she didn't say anything. She got back down on her hands and knees, raised her hammer, and the two women worked together for the next several hours, grimly destroying the evidence of a nightmare, with the only tools they had on hand.

A hammer, a crowbar, and the human heart.

Chapter Eighty-eight

After Connie had gone home, Ellen piled the last of the broken floorboards on her back porch because reporters were still camped out front. She stepped back inside the kitchen, shut the door against the cold, and closed the window, breathing in deeply. The gasoline smell was gone, but the subfloor was a mess. Removing the top boards had only exposed the older floor beneath, and she hadn't been able to pull out all the nails. They popped up here and there, making an obstacle course for Oreo Figaro, who walked gingerly to his food dish.

Ellen crossed to the refrigerator, careful not to step on a nail or a cat, and opened the door. She was about to reach for a bottle of water when her hand stopped in midair. Staring her in the face was the Pyrex bowl of lime green Jell-O, with a shiny cavern dug in the middle.

It's good, Mommy!

She grabbed the water bottle and slammed the door closed, determined to get through the rest of the day. The house had fallen quiet, a hollow echo of how she felt. She checked the clock on the wall—2:25. Odd that Marcelo hadn't called, and she had yet to call her father. She left the room with the water, twisted off the cap, and took a slug, then went into the living room, hearing only the sound of her footsteps on the floor. She found her purse and dug inside for her BlackBerry, but it wasn't there. She must've dropped it in Marcelo's car.

She looked up, aggravated, and through the windows she could see a commotion on the sidewalk. Reporters and photographers clustered around a taxi pulling up in front of the house, and in the next second, emerging from the crowd was her father.

Dad?

Ellen ran to the door as he waved off the press, taking the arm of an attractive woman in a chic white wool coat, probably his new wife, whose name Ellen had almost forgotten.

"Honey, what the hell?" her father asked, stepping inside, his hazel eyes round with disbelief. He stamped snow from his loafers. "This is crazy!"

"I know, it's awful." Ellen introduced herself and extended her hand to his wife. "Barbara, right?"

"Hello, Ellen." Barbara smiled with genuine warmth, her lipstick fresh and her teeth white and even. She was petite with smallish features, tasteful makeup, and highlighted hair coiffed to her chin. "Sorry we have to meet in these circumstances."

"Why didn't you call?" her father interrupted. "Thank God for the Internet, or we wouldn't have known a damn thing."

"It just got so crazy, all of it."

"We're in the hotel, and I went online to check the scores, and there's my daughter's picture and my grandson's gone! We got on the next plane."

"Why don't you go sit down, and I'll explain everything." Ellen gestured them toward the couch, but her father waved her off, agitated and acting oddly like a much older man.

"We came straight from the airport. I've been calling your cell."

"Sorry, I left it in a car." Ellen had to catch them up but she wasn't going to begin with Marcelo. "It's been difficult, Dad."

"I can imagine," Barbara said with obvious concern, but her father was distracted to the point of disorientation.

"So where's Will?" He looked around the living room, his head wobbling slightly. "Is he really not here?"

"He's really not here." Ellen stayed calm, only because he was so upset. She'd never seen him so shaken, so out of control.

"That can't be. Do the cops have him or what?"

"He's with his father, and they're already talking to shrinks and pediatricians, so I'm praying he'll be okay."

"Where is he? Where'd they take him?"

"He's in a hotel in town."

"I want to see him." Her father set his jaw, the soft jowls bracketing his mouth like a bulldog's.

"We can't, Dad."

"What do you mean, we can't?" Her father's eyes flared. "He's my only grandchild. He's my *grandson*."

"If we try to see him, they'll get a restraining order. I'm hoping that if we work with them, then we can—"

"That can't be legal! Grandparents have rights!" Her father's face reddened with emotion. "I'm calling a lawyer. I won't put up with this. Nobody takes my grandchild away from me!"

"I have a lawyer, Dad. He says what they're doing is legal."

"Then you didn't get yourself a good enough mouthpiece." Her father jabbed his finger toward her chest, but Barbara put her hand on his jacket sleeve.

"Don, don't yell at her. We talked about this. You know what she's been through."

"But they can't take him away!" Her father threw up his hands, his expression caught between bewilderment and pain. "I go away for one minute and when I come home, my grandson is gone? How can this be legal?"

"Dad, relax." Ellen stepped forward. "Sit down, have a cup of coffee, and I'll tell you the story. You'll understand the situation better."

"I understand the situation just fine!" Her father whirled around, his finger pointing again. "I remember when you came to see me, you thought that kid in the picture was Will. So I got it wrong. Ya happy, now?"

"What?" Ellen asked, stricken.

"Don!" Barbara shouted, so loudly that he stood stunned for a moment. "Shut up. Right now." She faced him head-on, despite her tiny frame. "I can't believe what I'm seeing. I can't believe this is the man I just married. I know you're a better man than this."

"Wha?" her father said, but accusation had left his tone.

"This isn't about you, or even Will." Barbara raised a manicured hand. "This is about your daughter, your only daughter. Start focusing on the child you have, instead of the one you don't."

"But she shouldn'ta said anything. She shoulda just shut up!"

Ellen felt slapped, and Barbara's mouth dropped open.

"Don, she did what any good mother would do. She did what was right for her child, even though it cost her."

Ellen recovered, listening. Barbara had given the clearest and best statement of why she'd followed up on that damn white card. She'd never thought of it exactly that way.

Her father's gaze shifted from Barbara to Ellen, suddenly very sad. He raked his thin hair with trembling fingers. "I'm sorry, El. I didn't mean it."

"I know, Dad."

"It's just that Will was my . . . chance."

"What do you mean?" Ellen asked, mystified, and tears came to her father's eyes. The only other time she'd seen him cry was at her mother's funeral, and the sight caught her by the throat.

"He was my chance, El. My second chance."

Ellen touched his arm, sensing what he'd say before he said it. She gave him a big hug, and he eased into her arms, with a little moan.

"Everything I did wrong with you, I was gonna do right with him. I wanted to make it up to you. To your mother."

Ellen thought her heart would break, and in the next minute, her eyes brimmed with tears, and she found herself crying like a baby in her father's arms.

"I'm so sorry, honey," he whispered as Ellen sobbed and breathed in his expensive aftershave, and she drew real comfort from his embrace in a way she never had before. The deepest pain in her heart eased just a little, and she let herself feel how very powerful is something so simple, yet so profound, as a father's love.

And she thanked God he was alive.

Chapter Eighty-nine

It wasn't until they had gone and Ellen was rinsing their coffee mugs that the phone rang in the kitchen. She turned off the faucet, crossed the room, and checked caller ID, which showed the newspaper's main number. She picked up. "Hello?"

"Ellen?" Marcelo asked, worried. "Are you okay? I've been calling your cell."

"I think I left it in your car. I was going to call you, but my father and my new stepmother just left."

"How are you?"

"Good, okay." Ellen glanced over and saw that the Coffmans still weren't home, their house dark. "You probably want me to look at that story, huh?"

"Only if you feel up to it."

"I'm not sure."

"Then let it go. I loved what you wrote for the homicide piece."

"Good, thanks." Ellen felt a warmth she couldn't deny.

"I'll be done here around nine. Happily, there's news besides you."

"You'd never know it from the crowd outside."

"Would you like company tonight? I don't think you should be alone."

"I'd like that."

"I'll be there." Marcelo's voice softened. "Take care of yourself, 'til then."

"See you." Ellen hung up and left the kitchen by the other exit, feeling an odd sensation when she reached the upstairs landing. It was exactly the spot where Carol had set Will down, before she'd made her final stand.

Ellen felt a tightness in her chest, then forced herself to step over the spot and climb the stairs. She caught a glimpse of the scene outside on the sidewalk, and the reporters were still there, smoking cigarettes and holding cups of take-out coffee against the cold. The afternoon sky spent its last hour before twilight descended, dropping purple and rose streaks behind the cedar shakes and satellite dishes, a suburban night in winter.

Ellen's clogs clattered on the wooden stair, echoing in the silent house, and she wondered how long she'd go on noticing every noise that she'd never noticed before. She lived in a house of echoes now. She'd have to exchange her clogs for slippers if she wanted to keep her sanity.

She reached the top of the stair, which ended in front of Will's room, and faced his door, which was closed. Not that it helped. Butterfly stickers, scribbled drawings, and a WILL'S ROOM license plate covered the door, and Ellen reached almost reflexively for the doorknob, then wondered if she should go in.

"Mrrp?" Oreo Figaro chirped, rubbing against her jeans, his tail curled around her leg.

"Don't ask," she told him, twisting the doorknob. She opened the door, and the Cheerios-and-Play-Doh smell caught her by the throat. She willed herself not to cry, and her gaze traveled around the room, dark except for the white rectangle of the window shade, bright from the snow and the TV klieg lights outside. She didn't know how long she stood there, but it was long enough for the daylight to leak away, so stuffed animals dematerialized into shadowy blobs and the spines of books thinned to straight black lines. Stars glowed faintly from the ceiling, and the WILL constellation took her back in time, to the countless nights she'd held him before bed, reading to him, talking or just listening to his adorable up-and-down cadence, the music of his stories from school or swimming, told in his little-boy register, like the sweetest of piccolos.

She watched almost numbly as Oreo Figaro leapt noiselessly to the foot of Will's bed, where he always slept, curled next to a floppy stuffed bunny whose ears were silhouetted in the light from the window shade. Will had gotten that bunny at a party that Courtney had thrown for her at work, when she adopted him. Sarah Liu had given it to him.

Anger flickered in Ellen's chest. Sarah, who was supposed to be her colleague. Sarah, who would later sell both of them out, for money. Sarah, who stole from her the choice about when or whether to give Will up. He could be here right now, home where he belonged, cuddled up with his cat, instead of in a strange hotel room, lost and confused, in all kinds of pain, going home to a house without a mother.

"You bitch!" Ellen heard herself shout. In one movement, she lunged into the room, grabbed the stuffed bunny, and hurled it into the bookshelves, where it hit a toy car. Oreo Figaro leapt from the bed, startled.

Anger flamed in Ellen's chest, and she hurried from the room.

On fire.

Chapter Ninety

Ellen stood on the snowy brick doorstep and knocked on the front door of the gorgeous Dutch Colonial. The ride to Radnor hadn't dissipated her anger, even with newsvans trailing her, and she knocked again on the door, drenched in the calcium white light of the klieg lights. Reporters recorded her every movement, but she didn't care. They were doing their job, and she was doing hers.

"Hello?" Sarah opened the front door, and her dark eyes flared in alarm. She shielded her eyes from the klieg lights with a raised hand. "What are you doing here?"

"Let me in. We're on TV, girlfriend."

"You have no right to come here!" Sarah tried to shut the front door, but Ellen straight-armed it open.

"Thanks, don't mind if I do." She powered over the threshold into a warm, well-appointed living room, furnished with gray suede sectionals and a thick pile matching rug, where two young boys were sitting on the floor, playing a noisy video game on a widescreen TV.

"Wait! My kids are here."

"I can see that." Ellen masked her emotions to wave to them. "Hey, guys, how you doing?"

"Fine," one answered without looking up, but Sarah shut the door and motioned to them.

"Boys, go to your room," she said, staccato, and they set down the game controllers and rose instantly, astounding Ellen. She couldn't get that kind of obedience from her hair, much less her son. They left the room, and Sarah picked up the controller, hit the red button for off, and set it down on top of the TV, which had gone black.

"Sarah, how could you do it?" Ellen kept her temper in check. "Not just to me, but to Will? How could you do that to Will?"

"I didn't do anything to him, nothing wrong anyway." Sarah edged backwards, tugging at the corner of her skinny black sweater.

"You cannot believe that."

"I do, and it's true. Your son is where he belongs, with his real parents." Sarah didn't look regretful in the least, her mouth still tight. "I did the right thing."

"You didn't do it because it was the right thing. You did it for the money." Ellen took a step closer, fighting the impulse to hit Sarah in the face. "You couldn't wait to quit your job, now that you're rich."

"It doesn't matter why I did it, what matters is that he wasn't legally yours. He was Timothy Braverman."

"I might have told them, but you took it out of my hands."

"No, you wouldn't have. No mother would."

"Maybe you wouldn't, but I might have, and because of you, Will was taken in the worst possible way." Ellen's anger bubbled to the surface. "No explanation, no phasing in, just *taken*. It's the kind of thing that can mess him up for life."

"All I did was tell the truth."

"Don't pretend you have the moral high ground, because you don't. Was it moral to spy on me? To search my computer? You even tricked my son into telling you where I was!"

"He wasn't your son. He was their son."

"He was *my* son."

"Not legally."

"He was my son until I said different." Ellen felt angry tears, and at some level, even she knew she was yelling at the wrong person. She wasn't angry at Sarah, she was angry at everyone and everything. Angry that it had happened in the first place. Still she couldn't stop herself. "I would never do anything to hurt your children, no matter what."

"You're not worried about Will. You're worried about yourself."

"You know what, you're right. I love my son and I want him home and I'm never going to have him again. But most of all, I want him to be happy. If he's happy, I'm happy, and thanks to you, he's in pain and—"

There was a noise behind them, from the other end of the living room, and Ellen turned around, shocked at the sight. It was Myron Krims, Sarah's husband, but he was in a wheelchair. She had met him only once, years ago, and he had been walking fine. Then he was one of the top thoracic surgeons in the city, but he was clearly ill. His black sweater and khakis were swimming on him, and his hair had gone completely gray. Circles ringed his eyes, and his aspect looked vague.

"Dear?" Myron asked, his voice shaky. "I've been calling you."

"Excuse me." Sarah hurried to her husband, and Ellen watched as she bent over him, whispered something in his ear, then wheeled him out of the room. Sarah returned after a moment, her face a tight mask. "So. Now you see."

For a minute, Ellen didn't know what to say. "I had no idea."

"We don't advertise."

"What happened?"

"He has MS." Sarah straightened a suede pillow that didn't require it.

"For how long?"

"For the rest of his life."

Ellen reddened. "I mean, how long has this been going on?"

"None of that is your business. It's nobody's business but ours."

Ellen saw a premature fissure in Sarah's forehead and wondered why she'd never noticed it before. All this time she'd thought she was the only one on a single income, but she'd been wrong.

"I was doing what was right for my family." Sarah's voice remained controlled, and her gaze unwavering. "I was doing what I had to do."

"You could have told me." Ellen felt disarmed, grasping. "You could have warned me."

"What would you have said? Don't take the money?" Sarah snorted. "It was my family or your family. I chose my family. You would have done the same."

"I don't know," Ellen answered, after a minute. She was thinking back to what the cop had said at the ER waiting room. *It's no-win.* Suddenly she didn't know anymore what was right or moral, what was legal or fair. She no longer took satisfaction in confronting Sarah. She wasn't composed enough to analyze the situation. She couldn't even tell what she would have done in Sarah's position. She knew only that Will was gone, and there was a deep rent in her chest where her heart had been. Her shoulders sagged, and she felt herself sinking onto the couch. Her face dropped into her hands, and in the next second, the cushion dipped down as Sarah sat beside her.

"I tell you this," Sarah whispered. "I am sorry."

And at that, Ellen let slip the few tears she had left.

Chapter Ninety-one

Ellen got home, hollow and spent, raw and aching. She tossed her bag and keys on the windowseat, and stamped powdery snow from her snowy clogs. She took off her coat and hung it up, but it fell onto the closet floor. She didn't have the energy to pick it up. She was thirsty but didn't get anything to drink. She was hungry but didn't bother to eat. She didn't even have the strength to be mad at the reporters, following her back from Sarah's, plaguing her with questions. Oreo Figaro came over to rub against her shins, but she ignored him and went upstairs to read Sal's piece.

She clopped slowly up the stairs, the sound of her clogs like the ticking of a clock slowing down. She had never felt like this in her life. She was empty, a ghost of a person. She went into her office on autopilot, flicked on a light, and crossed to the computer. She sat down and moved the mouse, and her computer monitor woke up with a screensaver of Will posing with Oreo Figaro.

Please, no.

She opened up Outlook and watched the boldfaced names pile

into the Inbox. She waited for Marcelo's email to load and braced herself to read the article. But Marcelo's wasn't the email that caught her eye. She moved the mouse, clicked on another email, and opened it, reading quickly.

And then she screamed.

And when she stopped screaming, she reached for the phone.

Chapter Ninety-two

Ellen shot up like a rocket, sending her desk chair rolling back across the floor, and ran to the door, then tore down the stairs.

Clop, clop, clop, clop, like a racehorse she sounded. She reached the living room, grabbed her purse and keys from the windowseat, snatched her coat from the closet floor, then flung open the door and hit the icy air.

She slammed the door shut behind her and went flying down the steps, spraying snow everywhere, her heart in her throat, heedless of the reporters, who surged forward as they had five minutes ago, raising cameras that had been at rest and flicking on generators to power up klieg lights and microphones.

"Hey, where you going now?" a reporter called out, filming her, and the others joined in. "Ellen, what's going on?" "You going back to Sarah's?"

Ellen tore through the snow on her front yard, staying on her property where the press couldn't follow, struggling in the deep snow to get to her car, as the reporters shouted questions from the sidewalk.

"Can't you give us a statement?" "Ellen, come on, give us a break!" "What's all the activity? You going to see Will?"

Ellen chirped the car door open, jumped in, and switched on the ignition. She threw the car in reverse while she hit the button to lower the driver's window. "Move, move, everybody!" she hollered, gesturing frantically out the window, her heart pounding. "Get out of the way! Get out of my way!"

"Where are you going?" "Have you heard from your son? Are they letting you see him?"

"Move, move, MOVE!" Ellen reversed out of the driveway, hitting the gas until they jumped out of the way. Some shouted questions while others sprinted to their cars and newsvans, ready to follow her again.

"Ellen, they're staying at the Four Seasons, did you know? Is that where you're going?"

"MOVE!" Ellen put the car in drive and hit the gas, spraying road salt and snow, speeding to the corner, and turning left so fast that she almost fishtailed on Wynnewood Road. She kept control of the car and accelerated up the plowed street in almost no traffic, and by the time she hit City Line, she was being followed by newsvans with microwave towers and an array of pursuit vehicles. The traffic light ahead turned red, but she hit the gas and powered through the inter-section. She passed a snowplow, a bus, and even an ambulance at speed.

Nothing was going to stop her.

Not now, not ever.

Chapter Ninety-three

Ellen hurried from the waiting room behind Special Agent Orr, passing the thick gold seal of the FBI, the framed picture of the president and the attorney general, the Ten Most Wanted posters, and whatever else was hanging on the off-white walls. She followed Special Agent Orr down the glistening hallway and reached a wooden door with a plaque that read CONFERENCE ROOM.

Special Agent Orr twisted the knob. "Here you go, Ms. Gleeson," he said, admitting her, then leaving.

Ellen stepped inside, getting her bearings. She had driven the farthest to get here, so they were all already in place. Special Agent Manning stood up at the head of the table, and on the near side, Ron Halpren stood up, too, with an uncertain smile. He was dressed in a tux from a benefit dinner, and Ellen shook his hand.

"Sorry to disrupt your night, gentlemen," she said, sitting down next to Ron. She nodded at Special Agent Manning, who retook his seat at the head of the table. "Thank you, too, Special Agent."

"It's my job." His smile was only polite and he was dressed casually, with a blue FBI windbreaker over a light Oxford shirt. Behind him was a large smoked-glass window that overlooked the snowy city at night. "I just hope this isn't a wild goose chase."

"It isn't." Ellen looked at the other side of the table, where Bill Braverman sat glaring in a sport jacket and polo shirt, next to his lawyer, Mike Cusack, who dressed like him.

"So why are we all sitting here?" Bill demanded, his eyes flashing with anger.

Ellen composed herself, folding her hands on the conference table, and took a deep breath.

Chapter Ninety-four

"Okay, here goes." Ellen paused, her heart in her throat. She was about to drop a bomb, and she met Bill's eye with sympathy. "The fact is, you're not Will's father."

"That's a lie!" Bill shot back.

"It's true, and I have proof."

"You're insulting me *and* my wife!"

Cusack placed a restraining hand on Bill's arm. "Please, allow me."

"Why should I?" Bill tore his arm away, glaring at Ellen. "You don't fool me for one minute! What kind of scam is this?"

"It's not a scam."

"Ms. Gleeson," Cusack broke in, looking askance. "You should be aware that intentional infliction of emotional distress is civilly actionable, and we won't hesitate to file suit against you."

Ron frowned. "I won't let you threaten her, Mike."

"But this is an Internet scam, obviously." Cusack raised a graying eyebrow. "Don't tell me you were taken in by that stupid email. Are you sending money to Ethiopian ambassadors, too?"

"It's not a scam, I assure you," Ron said, his tone even and reasonable.

Special Agent Manning cleared his throat. "Let's settle down and let Ms. Gleeson tell us what this is all about."

"Thank you." Ellen gathered her thoughts. "To make a long story short, when I was in Miami, I got DNA samples from both Carol and Bill Braverman. I followed them to a restaurant, and I collected some cigarette butts that Bill left in an ashtray—"

"You did *what*?" Bill interjected, rising, but Cusack pressed him back down.

"—I also got a Diet Sprite can that Carol drank from, and I sent them both to a lab that I found on the Internet."

"This is ridiculous!" Bill slammed the table with a heavy hand, but Ellen stayed the course. She couldn't blame Bill for his reaction, but neither was she backing down.

"I got the results emailed to me, and Ron forwarded the email with the results to you. Honestly, I'd forgotten about the tests, and I had no doubt that Will was really Timothy, after that night in my kitchen. Rob Moore said that his girlfriend was Amy Martin, and I knew that Amy was the one who put Will, or Timothy, up for adoption."

Next to her, Ron added, "It's a perfect chain of custody."

"It is," Special Agent Manning said, and though Ellen didn't speak law enforcement, she got the gist.

"The results of the test came back, and they show that Carol was clearly Will's biological mother. But Will has none of Bill's DNA. The results are that Bill is not Will's father."

"You're saying that Carol cheated on me?" Bill's eyes flew open.

"I'm sorry, she must have." Ellen felt terrible for him, but still. "You said your marriage wasn't the best."

"She wouldn't!" Bill flushed red. "She didn't, and she certainly wouldn't fool me into thinking another man's child was mine!"

"I'm sorry, I really am." Ellen took a second to compose herself, then said the words she'd been rehearsing all the way here. "Will is not your son, so you have no legal right to him. My adoption remains legal, and I want my son back."

Ron added, "My research showed the law would be the same in almost all jurisdictions, including Florida. As Carol has no living parents, Ellen is entitled to keep Will."

"This is a trick!" Bill shouted, jumping to his feet.

"Based on an *Internet* DNA test?" Cusack remained in his chair, his expression only slightly less hostile. "What do you take us for?"

Special Agent Manning waved Bill into his seat, and he complied, albeit angrily.

"It's a legitimate lab," Ellen said, willing herself to remain calm. She had discussed the way this meeting would go with Ron, who was her first phone call after she read the email. "But if you want to run another test to confirm the results, you're welcome to."

"I'm *welcome* to?" Bill repeated, incredulous.

"I will agree to a lab of the FBI's choosing, with the test to be administered under their supervision."

"I won't take any damn DNA test!" Bill's jaw set with determination. "Timothy's *my* son, and I'm keeping him!"

Ron raised a finger in his professorial way. "As a legal matter, we could require you to take a DNA test. If we take this matter to court right now, any judge would order you to do so, and my client and I are more than prepared. In fact, bear with me." Ron reached into an accordion-style briefcase sitting on the floor, extracted a manila folder, then opened it, slid out some papers, and handed them to Special Agent Manning, Bill, and Cusack. "These papers are ready to file. I have an emergency judge standing by. It's your choice, Mr. Braverman. If you and Will don't voluntarily take the DNA test, the court will order you to do so. I'll also ask the court to place Will in protective custody in the interim, so that you don't leave the jurisdiction with him."

"You *have* to be kidding!" Bill grabbed the papers from the center of the table and skimmed the front page, his eyes darting rapidly left and right, his mouth pursed in fury.

But Ellen could see that Cusack, sitting next to him and reading the papers, lifted his eyebrow again.

Ron added, "Mike, if you'd like a minute alone with your client, Ellen and I would be happy to step outside."

Cusack looked up after a minute, deep in thought. "Yes, thank you. I'd like to confer with my client."

Ellen and Ron rose from the table, left the conference room, and went into the hallway, where they closed the door behind them and Ron placed a fatherly hand on her shoulder.

"Ellen, don't get excited." His brow furrowed. "You have to remember that the Internet lab could be wrong. Even the most reliable labs get false results on tests, all kinds of tests, and I don't want you to get your hopes up."

"They're *not* that fly-by-night," Ellen said, but she knew better. "Jerry Springer uses them."

Ron smiled. "Remember, plan for the worst and you'll be happily surprised."

"Way to kill the mood, counselor."

Fifteen endless minutes later, the door to the conference room opened, and Special Agent Manning stuck out his head. "We're ready for you," he said simply.

Chapter Ninety-five

Ellen filed into the conference room with Ron behind her and took her seat at the table across from Cusack. Bill had deserted his chair but was standing by the window, his arms folded and his expression grim. Ellen saw the strain around his eyes and knew that he was more anguished than angry, and her heart went out to him.

Cusack began, "We've decided, in a spirit of cooperation, to undertake a DNA test. The FBI has recommended a lab that it uses all the time, and we'll be taking the samples of Bill and Timothy tonight."

"We'll fast-track it," Special Agent Manning interjected. "We should have the results by Monday."

Ellen felt her heart pounding but didn't show any emotion, for Bill's sake.

Cusack continued, "However, we don't believe it's necessary to place Timothy in protective custody with the Bureau, pending the results. Timothy is at the Four Seasons with a babysitter that comes highly recommended. Bill would like to keep the boy with him at the hotel and he won't leave the jurisdiction. We trust you'll agree." Cusack fell silent, awaiting Ellen's response.

So did Bill, by the window, his arms folded, and Ron, who cocked his head, his smile characteristically gentle.

"What do you want to do, Ellen?" he asked. "You can leave him with Bill until the tests come back, or the FBI can make him comfortable in a hotel."

Special Agent Manning added, "The Four Seasons isn't in our budget." He chuckled, *huh huh,* but nobody else did.

Ellen's eyes met Bill's from across the room, and she felt their shared bond. This situation was no-win, at every turn. As for protective custody, it had been Ron's idea. She didn't really want Will to stay with a cop. It only took Ellen a minute to make her decision:

"I trust that Bill will take good care of him, and right now, that's what's best for him. I don't want to disrupt him again if the test is wrong."

"Thanks," Cusack said, and Ron nodded.

But Bill didn't reply, just turned away and gazed out the window into the cold, dark night. He was facing the prospect of losing his son.

And Ellen knew exactly how he felt.

Chapter Ninety-six

A new snow had fallen, covering the minivans, swing sets, and lawn furniture in pristine white. The afternoon sky was sunny and bright blue, and the wind frigid and fresh, as if the deep freeze had killed every last germ, leaving only the healthiest and most wholesome air. Ellen breathed it in, standing on her porch with no coat like a crazy lady, folding her arms against her chest, her hair freshly shampooed, her sweater dry cleaned, and her socks laundered and matching. She even had on new clogs.

"Ellen, we could wait inside," Marcelo said, standing on her right.

"Nah, let's stay here," her father said, on her left.

"I agree," Barbara said, next to her father in her lovely white coat.

Behind them, Connie stood with her husband, Chuck. She said, "Wild horses couldn't drag me off this porch."

They all smiled, Ellen most of all, despite the reporters, TV anchorpersons, and photographers who mobbed the sidewalk in front of her house and spilled into the street, shouting questions, taking videos and pictures, and requiring five uniformed cops to keep traffic moving.

Marcelo smiled, puzzled. "Let me get this straight. It's freezing outside, but we're on the porch?"

"Right," Ellen and her father answered in unison, then they looked at each other.

"Great minds," her father said, and Ellen laughed.

Marcelo threw an arm around her shoulder. "You know what? I like it."

"Good," she said, snuggling against him.

Suddenly a black sedan turned onto the street, and Ellen felt her heart start to thunder. She stepped forward for a closer look, and the sedan slowed when it reached the photographers, who started hoisting videocameras to their shoulders. The sedan's emergency lights went on, flashing yellow as it braked in front of the house.

"My God," Ellen said under her breath, already in motion, and the press surged forward, pointing their cameras and microphones to the sedan. The doors were opening, and Bill emerged from the driver's side and Cusack from the passenger's. Reporters swarmed them with cameras and microphones, and Ellen ran down the front walk toward the crowd, and in the next instant she heard a little voice from its center.

"Mommy! MOMMY!"

"WILL!" Ellen shouted, tears blurring her eyes as she hit the crowd and elbowed her way through, reaching the sedan just as Bill unlatched Will from the car seat and carried him through the crazed reporters to her.

"MOMMY!" Will screamed, his arms reaching for her, and Ellen took him in her arms and hugged him so tightly she almost squished him.

"It's all right, it's all right now," she said, as Will burst into tears and wrapped his arms around her neck. Reporters shouted questions and stuck cameras in their faces, but Ellen caught Bill's eye, and his expression was pained. She called to him, "Want to come in, have a soda?"

"No thanks," Bill called back, then gestured vaguely at Will. "I got him new shoes."

"Thanks." Ellen felt a stab of sympathy. "Another time, then?"

"See you," Bill said, his eyes on Will's back. Grief flickered through his expression, then he turned away amid the clicking cameras, and so did Ellen, with a guilt that vanished in happiness when Marcelo, her father, and Chuck arrived at her side and ran interference as she hurried back up her front walk, hustled across the porch to the open front door, and swept inside the warm, snug house.

Will didn't touch the ground until half an hour later, after being passed from mother to grandfather to mother to new stepgrandmother to mother to Marcelo to Connie and Chuck then back again to Ellen, until he had stopped crying and everybody held him tight, kissed him too much, and reassured themselves by feeling his weight in their arms that he was really, safely, and finally back home.

Ellen felt her heart truly at peace for the first time since she'd first seen that white card, so long ago. She set Will down in the living room, but, oddly, he frowned, even as he stood at the center of an adoring circle. His glistening eyes scanned the room, ignoring the twisted streamers of green crepe, the green helium balloons on the ceiling, and even the pile of wrapped gifts from a love-crazed family.

"What's the matter, sweetie?" Ellen asked, puzzled. She reached down and ruffled his soft hair with her fingers. She thought she might never stop touching his hair.

"Where's Oreo Figaro, Mommy?"

"Oh. He was here a minute ago," Ellen answered, looking around, and in the next second, they both spotted the cat under the dining room table, running from all the commotion, a black-and-white blur with a tail like an exclamation point.

"There he goes!" Will hollered, taking off after the cat, who bounded into the kitchen.

"Uh-oh." Ellen went after Will, and everyone watched him, collectively holding their breaths. They had all discussed how he would react to seeing the kitchen again, and she had talked to a child psychologist who'd told her to let Will take the initiative in asking questions. The therapist had also approved her redecorating idea, and she prayed Will would, too. She held her breath when he reached the kitchen threshold.

"Mommy!" Will hollered, surprised. "Look in here!"

"I know, it's a surprise for you." Ellen came up behind him and rested a hand on his head. She and Marcelo had worked in the kitchen all weekend, installing laminated wood over the subfloor and painting the walls to cover the bloodstains. The wall color had been the easiest choice, although when sunlight flooded in through the back window, the room looked like it was growing. She doubted she'd ever get used to a bright green kitchen, nor should she.

"It's my favorite!" Will exclaimed, then grabbed the cat, and gave him a kiss. "I love you, Oreo Figaro."

"I love you, too," Ellen replied, in her Oreo Figaro voice.

Will giggled and set the cat back on the floor. "Can I open my presents now?"

"Yes, but gimme a kiss first." Ellen bent over, and Will threw his arms around her neck. If she was expecting a big reunion kiss, she wasn't getting one, not when there were gifts waiting to be unwrapped. Will ran out of the room, and she called after him, "Love you!"

"Love you, too!"

Ellen went to the cabinet and got a trash bag for the gift wrap, then straightened up, remembering that the last time she had stood here, she had killed a man. She turned to the wall where Moore had slid down, as if to reassure herself that it wouldn't still be bloodied.

But it was.

A sudden horrific flashback shot out of nowhere. Before her eyes,

Moore slumped against the wall. Bright red blood spurted from a deep hole in his forehead. A crooked grin crossed his face.

Ellen froze, remembering. That smile was crooked because it turned down on the right. Like Will's.

She put it together, stunned. She hadn't noticed it then, because she was sure that Bill Braverman was Will's father. But now that she knew that he wasn't, the crooked grin assumed a new significance. Then she remembered what Moore had said that night to Carol.

You shoulda said to him, "Honey, wifey-poo isn't the good girl you think."

Ellen stared at the wall, but it had turned green again. She stood a moment, shaken, trying to collect her thoughts, trying to process what she had just learned.

If Bill wasn't Will's father, she had at least a guess who was.

Epilogue

About a year later, there was another winter snow and another party with wrapped presents, balloons, and crepe streamers crisscrossing the living room, which this time was packed with noisy, sugar-fueled classmates of Will's. They ran back and forth, played with new toys, ate grocery-store sheet cake, and generally wreaked havoc for his fourth birthday.

"Watch out!" Will shrieked, running with a new laser sword, and Ellen grabbed it from him on the fly.

"Don't run with this."

"Please!"

"No, you'll hurt somebody."

"Aw, Mom!" Will took off after his friend Brett, and Ellen's father came over, his eyes glittering with mischief.

"I'll take that weapon, my lady."

"What for?" Ellen handed it over.

"You'll see. This will do nicely." Her father examined the laser sword, and Barbara joined him in her elegant white pantsuit, a multicolored party hat perched atop her head.

"Ellen, don't let him have that. He'll embarrass us all."

"Too late for that," Ellen said with a smile. She had come to love Barbara, who wisely hadn't tried to replace her mother, because no one could. But somewhere along the line, she had opened her mind to the possibility that if you could love a child no matter how he came to you, then you could also love a mother, no matter how she came to you.

"I need this for my golf lesson." Her father gestured across the crowded room to where Bill Braverman and his pretty date were talking with Connie and Chuck. Her father called to him, "Bill, come here. I need your expertise."

"Coming." Bill strode over in his out-of-place linen jacket, pants, and tassel loafers, making his way through the kids and ruffling Will's hair.

"Look how fast I go, Bill!" Will called after him.

"Good for you!" Bill entered the dining room, grinning, but her father was all business.

"Show me what you were saying before, about my grip." Her father flipped the sword around so that the point faced the floor, then wrapped his fingers around the hilt, swinging it like a golf club. "You said it was my elbow, right? Not tucked in enough?"

"Not exactly, let me show you." Bill focused on his task, and Barbara moaned.

"Please, guys, anything but golf."

"There is nothing but golf," Bill said, smiling, then turned to Ellen. "By the way, I have those papers for you to sign, for Will's trust. When he's of age, he can decide how much he wants to set aside for Charbonneau House."

"Great, thanks." Ellen smiled, and in the next second she felt an arm encircle her waist and tug her into the kitchen. Before she knew it, Marcelo had taken her into his arms, hugged her gently, and given her one of his best kisses.

"This is a wonderful party," he purred into her ear. "Very romantic."

"It's the Snickers bars. Snickers equal romance." Ellen put her arms around him, stretching out her hands over his shoulder. Her engagement ring sparkled prettily in the sunlight, and she never would have guessed that green would make such a nice backdrop for a diamond. It gave her a new appreciation for photosynthesis.

"You're doing it again, aren't you?" Marcelo asked, chuckling.

"Doing what?"

"Looking at your ring."

"Just kiss me," Ellen said with a smile, but suddenly Will burst into the kitchen and stopped himself before he ran into them.

"Marcelo," he said, looking up, "are you gonna kiss Mommy?"

"If you say it's okay, Will."

"Do it! She likes it!" Will hugged Marcelo around the leg, then ran out of the kitchen, and Ellen smiled.

"Good move, asking permission."

"I know who the boss is." Marcelo kissed her softly and sweetly, then whispered, "*Eu te amo.*"

And for that, Ellen didn't need a translation.

Acknowledgments

I have always been a fan of "write what you know," and this novel arises from a new sideline of mine: newspaper columnist. More than a year ago, I began writing a weekly column for *The Philadelphia Inquirer* called "Chick Wit." (Check it out online at my website, www.scottoline.com.) To stay on point, this novel grew naturally from my observations of the rewards and stresses of a reporter's life—especially in bad economic times—but it's important to head this disclaimer: *Look Again* is fiction.

I made it up, every word.

The newsroom herein is not *The Philadelphia Inquirer*'s, and the fictional owners of the newspaper, as well as its reporters, staff, and editors, are not anyone at the *Inquirer*. And though, like every newspaper, *the Inquirer* has suffered in this economy, the paper is nevertheless thriving due to the talent, hard work, and business savvy of its amazing publisher, Brian Tierney, with the help of Pulitzer Prize winner and great guy Bill Marimow and marketing whiz Ed Mahlman, as well as my friend and editor Sandy Clark, who has been a warm and loving guide in new terrain. I owe much to her, so thanks, Sandy.

I needed to do lots of research for *Look Again,* and I owe a huge debt to the following experts. (Any and all mistakes are mine.) A big hug to brilliant Cheryl Young, Esq., a divorce and family lawyer who is an expert on the intricacies of the law, as well as having an understanding of its very human implications. Big thanks, as always, to Glenn Gilman, Esq., and detective extraordinaire Art Mee. Thank you very much to Dr. John O'Hara of Paoli Hospital, as well as Brad Zerr, who put me in touch with Dr. Glenn Kaplan, head of Pediatric Surgery at Paoli Hospital in Paoli, Pennsylvania, and Tina Saurian, nurse manager of the Maternity Unit. Thanks, too, to Dr. Paul Anisman, chief of Pediatric Cardiology at Nemours/Alfred I. Dupont Hospital for Children in Wilmington, Delaware. Dr. Anisman showed me around and answered all my dumb questions, so I got to see firsthand the wonderful work he and his staff do for babies and children from around the world.

Thanks, too, to Rosina Weber of Drexel University, as well as dear pal and now Harvard prof. James Cavallaro, Esq., and his great wife, Madja Rodigues. Thanks to Dr. Harvey Weiner, director of Academic and Community Relations at Eagleville, for his expertise and for the good work he does for those suffering from drug and alcohol addiction. Thanks, too, to William Fehr, consultant and pal of Mama Scottoline. Thanks to Barbara Capozzi, Karen Volpe, Joey Stampone, Dr. Meredith Snader, Julia Guest, Frank Ferro, Sandy Claus, Sharon Potts, and Janice Davis.

I owe biggest love and thanks to the brilliant and enthusiastic gang at St. Martin's Press, starting with my editor, Jennifer Enderlin, whose comments on an early draft of *Look Again* improved the novel a thousandfold. (Not to mention that she thought of its terrific title, after I had been tearing my hair out for weeks.) And massive hugs all around to genius CEO John Sargent, ultrachic publisher Sally Richardson, the indomitable Matthew Shear, marketing maven Matt Baldacci, musical sales whiz Jeff Capshew, dynamic duo John Murphy and John Karle in publicity, Courtney Fischer, and Brian Heller. I've been overwhelmed by the wonderful energy, talent, and teamwork that St. Martin's has shown me; it's not a publishing house, it's a powerhouse, and they pull together like crazy for a common goal, namely this book. I couldn't feel happier or luckier to be at SMP, and I am indebted to all of you. Thanks so very much.

Deepest thanks and love to my genius agent and dear friend Molly Friedrich, Amazing Paul Cirone, new mom Jacobia Dahm, and to our newest addition, the lovely and talented Lucy Carson! Welcome, Lucy! This little tribe at the Friedrich Agency has nurtured me for a long, long time, and I feel enveloped in their embrace.

Thanks and big love to my wonderful assistant, Laura Leonard, who helps me in every single thing I do and is simply indispensable to my life.

And to my family, who are my life.

LOOK AGAIN

by Lisa Scottoline

About the Author

- A Conversation with Lisa Scottoline
- At Home with the Author

Keep on Reading

- Ideas for Book Groups
- Reading Group Questions

For more reading group suggestions,
visit www.readinggroupgold.com.

 ST. MARTIN'S GRIFFIN

A Conversation with Lisa Scottoline

Is it true that you had the idea for writing *Look Again* when your daughter went to college? What about that experience triggered the idea for this novel?

Yes. *Look Again* started in my mind when I was driving my daughter home from college and, like most parents, we have some of our best conversations in the car, probably because she's a captive audience. And I realized as much as I loved being with my daughter, she was about to graduate from college and I was about to let her go into the great beyond, which doesn't come easily to any of us, least of all an Italian mother. It got me thinking that the fact that I didn't want to let her go was to suggest that somehow I own her, and we don't own our children. The germ of the idea became *Look Again* because the novel really raises the question: Who does this child ultimately belong to? Is it either parent? Or is it actually, in the end, the child himself?

You say you've always been a fan of "write what you know." How did your being a single mom influence *Look Again*?

I've been a single parent almost all of my life, with one really terrific daughter, and I do draw upon my memories of raising her, as well as something more fundamental. I wouldn't suggest that the relationship between a single parent and a child is different or better than that between a parent who is married and has a child, but I do know this much: As a single parent, I was always aware that I was the person my daughter depended on, and I still am. And twenty years ago, I began to write because I wanted to stay home and raise her, and those first few years before I was published, and even thereafter, were some lean times, without any backstop. I'm not complaining, mind you, because on the contrary, those were some of the happiest times of my life. I was raising my daughter during the day and writing novels at night, feeling com-

> *"Writing from what you know has a special meaning when you're writing...what you love."*

pletely fulfilled, from my heart out to my very skin. We
shared a special connectedness, and we still do. For me, I
felt a heightened responsibility to her, since I was the one
on the front line when she got sick, or fell down, or
brought home her first drawing of a rainbow. Writing
from what you know has a special meaning when you're
writing what you live and what you love. All of that love
and life is in *Look Again*.

**This story certainly shares similarities with others you've
written (for one thing, it's another suspenseful page-
turner) but it seems to take on new social issues in a
new way. Do you see *Look Again* as something of a
departure for you?**

Look Again is a departure because the main character
isn't in the legal field, but the real truth is that, though my
books have been defined as legal thrillers, they aren't at
all. I never saw them that way, and I still don't. I see them
as stories about women who are strong, clever, and fully
realized and, as such, get themselves into trouble and
then out again. Maureen Corrigan calls them "female
adventure novels" in her book, and I'm honored by that.
My characters are never defined by their occupation any
more than I am, and I think it's a new, more modern way
to look at character, to look beyond what they do for a
living to who they really are inside, at soul level. In my
own case, I'm a mother before I'm a writer or a lawyer,
and so it was wonderful for me to write about a character
who has trouble seeing herself as a mother initially, not
only because she adopted her child but because she has
some insecurities herself, and then eventually she comes
to understand that if you're mothering, you're a mother.

As for social issues, every single one of my books always
concern questions of what is justice and what is law,
which is just another way of saying what is right and what
is wrong, or what is good and what is evil. This struggle

lies at the heart of Ellen Gleeson's decision whether to keep her son. I loved the complexity of her dilemma, and at the same time loved how accessible it was so that everybody picking up the novel could easily see themselves in her situation, from page one.

When writing your books, do you know how they're going to end, or is the ending a surprise even to you? And what was the case with *Look Again*?

When I started the book, I didn't know how it was going to end; in fact, I didn't even know how it was going to middle. I don't write with an outline. Instead, I write the book one step at a time, and try to determine what would logically happen next. This formula works for me, and I find that it allows me more flexibility when I'm writing and a natural order to the book. It also keeps the writing process very exciting for me, because I'm anxious to figure out the end as well.

What's the question you get most often at your book signing events or from fan e-mails?

I love to answer "where do you get your ideas," and I get that the most. Ask me that the next time you see me. Also I get tons of comments and questions about my characters, which makes me happy because I think relationships are the beating heart of this book, and all my others. I try to write fast-paced, page-turning novels but I'm very conscious of the need for strong, well-developed characters. Thankfully, my readers have really responded to the characters I've created and they seem to be able to relate to them. I try to write about ordinary people who face extraordinary situations and come out the other side even better and stronger, and I suspect that many of my readers can see themselves in these characters. I can, I know.

"I try to write about ordinary people who face extraordinary situations."

What are your favorite elements to explore when writing fiction?

The same things that draw me into books I enjoy reading are the same things that I enjoy writing. I love a book that grabs you and makes you want to turn the page, I love books that have fully realized and well-developed characters, and I love writing about themes that are most important to me, such as love, family, friendship, and the perfect tomato sauce!

What constitutes a satisfying conclusion to you in fiction—whether reading it or writing it?

For me, a satisfying conclusion to a book, whether I'm reading or writing it, is when I'm anxious to reach the end of the book, but sorry when it is actually done.

Your book *Why My Third Husband Will Be a Dog* (available from St. Martin's Press) is a collection of pieces you wrote from your popular *Philadelphia Inquirer* column. What made you want to write this column?

In my novels, my trademark heroine is always a strong, smart, sexy female character, but she isn't a superwoman. She's an ordinary woman whose inner strength, intelligence, and humor make her extraordinary, much like the women I know and, I suspect, much like the women who read my work. I think of these characters as tea bags, as in that great Eleanor Roosevelt quote: "A woman is like a tea bag. You never know how strong she is until she's in hot water." Writing the column gives me the opportunity to celebrate, in a humorous way, the everyday lives of real ordinary, extraordinary women by sharing my own experiences. *Why My Third Husband Will Be a Dog* includes more than seventy vignettes on everything from motherhood and love to wrestling with Spanx and trying to keep our roots touched up. You'll laugh, you'll cry, and you'll swear off pantyhose.

Lisa and Penny, her people-pleasing golden.

APRIL NARBY

> "A woman is like a tea bag. You never know how strong she is until she's in hot water."
> —Eleanor Roosevelt

Lisa with Mimi, the inspiration for Oreo Figaro.

APRIL NARBY

Lisa's to-be-read pile is her dining room.

APRIL NARBY

Lisa with Ruby, her beloved but highly controlling corgi.

APRIL NARBY

Ideas for Book Groups

I am a huge fan of book clubs because it means people are reading and discussing books. Mix that with wine and carbs, and you can't keep me away. I'm deeply grateful to all who read me, and especially honored when my book is chosen by a book club.

I wanted an opportunity to say thank you to those who read me, which gave me the idea of a contest. Every year I hold a book club contest and the winning book club gets a visit from me and a night of fabulous food and good wine. To enter is easy: All you have to do is take a picture of your entire book club with each member holding a copy of my newest hardcover and send it to me by mail or e-mail.

No book club is too small or too big. Don't belong to a book club? Start one. Just grab a loved one, a neighbor, or a friend, and send in your picture of you each holding my newest book. I look forward to coming to your town and wining and dining your group. For more details, just go to www.scottoline.com.

"Don't belong to a book club? Start one."

The Wednesday Evening Ladies' Literary Guild of Mineola, N.Y., submit their photo for Lisa's Book Club Contest.

Tour time is my favorite time of year because I get to
break out my fancy clothes and meet with interesting
and fun readers around the country. The rest of the
year I am a homebody, writing every day, but thrilled
to be able to connect with readers through e-mail. I
read all my e-mail, and answer as much as I can. So,
drop me a line about books, families, pets, love, or
whatever is on your mind at lisa@scottoline.com.
For my latest book and tour information, special
promotions, and updates you can sign up at
www.scottoline.com for my newsletter.

Lisa Scottoline

*The Delaware Valley Book Club,
last year's Book Club Contest winner,
enjoys a night out with Lisa.*

Reading Group Questions

1. *Look Again* really examines the notion of parenthood. What do you think makes someone a parent? Do you think the bond a child has with a nonbiological parent can be as strong as one they would have with a biological parent? Why?

2. Lisa's favorite quote is one from Eleanor Roosevelt: "A woman is like a tea bag. You never know how strong she is until she's in hot water." How does Ellen prove that she is a strong woman? Does Ellen remind you of anyone you know? Could you relate to Ellen, and did you like her? Why or why not?

3. As a journalist, Ellen has a heightened need to find the truth. In this circumstance, was this a good thing, or a bad thing? What would you have done in Ellen's place? Would you have looked for the truth, even if it meant losing your son? What do you think were Ellen's motivations?

4. The idea of "letting go" a child helped shape the whole premise of the book for Lisa, which led her to thinking about who really "owns" a child. Who do you think "owns" a child, and what exactly does that mean? If children actually "own" themselves, what then is the role of parents, and what are the limitations on parenthood?

5. If the child you raised and loved with all your heart actually belonged to someone else, and you were the only one who knew, would you give the child up? How do you think those around you would react? Who in your life would agree with your decision, and who would have done the opposite?

6. How would you describe Ellen's relationship with her father and how do you think it changed over the course of the book? Ellen considered her mother her go-to parent. Do you think everyone has a go-to parent, and what defines them as such?

7. What effect do you think all the drama in Will's life will have on him in the future? Do you think things ultimately worked out to his benefit or detriment and why?

8. How do you feel about single parents adopting children? What kind of, if any, additional requirements do you think should be put on single parents before they can adopt? How do you feel about open adoption? Is it better or worse for children? Is it better or worse for the adoptive parents? The biological parents? At what age do you think a child should be told they are adopted?

SAVE ME

In loving memory of my dear friend Joseph Drabyak,
who understood the pleasure, and the power, of books

You give something up for ev'rything you gain.

—Bob Dylan, "Silvio"

Always use the proper name for everything.
Fear of a name increases fear of the thing itself.

—Albus Dumbledore, *Harry Potter and the Sorcerer's Stone*

Chapter One

Rose McKenna stood against the wall in the noisy cafeteria, having volunteered as lunch mom, which is like a security guard with eye-liner. Two hundred children were talking, thumb-wrestling, or getting ready for recess, because lunch period was almost over. Rose was keeping an eye on her daughter, Melly, who was at the same table as the meanest girl in third grade. If there was any trouble, Rose was going to morph into a mother lion, in clogs.

Melly sat alone at the end of the table, sorting her fruit treats into a disjointed rainbow. She kept her head down, and her wavy, dark blond hair fell into her face, covering the port-wine birthmark on her cheek, a large round blotch like blusher gone haywire. Its medical term was *nevus flammeus,* an angry tangle of blood vessels under the skin, but it was Melly's own personal bull's-eye. It had made her a target for bullies ever since pre-school, and she'd developed tricks to hide it, like keeping her face down, resting her cheek in her hand, or at naptime, lying on her left side, still as a chalk outline at a murder scene. None of the tricks worked forever.

The mean girl's name was Amanda Gigot, and she sat at the opposite end of the table, showing an iPod to her friends. Amanda was the prettiest girl in their class, with the requisite straight blond hair, bright blue eyes, and perfect smile, and she dressed like a teenager in a white jersey tank, pink ruffled skirt, and gold Candie's sandals. Amanda wasn't what people pictured when they heard the term "bully," but wolves could dress in sheep's clothing or Juicy Couture. Amanda was smart and verbal enough to tease at will, which earned her a fear-induced popularity found in elementary schools and fascist dictatorships.

It was early October, but Amanda was already calling Melly names like Spot The Dog and barking whenever she came into the classroom, and Rose prayed it wouldn't get worse. They'd moved here over the summer to get away from the teasing in their old school, where it had gotten so bad that Melly developed stomachaches and eating problems. She'd had trouble sleeping and she'd wake up exhausted, inventing reasons not to go to school. She tested as gifted, but her grades hovered at C's because of her absences. Rose had higher hopes here, since Reesburgh Elementary was in a better school district, with an innovative, anti-bullying curriculum.

She couldn't have wished for a more beautiful school building, either. It was brand-new construction, just finished last August, and the cafeteria was state-of-the-art, with modern skylights, shiny tables with blue plastic seats, and cheery blue-and-white tile walls. Bulletin boards around the room were decorated for Halloween, with construction-paper pumpkins, papier-mâché spiders, and black cats, their tails stiff as exclamation points. A wall clock covered with fake cobwebs read 11:20, and most of the kids were stowing their lunchboxes in the plastic bins for each homeroom and leaving through the doors to the playground, on the left.

Rose checked Melly's table, and was dismayed. Amanda and her friends Emily and Danielle were finishing their sandwiches, but Melly's lunch remained untouched in her purple Harry Potter lunchbox. The gifted teacher, Kristen Canton, had emailed Rose that Melly sometimes didn't eat at lunch and waited out the period in the handicapped bathroom, so Rose had volunteered as lunch mom to see what was going on. She couldn't ignore it, but she didn't want to overreact, walking a familiar parental tightrope.

"Oh no, I spilled!" cried a little girl whose milk carton tipped over, splashing onto the floor.

"It's okay, honey." Rose went over, grabbed a paper napkin, and swabbed up the milk. "Put your tray away. Then you can go out."

Rose tossed out the soggy napkin, then heard a commotion behind her and turned around, stricken at the sight. Amanda was dabbing grape jelly onto her cheek, making a replica of Melly's birthmark. Everyone at the table was giggling, and kids on their way out pointed and laughed. Melly was running from the cafeteria, her long hair flying. She was heading toward the exit for the handicapped bathroom, on the right.

"Melly, wait!" Rose called out, but Melly was already past her, so she went back to the lunch table. "Amanda, what are you doing? That's not nice."

Amanda tilted her face down to hide her smile, but Emily and Danielle stopped laughing, their faces reddening.

"I didn't do anything." Emily's lower lip began to pucker, and Danielle shook her head, with its long, dark braid.

"Me, neither," she said. The other girls scattered, and the rest of the kids hustled out to recess.

"You girls laughed," Rose said, pained. "That's not right, and you should know that. You're making fun of her." She turned to Amanda, who was wiping off the jelly with a napkin. "Amanda, don't you understand how hurtful you're being? Can't you put yourself in Melly's shoes? She can't help the way she is, nobody can."

Amanda didn't reply, setting down the crumpled napkin.

"Look at that bulletin board. See what it says?" Rose pointed to the Building Blocks of Character poster, with its glittery letters that read CARING COMPASSION COMMUNITY, from Reesburgh's anti-bullying curriculum. "Teasing isn't caring or compassionate, and—"

"What's going on?" someone called out, and Rose looked up to see the other lunch mom hurrying over. She had on a denim dress and sandals, and wore her highlighted hair short. "Excuse me, we have to get these girls out to recess."

"Did you see what just happened?"

"No, I missed it."

"Well, Amanda was teasing and—"

Amanda interrupted, "Hi, Mrs. Douglas."

"Hi, Amanda." The lunch mom turned to Rose. "We have to get everybody outside, so the kitchen can get ready for B lunch." She gestured behind her, where the last students were leaving the cafeteria. "See? Time to go."

"I know, but Amanda was teasing my daughter, Melly, so I was talking to her about it."

"You're new, right? I'm Terry Douglas. Have you ever been lunch mom before?"

"No."

"So you don't know the procedures. The lunch moms aren't supposed to discipline the students."

"I'm not disciplining them. I'm just talking to them."

"Whatever, it's not going well." Terry nodded toward Emily, just as a tear rolled down the little girl's cheek.

"Oh, jeez, sorry." Rose didn't think she'd been stern, but she was tired and maybe she'd sounded cranky. She'd been up late with baby John, who had another ear infection, and she'd felt guilty taking him to a sitter's this morning so she could be lunch mom. He was only ten months old, and Rose was still getting the hang of mothering two children. Most of the time she felt torn in half, taking care of one child at the expense of the other, like the maternal equivalent of robbing Peter to pay Paul. "Terry, the thing is, this school has a strict zero-tolerance policy against bullying, and the kids need to learn it. All the kids. The kids who tease, as well as the allies, the kids who laugh and think it's funny."

"Nevertheless, when there's a disciplinary issue, the procedure is for the lunch mom to tell a teacher. Mrs. Snyder is out on the playground. These girls should go out to recess, and you should take it up with her."

"Can I just finish what I was saying to them? That's all this requires." Rose didn't want to make it bigger, for Melly's sake. She could already hear the kids calling her a tattletale.

"Then I'll go get her myself." Terry turned on her heel and walked away, and the cafeteria fell silent except for the clatter of trays and silverware in the kitchen.

Rose faced the table. "Amanda," she began, dialing back her tone, "you have to understand that teasing is bullying. Words can hurt as much as a punch."

"You're not allowed to yell at me! Mrs. Douglas said!"

Rose blinked, surprised. She'd be damned if she'd be intimidated by somebody in a Hannah Montana headband. "I'm not yelling at you," she said calmly.

"I'm going to recess!" Amanda jumped to her feet, startling Emily and Danielle.

Suddenly, something exploded in the kitchen. A searing white light flashed in the kitchen doorway. Rose turned toward the ear-splitting *boom*! The kitchen wall flew apart, spraying shards of tile, wood, and wallboard everywhere.

A shockwave knocked Rose off her feet. A fireball billowed into the cafeteria.

And everything went black and silent.

Chapter Two

Rose woke up lying on the floor against the wall. She opened her eyes. Overhead sprinklers poured water, like cold rain. Acrid black smoke clouded the air. She rolled over onto wet debris and broken glass. Her head pounded. Her ears rang.

what happened what is going on

She propped herself up to a sitting position, in the water. Her face hurt. She touched her cheek. Fresh blood covered her fingerpads. Dust caked her polo shirt and khaki capris, getting drenched from the sprinklers. Her legs splayed out in front of her, with a bloody cut on her ankle. She shook her head to clear her brain. She couldn't hear anything but the ringing in her ears.

She looked through the water and smoke. An inferno raged in the kitchen. Fire blazed from its doors. Hot orange flames spread upward. A jagged hole gaped in the kitchen wall. Rebar twisted from it like black tentacles. Wood studs lay splintered and broken.

Rose couldn't process what she was seeing. The perfect suburban cafeteria was a war zone. Acoustic tiles hung from the ceiling. Shattered skylights rained glass shards. The air felt furnace-hot. A burning smell filled her nostrils. Bits of flaming material blew around like a nightmare blizzard.

The kids!

Rose looked wildly around through the smoke. Amanda sat stunned on the floor nearby, then got up stiffly. Her mouth formed a terrified circle. Tears ran down her face. A cut bled on her arm. Emily lay near the door, crying in a little heap on the floor, like dirty laundry. Only Danielle was in motion, fleeing toward the door.

Suddenly, Rose could hear everything. Amanda was screaming. Emily was sobbing. Alarm bells were ringing. Fire roaring, sprinklers whirring, water *whoosh*ing. Flames billowed from the kitchen. Whoever was in there would have been killed. She had to get the kids out before they were, too.

Oh my God. Melly.

Rose stumbled to her feet, unsteady. Her knees buckled. Her head thundered. The room whirled. She struggled to get back up. The handicapped bathroom was across from the kitchen, where the explosion had been. Fear gripped her heart. Melly could have been killed in the blast.

Please God no.

Rose raced through the other possibilities. Melly could be trapped in the bathroom. If she hadn't gotten out, no one would come to save her. No one knew she was in the bathroom. Even if she got out of the bathroom, she wouldn't know how to get out of the building.

Rose staggered to her feet, panicky. She didn't know what to do. The smoke was getting thicker, the air hotter. Flames licked from the kitchen doors into the cafeteria. A skylight popped, showering glass.

Amanda and Emily were slowly moving around. Screaming. Crying. Stunned. They needed help. They were right in front of her. They were just kids. They couldn't save themselves.

Melly was in the bathroom, far away. Out the opposite side of the cafeteria and down the hall, at the very end.

Rose's mind reeled. If she got Amanda and Emily out of the cafeteria to the playground, she wouldn't have time to go after Melly. If she went to save Melly, she'd have to leave Amanda and Emily, who were right in front of her. She couldn't do that, and she couldn't leave her own child to die.

It was the choice from hell, in hell.

Rose could save Melly, or she could save Amanda and Emily. She had to choose.

Now.

Chapter Three

"Come on!" Rose grabbed Amanda by the arm. She didn't choose, she merely acted. Danielle was already running out of the cafeteria.

"Mommy!" Amanda screamed. Smoke blew everywhere. Fire licked across the ceiling, superheating the air. Tiles dropped in flames. Sprinklers whirred, making more smoke.

"We have to get out, after Danielle!" Rose kept one hand on Amanda and ran with her to Emily, lying on the floor by the exit, crying.

"Mommy!" Amanda screamed again, as Rose hoisted Emily up by her arm. Her leg was cut, but she wasn't seriously injured.

"Come on! We have to go!" Rose hurried Amanda and Emily toward the exit doors, which were propped open. The hallway beyond was smoky and packed with older kids, Danielle among them, hurrying toward the doors to the playground. A teacher with blond hair stood at the threshold to the playground, getting kids outside.

"Go to the playground!" Rose whipped Amanda and Emily into the hallway, where they were swept along with the others. "Follow Danielle! Run! I have to get Melly!"

Rose turned around and ran back into the fiery cafeteria, dodging flaming tiles. Heat seared her throat. Smoke stung her nose and eyes.

Water soaked her long hair and clothes. A ceiling stud crashed. Insulation flared.

She tore past the fireball in the kitchen, almost slipping on the wet floor. She ran through the cafeteria, bolted through the exit doors, and veered around the corner into the hallway. She skidded to a stop, stunned. Fire blocked her path.

No, no, no!

The hallway ceiling had collapsed. Debris burned on the floor. Smoke billowed black and thick. Sprinklers squirted sideways, uselessly. Aluminum ductwork hung at bizarre angles. The handicapped bathroom was on the other side. The flames blazed too high to jump and would get higher still. Ceiling tiles, insulation, and studs burned.

Rose spotted a piece of wood sticking out of the debris, grabbed the end, and yanked. It came free, trailing burning debris. She coughed and coughed. Tears flowed from her eyes. She swung the stud like a flaming baseball bat, knocking aside smoky insulation to make a path.

Sparks flew. Smoke filled her nose. She spit dry filth from her mouth. Stirring the debris fed the fire. It roared in response.

She redoubled her efforts, whacking to clear a path. She could barely see or breathe. Her throat felt tight, closing. Her eyes streamed with tears. The stud caught fire at the end. She kept whacking until she'd cleared a fiery path. If she waited any longer, she wouldn't be able to run through.

She dropped the stud, got a running start, and leapt over the fire. Flames licked at her clogs and ankles but she was too adrenalized to feel anything. She charged ahead, running through an oven. It lasted forever, but she got through, the fire behind her.

She raced through the smoke to the end of the hall. A conflagration raged to her left, the kitchen and the teachers' lounge ablaze.

She reached the handicapped bathroom. Smoke was being sucked under its door. Melly would suffocate.

"Melly!" Rose tried the lever, hot to the touch. The door was locked, so Melly had to be inside.

"Melly!" Rose shrieked, frantic. She yanked on the lever. It didn't open. Tears of fright poured down her cheeks. She coughed and coughed. Black smoke rolled along the floor, enveloping her.

Fire flared closer. She pulled on the lever with all her might. She felt hotter and hotter. She couldn't breathe, her lungs choked with smoke.

"Melly!" Rose screamed, at the top of her lungs.

There was no reply.

Chapter Four

"Help!" Rose screamed. Nobody was in the corridor. The alarm bells rang continuously. Sirens sounded far away. She was on her own.

She threw herself against the bathroom door. It didn't budge. She raked at the hinges to see if she could take the door off, but no. She told herself to stay in control. She couldn't surrender to panic. She coughed and coughed. Tears blurred her vision.

She knelt down to look at the lever. It had a hole underneath. It locked from the inside, by pushing a button. She could unlock it if she could stick something in the hole. She tried her finger. The hole was too small. She needed something thin enough to fit through.

She looked wildly around. Smoke billowed everywhere. The blaze in the teachers' lounge was spreading. She had to hurry. She got up, bolted to the library, and burst through the doors. Smoke filtered the air, less than in the hallway.

She ran to the librarian's desk and tore open a drawer. It held pens, pencils, rulers, orange Tic-Tacs. She grabbed a pair of scissors. The blades were too big. She threw them aside. She whirled around, then saw a coat rack holding a red cardigan and a few wire hangers.

She ran to the rack, snatched off one of the hangers, and twisted it out of shape on the run. She bolted out of the library, horrified at the sight in the hallway. The fire was spreading to the handicapped bathroom. Fingers of flames stretched from the teachers' lounge. Black smoke enclosed the door.

"Melly!" Rose shrieked, agonized. She ran to the bathroom and threw herself on her knees in front of the door. She couldn't see the hole for the smoke and her tears.

She wrenched the hanger out of shape, slicing her palm with the pointy end. She bent the wire and tried to shove the end into the hole. Her hand shook too much. She tried again and again, her face next to the lever. She finally rammed it through. She felt a *click*.

She yanked on the lever. The door opened wide. Heat surged behind her, the flames sucked forward by new oxygen. Smoke filled the bathroom.

"Melly!" Rose screamed, but Melly sat slumped beside the toilet in the clouds of smoke, her head to the side, unmoving. Her arms hung down. Her feet flopped apart.

Rose rushed to her side and scooped her up. She couldn't tell if Melly was breathing, but black soot covered her cheeks and ringed her nostrils and mouth. Her body was limp, her eyes closed. Rose knew CPR but had to get her out while she still could.

She gathered Melly up, staggered to her feet, and ran out of the smoky bathroom. She bolted to the library, burst through the doors, and tore through the stacks to the exit, which led her down one smoky hallway, then another. She'd never been in that part of the school. She followed the sound of teachers shouting. Melly remained silent, lifeless.

Rose barreled toward the noise and saw an EXIT sign over double doors. Twenty feet away, then ten. Then five. She exploded through the doors into a stairwell, where a teacher was evacuating older kids, hurrying down the concrete stairs toward the exit for the teachers' parking lot.

"It's my daughter!" Rose shouted on the run, and the teacher blanched.

"Let her through!" she called to the kids, who parted as Rose wedged her way out of the exit and into the sunshine.

"Help!" Rose screamed, and the school librarian and a teacher came running. Smoke clouded the parking lot, and beyond it thronged teachers, staff, and students, abuzz with shouting, crying, and head counts.

Rose raced to a patch of grass, laid Melly on the ground, and put an ear to her chest to listen for a heartbeat. She couldn't hear breathing because the alarms were too loud. She put her cheek to Melly's face to feel breathing, but no. She began CPR, tilting Melly's head back, opening her mouth, and breathing for her, ignoring the stench of smoke on her lips.

Suddenly, Melly started coughing. Soot puffed from her mouth, a horrifying sight.

"Honey!" Rose cried with joy, but Melly's eyelids fluttered and her eyes rolled backwards into her head. "Melly, wake up! Please!" She shook Melly to rouse her, to no avail.

"Here's the ambulance!" The school librarian touched Rose's arm. The teacher stood behind. "Let us help."

"Thanks!" Rose scooped Melly into her arms, and the librarian steadied her as they ran through the parked cars.

The crowd surged forward, craning their necks, but the teacher and custodians with walkie-talkies shooed them back. Parents and neighbors held up cell phones and BlackBerrys, snapping pictures and taking videos. The ambulance sped onto the long driveway, and people shouted to flag it down until it veered into the teachers' parking lot.

Rose and the librarian hustled to meet the ambulance, which zoomed to a stop. A paramedic in a black uniform jumped from the cab and raced toward Melly. The back doors flew open, and two other uniformed paramedics, a male and a female, hustled out with a stretcher and a portable oxygen tank.

"She's my daughter." Rose met a male paramedic at the curb. "She's breathing but she's not conscious."

"I got her." The male paramedic took Melly from Rose as the two others materialized at his side. He laid Melly on the cushioned stretcher while the others hurried to fit a translucent oxygen mask over her face and secure her with two orange straps. They all rushed the stretcher to the ambulance, sliding it inside.

Rose was about to climb in behind, but shouted to the librarian,

"Please get word to my husband, Leo Ingrassia. He's a lawyer, his office is in King of Prussia."

"Will do!"

Rose hoisted herself inside the ambulance, hurried to Melly's side, and picked up her hand. It felt limp and oddly cool to the touch, but she clung to it, making a human tether to keep Melly in this world.

Please God let her live.

Chapter Five

"I'm locking, Jim!" the female paramedic shouted to the driver, to be heard over the sirens and the radio crackling in the cab. She twisted a large handle under the steel corrugation on the ambulance doors. "Go, go, go!"

"Is my daughter going to be okay?" Rose shouted, lifting up her oxygen mask to speak. They'd made her wear one and sit belted to a cushioned jump seat, but she could still reach Melly's hand. She held on as the ambulance lurched off. "I did CPR, and she was awake. Why is she unconscious?"

"Please keep your mask on." The female paramedic hurried to Melly's side. "You can ask the ER doc all your questions."

The male paramedic scrambled to Rose, shouting, "Let me see that ankle, Mom."

"I'm fine," Rose yelled, under her mask. "Take care of her, please."

"We have to treat you, too. You've got burns on your ankle and hand." The male paramedic slipped on exam gloves, grabbed a square white bag that read ROEHAMPTON STERILE BURNS DRESSING, and squatted at Rose's feet. "I'll start here. This might be uncomfortable."

"Please, take care of my daughter instead."

"My partner has her, don't worry. We have to treat you. It's the law." The male paramedic zipped open the white bag, but Rose kept her eyes glued to Melly, who looked so pale under the oxygen mask. The female paramedic was attaching circular electrodes to her chest, leading to an EKG monitor that began spitting out a spiky graph, almost instantly.

Rose shouted to the female paramedic, "She was trapped in a bathroom full of smoke. That means she was deprived of oxygen. How do you know if there's brain damage?"

"I'm doing everything I can." The female paramedic grabbed a transparent saline bag, hung it on a hook, and reached for Melly's hand, glancing over at Rose. "Sorry, may I have her hand? I need to start an IV line."

"Sure." Rose let go of Melly's hand, trying not to tear up. She held onto her stretcher instead, watching the female paramedic tapping Melly's skin to find a vein, then sliding the IV needle in, with a speed born of skill and practice.

"I'm dressing your burn now." The male paramedic unrolled yellow dressing and wrapped it around her ankle, keeping his balance in the moving ambulance. "It doesn't look too bad."

"Do you think my daughter has brain damage?" Rose shouted at him, through her mask. "Is that why she's unconscious?"

"Don't worry, the docs will do everything they can. Reesburgh is a great trauma center. Our job is to get her ready, so they can hit the ground running."

Rose could see they needed to work, so she shut up and kept an eye on Melly while the male paramedic finished dressing the burns on her ankle. The female paramedic was wrapping a blood pressure cuff around Melly's arm, but Melly's eyes were still closed, and she didn't move or react. A layer of coarse soot blanketed her face, arms, and legs, obscuring the Gothic lettering on her Harry Potter T-shirt and the flowery pattern of her shorts. A deep gash bled through her hairline, blackening its dark blond strands. Her eyelids looked swollen, and tears made heartbreaking tracks in the filth on her cheeks.

"Here, Mom," the male paramedic said, offering her a Kleenex.

Rose hadn't known she was crying. She nodded thanks, swabbing at her eyes, and the Kleenex got damp and sooty. The female paramedic blocked Melly from view, and the male paramedic dressed the burn on Rose's hand. She looked around the back of the ambulance, noticing things that didn't matter:

The windows in the back doors were tiny. There were six round dome lights in the ceiling. The first-aid bag was orange, and the plastic defibrillator was yellow. A half-open cabinet held plush teddy bears, with the sales tags still on.

Rose felt a wave of sadness. She wouldn't have expected to find toys in an ambulance, but she should have. Children got hurt every day in this world. Now it was her child, and her world.

Her gaze fell on a chart posted above eye-level. It read, EMERGENCY MEDICAL SERVICES FOR CHILDREN, and she found the line for School Age, 6–12 Years. It read, Respiratory Rate, 18–30. Heart Rate, 70–120. Systolic Blood B/P, Over 80. She looked over at the monitors attached to Melly, displaying her vital signs in multi-colored digits, but she wasn't able to decipher them.

She looked at the other wall, but there was only another chart. PEDIATRIC ASSESSMENT, said the top, and underneath, GLASGOW COMA SCALE. She read the three criteria for a coma. Eye Opening, Best Verbal Response, and Best Motor Response. The chart assigned point values to each of the criteria, and she applied the criteria to Melly, like a nightmare laundry list. Melly's eyes remained closed. Zero points. She had no verbal response. Zero points. She had no motor response. Zero points. Melly had no points. Zero, zero, zero.

Rose felt a bolt of fright. New tears filled her eyes. She craned her neck but couldn't see Melly. The female paramedic was bent over her, lifting her eyelid and shining a light in her pupils.

Rose kept her fingertips on the stainless steel of Melly's stretcher. The male paramedic dressed the burn on her hand. The female paramedic shifted position, and Melly's hand popped into view. Blood and bruises covered her little palm, and Rose realized that Melly must have bloodied her hands, banging on the bathroom door. Trying to get out. Pounding with her fists. Waiting to be rescued. Calling for her mother.

Mommy!

Rose wanted to scream at herself. If she had run to the handicapped bathroom first, Melly would be fine now. It was a matter of time, of minutes and seconds. Of oxygen deprivation to the brain. Of points on the Glasgow Coma Scale. Why had she spent those minutes on Amanda, and not on her own daughter? Why had she chosen to save Amanda over Melly?

She held tight to Melly's stretcher. Any mother would have saved her own child. So what if Amanda was standing closer? What difference did that make? What was she thinking?

Rose wiped her eyes. She'd thought she hadn't chosen, but she had, and she'd chosen wrong. She loved Melly more than life. If Melly didn't come through this, she would never forgive herself. She could never justify it to herself or Leo. He was Melly's stepfather, but he loved her like his own. He'd been her only father since she was four, when her father died. A wave of guilt washed over Rose, and she felt as if she were drowning in it, going under.

The ambulance raced down Allen Road. The hospital was only twenty minutes away. She tried not to count the seconds. The male paramedic finished treating the cut on her cheek. Her chest felt tight. She wasn't even sure she was breathing. She could only pray.

"Here we are, good luck!" The male paramedic hurried to the door, the ambulance lurched to a stop, and everything else happened in a blur. The back doors of the ambulance opened into the blinding sun, and the paramedics hurried Melly's stretcher out of the back, with Rose right behind, with portable oxygen. The legs on the stretcher snapped down, and they were all running to the entrance of the emergency department, where the doors slid open and a crowd of medical personnel fluttered to them like angels, bearing Melly away.

Rose didn't let go of her until the very last minute.

Chapter Six

Rose slumped in a cushioned seat, alone in the empty waiting room. Smoke clung to her damp clothes and hair. Her throat felt dry, and her eyes smarted despite the drops they'd given her. Melly had been in one of the ER examination rooms for half an hour, and still no word. The doctors hadn't wanted to discuss Melly's condition until they'd examined her thoroughly, and Rose had been sent to the waiting room after the nurses had cleaned her up and given her a tetanus shot. She'd left her purse and cell phone in the car, so she'd used the hospital phone to call the sitter, who'd said she could stay with John until tonight, if needed.

Rose sighed, telling herself to stay calm. Framed prints of generic pastures covered the pastel blue walls, and the sun streamed through the windows, whiting out the screen of the muted TV. She didn't bother picking up the wrinkled copies of *People, Time,* or the other magazines on the coffee table. She watched idly as dust motes floated through a shaft of sunlight, rudderless. A pot of stale decaf sat in a Bunn coffeemaker on a side table.

Her gaze fell to her lap. Her right hand was freshly bandaged, and the left had residual soot etched into the back of her hand, black and thick as ground peppercorns. She flashed on Melly, covered with the same grime, and imagined her beating on the bathroom door, calling out, like Amanda.

Mommy!

Rose got up and crossed to the bathroom, walking gingerly because of the bandage on her ankle. She closed the door behind her, using her good hand to flick on the light. A mirror hung over the sink, and in her reflection, she looked like a cleaned-up coal miner. Soot underlined her crow's feet, the wrinkles under her eyes, and each nostril, like parentheses. A small cut on her left cheek glistened with Neosporin, and her forehead was as gray as a stormcloud. Her long, dark hair was a dirty mop, weighed down by dust, water, and filth.

She didn't want to miss the doctor, so she opened the bathroom door in case he came back. She twisted on the faucets, popped the bulb of antibacterial soap, and washed her face as best she could. She dried off with paper towels, checked the mirror again. She looked nothing like the model she'd once been, if only in catalogs. Her blue eyes, wide-set, large, and bloodshot, tilted down at the corners, and her nose, slim and straight, had turned red at its bony tip, from crying. Her mouth, wide with thinnish lips, was drawn into a frown. She remembered what her ex-husband Bernardo always used to say.

You look like somebody's mom.

She sighed at the memory, bittersweet. Bernardo Cadiz was a handsome photographer she'd met on a shoot, and he'd always wanted more for her career, a better agent, bigger bookings, an exclusive with Almay or Dove. Rose knew she wasn't pretty enough for the big leagues, though her Black Irish features and wholesome suburban look made her perfect for the Land's End and L.L. Bean catalogs, and she regularly dolled-up as Snow White to model adult Halloween costumes. She wasn't vain about her looks, because they were God-given; she viewed them as a way to earn a living. She'd never wanted a big career; what she really wanted was to *be* somebody's mom, and when they'd gotten married, Bernardo had promised he'd leave behind his partying ways and downtown friends. What had happened after Melly was born surprised no one but her.

"Rose?" a voice called out, and she turned to see her husband, Leo, looking around the waiting room for her. "Honey?"

"In here," Rose called back, her heart full at the sight of him. If Bernardo Cadiz had been all style, Leo Ingrassia was all substance, and he still looked like the Italian-American altar boy and second-string left tackle he'd been in high school. He was average height, stocky and powerfully built, and his face was honest and open, with rich brown eyes, round in shape, a coarse nose that was on the big side, and a full, generous mouth. His jet-black hair was thick, curly, and unruly, which suited him, because he was the least vain person she'd ever known.

"My God, honey! Look at you!" Leo's eyes went wide with alarm, and he threw open his arms, reaching for her. "Are you okay? How's Melly?"

"I don't know, it's awful." Rose buried herself in his embrace, laying her cheek against the stiff starch of his oxford shirt.

"I was on the way home when Julie called. Where is she? What happened?"

"She's with the doctors." Rose hid her face in his shoulder. "She wasn't conscious, and I'm worried about brain damage."

"But they said you rescued her."

"No, well, kind of." Rose faltered, tears springing to her eyes. She didn't know how he'd react if he knew she hadn't gone immediately to Melly. She pulled away. "Leo, listen—"

Suddenly someone cleared his throat, and they turned around. A doctor she didn't recognize entered the waiting room, his expression grave behind his steel-rimmed glasses. He had the lean look of a runner, and he was tall, African-American, and in his late fifties, the short hair at his temples shot through with silver.

"Hello," the doctor said. "Are you the parents of Melinda Cadiz, the little girl from the school fire?"

"Yes," Rose answered, reaching for Leo.

"I'm Dr. Holloeri." He extended his hand and broke into a smile. "Your daughter is resting comfortably, and she's looking good, so far."

"Thank God!" Rose's body flooded with relief. Tears filled her eyes but she blinked them away.

"Leo Ingrassia." He shook the doctor's hand. "Doc, what's the matter with her? Is there brain damage?"

"No," Dr. Holloeri answered. "However, she suffered significant smoke inhalation. It causes the throat to swell, restricting the airflow to the lungs, and this can be dangerous in a child. There can be swelling in the throat and trachea for up to forty-eight hours after exposure. We need to monitor her levels for the next day or so."

Rose wiped her wet eyes, and Leo put his arm around her.

Dr. Holloeri continued, "One concern would be if she were exposed to fumes from plastics or other toxic materials. That can cause problems as she gets older, but I won't go into the technicalities. Right now she looks good."

"Can we see her?" Rose asked, recovering.

"Not yet. She's asleep, and we gave her a sedative."

"A sedative, is that a good idea?" Leo asked, and Dr. Holloeri turned to him.

"Yes. The sedation is light, and her physical symptoms are uncomfortable."

"Can't we see her, anyway?" Rose asked, again. "Even if she's sleeping? It's for my sake, not hers."

"Mom, you'll do her more good to go home now, clean up, and come back." Dr. Holloeri glanced at the wall clock. "I figure, say, about two hours. By then, she'll be coming around, looking for you. After she wakes up, she'll want you for the duration, and I'm guessing you'll want that, too."

"I do."

"Good." Dr. Holloeri touched Rose on the shoulder, and his eyes softened behind his no-nonsense glasses. "You saved your daughter's life today. If she'd spent another five minutes in that smoke, we'd be having a much different conversation."

Leo looked over, with a surprised smile. "Babe, jeez. That's amazing."

"No, not really." Rose reddened, secretly ashamed. She felt like an imposter, knowing that she'd rolled the dice with her daughter's life. It was dumb luck that had saved Melly.

"Okay, take care." Dr. Holloeri smiled. "I ought to get back to work."

"Thanks so much." Rose gave him a hug.

"Yes, thanks." Leo shook his hand again. "We really appreciate all you've done for her."

"You're very welcome. Stay well, folks." Dr. Holloeri left the waiting room, and Rose and Leo followed, bade him another good-bye, and passed through the automatic doors at the ER exit.

Rose took Leo's arm as they stepped outside, and her nose and throat stung in the humid air, an Indian summer that just wouldn't quit. The sun burned over the pin oaks surrounding the entrance, their large, spiky leaves turned splashy red and rich rust. They shed brittle leaves on the walkway, where a small crowd stood, their heads swiveling to Rose and Leo. One of them was a TV anchorwoman in thick foundation and a bright red suit.

"Hello, Ms. McKenna!" the TV anchorwoman called out, flashing a camera-ready smile. She made a beeline for them, a microphone in her manicured hand, and she was followed by a producer-type and a photographer, who rested a bulky videocamera on his shoulder. "I'm Tanya Robertson, at Channel 9. I'm so honored to meet you. You're so brave!"

"Oh, no, please." Rose stiffened, aware that nurses, orderlies, and a uniformed security guard were watching, since Reesburgh didn't get many visits from TV celebrities.

"Okay if we film?" Tanya grinned, raising her microphone. Behind her, the cameraman pressed a button with his thumb, and the videocamera whirred to life.

"No, please, I'm a mess." Rose put up a hand.

"Come on, you look great. How's your daughter Melinda? Her nickname's Melly, right? Is she out of the woods?"

"She's much better, thanks." Rose looked around for an escape route, but the producer and cameraman blocked the path.

"We understand that you saved her life. Tell us how."

"No, thanks." Rose wanted to forget about today, not relive it for TV.

"Aw, my wife is too modest." Leo squeezed her tight. "In five more minutes, our daughter would have been dead."

"Really?" Tanya's mascaraed eyes flew open, and the cameraman filmed away, the black lens hood moving forward and back. "Ms. McKenna, what did you do to save your daughter?"

"Nothing, no. Please." Rose cringed.

"Tell us!"

"I did what any mother would do." Rose took Leo's arm. "Now, excuse us. We have to go."

"But you're a hero, a hero mom!" Tanya practically cheered. "Don't be so modest. Your hubby's right."

"Let's go, hubby." Rose walked past her, and Leo fell into step.

"Wait, wait!" Tanya hurried to follow them, keeping her microphone pointed at Rose, her crew at her heels. "Ms. McKenna, your story is the silver lining. There were three fatalities in the explosion, a teacher and two cafeteria workers."

Rose stopped in her tracks, horrified. Leo looked over, equally stricken, but he got them moving when the TV reporter started in again.

"Ms. McKenna, your story can lift so many hearts. How did you feel when you rescued your daughter?"

"Please, no questions," Rose answered, shaken. She was thinking how easily it could have been Melly who'd died today.

"No comment," Leo said, on the fly, and they left Tanya talking into the camera, saying:

"Some people think we report only bad news, but here's some good. Today at Reesburgh Elementary, a hero mom risked her life to save her daughter. That's our reluctant hero, leaving the hospital, and her name is . . ."

Rose walked down the pavement with Leo and spotted Melly's teacher, Jane Nuru, hustling from the parking lot toward them, waving.

"Rose, Leo!" Mrs. Nuru called out, and Rose waved back, touched that she'd come. Mrs. Nuru was usually in complete control, but her forehead was knit with anxiety, her graying topknot slipped off her head sideways, and her blousy blue pantsuit looked rumpled. She met them on the walkway with a brief hug. "Rose, you poor thing! How are you and Melly?"

"Melly will be fine, thanks. She'll have to stay a day or two, because of the smoke inhalation, but she's okay."

"Thank God!" Mrs. Nuru shook her head, jiggling her Halloween earrings, funky skeletons on a string. "I was so concerned about her, and so was Mr. Rodriguez. We tried to reach you, but there was no answer on your cell. What happened?"

"She was in the bathroom, but she's fine now." Rose didn't go into detail because Tanya and her TV crew were standing close enough to eavesdrop. "I'll explain another time."

"And are you okay?" Mrs. Nuru's eyes flashed a worried blue. "What's the cut on your face?"

"Fine, it's all nothing."

"Goodness!" Mrs. Nuru looked at Leo, her hand fluttering to her chest. "Leo, would you ever think? What a tragedy."

Leo shook his head. "It's terrible. Both of my girls went through hell, and three people are dead."

"It's just horrible. Horrible!" Mrs. Nuru pursed her lips, her pinkish lipstick almost gone. "Marylou Battle was the teacher; she's been subbing since her retirement. My sons had her, everybody loved her. She was in the teachers' lounge. The cafeteria workers were Serena Perez and Ellen Conze. They were killed instantly in the explosion."

"That's awful." Rose felt stricken. She didn't know them, but she felt for their families, heartbroken today.

"So, Rose, tell me." Mrs. Nuru cocked her head. "What happened to Amanda? When I left, they didn't know where she was."

Rose blinked. "What do you mean?"

"The last time anybody saw Amanda, she was with you."

Chapter Seven

"Amanda ran out to the playground, with the others," Rose answered, puzzled.

"No, she didn't. We hadn't found her, at least as of twenty minutes ago, when I left to come here." Mrs. Nuru's face fell into deep lines, draping her downturned mouth. "So far, she and Melly are the only two in our class not accounted for. I had my class list, I did the head count. It was thirteen girls, twelve boys, with Raheem absent, from strep." Mrs. Nuru turned to Leo again. "We drill on these emergency procedures. We do fire drills, lockdown drills, sheltering drills. We have a fire drill once a month, it's state law, but we've only had one in the new building, and everything's different when it's a real fire."

"Naturally." Leo nodded, but Mrs. Nuru didn't need encouragement to continue, so nervous that her words almost ran into each other.

"We can't account for Amanda yet. We haven't found her. Nobody knows anything about her. It scares me half to death. Mr. Rodriguez is beside himself. You say she went to the playground?"

"Amanda? Yes. She went to the playground with Emily. They ran out after Danielle."

"Really?" Mrs. Nuru's forehead furrowed again. "Emily and Danielle were with the others, but not Amanda."

"Did you ask Emily? She was with Amanda. She should know."

"We didn't get to speak with her. She and Danielle were taken to their family doctors. It's confusing, back at school. All the parents were caught unawares. Some moms have already picked up, and others gave verbal approval to send their children home with friends. Excuse me." Mrs. Nuru slid a phone from her pocket, hit a button, and started texting. "I'm telling Mr. Rodriguez you don't know where Amanda is."

"Maybe she went home with one of her brothers?" Rose was thinking aloud. "They're older, and Eileen works, doesn't she?" She had seen Amanda's mother, Eileen Gigot, on Parents' Night, but they hadn't met. By then, the bullying had started, and Rose had called Eileen to talk about it, but she hadn't gotten a return call. "Amanda has a slew of friends in class, too. She could have gone home with any one of them."

Leo looked over. "What caused the explosion, Mrs. Nuru?"

"Don't know yet. The bomb squad was there when I left, and there were fifteen firetrucks putting out the fire."

"Bomb squad?" Leo shook his head, incredulous. "We used to get bomb scares in Worhawk, but I didn't think Reesburgh—"

"Excuse me, wait, Leo." Mrs. Nuru turned to Rose, her phone in hand. "Tell me, did you actually *see* Amanda go to the playground?"

"No, not exactly." Rose lowered her voice so Tanya couldn't hear. "I brought her and Emily to the hallway, to go out with the other kids going toward the playground. A teacher was there, at the doorway to the playground."

"Who? Which teacher?"

"I don't know. I didn't know her."

"What did she look like? Short hair, long hair?"

"Blond. That's all I saw." Rose rubbed her forehead, suddenly tired. "I'd recognize her if I saw her."

"I don't understand." Mrs. Nuru's eyes narrowed. "Did you take Amanda and Emily to the playground, yourself?"

"No, I didn't. I brought them to the hallway."

"Did you have Melly with you?"

"No. She was in the handicapped bathroom. Amanda had been teasing her. I got Amanda and Emily to the hallway. Danielle had gone out already. Then I went back for Melly." Rose avoided Leo's eye. He'd be surprised to hear she'd left Melly for last, but she couldn't deal with that now.

"I see." Mrs. Nuru nodded. "You didn't take them out to the playground because you went back for Melly."

"Right," Rose answered, and for an odd second, she felt as if she'd said something wrong.

Leo reached for her hand. "Babe, isn't the door to the playground at the end of the hallway?"

"Yes."

"So all Amanda and Emily had to do was to go out with the other kids, right?"

"Yes, right."

Mrs. Nuru frowned. "Rose, Mrs. Snyder heard from Terry Douglas that you were keeping Amanda in the cafeteria, to discipline her. You know that lunch moms aren't supposed to discipline the students. That's for teachers only."

"Oh, come on." Leo scoffed, but Rose squeezed his arm.

"I didn't discipline her, I only spoke to her. I wanted to deal with the teasing on the spot. We talked about the building blocks of character, that's all."

"Perhaps, but now you understand the problem." Mrs. Nuru lifted a graying eyebrow. "If you hadn't detained her, she would've been on the playground when the explosion happened, like the others."

Rose blinked, surprised.

"Are you kidding?" Leo asked, bristling.

"Procedures are procedures, Mr. Ingrassia." Mrs. Nuru stiffened. "Lunch moms have to follow them. You know, before you came, we had paid cafeteria aides. But the aide budget got cut, and this is the kind of thing that happens, which they'll never understand in Harrisburg."

They were interrupted by the sound of sirens, and Rose, Leo, and Mrs. Nuru turned as a group. Traffic had parted on Allen Road to allow an ambulance to speed to the hospital entrance. People in the parking lot were pointing to the street, and a man on the walkway flicked his cigarette to the pavement.

Rose tried to catch Leo's eye, but he was looking at the ambulance, his mouth a grim line. She took his hand just as Tanya came up from behind, aiming her microphone.

"Ms. McKenna, excuse me, since you're still here, would you reconsider giving me a sit-down interview?"

"No."

"Not now, I'm talking tomorrow or the next day. We could do a feature on you, one-on-one, in your home."

"No."

Leo turned to the anchorwoman. "My wife answered you nicely, but I'm not as nice. Leave us alone."

"Okay, fine." Tanya pointed her microphone at Mrs. Nuru. "Excuse me, are you one of the other parents?"

"I'm not going to speak with any reporters."

"I just wanted to know if—"

"I said *no*."

"Fine, thanks." Tanya turned and walked away as the cell phone at her waistband started ringing. The ambulance zoomed down the driveway toward the emergency department, and everybody watched, including Rose, Leo, and Mrs. Nuru, who covered her ears because of the siren.

"Hey, folks," Tanya called out, snapping her phone closed. "You might like to know that another student was found in the school. The name hasn't been released yet, pending notification."

"*What?*" Mrs. Nuru took her hands from her ears.

"Boy or girl?" Leo asked, but Tanya was already hustling toward the curb as the ambulance sped toward the entrance, followed by a blue minivan with its flashers on.

Rose watched, numb. Her mouth had gone dry. She didn't blink. She wasn't sure she even breathed. She pretended she hadn't heard what Tanya had said. That she hadn't been lunch mom today. That she was home with John, cuddling him. Leo's hand closed around hers, his fingers warm and rough.

There was a commotion behind them, and the emergency room doors *whoosh*ed open. Rose, Leo, and Mrs. Nuru stepped aside as a trio of nurses in patterned scrubs hurried outside. The ambulance lurched to a stop, cutting its siren. Its back doors flew open, and a paramedic jumped out, whirled around, and reached for the stretcher behind him. A second paramedic leapt from the back, and they slid the stretcher into the sunlight.

Rose almost fainted at the sight.

Chapter Eight

Amanda lay on the stretcher, unconscious. Orange foam blocks sta-bilized her head, positioned on both sides of her neck, and blood clotted in her silky blond hair. Her forehead was a mass of bandages soaked with blood, bright red in the sunlight. Soot and blood spat-tered her face under the oxygen mask. Filth blanketed her shirt and skirt. Her arms and legs flopped askew. One glittery Candie's sandal was lying sideways at the foot of the stretcher.

No, no, no. Rose couldn't speak, stricken.

"Oh my God," Mrs. Nuru said, hushed, and Leo put his other arm around the teacher. The three of them huddled in shock as the nurses rushed the stretcher toward the emergency room, where the automatic doors opened, admitted them, and closed behind them.

"I wonder what happened," Leo said quietly.

"Let's go see." Mrs. Nuru turned to the entrance, with Rose and Leo following, when the passenger door of the blue minivan flew open, and a woman jumped out, shouting.

"*You!*" the woman screamed. She hit the ground running and charged to the walkway, her blond hair flying and her features so contorted with rage that it took a moment for Rose to recognize her. It was Amanda's mother, Eileen Gigot.

"What's going on?" Leo gasped, astonished, as Eileen rushed toward them, shrieking at Rose.

"*You!* What kind of *person* are you? What kind of *mother* are you?"

Rose edged backwards, reeling, and Leo blocked Eileen's path, putting up his hands.

"Please," he said, his tone calm. "You're upset, and I don't blame you, but there's no call to—"

"You abandoned *my little girl!*" Eileen shouted at Rose, ignoring Leo. "You didn't care if she lived or died! You took care of your daughter, not mine!"

"No, I didn't. I took Amanda to the hallway—"

"Liar! Terry told me the whole thing! You yelled at Amanda! You had it in for her from the beginning, calling me to complain! Well, are you happy now? They found her on the first floor! She got hit on the head with something! She could *die!*"

Rose's mouth dropped open. She felt sick to her stomach. Mrs. Nuru and everyone else on the walkway stared at the scene, appalled. Tanya held out her microphone, and the cameraman aimed his videocamera at Eileen, who was still shouting.

"You were only worried about your own daughter! You didn't care what happened to mine!"

"Please, that's enough." Leo raised his hands, but Eileen smacked them aside.

"Screw *you!* You're as disgusting as she is!"

"Eileen!" shouted another woman, running from the minivan. She reached Eileen, wrapped her arms around her, and tried to tug her away. "Forget them, they're not worth it. We need to go see Amanda. Come on."

"It's *your* fault!" Eileen shrieked, as she was hustled past Tanya and the cameraman. "Her blood's on your hands!"

"Let's get out of here." Leo hurried Rose toward the parking lot, and she fled the scene like a murderer.

Chapter Nine

Rose sat at the kitchen table, chin in hand, feeling horrible, while Leo ate Thai leftovers. He believed that food cured everything, having grown up in his family's restaurant, and she wished she had a similar panacea. She'd showered and changed into a blue cotton sweater and clean jeans, but she couldn't stop thinking about Amanda. She'd brushed her teeth, but the taste of smoke lingered on her tongue. She kept hearing Eileen Gigot, yelling in front of the hospital.

It's your fault!

She'd told Leo everything that had happened in the cafeteria, and if he'd been angry that she'd left Melly until last, he'd been too kind to say so. It felt strange to be at home without her and John, who was still at the sitter's because they were going back to the hospital. Rose missed his warm little presence, always around her, happily cuddled on her lap or bouncing along on her hip. She hadn't known she could love a child as much as she loved Melly until John had been born, but then she learned that when it came to the human heart, one size fits all.

Mommy!

Her gaze flitted around the kitchen, and though it was the reason she'd fallen in love with the house, it gave her no pleasure today. It was big enough to eat in and was ringed with white cabinets, except for bay windows filled with French lavender, their tall green shoots showing tiny purple flowers. Ordinarily they scented the air, but Rose couldn't smell anything but smoke. Mint-and-white tile made a muted backsplash, the appliances were stainless steel, and the table was rough pine. Underneath was their little spaniel, Princess Google, who rested her soft red-and-white head on Rose's loafer, having sniffed her ankle bandage with curiosity.

Her blood's on your hands!

"Don't take this on, babe." Leo steered his tablespoon into his rice like a shovel into fresh snow. His tie was off, and his shirtsleeves folded up. "You didn't do anything wrong. By the way, a reporter called while you were upstairs, so I took the phone off the hook. The hospital has our cells."

"Good." Rose tried to rally, sipping some water, but her throat stung. "I pray to God that Amanda is okay."

"You got her out, and it's not your fault that she ran back in."

"You think that's what happened?"

"It has to be, doesn't it?" Leo stopped his spoon in mid-air, dripping red curry sauce. "They found her somewhere on the first floor."

"That can't be what happened." Rose felt sick at the thought of Amanda lying there, fire raging around her. "If she tried to run back in, the blond teacher would've stopped her."

"Either the teacher was gone by then, or she didn't see her. Amanda's short for her age, isn't she?"

"Yes."

"So she got through, somehow. She could have come into the hallway on the opposite side, away from the teacher. With the hallway full of kids in between, it would be easy to miss her." Leo scooped more sauce onto his rice. "The teachers and staff on the playground missed her, too. You heard Nuru, it was confusing. They had only one fire drill in the new school, so I don't blame them. But I don't blame *you* either, that's for damn sure."

Rose tried to imagine the scene on the playground. It would've been like the teachers' parking lot, only worse. Smoke, tears, shouting. "Mrs. Nuru said she was out there, with the class list."

"Yep. Nuru missed her, too. That's why she's pissing on you."

"That's not nice."

"But it's true." Leo scoffed. "I was surprised at her. Giving you grief about procedures. I mean, really."

"Maybe Amanda ran out of the cafeteria, then ran back in, before she went outside. Maybe the blond teacher didn't see her."

"Anything's possible. All I know is, it's not your fault."

"My God." Rose ran shaky fingers through her wet hair. She could still feel the grit, near her scalp. "Nobody can blame me for going back for Melly, can they?"

"Of course not, that's ass backwards." A flicker of disapproval crossed Leo's face, and Rose sensed they should clear the air.

"Are you mad that I got the other kids out first?"

"Look." Leo shifted forward, his forearms on the table. "I understand why you did. They were in front of you. You couldn't turn your back on them."

"Right." Rose felt relieved.

"It was luck of the draw, who was closer. Bottom line, I'm glad Melly's okay. We dodged a bullet. You wouldn't normally put another kid ahead of your own."

"No." Rose flushed. It sounded awful, put that way.

"Plus it was an emergency. You had to react on the spot. Explosion. Fire. Ka-*boom!*" Leo glanced away, then his gaze shifted back to her and he set down his fork. "But I'm curious about one thing."

"What?" Rose wasn't sure she wanted to know.

"Imagine this hypothetical. Let's say that you're supposed to take somebody's kid home, in your car. But you only have one car seat. Two kids, but one car seat." Leo wiggled two fingers. "Which kid gets the car seat? Your kid or hers?"

"You want me to say that my kid gets the car seat."

"Uh, hello, yes." Leo laughed uncomfortably.

"What would you do?"

"I'd give it to my kid, no question."

"I might not. Maybe. I'd feel guilty about it if I did."

"Why?" Leo asked, incredulous.

"Because if there were an accident on the way home, and something happened to the other child, I'd feel responsible for her. And I'd feel horrible if my kid got hurt, too."

"And we always treat other people's things better than our own, right?"

"Right."

Leo shook it off. "On that we agree to disagree, and anyway, that's not this case. You took care of the other kids, you went back for Melly, and in the end, you saved all of them. You were multi-tasker extraordinaire."

"Not at all." Rose shook her head. "What about Amanda?"

"You got her to safety. But next time, give Melly the car seat." Leo smiled, but Rose couldn't.

"Here's what's killing me. If I had delivered Amanda all the way to the playground, she'd be fine now."

"But then you wouldn't have had the time to go back for Melly. That's five minutes more, like the doctor said." Leo gulped some ice water. "Also, the way you told me, there's more variables, like the fire in the hallway could have been too high for you to get through. It was no-win, and somehow you managed to win."

"Not with Amanda hurt." Rose flashed on Amanda, on the stretcher. The fresh blood on her bandages. "You saw her."

"But what caused Amanda to get hurt? Who's at fault? How about the blond teacher who didn't see her run back in? How about the other lunch mom? What's her name again?"

"Terry. How's it her fault?"

"How many lunch moms are there?"

"Two."

"Okay, two. Two lunch moms for two hundred kids isn't much." Leo nodded. "And I would imagine that the lunch moms are supposed to stay in the cafeteria until lunch is over, right?"

"Yes, until all the kids are out, then we go home."

"So Terry didn't follow procedure. If she'd stayed in the cafeteria instead of leaving to tell on you, she could have taken Amanda and the other girls to the playground while you went to rescue Melly." Leo eyed her, trying to see if his message was hitting home. "All of these causes are only 'but for' causes. By which I mean, *but for* Amanda's running back into the building, she wouldn't have been hurt. *But for* Terry's leaving her post, Amanda wouldn't have been hurt. *But for* you talking to the kids about bullying, Amanda wouldn't have been hurt. *But for* the bomb or whatever blew up, Amanda wouldn't have been hurt. You get the idea? If you say yes, I'll stop."

Rose smiled. "Yes."

"No single 'but for' cause, including you, caused what happened."

"Then what did?"

"All of the above. The perfect storm of a terrible situation. No one thing. Everything went wrong, and that's why Amanda and Melly are in the hospital and three people are dead." Leo reached across the table and touched her hand. "For you to take the blame on yourself, to the exclusion of everything else, makes no sense."

"Eileen thinks I didn't even try."

"Eileen doesn't know the facts and she wants someone to blame. She doesn't know us, either." Leo cocked his head. "Please, who do you think Eileen would rescue? Melly or Amanda?"

Rose didn't reply. "That poor kid."

"Which poor kid? Melly or Amanda? Don't get mixed up."

"Amanda is the poor kid. Melly is fine, Amanda isn't."

"Point taken." Leo paused, his eyes softening. "Listen, I know it's terrible, but you have to be realistic. Amanda might not make it."

Rose suppressed the emotion that welled up. "I'd hate to be responsible for that."

"Then don't. You're not. We just went through the analysis."

Mommy!

"Please stop beating yourself up, Ro." Leo pushed out his chair and got up heavily from the table. "You're supposed to save your own child. That's why we each get a mother. My mother would've saved me, no question. My mother would've walked on bodies to save me, and you're an even better mother than she was."

Rose managed a smile. Leo was a great man, and she was lucky to have him, especially when the chips were down.

"Come on, sweetie." Leo picked up his silverware, let it clatter onto the plate, and lifted his dish. "The baby's at the sitter, but the clock is running. Let's go to the hospital."

Chapter Ten

Rose looked out the window of Leo's sporty Audi, dismayed as they pulled into the hospital parking lot. They'd picked up her car at school and dropped it back off at home, since Leo didn't want her driving herself to the hospital. It turned out he'd been right, but for a different reason. The main entrance was crowded with people, security guards and reporters with videocameras. Klieglights on metallic stalks sprouted above everyone, like steel sunflowers.

"We got company," Leo said, cutting the ignition. The air conditioning hissed into silence.

"Do you think that Amanda—" Rose started to say, but the sentence trailed off.

"No. I checked online before we left the house."

"I wonder how she is."

"We'll see. First, we gotta get through the media. Here's some free legal advice." Leo patted her leg. "Stay with me. Say nothing. Keep moving. Don't put your head down, it makes you look guilty."

"I feel guilty."

"You shouldn't. Please, remember, we're going to visit our daughter. It's not about Amanda, it's about Melly, who almost died today."

Rose flashed on the smoke in the bathroom. "You're right."

"As usual." Leo flashed her a grim smile, and they got out of the car. The air was barely cooling, though the sun had dropped behind the trees. The streetlights along Allen Road were beginning to glow, as was the red neon CVS sign, the McDonald's, the Olive Garden, and the Target. Rose drove the main drag so often she felt as if she'd lived here five years, but she hadn't been to the hospital until today.

Leo took her arm and walked with her toward the entrance. Heads started to turn as they approached, then klieglights and video-cameras. She held her chin up and kept pace with him, moving forward even when Tanya and her TV crew came running toward them, followed by other reporters and photographers.

"Hello, Ms. McKenna!" Tanya called out, on the run. "A few questions, please. What happened with Amanda in the cafeteria this morning? This is your chance to set the record straight."

"No comment." Rose masked her worry. She hadn't realized there was a record.

"Ms. McKenna, talk to me and get your story out. My offer's still good on that one-on-one. Tell me what happened, from your point of view. Can't we set that up?"

"She said no comment, thanks." Leo put up his hand, keeping them both walking ahead, but Tanya fell into step with them.

"Ms. McKenna, if you don't tell your side of the story, it leaves everyone to speculate. Eileen Gigot alleges that you chose to rescue your child to the detriment of three other children, including Amanda. Is that true?"

Oh no. Rose kept her chin up, even as other reporters joined the flock, yelling more questions.

"Ms. McKenna, did you complain to anyone about Amanda, calling her a bully?" "Ms. McKenna, did you place Amanda Gigot in a time-out?" "Ms. McKenna, over here!" "Rose, has Amanda ever struck your child?" "Ms. McKenna, did you move here because you claim your daughter was bullied?" "Any comment, Ms. McKenna? How about you, Mr. Ingrassia?"

Leo ignored the reporters, holding Rose close as they threaded their way through the crowd. She recognized parents from Melly's class, and they craned their necks, their expressions collectively solemn. She lowered her head as Leo steered her up the walkway, followed by reporters, shouted questions, and videocameras. They reached the entrance, where a few women stood together.

"Rose McKenna?" one woman called out. She had short black hair and wore a blue dress with a laminated Homestead ID on a yellow lanyard around her neck, as if she'd come from work.

"Yes." Rose approached, tentatively.

"I'm Wanda Jeresen. My daughter Courtney is in Nuru's class, too, and Amanda is my goddaughter. I want to know how you justify what you did." Wanda's dark eyes flashed under light makeup, and her tone was angry, but controlled. "Terry and Eileen told me you ran to the bathroom to get Melly instead of helping her and Emily."

"No, that's not true," Rose answered, and the crowd of parents and reporters closed in around them.

"Excuse me." Leo put up a flat hand, turning to Wanda. "If you want to talk, we're happy to do that, but not here."

"Why not?" Wanda shot back. "I'd want an answer, here and now. We all do. I called you at home, but you didn't answer."

Leo raised both hands. "Hold on now—"

"Why am I talking to you anyway?" Wanda turned back to Rose. "Can't you speak for yourself? You have to hide behind your husband? Don't you think you owe me, or anybody, an explanation? We're mothers, so talk to me, mother-to-mother."

"Okay, well, that's not the way it happened—"

"Then how did it happen?" Wanda's dark eyes glittered. "Danielle had to run out of the fire, all by herself. I called and talked to Barbara, her mother. She didn't even see you. You went to get your daughter and ignored her and Emily."

"No, wait, listen." Rose put up a hand. "I fell unconscious, and when I woke up, Danielle was running. Ask Emily, I took her and Amanda to the door."

"Nice try, but I called Jerusha, too. Emily's mother. We've been friends since the girls were in first grade. All Emily remembers is that you went to get Melly. She even remembers you saying that's what you were doing. You told her that, didn't you?"

"Yes, but—"

"No buts about it! And thank God that Danielle ran. If she hadn't run, she'd be upstairs now, like Amanda. Or dead!"

"Wanda, hold on!" another woman shouted, making her way through the crowd. She had glasses and long dark hair, and wore a striped top with jeans and flats. "Rose, I'm Cathy Tillman, Sarah's mother, from class. Tell me, since when is it okay to *desert* a child?"

"I didn't desert her. I helped her. The first thing I did was take Amanda and Emily to the hallway leading to the playground."

"What about Danielle?" Wanda demanded, hands on hips.

"Danielle had already gone. She was in the hallway with the others. I told Amanda and Emily to follow Danielle—"

"Follow *Danielle,* that's *it*?" Cathy interrupted, her light eyes round with astonishment behind her glasses. "You don't put an eight-year-old in charge of another eight-year-old. They're just kids, and it was an emergency. You should have taken them out to the playground yourself. Danielle wasn't the lunch mom, you were. That's your responsibility."

"Right," Wanda joined in. "I heard what happened. You punished Emily and Danielle for something they didn't do, and so what if Amanda was joking around with your daughter? Kids are kids. You have to let them fight their own battles."

Cathy leaned closer. "Let's talk turkey. You're just jealous of Amanda because she's popular and Melly isn't. Harry Potter this, Harry Potter that. Melly's a freak!"

"She is not!" Rose's temper flared. "She reads, that's all!"

"Oh, please!" Cathy's hand shot out, waving Rose off, but it startled her and she stepped backwards, bumping into a tall cylindrical ashtray, then losing her balance and falling to the hard concrete with the ashtray spilling sand, cigarette butts, and gum wrappers.

"That's it!" Leo bellowed, pulling a stunned Rose to her feet.

Cathy burst into nervous laughter. Wanda's mouth dropped open. The reporters surged forward, the photographers held their cameras overhead, and the crowd reacted with gasps, chatter, and a hoot or two.

"Let's go!" Leo hurried Rose through the glass doors into the hospital. The lobby was like a refuge, quiet and cool, filled with potted plants and soothing framed landscapes. A few older people sat in sectional furniture, one holding Get Well balloons weighted with a small sandbag. Leo touched Rose's arm. "My God. Are you okay, honey?"

"Yes." She brushed cigarette ashes from her jeans. "And Melly's not a freak."

"I know." Leo smoothed down his suit jacket. "Sorry about that. I should've seen that coming."

"It was an accident."

"Right. Yes, but they still laughed about it."

Shaken, Rose tried to recover. "You told me not to talk to them, but I thought they deserved an answer."

"They didn't want an answer. They wanted to vent." Leo put an arm around her. "Damn, I should have anticipated this. Hubby let you down."

"Hubby never lets me down."

Leo gave her a quick kiss. "You good to go?"

"Yes."

"Okay, then we need an information desk." Leo looked around.

"There." Rose pointed, and they went to the information desk, where they gave their name and asked for Melly's room.

"She's in 306," answered the receptionist, who was an older woman with a button that read VOLUNTEER. "She's one of the little girls from the school, isn't she?"

"Yes, she's our daughter." Rose leaned over the counter. "Where is the other little girl, Amanda Gigot?"

"Let me see." The receptionist hit a few keys. "Yes. She's in 406. That's Intensive Care."

Rose felt her stomach tense.

Leo leaned on the desk. "What floor did you say is Intensive Care? The fourth?"

"Yes, but you can't visit. Only immediate family is permitted."

"I understand, thanks." Leo took Rose's arm, and they left for the elevators.

"Do you want to visit Amanda?" Rose asked, incredulous.

"No, I want to avoid the fourth floor."

Chapter Eleven

Rose stood at Melly's bedside, suppressing a surge of emotion. It was one thing to know that Melly was in a hospital, and another to see her lying there, asleep. She took up only half of the bed, and her feet made little mounds in the white coverlet, midway. Her hospital gown was too big, and its scoop neck exposed her collarbones. Her eyes were closed, and even though she was only sleeping, she could so easily have been gone, forever. Rose watched her chest move up and down, to make sure she was breathing. There wasn't a mother in the world who hadn't done the same thing, more than once.

Mommy!

Melly's head lay tilted to the right, displaying her birthmark in a way that would have mortified her, if she'd been awake. It was as red as fresh blood, covering her left cheek at its upper edge, roughly roundish in shape, about the size of a small plum. A greenish oxygen tube lay across it under her nostrils, and her index finger was covered by a plastic cap that connected her to a boxy monitor, flashing her vital signs in multi-colored digits.

"She looks good," Leo whispered, a wet shine in his eyes.

"Thank God she's alive."

"Let me get you a seat." Leo picked up a wooden chair and moved it close to the bed, near the thick plastic guardrail. Behind them, a TV mounted on the wall played on mute. "Here, sit."

"Wanna share? I'll move over."

"No, you."

"Thanks." Rose sat down, resting her hand on the bedrail. As happy as she was that Melly was alive, she couldn't forget that a different scene would be playing out a floor above them, in Intensive Care. She tried to shoo away thoughts of Amanda, but the images were too fresh in her mind.

"Oh no. We left your overnight bag in the car."

"It's okay." Rose flashed again on Amanda, on the stretcher. The bandages on her forehead had been blood-soaked, and Eileen had said she'd gotten hit on her head with something, so she might even need brain surgery.

"You'll have to brush your teeth with your finger, like I did in the old days, when I used to stay at your apartment. That was before the guest toothbrush. Remember the guest toothbrush?"

"Yes." Rose thought of the soot on Amanda's face. She'd been in the school a lot longer than Melly, but probably not in as enclosed a space. She could have brain damage, not only from whatever fell on her head, but from the oxygen deprivation.

"You can sleep in your clothes, too. Do you want me to ask for a cot, or do you want to sleep in the same bed with her? Babe?" Leo took her hand. "You with us?"

"Yes, sure."

"Take a look at your daughter. Now. Do it."

Rose looked at Melly. "She's sweet, huh?"

"She's a great kid. My bonus kid."

Rose smiled. Leo always said that, and she loved hearing it.

"Remember when we met, on the train? I went to the food car, starved and beat, and there you were, this stunning young mother with her brainy little girl, who recommended I try the hot dogs. We bonded over our shared love of sodium nitrate."

Rose smiled. It was true. They'd all met on the Acela between New York and Philadelphia. She wouldn't have talked to Leo if it hadn't been for Melly. She didn't think he was her type. She'd been into bad boys, and Leo was not only a good boy, but an altar boy.

"You did the right thing today. You saved her life. Don't listen to those crazies out front, or anybody else. We love Melly and we're blessed to have her. Looking at her, being here now, would you change anything you did?"

"No." Rose heard the truth in his words, but she still felt torn. "I keep thinking of Amanda and Eileen, just one floor up. How can I not?"

"I'll tell you." Leo let go of her hand. "Because it could get worse, honey, and you need to keep your head on straight."

"What do you mean?"

"Let's not talk about it now." Leo shook it off. "Like I said outside, this isn't the time or the place."

Rose didn't like his expression. The shine had left his eyes. "No, what do you mean?"

"We could get sued, babe. Eileen could come after us. Best case scenario, Amanda is fine, but she'll have monster medical bills. Eileen's a single mom. How will she pay?"

"She wouldn't win if she sued, would she?"

"She could. When you volunteer at school, you're exposed to liability."

"You are? I am?"

"Look, I'm a humble general practitioner, but I don't see why you wouldn't be. You took on the responsibility for her kid, and she got hurt, end of story." Leo jerked a thumb to the hospital window. "And those women out front, the *moms,* will be the first witnesses testifying against you."

Rose felt her chest tighten. She sensed he was right, but it felt wrong to worry about being sued when Eileen was worrying about her child dying.

"Eileen could sue the school, too, for letting her run back into the building, and don't even think about what happens when they find out whatever blew up. Plus the family of the cafeteria workers could sue, and so could the teacher's." Leo spoke in his professional voice, albeit softly. "This could be a holy mess for the next few years, while the litigation goes on and on. Win or lose, we'd get hit for the legal fees, because I couldn't represent us. It could cost us everything we have. We could lose the house."

Rose's mouth went dry. The thought of losing the house shook her. Leo made a good living, but she had stopped working. They didn't have much in savings apart from the kids' college funds, and they had loan payments on two cars and a hefty new mortgage.

There was rustling from the bed, and they both looked over. Melly shifted under the covers, moving her head back and forth, and they lapsed into silence, waiting for the moment to pass.

"Uh-oh," Leo said, nudging Rose. "Look at the TV, babe."

She turned around to the TV, then did a double-take. The screen showed her own face, then a shot of the firetrucks and burning elementary school. "Oh my God," she said, appalled.

"I know."

Rose felt her heart sink. The TV screen changed to Tanya, talking into a microphone. The closed captioning read, A LOCAL MOM IS A HERO TODAY, then the film was of Rose again, at the hospital after they'd gotten the news that Melly was fine. The captioning said, I DID WHAT ANY MOTHER WOULD DO.

"Mom?" said a voice from the bed, and Rose turned.

"Melly!"

Leo got up and hit the POWER button on the TV, willing the screen into blackness.

Chapter Twelve

Rose lay in darkness, cuddling with Melly in her hospital bed, by now accustomed to the smoky smell in her hair. Leo had left at the end of visiting hours, gotten John from the sitter, and taken him home. Melly had been quiet during the evening, drowsy as a result of the drugs.

"You sleepy, honey?" Rose asked, and Melly looked over, resting her head on Rose's left arm.

"A little. Are you going to sleep here?"

"I sure am. Want more water, or Jell-O?"

"No."

"How's your head?"

"Okay.

"Mom?" Melly's voice sounded raspy, from the irritation. "When I was in the bathroom, the floor felt like an earthquake."

Rose thought back. "Yes, it did."

"Why?"

"Because of the explosion in the kitchen." Rose and Leo had explained to Melly generally what had happened, but she wasn't ready to hear about the deaths yet, or Amanda.

"Was it a bomb? It sounded like a bomb."

"They don't know for sure. Whatever it was, the fire is already out, and they'll make it safe to go back."

"Is it from a terrorist?"

"I doubt that very much." Rose cursed modern times. When she was little, the only bombs she saw were in cartoons, round black bowling balls with wiggly cotton strings.

"It was a *big* noise."

"Sure was. Did it scare you?"

"Yes. I didn't come out of the bathroom."

"I know. Is that why?"

"No. Remember Fire Safety Week?"

"Not really." Rose remembered nothing, and Melly remembered everything.

"At our old school, we went to the firehouse on Fire Safety Week. You came, and we climbed on top of the firetruck, and they gave me a green sticker for my bedroom window and for Googie. It says, Save Our Dog."

"Okay."

"They said, don't open the door if it's hot. The bathroom door was hot, so I didn't open it, then I couldn't breathe. I hit the door and hollered so people would know I was inside, but nobody came to get me."

Rose felt a pang. "Well, it's all right now."

"How did I get out?"

"I got you out."

"Is that how you hurt your hand?"

"No," Rose lied. She'd burned it when she'd picked up the burning stud. "It got burned in the cafeteria, but it's nothing."

"Remember when Quirrell gets burned by Harry's scar? He gets burned on his hands, too."

"This wasn't that bad." Rose flashed on the mothers making fun of Melly's love of Harry Potter, then put it out of her mind. She and Melly had read the Potter books aloud before bedtime, and it was easy to see why Melly identified with a kid with a scar on his face.

"I'm sorry I ran to the bathroom, Mom."

Rose felt a twinge. Sometimes she thought motherhood was full of twinges. "It's okay, I understand why you'd be upset. Does Amanda tease you like that a lot?"

Melly fell silent.

"Huh, Mel? Does she?"

Melly didn't answer. She wasn't a whiner. She hadn't complained about any of the teasing at their old school because she thought if they did anything about it, it would get worse, and she'd been right.

"Mel, I won't do anything, I promise. I just want to know." Rose looked over, but she could barely make out Melly's profile in the dark. "What does Amanda do?"

"Yesterday we were finger-painting with Ms. Canton."

"Okay," Rose said, keeping her tone drama-free. Melly, Amanda, and two other children in Mrs. Nuru's class were in the gifted program, spending an hour in the afternoons with Kristen Canton, twice a week.

"I was painting a picture of Dumbledore, and Amanda put poster paint on with her finger and painted on her cheek, like with the jelly. Ms. Canton told her it's not funny or caring, and how we're a community. I *love* Ms. Canton."

"Me, too," Rose said, hearing Melly's voice warm.

"Her favorite Harry Potter is *The Sorcerer's Stone,* and she has a cat named Hedwig and a Hermione wand. She says it looks just like it came from Ollivander's. It doesn't light up, but it sounds cool."

"I bet." Rose felt lucky that Melly had found a fellow Harry Potter fanatic in the gifted teacher. "Maybe we should get some sleep, honey."

"I'm not tired."

"Okay, we'll just rest." Rose held her closer, feeling her body grow heavier. In the next few minutes, Melly fell quiet, her breathing grew regular, and she fell asleep.

Rose lay awake in the dark, and found herself wishing that Melly had never had the birthmark. It wasn't the first time she'd fantasized about how their life would be different, without. The birthmark had come to define Melly and their family, and they all revolved around the red circle as if it were the sun itself, setting them all in mad, dizzying orbit.

Rose let her thoughts run free, knowing it was forbidden, like a family dog running through an electric fence. It was the birthmark that had started the sequence of awful events today, whether Leo would say that was a *but for* cause or not. Funny, Rose hadn't even seen the birthmark when Melly was first put on her chest, as a newborn. In her first instant as a mother, Rose felt suffused with such wonder and happiness that she saw only a beautiful baby. The nurses all cooed happily, but Bernardo had asked the doctor, in disgust: *What the hell is that red thing on her face?*

His awful words had a hang time in the cold delivery room, chilling Rose to the marrow. The doctor had replied that it was a *nevus* even before he'd announced that the baby was a girl, and the nurses had receded, their tones newly subdued and their smiles stiffening at Bernardo's reaction. Rose had gotten what she'd always wanted, a baby girl looking at the world with eyes the hue of heaven itself.

I love you, Rose had told the baby then, and when she saw the stain on her cheek, she'd added silently, *I love all of you.*

Rose's parents were both gone by the time Melly was born, but her in-laws had flown in to see the baby, bringing their *She'll grow out of it, don't worry.* But the baby didn't grow out of it, and Bernardo obsessed more and more on the birthmark, as if it marked him. He was a photographer, but rarely took pictures of Melly, and then only from her right side. Toddlers would stare at baby Melly in her stroller, and he would pull down the Perego's top, hiding her in their walks through the West Village. Children would ask questions, and Bernardo would ignore them, leaving Rose to answer with the medical facts, much as Melly would later, fielding questions like the most patient of family doctors.

The teasing had started in pre-school, and Rose had watched as Melly's grin disintegrated, bit by bit. She became withdrawn and quiet, wanting to stay home and avoid strangers, begging to quit Mommy & Me and Gymboree. Meanwhile, Bernardo scheduled her with Manhattan's best dermatologists, who judged the birthmark too big for surgery, then he dragged them all over the city for more opinions and different treatments, shooting the birthmark with pulse-dye lasers, treating it with bipolar radio-frequencies, and even covering it with custom-made foundation, to no avail.

It was a thicker *nevus* than most, and all the time, Rose had hated the message they were sending Melly. Their marriage cracked under it and other strains, mainly Bernardo's partying, and they divorced when Melly was three years old. Bernardo was killed the very next year, crashing his Porsche, and around that time, Rose and Melly met Leo on the train. They'd fallen in love and married the next year, and she'd left the city to move to southeastern Pennsylvania, near where Leo had grown up in Worhawk. On her own, she felt free to help Melly accept herself, even after her fifth Halloween, when she wouldn't take off her Dora the Explorer mask.

Mommy, I hate being me.

Rose stared at the ceiling, then closed her eyes, and her thoughts returned to the room above. She wondered if Eileen was holding Amanda right now, or if that wasn't permissible in Intensive Care. She tried to put it out of her mind, but gave up. She eased Melly off her chest, rolled quietly out of bed, and left the room. The hallway was empty at this hour, and there was only one nurse behind the desk. Rose crossed the polished hall, and the nurse looked up.

"Oh my God, I know you!" The nurse's eyes sparkled. She was young and tanned, with short, sunbleached hair and a line of gold studs in one ear. "You're the mom who saved her daughter, aren't you?"

"Well, yes." Rose felt her face warm.

"I have a baby at home, and I give you so much credit. How'd you do it?"

"It's a long story, but I'm wondering if you could help me." Rose leaned on the desk. "There's another little girl who was caught in the fire. Her name's Amanda Gigot, and I was wondering how she's doing. Last I heard, she was in Intensive Care with a head injury. Can you find out how she is?"

"Hold on." The nurse turned to a computer keyboard and pressed a few keys. "She's still in Intensive Care."

"Is there any way I could get some details on how she's doing, or maybe you can?"

"We're not supposed to divulge that information."

"Please?" Rose put her hands together in mock prayer.

"Let me see." The nurse shifted her gaze down the hallway, then picked up a desk phone and hit a few buttons, turning slightly away.

"Suz, what up? Can you give me some info on the girl up there from the school? Name's Gigot?"

Rose waited while the nurse nodded on the phone, listening for a few minutes, saying only "uh-huh" from time to time. When the nurse hung up, her expression was unreadable.

"Well?" Rose asked, breathless.

"I'm sorry, I can't really say."

"Please?" Rose begged, but the nurse shook her head.

"Sorry," she answered, looking away.

Chapter Thirteen

It was morning, and Rose had watched the light in the hospital room change from darkness to dawn, as the outlines of the TV, wooden chairs, and night table acquired definition in increments. She had barely slept, worrying about Amanda, and said more than one prayer for her.

Well, are you happy now?

Outside the closed door, there were sounds of people talking, metal carts rattling, and an unidentified beeping, something mechanical. She caught a whiff of breakfast being served, an eggy smell rather than the proverbial coffee aroma, and either way, she wasn't hungry.

We could lose the house.

Melly was still asleep, so Rose leaned over carefully, slid a hand into her jeans pocket, and pulled out her BlackBerry, checking the time. 8:26 A.M. She wished she could call Leo, but the cell phones supposedly interfered with the medical equipment. Last night, she'd texted him, and the red stars on her phone meant that she had new texts, emails, and calls. She pressed the button to see if he'd texted back.

Babe, Hope Amanda pulls through. Call me. Love you.

Rose thumbed the rollerball to check her email and skimmed the list of senders. They were parents of kids in Melly's class, who must've gotten her email address from the class list. She opened the first email:

You have a helluva lot of nerve acting like you're a hero when you were happy with letting those kids die. All you did was save your own hide and child

Rose swallowed, closed the email, and opened the next.

I will never understand how some people can be so blind to the needs of others. God will judge what you did

She closed the email, and didn't want to read the next one, but the sender's name caught her eye. **Barbara Westerman.** Danielle's last name was Westerman, so Rose clicked Open:

I am outraged that you would care so little about my daughter's safety. She was terrified and had to run out of the building all by herself. She could have died or been gravely injured, like Amanda! We don't need selfish people like you in Reesburgh, and you should go back to

Rose closed the email, shaken. She clicked over to her phone calls. The log showed new calls from Unknown Numbers, and she didn't call her voicemail to listen to the messages. She had a sense of what they'd say.

Melly was shifting in bed, her eyelids fluttering and her oxygen tube slipping, so Rose readjusted the oxygen, forwarded the last three emails to Leo, turned off the BlackBerry, and slid it back into her jeans pocket. She turned to Melly and brushed a stray hair from her forehead, just as the door to the room opened and a young orderly stuck his head inside.

"Anybody hungry?" he asked, with a smile.

"Sure, come on in, thanks." Rose motioned to him, then returned her attention to Melly. It was the first chance she'd had to get a look at Melly in the daylight, and she eyed her with more care than usual, like Dr. Mom:

Her eyes, large and blue, still looked bloodshot, and her skin, which was on the fair side, seemed reddish, whether from the antiseptic used to clean it or from the smoke's irritation. Her nose was small and turned slightly up, but showed redness around the nostrils, which was to be expected, and her lips, also thin like Rose's, looked dry and parched. Bernardo had always said that Melly looked exactly like Rose, except in a dark blond Bernardo wig, and Dr. Mom decided she looked fine.

"Hi, Mom." Melly raised her arms and hugged Rose around the neck. "I love you."

"I love you, too, Mel. I hope you got some good sleep. You conked out." Rose eased Melly back onto the bed. "Do you feel like waking up and eating a little breakfast? Or do you wanna rest?"

"I want to wake up." Melly rubbed her eyes. "Can we go home?"

"Not yet, not until the doctor says."

"Breakfast!" The orderly placed the tray on the night table, then blinked when he spotted her birthmark. He pointed at the scrambled eggs under their steamed-up cover of thick amber plastic. "Eat up. Help you grow up big and strong."

"Thank you," Melly said, raspy, getting into a sitting position as he left the room, closing the door behind him. She lifted the lid, releasing the smell of institutional eggs. "Is this all for me?"

"Yes."

"My throat hurts. Do I have to go to school today?"

"No, it's Saturday. You'll feel better soon. Drink this." Rose opened the water bottle, poured some in the flexible cup, and helped her sip some.

Melly swallowed, grimacing.

"It'll be okay soon."

"Do you have my *Beedle the Bard* book?"

"No. Sorry." Rose had forgotten to ask Leo to get it in the car. There was another knock on the door, and she looked over. "Come in."

The door opened, and Kristen Canton, the gifted teacher, popped her head inside the room. "Hello!" she called out, with a grin.

"Kristen!" Rose got up to greet her, calling her by her first name because she was only twenty-five, and preferred it. "How nice of you to come."

"I'm so sorry I didn't get here yesterday." Kristen gave her a warm hug, then whispered in her ear, "I've been upstairs."

"Oh." Rose released Kristen, and close-up, she could see that the pretty young teacher was a wreck. A normally bouncy redhead with warm brown eyes, a small, straight nose, a sprinkling of adorable freckles and an omnipresent grin, Kristen wore a forced smile today, and her eyes looked puffy under fresh makeup.

"Ms. Canton!" Melly shouted.

"Hey, girlfriend!" Kristen crossed to the bed. Her hair had been gathered into a messy ponytail, and her usually hip shirt-and-jeans combo had been replaced by a gray hoodie, which she had on with black yoga pants and flats. "How you doin'?"

"Good!"

"Great. I'm so happy to see you're all right. I'd hug you but I'm a little sick."

"There was a fire in the school, Ms. Canton. My mom found me."

"What a great mom!" Kristen winked at Rose, then turned back to Melly. "Guess what? I have a get-well present for you."

"What is it?"

"Check it out." Kristen slipped a hand into her shoulder bag, pulled out a longish box with flowery gift wrap, and presented it with a flourish. "Ta-da!"

"Yay!" Melly tore off the gift wrap, which covered a forest green box. She flipped open the lid, and inside was a green velveteen channel that held a magic wand, of fake wood. "Mom, look! It's a Hermione wand!"

"Honey, what do you say?" Rose smiled, touched.

"Thank you, Ms. Canton!" Melly took out the wand and started waving it around, letting the box and wrap fall to the bed. "*Alohomora!* I opened a lock, just like Hermione."

"Good for you."

"Thank you so much. I have Harry's wand but not Hermione's. Now I can put out fires."

Kristen grinned. "Like in *Deathly Hallows*."

Rose didn't remember. "There's a fire in *Deathly Hallows*? Remind me, Mel."

"Hermione puts out the fire in Mundungus's eyebrows after Harry sets him on fire by accident. Water squirts out the top of the wand." Melly waved the wand around, almost hitting her metal IV pole. "I don't know the incantation, though."

"Me, neither," Kristen said, frowning.

Rose smiled. "You haven't memorized every spell in Harry Potter?"

"I'll put out the fire in the school!" Melly looked over, then her face fell. "Did the school burn down, Ms. Canton?"

"No," Kristen answered, growing serious. "The school is fine. Only the section with the cafeteria was damaged, and we're going to fix it, as good as new."

"Was it from a bomb?"

"No, there were no bombs."

Rose looked over. "Kristen, do they know what caused the explosion?"

"They think it was some kind of gas leak and faulty electrical wiring. Mrs. Nuru says they rushed construction to open on time, and the punch list didn't get done." Kristen checked her watch and turned back to Melly. "Oops, sorry, it's late and I've got to go, sweetie. See you at school." Kristen gave Melly another hug. "Good-bye."

"Bye, Ms. Canton." Melly released her, waving the wand, and Kristen shot Rose a meaningful look.

"Rose, will you walk me out?"

"Sure." Rose turned to Melly. She knew it had to be about Amanda and she wanted to know what was going on upstairs. "Honey, I'll be right back. Ms. Canton and I will be outside the door. Call if you need me."

"Okay, Mom. Thanks for my wand, Ms. Canton!"

Chapter Fourteen

Rose led Kristen to a window well near Melly's room, but away from the nurses' station. Sunshine poured through the glass, bathing the young teacher in light as she leaned against the ledge and heaved a heavy sigh. Now that they were alone, she dropped her perky mask, and the naked sadness in her eyes made her look like a little girl.

"They don't prepare you for this, in school," Kristen said, exhaling. She shook her head, and her long, dark red ponytail slipped from side to side. "They don't tell you that something horrible could happen to kids. I've been the gifted teacher for two years, and until now, my biggest worry was my math skills. I'm like, how can I help these kids with broken fractions, when I don't understand them myself?"

Rose patted her back, sympathetic. "I know, this is tough."

"I'm happy that Melly's okay. It did me good to see her."

"Thanks so much for the gift."

"No worries. I love that kid. She's awesome."

"She loves you, too. She looks forward to school, because of you." Rose couldn't wait to ask. "Kristen, how is Amanda? I'm so worried about her. She was in a coma, last I heard."

"She's worse," Kristen answered softly. Her pretty features contorted with pain, and she heaved a sudden sob, her hands moving to cover her face. "They just gave her last rites."

Oh my God, Rose sagged next to her on the window ledge, feeling as if she'd been punched in the gut.

"The family is all up there," Kristen said, between sobs. "The two brothers, their priest, the grandparents. They're a mess, a total mess."

Rose hung her head. Air conditioning blew onto her face, through a grate on top of the window well.

"I'm sorry, I just feel so lost, she's just a little kid." Kristen's shoulders shuddered. "It's so awful to see her that way."

Rose ached for Eileen and the family, and her regrets rushed back at her. She should have saved Amanda when she had the chance. It wouldn't have taken that long to get her out of the building. Both girls could be fine now, alive and well.

"I'm so sorry." Kristen's sobs began to subside, and she fumbled in her purse, found a soggy tissue, and dabbed underneath her eyes. "Things like this aren't supposed to happen."

"No, they're not," Rose said, but she knew better. Things like this happened all the time. Ambulances stocked teddy bears for a reason.

"I was so excited to get the job, running the gifted program." Kristen sniffled. "Reesburgh is such a great district, and they were like, make it your own, go with it, develop your own curriculum and enrichment programs. It was the job everybody wanted. Now I'm sorry I got it."

"Don't say that." Rose put an arm around the young teacher's shoulder. "You do such a great job. Melly loves the gifted program and all the things you do, like when you bring in a speaker, that guy with the falcons or that poet. And Senator Martin and the Phillie Phanatic? The kids adore you, you relate so well to them."

"That's the problem, you know." Kristen blew her nose noisily, causing her face to flush under her fair, freckled skin. "Mrs. Nuru says I'm too close to the students, that I lack professional distance. She says that I . . . I don't know, oh, forget it."

"What?"

"She thinks that I'm too close to Melly and that's why she got so upset when Amanda teased her at lunch, or when we meet, in gifted. She says Melly's too sensitive, and I shouldn't encourage it."

Rose stiffened. "That's blaming the victim. What Amanda did was downright cruel, and you weren't even there."

"I agree, but not everybody does." Kristen blew her nose, with finality. "They're all talking about it. Everybody has an opinion, because of what happened."

"What happened? You mean that I got Melly out, and not Amanda?"

"Forget it, I shouldn't have mentioned it." Kristen rolled her eyes. "God, I'm such a motor mouth."

"Kristen, no matter what you heard, I want you to know that I thought I got Amanda out of the building. I took her and Emily to the hallway door before I even went to get Melly, and I thought she'd keep going—"

"Wait, stop." Kristen raised her hands. "I'm not accusing you of anything, and I know you. I know you wouldn't just leave Amanda in a burning school. If you tried to get Amanda and the others out, then went back for Melly, no one can blame you. I don't blame you. You couldn't leave *Melly.*" Kristen blinked. "That's crazy! You were in a terrible position. You did your best."

Rose felt a warm rush of gratitude. "They think I chose Melly over Amanda, but I didn't."

"Don't let them get to you. No one has the facts, and I heard Emily's traumatized. Eileen's losing Amanda, and it's so horrible that she's totally crazy. Everybody's crazy! Her, Mrs. Nuru, Mr. Rodriguez, all of them. You don't know the half of it. My mother would say, we're 'undone.' I'm 'undone,' and so are you." Kristen looked up, her tired eyes glistening. "Have you told Melly about Amanda and the others?"

"Not yet, no." Rose didn't want to fast-forward to that conversation. "I'd like to get her home first, and get her feet under her."

"Good. I'll be glad to come over when you tell her. Call me, whenever. You have my cell number. I think it's on my email to you."

"Thanks," Rose said, grateful. "I'll talk to Leo, to see what he thinks."

"We'll have grief counselors at school, and the guidance counselor. Mrs. Nuru's been through this, and she says the counselors really help. She's lost three students in her time. One to leukemia, one to bone cancer, and another died in a car crash with a drunk driver."

Rose reeled. Leukemia. Cancer. Car crash. Now, Amanda. It made a blotchy red birthmark seem like nothing. She felt tears rising, then willed them away. At least her child was alive. "How the hell do you outlive your child?" Rose asked, half to herself.

Mommy!

"Don't ask me, I have both my parents, and my only kid is a cat." Kristen looked down the hall, distracted, and Rose turned to see Mr. Rodriguez striding toward them. He'd been a teacher for thirty years before he became principal, and he was in his fifties, if less than fit. Six feet tall with a blocky build, he came off like everybody's favorite uncle in a navy polo shirt that showed a paunch hanging over gray suit pants.

"Rose." Mr. Rodriguez smiled when he reached her, but his brown eyes showed the strain. He ran a hand through short, dark hair. "I'm sorry about what happened, and I'm sorry it took me this long to come see you. How is Melly? I hear she's on the mend."

"Yes, thanks. We're hoping she goes home tomorrow."

"Wonderful." Mr. Rodriguez's brow relaxed, his relief genuine. "Where's Leo?"

"Home with John, the baby."

"Of course. Great guy. I'm so happy you were there for Melly. Your acts were positively heroic."

Rose flushed. "I only wish I could have saved Amanda, too. I did take her and Emily to the hall leading to the playground."

"I'm sure." Mr. Rodriguez frowned deeply, his dark eyebrows joining like gathering nimbus clouds. "I was just upstairs. You should know that Amanda's been given last rites."

"Kristen told me. I'm so sorry."

"It's just tragic." Mr. Rodriguez sighed. "Fortunately, Eileen's got a lot of support, and her family will get her through whatever she has to face, whenever the time comes."

"I can't imagine losing a child."

"Nor can I. My daughters are my life. I've had challenges in my career, but never like this. Eileen will have to go on, for her boys."

Mr. Rodriguez nodded, as if trying to cheer himself up. "You'll find that there are real advantages to being a member of such a small community. We support each other in Reesburgh. Most of the people here have watched the Gigots grow up, and you'll see how tight we are, when we reopen on Monday."

"Back to school, so soon?" Rose asked, surprised.

"Routine is really the best thing for the students, and school becomes a constant in times of stress. We'll eat in the classrooms during the clean-up and put up plywood fencing so they don't see the cafeteria. We'll start with half a day on Monday and dismiss at noon." Mr. Rodriguez stuck his hands in his pockets, jingling his change. "We're asking the parents to drive the kids in, and we'll have a special assembly in the morning for Marylou, Serena, and Ellen."

"When are the funerals?" Rose felt a step behind, playing catch-up.

"They'll hold the wake on Sunday night, at Fiore's, with private burials on Monday. We'll have grief counselors in the auditorium for the next two weeks. The healing can begin, right away."

"It seems soon, doesn't it?"

"Feel free to keep Melly home if you wish, we'll count it as excused, but if she's well enough, I'd send her. We need her to assimilate into the school community, and I'll look out for her, and so will the staff." Mr. Rodriguez turned to Kristen. "You have a special relationship with Melly, don't you?"

"Yes, I'll take care of her."

Mr. Rodriguez turned back to Rose. "Please, don't think I'm callous. Under state law, we have to hold class a certain number of days, come hell or high water. We can't afford to lose the days now, in case we get as much snow as we did last winter."

"But it was such a big fire." Rose flashed on the horrific scene in the cafeteria.

"Perhaps it seems that way to you, but in fact, it was fairly confined. The only damage was to the cafeteria, teachers' lounge, and hallway, and those will all be closed."

"What about water damage? The sprinklers went off."

"The sprinkler system is zoned. The sprinklers went off only where there was fire." Mr. Rodriguez straightened, his manner turning official. "I spent all afternoon yesterday with the county Fire Marshals, the Fire Chief, the state police, and the district supervisors. We even hosted the FBI. Quite the command center, for a tragedy of this scope."

"My condolences, too."

"Thank you." Mr. Rodriguez pursed his thin lips. "The Fire Marshals have already certified the rest of the building as structurally sound, and we hope to rebuild the cafeteria by the end of February."

"This time they better get the wiring right."

"Excuse me?" Mr. Rodriguez frowned. "What makes you say that, Rose?"

Rose blinked. "I heard there was faulty wiring, maybe something left off the punch list."

"Where'd you hear that?"

Rose hesitated, sorry she'd mentioned anything, but Kristen answered, "I told her."

Mr. Rodriguez turned to the teacher, his eyes hardening. "Kristen, this is a difficult situation, with three fatalities, and there shouldn't be any idle speculation about its causes, especially from my own staff. The cause of the explosion and fire haven't been determined as yet."

Rose interjected, "I asked her. She wasn't speculating."

"Just the same." Mr. Rodriguez's gaze bored into Kristen, then shifted back to Rose, his brow relaxing just a little. "We've all been instructed by legal counsel not to discuss the particulars of this tragedy with anyone. You can imagine, with three families grieving and two children in the hospital, even Melly, that we need to keep an even keel, going forward." Mr. Rodriguez squared his shoulders. "Rose, I have my work cut out for me, this weekend. I'd like to say hello to Melly, if that's okay with you, and then we'll go. Kristen, you'll leave with me, please."

"Sure." Kristen nodded, nervously, and Rose couldn't process it all fast enough. Everybody lawyering up. Amanda, dying upstairs. School, opening after the weekend. It was a lot to wrap her mind around, and it would be even harder for Melly.

"Right, let's go see Melly," Rose said, summoning her composure and leading them to the door, but when they opened it, Melly was sound asleep.

Mr. Rodriguez looked over, a twinkle in his eye. "Usually this happens *after* I speak," he said, with a tight smile.

Chapter Fifteen

"Sure you're not thirsty?" Rose asked Melly, sitting at the edge of her hospital bed, when they were alone. She felt devastated that Amanda had been given last rites, but she masked it for Melly, who was waking up, having napped only briefly.

"No."

"No water?"

"I drank some." Melly touched the oxygen tube under her nostrils with her fingernail, polished pink, now chipping. "Did Ms. Canton go home?"

"Yes. She told me to say good-bye. Mr. Rodriguez came to meet you, but you were asleep, so I didn't wake you."

"Maybe because she's sick. That's why she wasn't in school." Melly let go of the oxygen tube. "Do you have my DS?"

"No. It's in the bag I left in Leo's car, with the book. Sorry. I don't have my laptop either."

"It's okay. I miss my friends on Club Penguin. We always talk on Saturday morning."

"I know." Rose limited Melly's time on Club Penguin, a safe chat site for children, though for a kid self-conscious about her looks, the site was a godsend.

"Can we watch TV? Cartoons are on."

"No, let's not." Rose didn't want to take a chance that any news-break or screen crawl could update the school fire, especially the fa-talities.

"So what can we do?"

"I can run down to the gift shop and see if they have any maga-zines, and we can read together."

Melly brightened. "Do they have *Teen People*? It's my friend's fa-vorite magazine."

"Which friend?"

"A girl on Club Penguin. She likes all those magazines. She likes Harry Potter, too, but she only read *Chamber of Secrets*."

"Okay, I'll go get the magazine." Rose rolled the night table out of the way and stood up, just as the door opened. It was Leo, and he had John asleep on his shoulder, in his yellow onesie and a white re-ceiving blanket. Oddly, Leo looked dressed for work, in the white oxford shirt, tan Dockers, and penny loafers of the American lawyer on a Saturday.

"Hey, boys! Let me see my Johnnie Angel." Rose got up and took the sleeping baby, who filled her arms. John was big for his age, making a nice warm bundle, and he resettled his head on her shoul-der. She was happy to see him, even if it wasn't the greatest idea to bring a sick baby to a hospital. She stroked John's tiny back in the soft blanket, cuddling him, and given what was happening with Amanda, she felt vaguely more comforted than comforting.

"Hey, girls!" Leo dropped the diaper bag on the chair by the door and went over to Melly. "How's my melba toast?"

"Leo!" Melly knelt in bed and threw open her arms, and Leo gathered her up in a bear hug, ending with his trademark grunt.

"I'm so happy to see you, kiddo."

"Leo, I have oxygen."

"Great." Leo laughed. "I love oxygen."

Rose watched them, counting herself lucky that Melly loved her stepfather so much, whether she called him Daddy or not. Her family was finally complete, even if it wasn't exactly the way she'd planned it, and she felt a deep stab of guilt over her own happiness, when she knew that upstairs the scene would be one of profound grief. She went over and impulsively kissed Leo on the cheek, catching a whiff of his spicy aftershave, also unusual for a Saturday. "Why do you smell so nice?"

"Because I'm a sexy beast?" Leo smiled crookedly, but Rose saw a flicker of regret behind his eyes.

"You're not going in, are you?"

"I have to, babe." Leo's brown eyes met hers, his emotions now plain. "I'm going to trial, in *Granger Securities*. I'm so sorry, honey, but it can't be helped. We were number ten in the trial pool, but everything settled and we're up on Monday. I got the call an hour ago, from the law clerk."

"On a Saturday, they call?"

"Yep. It happens. Judges can't afford down time in their dockets."

"But what about John? They won't let him stay here tonight, and if they find out he's sick, they'll throw me out."

"I couldn't get a sitter." Leo shook his head. "Babe, believe me, if I could avoid this, I would, but I can't. My hands are tied. You know how big this case is."

"I know." Rose did, it was true. He'd been talking about *Granger Securities* for three years. "But what about Jamie, couldn't she sit?"

"No, she's busy. I even called the backup sitter, and she has exams. I told her she can study at our house, but she said no. Plus I asked the neighbor, Mrs. Burton. She's going out, and I don't know anybody else. I'm out of options."

"What about the sitter from the old neighborhood. Sandy?"

"No answer." Leo shrugged. "I'd take him with me to the office, but I have witnesses flying in from Denver, and it's all hands on deck. I have to work all weekend, and next week will be sheer hell."

"Oh, Jeez." Rose was getting that Peter and Paul feeling again, torn between the two children. She didn't want to go home with John and leave Melly alone in the hospital. "On the bright side, he's cooler. Is his fever gone?"

"Yes, but I packed the Tylenol and amoxicillin, just in case. Also I fed the dog and left the dog door open."

"Leo, Leo!" Melly called from the bed. "Ms. Canton gave me a Hermione wand!"

"Lemme see."

"I forget the incantation to make water come out, though. Oh, wait. *Aguamenti!*" Melly grabbed the wand and waved it around, and Leo ducked.

"Cool. Let me try. I don't speak Harry Potter." He took the wand and waved it in the air. "Bibbity, bobbity, boo! What's the spell for a babysitter?"

Melly frowned. "Leo, Mom says I can't watch *iCarly.*"

"She said that? She's such a meanie." Leo turned to Rose, waving the wand. "Let's make her change her mind. Presto!"

"No TV." Rose flared her eyes meaningfully, but Leo scoffed.

"Come on, she won't see anything bad on Nick."

"What's anything bad?" Melly asked, and Leo caught himself, cringing.

"Nothing."

"Step outside with me, will you, Merlin?" Rose went to the door with John, then turned to Melly. "Honey, stay in bed. We're going into the hall a minute, to talk."

"Later, tater!" Leo kissed Melly and gave her back the wand, and Rose led him outside to the window well, dreading the task at hand. Her heart felt so heavy, and she leaned against the ledge, with the air conditioning cold on her back.

"Leo, there's terrible news about Amanda. They gave her last rites. She may already be—" Rose still couldn't finish the sentence, and from the expression on Leo's face, she didn't have to. His forehead collapsed into folds, and he winced.

"Aw, no." He wrapped his arms around her and John, holding them close and rubbing her back. "That's terrible, so terrible. That poor kid."

"I know. I just feel so awful for her, and for Eileen. I wish we could do something."

"We can't."

"You sure?"

"Of course." Leo released her, squinting against the sunlight. "There's nothing we can do."

"Just to tell them we're thinking of them."

"You'd make yourself feel better, but not them. You're the last person they want to hear from right now."

Rose felt stung, if only because it was true.

"Plus anything you say can look like an admission of guilt, later." Leo frowned. "Let it go. Can you let it go?"

Rose had been here before. She could never let anything go. She didn't even know what letting go meant.

"Listen." Leo rubbed her arms, and John stirred, but stayed asleep. "I got a bunch of calls from reporters today, and there are messages at work, too. We have to be smart about this. I realize that this trial comes at the worst time, but it's out of my control."

"Can't you get an extension from the judge? You have a child in the hospital."

"Melly's coming home tomorrow, right?"

"Yes, around noon."

"Then no." Leo gave her a quick kiss on the cheek. "Look, I have to leave. Tonight, take John and go home."

"I don't have a car."

"Yes, you do. I parked yours out front."

"Thanks. How did you do that?"

"By cab. Listen, Melly will be fine tonight. I put her new book in the diaper bag, plus the DS. You can call her every hour. I'll call if I can, too."

"Leo, no." Rose felt so confused. Her head thundered. "I can't go home and leave her alone. She just went through a major trauma."

"Then go home until one of the sitters frees up, and maybe you can come back."

"I don't want to leave her alone. She could have died. Amanda is dying. This is real, and it matters." Rose felt herself get worked up. She flashed on the teddy bears in the ambulance. "These kids are real, not packages you can drop off. They live and they die."

Leo blinked. "I know that."

"Melly's always accommodating John. It's never the other way around."

Leo frowned in confusion. "That's because he's the baby."

"Or is it because he's *your* baby?"

"What?" Leo's lips parted. "Are you crazy?"

Mommy!

Rose blinked. Maybe she was. She felt it, a little. She was responsible for a child's death. She couldn't take anything back. She couldn't replay anything. It was too late to make a different decision. Time wasn't her friend, it had never been. It didn't care about children, life, or death. It just ticked ahead, moving on, ever forward, always later.

"Ro, it's not a choice between Melly and John, or between Melly and Amanda. You're all over the place. Hang on to yourself." Leo touched her arm, and John shifted, his nose bubbling. "I love both kids the same, you know that. Right now, the only family that matters is ours. Not theirs, ours. You, me, Melly, and John. Even Googie. That's the family that means everything to me."

"Is that why you're going to work?"

"*What?*"

"You heard me." Rose knew she was wrong, even as the words escaped her lips. She was digging herself a hole and she didn't know why, but she couldn't stop herself, either.

Leo's eyes widened, a bewildered brown, the hue of earth itself. He shut his mouth, pursing his lips, and she could see he didn't want to say anything he would regret. Without another word, he turned on his heel and strode back to the hospital room, where she knew he would put on a happy face and give Melly a good-bye kiss.

Rose remained frozen in the sunlight, and when Leo emerged from Melly's room, she didn't apologize or try to stop him.

She let him walk down the hall.

Away.

Chapter Sixteen

Rose began walking and rocking John, who was fussy and unhappy. He'd slept most of the afternoon, but his second dose of Tylenol was wearing off and he must've been hungry. She replaced his pacifier and sang him "Oh Susanna," her go-to song, but it wasn't working. She didn't know what had happened to Amanda, and she felt cut off from the world, tense, and out of sorts.

John wailed, and Melly looked up from her *Beedle the Bard* book. "Mom, what does he want?"

"I don't know. His ear must hurt."

"Why don't we tell the doctor?"

"They're all busy, and he's not their patient."

"Why not?"

"That's not how it works."

" 'Oh, don't you cry for me.' " Rose sang and swayed, but John kept crying. She walked him to the window, but he wouldn't be distracted by mere trees and a setting sun. She had to quiet him before the nurses got wise to their pajama party. She paced back to the bed. "Melly?"

"Yes?" She looked up from the book, pressing her oxygen tube dutifully into place.

"I'm going to go downstairs and get us some more food. I'll be right back, okay?"

"Okay."

"If you need anything, you can always ask the nurse." Rose picked up her purse and slung it over her shoulder, then grabbed the remote control and tucked it under John. She wiped his nose with her sleeve, then slipped out of the room. An older nurse and a young intern looked up from behind their counter, and Rose flashed them a smile. "We're going down for some food, and my daughter Melly will be alone. Can you keep an eye on her?"

"Sure," the nurse answered. "Take the stairs, it's quicker. The cafeteria is to the right, at the bottom, first floor."

"Thanks."

John cried, and the intern winced at the sound. "No lung trouble on him, eh?"

Rose faked a laugh and wished parenthood on him, then headed down the hall toward the stairs. Visitors and orderlies turned as she passed, and when she went through the stairwell door, John quieted abruptly, at the change in scenery. He sighed a baby sigh, his chest heaving, and he looked around in wobbly wonderment. The tip of his nose was red, his cheeks pink and chubby, and his curly brown hair damp where he had sweated. His brown eyes shone with tears, but were round and lively, like Leo's.

Is it because he's your baby?

"There you go, honey bun." She rubbed his back between his tiny shoulder blades, and his sleeper felt warm and nubby under her palm. "It's all right, honey. Everything's all right."

John smiled at her, and Rose felt her heart fill with love. She gave him a kiss, then climbed down the stairs, cradling him close to her chest. She adored John, and she adored Leo, and she felt terrible about what she'd said about him favoring the baby. It was a terrible thing to say, and it wasn't even true. She must have been crazy.

Mommy!

She stopped on the stairwell, slid her BlackBerry from her pocket, and thumbed her way to the phone function. She didn't think she'd screw up any cardiac monitors if she called from here, but there was only one bar left on the screen. She thumbed her way to the text function, texted I'M SORRY LOVE U, and hit SEND. But the text didn't transmit, either because of the low battery or poor reception.

She hit the first floor, opened the door, and entered the bright, glistening lobby. It was an uncrowded, sleepy Saturday night, and for that she was grateful. She passed a sign for the cafeteria and followed it past bronze plaques that listed major donors and corporate sponsors, knowing she was getting closer to the cafeteria by the comforting aromas of grilled cheese and tomato soup. She kept going, and the hallway wound around to an institutional cafeteria signed THE GROTTO, where papier-mâché salamis and ersatz wheels of provolone hung above a stainless steel lineup of trays and silverware. She grabbed a red plastic tray and got in line behind a man and a woman, sliding the tray along with one hand and holding John with the other, giving him a kiss on the cheek.

"Let's see what they have, huh? Hot dog, grilled cheese, mac and cheese." Rose talked to John all the time, like the narrator of their everyday life. She didn't know why she did it, but she'd done it with Melly, and she knew he understood the gist. Science didn't give babies enough credit, and every mother knew it.

"Johnnie, look at all this good stuff." Rose eyed the hot sandwiches wrapped in aluminum foil and picked two grilled-cheese sandwiches for them, hoping to find something easier on the throat for Melly. John started pumping his fists happily, which he did when he was hungry, and it caught the attention of a female cafeteria worker, whose nametag read DORIS.

"What a cute little guy!" Doris walked over with a tray of wrapped hamburgers, flat and silvery as flying saucers. "Is he a good baby?"

"The best. Easy as pie." Rose thought of the cafeteria workers killed in the explosion, then shooed it away. She plucked a French fry from the bag and offered one to John, who closed his little fingers around it and throttled it before it got to his mouth, where he stuffed it in, sideways. "Yummy, huh?"

"He loves my cooking." Doris smiled.

"He sure does." Rose went down the line, looking for pizza. The man in front of her skipped ahead to the coffee station, and she closed up behind an older woman with a short, steel-gray ponytail, who was squinting at the vats of soup, the deep lines in her face illuminated by the under-counter lights.

"Excuse me, can you read that, dear?" the older woman asked, frowning at Rose. "I forgot my reading glasses. Does that say 'vegetable'?"

"Yes, it's vegetarian vegetable."

"Thank you." The woman smiled, her hooded eyes lighting up when she saw John. "Goodness, a baby! How I miss those days! She's adorable."

"Thanks." Rose didn't bother to correct her, and Doris tried to get the older woman's attention.

"Ma'am, did you want some soup?"

"Yes, please, just one. Vegetable. Small."

"And you want the burgers, too. All eight?"

"Yes, I've got to feed a lot of people."

"Good for you," Rose said, trying to leave. The heat lamps shone blood-red onto pizza slices in cardboard triangles, and next to that were glass shelves of cherry Jell-O and chocolate pudding, which she slid onto her tray for Melly.

"They sent me down for the food. I'm the one who pays, naturally. I'm always the one who pays." The older woman chuckled, and Rose took three bottles of water from a well of chipped ice.

"That's nice of you," she said, to be polite.

"My grand-niece is in a bad way," the older woman said to Doris, who was putting the hamburgers in a large paper bag. "She got hurt real bad, in that fire at the school."

Rose froze. The woman had to be talking about Amanda. It was a coincidence, but not that strange. Reesburgh Memorial was a small hospital in a small town. It meant that Amanda was still alive. Her heart leapt, and she wanted to hear more. She handed John another French fry to keep him quiet, eavesdropping.

"Sorry for your trouble." Doris pitched ketchup packets into the bag. "I saw that fire on the news. They broke in right in the middle of my stories."

Rose kept her head down. She wanted information, but she didn't want to be recognized.

The older woman was saying, "The doctors thought she was going to pass this morning, but she proved 'em all wrong. It's a rollercoaster, up and down, down and up, day and night."

"I'm so sorry." Doris frowned. "I'll say a prayer."

"Thank you. We drove across the state from Pittsburgh, when we heard. They won't let us in to see her, for more than fifteen minutes every hour."

"Rules are rules." Doris handed the bag to the cashier, then turned to Rose. "Would you like to go first, miss? You have the baby, and this lady has a large dinner order."

"Yes, thanks, I should hurry." Rose went ahead to the cashier, keeping her head down, but she could still overhear the conversation.

"I believe in the power of prayer," the older woman was saying. "I pray every day. Ever since my husband passed, it brings me peace and tranquility. You ask me, the rest of my family could use some good old-fashioned religion. My nephew, he's a lawyer, and he's just plain angry all the time. He's up there now, ranting and raving. Hard to believe he was raised a Christian."

"I hear that." Doris put a floppy packet of napkins in the bag.

"He wants to sue the school and everybody in sight. He says, 'Heads will roll!'"

Oh no. Rose got her wallet from her purse, but the cashier was taking forever, pecking the register keys. Another cafeteria worker, a tattooed teenager, came over and helped the older woman. Rose kept her head down, and the cashier stuffed the food in a bag, firing lids for the Jell-O and pudding, while the machine came up with a total.

"That'll be $18.36," the cashier said finally.

"Keep the change." Rose left a twenty, grabbed the food bag, and hurried from the cafeteria. She hit the hallway, her thoughts racing. She wanted to call Leo and tell him that he'd been right. People were lawyering up. Amanda's family, the school district, and God knows who else.

She took her phone from her pocket, juggling John, purse, remote control, and food bag. She glanced at the screen but it was still a single bar, so she headed for the hospital entrance, figuring she'd get better reception outside. But when she looked up through the glass doors, she stopped in her tracks.

Reporters mobbed the walkway, drinking sodas and smoking, their videocameras and microphones at rest. She turned on her heel and hustled back to the stairs.

Chapter Seventeen

Rose lay next to Melly on her bed, with John snoring on her chest, induced to slumber with Tylenol and carbs. The TV played softly on the Nickelodeon channel, and the saturated colors of the cartoons flickered around the darkening room. She checked her watch. 8:15 P.M. Her phone battery had gone dead, and she hadn't heard from Leo on the hospital phone. She'd called him and left a message, then she'd called every sitter she could think of, with no luck. She could hide out in the room for only so long after visiting hours.

Rose turned to Melly, watching TV. "Mel? We have a problem, and I need your help."

"What?" Melly looked over, her long hair messy on the pillow and her eyes tired.

"I can't stay much longer with John, and Leo can't take him, so I might have to go home for tonight."

Melly frowned. "Do I go, too?"

"No, you stay here. Later tonight, if I can get a sitter, I can come back, but if I can't, I'll be back in the morning. You'll have to be alone tonight, like a big girl, but I think you'll be fine. I'm not worried about it." Rose always said she wasn't worried when she was, which was professional parenting.

"I would be here, all by myself?"

"You won't be alone. There are nurses and doctors right outside the door. They sit there all night, at their desk. We can go meet them, right now."

"I don't want to."

"Okay, well, before I go, I'll make sure they'll check on you. That's their job, to check on the patients."

"Why can't I go home with you?"

"You can tomorrow, but not tonight. They want to keep an eye on you, to make sure your oxygen level is okay."

"But I was good, Mom. I kept it on." Melly fingered the oxygen tube, wounded.

"Yes, you were, but they need it on all night, one more night."

"Why do you have to leave?" Melly boosted herself up on the pillow.

"They don't let babies stay, and I can't get a babysitter. You heard me on the phone. I have a problem, and you could really help, if you'd just stay here by yourself." Rose went into bribe mode. "You can watch TV as late as you want, but only *Nick at Nite*."

"Really?" Melly perked up as the door opened, and the nurse entered, with a smile.

"Hello, ladies," she said, cheery. She was a young brunette, heavyset, with a broad smile. Her pink scrubs were covered with a puppy print, and taped to her stethoscope was a laminated photo of a white poodle. "I'm Rosie, the night nurse."

"Ha!" Melly laughed, sitting up. "Same name as you, Mom."

"Right." Rose edged out of bed, holding the sleeping baby. "My name's Rose, too. And we both love dogs, right?"

"Guilty as charged. I have a poodle named Bobo."

Melly perked up. "We have a Cavalier King Charles spaniel. Her name is Princess Google Cadiz McKenna Ingrassia."

The nurse laughed. "That's a long name."

"We have a lot of names in our family. We just call her Googie because she has googly eyes."

"Cute!" The nurse lifted the blood pressure cuff from a wire basket in the wall. "Melly, I'm going to take your blood pressure. You know how this works?"

"Yes. It hurts."

"Not the way I do it." The nurse picked up Melly's arm, and her gaze shifted to Rose. "I'm sorry, but you can't stay here at night, with the baby."

"I know, I'm leaving." Rose smiled, to send the right signal to Melly. "I was telling Melly that you'll be right outside the door, and she shouldn't be worried about a thing. I'm going to let her stay up and watch *Nick at Nite*."

The nurse nodded, wrapping the cuff with care. "That's right, Melly. We're going to have fun. I like your nail polish. I love pink."

"Me, too."

"Know what?" The nurse strapped the cuff closed with Velcro. "I have some nail polish at my desk, and we can do each other's nails, later on."

"Yay!" Melly grinned, scrambling to her knees. "I know how to do it, all by myself."

"Really?" The nurse pumped up the cuff. "We'll have a good time, you and me."

"Do you like pudding?"

"I love pudding! See my hips?" The nurse chuckled, eyeing her watch. "I like it all gooey and yummy and chocolaty." She released the cuff. "All done. You're doing great, cutie patootie."

Melly smiled, surprised. "Hey, that didn't hurt. How did you do that?"

"That's my secret."

Melly turned to Rose, bright-eyed. "Mom, you can go now."

"Okay, good idea." Rose cuddled John to her chest, gave Melly a quick kiss on the cheek, hoisted her purse and diaper bag to her shoulder, then noticed the remote control on the chair. She picked it up and wedged it into the diaper bag, just to be on the safe side.

"There was a fire at my school," Melly told the nurse.

"I know, I heard."

"My mom got me out."

"She's amazing. You know why?"

"Why?"

"Her name is Rose." The nurse winked, then turned to Rose. "Bye now, other Rose!"

"Bye, and thanks!" Rose went to the door. "Sweetie, I'll call you on the phone in about an hour."

"Okay, Mom!"

"Have fun! Love you!" Rose hurried down the hall and took the stairs, trying not to jostle John. She got her car keys from her purse, held John close, put her head down, and barreled through the doors.

Heads started to turn as soon as she hit the pavement, and the crowd surged toward her. Klieglights burst into brightness, cameramen hoisted videocameras, and microphones were brandished. Leading the crowd was Tanya Robertson, and she thrust her microphone at Rose.

"Ms. McKenna, how's Melly? Is she still being discharged tomorrow? Can't we get that one-on-one interview? Just say the word!"

"No comment." Rose looked around for her car, but the klieglights blinded her, and the commotion woke John, who burst into tears.

Tanya persisted, joined by the other reporters. "Any comment on the condition of Amanda Gigot, Ms. McKenna?" "Did you administer CPR to any child besides yours?"

Rose spotted her blue Explorer in the lot and picked up a jog, holding the crying baby to her chest.

"Is it true that you have complained to school officials about the behavior of Amanda Gigot toward your daughter?" "Has the Gigot family or their lawyer contacted you?"

Rose chirped the door unlocked, buckled John into his car seat, jumped behind the wheel, and hit the gas, leaving their questions behind.

Chapter Eighteen

It was dark by the time Rose got home and pulled into the driveway. Her neighbor across the street was putting out his trash, and she waved to him. He didn't wave back, though he had to have seen her. She cut the engine, got out of the car, went around the backseat, and lifted John, still asleep, from his car seat. Stale Cheerios fell to the driveway as she hoisted him to her shoulder, grabbed the diaper bag, and closed the door. She walked the sidewalk to the house, grateful for the darkness, the starless night like a cloak, hiding her from view.

She went up the sidewalk, then the flagstone path to the house, a four-bedroom colonial of solid gray stone, with a half circle of white roof sheltering the entrance. It seemed impossible that they could lose the house, but everything that had happened since Friday seemed impossible. She found her house key and let herself in, waking Princess Google, the world's worst watchdog.

She set her bags on the couch and went straight upstairs with John, walking evenly so she wouldn't wake him. She switched on the hall light, changed him, and put him down. He stayed asleep, his arms open, his fists balled, and his legs flopped apart like a frog's. She tiptoed from the room and was going downstairs to try to find a sitter when the phone started ringing. She ran to the wall phone in the kitchen, and the caller ID read REESBURGH MEMORIAL.

Rose picked up instantly, alarmed. "Yes?"

"Mom?" It was Melly.

"Honey! I was going to call you soon. How are you doing?"

"They put a little girl in my room."

"Oh well." Rose should have thought of that, as a possibility. "That happens, sometimes."

"That's what Leo says. He called to say hi."

"That was nice."

"The mom is sleeping over with her. She's on the other side of the curtain."

Rose heard noise in the background. "What's that sound?"

"She has the TV on, really loud. I can't even hear *Nick at Nite*. I don't know where the nurse went and we didn't do our nails."

Rose hated that Melly was there alone. "I guess she got busy. Do you see the button—"

"Mom, it said on their TV that Amanda was in the hospital. I heard it. They said her name, Amanda Gigot. Is Amanda in the hospital?"

Oh no. "Yes, she is."

"*This* hospital?"

"Yes."

"Is she sick?"

"Yes. She has what you had, from the smoke." Rose didn't want to lie, but she couldn't tell the whole truth, not with Melly by herself. "She needs more oxygen, and they're keeping an eye on her."

"I don't want her to come in my room, Mom."

"She won't."

"She better not." Melly sounded anxious. "I'm already sharing it with a little kid. I shouldn't have to share it with Amanda, too. Mom, can I come home?"

"Not yet."

"But I don't want to stay here, all by myself."

Rose felt a guilty pang. "I'm going to call some babysitters and see if I can get someone to stay with John, so I can come back to the hospital. Okay?"

"Please come soon, Mom."

"I'll try. In the meantime, can you rest a little?"

"No, the TV is so loud. If you were here, you would say, 'turn that down!'" Melly did a fair impression of Rose as fishwife.

"Let me see if I can do something about that TV, then get a sitter." Rose checked her oven clock. 9:25 P.M. "I'll call you as soon as I can. I love you."

"Love you, too."

"Hang in there. Bye." Rose hung up, then hit redial to get the main switchboard at the hospital. The operator picked up, and she asked, "Can you transfer me to the nurses' station on the third floor?"

"Certainly," the operator answered. There was a click, and the phone rang and rang. Nobody picked up, so Rose hung up and redialed.

"I'm the one calling the third floor," Rose said, when the operator answered. "My daughter is in the hospital, and I want to speak with the nurse outside her room. Her name is Rosie, and the TV in—"

"Hold the line."

"No, wait!" Rose heard the same clicks and the same ringing. She waited ten rings and hung up. She took her phone from her pocket and plugged it into the charger near the toaster. The phone came to life, the red star telling her there was a message, so she pressed to the phone function. The last call was from Leo's cell, and she pressed voicemail, for his message:

"Babe, I got your text, and I'm sorry, too. I'm up to my ass in alligators here, so don't wait up. Hope you found a sitter and give the kids my love. You, too."

Rose pressed END, happy to hear his voice, then pressed her way to her address book, thumbed to her B-list babysitters, and got busy. Almost half an hour later, she hadn't been able to beg, borrow, or steal a sitter. She checked the clock, and it was almost ten o'clock. She felt terrible, but she had to call Melly with the bad news. "Honey?" she said, when Melly picked up.

"Mom! When are you coming?"

"I'm so sorry, sweetie, but I can't. I tried, but I can't get a sitter. I'll keep trying, and if I get lucky, I can—"

"Mom, please? I don't like it here."

"Did the nurse come back?" Rose could hear the TV, blaring in the background.

"She did but she had to go. Mom, please. Please come."

"Did you tell her about the TV?"

"No, I felt funny."

"Mel, see the button on the side of the bed? It's a white plastic thing and it's attached to a white cord. Can you press it?"

"Yes. I'm pressing it, but the nurse isn't coming."

"Keep pressing it, and she will."

"She's not, Mom." Melly started to cry, softly.

"Honey, don't cry, everything's all right. Don't be upset. When the nurse comes, put her on the phone. I'll tell her to tell the lady to lower the TV." Rose heard Melly sniffling, then some noise and talking, and it sounded like the nurse was in the room. "Melly, put the nurse on. Melly? Hello?"

"Yes," replied a cool voice, clearly not nurse Rosie.

"Hi, this is Rose. Who is this?"

"It's Annabelle. Are you the mother?"

"Yes, please, help her. She was in that school fire yesterday, and the woman in her room is blaring the TV. The news is upsetting her."

"Relax. I have it under control. Hang on, please." The nurse sounded calm, and in the next minute the background noise stopped and the TV silenced, but Melly was still crying softly, which broke Rose's heart.

"Hello, Annabelle?" she said. "Are you there?"

"Pardon?"

"Can you just comfort my daughter? She's a good kid, she's just scared, and she's been through a lot in the past few—"

"I'm sorry, but we have to hang up. There are no calls permitted this late."

"No, wait. Don't hang up. I want to talk to my daughter."

"There's an automatic cut-off for phone calls after ten. I'll take good care of her."

Rose felt her temper flare. "Let me say good night to her, for God's sake."

"Please, hold on."

"Melly? Melly?" Rose said, but the line went dead. She tried to call back, but there was no answer. She tried the switchboard and asked again for the nurses' station, but the phone rang and rang, all over again. She hung up, noticing the red light was blinking on her phone, which meant incoming email.

She pressed the button to see the list of senders, but they were all messages sent from Facebook. She scanned the names in the messages: Kim Barnett, Jane Llewellyn, Annelyn Baxter, moms from the class and school committees. When she'd moved to Reesburgh, she'd friended everyone in the class. She clicked the first name, and the email came on the screen:

Kim Barnett has sent you a message on Facebook. "I KNOW THE GIGOT FAMILY AND THEY ARE HEARTBROKEN! HOW DO YOU LIVE WITH YOURSELF?"

Rose set down the BlackBerry. Reesburgh was a small town, and the Internet made it even smaller. She didn't need to read any more.

She got the gist.

Chapter Nineteen

Rose stood at the kitchen counter, drinking Diet Coke and waiting for the TV news. She didn't relish seeing the story of the school fire, but she wanted to know what Melly might have seen or heard. She scratched the sleeping dog with her foot while the turbocharged theme of Philly News started. A handsome anchorman came on the screen, with a photo of the burning elementary school behind him, above a banner, FATAL SCHOOL FIRE.

"Good evening, Tim Dodson here. In our top story, life in Reesburgh is getting back to the new normal, after a cafeteria fire in an elementary school that left three dead, a beloved teacher and two female cafeteria workers. Tanya Robertson is on the scene at Reesburgh Memorial Hospital, where young Amanda Gigot remains in Intensive Care, fighting for her young life . . ."

The screen changed to Tanya, holding a bubble microphone to her lipsticked lips, standing in a pool of manufactured light. "Tonight, the two students injured in Friday's school fire remain in this hospital. They're little girls from the same third-grade class, but that's where the similarity ends. The lucky one, Melinda Cadiz, age eight, will be going home tomorrow after being treated for smoke inhalation. Melinda, called Melly, was rescued from the flames by her mother, our reluctant hero Rose McKenna. We were the first to show you that viewer video yesterday, of Rose running out of the smoky school, with her daughter in her arms."

Rose shuddered, but wasn't completely surprised. So many people had phones and BlackBerrys. She'd carried a flip camera around since the day John was born.

Tanya's expression darkened, and a school photo of Amanda popped onto the screen. "Not so lucky is Amanda Gigot, also age eight, who remains in a coma, after a head injury and significant smoke inhalation. Amanda's the only daughter after two sons, and the Gigot family is headed by hard-working single mom Eileen Gigot, whose husband was killed in a forklift accident seven years ago. The entire extended Gigot clan is now by Amanda's side, hoping and praying for her recovery."

Tanya changed her tone, to investigative mode. "Authorities say that the school is set to reopen on Monday, but a spokesman for the Gigot family tells me they're considering legal action against the school, the school district, and the school's general contractor for negligence. The Gigot family has already filed for an emergency injunction, trying to stop the school from demolishing the damaged cafeteria until the cause of the fire can be independently determined. They've also called for the county District Attorney to investigate the matter for possible criminal charges."

Rose shook her head. So the Gigots really were going to sue, and she hadn't known about the injunction. She thought back to her talk with Mr. Rodriguez. No wonder he'd been angry at Kristen for talking about the cause of the fire. Things were about to go from bad to worse, and she hoped that didn't include suing her and Leo.

"We'll keep you posted on developments in this heartbreaking story, and I'll have my exclusive interview tomorrow, my one-on-one exclusive with Eileen Gigot. Back to you, Tim."

Rose took a final slug of soda. The story was getting bigger, spreading like the fire itself, and she didn't know how long it would burn. She switched off the TV, troubled. Her gaze fell on her black laptop, which she kept on the kitchen table, off to the side. She pulled up a stool, sat down, and hit a key. A screensaver came on of Leo, Melly, John, and her, grinning in a cottony mass of matching sweatshirts on the beach. She went online, plugged in the website of the TV station, and its website popped onto the screen. PHILADELPHIA'S BIGGEST NEWS, read the top of the page, and underneath were headlines, among them, SCHOOL FIRE IGNITES CONTROVERSY, above the banner, Share, Print Email, Buzz up, Twitter, Facebook.

She skimmed the story, which said nothing that hadn't been reported on TV, but at the bottom was a bright red banner, SEND US YOUR VIEWER VIDEOS! There were a bunch of thumbnails: scenes of the burning school, frozen in time, with the title on top. The Most Watched was *Hero Mom.* Rose clicked *Hero Mom* and watched. The video showed kids and teachers milling around the teachers' parking lot, with the sound of head counts and other snippets caught on audio—"it's only in the cafeteria," "the fourth grade got out first," "because it's a new school, so they didn't have the drill down yet."

Suddenly the camera turned, jittery, to the building, where students streamed from the double doors by the library, and Rose recognized the older kids she had seen in the stairwell. Their flow stopped abruptly, and she saw herself running out of the building, her expression stricken, with Melly limp in her arms, her legs swinging. "Help!" she heard herself scream, on the video. Her cry was barely picked up by the audio, but Princess Google woke up, blinking and cocking her head.

Rose watched herself run and lay Melly down on the grass, then the view was obstructed by heads and feet as the crowds surged forward, until there was the ambulance siren and the tape ended. The video left her heart pounding. The sights, the sounds, the very picture took her back to the fire. She sat there a moment, staring at the titles of the other clips: *Hero Mom Carries Daughter to Ambulance. Mom Gives CPR to Daughter. Cafeteria Fire.* She moved the cursor over *Cafeteria Fire,* and hit PLAY, and the first frame of the video wasn't a sunny parking lot, but a nightmare.

Rose swallowed hard at the sight. The view was from the playground, and the screen showed the front of the school, with the cafeteria front and center. Smoke billowed from the playground exit and from holes in the cafeteria walls and roof, where windows and skylights used to be. The air grew increasingly gray and hazy, and frantic children popped from the fog, being shepherded by teachers, janitors, and staff. The audio picked up a cacophony of screams, shouts, tears, yelling, and people shouting "oh my God," "look at that," "this way, this way," and "help!"

Rose watched, galvanized, and suddenly she saw a terrified Danielle running out of the smoke, and after her, Emily, running in tears. Teachers surged forward to meet them, and the older students kept coming out of the smoke, hustled out in lines, until the video ended.

Rose remained motionless at the laptop, her hand still on the mouse. She wished she could play it again and have it end with Amanda fleeing the building, her blond hair flying behind her, her tanned legs churning, her arms open as she ran into the waiting embrace of Mrs. Nuru.

Mommy!

Rose didn't move for the longest time. Princess Google fell back asleep on the floor, and the kitchen went completely silent. A light rain began to fall outside, and the leaves of the trees rustled with the drops, making the softest of sounds, an undercurrent of hush.

Tears came to Rose's eyes. She'd been holding them back for so long, but this time, she let them flow.

Chapter Twenty

Rose woke up, hearing her name called softly, then feeling a gentle touch on her back and a soft kiss on her cheek. She had fallen asleep in front of the laptop, on her folded arms. She lifted her head, blinking. "Leo?" she said, muzzy from sleep.

"Hi, honey." Leo knelt beside her, so that they were eye level, and he put his arm around her. "I was worried about my best girl, so I snuck out."

"Aw." Rose let herself be hugged, their heads touching. Princess Google pressed between them, pawing for attention with moppet feet, her tail flopping back and forth. "That's so sweet of you."

"I can sleep here if you want to go back to the hospital. I'll work from home tomorrow morning, then come by the hospital at noon and pick up you and Melly. Sound like a plan?" Leo kissed her again, and Rose felt the delicious scratchiness of a late-day beard.

"Yes, thanks. I'm sorry I was a jerk."

"I'm sorry you were, too." Leo smiled, and Rose smiled back.

"I don't like when we fight."

"Me, neither." Leo kissed her again, more deeply. His mouth was warm, soft, and familiar. A best friend, and a best lover.

"I love you."

"I love you, too, which brings up an option I didn't mention. We forget the kids and go upstairs and make love like people who have orange crates for furniture and read the liner notes on CDs."

Rose smiled, then felt it disappear. "Amanda's doing better, but still in a coma. Melly heard about her on TV."

"Oh no." Leo frowned, and Princess Google jumped up on his leg again. He scratched behind the ear, burying his knuckles in her fluffy coat. "You'd better get to the hospital. Unless you want me to."

"Thanks, but I will." Rose stretched, feeling stiff. "The Gigots have a lawyer in the family, and they're suing to stop the school from opening and cleaning up the site. Think they'll sue us, too?"

"Here we go." Leo stood up, then steadied her to her feet, his lips pursed. He looked tired, his tie gone and his shirt unbuttoned, showing the collar of his undershirt. "The state and the school district have deeper pockets than we do, but as I said, I'd name us, too."

"So what can we do? What does it mean, exactly? Can we really lose the house? Do they just take it, and sell it?" Rose couldn't wrap her mind around it. "What about the mortgage? Do we owe the bank then, too?"

"Relax." Leo held up a hand. "I have to look at the insurance policy and see if we're covered. I refuse to worry about it now. It's late, and we're both beat."

"Would you represent us?"

"Not now. Please." Leo held up his hand, his expression tense. "I can't deal. One thing at a time."

"I'm sorry."

"It's okay. I said for better or worse, and I meant it."

"Then I'm a lucky woman." Rose hugged him tight, and Leo held her close for a second.

"Is this sex?" he asked.

Rose laughed.

Leo gave her a final squeeze, with his trademark grunt, like a punctuation mark. "Want some coffee before you go?"

"Good idea."

"I'll get it." Leo made a beeline for the coffeemaker. He was a coffee fetishist, always on a quest for the perfect cup, trying out French Presses, Cuisinart brewers, and now a single-cup Keurig. He slid a mug under the spout and hit the blue button, and Rose leaned against the counter.

"How's trial prep going?"

"Not bad. I have a ton to do, but I'm on it."

"Melly gets discharged at noon. Can you really be there?"

"Yes, I planned on it. I don't want you running that gauntlet of press alone."

"Thanks." Rose knew it wouldn't be easy for him. His office was an hour's drive away. "Also, I know you can't swing it, but the wakes are tomorrow night for Marylou, Serena, and Ellen."

"You're not going, are you?" Leo turned, frowning. Behind him, coffee poured into the mug in a stream, releasing a rich aroma.

"Yes, I have to. I lined up a sitter."

"You shouldn't, babe."

"What will it look like if I don't?" Rose gestured at her computer. "You should see the email I'm getting. They think I'm heartless."

"All the more reason you shouldn't go. If we're getting sued, we have to clam up and lay low."

"But the whole town will be there. Everyone loved the teacher. You heard Mrs. Nuru."

"My point exactly."

"We'll look disrespectful."

"So send flowers, lots of flowers." Leo handed her the coffee mug, and Rose set it down, letting it cool.

"I don't know."

"Well, I do. Don't go. Please. As a favor to me."

"Come on. Don't be that way."

"What way?" A wounded look crossed Leo's tired eyes. "You don't know what can happen, or what they'll do, what you'll do."

"What would I do? I won't do anything wrong."

"You could say the wrong thing." Leo started to take a sip of coffee, then stopped. "Like how guilty you feel, or how sad that you couldn't get them both out of the school. All the things you say to me."

Rose blinked. "I might say that, but only to you or a friend."

"Like who?"

"I don't know. I guess Kristen, maybe. She'll be there."

"The gifted teacher? Who works for the district that's about to be sued, who would testify against you or lose her job?" Leo's eyed flared. "Babe, we don't have any friends. Nobody knows us, and what they know, they don't like."

"We can't just accept that. It could be our chance to show them that we're not what they think."

"No way." Leo's tone flattened. "It ain't gonna happen."

"It *has* to, Leo. You can go to the office every day, but this is my world. I have to make it work, for my sake and for the kids."

"Not now, not tomorrow night. Stay home, will you? Haven't you done enough?"

Ouch. Rose stood, stunned.

"Oh, jeez." Leo rubbed his forehead, irritably. "I didn't mean that. I'm sórry, really."

Rose turned away, hurt, and headed for the living room. "I'm going to the hospital. See you tomorrow."

Chapter Twenty-one

Rose walked down the quiet hall of the hospital, empty at this hour. There had been no press out front, and a janitor in baggy blue scrubs was shining the floor with a large rotating polisher. The nurses' station held only the goateed intern, who was on the computer and barely nodded at Rose when she approached the counter.

"I'm Melly's mother, back to stay the night."

"No problem." The intern glanced up from the computer, and Rose could see tiny playing cards reflected in his glasses.

"I understand there's another child in the room."

"Not anymore. A new bed opened up, and her parents wanted a private."

"Great." Rose looked around. "Is Rosie here, the nurse?"

"Saw her a while ago, but not sure where she is now."

"Okay, thanks. See you." Rose crossed the hall to Melly's room and opened the door. It was still and dark, except for the vital-signs monitor, pulsing red, blue, and green digits.

"Mom?" Melly asked softly, and Rose felt a rush of tenderness, shedding her purse on the chair and coming over to the bed.

"How'd you know it was me?"

"You're my mom."

Rose smiled. "How you doin', night owl?"

"You came back."

"Leo's with John. Why aren't you asleep?"

"I'm not tired."

"Well, I am." Rose lowered the guardrail, kicked her loafers off, and eased onto the bed. "Roll over, Beethoven."

"They said on the TV that cafeteria ladies died in the fire."

I hate TV. "That's true, sweetie, and a teacher died, too. Marylou Battle."

"I don't know her."

"I didn't think so."

"Did they burn up?"

Rose shuddered. Another truth she couldn't tell, another necessary lie. "No, the smoke got them."

"The smoke almost got me, too."

"But it didn't, in the end."

Melly fell silent, her breathing shallow. The oxygen tube was in place under her nose, and she'd been taken off the IV. "Did they go to heaven with Daddy?"

"I'm sure they did, Mel," Rose answered. Bernardo had died when Melly was four, and she brought him up often, though he hadn't bothered to see her much, after the divorce.

"If Amanda dies, will she go to heaven?"

"Yes." Rose swallowed hard, caught unawares. "Absolutely."

"I think so, too," Melly said, after a moment.

Chapter Twenty-two

"You look cute!" Rose was trying to make the best of things. She hadn't gotten a change of clothes for Melly, so she'd had to buy her a pink Hello Kitty sweatsuit and flip-flops in the hospital gift shop.

"Nobody in third grade wears Hello Kitty." Melly sulked at the end of the bed. She'd taken a shower and shampooed her hair, so the smell of smoke was almost completely gone. "It's for babies."

"You can take it off when we get home."

"What if kids from my class see, like Amanda? She's in the same hospital, you said."

"She won't see." Rose hadn't heard anything about Amanda, and she was hoping no news was good news. She hadn't slept well and couldn't wait to go home, having signed the hospital's discharge forms and gotten a flurry of papers with instructions for aftercare.

"I wish I had my Harry shirt. The nurse said they had to throw it away, but I wish they didn't."

"We'll see if we can get you a new one."

"They don't make that one anymore, Mom. It was from the first movie."

"We'll look on eBay." Rose wondered if the Harry Potter shirts were such a good idea, anymore. "Now, listen, if there are reporters outside, don't say anything to them. They'll know your name and they'll call it out, but don't answer."

"Okay." Melly looked over as the door opened, and Leo came in, dressed for work and holding John, awake and gurgling, in a blue onesie. "Leo, did you bring my clothes?"

"No." Leo looked from her to Rose. "Was I supposed to?"

"No, hi." Rose was sorry they'd fought, but she still felt distant. John smiled and reached for her with wet, outstretched fingers, and she took him and gave him a kiss without meeting Leo's eye. "How's he doing?"

"All better. No fever. Slept like a baby. Ha!"

"Hugs, Leo!" Melly called out, and Leo scooped her up and gave her a big kiss on the cheek.

"Wow, I like your cat shirt. Very fashionable."

"Yuck." Melly wrinkled her nose. "I wish I had my Harry shirt."

"Aww, this is nice for a change. It's pink, like cotton candy. You know I love cotton candy." Leo buried his face in her neck and blew raspberries, sending Melly into gales of giggles. The sound made John laugh, and he reached for Melly, his chubby hand outstretched and flapping happily.

"Let's go home." Rose picked up her purse and went to the door. "Is there a lot of press outside?"

"Some." Leo carried Melly out of the room and down the hall to the elevator, where he set her down. "Want to press the button, tater? Go for it. When we get inside, hit L."

Melly pressed the DOWN button, then led them into the elevator cab when the doors slid open. They piled inside, and she hit the lobby button. "*Descendo!*"

"You okay, babe?" Leo asked lightly, after the doors closed, but Rose busied herself with John's pacifier.

"Fine. You?"

"Good. By the way, I brought your phone. It was on the counter." Leo slid her BlackBerry from the pocket of his khakis and handed it to her.

"Thanks." Rose accepted it with a pat smile.

"You going out tonight, still?"

"Yes." Rose knew it was code for the wake, but they never fought in front of Melly, who undoubtedly knew whenever they were fighting. The kid wasn't gifted for nothing.

"Too bad," Leo said, pleasantly. "I wish you wouldn't. You might want to rethink it."

"I don't think so."

"I'll walk you to the car." Leo pursed his lips as they reached the ground floor. "Ready, everybody?"

"Ready!" Melly said, and Leo took her hand. When the doors slid open, they filed out into the carpeted lobby, which was quiet except for a few people sitting on the sectional furniture. Outside the glass entrance was a throng of reporters and cameras.

"Melly, just walk and keep going, no matter what." Rose hoisted John higher, and Leo picked up Melly on the fly.

"Let's go. Melly, where's your wand?"

"In the diaper bag."

"Too bad. Can you make those reporters disappear, anyway?"

"Let's put on our invisibility cloak!"

"Now you're talking." Leo smiled.

"It's on! Go, Leo!" Melly looped one hand around his neck and pointed forward with the other, and they moved as a pack out the entrance and into the sunlight. The reporters flocked to them with cameras, microphones, and questions.

"Any comment, Rose?" "How are you feeling, Melly? Are you friends with Amanda?" "Melly, you going to school tomorrow? What was it like when your mom came to save you?" "Melly, were you afraid in the cafeteria?"

Tanya Robertson caught up with Rose, running alongside, bubble microphone outstretched. "Ms. McKenna, please, I've done an interview with Eileen. You'll want to respond to what she's saying. This is your last chance."

"No comment." Rose kept moving, hugging John close.

"Back off!" Leo said, and Melly buried her face in his neck.

Rose hurried ahead, chirped the doors unlocked, and hustled John into his car seat while Leo took Melly to the other side, buckled her in, and closed the door behind her, as the press swarmed the car, firing questions.

"Mr. Ingrassia, what do you have to say about the injunction the Gigots have filed?" "Did you join in the injunction? Will you be suing the district as well?" "Is Melly going back to school tomorrow?"

Rose jumped inside the car and shoved the key in the ignition. Her phone started ringing, but she ignored it. Reporters edged away as she backed up, and she hit the gas and drove toward the exit, leaving them behind, relieved. She stopped at the first traffic light, slid the phone from her purse, and checked the display. The call was from her best friend, Annie Assarian, so she pressed REDIAL. "Hey!"

"Girl, I've been calling you and leaving messages. What's going on? There's all kinds of nastiness on your Facebook wall. Is Melly okay?"

"Fine." Rose kept her tone light because Melly was listening. "Can I call you back? I'm driving."

"I'm in Philly this week and next on a movie shoot, and we just finished for the day. You wanna have drinks?"

"I can't go out."

"How about I come over? I have my car."

"I'd love that, if it's not too much trouble."

"I'll be there as soon as I can."

"Great." Rose brightened. "See you then." She hung up and set the phone in the cupholder as the traffic light changed to green. "Guess what?"

"Aunt Nemo's coming? Yay!"

Rose smiled. "How did you know? Did you hear?"

"You always smile when you talk to her."

"I bet I do." Rose felt better. She didn't get to see Annie that much anymore, and she fed the car some gas, wondering if there was any food in the fridge.

"Mom, think I'll ever get a friend like Aunt Nemo?"

"I know you will, honey," Rose answered, though her throat caught.

Chapter Twenty-three

Rose made pizza bagels for the kids, then put John down for a nap and installed Melly in the family room with Princess Google and a Harry Potter DVD. Sunshine poured through the lavender in the bay window, and while the two women cleaned up the kitchen, Rose told Annie the whole story.

"You didn't do anything wrong, Ro." Annie shook her head, a stiff cap of onyx curls. Her eyes were large and a rich brown, with a faint almond shape that hinted at her biracial parentage. Her warm skin tone freed her from makeup, though she was one of the most-sought-after makeup artists in New York.

"Still, I feel terrible." Rose rinsed a dish and loaded it into the open dishwasher. "I wish I had gotten them both out."

"You did, essentially. Amanda ran back in, and you couldn't have known that."

"I should have."

"You're not superhuman. You're just a model."

Rose smiled. She had stopped thinking of herself as a model, ages ago.

"I'd have done the exact same thing, if it were Joey or Armen." Annie had two boys with her husband Simon, a sculptor and art history professor at NYU.

"You would?"

"Totally." Annie twisted the plastic bag of bagels closed and put it back in the freezer. "Meanwhile, these were good, for frozen."

"I know, they're fine, right?"

"Totally." Annie yanked up the skinny strap of her purple boho sundress, which showed off tattooed arms encircled with fire-breathing red dragons, Chinese symbols, and an orange koi that had reminded a younger Melly of the cartoon Nemo, so a nickname was born for her godmother.

"Remember when we had to have Murray's? They were the cool bagels." Rose rinsed tomato sauce from a tablespoon. "We'd stand in line every Sunday morning with all the investment bankers?"

"I still do that." Annie smiled.

"Well, I still do this." Rose dropped the spoon into the silverware holder in the dishwasher, keeping it with the other spoons.

"Oh no!" Annie burst into laughter. "Set that spoon free. Let it hang with the knives and forks."

"I'm telling you, sort the silverware before you wash it, then it saves time when you put it away."

"It saves *no* time," Annie shot back. It was an historic disagreement, from their years sharing a one-bedroom in the East Village, which was so small that they stored their boots in the oven.

"Melly agrees with me. She thinks Aunt Nemo's crazy."

"Aunt Nemo *is* crazy, but that's not why."

"But for real, tell me the truth. You would have done the same thing?"

"Yes."

"You don't think I'm a horrible person?"

"I *know* you're not. You're the sweetest person I know."

Rose smiled. "Should I keep fishing for compliments?"

"Go right ahead. I love you, and you know it." Annie's smile vanished. "And I *hate* how Melly gets bullied. If Amanda hadn't been teasing her, they both would have been outside on the playground when the fire started. Ever think of that?"

"I did, but Leo would say that's only a *but for* cause."

"Whatever. All I know is that Melly could have died of smoke inhalation because of that brat."

Rose winced. "Don't say that."

"I know it seems mean, but what about you guys? You moved once already because of the bullying. You can't move again. You're running out of planet." Annie picked up the sponge and wiped the kitchen table. "When I read what they were saying about you on Facebook, it made me nuts."

"Was it bad? I'm afraid to look."

"You should remove all those posts. Those people are insane."

"They're just upset about Amanda."

"Please. Did you read them? Those women are jealous of you, just because of the way you look." Annie finished wiping the table and rinsed out the sponge. "You're going through hell, but nobody ever feels sorry for the pretty one."

"That's not what's going on, and I'm only 'catalog material,' remember?" Rose was quoting her old modeling agent.

"What an idiot he was! You were better than the other girls. Not only were you gorgeous, you were the only one who was nice to everybody, even the makeup gypsies."

Rose didn't reply. She liked the past to stay past. She needed it to.

"You know, if Melly hadn't come along, you'd be making a fortune. Even Bernardo said so. It was the only thing he was right about."

"Nah, they all use actresses now. I got out just in time, and luckily, Melly did come along. Anyway, let's talk about here and now. What if we get sued? We could lose the house. Now that scares me."

"Oh, man. That would scare me, too." Annie frowned under her dark curls. "You can't get sued for saving your own kid, can you?"

"Leo seems to think you can, but it's not his field." Rose screwed the cap on the jar of tomato sauce and returned it to the fridge. "He doesn't want me to go to the wakes, but I really feel like I should pay my respects, and it's tonight. It's too bad that the one night you're in town, I ditch you. Sorry."

"Oh, you're not ditching me. I haven't seen you in, like, six months. I'm going with you."

Rose felt touched. "You are?"

"Sure. You shouldn't go alone, and I have nothing else to do."

"But you don't even know these people."

"Neither do you." Annie smiled, crookedly. "Besides, I go to lots of parties where I don't know anybody."

"It's a wake, not a party, and don't you have to get back to Philly?"

"I'll follow you there in my car, then leave. Lend me a sweater, to cover my tats."

Rose smiled. "Now, *that's* a best friend."

Chapter Twenty-four

Rose braked in the traffic for the funeral home, which anchored Old Town, the historic district of Reesburgh, bisected by Allen Road. The late-day sun tarnished the quaint brick homes, with their Victorian porches, and next to them was a stop-time corner grocery, a mom-and-pop drugstore, and a funky independent bookstore called READsburgh.

Rose circled the block looking for a parking space, with Annie following in her car, and they ended up finding them about ten blocks away from Fiore's. She parked and slipped on sunglasses, having worn her hair tucked under a raffia hat. "Quite a crowd, huh?" she said, getting out of the car.

"Yes." Annie sniffed the air. "Hey, do you smell that? Is that French fries?"

"It's potato chips from the Homestead factory. You smell it stronger here in Old Town, because it's closer to the plant, downwind."

"How many carbs in one breath?"

"Don't ask." Rose fell into step with her on the sidewalk. The humidity was still high, making her black linen dress uncomfortable. They passed a series of graceful brick homes with restored façades and generous wrap-around porches, surrounded by tall, ancient trees in resplendent autumn leaf.

"Where are we?" Annie's neat head swiveled left and right. "Mayberry?"

Rose smiled. "This is called Bosses Row, where the Allen brothers lived when they started Homestead. The company used to be family-owned, but it's not anymore."

"No surprise. Families aren't even family-owned anymore. Look at these houses. They're beautiful."

"They're over a hundred and fifty years old."

"Yes, massa. Remind me to take potato chips back to the boys. I'll say they're from Tara."

"You have this place all wrong." Rose shook her head, walking along, her black flats slapping against the pavement. "It's not homogeneous at all. It's a company town. Most people who live here work at the Homestead plant, and there's plenty of professionals, too. That's what I like, it's a cross-section of people. Normal people."

"Snore."

Rose laughed. "You're a snob."

"I'm a New Yorker." Annie tugged at her black cardigan. "And I'm so hating on this sweater. You wear this?"

"Sure. It's useful."

"It's so boxy, it makes me feel like a nun. Are you dead below the waist, too?"

"Uh-oh." Rose spotted a group of reporters on the pavement ahead of them, with cameras and klieglights. "On the left, ahead, is the press. When we get in the line, stay to the right."

"Gotcha." They reached the end of the receiving line, which flowed down Fiore's flagstone walkway and onto the sidewalk. There had to be a few hundred people here, somber and teary-eyed. Rose hadn't realized how many people these deaths had affected, but she should have. A single life, and death, could touch so many people, and a teacher was forever.

"Sorry, it could take an hour to get inside."

"I don't mind. I'm used to waiting on line." Annie shrugged. "The air is adding years to my life."

Rose felt a wave of sadness for Marylou, Serena, and Ellen. She flashed on the billowing smoke, the raging fire, and Amanda.

Mommy!

"Are you okay?" Annie pulled her closer, by the elbow. "You look so sad. You didn't know any of them, did you?"

"No." Rose understood what she was feeling, but there was too much to say, and she'd never said any of it to anybody, not even Annie. "I keep thinking of Amanda."

"I understand."

Rose noticed a few of the teachers leaving the funeral home, making their way down the driveway to the sidewalk, a downhearted group that included Mrs. Nuru, dabbing her eyes with a Kleenex. "That's Melly's teacher," Rose said, leaning over to Annie. "I should go say hi."

"Go. I'll hold our place."

"Thanks. Be right back." Rose crossed to Mrs. Nuru, who stopped and smiled stiffly at Rose, her hooded eyes glistening.

"Hello, Rose. How's Melly?"

"Home, thanks. I'm so sorry, and Leo sends his condolences, too."

"Thank you."

"Is Kristen here?"

"She came and left. The school staff all came early, at the invitation of the families." Mrs. Nuru pursed her lips. "I heard from Mr. Rodriguez that she told you what I said about the faulty wiring. That was imprudent of me, and of her. I trust you'll keep it confidential."

"Of course."

"Kristen is young, and she has lots of growing up to do. She needs to learn judgment."

"Do you really think so?" Rose asked, defensively. "I think she's such a great teacher."

"Experience tells, in my opinion." Mrs. Nuru sniffed, glancing at the other teachers. "I should go, they're waiting. Will Melly be in school tomorrow?"

"I'm not sure I'll send her." Rose remembered that Mrs. Nuru thought Melly was too sensitive, so she didn't elaborate. "I haven't decided yet."

"If she's well enough, I'd send her. If you decide not to, give her my best."

"Will do, thanks. Bye now." Rose turned and went back to the line, trying not to notice that people started whispering among themselves when they spotted her.

"Everything okay?" Annie asked, when Rose got back to the line.

"I guess. She's upset. They all are." Rose was troubled by what Mrs. Nuru had said about Kristen, and now heads were turning and people were talking about them. "Um, look around."

"I know, I noticed before you did. And here comes the press."

Rose turned to see Tanya Robertson approaching from the left. Her crew followed, switching on klieglights, and the cameraman started filming, his camera perched on his shoulder.

"Ms. McKenna, please." Tanya thrust her microphone forward. "Can't we chat for a moment?"

"No comment." Rose put up a hand, though she knew it would make her look bad on TV. "Please, show some respect."

"We're on public property, and if we could speak one-on-one, as I did with Eileen, this would go much easier. Did you see my interview with her? Do you have a response to her allegations about you?"

"I said, no comment." Rose didn't look over. She didn't know Eileen had made allegations against her. The women in front of her edged away, and other people in the line kept turning around, whispering, and staring at them.

Tanya held her microphone out. "Eileen alleges that you intentionally left Amanda because you think she teases your child, and you've even called her about that. Do you have animosity for Amanda?"

"Stop it!" Annie interrupted, stepping over. "Are you *insane*? If you knew this woman, you'd never say anything like that!"

"Annie, no, it's okay." Rose put a hand on her arm, but Annie wasn't listening.

"This is harassment. I'm calling the cops. Where are the cops?" Annie looked around, then tried to flag down a funeral home employee in a gray suit, who was directing traffic. "Sir? Sir!"

"Annie, that's okay, no." Rose wanted to defuse the situation. Everyone was watching, and a short woman in a black pantsuit got out of line and stalked toward them, her forehead creased with anger.

"How can you show your face here?" the woman shouted, and people reacted with shock, chatter, and nervous laughter.

Rose edged away from the woman. The situation was getting out of hand, and she hadn't counted on the press being there. "Annie, we should get—"

"Aren't you ashamed?" The woman kept charging toward her, then pointed down the street. "Get out of here. You don't belong here."

"What?" Annie shouted at the woman, in disbelief. "What's the matter with you? She didn't do anything wrong, and she has every right to be here. What is this, Salem?"

Tanya held the microphone out, recording audio. The cameraman zoomed in, the large black lens telescoping forward and back.

The woman was yelling, "She abandoned a *child* in the fire, to burn alive!"

"You're wrong!" Annie yelled back. "She tried to get the girl out, but she must have run back in!"

"How dare you blame that child? She's a child! A little girl!"

"Ladies, please!" The funeral home employee came over, waving his hands. He was bald and on the slight side. "This is inappropriate at such a time. Please."

"Sorry, we're leaving." Rose took Annie's arm, but she pulled it away and pointed at the woman.

"This woman is insane!" Then Annie pointed at Tanya. "And *this* woman is harassing us to sell commercial time on TV, so a grateful nation can have enough toothpaste, beer, and deodorant!"

"Let's go." Rose hustled Annie away, but Tanya and her crew followed on their heels.

"Ms. McKenna, what do you say to the court's denial of the emergency injunction? Do you think the school is reopening prematurely? Do you expect to be sued by the Gigots? Are you suing the school? Will you attend the candlelight vigil Monday night?"

Rose and Annie broke into a jog toward their cars.

Chapter Twenty-five

Rose parked in Allen's Dam, the public park outside of Old Town, its tall trees ablaze in rich reds, oranges, and golds, a conflagration of hues that only reminded her of the fire that had brought so much destruction and death.

Annie climbed into the car and sat in the passenger seat, having followed her in her car. "What a disaster!"

"I feel like such a screw-up." Rose took off her sunglasses and tossed them onto the console. "I shouldn't have gone."

"Of course you should have. You're a member of the community. The problem was, where were the cops? In the city, we would've had a swarm."

"There are no cops. Only state police."

"What?" Annie looked over, incredulous. "Of course there are cops."

"No." Rose shook her head. "Not every town in America has its own police force. I didn't know that either, but it's true. Most of the rural townships don't have a police force, or they share. The area's too sparsely populated, and when the economy tanked, they cut the funds for it."

"For police?"

"Yes."

"How about fire?"

"We have a fire department, and if there's a crime, we're supposed to call the state police. The realtor said they'd come, but it could take a while. She didn't even know anybody who'd called them, except for hunting out of season."

Annie shook her neat head. "I wouldn't feel safe without cops."

"I do, now. There's no crime here. Most people don't even lock their front doors. It's paradise. At least it was, until recently."

"Whatever, I'm sorry I lost it at that woman." Annie frowned, and the corners of her mouth tugged downward, as if by strings. "I hope I didn't make it worse for you. It'll pass, it has to."

"It's okay." Rose rubbed her forehead, thinking. Leo had a small cabin near Lake Harmony, which Melly loved, and their neighbors at the lake, Mo and Gabriella Vaughn, were like her honorary grandparents. "Maybe we should take a break, up to the cabin. Leo's busy anyway, and we could all use a little R&R while it's still hot, and Melly loves the Vaughns. What do you think?"

"No."

"Why not?"

"I know you love the Vaughns, but it'll all be here when you get back. You can't run from this, Ro."

"I'm not running," Rose said, stung.

"I think you are."

"What am I supposed to do? How can I send her to school on Monday? They'll take it out on her."

"I think you should send her. Tell you why." Annie cocked her head, her expression thoughtful. "This whole thing, with the fire, the deaths, and Melly and Amanda, it's all of a piece. Getting through it is going to be a recovery process. All grief is, and all trauma. That recovery process is starting at school tomorrow, with the memorial service."

Rose set her ego aside, listening. Annie was honest, if blunt.

"If Melly's not a part of that, she's more on the outs than ever. She'll be a step behind everybody else, and that sucks. Like when you start the day late, you know that feeling? You never quite catch up. You spend the day unsettled, off-balance, left behind. True?"

"Yes."

"You say she has a relationship with this Kristen. She'll look out for her."

Rose mulled it over. "Mrs. Nuru thinks I should send her, but she's mad at Kristen and thinks she favors Melly. It's gotten political, all of a sudden."

"Great." Annie curled her upper lip. "I like the one who likes Melly. I'm Team Kristen."

"Me, too." Rose smiled. "I wish I could ask her about all of this. She said she'd look out for Melly, but that was before they came down on her. I'm not sending Melly, unless Kristen keeps an eye out for her."

"So call and ask her."

"I have her number somewhere at home." Then Rose realized something. "You know what? Kristen's apartment is two blocks from here. I dropped cupcakes off there once."

"So why don't you just go over? If she likes Melly that much, she won't mind. You have the sitter until nine, you might as well use her." Annie checked her watch. "I should go, too. Forget the chips for the boys. Mom's tired."

"Okay, it's a plan." Rose leaned over and gave her a hug. "You're the best. Thanks so much for coming."

"I'll be in Philly all week. Call me if you need me. Give everybody kisses for me, would you?"

"Yes. Same to Simon and the boys. Love you."

"You, too." Annie opened the door and climbed out of the car, her eyes glittering with mischief. "By the way, I'm keeping this sweater. I'll give it to the homeless lady on my corner."

"No!" Rose smiled. "Gimme back my sweater."

Annie laughed. "Why, you going to a funeral?"

Rose blinked, caught up short, thinking instantly of Amanda.

Annie's smile faded. "Oops, sorry. I just stuck my foot in my mouth, didn't I?"

"Nah, and keep the sweater." Rose tried to rally. "Then maybe I won't need it, right?"

"Right!" Annie said, closing the door.

Chapter Twenty-six

Rose walked up the brick walkway to Kristen's house, a boxy duplex on a street of older rowhouses. A man in a white undershirt and jeans was washing a red Ford pickup in the driveway, and he shut off the hose when he saw Rose.

"Whoops, didn't mean to spray you," he said with a grin. "Hi."

"Hello, I'm here to see Kristen. I'm a parent of one of the kids in her class."

"Jacob Horton. I live on the first floor. Just a heads-up, Kristen came home, upset. She was over at Fiore's."

"Thanks, bye." Rose went to the set of exterior steps, climbed to the second floor, reached the wooden landing, and knocked on the screen door. "Kristen!" She waited but there was no answer, so she knocked again. "Kristen?"

The door opened, and Kristen stood in the doorway, dressed in a black cotton dress, wiping tears from her eyes. "Rose?"

"Can I come in, for a minute?"

"Okay." Kristen sniffled and stepped aside, and Rose entered and gave her a big hug.

"I know it's a hard time for you and the other teachers."

"It's so awful, everything's so awful." Kristen hugged her back, then released her, wiping her eyes. "The wakes were so sad, and Mrs.

Nuru and Mr. Rodriguez are so angry, and there were even reporters there, asking me a zillion questions, like how Melly and Amanda got along."

"I know. I was there." Rose looked around, her eyes adjusting to the light in the small living room. A black suitcase rested on a red-checked couch, and T-shirts and shorts sat stacked in a pile on top of a painted bookshelf, ready to be packed. "Are you going somewhere?"

"I'm sorry, I'm leaving. I can't take it anymore. I quit."

"*What?*" Rose asked, aghast. "When? *Why?*"

"It's all too much. I messed up here, I talk too much, and I can't work here, watching everything I say, walking on eggshells." Kristen's eyes welled up again, her freckled skin mottled with emotion. "Mr. Rodriguez said I have bad judgment and loose lips sink ships. I give up. I'm not cut out to be a teacher, at least not here, not anymore. I'm going."

"Wait, slow down." Rose thought of Melly. "I was just saying this will pass, it has to."

"No, it won't, and it doesn't have to."

"Yes, it will, Kristen. You're young and you don't realize. Time changes things. Things you don't think you'll survive, you do. I know, I've lived it."

"Sorry, I've made my decision. I'm leaving. I'm sorry." Kristen turned on her heel, picked up two T-shirts, and tossed them into the suitcase, startling a white cat that bounded out of the room, his tail high.

"But what about Melly? And what about the other kids in the program? They just went through a trauma, and Amanda's still in the hospital. They need you, now more than ever. Melly needs you."

"I'm just the gifted teacher, and not that experienced, as Mrs. Nuru keeps reminding me."

"But the kids love you. Melly loves you."

"I have your number, I'll call her." Kristen placed a quilted toiletries case into the suitcase. "I'll stay in touch with her."

"It's not the same."

"Don't you think I know that? Don't you think I feel guilty enough?" Kristen picked up some socks and wedged them into the case. "I have to live my own life."

"Kristen, please stay. *Please.*"

"Don't you see, if I stay, I make it worse for her?" Kristen turned, stricken. "They think I favor her, and now they'll be looking for it in everything I do. It's best for her if I go."

"That's *not* what's best for her. I know what's best for her."

"Look, I'm sorry, I really am, but this is messing up my life, too."

"Then why don't you slow down, see how you feel in two weeks?"

"No. I emailed Mr. Rodriguez my resignation. I said to tell people I had a family emergency. It's a done deal."

"You're really leaving *now*?" Rose asked, incredulous.

"Yes. I'm going to my parents', and I'd appreciate it if you'd keep it confidential. I don't want any of these crazy parents emailing me or posting any more crap on my Facebook wall. No more reporters, either." Kristen's pretty features softened, and she became her old sweet self. "I really am sorry, so sorry, for everything, but I have to go now. Please, go. I'll call Melly in a day or two."

"Do you swear? You'll break her heart if you don't. You owe her that much. She's a person, with feelings."

"I said I will, and I will." Kristen crossed to the door, and opened it wide, and Rose went to the threshold, bewildered.

"You're not who I thought you were."

"None of us is," Kristen said, unsmiling.

Chapter Twenty-seven

Rose steered down Allen Road, the window open, her elbow resting on the door, and a breeze blowing through her hair. She'd called Leo to tell him about Kristen, but he hadn't answered, and she'd left a message. Kristen was leaving Melly without her only ally, and Rose wasn't sure what to do. She didn't know whether to send Melly to school or how to tell Melly that Kristen was leaving, and in the end, either way, it would be a terrible blow.

Rose stopped at a red light, and the traffic had lessened, once she was on the outskirts of town. The sky was darkening, and she scanned the neat houses with their glowing lights, a typical Sunday night in the suburbs. Parents and kids would be hunkering down around kitchen tables, doing math and French homework, or building volcanoes with baking-soda lava or teepees ribbed with Popsicle sticks. Not all the Sunday night scenes would be so idyllic, and Rose knew that, too. That, she had lived, too.

She hit the gas, and the homes disappeared among the commercial outskirts and the chain stores like the CVS, Giant, Costco, Walmart, and Target. Beyond them, she could see the distant outline of the school, with its long, low roofline and large wings on either side. The wings held the classrooms, and the entrance and administrative offices were nearer the left wing, on the north side. The cafeteria was also near the left, but it was built on the front of the school like an addition, with no second floor because of the skylights. Rose stopped at a traffic light, and from this distance, she could pretend that nothing had ever happened. No fire, no women in coffins, no daughters in hospitals, no angry parents, and no young teacher quitting a promising career, leaving Melly on her own.

Rose fed the car gas when the light changed, braking as she approached the school. As she got closer, she could see that the street in front was marked off by orange cones and sawhorses. Pickups and construction vehicles sat parked along the curb, ending in a rusty dumpster. The few cars around her slowed down, rubbernecking, and she found herself pulling over in front of the school, parking behind a dusty pickup with a bumper sticker, UNION CARPENTERS HAVE BETTER WOOD. She cut the ignition, and the breeze through the window smelled like burned things.

She scanned the school and understood what Mr. Rodriguez had meant. Most of the building looked the same, its brand-new brick façade and classroom wings perfect, and only the cafeteria had been damaged, like a black eye on a pageant queen. The cafeteria windows were empty holes, dark smudges marred the windowsills and brick, and a blue plastic tarp covered the roof.

Rose thought of the people who had died inside, and the long lines at Fiore's, and to her mind, public property had become hallowed ground. It seemed impossible that there would be recess tomorrow, with kids throwing basketballs, jumping rope, and playing kickball. She could almost feel the flames licking at her ankles, all over again. She flashed on Melly, slumped in the bathroom, Emily, crying, and Danielle, running terrified. Her thoughts ended where they always did, with Amanda.

Mommy!

She got out of the car, closed the door behind her, and walked through the playground toward the cafeteria, which had been cordoned off in different sections with yellow caution tape, sawhorses, and a temporary fence of orange netting. She stood behind the sawhorse, eyeing the scene.

Klieglights lit up the façade of the cafeteria, making supersized shadows of the workmen as they went back and forth from the cafeteria to the dumpster with wheelbarrows, tarps, and trash bags of charred debris. Some of the workmen were building a plywood wall, probably the one that Mr. Rodriguez had mentioned, and a workman in a T-shirt and Carhartt overalls smiled as he walked to the pickup in front of her car. He was carrying a heavy-duty laptop, and he stowed it inside, slammed the door, and came over to her, with a confident stride.

"Can I help you?" he asked, in a friendly way. In the reflected light, Rose could see that he had an easy grin, a longish nose, and dark eyes under a white plastic hardhat with a Phillies sticker. "Name's Kurt Rehgard." He stuck out a large hand, and Rose shook it, feeling her fingers crunch.

"Rose. I'm just looking around."

"Been a lot of that today."

"I bet." Rose eyed the bustling scene. "You guys are working late."

"All night. The bigwigs want this school up and running, time is of the essence, and we don't mind, I'll tell you that. We're all loving the OT, especially in this economy." Kurt gestured to the work crews behind him. "My crew is all from Phoenixville, the electrical contractor's from Pottstown, and the GC's from Norristown. The district wanted all new on site, on account of the lawsuits they expect."

"There's more than one lawsuit?" Rose felt her chest tighten.

"Hell, yeah. Everybody's pointing fingers and who's responsible for what, who caused this, who did that."

"I heard it was a gas leak and faulty wiring."

"I'm not supposed to say, on pain of death." The carpenter drew a dirty finger across his throat. "You a reporter?"

"No way." Rose smiled. "Just a mom. You were saying, about the lawsuits?"

"Startin' in already. The first electrical contractor says it was the GC's fault, and the first GC says it was the gas company's fault, and the HVAC guys are in trouble because the ductwork was too close for code, and somebody said the fire used it to spread so fast." Kurt shook his head. "All the fire marshals, building inspectors came around, even the FBI, because of the fatalities. Then the lawyers and the so-called experts they hired, all taking pictures. It's a damn circus."

Rose's head was spinning. It sounded like the lawsuits that Leo talked about at dinner, and she hoped they wouldn't be caught in the middle, becoming the lawsuit that people talked about at dinner.

"You say your child goes here?"

"Yes. My daughter's in third grade, and school's open tomorrow, which seems kind of strange to me."

"Not at all. It's not unsafe or anything. The kids can't go in the cafeteria, and there'll be fire and water damage crews in the hallways, but your kid will be safe in the rest of the building. Don't worry." Kurt cocked his head. "I thought you were a lawyer, that's why I came over. That, and to see if you were married."

"Thanks, but I am married. To a lawyer."

"No!" Kurt pretended he'd been shot, staggering backwards comically. "Dump his lame ass!"

Rose laughed.

"Hey, if you like, I'll show you inside. You'll see, it's safe. You want a quick tour?"

"I'd love to," Rose answered, intrigued. "Is that kosher?"

"The bigwigs are gone, and my guys don't care. Act like a lawyer."

"I can do that." Rose ducked under the tape.

Chapter Twenty-eight

Rose followed Kurt beyond the cordon, past a paint-spattered boom-box blasting vintage Aerosmith. Heads turned as they stepped into the klieglights and tramped across the playground, churned to muddy spots by the wheelbarrows and foot traffic. She smiled in a professional way, though she knew they weren't fooling anybody. Workmen looked up and nodded hello before they returned to their tasks. Their faces were streaked with sweat, and they seemed not to recognize her, either because they weren't local or they'd been working nonstop, with no time for TV news.

Rose asked, "I guess you rebuild the cafeteria after you throw all this stuff out, huh?"

"Basically, yes. I'm with Bethany Run Construction, and we'll do the demo, then the framing and construction. Here, follow me." Kurt led her to the threshold of the playground exit, where the blackened double doors had been propped open with cinderblocks. Calcium-white light flooded the area, illuminating the hallway. Soot blanketed the walls, and the glass ceiling fixtures had been shattered.

"My God," Rose said half to herself.

"The hall is messy, but structurally sound. There's nothing unsafe about it, see? Got certified right off. It'll be good to go as soon as we clean up the water." Kurt walked ahead, gesturing at a series of noisy black machines. Hoses sprouted from each one, affixed to corrugated black mats that were duct-taped to the grimy floor. "Bet you're wondering what these puppies are."

Rose was drawn to the cafeteria, which was a hellish sight. The tables, chairs, and decorated bulletin boards had been removed, leaving a black shell of a room. Smoke had blackened the walls, obscuring the cheery blue-and-white tiles, and the ceiling was gone, exposing steel joists, aluminum ductwork, and electrical wiring.

"I'll explain, hold on. It's so damn noisy, I can't stand it." Kurt stepped to the first machine and pressed a red POWER button. The machine shuddered into silence, though the others thrummed loudly. "See, these are Injectidry machines. They're on day and night. The water sprinklers went off here, and the machines suck the moisture out of the subfloor, so it doesn't warp."

"Got it," Rose said, but she couldn't tear her eyes from the cafeteria. The floor tiles were cracked, and charred rubble lay in piles where it had been swept; broken ceiling tiles, split wooden beams, and filthy debris. The skylights were gone, and the blue tarp covering square holes they left behind made an azure glow, like a tropical sky.

"Those machines over there, they're different." Kurt pointed down the hall to a series of tall gray machines, also boxlike and attached to a generator. "They're dehumidifiers on steroids. Not the kind you have in your basement when the sump pump goes out, if you get me. They make sure no toxic mold gets a chance to form, in case you were worried about that for your kid. Did you say you have a boy or a girl?"

"A girl." Rose took a step toward the cafeteria, where the front wall of the kitchen had been demolished. She could see through to the industrial ovens and stainless steel shelving in the kitchen, which lay twisted and in pieces, like the residuum of a twenty-car collision. She could imagine how the blast had killed poor Serena and Ellen.

"I have a niece that I've taken to Disney World, my sister's kid. Her dad's in Iraq, so I'm spending a lot of time with her. I taught her to throw, and she goes to the Phils games with me, too." Kurt gestured at the hallway. "See, it's all sound. I'd send my own niece here. You got nothing to worry about."

"Great." Rose took another step down the hall, and from the new perspective could see that the explosion had blown away the wall between the kitchen and the teachers' lounge, which was only partially blackened, but full of broken cabinetry and a yellow Formica counter that had been cracked into pieces, like a nightmare puzzle.

"We'll have this fixed up good as new. Better." Kurt leaned over, lowering his voice. "You ask me, they opened too soon. You can't rush a job, especially the electrical. It always bites you in the ass."

"I bet." Rose came out of her reverie. "It's sad to see where somebody died."

"Nobody suffered, if that helps you. The explosion was in the gas line in the back wall of the kitchen, a three-quarter inch pipe that feeds the oven in the kitchen and the teachers' lounge. It took out everything instantly."

"How terrible," Rose said, heavily. "A gas leak? Why didn't they smell it?"

"It was in the wall, and maybe they did, for all we know. Tell you something about the smell of gas, you get desensitized. You smell it in the beginning, then you stop noticing it." Kurt seemed to catch himself. "That's not the official cause, they didn't say that yet, and you didn't hear it from me."

"Hear what?"

Kurt laughed. "Let's go." He motioned, leading Rose back down the hall, out the exit door, and into the blinding klieglights. She put up her hands, shielding her eyes, and he held her elbow. "Watch out for that pile of junk."

"Oops!" Rose looked down at a heap of blackened debris on a tarp, a heartbreaking sight. Twisted pieces of rebar and busted dry wall mixed with a *Toy Story* lunchbox, a crushed juicebox, and a broken Sony PS2. She flashed on Amanda, showing her new iPod to the girls at the table. Suddenly, it struck her why Amanda had run back into the school. The blond teacher could have missed her running back in, like Leo had said, because she'd been on the other side of the students being evacuated to the playground.

"An iPod," Rose blurted out, and Kurt looked over.

"Excuse me?"

"Nothing," Rose answered, saddened. Amanda lay in a coma tonight, because of a shiny new toy. And because of her.

"Here, take my card." Kurt dug in his pocket, extracted a wrinkled business card, and handed it to her. "Call me if you need a deck, or if you dump that husband of yours."

"Thanks." Rose smiled.

"Feel better, now that you've seen the school?"

"Yes," Rose lied, and when she turned away, she dropped the smile.

Chapter Twenty-nine

"Hi, sweetie." Rose entered Melly's bedroom, where she was reading in bed, with Princess Google. The butterfly lamp on the night table cast a warm glow over her yellow comforter, whitewashed bureau, and matching desk, but the rest of the room was a Harry Potter shrine. A black Hogwarts banner hung above the headboard, and the bookshelf contained the thick books, figurines, a Sorting Hat, and new Hermione wand. The lower shelves held B-list books, which was everything not Harry.

"Hi, Mom." Melly peered over the top of *Beedle the Bard.* Her hair had been brushed out and lay wavy on the pillow.

"How was your night?" Rose sat down on the edge of her bed and gave her a kiss. "What did you and Julie do?"

"We watched *Up.*"

"Sounds good." Rose had told the babysitter, DVDs only. "Did you like it?"

"Yes." Melly placed her laminated bookmark carefully in the page, making sure the blue tassel showed, and closed the book.

"Good. Hi, Googs." Rose scratched Princess Google, and the spaniel raised her small, flat head and tucked into a ball of red-and-white patches.

"Googie's so cute."

"She is. Did she eat any underwear?"

Melly smiled. "No, she was good, Mom. I let her out in the backyard. Two times."

"How was John?"

"He pooped, and his face got all red."

"Great. Just so he didn't eat any underwear."

Melly giggled. "You're silly."

"Thanks."

"Was the funeral sad?"

"Yes. It's hard when people pass."

"Like Daddy." Melly frowned, showing a tiny buckle in her smooth forehead.

"Right." Rose felt a surge of love and worry, eyeing Melly, who looked so happy and comfy in Leo's Phillies T-shirt. "We have to make a decision about whether you should go to school tomorrow."

"Is it open?"

"Yes. The cafeteria isn't open, but the classrooms are. I was just there to see it."

"I know, I can smell." Melly scrunched up her nose. "You smell like fire."

"Gross." Rose hadn't realized. "Anyway, it's a half-day tomorrow. They're going to have an assembly in the morning, about the people who died, then go back to class, then you'll come home."

"Okay, I can go."

"Do you feel well enough?"

"Yes." Melly shrugged. "I'm not sick. The doctor said."

"I know, but if you feel tired or you just want to rest another day, you can stay home." Rose was stacking the deck, but she couldn't help herself. She was worried about the reception that Melly would get tomorrow. "How's your throat?"

"Okay. I can go. I'll go."

"Well, then let me say this. You know that Amanda was caught in the fire, and you should know that there are some people who blame me about that."

"Why?"

Rose kept it simple. "They say I saved you instead of her."

"I'm your kid."

Rose smiled. "I know, but really, I got Amanda to the door of the cafeteria, and when I went to get you, she ran back into the cafeteria. I think, after her iPod."

Melly blinked, and it seemed not to register that she'd been left for second. "I heard her talking about that iPod. It was her big brother's. He got it for his birthday."

"Anyway, the other kids might say things to you, about that. Try to ignore them, and don't answer, okay? Like the reporters, in a way."

"I'll tell Ms. Canton. She'll tell them not to."

Rose felt her heart sink. "Mel, listen, I have some news for you about Ms. Canton. She had an emergency with her family, and she had to leave school and go home."

"When is she coming back?"

"She's not. She had to move home, to be with her family."

"Why?" Melly frowned, confused.

"I don't know more than I told you. Somebody in her family is sick, and she has to take care of them. She went home for good."

"Forever?" Melly's eyebrows flew upward, and Rose nodded, not hiding her disappointment.

"Yes. I know you like her, and you know she likes you, so much. But she can't help it, she has—"

"She *has* to come back." Melly raised her voice, anxious. "She's the best teacher I ever had."

"She won't be able to come back, but I hope she can call us, to talk and say hi to you, if she's not too busy."

"But I like her. I *want* her to be my teacher." Melly's lower lip buckled, and Rose gave her a big hug.

"I know, sweetie. I'm hoping they'll get a new teacher you'll like as much as her. You know, you don't have to go tomorrow if you don't want to."

"I want to, I just want her to be there." Melly's blue eyes glistened the way only a child's can, showing all the hurt, unguarded and guileless. "Why didn't they tell us this before?"

"Nobody knew. Things like this happen, in life. Unexpected things, and people have to take care of their families." Rose shifted on the bed, waking Princess Google, who moved her head to Melly's leg and gazed up at her with round, melty brown eyes. "Look. Googie knows you're upset."

"I know. It's okay, Googs." Melly stroked the dog's head, her fingernails bright with pink polish, probably from the babysitter. "Don't be sad, Googie Girl. Everything will be okay. Everything will turn out okay."

Rose fell silent, listening and watching, and it struck her that Melly was comforting herself.

"Don't worry, Googie. Don't worry." Melly kept petting the dog, who closed her eyes.

"I think you're making her feel better."

"I tell her all the time, don't worry. But she still does."

"It's hard not to, sometimes."

"She knows that." Melly ran her hand down the spaniel's coat to her feathery tail. "See, Mom, how this part is all white? Like a wiggly line down her back? That's like a river, all along on her back, and the red parts are down the side."

"I see." Rose smiled, and Melly walked her fingers up to the spaniel's fluffy neck, then scratched her ears.

"She likes it when I scratch here. She has mats in back of her ears, and I try to get the mats out. She doesn't like the mats. She likes to look her best, so I help her." Melly touched the russet patch on the spaniel's head. "This is from the Countess's thumb, in England."

Rose had taught Melly that, one of the breed's characteristics. "Remember what it's called?"

"Her 'Blenheim spot,' because the Countess of Marlborough used to rest her thumb there, waiting for her husband to come home from the Battle of Blenheim."

"Good for you."

"The Countess lived in Blenheim Palace, in England. Harry Potter is from England, too."

"Right." Rose smiled.

"That's what I like about Googie. We both have a spot."

Rose blinked. Funny, she'd never made the connection. They'd gotten a Cavalier because she'd had one as a child and they were great with kids.

"I tell her not to be sad about her spot. The Countess gave it to her, and that's just the way she is." Melly shrugged, stroking the little spaniel. "I tell her, the spot is part of her. Just like Harry Potter. She has other spots, too." She pointed to the small spots on the dog's leg. "I told her she shouldn't worry about any of her spots."

"What does she say?"

"She says she doesn't. Other people do." Melly kept petting the dog, whose eyes stayed closed, fringed with red eyelashes. "When I see her, I don't see the spots, I just see her. And she's beautiful."

Rose felt her throat catch. "I feel the same way. She's the most beautiful dog I ever saw."

Melly looked up. "Am I beautiful, Mom?"

"You sure are."

"As beautiful as you? You were a model, in magazines."

"Yes, and you know what I learned from all that?"

"What?"

"That beauty doesn't really have anything to do with what we look like. It's who we are inside, and what we do, in life. Googie's beautiful because she has a beautiful little spirit inside her, and so do you."

"And so do *you,* Mom." Melly smiled sweetly, and Rose smiled back.

"Thanks, honeybun."

"I can go to school tomorrow."

"Okay, good idea," Rose said, hoping it sounded like the truth.

Chapter Thirty

Rose tucked Melly in, checked on John, changed into jeans and a T-shirt, then went downstairs. She padded into the kitchen and hit a button on her laptop, and while it woke up, placed a decaf pod in the coffeemaker, got a mug from the cabinet, and hit BREW. Hot coffee spurted into the mug, and she thought of Leo. He hadn't called her back yet, and she knew he must be busy, so she texted him.

Love you. Canton quit. Call anytime.

She grabbed the mug of coffee, took it to the laptop, and sat down. She logged onto Facebook and looked at the first three messages on her wall. She didn't know the people who had posted, but she recognized the names from class, and the messages were familiar:

I think you are a terrible person . . .
You should leave and go back . . .
I saw you at Fiore's and you must be crazy if you think . . .

Rose didn't read any further. She logged onto Account Settings, then Deactivate Account, and clicked Yes, ending her Facebook account. She sipped her coffee, strong and bitter, then logged into her email account and read the list of senders. She didn't know any of them, and their email wasn't friendly:

You are so fake . . .
I will not let my son . . .
If I am unlucky enough to see you at school . . .

Rose was about to delete them but spotted an email from **Principal Lucas Rodriguez** to the **Reesburgh School Community**, and she opened it:

We all mourn the loss of Marylou Battle, Serena Perez, and Ellen Conze, and we will have an assembly in the gym to honor them, on Monday morning (students only). We'll also hold a meeting for parents (parents only) in the auditorium, at 9:00 a.m., and administrators and dignitaries will be there to answer any questions you may have. Please drive your child to school and try to calm any emotional reactions. It's time to put the past behind us and move on. . . .

Rose read between the lines. Mr. Rodriguez wanted peace at school tomorrow, and so did she. She went into her email account and navigated around until she figured out how to deactivate it, then did. It left her with one thing to do. She logged onto the website for the TV station, which burst into the screen with PHILADELPHIA'S BIGGEST NEWS at the top. She skipped the SCHOOL FIRE EXPLODES IN CONTROVERSY and scrolled down until she found Tanya's one-on-one interview with Eileen Gigot. She wanted to know what was going on to prepare Melly, if she had to. She plugged in the earphones she used when John was sleeping, and clicked the play arrow on the video.

"I'm Tanya Robertson," the anchorwoman said. She was sitting across from Eileen at a dining room table, in front of family photographs and a breakfront. "Tonight, I'm with Eileen Gigot, the mother of young Amanda, who remains in Intensive Care, as a result of being trapped in the school fire at Reesburgh Elementary." Tanya turned to

Eileen. "Thanks for agreeing to meet with me. I know this is a difficult time for you, and I will keep this short. First, how is Amanda?"

"She's still in a coma, and we're praying for her." Eileen looked
exhausted, and smiled wanly. She wore little makeup, and her short
blond hair was pulled into a ponytail. She looked like an adult version of her daughter, except for the dark circles under her bloodshot
blue eyes and the despair that formed deep wrinkles at the corners
of her mouth.

"I understand that you're a single mother, a widow, and in addition to Amanda, you have two sons at home, Jason, thirteen, and Joe,
ten. Can you tell our viewers how they're coping with this terrible
accident involving their sister?"

"The boys always help, because I work. I'm a secretary in an accountant's office, in Reesburgh. They pull their own weight and
then some. Amanda's the youngest, and they act like she's a mascot,
or their pet."

Rose felt her gut clench. Eileen had been going through hell. And
now this, with Amanda.

Tanya continued, "Now, you've made certain allegations regarding alleged negligence by the school district, the general contractor,
and the subcontractors."

"Yes, but I can't elaborate on that. My lawyer has said we shouldn't
discuss it, and we'll do our talking in court." Eileen stiffened. "We're
not going to let this happen to another family, is all I'll say."

"Of course." Tanya shifted closer. "When we were talking earlier,
you told me that you're upset with the way the school handled evacuating the children to safety. Can you elaborate on that?"

"Again, I can't go into detail, on my lawyer's advice. But I don't
think they had enough safety procedures in place. They only held one
fire drill." Eileen held up an index finger. "Also, when the fire started,
the school left it to certain volunteers to get the children out. Those
volunteers did not follow correct procedures. That's why Amanda was
trapped in the fire."

Rose gasped.

"What do you mean?" Tanya asked.

"Again, all I can say is that these volunteers are other mothers, and I have been advised not to name names. But one of these mothers made sure her child was brought to safety, and Amanda and the others were left on their own." Eileen faltered, pursing her lips. "I just wish I had been there, like the moms who don't work. I keep thinking, if I had, Amanda would be healthy and happy today."

"I understand." Tanya leaned over. "You also told me that this mother called you and complained that Amanda was bullying her child."

"Yes, she did call me to complain." Eileen scowled, deeply. "But Amanda is *not* a bully. She'd never tease or raise a hand to another child, ever. She's just a little girl, a wonderful child, and everybody knows it. If she occasionally acts up, all kids do, especially one who's lost her daddy. Kids work this stuff out, and moms who interfere are the worst."

Rose's mouth dropped open.

Tanya said, "But to return to your point, do you think this mother intentionally left Amanda behind?"

"I'm not allowed to say more. I have turned this matter over to the District Attorney and asked him to press criminal charges."

Rose felt her heart stop. She remembered Mr. Rodriguez talking about criminal charges against the school district. But could there be criminal charges against her, too?

Tanya asked, "Are you saying that you have filed a criminal complaint against this volunteer, for intentionally failing to help Amanda?"

"The District Attorney said—" Eileen caught herself, then stopped talking. "Well, I was instructed not to speak about it. I won't, any further."

"Thank you, Mrs. Gigot." Tanya turned to the camera with a satisfied smile. "Back to you, Tim."

Rose yanked out the earphone, jumped up, and got her phone.

Chapter Thirty-one

"Leo?" Rose said, anxious, when he finally picked up.

"Babe, I was going to call you, but I'm crazy busy. Got people with me in the conference room. Hold on a sec." Leo covered the phone. "Folks, gimme five minutes. Be right back. Mark, hold the fort."

Rose waited while there were some voices, then the sound of a door closing, and she used the time to take a deep breath.

"Okay, I'm back," Leo said, himself again. "So Canton quit?"

"Yes. She couldn't take the pressure."

"What's wrong, babe? You sound weird. Did something happen at the wake?" Leo's voice carried no judgment, and Rose loved him for it.

"Yes, but that's not the problem. Did you see the TV news tonight?"

"Are you kidding? I don't have time to pee."

"Eileen implied that she asked the D.A. to bring criminal charges against me. What does she mean? What did I do that's criminal?"

"Really." Leo paused. "I expected a civil lawsuit, but criminal charges?"

"What is she talking about? Should we call the D.A. and ask?"

"No, that's the worst thing to do. Wait, hold on again." Leo paused, then his voice sounded muffled. "They're in the file on my credenza, with the eagle statue."

Rose waited, panicky. It was bad enough to lose the house. It was impossible to go to jail. It seemed inconceivable, but then again, so did school fires and a little girl in a coma.

"Honey, did she say the District Attorney? Are you sure?"

"Yes, the D.A. That's criminal, right? That's different from civil, right?"

"Yes, sure. Criminal charges are criminal, with criminal penalties. A negligence suit would be civil, that's money damages only. Wait, wait." Leo covered the phone again, his tone newly tense. "The *back* credenza, under the eagle. Next to the softball trophy."

"Does this mean they won't try to charge me with something or they will?"

"Please, hold on." Leo sighed heavily. "A credenza is a file drawer. Is this a hard one? How's Melly?"

"She's sad about Kristen."

"Babe, tell you what. The trial looks like it'll take two weeks, and we're all staying in Philly, at the Omni near the courthouse. But we need to get ahead of this criminal thing, if they're talking about charges against you. Let me get a hold of somebody who can answer your questions. Dean will know a criminal lawyer. I'll let you know."

"Okay, thanks."

"Hang in, and I'll get back to you. Love you."

"Love you, too," Rose said, relieved, but Leo had already hung up.

Chapter Thirty-two

Pewter clouds hid the morning sun, and Rose carried John on her hip and held Melly's hand as they wound their way through the school parking lot, which was full to bursting. It hadn't been designed for every parent to drive, and she'd had to park on the grass because they were running late, to boot, having had one of those hectic mornings.

She'd had to dress up, in a blue cotton shirtdress, because Leo had gotten her a meeting with two lawyers, and she'd changed the bandages on her hand and her ankle. Melly had tried on three different outfits, implicitly anxious about her return to school, and she'd decided on a flowery T-shirt and pink cotton shorts. Rose hadn't rushed her, secretly relieved that Harry Potter had stayed home.

She shifted John higher onto her hip, and he was back to being his sweet self, bouncing happily along, kicking his chubby legs and sucking his light-blue pacifier. He'd slept well, and looked natty in a blue-striped polo and denim pants, which fit him like Mom jeans. She was taking him to the lawyers' office with her, because she took him along whenever possible. She hadn't had children to leave them home with a sitter.

She kept walking, pleased to see that the press stood off school property, behind a cordon, and that Tanya and her TV crew were nowhere in evidence. The last of the parents and children were heading to the entrance, where Mr. Rodriguez stood on a receiving line with the vice principal, guidance counselor, gym teacher, computer teacher, and the librarian who'd helped the day of the fire. The air still smelled faintly, though Rose wondered if she was the only one who noticed. She found herself thinking of the charred Sony PS2, then Amanda. She'd checked online and there'd been no more news about her condition, and Rose had avoided all the news stories about her, including HERO MOM?.

"Mom, come on." Melly tugged her hand. "We're going to be late."

"How you doing, sweetie? You okay?"

"Fine." Melly faced forward, and the slight breeze blew her hair from her cheek, revealing her birthmark. Reflexively, she patted it back down.

"Don't worry. Everything's going to be okay."

"I'm not worried."

"They'll have an assembly in the gym, then you'll go to class for a little while and come home before lunch. I'll come get you, and maybe we'll do something fun. Wanna eat out?"

"Okay."

"Mrs. Nuru wanted you to come in today." Rose felt Melly's fingers tighten on her hand. "She likes you a lot, you know."

"Maybe Ms. Canton will be there, like a surprise."

Rose felt a twinge. "No, she won't, Mel. But she'll call you."

"When?"

"Soon, I hope. When she can." Rose fell in behind a first-grade boy and his mother, and he glanced behind him to see who was there. When he realized he didn't know them, he turned away, then back again, an obvious double-take at Melly's birthmark. "Mel, don't let it bother you if people bug you today. It could happen, with the fire and all."

"Will Amanda be there?"

"No, she's still in the hospital."

"What about Emily and Danielle?"

"Yes, I assume. You can just steer clear of them, if you want. Are you worried about them bothering you?"

"No. I'll use my *Protego* charm. It makes a shield against them. Or sometimes I just tell myself they're just Slytherins. Amanda is like Draco Malfoy, and Emily and Danielle are Crabbe and Goyle."

Rose was about to reply, but Mr. Rodriguez was coming toward them in a jacket and tie, his suit pants flapping. "Melly, here's Mr. Rodriguez."

"Hello, Rose! Hi, Melly!" Mr. Rodriguez made a beeline for them, and Rose met him, shaking his hand.

"Good to see you again."

"You, too." Mr. Rodriguez bent down to talk to Melly. "I'm glad to see you on your feet, and I'm glad you came to school today."

"I'm not sick, and I have to go to school. Is Ms. Canton coming?"

"No, she had to go home," Mr. Rodriguez answered, without missing a beat. He tousled her hair, which Rose knew she hated, because it exposed her birthmark. "Mrs. Nuru's inside waiting for you, and she's proud you came, too." He held out his hand, palm up. "Wanna walk with me?"

"Can my mom come?"

"She's going to her own assembly, with the parents." Mr. Rodriguez's hand remained extended, like an unanswered question.

"Melly, go with Mr. Rodriguez, and I'll see you later, okay? Love you." Rose let go of Melly's hand and bunny-dipped to give her a clumsy kiss, which she returned with an awkward hug, wrapping her arms around Rose and the wiggling baby.

"Bye, Mom. Bye, John."

"Bye, sweetie. We love you."

Rose lingered, watching Melly trundle along, her pink-and-purple Harry Potter backpack bumping up and down. The vice principal, the guidance counselor, the librarian, and the gym teacher all came forward to meet her, greeting her with open arms and broad smiles. Rose felt a rush of gratitude for their kindness, praying that Melly would be okay. Sometimes, it was the most a mother could do.

Mommy!

Ten minutes later, Rose had joined the parents waiting in the hallway to go into the auditorium. Windows filled the corridor with light, reminding her of the skylights in the cafeteria, before they'd exploded into shards, but she told herself to get a grip. John made an adorable armful, smiling up at her and reaching up to play the got-your-nose game. She caught his outstretched hand and gave it a kiss, glad of something to do.

The line of parents shifted forward, and Rose shifted, too, wiggling her index finger with John's finger curled around it. He giggled behind his pacifier, and she would have talked to him, doing her life narration routine, but she didn't want to draw attention to herself. She didn't know the parents ahead of her in line; two were men in casual dress with the yellow ID lanyards of Homestead employees, and the other was a woman in a pantsuit, paging through her email with a skilled thumb.

They reached the doors to the auditorium, which were propped open, and Rose could hear the harsh noise of a microphone being bumped around and someone saying, "testing, one, two, three." The men went inside, then the woman with the BlackBerry, and Rose with John. The auditorium was packed to bursting, with standing room only, and the air conditioning struggled to cool so many bodies. Rose found a place in the crowd under the balcony, happy to be less conspicuous. She dreaded seeing Danielle's mother, or Emily's, and wanted to avoid any confrontations.

The stage curtain was closed, with its blue-and-white pattern in school colors, and the gym teacher was at the podium adjusting the microphone while Mr. Rodriguez ushered a group of public officials into brown folding chairs. The audience talked, finished cell phone calls, or wrote last-minute texts and emails, the artificial light from their various hand-helds illuminating their faces from below.

Mr. Rodriguez took the podium, tapping the microphone and making a *bonk* sound. "Good morning, everyone," he began, and though Rose couldn't see his expression at a distance, his voice sounded heavy with the gravity of the occasion. "Thank you all for coming. I know these last few days have been very difficult for all of you, as they have for all of us in the school community. We have a lot to get to, so let's get started, because I know many of you have questions and we want to address as many as we can in this next hour."

"Damn!" said a well-dressed woman, standing near to Rose. She was typing on her iPhone, her head down. "I'll never get used to this thing. My daughter wants a dress for her American Girl doll, but I can't work this touch screen, to order one."

Rose didn't say anything. She didn't want to risk being recognized, and she never talked while someone else was speaking. It was a pet peeve of hers, and she was always surprised at how rude people could be, even adults. She kept her eyes forward.

Up on the stage, Mr. Rodriguez was saying, "However, we cannot begin our program until we honor these three precious lives we have lost, each of whom was special to our community in her own way. I'm speaking, of course, of Marylou Battle, Ellen Conze, and Serena Perez. To lead us in a moment of silence, let me introduce a man who needs no introduction, the Mayor of Reesburgh, Leonard Krakowski. Mayor Krakowski?" Mr. Rodriguez stepped aside, gesturing at Mayor Krakowski, a short, bald man in a dark suit and tie, who seemed to scoot to the podium.

"I miss my buttons." The woman with the iPhone kept talking, still fussing with the keypad. "But I love this gadget, otherwise. I'm a real gadget hound. You have an iPhone?"

"No," Rose answered, to shut the woman up.

Mayor Krakowski bent the microphone down to his height, then cleared his throat. "Good morning, ladies and gentlemen. Like all of you, I am positively grief-stricken over the loss of these wonderful women, and over the weekend, I took the time to mourn them and reflect on the meaning of their lives, and of all of our lives. Ironically, it's a tragedy like this when a town like Reesburgh can be at its best, because we all come together, as a family."

"Do you have a daughter or son?" The woman kept tapping her iPhone, but her voice made heads turn in the back row.

"A daughter," Rose whispered, getting nervous.

Mayor Krakowski continued, "Let us pause for a moment of silence this morning, to honor these fine women and reflect upon all they meant to all of us, and to our community as a whole." He bent his head, as did most of the crowd. There was the sound of a sniffle or two, though the woman with the iPhone kept fussing with the touch screen. Rose looked down, cuddling John so he'd stay quiet, but there was rustling in the back row as more people turned around and glanced in their direction. She hoped they were looking at the woman next to her.

"Is your daughter into American Girl, too?" the woman asked, turning to her.

"Shh," Rose whispered, but the woman's eyes widened slightly.

"Oh, my! You're the one who left Amanda."

Rose snapped her face front, mortified. Her cheeks flushed, her mouth went dry. She didn't know what to do. She didn't know whether to stay or leave. More heads turned in the back row, and Rose knew it was about her.

Mayor Krakowski raised his head, finishing the moment of silence. "Thank you, and allow me to introduce another person who needs no introduction, Senator Paul Martin. Senator Martin?" He stood aside as Senator Martin rose, tall and slim in a dark suit, with tortoiseshell glasses. His thick, graying hair caught the auditorium lights as he took the podium, raised the microphone, and said, "Good morning, Mayor Krakowski, Mr. Rodriguez, members of the school board, parents, and friends."

Rose kept her eyes to the stage, pretending not to notice that the woman with the iPhone had turned away and was murmuring something to the woman beside her, who had been digging in her purse. The woman with the purse looked over and both of them edged away. More heads were turning around in the audience, as word spread to the back rows. They were all looking at her, talking about her.

Senator Martin continued, "I feel honored to address all of you this morning, on the loss of an amazing teacher, Marylou Battle, and two very dedicated cafeteria workers, Ellen Conze and Serena Perez. I see the expressions of loss and grief on your faces today, and I know that all of you will pull together and stay strong for your families, and particularly your children. Reesburgh is small, but strong, proud, and the very definition of community, and having been at Homestead like many of you, I know that you will persevere through this tragedy."

Rose ignored the commotion to her right, where the women were talking to someone else, their heads together, their whispers behind manicured fingers. She held John closer, hugging him protectively, as people in the seats twisted around to get a look at her. People standing in the back were shifting away from her, leaving her alone. She felt surrounded by shuffling, rustling, and murmuring, but nobody said anything to her.

Rose swallowed hard. She realized that there weren't going to be any more yelling matches, like at Fiore's or the hospital. People would ignore and avoid her until she became invisible, someone they talked about, but not to. And she understood, for the first time, how Melly felt.

Every day of her life.

Chapter Thirty-three

Rose was let into a small conference room, dominated by a floor-to-ceiling panel of windows and a round walnut table covered with papers, briefs, and a laptop. The two lawyers rose instantly, their backlit silhouettes markedly different; the man on the left was reedy and tall, and the one on the right was stocky and short. Until Rose's eyes adjusted to the light behind them, she couldn't see their features at all, and it added to her feeling of surrealism, that she found herself meeting with two faceless lawyers, one of whom represented criminals.

"Thanks for seeing me on such short notice," she said, hoisting John higher on her hip, and the tall lawyer strode around the table toward her, extending a hand with long fingers. His polished smile came into focus first, then his light eyes behind hip rimless glasses, and a lean face framed by thick, reddish hair cut in expensive layers.

"Oliver Charriere." His handshake was strong and brief, and he looked more styled than dressed, in a superbly tailored Italian suit with discreet pinstripes. "Great to meet you."

"I'm Tom Lake," said the other, who had a big folksy grin and the handshake of a weightlifter. His hair was short and bristle cut, his eyes brown behind aviator frames, and his tan suit strained at the seams. His neck was so big that the collar of his blue shirt cut into his jugular. "At this point, we usually say we're Mutt and Jeff, but I can see you're too young to get the joke."

"Not at all, but thanks." Rose smiled.

"Coffee?" Oliver asked, gesturing.

Tom smiled. "He takes your drink order, and I make the doughnuts. I've been baking all morning."

Rose chuckled. "Coffee would be great, thanks."

"Cream and sugar, correct?"

"Yes. How did you know?"

"My Spidey sense." Oliver crossed to the credenza, which held a tall coffee container and a flat box of doughnuts. He picked up a styrofoam cup and raised it to the coffee dispenser, pressing down the button on the lid. "Women like cream and sugar. Very few women drink black coffee, and I can tell who they are with my eyes closed. You're too lovely to be one of them."

Tom snorted. "Believe it or not, Oliver's inherent sexism helps when he picks a jury."

"If not a wife," Oliver added, and they laughed.

"Allow me." Tom rolled a maroon Aeron chair from under the table for her. "Please, sit down. You okay with the baby?"

"Yes, thanks." Rose took a seat, resettling John, who smiled up at her, then sucked his pacifier with such vigor that it moved up and down. "Thanks for letting me bring him."

"Not at all, we allow pets." Oliver strolled over with the coffee, and Tom shot him a comically dirty look.

"Please, show respect. That's Leo Ingrassia's son."

"Right." Rose felt herself relax. "And he bites."

"So do I." Oliver set the coffee on the conference table in front of Rose, then leaned over slightly, unfastened a button on his jacket, and sat down opposite her.

Tom took a seat next to him, sitting down heavily. "And so begins our lesson on the difference between criminal lawyers like my partner, and civil lawyers like me. He's an obnoxious peacock, and I'm straight."

Rose laughed.

Oliver shook his head, then glanced at Tom. "Same old jokes, over and over. You're fired."

"You can't fire me, I quit, and we're here for her." Tom pointed an index finger at Rose. "So you're married to Leo, the lucky bastard, and he knows Dean. I was in JAG with Dean's brother. It's lawyers all the way down. Let's get started." Tom looked over at Oliver with a crooked grin. "Should I clear the deck, first?"

"Oh, please. Not again."

"Yes, again. Clean up time!" Tom stuck out his arm, placed it against the clutter of stapled briefs, newspaper clippings, and Xeroxed legal cases, then swept it off the edge of the table and onto the maroon rug.

Rose burst into laughter, and Oliver rolled his eyes behind his cool glasses.

"Rose, please, don't encourage him. Now, you probably already know this, as a lawyer's wife, but let me explain one thing at the outset. You need to see both of us this morning, a criminal lawyer and a civil lawyer, because criminal charges may be filed against you, by the D.A., and you may also be sued in civil court, for damages. They're two different things. Understood?"

"Yes."

"Here's how we'll run this meeting this morning. Criminal law is more important than civil because locks and keys are involved. That means I'll talk first, while Tom tries not to pick his nose. Still with me?"

"Yes." Rose kept her smile, even though she didn't like the joke about the lock and keys.

"We're both familiar with your case. We've seen the TV and online video, but tell us what happened at school last Friday. Omit nothing."

"Well, I was lunch mom," Rose began, and told them the whole story, from the jelly circle to the debris she'd seen at the school last night. Oliver took notes on the laptop, and Tom wrote on a fresh yellow legal pad, pressing so hard that he embossed the paper with his handwriting. When she finished, she braced herself, managing a smile. "Okay, what's the verdict, gentlemen?"

Oliver leaned back in his chair. "First, don't look so worried. You're in excellent hands with us. We're smarter than we look. At least I am."

"Good." Rose shifted John onto her lap, and he leaned backwards, lying in the crook of her arm and gazing up at her, in his sweet way.

"Let me lay out the criminal side for you. Under Pennsylvania law, specifically 18 Pa.C.S.A. Section 301(b)(2), criminal liability can be imposed for an act, or for the failure to perform an act, when one is imposed by law." Oliver spoke with authority and confidence. "In other words, you're not criminally liable for an omission, unless your duty to act is imposed by law. Understood?"

"Yes."

"There are circumstances in which adults do have a duty to a child imposed on them, and one such time is when there is a 'status relationship' to the child." Oliver made quote marks in the air. "Parents, for example, have that duty to their children, merely by virtue of their status. Make sense?"

"Yes." Rose glanced at John, and he was dozing off, sucking away.

"Now, the duty isn't only for parents. It can apply to anyone in control and supervision of a child, like a babysitter, a day-care worker, or a boyfriend or girlfriend who lives with the child. In Pennsylvania, that was established in the *Kellam* case."

Rose nodded.

"If someone can be said to have assumed a status relationship to the child, that forms a basis for criminal liability, in this and most other jurisdictions."

"Like being lunch mom?"

"Yes, exactly, and many other volunteer situations in schools, volunteers in the library, computer lab, music room, also coaches and chaperones on field trips."

"Really?"

"Yes."

"Jeez." Rose considered the implications, with dismay. "You mean if anybody in one of those situations screws up, they can be charged with a crime?"

"Let's not speculate that broadly. To be precise, all of those situations are fraught with liability, not only civil but criminal."

Rose had had no idea. She smoothed John's hair into place, but had the feeling she was comforting herself again.

"To digress, every summer, I'm asked to speak to baseball coaches. The first hour they have a doctor tell the coaches—all parents, like you—about medical care in case of emergency. Then, the second hour, I advise them to forget everything they just heard. I tell them that the only thing they should do in an emergency is call 911. That's it. Period."

"Why?"

"Because they could incur civil and criminal liability, otherwise."

Rose thought it was awful that they'd come to this point, as a civilization. It was hardly civilized. "Does criminal liability mean go to jail?"

"Not always, but usually."

"Am I going to jail?" Rose asked, her heart in her throat, but Oliver held up a hand.

"Wait. Stop. Don't get ahead of us, please. When you became a lunch mom, you arguably assumed such a status relationship to the children."

"'Arguably'? What does that mean?"

"It means that if I were to represent you, we'd argue you didn't, but it's a tough argument to win, and criminal liability arises under *Kellam* when you have prevented others from rendering aid."

"But I didn't do that."

"Yes, you did. You just told us you kept the girls in the cafeteria after dismissal to recess." Oliver's gaze was direct, yet without judgment, behind his tiny glasses. "They couldn't go outside where there were teachers and others to help them. Then the other lunch mom, Terry, left."

"That was her decision." Rose shook her head. "I didn't want her to go."

"True, but that's not legally significant. At the point at which she leaves to tell Mrs. Snyder, you detained the children and put them in a position where they couldn't be helped by others. Then, the D.A. will say, you failed to adequately help them, under *Kellam*. And it doesn't help that there's a suggestion your actions were motivated by dislike for Amanda, since she teases Melly."

Rose felt her stomach twist. "Can you contact Emily and her parents, or Danielle and hers, and try to get the facts? They can say I took them to the door."

"We'll try but they won't talk to us, I'm sure. If they're thinking of suing you or the school, they won't be permitted to talk to us."

Rose nodded. She should have known. It was a nightmare, replayed. They'd never get the truth now. Justice would be kept at bay by the lawyers.

"In addition, under *Kellam,* their testimony can hurt you. The kids will say you had them in time-out, yelling at them. One of them cried, right?"

"Yes," Rose admitted, miserable.

"*Kellam* is a bad case for you, though the facts are very different. Mr. Kellam was a child abuser."

"How long did he go to jail for?"

"Ninety to 240."

"Days?"

"Months."

Rose gasped. "That's twenty years!"

Tom pursed his lips, and Oliver held up his hand, again. "Look, there's nothing saying you'll be charged."

"How do we know if I'll be charged?" Rose felt panicky. "Who decides?"

"The D.A."

"So can we ask him what he's going to do?"

"No. Better to wait and see—"

"But this is my life, and the uncertainty is awful!"

"The uncertainty is better than provoking him. Keep your eye on the ball. We want this to blow over. The D.A. will be hard pressed to charge a pretty mommy with a crime, unless public pressure is too great not to do so. Lucky for us, it's not an election year."

Rose wasn't feeling so lucky. "If they charge me, do they arrest me?"

"We'd ask for bail, and we'd get it. You're not a flight risk."

Rose's mind reeled. Bail. Arrest. Flight risk.

"Also there's a separate statute, for criminal endangerment of a child, that we need to worry about." Oliver turned to the laptop and hit a few keys. "The criminal endangerment statute provides that a parent or guardian or 'other person supervising the welfare of a child'"—Oliver made quote marks again—"may be criminally liable for endangering the welfare of the child. And the Pennsylvania Supreme Court, in the *Gerstner* case, has interpreted the term to include babysitters and others who have 'permanent or temporary custody of the child.'" Oliver turned back to her, his gaze steady. "Much of this jurisprudence evolved under child abuse law, which is clearly not this case, but the law is the law."

"So how does that apply to me? As you said, I'm no child abuser."

"Of course not." Oliver leaned over. "But again, not legally significant. You were in supervision, it was exclusive, and you didn't take the kids all the way to the playground. I don't blame you, but that's not the point."

Rose couldn't believe her ears.

"Assume the facts that they have are true, namely, that you chose your child over the others, abandoning Amanda and the other two. That's straight-up endangerment."

"But that's not what happened."

"I know, but that's a matter of proof. They'll have to prove their set of facts, and even though we don't technically have the burden, we'll have to prove ours. Now, is there surveillance videotape in the cafeteria or elsewhere in the school?"

Rose hadn't thought of that. "I don't know, I doubt it. They videotape on the buses. Melly doesn't take the bus."

"Understood." Oliver nodded. "The D.A. will need more information to charge you, and they'll try to get it, in the days to come. If one of the assistant D.A.s calls you or drops by, say nothing and call me. In the meantime, say nothing to anybody about this case. Don't talk about it at all. Understand?"

"Yes."

"If it starts to look like they'll charge you, we'll have an opportunity to tell them the way it really happened. I don't think a jury that has all the relevant facts would convict you beyond a reasonable doubt."

"Are you sure?"

"No, but I've been doing this for twenty-six years and I'm not bad at it. It helps that Amanda is still alive. The D.A. will be far less likely to charge you if she lives. If she doesn't, you could be looking at third degree murder."

Rose felt vaguely sick. It was a double-whammy. Amanda dying, and her being arrested.

"Keep calm and carry on. That's my motto, which I stole from British royalty." Oliver permitted himself a crooked smile. "Third degree murder is like gross negligence. It's killing done with legal malice, but without the specific intent to kill." He turned to the laptop again and hit a few more keys. "Malice is defined as 'principal acts in gross deviation from the standard of reasonable care, failing to perceive that such actions might create a substantial or unjustifiable risk of death or serious bodily injury.' That's *Yanoff*."

"This is a nightmare."

"No, this is a situation that we can deal with, and we will. For the present, some things are up in the air." Oliver smiled. "Now, it's time to turn the floor over to my genius partner, who will tell you the relevant civil law and also a brilliant legal strategy we came up with."

Rose turned to Tom, who was at the credenza, pouring water into another styrofoam cup. She'd been so focused, she hadn't noticed that he'd left the conference table.

"Hold on." Tom returned to the table and placed the cup of water in front of her. "Have some."

"Thanks."

"Ready?" Tom asked, his tone sympathetic as he sat down in his chair.

"Sure," Rose lied. "I'm all ears."

Chapter Thirty-four

Rose took a sip of water while Tom glanced down at his handwritten notes, flipped through the pages, then looked up.

"Rose, let me ask you a few questions, for starters."

"Okay."

"When you were lunch mom, were you given any instruction in any emergency or fire procedures at the school?"

"No."

"Were you asked to take part in a fire drill at the school?"

"No."

Tom made a note. "Have you ever seen a fire drill at the school?"

"No. It's a brand-new school. We just moved here, in June."

Tom made another note. "Ever been in a school fire drill elsewhere, as an adult?"

"No."

"New topic. You said there are lunch-mom procedures." Tom looked up, his expression businesslike and his elbows resting on the table. His fingers throttled his Bic pen. "How were these procedures communicated to you?"

"One of the other moms told me."

"Who?"

"Uh, Robin Lynn Katz."

"She's another parent, isn't she? She's not employed by the school or the school district?"

"No. Yes. She's a mom." Rose was getting confused. She tried to adjust to the cadence of his speech, so different from Oliver's.

"How did Robin Lynn Katz find out about the procedures, if you know?"

"I don't know."

"Are the lunch-mom procedures written anywhere?"

"Not that I know of."

"In any event, you were never given written instructions about them, correct?"

"Correct. No."

"Were you given any instructions by anyone at the school with respect to emergencies or fire safety procedures?" Tom gestured at Oliver, who remained silent, listening. "Like Oliver was saying, with the baseball coaches."

"No."

"New topic." Tom checked his notes. "Let's talk about the blond teacher at the door to the playground. You sure she was a teacher and not a mom?"

"Yes."

"Why?"

"I don't know. She appeared to be getting them outside, in some official way. She acted like a teacher."

"Good enough." Tom made a note. "When you ran back into the cafeteria, was she still there?"

"As far as I know, yes."

"Did you see her? In other words, you didn't see her go out, did you?"

"No."

Tom made another note. "Now. Reesburgh is a new building, finished in August, correct?"

"Yes."

"And you told us what Kristen Canton told you, about the gas leak and the faulty wiring. The carpenter, Kurt Rehgard, told you the same thing. Were they the only people who told you about that?"

Rose thought a minute. "Kristen told me that the teacher, Jane Nuru, said something about them rushing the job and not doing the punch list."

"Right. You mentioned that. Sorry. My error." Tom made a note. "Okay, shifting gears again, tell me how you get in and out of the school, particularly through the playground door."

Rose didn't understand. "You walk?"

"No." Tom shook his head. "I'm being unclear. In my son's middle school, only the main entrance to the school is unlocked, and it leads to the office and only to the office. All visitors check in."

"Right. Reesburgh works the same way."

"You need a keycard to get in the other doors?"

"Same as Reesburgh." Rose thought a minute. "One time I went into the side entrance and it was locked. The teachers have the keycards. They wear them around their necks."

"Good." Tom made another note. "In my son's school, the doors lock automatically when they close. Also the fact, in Reesburgh?"

"Yes."

"So think back to that morning. Tell me about the kids in the hallway, running out to the playground. Are they moving in a continuous stream?"

"Mostly."

"But not always?"

"No, I think. I don't know." Rose could imagine how scary it would be to get cross-examined by Tom, and felt glad he was on her side.

"Does each kid open the door himself, on the way out?"

"I'm not sure."

"See it now." Tom held up his hand, almost like a hypnotist. "Close your eyes. Focus on the kids. What do you see?"

Rose obeyed. She saw smoke. Fire. The kids, a moving stream of heads.

"Do you see the door closing in anybody's face? Do you see them hitting the bar in the middle to open it?"

Suddenly Rose knew the answer, and she opened her eyes. "No. The door was open the whole time, propped open."

Tom broke into a grin.

Oliver looked over with a sly smile. "Bingo."

Rose didn't understand. "Does that matter?"

"Patience, grasshopper." Tom cocked his head. "Why was it propped open, if you know? Is that typical? Have you seen that before?"

"Yes, I have seen that, when I pick Melly up." Rose shifted, and in her arms, John stirred but stayed asleep. "It's been hot this month, and they keep it propped open, to make it cooler in the hallway."

Tom frowned. "But what about the air conditioning?"

"The hallways aren't air-conditioned. Only the classrooms."

"Yes!" Tom turned to Oliver and raised his hand for a high five. "Hit me, bro!"

Oliver recoiled, smiling. "Quiet. You'll wake up the puppy, and I don't high-five. Also, *never* call me *bro*."

Tom grinned at Rose. "Boy, am I feeling better!"

"Why?"

"Here's why." Tom set his notepad aside. "First, the basics. There's no duty to rescue in civil law. In other words, you had no duty to rescue Amanda. But under common tort law, in Pennsylvania and mostly everywhere else, once you undertake to rescue someone, you have to do so with reasonable care. The only exception is for doctors under the Good Samaritan statutes, but they don't apply to you."

"Okay."

"So the question for the jury would be, what is reasonable care in these circumstances? The jury will have to ask themselves, what would *I* do?" Tom put a finger to his head, mock-thinking. "Would I take Amanda and the others out to the playground all the way, and risk losing my own child in the fire? Or would I do what Rose did, strike an on-the-spot compromise that tries to save all of them? Or would I ignore Amanda and the others altogether and go save my kid?"

Rose's mouth went dry. She picked up her water and sipped some.

"I've listened to your account, and we have an obvious proof problem between what you say you did and what everybody else says you did. We'll have to overcome that, but the best way to get you off the hook is to put someone else on it."

"Who?"

"The school, and the state. We can either wait for Amanda and her parents to sue you and the school, or we can take a more aggressive position and file suit against the school."

"What? No." Rose recoiled. "I like the school."

Tom raised a hand. "Keep an open mind."

"I would never want to sue the school."

"Why not?"

Oliver clucked, shaking his head. "She's cream and sugar. Black coffee would sue, no question."

Tom ignored him, leaning over. "You're injured. Your kid was injured. She almost died. You'll have expenses you haven't gotten the bills for yet."

"Yes, but—"

"Hear me out, please. Leave aside the faulty wiring for a minute, because we don't have all the facts on causation, and right now I want to focus on you. You need to change the way you see yourself." Tom pointed at her. "Let me paint you a picture. You're thrown into the school as lunch mom, with no instruction on fire safety, either written or oral, and you could have died. So could your daughter."

"I don't want to sue anybody, least of all the—"

"The teacher at the door doesn't notice that a kid is running back inside, which is clear negligence, and the exit door is left propped open, which is a patently unsafe procedure, because a kid could run back inside undetected, and she did, and that's why she was grievously injured."

Rose listened, trying to keep up with him. "But how did anything the school did cause harm to me, or Melly?"

"You weren't told the procedures in case of fire emergency, which put you in jeopardy. You could've been killed."

"Okay, but what about Melly? How did the school do anything to her?"

"It has no fire procedures in place to convey to volunteers, to save kids in a fire emergency. Also, the school could have three or four lunch moms, not just two. That would have helped, right? Or maybe one of the lunch moms should stand in the hallway to the bathroom, to see what's going on." Tom shook his head. "Rose, you should sue the school for the same reason that the Gigots might sue the school. You stand on the same footing. Melly equals Amanda, legally speaking."

"But Melly is fine, and Amanda might die."

"That makes no difference, again, legally. That's a damages question, and goes to extent of recovery."

"What does that mean?"

"Money." Tom spread his hands, palms up. "Look, we don't have all the facts on causation yet, for sure. Our firm investigator is a former detective and fraud investigator, and he's very experienced. He'll get started fleshing out all the details, obtaining the fire and state police reports, and he'll do his own investigation. When we find out who's really at fault—the school, the general contractor, or the electrical contractor, the inspector, whoever—we'll develop and refine our theory."

"Still." Rose shook her head. "I don't want to sue the school. You don't know what it's like. They'll crucify my daughter. I sat in an assembly like I was radioactive. We just moved, and we can't move again."

"Okay. Relax. Fine." Tom pursed his lips. "You're in charge. You make the decisions, we only make the recommendations."

"Good."

"But if you get sued, this is the best argument you have, and I think you might prevail with it, even if Amanda dies. You weren't at fault, you were a victim, the same as Amanda and the others. All of you were victims of a school system that saves money by throwing unpaid and untrained moms and dads, normal people like you, into a situation they're ill-equipped and ill-prepared to handle." Tom leaned forward again, his gaze intense. "You cannot do more with less, not now and not ever. Bet on it. This economy is in trouble, and the more our state government tries to cut corners in school budgets, the more *children will die.*"

Rose blinked. Tom fell silent as the words sank in, and the only sound in the conference room was John sucking on his pacifier, in a baby dream.

Oliver clapped softly. "Best jury speech ever. I love the send-a-message closing."

Tom looked over, then grinned. "I got myself all worked up, right? But I can feel it. It's a winner."

Oliver turned to Rose, with a smile. "Now you see why he's my partner. He seeks and destroys."

"But I still don't want to sue," Rose said, shaken. "I have to make a life for us in Reesburgh. They're already against us. I had to disable my email and they posted about me on Facebook."

"I see that all the time now, in my cases." Oliver nodded, knowingly. "The mob doesn't need burning torches and clubs anymore. It's trial by Facebook. That's why you have to be realistic. Your duck-and-cover posture isn't the best. If we don't file suit against the school, then at least you know you have a defense, and it could work. Understood?"

"Yes."

"I do recommend, however, that we get the word out in the press. We can leak it or go with a press release, or both. We have to start to shift public opinion in your direction. You have a side of the story, and you need it out there."

"Why?"

"If you're charged, the first thing I'd do is ask for a change of venue, and I won't win. There's enough press to make you look bad, but not enough to make you look bad enough."

Rose felt bewildered. "I wouldn't know how to leak something or send a press release. I thought you told me not to say anything."

"You don't, we do. We have people, sources. We write the release and put it out there. You say nothing." Oliver seemed to think aloud. "You need an official statement, especially in a place like Reesburgh. It's a small town, and views become self-reinforcing. We have to reverse the tide."

Tom's lips made an unhappy line. "Rose, if you were my wife, I'd give you the same advice. You need to get ahead of this situation, public relations–wise, whether it's civil, criminal, or both, and whether you file a lawsuit or defend one. You're getting killed in the press, and that taints the jury pool against you, civil and criminal."

Rose hadn't even thought of that. There was a lot to process, it was overwhelming.

"Look, Rose." Tom's expression softened. "You need to act, but you have a day or two. Think it over. Talk to Leo. If you want to get a second opinion, feel free to do that, too. Get back to us as soon as you can."

Oliver rose slowly, buttoning his jacket. "You're in a terrible bind. You don't want to sue the school, but if you did, it would help your criminal case, too. It would make a statement that you're not at fault. It could even deter the D.A. from charging you. The best defense is a good offense, to cite a cliché."

Tom got to his feet. "This comes down to one thing. Them or you."

Rose cuddled John and stood up. "Well, thanks so much, gentlemen. I do appreciate the time, and the advice."

"Last word. Think about what you hold dear." Tom gestured at John. "That little guy. Your daughter. Leo. Your home. That's what you need to protect. Not the school."

Rose heard the truth in his words, though it tore at her heart. She was remembering how kind Mr. Rodriguez and the staff had been to Melly this morning.

"Never hesitate to shoot." Tom eyed Rose, hard. "It's self-defense."

Chapter Thirty-five

Rose hit the gas, keeping her eyes on the road, relieved she could find an excuse to avoid Melly's gaze. The notion of being sued was bad enough, but she couldn't begin to think about going to jail. Meeting with the lawyers had left her shaken, but letting it show would defeat the purpose of their lunch outing, so she put on a happy face. "Mel, how was your morning?"

"Fine."

Rose braked for a yellow light, turning red. She'd picked Melly up at school without incident, and the other parents ignored them as they went to their car. The press stayed behind the cordon, and even though they snapped photos of the car as they drove past, nobody followed them. "What did you do in school?"

"More *Flat Stanley.*"

"Was it fun?"

"Ms. Canton wasn't there. She's not coming back."

"I'm sorry."

"She had to take care of her mom. She's sick."

"I see. Did Mrs. Nuru say when they're getting a new gifted teacher?" Rose glanced over, and Melly kept her head to the window, which was open.

"No."

"Did you spend much time with Mrs. Nuru?"

"No. Sammy and Seth got in a fight. They always do."

"What happened at assembly?"

"Nothing. It was sad."

"Mine was, too." Rose thought back to the parents' assembly. Aside from feeling like she had leprosy, it was an hour of boilerplate assurances that the school would return to business as usual, which was the best thing for the children. "We had a moment of silence. Did you?"

"Yes."

"What else did they say? Anything?"

"That we shouldn't be scared and there's no more fire, and we'll get a new cafeteria and still have the Halloween parade." Melly looked over. "I want to be Hermione again, okay?"

"Sure."

"Now I have the Hermione wand, it makes it better."

"Perfect," Rose said, though she was beginning to feel otherwise. As great as Harry Potter was, she was worrying that it was just another thing to set Melly apart.

"They said we should make get-well cards for Amanda, so we did. Mine was really good."

"That was nice. I'm proud of you." Rose smiled, meaning it. It couldn't have been easy to make a card for your bully. "So, where should we eat?"

"I don't know."

"What do you feel like? I didn't have time to make any sandwiches this morning." Rose eyed the McDonald's, Saladworks, and the other fast-food joints. This section of Allen Road was one strip mall after another, all with tan stucco façades and fake-English names like Reesburgh Mews, Reesburgh Commons, and Reesburgh Roundabout. Traffic was busy, with school dismissed early and the noontime rush. "Want a Happy Meal? Or chicken? Want a hamburger?"

"Ms. Canton doesn't eat hamburgers. She eats veggie burgers. We ate together. It was really good."

"When was that?" Rose hadn't heard anything about Kristen and Melly eating together. The traffic light changed, and she hit the gas.

"She showed me how to make a veggie burger."

"Really, when?"

"At lunch. She gets a veggie burger out of the freezer, puts it the microwave, then she puts a Stackers pickle on top, and ketchup." Melly made a motion with her hand. "Stackers pickles are flat. She said we can buy them at the Giant, and the veggie burgers, too. She showed me the box, and it says Amy's Burgers, but I said they were Kristenburgers, and she laughed."

Rose still didn't understand. "Why were you eating with her?"

"She saw me going to the handicapped bathroom and she said I could." Melly turned, her eyes hopeful. "Can we get Stackers pickles at the store? And Kristenburgers?"

"Sure." Rose wanted to know what had happened, though. If it was what had prompted Kristen's email to her, about lunchtime, she didn't know the details. "Why were you going to the bathroom? Was there a problem? I'm not going to do anything. I just want to know."

"Ms. Canton said I needed a break. She calls it 'me time.' She says she eats alone on Friday, like me. She doesn't mind, because that's her 'me time.' "

Rose knew the weekly schedule, but that wasn't the point. On Friday, the teachers ate in the classrooms, because they made folders that got sent home with the kids, containing work from the week prior. Kristen, as a gifted teacher, wasn't responsible for making any folders, but that still didn't explain why she was eating with Melly. "So why were you eating with her? What happened?"

"She says I needed 'me time' from Amanda and Emily."

"Were they teasing you?" Rose tried to put it together, like a puzzle.

"They were saying that Harry Potter is for boys, and I said, he's not. They only saw the movies, so they don't know. He saves Hermione from the bathroom. Remember, Mom? Like you saved me. I knew you'd come."

Rose felt a twinge. "I love you, Mel."

"I love you, too." Melly twisted to the backseat and waved to John, who was asleep. "I love *you*, John!" she whispered, then turned back to Rose, cheered. "He's cute, isn't he?"

"He's very cute." Rose brightened. "I have an idea. How about we get some lunch, go over to the park, and have a picnic?"

"It's not a sunny day."

"You don't need the sun for a picnic. It won't rain."

"Okay." Melly nodded. "Then can we get the Kristenburgers?"

"Yes."

"Yay!" Melly cheered, and Rose steered the car into the turn lane.

Two hours later they'd had a picnic at Allen's Dam, found the reddest fallen leaf, and gone to the grocery store. Rose wanted to make one last stop before home, in one of the strip malls. She pulled into the lot, cut the ignition, and turned to Melly. "I thought we'd get some books."

"Goodie!" Melly turned to John, who was babbling away in the backseat. "Johnnie, books!"

"Careful, it's a parking lot. You have to hold my hand." Rose grabbed her car keys and purse, and Melly was already in motion, climbing out of the car and closing the door. Rose went around to the backseat, unclipped John from his car seat, found his pacifier, and lifted him into her arms. "Hey, buddy, how're you?"

"Bababsbsbsb," he answered, and Rose kissed his cheek as Melly came around and took her other hand.

"Mom, can I lock the car?"

"Sure." Rose handed her the car keys.

"*Colloportus!*" Melly pointed the key fob at the car.

"Good job." Rose knew the basic Harry Potter incantations, since it was Melly's second language. She dropped the keys into her purse and took Melly's hand. "I want to get a book for me, and you can pick some out, too."

"There's a new one about Quidditch. My friend on Club Penguin told me. She's Harryfan373 and I'm HarryP2009. She loves it!"

"Mel, do any of the kids in your class like Harry Potter? I would think there'd be a few."

"William does."

"Nice. Did you talk to him about it?"

"No. I only know because he has a Gryffindor beanie, too. It's maroon like mine."

"So maybe we can make a playdate with him."

"Mom." Melly rolled her eyes. "He likes the video games, not the books."

Rose walked her toward the store. "A woman at assembly told me her daughter loves the American Girl books. She said they're good."

"They're not." Melly kicked a stone, sending it skidding across the rough surface of the asphalt.

"Have you ever read one?"

"No."

"Do kids in your class read them?"

"All the girls do. They have the dolls, too."

"Really?" They reached the bookstore, and Rose opened the heavy door. "So how's it work? You read the book and you get the doll that's in the book?"

Melly let go of her hand, skipping ahead. A woman standing at the octagon display of hardcovers looked up from behind her reading glasses, her gaze lingering a fraction too long on Melly's face. Oblivious, Melly was already heading toward the Harry Potter books, in Fantasy. A cardboard Dumbledore presided over the section, his magic wand in hand. Behind him was a Hogwarts flag, its shield covered with fake spiderwebs.

"Mel, come check this out," Rose called out, and Melly turned, her eyes bright and alert. She came alive in bookstores.

"Check what out?"

"This way." Rose gestured at the children's books section, a pastel-hued kingdom of pink mushrooms, cartoon parrots, and a papier-mâché cottage. "They probably have American Girl books, and we can pick some books for John."

"I don't want American Girl, Mom."

"What about John? He needs books, too." Rose smiled in an encouraging way, then walked toward the children's department. "Follow me. Let's do this, then go over to Harry Potter."

"Okay." Melly skipped ahead.

"Do you see the American Girl?"

"Over here." Melly stood at a yellow shelf, her knees bent so they bowed backwards. It was her characteristic stance; she was double-jointed, one of the reasons she didn't do well at sports.

"Find anything that looks good?"

"Nah."

"Lemme see." Rose came over and slid an American Girl paperback from the shelves. On the cover was a dark-haired girl in an old-fashioned straw hat. *"Rebecca and the Movies."*

"She looks dumb."

"Okay." Rose shrugged, which was reverse psychology, the hallmark of professional parenting. "Maybe there's a better one."

"Here." Melly slid one off the shelf and eyed the cover, which showed a girl with straight blond hair and a big smile, touching a butterfly.

"Lanie's Real Adventures." Rose thought it looked fine. "Wanna give it a try?"

"Amanda likes Lanie. She has a Lanie doll, too."

Oops. "Amanda looks like Lanie, doesn't she?"

"Yes." Melly put the book back on the shelf, wedging it between the others with care. "Get it, Mom? You like the books that look like you. You get the doll that looks like you. You go on the website and make the doll that looks like you. Like Build-A-Bear, only with dolls."

"Oh." Rose wanted to kick herself, realizing the problem. None of the American Girls had a birthmark. She spotted one hugging a cute tricolored dog and picked it from the shelf, trying to recover. "Look at this one, about Nicki. She likes dogs, and we like dogs."

"Bbsbssbsb." John pumped his arm, and Rose put on a smile.

"He likes it. Let's get it."

An hour later, Rose pulled into the driveway at home, with sleeping kids, groceries, and a shopping bag of books. The clouds had darkened, and it looked like rain, so they were just in time. She cut the ignition and was about to wake Melly when she noticed a strange car parked in front of the house. It was a navy blue Crown Victoria, and in the next minute, two men in suits were getting out of the front seat and walking toward her car. They didn't look like reporters or door-to-door salesmen, if there was such a thing anymore. She stayed in the driver's seat and slid the key back in the ignition.

"Excuse me, Ms. McKenna?" one of the men called out, reaching into his pocket as he approached. He was young-looking, his sandy hair stiff with product, and he had on a dark suit and an edgy patterned tie. He held up a slim black billfold that flopped open to reveal a heavy, gold-toned badge.

Rose felt her heart stop.

"I'm Rick Artiss, with the District Attorney's Office, Reesburgh County. Can I speak with you a minute?"

Chapter Thirty-six

Rose's mouth went dry. Melly slept in the passenger seat, and John snored in the back, but for a split-second, she forgot they were there, that they even existed, and she was transported back to another time. Everything came rushing back, conflating the days of her life, collapsing the past into the present, making them one and the same, as impossible to separate, one from the other, as waves in an ocean.

"Mrs. McKenna?" The young assistant district attorney was frowning, and so was the other man with him, older and taller, in horn-rims, a dark suit, and a preppy striped tie. Behind them, one of her neighbors, Sue Keller, was walking down the sidewalk with her dog, an old gray poodle.

Rose blinked, recovering. It wasn't the lawyers or the neighbor that snapped her out of her reverie, but the poodle. His name was Boris, and he'd growled at Princess Google last week, scaring her and Melly. The incident anchored Rose in time, and she came zooming back into the present, shaken and seared, as if she'd traveled through the atmosphere of Earth itself.

"Whoa, don't be afraid." The young assistant district attorney closed the billfold and slipped it into his back pocket. "We're just lawyers. We just want to talk with you for a minute or two."

Rose signaled to him with a jittery index finger, mouthing *hold on a sec.* She thought of Oliver and Tom, who'd told her not to talk to the prosecutors, but she didn't want to look guiltier than she did already. She slid the key from the ignition, trying to get in control.

"Mom?" Melly started to stir, and Rose leaned over.

"Melly, go back to sleep. Everything's all right."

"Okay," Melly said, drowsy, and Rose reached for the door handle, got out of the car, and closed it behind her.

"Sorry, we didn't mean to startle you." The young assistant district attorney backed up, deferring to his older colleague, who stepped forward with a confident air. Deep crow's feet creased his eyes behind his bifocals, and a bald spot left him with a sparse fringe of grayish-brown bangs.

"Sorry, young Rick comes on like a carjacker," he said, extending a hand. "I'm Howard Kermisez, also an assistant district attorney with the county. Call me Howard."

"Rose McKenna." She shook his hand, managing a smile. Sue Keller eyed the scene as she walked by, with Boris sniffing the breeze.

"We didn't mean to scare you. We thought you saw us. Sorry about that." Howard leaned over, peering into the car. "And that must be Melly."

"Yes." Rose edged reflexively in front of the window, blocking his view.

"Welcome to Reesburgh. It's great to see new folks moving in, especially babies. This is a great town, in a great state." Howard smiled in a pleasant, if impersonal, way. "How are you and your husband enjoying it? He's from Worhawk, I understand."

"We love it, thanks. But excuse me, I have to get the kids inside." Rose gestured behind her, as if that explained it all. She couldn't go to jail because she had to make dinner, then there were fractions to practice, and another Flat Stanley to be pasted into the scrapbook, from a cell phone picture taken at the picnic. Melly had already thought of the caption: Flat Stanley Meets a New Newt.

"Of course, you're busy now, I can see that. I have three sons. They're older, but you know what my wife says? Little kids, little problems, big kids, big problems." He smiled coolly, again. "So we won't take long. We just have a few questions. You were volunteering at the elementary school last Friday, when the fire broke out, weren't you?"

"No, wait, listen. I've been told not to speak with you. My lawyers are Oliver Charriere and Tom Lake." Rose almost blanked on Tom's last name, she felt so panicky. "You should call them if you have any questions for me. I have their card. Hold on."

"I'm not sure we need to get formal about this."

"I'd prefer it that way." Rose opened the car door, grabbed her purse, extracted the card, and handed it to Howard. "Now, excuse me, but I should really get the kids some dinner."

"Sure, okay." Howard's smile flattened. "I know Oliver well. I'll give him a call, then get back to you."

"Great," Rose said lightly, as if it were a date, not an arrest. She opened the car door, and Melly was sitting upright in the seat, awake.

"Mom, who are those guys?"

"Just lawyers." Rose reached in, unbuckled Melly's harness, and let it retract. She wanted to get the kids inside and call Oliver, right away. "Let's go, honey. Got your backpack? Get your backpack."

"Like Leo?" Melly stretched slowly.

"Not as much fun as Leo." Rose glanced over her shoulder, and the Assistant District Attorneys were getting back into their car. Sue Keller and Boris were on their way back, for the return trip. "Hurry up, let's go."

"Are you okay, Mom?"

"I'm fine, I just have to go to the bathroom. Let's go, okay?" Rose hurried to the backseat, opened the car door, and unbuckled John's car seat.

"Mom, don't forget the bag from the bookstore."

"I'll get it later." Rose slipped the seat belt over John's head and lifted him up to her shoulder, where he flopped, staying asleep.

"But I want my books."

"Then can you get the bag?" Rose checked over her shoulder. The sedan was still parked in front of the house. They hadn't even started the engine.

"It's heavy." Melly had her backpack and was struggling with the bag of books.

"If you can't do it, leave it. I'll come back for it." Rose glanced behind her, worried. Still, the sedan hadn't moved. She felt her heart start to pound. Prosecutors, lawyers, charges. She had been here before. "Mel, please, hurry up."

"Mom, you don't have the Kristenburgers."

"I'll come back for the groceries."

"Can we still have them for dinner tonight? You said."

"We will, just hurry. I have to go to the bathroom, please." Rose hurried down the sidewalk, reaching the sedan. The prosecutors were inside talking, and she slowed her pace so she didn't look like a fleeing felon. "Mel, do you need help?"

"No. I can do it myself."

"Okay, hurry." Rose could see that Howard Whatever was pressing a number into his cell phone, and she wondered if he was already calling Oliver. Meanwhile, Sue Keller was catching up to them, with Boris yanking her forward. The cranky dog was getting close, so Rose hurried back to Melly. "Let me help, sweetie."

"I was doing it, Mom. I can do it."

"I know." Rose bunny-dipped with John and picked up the plastic bag of books. "I don't want Boris near you. Remember last time?"

Melly turned. "Oh, right. Norbert the dragon. Tried to bite me and Googie."

"Yes. Come on." Rose herded Melly up the sidewalk and past the sedan, where Howard was talking on his cell. The younger prosecutor sat in the driver's seat, watching her. She turned with Melly onto their front walk and went up the flagstone path.

"Mom, we didn't lock the car."

"I will later. When I come back out."

"*Colloportus,*" Melly said, anyway.

They reached the front step, where Rose set down the bag of books and handed Melly her purse. "Can you get the keys and open the door? I can't with my hand."

"*Alohomora!*"

"No unlocking spells, please. Use the key with the red thing on it."

"I know, I see you do it, all the time." Melly dug in the purse, found her keys, slid the key in the lock and twisted it, then pushed open the door. "Did it!"

"Good for you. Close the door. I'll be right back." Rose left Melly in the living room with the new books, went upstairs and put John down, then hurried into her bathroom with her purse. She got out her phone, and Oliver's number was still in the text function. She highlighted it and pressed CALL. "Hello?" she said, as soon as a woman picked up. "I'd like to speak to either Oliver or Tom. I'm a new client. Rose McKenna. I was there today."

"I'm sorry. Tom is in court, and Oliver is on the phone. May he return—"

"Is he on the phone with an Assistant District Attorney from Reesburgh?"

"I'm sorry, I'm not permitted to give out that information, but I can ask him to return your call."

"Thanks." Rose left her name and cell number, then hung up and dialed Leo's cell. It rang and rang, then the voicemail came on. She told herself to calm down when the beep sounded, and she left a message: "Leo, I met with the lawyers, and two assistant D.A.s were here at the house. Give me a call when you can. Love you."

Rose pressed END, then sank to the edge of the bathtub, her thoughts bounding back in time, a wild animal set free. She knew these woods. She had brought it on herself. She had it coming, truly. Her heart raced, she broke a sweat, and her gaze flitted around the picture-perfect bathroom, finding the his-and-hers pedestal sinks and the cornflower-blue accents in the shower curtain, which matched the hue of the thick bathtowels.

She had picked everything out for the new house, and seeing it all now, she knew she didn't deserve any of it; neither the pretty Italian floor tiles, nor the overpriced shampoos on the rim of the tub. She'd wanted to start over, to have one last starting-over in a lifetime of starting-overs, of endless moving from apartment to apartment, and from base to base. The only difference in each place was the color of the bathtowels.

Rose blinked. Her mother lay on the bathroom floor in her robe, passed out again. She'd need to be awakened, picked up, washed off, sobered up. Long, dark hair hid her once lovely face. The bathtowels in that apartment were yellow. Then pink, then white. The bathtowels were the only thing that changed in the apartments where her mother lay on the floor, until one day, she couldn't be awakened, at all.

Mommy!

"Mom?"

It was Melly, at the door. The door knob was twisting.

"Yes, honey?" Rose asked, coming out of her reverie.

"Why is the door locked?"

"Here I come." Rose got up and caught sight of her reflection, but didn't recognize herself. Her eyes, dark and blue, looked haunted.

"*Alohomora.*" Melly giggled, on the other side of the door.

Chapter Thirty-seven

Rose was cleaning up the dinner dishes when her phone rang, and she dried her hand hastily, reached for the cell phone, and tucked it into the crook of her neck. "Hello, yes?"

"Rose. It's Oliver. I heard you got a visit today."

"Yes. Did they call you? What did they say?" Rose peeked around the corner and double-checked that Melly was out of earshot in the family room, sitting at the computer desk and printing the Flat Stanley picture. John was in his high chair in the kitchen, mashing his rotini, his hand a small starfish. His palm made a *bum, bum, bum* sound when he banged the tray.

"They want a meeting tomorrow. Our offices, at ten in the morning. Can you make it?"

"My God, so soon?" Rose felt stricken. "What's going on?"

"Remain calm and carry on, remember?"

"Does this mean they're thinking of charging me?"

"It means they're investigating the facts."

Rose's gut tensed. "But why so soon?"

"The sooner, the better for us. We want to meet with them while Amanda's still alive."

Rose shuddered. "Why?"

"As we discussed, now there's less public pressure to charge you, and less pressure from the Gigot family. At present, the worst-case scenario is still a hypothetical. Understand?"

"Yes, but why are they moving so quickly?"

"Lots of reasons. They could be following up when your memory is fresh, or trying to show how responsive they are and how hard they work. Or they want to have their ducks in a row, in case Amanda dies."

"Do you have to talk that way?"

"What way?" Oliver paused, his voice warmer. "Sorry. I really am a nice man. You recall."

Rose didn't smile. She eyed John, banging the tray. *Bum!*

"Rose, be of good cheer. I'd like them to hear your side of the story before they get entrenched. If we put on a strong enough case, I hope we can back them down."

"We have to put on a case?"

"Not in a strict sense. I'll explain when I see you. Can you come in around nine, so I can prepare you before the meeting?"

"Yes. Sure." Rose thought a minute. "What if I can't get a sitter that quick? What do we do?"

"Melly's in school, correct?"

"Yes."

"Don't get a sitter. I want Howard and his lackey to see what the jury will see. Bring the baby."

"You talk like he's a prop."

"Well said. He's a prop."

"Oliver, he's my son," Rose said, upset. It was getting worse and worse.

"Did you speak with Leo yet?"

"No."

"By way of housekeeping, am I correct in assuming that you'd like us to represent you, on both the criminal and the civil side?"

"Yes."

"Excellent. We're delighted, and I know I speak for Tom. If you tell me your email address, I'll email you an engagement letter and when you get a second, send us a check for the retainer, which is five thousand dollars."

"Okay." Then Rose remembered. "Wait. I disabled my email."

"Get a new account, and we'll keep it private. What do you want to do about the press release, or me talking to one of my sources? May I go forward?"

"I'm not sure. Let me think and talk to Leo."

"Sure. Let me know. See you. Take care."

"Thanks." Rose pressed END, then L to speed-dial Leo, and waited while it rang, then went to voicemail. She composed herself before leaving another message: "I'm meeting with the D.A. tomorrow morning. Please call."

She pressed END, and her gaze fell on John, happily sucking his fingers. She couldn't imagine what would happen to him or Melly, if she had to go to jail. Leo would have to hire a full-time caretaker, and even if John could adapt, Melly would be devastated. She'd already lost her father, now she'd lose her mother. And there'd be no backstop for her at school, now that Kristen was gone.

Rose felt a wave of sadness so profound that she had to lean on the counter until it passed. It killed her that her children, and Leo, would have to pay for what she'd done, and even so, she sensed that she was entering eye-for-an-eye territory, the ultimate payback. She pressed the emotion away, trying to stay anchored in the present. There were dishes to rinse, counters to spray-clean, and a baby to bathe; the tasks of home life, the very stuff of being a mother. She had always taken satisfaction in the tasks, because she knew that each one mattered; it was the little things that made a house a home, and moms did all the little things.

Rose went to John, pulled out his tray, picked him up, and hugged him close, breathing in his damp baby smells and feeling his reassuring weight. He looped his fleshy arm around her neck, and she rocked him, told him she loved him, and nuzzled his warm neck with her nose, trying not to think about how much longer she'd have him, or he'd have her.

"Let's go say hi to your sister," she whispered into his ear, swallowing her emotion. She carried him into the family room, where Melly looked up from the computer printer, her blue eyes expectant.

"Mom, was that Ms. Canton on the phone?"

"No, sorry."

"When is she going to call?"

"I'm not sure, but soon, I hope."

"She said she would.".

"She will," Rose said, uncertain.

After the kids were in bed, she went back down to the kitchen, cleaned up, and sat down in front of the laptop, logging onto the web and checking philly.com for news of Amanda. The earlier stories hadn't changed, which meant that she was still alive.

Thank you, God.

Rain fell outside the window, and the sky had grown dark, a backdrop like a final curtain, of dark velvet. She could see the peaked roof of the house next door, which had in-ground floodlights that shone upward at its brick façade, lighting the place like a stage set. The tall trees in the sideyard were shedding leaves, but night and rain had obliterated their colors, so they looked black and shiny.

She wondered which leaf would fall next, playing a waiting game with herself, which felt uncomfortably familiar. She'd been waiting to see what would happen to Amanda. Waiting to see if she'd be charged with a crime or sued. Waiting for decades, since it had happened.

It had been a night just like this, and the rain was a slow, steady downfall. Her downfall. Rose could call up the memory of that night, without thinking. In fact, it took thinking *not* to call it up. She could see it now as if it were in front of her. It had happened around this time of year, too, but at the end of October. Halloween night, the leaves fallen, dead on the street.

Rose blinked, and the memory vanished. The kitchen was dim, the halogens under the counter working their suburban magic. The only sound was the patter of the raindrops on the roof and the thrumming of the dishwasher, which shifted gears. The blue digits glowed on the door, counting down until the end of the cycle. She watched the number change, 36, 35, 34, finally permitting herself to have the thought she'd been suppressing, almost constantly since the fire.

I need a drink.

She got up, went to the side cabinet, and reached into the wine rack, sliding out the first bottle she touched, then closing the door. The label read LOUIS JADOT, which would do just fine. She went into the drawer for the corkscrew, peeled the metal wrapping off, and did the honors with difficulty because of her bandaged hand. She poured herself a glass of merlot, and still standing at the counter, drained the glass like she used to, in the bad old days. It tasted more bitter than she remembered, but it could have been her state of mind.

"Don't tell anyone," she said, when Princess Google looked up.

She grabbed the bottle by the neck and set it on the table, then took the glass over to the laptop and sat down. She poured another glass, drank it, and her gaze fell on the laptop through the glass, an alcoholic wash of the newspaper's front page. HERO MOM? read the sidebar, and underneath that, *New Viewer Videos*!

She set down the glass, palmed the mouse, and muted the volume on the laptop. She clicked on the link for the videos, and it brought her to a list in bright blue, each one titled: School Fire, Cafeteria Fire in Local School, First Responders Arrive, Ambulance Leaves with Amanda Gigot, and so on, the list reading like a chronological description of her nightmare. Luckily, she was starting not to feel anything.

She poured another glass, drank it, and clicked one of the links, of the kids running from the school and onto the playground. She watched them come, numbing to their stricken faces, racing into the camera. The video ended, and the arrow froze, and she clicked and watched it again and again, until she felt absolutely nothing. She clicked on another video, titled Copter Shots, and watched the roof of the cafeteria smolder, then flare into flames. She slid the bar back and forth, forward and back, moving time backward and forward, so the past became the present, then they traded places and the present came before the past, her life a palindrome.

Rose came out of her reverie, realizing the cell phone had been ringing. The screen read LEO, so she reached for it and answered, "Hello?"

"Babe, is that you? You sound funny."

"I was sleeping. I went to bed early."

"Sorry. You wanna go back to sleep? How are you with this D.A. meeting?"

"Fine, but I need to go back to sleep."

"Sure, okay. Oliver's a great lawyer, so don't worry. Just listen to what he tells you when you meet with the D.A. Don't let them rattle you. If you wake up, call me, no matter how late. Love you."

"Love you, too." Rose hung up, set the phone down, and reached for the bottle.

Chapter Thirty-eight

Rose sipped her coffee, but it couldn't cure her cotton mouth from last night. They were in a larger conference room than yesterday, containing a long walnut table that held only a stack of fresh legal pads. The windows showed off a view of the woods behind the corporate center, with picturesque autumn foliage, a sharply blue sky, and a cool sun.

Rose stayed seated with John in her lap, while Oliver introduced himself to the two prosecutors. She had on a navy dress with a matching sweater, light makeup, and her hair in a half-ponytail, and John was in a white polo shirt and his Mom jeans, sucking his pacifier and clutching his Fisher-Price car keys. Long ago, she had posed almost the same way, for the Hanna Andersson catalog.

"Gentlemen, be my guest." Oliver gestured at the walnut credenza against the wall, which held two canisters of coffee, fresh bagels, and cream cheese, the delicious smells scenting the air. "Get yourself some coffee, and we have the best bagels of any law firm in the county."

"Thanks, but no," Howard said, evidently for both of them. He rolled out a chair for Rick, then unbuttoned his khaki jacket before he sat down, with a warm grin for Rose. "Hello again. Now that I can see the baby, he's cute, and the resemblance is remarkable."

"Thanks." Rose flashed a professional smile, wary. During their meeting prior, Oliver had warned her that Howard would use the friendly approach to get her to talk, and he'd told her to clam up, which should be easy, because she was terrified.

"Let's begin, shall we?" Oliver pulled up his chair and sat next to Rose. Their backs were to the window, forcing the prosecutors to squint against the brightness. Oliver had told her that the seating plan was intentional, but she hadn't reminded him that yesterday, she'd been the one squinting.

Oliver cleared his throat. "I suggest that we proceed as follows. Rose will tell you what happened at school, then you may ask questions, for clarification purposes. Understood?"

"Fine."

"Let's be clear. Rose is here today because she wants the truth to come out, and it hasn't, as yet. Between us, she's considering whether she will file a civil action against the school and the school district, for damages arising from their negligence."

Rose said nothing. Oliver hadn't told her he would say that, but she let her smile mask her dismay.

"I see." Howard lifted an eyebrow. His eyes were brown behind his hornrims, and there was a small scab under the softness under his chin, as if he'd cut himself shaving.

Oliver nodded. "Frankly, I have advised her to file suit, as has my partner Tom, but she and her husband have yet to decide. Her daughter Melly, as you may know, almost perished in the fire, and as you can see, she herself was burned on her hand and ankle." He gestured in Rose's direction, and John banged his plastic keys on the table. "In addition, Howard, let me ask you if the Commonwealth intends to file criminal negligence charges against the school and the school district in connection with the fire?"

"We're undecided, at this point." Howard's smile faded, and beside him, Rick looked down, as if the conference table needed examining.

"I would hope so." Oliver leaned back in the chair. "Who makes that decision, anyway? The District Attorney himself? And you make a recommendation to him, go or no?"

"Something like that." Howard looked annoyed.

"You've got 'em dead to rights, don't you? Even I've heard rumors there was faulty wiring and a gas leak. What did the Fire Marshal determine as the cause?"

"We haven't yet released that information."

"Of course, whatever, I'll play along." Oliver shrugged it off. "Obviously, the general contractor and all of the subcontractors—electrical, HVAC, and the like—were under the school and the district's exclusive control and supervision. I assume that the district chose them, and were I in your chair, I would examine the bidding method by which they were selected with a close eye." Oliver sniffed as if he'd caught a whiff of something stinky. "I know that state and local politics often play an unfortunate role in the awarding of major construction projects, and that should be investigated, too. If the district awarded the job to the low-ball contractor, they'd get haphazard construction, which resulted in foreseeable loss of life. That's criminal negligence."

Rose was surprised at how strong Oliver was coming on, and it was ratcheting up the tension in the room. Across the table, she could see Howard stiffen.

"Not to mention the elementary school's failure to have adequate safety procedures, which your discovery will reveal, if it hasn't already." Oliver gestured again at Rose. "My client is happy to speak with you now, however. We hope it will help you build a case against the people responsible for the deaths of three innocent citizens—and a little girl, if Amanda Gigot doesn't recover, God forbid. I assume you've been in contact with the Gigot family, and I would hope that your office isn't succumbing to their pressure to scapegoat Rose and her family."

"No, nothing of the sort." Howard frowned.

"Then I'm at a loss to understand why you visited my client at her home, yesterday. I would think she's the last person you would want to speak with, a mother who's as much a victim as the Gigot family. I trust you understand, whether we file suit or not, that's our position."

"I do." Howard shifted forward. "Now, if we could get on with—"

"Finally, of course, Rose is in no way waiving any of the constitutional rights that she may seek to assert later, such as self-incrimination, which we expect will not be necessary. Understood?"

"Yes."

"And, one questioner only. That's you." Oliver pointed at Howard. "If at any point, Rose wishes to break, we will. If she feels uncomfortable, we stop. If she wants to end, we do. Understood?"

"Yes," Howard answered, and Oliver turned to Rose, with a confident smile.

"Rose, why don't you begin?"

"Okay." Rose hoisted John higher on her lap and launched into the story. She told it in brief strokes, the way she had to Oliver and Tom, and Howard listened quietly, his expression sympathetic. When she got to the part where Melly was taken away in the ambulance, Oliver leaned over, raising his hand like a school crossing guard.

"And the rest is history," he said, to Howard. "So you see, no matter what the press or the Gigots may be saying, it's not as if Rose chose to rescue Melly over Amanda and Emily. On the contrary, she chose Amanda and Emily *over* Melly. There's simply no basis for any criminal charges against her."

Howard's gaze shifted from Oliver to Rose, then back again.

Rose held her breath. It was hard to believe she was sitting here, in front of a man who determined her and her family's fate. He wielded all the power and resources of the Commonwealth of Pennsylvania. He could send her to prison for twenty years.

Oliver kept talking. "I cannot imagine a jury in the world who would find anything blameworthy in her conduct, because she *is* a hero. The fact that Amanda was eventually injured is the fault of the construction deficiencies, the school's non-existent fire safety procedures, and the negligent supervision of the blond teacher in the hallway, who permitted her to run back in after an iPod."

Rose remained still. John banged the keys on the table, but everyone ignored him.

Howard looked deep in thought, eyeing Rose. "Just to clarify, where was the other lunch mom, Terry Douglas, when you asked Amanda and the other students to stay behind?"

Rose swallowed, hard. "She was—"

"Stop." Oliver raised his hand again. "I object to the phraseology 'stay behind,' and Rose has been clear about that. I won't have you go over and over it."

"I was clarifying."

"It's clear enough."

"Not to us." Howard shook his head. "The Commonwealth's concern is that Rose assumed and insisted upon exclusive control of the three children, including Amanda."

Rose felt her gut clench.

"We dispute that," Oliver shot back, coolly. "As soon as Rose regained consciousness, she delivered Amanda and Emily to the hallway and the supervision of the teacher there. She excluded no one, at any time. There was no one helping any child, except Rose." Oliver checked his watch. "We've been here an hour. That's an hour you should have spent interviewing the contractor, subcontractors, school district officials, and a teacher who let a child run into a burning building." Oliver rose, suddenly. "This meeting is over. Good-bye, and thank you for coming."

Howard looked up, pursing his lips. "Grandstanding doesn't help your client, Oliver."

"Oh, please." Oliver didn't bat an eye. "I'm not grandstanding, I'm merely standing. If you persist, I'm going to have to wonder why you're so intent on *not* investigating the school district and state officials who made the decision to hire whomever they hired. Please tell me it's not because they pay your and your boss's salaries, because the jury won't like that, not one bit."

"What?" Howard's eyes flared an angry brown, and he got to his feet, as did Rick. "What are you suggesting? That I'm in somebody's pocket?"

"I didn't say that, did I?" Oliver strode around the table, went to the door, and opened it calmly. "No more free discovery. Know that if you come after her, I'm coming after *you*."

Chapter Thirty-nine

Oliver eased into Howard's vacated chair across from Rose, exhaling with a smile. "So, now we can talk. How are you?"

"Worried sick." Rose sipped her coffee, which was cold. "Tell me how you think it went. Will he charge me?"

"That, I don't know." Oliver buckled his lower lip. "But you did well. Your account was brief and to the point."

"Thanks."

"This isn't in our control, and you have to understand that. We shot our wad, we bloodied his nose." Oliver paused. "I'm mixing my metaphors."

"It's okay."

"You heard the question he asked. That's our problem. The *Kellam* case, as I told you."

"Tell me if you think he'll charge me. Take a shot."

"We have to wait and see, about Amanda, and so forth, as I told you."

Rose gave up. "Why did you say all that, about me filing suit?"

"To back him down, to show him he's at risk if he moves against you." Oliver's smile vanished. "This is war, Rose. Make no mistake. Tom is right about that."

Rose didn't know what to say. She felt worried sick.

"This is no time to hesitate. You don't want to be sitting in cell-block C, thinking, 'I wish my lawyer had been more aggressive, I wish he'd fought harder for me.'"

Rose didn't want to admit it, but he was right. "So, do you think there's some payoffs going on, with the school district?"

"Of course not. I just said that to scare him. To let him know I'll go after him and his boss if I have to. I don't want him going after you instead of the district. I won't let that happen."

"Thanks," Rose said, meaning it.

"I do think we have to put our story out now. Let me proceed with a press release, please. I'll tell it from your point of view, and at the end, I can suggest that you're thinking about suing, not that you actually are going to."

"Why can't you put out my side of the story, without talking about me suing anybody?"

"It's not as newsworthy, and the first question they'll ask me is, is she suing? If I say no, you'll look weak." Oliver shook his head. "I'd rather say nothing than say that. Then at least they'll think you're contemplating suit."

"Then don't say anything. To the outside world, saying I'm thinking about suing is the same as saying I *am* suing. These are distinctions that only lawyers make, Oliver."

"Please, at least talk to Leo. See what he says."

"Okay, fine."

"You'll see a change for the better, as soon as we do. In the short run, it will get more intense, but we want to win, in the end. Keep the long run in mind."

"I will." Rose was about to get up, and John had fallen asleep, now that the meeting was over. She slid the plastic keys from his hand as his grip loosened. "Such a good baby."

"He earned his keep today, our little Exhibit A."

"His name is John."

"Exhibit J, then."

Rose didn't smile as she dropped the plastic keys into her purse, then raised John to her shoulder and stood up. "Thanks for everything today."

"You're welcome." Oliver stood up, too. "You know, I get it, seeing you with Exhibit J."

"Get what?"

"Why people want offspring. I never did, but all my wives did."

"Children are all that matters, Oliver." Rose met his eye and spoke to him from the heart. "This baby needs me, and so does Melly. They love their dad, but I'm their world. You have to keep me free, for them. Not for me, for them."

Oliver dropped his cynical expression, seeming to get real. "Listen. I'll try my best, but I can't guarantee anything."

"I know," Rose said, aching. She picked up her purse and left. There was something she wanted to do, and she had no time to waste.

Chapter Forty

Rose steered into the school parking lot, her face hidden behind sunglasses, but Tanya Robertson and the other press at the cordon recognized her car. They snapped photos and shouted questions she couldn't hear, with the car windows up and Disney lullabies on the CD player. John listened contentedly in his car seat, shaking his plastic keys, a toy worth its weight in gold.

She hit the gas, cruised as far from the press as she could go, and parked. The lot was almost empty because it was too early for dismissal, but she was a mom on a mission. She twisted off the ignition, grabbed her purse, got out, and slid John and his toy keys from the car seat. She gave him a big kiss on his fleshy cheek, and his tiny arm went around her neck.

"Bbsbb," he gurgled, with a wet grin that revealed a white flash of tooth nugget on his lower gum.

"A new tooth!" Rose hadn't noticed, with all the horrible stuff going on. She walked toward the school, reached the concrete ramp, and went inside through the door signed, ALL VISITORS MUST CHECK IN. It was the only door open to the public, and she thought of Tom. She couldn't imagine filing suit against the school, shook it off, and entered the office. The room was large, with a sunny panel of windows, soft blue walls, and matching patterned carpeting. An oak-like counter divided the office lengthwise, and the front part served as a waiting room, containing four blue-cloth chairs, an end table, and a wire rack with tri-fold brochures for the PTO.

"Hi, Jill." Rose slid her sunglasses onto her head and walked to the counter. The main secretary's desk was on the other side, a petite, friendly woman named Jill Piero.

"Hello, Rose." Jill looked up from her keyboard with a smile that hardened like ice. "How's Melly?"

"Fine, thanks." Rose wasn't completely surprised by the cold shoulder. "I was wondering if you could help me. Melly was really close to Kristen Canton, and she's so sad that Kristen's gone."

"Yes, it's too bad." Jill pursed her lips.

"Kristen said she'd call us to say hi to Melly, but so far she hasn't. Do you have a number where I can call her?"

"I don't know if we have it, but even if we did, I wouldn't be permitted to give that out."

"But Kristen was close to Melly, and she wouldn't mind."

"Sorry, no can do." Jill glanced behind her at the other secretaries, but they were both on the phone at their desks.

"Then can you call Kristen and ask her to give us a call? I'll give you my cell number."

"If we have a number for her, I will. I don't even know if we do."

"Can you check?" Rose thought a minute. "Or if you have a home address for her parents, I'd take that too. Then I could send her a note or maybe Melly could send her a card."

"Hold on." Jill turned and went behind the wall, which connected to the hallway to Mr. Rodriguez's office.

Rose could hear talking, but couldn't make out what anyone was saying. She waited a minute, but sensed where this was heading and decided to get proactive. She went to the right, down the hallway, about to find Mr. Rodriguez and ask him herself when she spotted the teachers' mailboxes, to her left. Neat oak slots lined the wall, and each one was open, many with mail.

Rose scanned the nameplates, in alphabetical order, and reached the C's. Kristen Canton. Her mailbox was lower than eye-level, and there was a thin packet of mail inside. The school must have been accumulating mail, to forward it when they had enough. She slid it out quickly and read the forwarding address, printed in ballpoint pen next to the crossed-out school address. **765 Roberts Lane Boonsboro MD.** She committed it to memory, went back to the counter, and waited for Jill, who returned after a few minutes.

"Sorry, we don't have her cell and we can't give out her parents' home address."

"Thanks for trying, bye." Rose left the office, flipped down her sunglasses, walked from the building, and slid out her phone, adding the Cantons' address to her list of contacts, so she wouldn't forget it. She started to go back to her car with John, but it was too nice a day to sit in a car, until dismissal. On impulse, she walked to the back of the building and through the teacher's parking lot, shaking off some unhappy flashbacks.

Here's the ambulance!

She went around the back of the building and ended up on the far side of the school. The township parking lot lay to her left, and the school buses sat parked against the cyclone fence like a row of yellowed teeth. She passed the grassy stretch of athletic fields, with their soccer goals outlined, and approached the cafeteria from the other side.

She was downwind, where the breeze carried the stench of burned plastic, and the sight filled her with renewed sadness. A new plywood wall concealed the cafeteria, which had been state-of-the-art, and she walked along on grass blackened and filthy with mud and charred debris. Workmen flowed in and out of the site through an opening in the plywood, pushing wheelbarrows of charred debris, or carrying building materials. One of the workmen, in a white Bethany Run T-shirt and Carhartt pants, was her carpenter friend from the night before, Kurt Rehgard.

Kurt looked over, recognizing her, with a slow grin. "Hey, Mrs. Lawyer," he called out, coming over as his buddies exchanged glances, behind him. "How's your daughter?"

"Back to school."

"I didn't hear from you, so I figured you're not getting that divorce." Kurt grinned. "And I know who you are, even with those big shades on. I saw your picture online. The article wasn't very nice."

"I didn't mean to keep it from you." Rose reddened, and Kurt met her gaze directly, his eyes flinty under his hardhat.

"Yes, you did."

"Okay, maybe I did." Rose felt unmasked. "I guess they know who I am, too. Your buddies."

"Those clowns?" Kurt gestured behind him. "No way. If they go online, it's for porn. I went to one year of community college, and they think I'm Einstein."

Rose couldn't smile. "I didn't leave that little girl behind. I thought I got her out, but she ran back in."

"I didn't think you'd just leave her there. I can tell. I'm a good judge of character. Also, you keep coming back here, looking so sad, like you're visiting a grave. It said online that that little girl's family wants to sue you. Are they for real?"

"Evidently."

"That's crap." Kurt frowned. "It's not your fault. I told you the wiring was bad, and the gas leaked, too. The GC was Campanile. Those are the guys who need to get their ass sued."

Rose made a mental note of the name. "Are they a good contractor?"

"Yes. Campanile is top-drawer, but mistakes happen, even with the best outfits. The electrical contractor messed up, and the building inspector shoulda caught the mistakes. He certified it, so he messed up, too."

"But the inspector would've certified it before the school opened, right?"

"Yes."

"So why did it blow up now, in October? School's been open for a month."

"You ever put a penny in a fuse box? A lotta guys, they do a jury-rigged job, down-and-dirty, to get it done when the client wants in. They tell themselves they'll come back later and do it right, but they don't. Or they forget. Or they get canned. If that's what happened, that's on Campanile, the GC, or the building inspector. Not you."

"What a mess." Rose shook her head, thinking down the line. "This is going to be the lawsuit from hell, and that's if they don't bring criminal charges."

"Against you? That's ridiculous. Tell you what." Kurt checked behind him again. "Let me do some asking around, and I'll see what I can find out about how it happened. Off the record."

"Really? Thanks."

"No sweat. When I read that article, I thought of my niece, the one I told you about. Kids are precious, and we gotta take care of 'em, and sometimes, like with Iraq and all, we gotta take care of each other's. You really stepped up for those kids."

"Thanks," Rose said, touched.

"S'all right. Gimme your phone number, for official use only." Kurt slid out his cell phone, Rose did the same, and they added each other's numbers to their contacts.

"Aren't we so modern?" Rose asked, and Kurt grinned.

"Hell, to me, that was phone sex."

Chapter Forty-one

Rose walked around the back of the school, shifted John to her hip, checked her phone for the address of Kristen's parents, then dialed information. She got their home phone and let the call connect, stopping in front of an empty parking space.

"You have reached the Canton residence," said the voicemail, and Rose waited for the beep, disappointed.

"Hello, I'm Rose McKenna, trying to reach Kristen. She taught my daughter at Reesburgh Elementary, and she was going to call us. We hope to hear from her. Please call when you get a sec, thanks." She left her home and cell number, pressed END, and dropped the phone back into her purse.

She checked the time on the phone, and it was 2:25—ten minutes until dismissal. The buses were lined up and idling at the long driveway, and SUVs and minivans were pulling into the parking lot. A group of walkers, who lived close to the school, were assembling at the entrance ramp, standing with babies in their arms or in strollers. They were talking, still abuzz from the morning, but none of them noticed Rose. Suddenly, she spotted a boxy white newsvan stop at the entrance to the parking lot, open the sliding door, and disgorge Tanya and her cameraman behind the cordon.

Rose stalled, hugging John, uncertain. She didn't want Tanya to get an early bead on her, so she stayed where she was, apart. The school's front doors opened, and fifth graders emerged, carrying heavy backpacks looped over one shoulder or banging against their legs. More kids started flowing out, headed for the buses or for parents who had walked or driven.

Rose eyed the kids for Melly's class, but they weren't out yet. She took a few steps forward, but one of the moms spotted her as she approached, then the others noticed, and she caught their collective frowns. One of them was Janine Rayburn, whose son was in Melly's class, and when Rose smiled at her, she turned away.

The kids in Mrs. Nuru's class started to leave the building, then Melly appeared. Her head hung lower than usual, though her back was characteristically straight, with the padded loops of her backpack placed on both shoulders; it was a habit of hers that touched Rose, because it told so much. Melly had to be perfect, controlling what she could because there was so much she couldn't.

"Melly!" Rose waved her free arm, and Melly hurried down the ramp, as the other moms followed her with their eyes, talking behind their hands.

"Hi, Mom, hi Johnnie!" Melly hugged her and John, but when she pulled back, Rose noticed a long reddish bruise on her arm.

"What's this?"

"Oh." Melly put a hand over the bruise. "Just a bump."

"How did you get it?" Rose asked, surprised. Melly wasn't the kind of kid who got a lot of bumps.

"I'm fine, Mom." Melly stood on tiptoe to kiss John, her blue eyes shining. "Hi, baby boy. Love you." John made a pass at her with his fingers, outstretched, and Melly giggled. "He almost got me that time!"

"What happened to your arm?"

"Did Ms. Canton call?"

"Not yet." Rose didn't tell her she'd called Kristen's parents, because she didn't want to get her hopes up. "Answer me, about your arm."

"I got in a fight, that's all."

"A *fight*? How did that happen?"

"I pushed Josh and he pushed me and I fell down."

"You pushed him first?" Rose felt incredulous. It was unprecedented. "Why?"

"Let's go home, Mom."

"Why did you push Josh?" Rose took Melly's hand, and they walked through the noisy parking lot. Kids shouted, minivan doors rolled shut, and hatchbacks came down. Engines started, and buses lurched off with hydraulic squeaks, spewing exhaust. Rose squeezed Melly's hand to provoke her answer. "Mel?"

"Josh said you let Amanda burn up like a French fry. So I pushed him and he pushed me back and I fell down."

"Oh no." Rose felt a stab of guilt. "Mel, you don't have to defend me. I don't care what people say about me."

"Okay."

"I'm sorry it happened."

"It's not your fault. You didn't do it."

"What did Mrs. Nuru say?"

"She didn't see."

"Did you tell her?"

"No." Melly shook her head. "Can we not talk about it anymore?"

"Okay." Rose squeezed her hand, and they reached the car. "Let's go home and get lunch."

"Can we have Kristenburgers?"

"You got it." Rose shifted John to the back of her hip, found her keys in her purse, and chirped the car unlocked.

"I wanted to unlock it, Mom."

"Sorry, honey. I forgot. Give me your stuff." Rose opened the front door for Melly, then took her backpack and lunchbox so she could climb in unencumbered. Melly clambered into the passenger seat, and Rose went to the back, opened the door, tossed the stuff onto the floor, and lowered John into his car seat, buckling him in. An SUV pulled into the space next to her, not leaving her much room to maneuver.

"Ms. McKenna, excuse me," said a woman's voice in the SUV behind her, and Rose turned around. The passenger slid down the window to reveal Tanya Robertson, squinting so hard in the sunlight that her false eyelashes stuck together.

"What are you doing here? You're not allowed on school property."

"It's about my 'More on Moms' feature. It's very popular, and I've already interviewed Eileen—"

"Get off of school property before I call somebody." Rose looked around for a teacher, but no one was close enough to see. "I told you, I'm not giving you any interviews."

"I'm not asking for one, about Amanda, anyway. I'm trying to help you."

"The hell you are." Rose turned away and went to the front door, but Tanya stuck her hand outside the window, with her business card.

"Call me. We need to talk about Thomas Pelal."

Rose stopped, stunned.

"Ms. McKenna? Do yourself a favor. Take my card. If I don't hear from you by five o'clock today, I'm going with my story."

Rose willed herself into action, got inside the car, closed the door, and twisted the ignition key with a shaking hand. She was being called to account, to atone. To explain, when there was no explanation. She had waited for it to catch up with her for years, and now, finally, it had.

"Mom?"

"What?" Rose hit the gas, aimed to the exit behind the other cars, and reached into her purse for her phone. "What, honey?"

"Do you think we should have Muenster cheese on the Kristenburgers or Swiss?"

"I don't know." Rose thumbed her rollerball in a panic.

"Mrs. Canton likes Muenster, and so do I. A kid in my class calls it monster. Monster cheese. I think that's so funny and cute."

"Me, too." Rose swung the car out of the school parking lot onto Allen Road, trying to find Oliver's office number in her phone. Her heart thundered in her chest. All hell was about to break loose.

"Mom, remember, you said the car is a no-phone zone."

"This is important, honey." Rose fed the car gas, thumbing to the phone function. Traffic flowed steadily, and she kept pace. Everybody but Reesburgh Elementary parents avoided Allen Road when school was dismissed. Her thoughts raced ahead. She wished she could reach Leo, but he'd be in court and wouldn't pick up. She could have texted him, but it wasn't the kind of message you left by text.

"You said, no phones, it's a rule. You told me to yell at you if you did it, like being on a diet."

"Well, this is an exception." Rose fed the car gas. The rollerball was stuck for some reason, and she couldn't get it to move to the phone function. Sunlight flooded through the car window, obliterating the small screen.

"Why is it an exception?"

"It's okay, just this once. It's a school zone, so don't worry." Rose finally got to the phone function and scrolled down to the call before last.

"So why does that matter, that it's a school zone?"

"People drive more slowly in a school zone." Rose rolled the rollerball to highlight the phone number, but it got sticky again.

"Mom, watch out!"

Rose slammed on the brake before they almost crashed into a minivan in front of them, its left turn signal blinking. They shuddered to a stop, the ABS stuttering and the tires screeching. The sudden movement tossed them all forward, then back into their seats.

"We almost hit that car!" Melly cried, her eyes agog, and in the backseat, John burst into tears.

Rose exhaled, coming to her senses. She set the phone down on the console and looked over. Melly looked bewildered, her frown deeper than any child's should ever be. Rose prayed she'd never see that look on her daughter's face again, but now she wasn't so sure. "Mel, I'm so sorry. Are you okay?"

"Yes." Melly nodded, still wide-eyed. "Are you?"

"Yes." Rose smiled, touched. She loved Melly so much it hurt. She could have cried out loud at what was going to come, for all of them. She checked John in the rearview, and he was crying full-blast, his tiny features clustered and his pacifier gone. "Aww, Johnnie, I'm sorry, I love you."

"What's the matter, Mom?"

"Nothing." Rose knew that Melly would find out, soon enough.

The minivan in front of them took its left turn, oblivious to the near disaster, and Rose hit the gas. She'd wait to call Oliver until Melly was out of earshot, but she knew there wasn't anything anybody could do. Some crashes could be averted, and some couldn't. This one was head-on, barreling faster than an express train.

Hurtling toward everyone she loved the most.

Chapter Forty-two

Rose closed her bedroom door, having put John down for a nap and left Melly downstairs, reading her new book. The ride home had given her a chance to think, and she had even more questions than before. What interest did Tanya have in Thomas Pelal? Would she even report on it, and could Rose sue her if she did, maybe to stop her? Or should Rose try and call her to talk her out of it?

If I don't hear from you by five o'clock today.

Rose checked the clock on the night table; it was 3:13. She sank onto the bed, pressed CALL, and waited for the call to connect to Oliver.

"Charriere and Lake," the receptionist answered, and Rose identified herself.

"Is Oliver or Tom there?"

"They're both in court, Ms. McKenna. May I take a message?"

"Can we interrupt them, either one? Can we reach them? It's an emergency."

"Are you calling from the police station? Are you under arrest?"

"No. It's almost as bad as that, though."

"Are you in physical danger?"

"No, not at all, sorry." Rose hated being so mysterious, but she didn't want to talk with anyone but a lawyer. "Do they call in? Can you leave them a message, asking them to call me as soon as possible?"

"Yes, certainly. They both just did call in, but if they call again, I'll make sure they get back to you, top priority."

"Thanks, bye." Rose hung up, tense, then pressed L for Leo, and waited for the call to connect. Leo's voicemail came on, and she left him a message. "Something's come up, and it's really important that you call me ASAP. I love you."

Rose thumbed her way to the text function and left him a text message, saying the same thing, then pressed SEND. She hated to think of how hurt he'd be, and what impact it would have on their marriage. The phone rang in her hand, and she jumped. The screen showed Oliver's office number, and she pressed answer. "Yes, hello?"

"Ms. McKenna?" It was the receptionist. "Sorry, I can't reach them or the paralegal. They're both in court, on separate trials. I'll keep trying."

"When's the next break?"

"As I said before, they just called, and I know they're both putting on witnesses this afternoon. I'll keep trying, as I say."

"Okay, thanks. Bye." Rose pressed END, sitting at the edge of the bed, feeling pressure building. She couldn't prevent what was going to happen, and it clarified her greatest fear. It didn't matter what the world thought of her. What really mattered was her family. She'd made mistakes in her life, and the worst part was that everybody she loved was about to pay for the biggest one. How they'd feel, how they'd be impacted. She had to tell Leo before he heard about it on TV.

Haven't you done enough?

Rose sighed, looking around the sunny, peaceful bedroom that they'd worked on together. She'd unpacked the moving boxes while Leo had painted the walls, a soft powder-blue that they'd joked would induce falling asleep, if not making love. They'd agreed on the matching blue rug, and refinished as a team an Irish pine dresser from a Lambertville antiques store. Above it hung a matching mirror and a panel of scribbles that a younger Melly had drawn for their wedding, which Leo had framed; crayoned circles in red, blue, and yellow that represented the three of them, a new family.

If I don't hear from you . . .

Rose tried to hold at bay the sensation that everything in the bedroom was about to explode, flying into smithereens like a picture-perfect cafeteria. Her phone rang again, and she looked down at the screen. LEO, it read. She didn't know how to tell him, but she would find a way.

She pressed ANSWER.

Chapter Forty-three

Rose spent the afternoon dreading the TV news, but going through the motions, making Kristenburgers again, cleaning her counter-tops, helping Melly take a picture of Flat Stanley with fallen leaves in the backyard, changing and feeding John, and fussing at Melly about being on Club Penguin too long. Leo had said he'd be home around eight o'clock, and she'd prepared him as best as she could without telling him over the phone. It was a conversation they could have only in person.

"Mel?" Rose called into the family room, checking the clock. It was 4:45. She wiped John's face, and he squeezed his eyes closed whenever the paper towel touched his cheek, which made her laugh, on any other day. She realized she wasn't narrating their life either, but that was no surprise. "Mel, I want you to go up and take a bath."

"Now?"

"Yes." Rose didn't want Melly anywhere near the TV at five o'clock. She held John tighter on her hip, opened the base cabinet, and tossed the paper towel in the trash, then left the kitchen, already formulating a plan for the next few days. "And I want to talk to you about something else."

"Okay, I'm signing off." Melly hit a key on the computer keyboard, and Rose went over and stroked her head. There was a window next to the desk, and sunlight poured through the window sheers, bringing out the gold in her long hair and casting a fuzzy square of light on the patterned Karastan, where Princess Google was lying flat, her feathery white legs stretched out like Superdog.

"Let's get you in the bath, and I'll tell you what I'm thinking."

"Okay." Melly rose from the computer, and Princess Google woke up, stretching her front legs, then trotting behind as they headed upstairs with John, who was making bubbles with his spit. "Mom, look, he's doing motorboat again. He loves it."

"He sure does." Rose followed Melly up the stairs, keeping her moving with a gentle hand. "He's talented."

"He's a baby wizard."

"Mel, you know what I was thinking?" They reached the landing, and Rose guided her upstairs, down the hall, and into the bathroom. "I was thinking that maybe we could take a break, like a few days, up to the lake."

"When?"

"Maybe even tomorrow."

Melly looked up, her eyes a surprised blue. "I have school."

"I know, but it's just for a few days." Rose sat down on the edge of the bathtub and held John closer as she leaned over and twisted on the faucet, then ran her fingers through the water to check the temperature. Princess Google settled onto the bathmat, curling like a cinnamon bun. "Wouldn't that be fun? We could take Flat Stanley to the creek and take pictures of him with the minnows. That would be cool."

"Would I miss school?"

"Yes, but just for a few days."

"Who would go?"

"Me, you, and the motorboat." Rose smiled in a way she hoped was reassuring. "Leo has to work. He's on trial. He'll be home tonight, but that's it for the week."

"Would Googie go, too?"

"Of course, the Googs. We can't live without her."

"Why do you want to go to the lake?"

Rose wasn't about to lie to her, at least not much. "There's just so much stuff going on, with what happened with Amanda. I think if we went away for a few days, things would cool down and then we could come back, next week."

Melly stood a little forlornly, her arms at her sides. The only sound was the water rushing into the tub. "Is it my fault? Because I pushed Josh?"

"No, not at all." Rose wished she could say, it's not your fault, it's mine. "It's okay to take a break, even if it's during school, like 'me time.' We could get you an excused absence. You were in the hospital, just two days ago."

Melly blinked. "Did Amanda die?"

"No."

"Do you think she will?"

"I don't know." Rose looked at Melly, eye-level, because she was sitting on the bathtub. "I pray she won't, and I didn't leave her in the fire, no matter what Josh said."

"I know, Mom." Melly wrapped her arms around Rose's neck, mashing John, but he didn't protest. "I love you."

"I love you, too, sweetie." Rose swallowed hard, then released Melly and stood up. "Let's go, okay?"

"Okay." Melly brightened. "Are Gabriella and Mo gonna be there?"

"They sure will, and we'll get to see them again. And we've never been up this time of year, so I bet all the leaves are pretty. There might even be foxes."

"And owls!"

"And raccoons."

"Yay!" Melly kicked off her sneakers, and Rose tested the bath water again.

"Good, then get yourself cleaned up. Call me when you're finished." Rose kissed her on the cheek, left the bathroom, and went downstairs with John, checking her watch. Five minutes to go. She went to the TV in the family room, dug the remote from between the couch cushions, and pressed POWER, then lowered the volume. The TV was large, forty-two inches built into a cherrywood entertainment center, and everything on the screen looked gigantic. A commercial was ending, and the massive face of a handsome male reporter appeared, his smile a canoe.

Rose sat down cross-legged on the rug, cuddled John on her lap, and offered him her index finger, which he brought to his mouth and gnawed on, teething. The TV screen segued from the male anchor to a huge picture of Tanya Robertson, her head larger-than-life and her lipsticked mouth big as a swimming pool. Behind her was a banner in pink that read MORE ON MOMS. Rose felt her heartbeat thunder.

"I'm Tanya Robertson, and I continue my 'More on Moms' report, which tonight examines the role of the parents who volunteer in our schools. You've heard the expression, 'Who guards the guards?' Well, we're wondering, 'Who guards the volunteers?' Many schools rely on parent volunteers, sometimes even in emergencies, as shown in the recent fire at Reesburgh Elementary. The life of Amanda Gigot still hangs by a thread at Reesburgh Hospital, where she remains in Intensive Care."

Rose's mouth went dry as the screen behind Tanya changed to footage of the fire at school, with children running from the building.

Tanya's expression turned to photogenic concern, writ large. "We're asking, how much do you *really* know about the volunteers who serve as lunch moms, softball coaches, library aides, or chaperones on field trips? How much do you *really* know about the moms who take care of your child in a life-threatening emergency, like at Reesburgh?"

Rose watched appalled as the film of the school fire was replaced by her own Facebook photo, from before she'd closed her account.

Tanya continued, "If you watched my first installment of 'More on Moms,' you saw my expanded interview of Eileen Gigot, but today we focus on Rose McKenna, one of the lunch moms the day the fire broke out at Reesburgh Elementary. At first, Ms. McKenna seemed like a hero because she saved her child Melly from the fire. Then little Amanda Gigot was found injured in the same fire. The Gigot family alleges that Ms. McKenna was negligent in her failure to rescue Amanda, and the District Attorney is investigating the matter."

Rose swallowed hard, aghast. The screen morphed to her at eighteen years old, in her mug shot. She was a mess, her dark hair disheveled and her eyes puffy from crying. Her expression was unfocused, her head tilted slightly. She looked drunk in the photo, but she was stone cold sober. She'd just had the worst moment of her life.

"We've discovered that Rose McKenna was arrested when she was eighteen years old and charged with suspicion of driving under the influence, after a fatal auto accident involving a six-year-old boy, Thomas Pelal. The accident occurred outside of Wilmington, North Carolina, and police determined that the little boy ran in front of her car and was killed. Though Ms. McKenna was arrested, the charges were later dropped. Ms. McKenna has declined any comment."

Rose gasped. It was true, but it wasn't the whole story, and the fact that she hadn't commented made it worse, as if she were hiding something.

Tanya said, "Here's what we're asking, at 'More on Moms.' Don't you have a right to know that information about Rose McKenna, if she were volunteering in your child's school? Would you want her taking care of your child? Shouldn't we do background checks on moms who volunteer? How about drug and alcohol testing? Some schools background-check paid aides, but why should we restrict it to paid personnel? Shouldn't anyone who cares for *your* child be proven safe, in addition to being drug- and alcohol-free?"

Rose felt tears in her eyes, watching her photo fade on the screen, replaced by a black question mark. The whole thing was worse than she had imagined. Or maybe it was just seeing the face of that sweet little boy broadcast before her eyes, in high-definition. She didn't need the photo to remember Thomas Pelal. What she had done haunted her, and she thought of him every day.

Tanya paused. "Don't you have a right to know *more* about the parents who take care of your children at school, on the ball field, or at the field trip to the pumpkin patch? What do *you* think? Weigh in at our website. This series has produced a record amount of email and tweets, so give us your opinion. I'm Tanya Robertson, looking out for *you*."

Rose clicked POWER, silencing the TV, but she could still hear the scream of little Thomas Pelal, just before she hit the brakes. It would echo in her brain, and her heart, forever.

Mommy!

Chapter Forty-four

Rose was packing in Melly's room when she heard the front door close, downstairs. Melly was reading in bed, with Princess Google curled up on the pillow beside her. Leo was home, and she steeled herself, glancing at the clock on the night table. It was 7:30, so he'd booked it from the city.

"Leo!" Melly called out, looking up from *Beedle the Bard.* "Leo! We're up here!"

"Shh." Rose folded Melly's pants in two and set them inside the open bag. "Don't wake John."

"Sorry." Melly placed her bookmark into her book, set it aside, and climbed out of bed. She looked small and skinny in the oversized T-shirt, and took off for the stairway. "Be right back."

"Okay, but make it fast." Rose wanted Melly asleep by the time she and Leo started talking, and she hid her worry. She'd been hiding her worry all afternoon. Or maybe since Thomas Pelal.

"Leo, here I am!" Melly whispered, standing at the top of the stairs. Below was the sound of Leo's heavy tread on the hardwood floor of the entrance hall as he walked to the coat closet, took off his suit jacket, and closed the door, then came to the stairs.

"Tater! How's my girl?"

"We're packing."

"Packing?" Leo climbed the stair, chuckling. "Where are you going?"

"The lake house, to see Mo and Gabriella. And raccoons!"

Rose cringed. She hadn't told Leo about the trip yet. She turned as Leo reached the landing and scooped Melly into his arms. Hurt flickered across his face, but it vanished when he let Melly go, replacing it with the suburban blank that parents reserve for their children whenever there's trouble.

"How you doing, tater tot?"

"Good! Did you win your case?"

"Not yet. I came home to say hi to my girls." Leo took Melly's hand, then spotted the bruise on her arm, frowning. "What happened?"

"I don't want to talk about it anymore."

"Okay." Leo came upstairs, and his gaze went to the open suitcase. He avoided Rose's eye, impassive. "Going to the lake house?"

"Yes, I'll explain later." She gave him a quick kiss on the cheek, which smelled of faded aftershave. "Sorry I didn't mention it to you."

"No matter." Leo went to Melly, helping her back into bed, next to the drowsy little spaniel. He picked up the comforter, tucked her in, and sat down next to her. "Mel, didn't you finish your book yet?"

"Almost." Melly showed him her bookmark. "I have ten more pages."

"What? Slacker, get on it. You've had that thing for a whole day." Melly giggled. "Mom wants me to read American Girl."

"Why should you read American Girl? You *are* an American Girl!"

"I know. I don't want to."

"Then don't. Read whatever you want. It's a free country. I'm a lawyer and I know. Tell Mom, your lawyer said you have First Amendment rights."

"I will!" Melly's eyes lit up when she looked at Leo, and Rose could see how much she loved him. They had actually succeeded in creating a family, despite divorce and death, and Rose couldn't bear to think they could lose it all. She dreaded the conversation to come, but it was time.

"Bedtime, Melly," she said, managing a smile.

"Kiss, Leo." Melly held out her arms, and Leo gave her a hug and a grunt, then got up, brushing down his pants.

"Get some sleep, you. I'll try to come home tomorrow night to see you, but I don't know if I can."

"We won't be here."

"Oh right. Sorry. Then here's another kiss to hold you over. Have fun at the lake. Bye now." Leo gave her another big hug.

"Leo, say good-bye to Googie, too."

"Bye, Googie."

"Kiss her!" Melly giggled, playing their game, because Leo would never kiss the dog.

"No way, I don't kiss dogs, only girls." Leo stroked the spaniel, who barely opened her eyes. "See ya, Googie."

Rose went to Melly's beside, gave her a quick kiss, and patted Googie. "Good night, sweetie. Sleep tight."

"Mom, did Ms. Canton call when I was in the bath?"

"No."

"Can we call her again?"

"I will, tomorrow."

"If she calls tonight, will you wake me up?"

Rose brushed Melly's hair from her forehead. "I doubt she'll do that, but if she does, I'll wake you up. Say your prayers."

"I will. I'll say one for Amanda."

"Me, too. Pleasant dreams."

Chapter Forty-five

Rose followed Leo downstairs, and they both went automatically to the kitchen. She lingered behind the table, while he walked ahead and opened the refrigerator. She didn't know how to start the conversation, suddenly uncomfortable with her own husband, in her own kitchen. The setting sun came through the window, making spiky shadows of the lavender shoots, like a bed of needles.

"You hungry?" she asked.

"No." Leo grabbed a Yuengling beer by the neck, turned around, and pulled out a chair, sitting down heavily. "I had a sandwich when I stopped for gas. Sit, please." He gestured.

"I'm sorry about the lake thing." Rose sank into her chair, behind the watery Diet Coke she'd had before she went upstairs. Her mouth was dry, and she took a sip, then forced herself to look at him directly. He held her gaze for a second, and she could see the hurt, plain in his eyes. "I decided on the spur of the moment."

"Right." Leo's mouth went tight, and he made much of opening the beer bottle, as if he hadn't done it with ease, a hundred times before. "You're not leaving me, are you?"

"No." Rose laughed, a release of nervous tension. "No, of course not."

"Good." Leo leaned back in the chair, regarding her in a remote way. "I got a call from Martin when I was on the way home. His wife saw it on the news and called him. Also Joan called me and told me."

Rose reddened. Joan was his secretary, and Martin was an old friend from Worhawk. "I'm so sorry."

"Joan said we're getting more than a few calls, from clients."

"Oh, no. I'm sorry, really. What will you say to them? Are you worried—"

"I'll deal with them, but what gets me is what's between us. It would have been nice to hear it from you when we met. Or when we got engaged. Or when we got married."

Rose felt vaguely sick. Leo's tone was controlled, and he was too kind to yell, which made it worse. Outside, the peaked tops of the trees bent in the wind, and the sky was turning a lurid pink, an unearthly hue.

"I can think of lots of times, going back, when you could have told me, but you didn't. Even this thing with Amanda, it would have been a good time to mention it."

"I know. I'm so sorry."

"It explained a lot to me, like why you were taking it all so hard, so personally. It explains why you've been feeling so guilty. So why don't you tell me now, the whole story?"

Rose swallowed hard. "Okay, well, to keep it simple—"

"Don't keep it simple. It's not simple, and I have time."

Rose nodded. "It happened on Halloween, and I was eighteen years old. I'd just had a fight with my mom."

"What did you fight about?"

"It was Halloween night, sorry, I said that already, and I was having some friends over, from my job. It was during my year off, after high school, when I was living with her and working, modeling to save money for college. She'd said she'd stopped drinking, and I actually believed her, God knows why. She'd seemed fine for almost a year, doing AA again, so I figured it was okay to have friends over." Rose paused, trying to remember, and trying not to remember, both at once. "We all had costumes, I was Cleopatra, and we were giving candy to the kids who came to the door, trick-or-treating. My mother said hi to us, everything was fine, then she went upstairs."

"Okay."

"Later, she came falling down the stairs, drunk, and, randomly, topless." Rose felt mortified, even at the memory. "She came down the stairs with no bra or anything, only in her panties and high heels, my high heels, oddly, and she hit on one of my guy friends. She actually tried to sit in his lap, with her breasts in his face, and it was, well, you get the idea." Rose shook it off. It wasn't anywhere near the worst part of the story. "Anyway, the party broke up, and I ran out crying. I got into the car, and drove to my old high school. I was in her car, I didn't have a car. I sat in the parking lot, which was empty. I stopped crying, I calmed down, then I left for home. I was upset, but not too upset to drive, and I hadn't been drinking."

"I know that. You don't have to tell me that. You never drink."

"Right." Rose never drank, except for the backsliding the other night in the kitchen. She'd spent her college years partying harder than she should have, then stopped after she'd graduated and started working, full-time. She'd wanted to be a mother, and not *her* mother. Her mother's drinking had driven her father away, when she was only ten. Rose hardly remembered him, and he never came around again, though he always sent checks, to support them.

"So what happened?"

"I was driving home, and most of the little kids were done trick-or-treating. It was like nine o'clock. Only the older kids were left, the hoboes and the basketball players, too cool to dress up. But still, I was going slow, the roads were slick from the rain." Rose could see the scene, in front of her. "Wet leaves were everywhere, so I was careful. She would never want anything to happen to her car, not a scratch. I could see everything. I was paying attention. I didn't even have the radio on. I was driving fine, I was—"

"Okay, you were being careful."

"Right, I was." Rose could see it happening all over again, in her mind, and she could tell him the story in real time, like a horrifying play-by-play. "Something flew out in front of me, a white blur. I heard a noise. I stopped right away, but the car skidded on the wet leaves, and I heard a scream. A child, a scream. It was him." Rose held back tears that came to her eyes. "Thomas Pelal."

"The little boy."

"He was six."

"Where were his parents?"

Rose could hear a change in Leo's voice, and he sounded almost professional. Already he was thinking like a lawyer, constructing a legal argument for her, finding a way to absolve her of responsibility. It had been his first instinct, even as angry as he was at her, and Rose felt so much love for him at that moment that she couldn't meet his eye.

"Babe?"

"His parents were up the street, talking to a neighbor. He was with his sister."

"How old was she?"

"Fourteen. She had gone up on their porch. It happened right in front of their house. He'd dropped a jawbreaker, one of those big ones they used to have." Rose formed a ball with her fingers, for some reason. Maybe because she'd seen the jawbreaker later, when the ambulance and the police came, with their sirens and lights. The jawbreaker made a yellow dot among the wet leaves, like a discarded sun. "It rolled into the street. He was going after it. I didn't see it roll, it was too small. He'd gotten it that night, in his Halloween bag."

"So then what happened?"

"I heard this sound. *Thud.*" Rose knew she wasn't telling the story in order, but it didn't matter. It would end the same way. "And I realized I'd hit a child because he screamed, 'Mommy!'"

Mommy!

"I jumped out of the car and ran around the front, and he was lying there, crumpled, on his side, turned away. He had on his costume, a white pillowcase with holes cut out for the neck and arms." Rose blinked, but the sight, and her tears, wouldn't clear. "God knows why I thought this, but I remember thinking, it was such a sweet, old-fashioned costume. I mean, here I am, in this Cleopatra outfit, all eye-makeup and turquoise polyester, bought at the store. And here he is in his little white pillowcase, a real pillowcase. He'd must've made it himself. He was a ghost."

Leo slid her a napkin across the table, and Rose accepted it, though she hadn't seen him get up to get it.

"So I tried to save him, I knew CPR, from lifeguarding. Blood was coming out of his mouth, but he was awake, alive, and his sister came running, but he was saying something." Rose's eyes brimmed, and she wiped them with the napkin. She didn't want to tell it, but now she had to. Just one time in her life, it had to come out of inside her. "I bent over, and got a hand under him, but the blood was bubbling, and he said something."

"Rose, it's okay." Leo's voice was back to normal, his eyes filled with concern. He stood up to come around the table to comfort her, but she held up a hand because if he hugged her, she might stop.

"His eyes opened, and they were blue, and he looked right at me, and said, 'Mommy.'" Rose wiped her eyes, the tears coming freely, her nose all clogged. "I was thinking, later, maybe it was because of the Cleopatra makeup, I looked older. In the dark, the way he was, he could have thought I was his mother, or maybe he wished I was. And, I know, it sounds awful, but, I answered him."

Leo blinked. "You did?"

"I still can't believe I did it, I don't even know why. I guess I wanted to comfort him, so he could feel like his mother was with him. It wasn't my place, but I did it."

"What did you say?"

"I answered as if I were his mother. I answered, as her. I said, 'I'm here, and I love you. Your mommy loves you, very, very much.'" Rose burst into tears. "And then, he died. Right there. Right then."

Leo came and put his arms around her, sitting down. "It's okay now, babe. It's all right."

"No, it's not. I killed that child."

"It wasn't your fault." Leo held her tight, his embrace warm and certain. "Accidents happen. Kids run out in front of cars. They do that."

"The mom and dad came running, they were hysterical. His mother screamed for him, 'Thomas!' It was an awful sound. Primal. I'll never forget it. I can hear it now." Rose kept shaking her head. "My mother was sure they'd sue, so she got a lawyer, and he told me never to call them, never to speak to them, so I didn't. I wanted to, I wanted to say I was sorry, as if that would help, but I didn't."

"Babe, relax. Drink something." Leo slid her watery soda to her, but she ignored it. Her tears slowed and she blew her nose, messily.

"I must look awful."

"You don't have to look pretty when you cry. I'm not that guy, so don't be that girl."

Rose nodded, blowing her nose with gusto. She balled up the napkin and set it aside, then drained her soda.

"Want another?"

"No, thanks." Rose heaved a deep sigh, and Leo released her.

"So why did you get arrested? Joan said there was a mug shot on TV."

Rose cringed. "They found vodka bottles in the car, three of them, empty. They were my mother's. I didn't even know they were there. When I braked, they came rolling out from under the front seat, so the cops thought I'd been drinking. They gave me a field sobriety test, and I passed, but they still booked me, on suspicion." Rose stiffened, remembering the fight the next day, with her mother. "And the Pelals never sued us. I kept waiting, expecting it, but they never did. I never heard anything from them, and I didn't contact them, either. I would have, but the lawyers said no, then we moved again. Away, up north."

"So that was that." Leo's mouth made a grim line.

"No, hardly. Sometimes I wished they had sued, and I'd been punished in some way. Then I would have felt like I paid for it, and told what happened, and how sorry I am, every day." Rose felt too upset to articulate her thoughts. "And now this thing, with Amanda, it feels like it's all coming back, full circle."

"It isn't. Don't be silly. It's not karmic."

"How do you know?" Rose looked over, sniffling. "I swear, for a long time, I thought that Melly's birthmark was payback. That my child was being punished for something I did to another woman's child. That Melly was marked, because I was marked. It's the stain of sin, my original sin."

"Stop, no." Leo put a hand up. "That's crazy."

"Not to me. Not in my heart."

"Honey, please." Leo frowned. "You can't carry that kind of crap around, all by yourself. That's what bothers me, that this came out the way it did. Why didn't you just tell me?"

"I didn't want to in the beginning, when we first met, and then we were so happy, right away, I didn't want to ruin it." Rose shook her head. "I never told anybody, if it makes you feel better."

"What about Bernardo?"

"No. No one, not even Annie. It seems wrong now, I know, but I kept it to myself, ever since."

"Not wrong. Distrustful." Leo looked pained, his forehead buckling unhappily under his dark curls. "It's like you don't trust me. You don't trust our relationship."

"Yes, I do."

"No, you don't. You didn't tell me, so you don't. Meanwhile, it's too big a secret to keep to yourself. Did you ever even have therapy about it?"

"A little, but it didn't help." Rose turned to him, finding her emotional footing. "Therapy or no, the fact never changes. I killed that child. I did that. It's a fact. I have to live with that, and I'm the lucky one. Thomas Pelal doesn't get to live, at all." Rose felt terrible, but honest, saying it out loud. "That's why they reported it on the news, and that's why they're right."

"Please." Leo pushed her empty glass aside, maybe just to push something. "They reported it for ratings. Don't buy in."

Suddenly Rose's phone rang, sitting on the table, and the screen lit up, Kurt Rehgard. She was so immersed in the conversation that at first she didn't recognize the name. "I'll get it later."

"Who's that?" Leo asked, glancing at the screen. "A reporter?"

"No, a carpenter, at the school."

"What? What's he want?"

"He said he'd do some asking around for me."

"What do you mean?"

"I was at the school, and I was talking to him about what caused the fire and he said he'd do some looking around and get back to me if he found anything out."

Leo frowned. "Why did you do that? And when?"

"It's nothing, Leo. I had time to kill before I picked Melly up today, so I went over to the cafeteria." Rose blinked. She was thinking about Thomas Pelal. "Look, it doesn't matter."

"It does to me. What's going on? Can you fill me in on my own life, for just a sec?"

Rose set down the soggy napkin. "I didn't even get to tell you about the meeting with Oliver and his partner. They told me that what actually caused the fire was going to be relevant to me, since they want us to sue the school."

"So why are you poking around?"

"Because I want to know."

Leo's lips parted. "Oliver has a firm investigator."

"I know, but I was curious."

"Curious?" Leo opened his hands, his dark eyes flashing. "You shouldn't do that, if you're going to be the subject of a lawsuit, or if we are. You should stay as far away from the scene as you can, and you shouldn't say anything to anybody about the fire or that day."

"All I did was chat with him."

"I know, but whatever you've been saying to this carpenter is discoverable. Admissible in court." Leo got up, shaking his head. "Rose, you're taking on everything, all on your own. You decide to go to that wake, no matter what I think. You chat up carpenters on your own. We're supposed to be partners, you and me. You're acting like a single mom, but you're not, anymore."

"No, I'm not," Rose said, surprised.

"What else don't I know? What else didn't you tell me?" Leo started to pace, then stopped, hands on hips. "I have to hear from my secretary that my own wife has a mug shot? I have to hear from Melly that you're going to the lake house? Now I learn that some carpenter is giving opinions on legal causation in a putative lawsuit against us? Great!"

"It's not like that," Rose said, but it wouldn't help to get into it.

"Can't you talk to me about what you're doing? Can't we make at least *some* of these decisions together? You're not thinking as a family."

"Yes, I am."

"How?"

"Well, for example, going up to the lake house. I thought, with all this terrible stuff coming out, that it would be harder on everyone if we stuck around, especially Melly. You saw that bruise. She got into a fight at school, defending me."

"Okay, that's my point."

"What is?" Rose thought the bruise would prove her point, not his.

"If she got into a fight, then we'll deal with that. We have to. Like you said, we have to make a home here." Leo gestured around the kitchen. "We moved here because you wanted to, and the bullying started all over again. We can't just take off, or you can't. Running away doesn't fix anything."

"Leo, you agreed to the move." Rose raised her voice, then lowered it quickly, glancing at the stairwell. "And I'm not running away, I'm taking a break."

"From me?"

"No, from everything here."

"But *I'm* here."

"No, you're not. You're on trial."

"This again." Leo raked a hand through his hair. "I wish you had told me, is all. I wish I'd known. I'm blindsided." He stopped pacing, with a resigned sigh. "You know what, I take it back. Go to the lake house. Take a few days, take a week. The time apart will do us good."

Rose didn't understand what was happening. It was one thing to go, and another to be sent. The situation was getting away from her. "Leo, it's not about you."

"I know." Leo leaned on the back of the chair and looked at her, dead even. "That's what I'm saying. It's about you and the kids. Your decisions, your reactions, your past, your *guilt,* and I'm on the perimeter. You cut me out, and it has nothing to do with my trial."

"Yes, it does. Everything's been happening so fast, I haven't seen you to catch you up."

"Babe, let me ask you this. If I had no trial, would you have asked me to go to the lake house? Did you even think of me?"

Rose hesitated. She didn't know what to say.

"Be completely honest. Trust me enough to tell the truth, for once."

Ouch. "That's not fair," Rose said, stung.

"Then tell me." Leo folded his arms. "Yes or no?"

"No."

"Thank you," Leo said, with a snort. "Thank you, at least, for that."

Chapter Forty-six

Rose stood in the backyard, letting the dog out before bed. It was dark, and the nighttime breeze felt cool, with a chilly hint of the autumn to come. The sky looked black and starless, but the lights from inside the house cast squares of brightness around the yard. Googie made a white spot near the back fence, her head down, her nose buried in the fallen leaves. Rose had gotten a return call from Oliver, and he'd said there was nothing they could've done to prevent the broadcast, anyway. He'd asked her again about the press release, but she still wanted to talk to Leo about it and told him so.

Rose felt raw and lost, after Leo had gone back to the city. She'd feared that his knowing about Thomas Pelal would end them, and she wondered if this was the beginning of the end. Leo had too good a heart to let Thomas Pelal be the reason for any split; he'd chalk it up later to her distrust, her childhood, their growing apart or whatever; but she wondered if this was the moment when his view of her changed, and years from now, whether she'd think back to tonight and say to herself, this was where our end began.

Rose sighed. The air carried the canned laughter of a sitcom from someone's TV, the mechanical rumble of a garage door rolling down, and an SUV being chirped locked. A couple was arguing somewhere, their shouts echoing, and Princess Google raised her head, sniffing the air, the tips of her ears blown back. Rose's phone started ringing in her pocket, and she pulled it out, hoping it was Leo. The glowing screen read Kurt Rehgard. She'd forgotten that he'd called earlier, after all that had happened. She pressed ANSWER. "Hello, Kurt?"

"Rosie, why didn't you call me back?" Kurt slurred his words slightly. "I gave you good info."

"Are you drunk, Kurt?" Rose asked, annoyed. Maybe she shouldn't have given him her number.

"Nah, come on, tell Matlock you have to get away. You can meet my new buddies."

"Sorry, I have to go." Rose pressed END. The phone rang again almost as soon as she hung up, but she saw it was Kurt and let it go to voicemail. She was about to slip the phone back into her pocket when she remembered he'd said something about good info. She pressed VOICEMAIL for her messages, then listened:

"Rose, I got some inside info on the fire." Kurt's words sounded clear and distinct in the call, earlier. "This will come out, sooner or later, but a buddy of mine heard one of the fire marshals talking, and they think the fire started when the loose wire in the wall sparked with gas and fumes from some polyurethane cans, that some slob left in the teachers' lounge, from shellacking the cabinets. So, if you ask me, it's the GC's fault, the general contractor, Campanile. They're ultimately responsible for clean-up. Call me and I'll explain. Take care."

Rose pressed END, slipped the phone back into her pocket, and put the fire out of her mind. The rift with Leo and the news about Thomas Pelal had put everything in perspective. She had to take care of her family, keep praying for Amanda, and let the lawyers and their investigator take care of the litigation and criminal charges. She'd call Oliver in the morning, tell him what Kurt had said, and let it be his problem. She'd use the time at the lake to get herself centered and wrestle with the question of what to tell Melly about Thomas Pelal.

"Googie, come!" Rose called, and the little spaniel looked up, her bugged-out eyes making blood-red spots in the dark. They'd be leaving first thing in the morning, and she wanted to straighten up the kitchen before she went to bed, so she went into bribe mode.

"Googie, treat!" she said, and the dog came trotting. Rose shooed her inside the kitchen and gave her a biscuit, then got to work, straightening the clutter of papers on the counter. She spent a half hour reading the unopened mail, taking the bills out and stacking them for payment, then setting aside the stack of school notices: a flyer for a Pumpkin Carving Contest, a permission slip that had to be returned for a field trip to go apple-picking, and a reminder about the school's Halloween Parade. She flashed on Thomas Pelal in his ghost costume, then skimmed the notice:

Parents, Please remember not to park in the faculty lot the morning of the Halloween Parade! In case of emergency, we need that to keep those extras spaces open . . .

Rose thought of the fire, the ambulance, then Amanda. She gathered up the papers, stacked them, and at the bottom found the school newsletter for September, which they'd given out on opening day. She remembered that day, when Reesburgh Elementary was brand-new and she'd had such great hopes for moving here. She hadn't known Leo felt differently. She looked at the flyer, with its proud banner headline REESBURGH READER. Under **Meet the Office Staff,** the front page showed Mr. Rodriguez, the guidance counselor, and the secretaries standing in front of the counter. She scanned the smiling faces, knowing she could never sue them, ever.

She turned the page, and a subhead read **Meet the Teachers and Staff,** with photos of the gym, music, and art teachers, then the head janitor and his staff, and the two cafeteria ladies, Serena and Ellen. Rose felt a pang, seeing their smiles. It was awful to think they'd been killed because somebody had been careless. She turned to the next page, to **Meet the Library Staff,** and a photo of the librarian and her aide, grinning in the neat stacks. Rose would never forget the kindness of the librarian who had helped her get Melly to the ambulance.

There were two photos under the headline, **Meet the Special Services and Gifted Teachers.** The one on the left showed three special services teachers, who helped kids with ADHD, ADD, and the like, and the photo on the right showed Kristen Canton, who looked pretty and carefree. Rose felt a nub of resentment that Kristen still hadn't called Melly and made a mental note to try tomorrow. Then she looked at the photos again. Both showed the various teachers standing in the teachers' lounge, in front of the counter. The room was small, and the pictures were taken from the door, showing the entire lounge. On the left was a galley kitchen, with a toaster, microwave, and coffeemaker, and next to that was an oven and a tall refrigerator. The room contained six round lunch tables, and there weren't any cans of polyurethane around, or any construction debris. The lounge looked perfectly clean and ready for use, and the cabinets looked shellacked. She turned the newsletter over to double-check the date, and it was dated the first day of school. The picture had to have been taken before school opened, to make it into the newsletter.

Rose thought back to when she had visited the school, the night after the fire. Kurt had taken her around, and it felt like so long ago. She'd been thinking of Amanda then, especially when she'd found the charred videogame. But she'd seen the cafeteria, the kitchen, and clear through to the teachers' lounge. The wall that had blown up had been between the kitchen and the teachers' lounge. That was where the gas leak and faulty wiring must have been. She didn't know what it meant, or if it meant anything, and anyway, it wasn't her problem anymore. She added it to the list of things to tell Oliver, put the newsletter into the pile, and deemed the kitchen cleaned.

"Bedtime, Googie." Rose shooed the dog to the stairwell, then checked the clock on the stove. 10:55, almost time for the eleven o'clock news. She was curious if they'd run the story about Thomas Pelal again, so she went into the family room, picked up the remote, and clicked on the TV, keeping the volume on mute. She didn't need to hear her past played out again, or risk waking the kids up.

Commercials came on for Boniva and Chevy trucks, then the male news anchor popped onto the screen, with a banner behind him that read WAREHOUSE FIRE. If they were going to rerun the feature, it would probably be at the end of the half hour, so Rose sat down on the couch, and the dog jumped up beside her, nudging onto her lap. The next story was of a gas-station shooting, and then an old bridge collapsed outside of Camden; Rose knew because of the banner, and she considered watching the news with the sound off all the time, because none of the stories had any emotional impact. She petted the dog's soft head, which felt like a baseball with fur.

The banner changed again, this time to BREAKING NEWS, and Rose felt impatient, since she had learned long ago that breaking news was neither breaking nor news. She watched as the screen went live to an aerial shot of a highway at night, with the shoulder surrounded by police cruisers, their red lights flashing. There must have been a traffic accident, and she thought instantly of Leo, driving back to the city. She reached for the remote and clicked the sound on.

The anchorman was saying, ". . . called to the scene of a fatal accident on Route 76, heading eastbound."

Rose frowned. Route 76 was the expressway, back to Philly.

"The two passengers in the car were pronounced dead at the scene. They have been identified as Hank Powell, twenty-seven, and Kurt Rehgard, thirty-one, both of Phoenixville."

What? Rose wasn't sure she'd heard correctly. It couldn't be possible. It must have been a different Kurt Rehgard. Her Kurt Rehgard had just called her. She had just listened to his message. She hit PAUSE and ran the TV broadcast back until the highway shots reappeared on the screen, then hit PLAY.

". . . identified as Hank Powell, twenty-seven, and Kurt Rehgard, thirty-one . . ."

Rose watched the rest of the report unfold, stunned. It had to be the same Kurt Rehgard. It was such an uncommon name, and he'd sounded a little buzzed. He'd been out partying with friends.

You can meet my new buddies.

She pulled out her phone, thumbed the rollerball until she got to the phone function, and checked the time of his call. 10:06 P.M. Then she checked the current time. 11:12 P.M. She realized what must have happened. Kurt had left the bar, buzzed, after he'd called her, and driven home with his friend. And now they were dead.

The news went on and on, then the commercials, but Rose didn't hear or see anything on the screen. There had been too much death lately, too much destruction.

It was a long time before she felt strong enough to stand.

Chapter Forty-seven

It was a sunny morning, and Rose hit the BREW button on the Keurig, already on her second cup of coffee. She'd hardly slept last night, thinking of Kurt, Thomas Pelal, and Amanda. Leo hadn't called, and she hadn't called to tell him about Kurt's death because she knew he was busy and it seemed random, after their fight. Melly was asleep upstairs, and John sat contentedly in his high chair, chasing dry Cheerios around his tray with wet fingers.

She went to her laptop and logged onto the newspaper, wondering when she'd gone from being a mom who had an interest in the news, to one who could follow her life in the headlines. She skimmed the home page and breathed a relieved sigh that there was no mention of Amanda, so the child must still be alive.

Thank you, God.

She glanced down the screen, found a link titled *Alcohol a Factor in Expressway Collision,* and clicked, scanning the five lines:

Two Phoenixville men, identified as Kurt Rehgard, 31, and Hank Powell, 27, both of Bethany Run Construction, were killed in a drunk-driving accident last night. . . .

She read the story but there was no further news, a photo of the men, or listing of survivors, which left her with the same empty feeling she'd had all night. She clicked to the Local News page, where her own photo ran beside one of Thomas Pelal. The sight stunned her: the two of them, side-by-side, joined together forever, villain and victim, life and death, present and past, juxtaposed.

Mommy!

Rose sank into the chair and read the story, REVELATIONS AFTER REESBURGH FIRE. The article said she had "caused the death of a six-year-old boy, when she struck him with her car," ending with a disclaimer that the charges had been withdrawn and she had been "convicted of no wrongdoing." The last paragraph was a quote by Oliver, who had been interviewed on the phone last night:

> "It must be noted that my client, Rose McKenna, was convicted of no wrongdoing in connection with the accident that killed Thomas Pelal. In addition, Ms. McKenna is a hero who was injured trying to save her daughter and three other children, including Amanda Gigot, from the school fire. Rose and her husband are currently contemplating litigation against the state, the school district, the school, and its contractors for negligent fire evacuation procedures and for faulty construction."

What? Rose's mouth dropped open. She'd told Oliver that she wanted to talk to Leo before she'd let him say that she was contemplating suing the school. She couldn't imagine how hurt and betrayed Mr. Rodriguez, Mrs. Nuru, and the rest of the faculty would feel, when they heard. She reached for her phone, pressed in Oliver's number, introduced herself, and asked for him.

The receptionist answered, "Oliver's in court today, Ms. McKenna. Same trial as yesterday."

"How about Tom?"

"Same thing, but they'll both call in."

"Please ask either one of them to call me on my cell as soon as possible."

"Certainly."

"Thanks," Rose said, pressing END. She checked on John, who was gumming a Cheerio. She glanced at the clock; 8:10. Time to call the school and let them know Melly would be absent. Rose pressed in the office number, hoping they hadn't read the papers yet.

"Office," a woman answered, and Rose recognized her voice.

"Jill, how are you? It's Rose McKenna, Melly Cadiz's mother."

"How can I help you?" The voice went stone cold, and Rose's heart sank.

"I just wanted to let you know that Melly won't be in today. I want to take her away—"

"That's fine. Thanks."

"I was hoping it could be counted as excused. Mr. Rodriguez said that if—"

"Not a problem."

"I'm not sure how long I'll be, maybe until the end of the week."

"Fine. If there's nothing else, I have to go." The line went dead, and Rose hung up. The secretaries and the rest of the office had heard she was suing. Her family had gone from outsiders to pariahs. Suddenly the house phone rang, and Rose checked Caller ID. Kristen Canton, it read, and she picked up.

"Kristen, how are you?" Rose asked, grateful that she'd called. "Melly's been asking about you."

"Sorry to call so early, but I didn't want to let another day go by without talking to her. I thought I could reach her before she left for school."

"That's okay, she's not going today." Rose's affection for the teacher returned at the sound of her voice. "We're taking a few days at the lake until things simmer down. How are you doing? Better, I hope."

"Finding my footing. Thanks." Kristen paused. "Sorry I was rude the night I left. I was upset."

"Me, too. I'm sorry I was so tough on you, and that I've been calling your house so much. Were your parents annoyed?"

"No, they're fine with it."

"Are they upset that you quit?"

"No, they get that, too, considering. They're really supportive. I'm gonna take some time for myself, just kick back and let my mom pamper me."

"I'm sure she loves that." Rose smiled. "Let me get Melly. I hear her padding around upstairs. Can you hold on a sec?"

"Sure."

"Great." Rose went to the base of the stairwell. "Melly, it's Ms. Canton on the phone, for you!"

"Yay!" Melly's bare feet pounded on the floor in the upstairs hallway, then she hurried down the stairwell in Leo's T-shirt, sliding her hand down the banister. Princess Google scampered behind her, feathery tail wagging.

"Exciting, huh?"

"Yes!"

Rose went back to the wall phone and hit the SPEAKER button, like they did when Leo called. "I'll put you on speaker, Kristen, and let you two yap away."

"Great. Melly?"

"Ms. Canton!" Melly climbed into her chair, while Rose crossed to the back door, opened it, and let the dog out into the backyard. Then she went to the cabinet, took the box of cereal off the shelf, grabbed a bowl and spoon, and set it all down in front of Melly. She wanted to get an early start on the drive to the lake, which took three hours.

"How are you, Melly?" Kristen asked, her voice sounding warm, despite the mechanical timbre of the speakerphone.

"Good! Is your mom still sick?"

Rose cringed, having forgotten that they'd lied to Melly about why Kristen had left.

Kristen answered, "She's doing better, thanks for asking."

"So are you coming back to school now?"

"No, I have to stay at home. I don't think I'll be back again, Melly. I'm sorry, but I can't help it." Kristen's voice went heavy with regret, and Melly looked disappointed, her lower lip buckling.

"It's okay," she said anyway.

"You know, Melly, I don't have to be your teacher for us to stay in touch. We can email, and I'll call you, and you can call me, too. I'll give my cell phone number and my new email address to your mom before we hang up, okay?"

"Okay. But I don't have email."

"You can use your mom's."

Rose didn't interrupt to say that she didn't have email, either. She went to the refrigerator, picked out the milk, and set it on the table.

"Melly, tell me how you are. How's school?"

"Good."

"Everything going okay?"

"Yep."

Rose noted that Melly didn't mention the fight with Josh.

Kristen said, "I hear you're going up to the lake. It sounds like fun."

"My grandparents live there, not my real ones, you know, and there's raccoons and foxes. I got *The Tales of Beedle the Bard*. I love it!"

"I knew you would. What's your favorite story?"

Rose hadn't realized the recommendation had come from Kristen.

Melly answered, "I like 'The Babbitty Rabbitty and Her Cackling Stump.'"

"That's a good one. My favorite is 'The Warlock's Hairy Heart.'"

"I love that, too!" Melly said, quick to agree. "I like the part where . . ."

Rose zoned out on the Harry Potter details and emptied the dishwasher, cleaned up John's tray, wiped his face and fingers, let the dog in and fed her, turned off the coffeemaker, and nudged Melly to start and finish her cereal during a conversation about wizards, healers, magical fountains, giants, witches, sorcerers, kings, and charlatans, all of which left Rose to conclude that the most magical beings in the universe were teachers.

Kristen was saying, "Melly, I'd better go, and I know you've gotta get to the lake. Rose, are you there? I'll give you my cell and email."

"Right here." Rose picked up her phone, but the battery icon had turned red and it needed charging. "Hold on," she said, moving John to her other hip and finding a scrap of paper and a pen. "Go ahead."

Kristen rattled off her number and email, then said, "Well, goodbye, both of you. I'll talk to you again, and you guys stay in touch."

"We will," Rose said, buoyed. "Thanks again. Stay well."

Kristen added, "Melly, have fun at the lake."

"I will, I'm taking my Hermione wand!"

"Good. See you!"

Rose hung up the phone, then crossed to Melly and gave her a hug. "You know what I was thinking? Maybe for our next family vacation, we can go to the Harry Potter theme park in Florida. Would you like that?"

Melly's eyes lit up. "Is that a real thing? One of my friends in Club Penguin said they have that, but I didn't think it was real."

"Sure it is." Rose gave her an extra squeeze.

"Yay! We can show Johnnie." Melly boosted herself up in her chair and grinned at John, who leaned over and reached for her.

"Then let's go to the lake!" Rose felt her spirits lift, but three hours later, everybody's good mood had evaporated.

Chapter Forty-eight

Rose was in the driver's seat with Melly in the backseat, unhappy. John was gurgling in his car seat, transfixed by his amazing plastic keys, and Princess Google was curled up next to him. They were an hour from the lake house, stuck on the Pennsylvania Turnpike in rush-hour traffic when Melly announced that she wanted to call Kristen back. But Rose had left her cell number on the scrap of paper at home.

"Why didn't you bring it with you?" Melly asked, frowning.

"I forgot, and it's not in my phone because she called us on the house phone. Why do you want to call her back anyway?"

"I want to tell her about the Kristenburgers and a drawing I made for her."

"We can tell her later, or email her."

"Do you have her email?" Melly asked, with hope.

"No. It's on the paper at home, too." Rose couldn't remember the email, which was an incomprehensible combination of letters and numbers, more password than email address. "We can write her when we get back."

"Can't we turn around?"

"No, honey. It's too far." Rose gestured at the traffic, red lights in a line like an airport runway, heat broiling from their hoods in wiggly waves. The clouds had cleared for another unseasonably hot day.

"I really want to talk to her, Mom. She loves Kristenburgers. I told her I would make them."

"We can tell her another time."

"And the picture I made for her, it was of Albus Dumbledore, and she loves him. I never got to give it to her."

"We can send it to her when we go home."

Melly looked out the window, quieting.

Rose felt a pang. She knew it wasn't really about the drawing or the Kristenburgers. Melly was having a hard time saying good-bye to Kristen. "You okay, sweetie?"

"Fine."

"Wait, I have an idea." Rose reached into her purse and extracted her cell phone. "I don't need her cell phone. I have her parents' number and I can call her at the house."

"Good!" Melly looked over, smiling. "But not while we're driving."

"We're stopped now." Rose double-checked. They were not only stopped, they were practically parked. She thumbed to her phone log, got the Cantons' home number, pressed CALL, and let it ring. The call was picked up almost immediately by an older woman, probably Kristen's mother. Rose said, "Hello, Mrs. Canton?"

"No, I'm sorry, who's this?"

"Rose McKenna, the mother of one of Kristen's students. We spoke with her this morning, and I wanted to tell her one more thing. Is she in?"

"Oh, you must be the woman leaving those messages."

"Yes, sorry, that's me. Thanks for giving them to her."

"I didn't. Is she the daughter?"

Rose didn't understand. She felt like they were having a conversation of non sequiturs. "Do you know where Kristen is?"

"No, I never met her or the Cantons. I'm the housesitter. I was sent by the agency. They do the interviewing."

"Is this her parents' home, the Canton residence?" Rose asked, confused. The address she'd written down the other day at school popped into her mind. "Roberts Lane, Boonsboro, Maryland?"

"Yes, this is the Canton residence, but the professor and his wife, Mr. and Mrs. Canton, are on sabbatical in Japan. I don't know the family."

"But isn't Kristen living there?"

"No. Nobody lives here this year, but me and two cats."

Rose felt mystified. Kristen had said she was home with her parents. "Do you have any address or number for Kristen?"

"No. You're the second person who called for her today, though. Now, if you'll excuse me, I'm in the middle of something."

"Sure, thank you." Rose pressed END, and Melly looked over, frowning.

"What's the matter? Did she go out?"

Rose didn't understand, and she didn't want to tell Melly that Kristen had lied. "The woman said she wasn't there."

"Maybe she went to her other house."

"What other house?"

"Her house in Lava Land."

"What's Lava Land?" Rose looked over, confounded. "Is Lava Land a real place? Is this a Harry Potter thing?"

"No, Mom." Melly giggled. "It's real, it's near a beach."

"Ms. Canton has a house at the beach? Where?"

"I don't know."

Rose gave up. It didn't matter where. "How do you know about her beach house?"

"She told me. She loves the beach. We talk about it. I like the lake, and she likes the beach. She says I'm a lake person, and she's a beach person."

The traffic loosened, and Rose fed the car some gas, then braked, checking John in the rearview mirror. His pacifier had dropped out, and he was gnawing on his keys, but he looked happy.

"Ms. Canton said we could come visit her in Lava Land, in the summer."

"Really." Rose kept her foot on the brake. The traffic had stopped again. There must be an accident somewhere; lately, there was always an accident somewhere. Something had gone wrong with the world, and now Kristen was behaving strangely.

"So how can we talk to her?" Melly asked.

"I don't know if we can. Let me think a sec." Rose tried to process what was going on. She hadn't realized how close Melly had gotten to Kristen. "You miss Ms. Canton, don't you?"

Melly turned her head away, to the window. "I'm fine."

"It's okay to miss people."

"You told me that, about Daddy."

"Right." Rose flinched. Melly could be so direct, sometimes it came out of left field. "Someone doesn't have to die for you to miss them. It's a loss for you, just the same. You don't get to see that person, or hear their voice." She was thinking of her father, whom she barely remembered, except for his voice. Low, deep, and gentle. "When you lose someone, it's a sad thing, and it helps to talk about it."

Melly remained silent, and Rose drove forward.

"Mel, what do you like about Ms. Canton? What will you miss?"

"Everything. We like to talk in class, and at lunch."

"Lunch?"

"Yes, like when she saw me in the handicapped bathroom. She would tell me to come eat and talk, with her."

"Over Kristenburgers, like on Fridays?"

"Yes." Melly nodded, still facing away. "She doesn't have anyone to eat with then, and she's left out."

Rose seized the proverbial teaching moment. "You don't have to be a kid to be left out, huh?"

"No." Melly looked over, breaking into a rueful smile.

"You don't have to talk funny or have special needs or wear glasses. Anybody can get left out for any reason, anytime. Or even for no reason."

"Or a *dumb* reason. Like Ryan. Josh won't play with him and calls him Rye Bread because of his name. How dumb is that?"

"Dumb. Ryan can't help his name, and he can't change it."

"I know, right?" Melly rolled her eyes. "He teases you if you have diabetes, like Sarah. She has to wear a pump, she showed us. And he teases Max because he can't eat peanut butter. He has an EpiPen all the time."

"See what I mean? That's just dumb. We can't control what people do or say, even if it's dumb." Rose hit the gas as the traffic started to move. They'd had some of their best talks in cars, and she knew other moms felt the same way. All across the country, kids were captive when that door locked, and cars became family therapy on wheels.

"That's what Ms. Canton says. I made a picture for her. Wanna see? It's in my backpack."

"Sure."

"Wait." Melly got her backpack from the foot well, extracted her binder, and slid out a drawing on a piece of yellow construction paper. "Look. It's me, Albus Dumbledore, and Ms. Canton."

"Wow," Rose said, looking over. Melly had crayoned two smiling girls, one big and one little, and they were holding hands with a figure in a peaked hat. "That's a great drawing."

"Thanks. I made it for Ms. Canton, but I didn't get to give it to her. The fire happened, and I didn't see her."

"Oh, right, you see her in the afternoons, so you didn't see her that day."

"Also she was sick. Mrs. Nuru said she wasn't going to be in, and we'd have a substitute."

"Oh." Rose had known that Kristen was sick the day of the fire, but she hadn't focused on it before. Now she put two and two together. Marylou Battle, the substitute teacher who was killed, must have been called in to substitute for Kristen.

"I'm worried I made Albus's beard too long. It isn't that long in the books."

Rose's mind went elsewhere. "Melly, let me ask you something. When you and Ms. Canton eat the Kristenburgers, is it in the teachers' lounge?"

"Yes."

"It's just you and she, because it's on Friday and she's on a different schedule from the other teachers?"

"Yes."

Rose thought a minute. The substitute teacher had been killed in the teachers' lounge, and the cans of polyurethane had been there, too. If Kristen had been at school that day, she would have been killed in the lounge. And if Melly had been with her, they both would have been killed. Rose's fingers tightened around the steering wheel.

"Do you think his beard is right, Mom?"

"Perfect," Rose answered, but she felt unsettled, uneasy. Kristen had lied about where she was and had left Reesburgh in a hurry, claiming she was upset about the fire and the reporters. But maybe that wasn't the real reason.

"She'll love this picture." Melly placed the drawing back in her binder and slid it into her backpack. "We can mail it to her."

"Sure we can," Rose said, preoccupied. The scenario was fishy, and a series of strange what-ifs popped into her mind. What if Kristen had known the explosion was going to happen? What if she'd made sure she wasn't in school that day? What if she'd been involved somehow, and she'd quit and run away, to avoid being caught?

"Are we almost there?"

"Almost." Rose returned to her thoughts, confused. It made no sense. A devoted teacher wouldn't blow up a school full of children. But then again, Kristen would have known that the kids would be outside the building, at recess, at the time.

"How long will it be?"

"About an hour." Rose would have thought it was crazy, except for the fact that Kristen had lied. Why would Kristen lie about where she was? And if she'd lied about that, what else had she lied about?

Rose had an odd sensation that something was wrong. She couldn't stop the questions from coming, and she couldn't deny that there was one person who would know the answers.

Kristen.

Chapter Forty-nine

Rose pulled into the driveway next to their cabin, a charming, three-bedroom Cape Cod with cedar shakes, which was nestled next to the Vaughns' in the middle of an autumnal woods. Leo had bought the place as a getaway, and when they'd married, he'd called it his dowry. The memory made Rose smile, but she put it out of her mind. She didn't want to think about Leo now.

She cut the engine, parked the car, and waved to Gabriella, who was in front of her house, kneeling as she worked in a garden overflowing with pink asters, poppy-red anemones, and tall black-eyed Susans, their black centers like so many punctuation points. It made a gorgeous sight, but Rose was still preoccupied, her mind on Kristen.

"Hey, Mrs. V!" Melly hollered through the open window, and Gabriella stood up, leaning on a bulb planter with a long handle.

"Melly!" Gabriella smiled, and her hooded eyes followed the car. Her silvery hair was in its chic wedge, and her baggy work shirt and gardener's pants hid a slim body that she kept fit, making her look more forty than sixty-five.

"Girl, you cannot look this good!" Rose called to her, opening the car door. She got out of the seat and stretched, breathing in fresh mountain air. Up here, the sun felt warm and the breeze was balmy, but all she wanted to do was get to her laptop.

"You're wonderful for my ego!" Gabriella came toward the car, tugging off her patterned gloves, black with soil at the fingertips. "What a treat to see you again. I was so glad when you called."

"We're here!" Melly flew out of the car and ran headlong into her arms, followed by Princess Google, caught up in the spirit.

"Melly!" Gabriella gave Melly a big hug and managed to pat the dog, jumping onto her pants in a bid for attention. "How are you, dear?"

"We're on another vacation!" Melly let her go and picked up the bulb planter. "What's this, Mrs. V?"

"A tool for planting bulbs. Give it a whirl, over there." Gabriella pointed to an open patch on their lawn, already raked clean of leaves. "Hold it by the handle, press down, and twist, then drop a tulip bulb inside the hole."

"Like this?" Melly ran over and jumped on the planter, like a pogo stick.

"Perfect." Gabriella beamed.

"Really?" Rose hoisted the sleeping John to her shoulder. "She'll break it that way, won't she?"

"I hope so, I hate that thing." Gabriella chuckled. "Mo got it for me, and I don't have the heart to tell him I'd rather use my hands."

"Ha! So good to see you!" Rose gave Gabriella a hug, breathing in the smells that clung to her work shirt, L'Heure Blue and Merit Lights.

"You, too." Gabriella hugged her back, then stroked John's small back, in his T-shirt. "He's gotten bigger since June."

"I feed and water, as needed."

"Give him to Grandma. I need a fix." Gabriella held out her arms. "I won't wake him."

"An earthquake wouldn't wake him. Please take him, then I can unpack the car. We stopped before we left and got some groceries." Rose handed John over and went around to the back of the car, and Gabriella followed, cuddling him against her cheek.

"I can't say I'm surprised to see you, after what I'm reading about you and this fire at the school." Gabriella eyed her with sympathy. "My heart goes out to you, and thank God Melly's okay."

"No matter what the papers say, I didn't leave that child—"

"Don't even say it." Gabriella raised a hand. "It goes without saying. You'll tell me all when you get a chance, but we know you better than that. We tried to send our love, but we could only leave a message and our email bounced."

"Thanks for trying, but it's a long story." Rose chirped the trunk open and took out three shopping bags, then the tote that held her laptop. "Let's get some lunch and catch up. I have fresh cold cuts."

"Good. Mo can keep Melly occupied. By the way, I'm down to three cigarettes a day. That's why I'm planting bulbs, like mad." Gabriella gestured at a cloth bag of bone meal and a lattice sack. "If this keeps up, we're Holland."

Rose smiled. "Let me get this stuff inside. I'll come out for the rest." She left the trunk open and walked on fallen leaves to the cabin's front door.

"I'll stay out here with Melly. Is Leo coming up?"

"No, he's on trial," Rose answered, and across the driveway, the Vaughns' front door opened and her husband Morris stepped outside, squinting in the sunlight. A former corporate banker in Princeton, he was tall and lean, with the permanent tan of a lifetime sailor and the elegant manners of a Yale grad. His craggy face broke into a broad grin when he spotted Melly.

"Is that Melly The Younger?" he called out, shielding his eyes, and Melly jumped off the bulb planter and went running to him, followed by Princess Google.

"Mr. V!" she squealed, and Rose grinned at him on the way to the front door.

"Hey, Mo!"

"Welcome back!" he called to her, just as Melly caught him in the waist.

Rose unlocked her front door, juggling the keys and bags, then hurried inside, greeted by a cedar smell. The first floor was one great room, which Leo always called the not-so-great room, with an old plaid couch and chairs, a small TV with bookshelves stuffed with old puzzles, board games, and paperbacks on the right, and on the left, a small kitchen with builder's-grade appliances. She hustled to the kitchen area, dumped the bags on the large farm table, and set the tote bag down, then slid out the laptop.

She opened it up, hit POWER, and waited for it to come to life and connect to the Internet. They were in the middle of nowhere, but Leo had made sure his wilderness came equipped with wireless. In minutes, the laptop connected to the web, and she went to MapQuest, clicked to Maps, and plugged in Lava Land, in Pennsylvania, taking a flyer.

We did not find an exact match for your search. Try again.

She knew it couldn't be Lava Land, but it had to be something similar. It sounded like LaLa Land, but nobody around here had a beach house in L.A. Instead she plugged in Lava Land and Maryland, because that was where Kristen's parents had their main house. She hit ENTER, and a box popped up, **We did not find an exact match for your search, but we found a similar location, LaVale, MD.** She clicked on the link, bringing up the region with LaVale starred, but the town was inland, not near a beach.

She typed in Lava Land, PA, and the window came up, **Lavansville, PA,** so she clicked. Lavansville was inland, too. She tried Lava Land, NJ, then clicked the mouse. A window popped up that suggested **Lavallette, NJ.**

"Lavallette," Rose said aloud, and it sounded almost like Lava Land. She clicked the link, and a map filled the screen. Lavallette, NJ, was on a narrow spit of land on the Jersey shore, near Toms River and Seaside Heights. It had to be a beach town. She went to whitepages. com, plugged in Canton and Lavallette, NJ, and in five seconds, she had a street address and an apartment number on Virginia Avenue. There was no phone number, but Rose didn't need one.

She had other plans.

Chapter Fifty

Rose hit the road after lunch with the Vaughns, who were happy to babysit for the day. She was heading east under clear, sunny skies, starting to feel better, stronger. The highway lay open ahead of her, and she hit the gas, whizzing past gorgeous autumn foliage, strip malls, and small towns. It felt good to be moving forward, taking the initiative instead of reacting all the time. She'd been so defensive, ducking for cover since the school fire, and even before, since Thomas Pelal.

Mommy!

Rose heard his voice and honored it, for once, not trying to shake it off. She'd felt horrible and guilty for so long, always dreading that her worst secret would come out, and now that it had, as awful as it was, she could finally exhale. The truth really had set her free, and she was willing to let the chips fall. Now Leo knew everything about her, and while she prayed he still wanted her, she couldn't control him or anybody else.

Her phone rang on the seat beside her, and Rose decreased her speed and picked it up. She recognized Oliver's number on the screen, but she didn't want to have this conversation on the fly. The traffic was light, and she pulled over to the shoulder, spraying gravel, and pressed ANSWER. "Hello, Oliver?"

"Rose, I'm returning your call. I hope you're feeling better since we spoke."

"I am, but not for the reason you think. Oliver, why did you say I was suing the school?"

"I said you were *thinking about* suing the school."

"Oliver, I asked you not to do that. We discussed it, remember?"

"No, you told me you were going to talk with Leo, and I ran into him at the courthouse. I told him about our conversation, and he gave me the go-ahead to say that you two were thinking about suing the school."

"Leo?" Rose asked, surprised. "He said that?"

"I thought you said if it was all right with him, it was all right with you."

"I didn't say that." Rose recovered. "I'm sorry if you misunderstood me. Just because I told you I wanted to talk with him, doesn't mean you can talk to him and get his go-ahead. Leo's not your client, I am."

"He recognizes a good defense strategy when he sees one, and I hope you've come around."

"No, and I won't." Rose didn't get angry. For the first time in a long time, she felt supremely in control. "The very suggestion that I'll sue the school is damaging to my family. The office was stone cold when I called today, and I can't imagine how Melly can attend a school that her parents are suing."

"They have no right to react or retaliate, and I'll send them a cease-and-desist letter, immediately."

"Oliver, they're human, they're people. They have feelings. You can't cease-and-desist feelings." Rose would have laughed, in another mood. "I've tried, and it doesn't work."

"Rose. You're in very serious trouble, have you forgotten? Civil suits and criminal charges may be brought against you, any day now. The smartest thing for you to do is pre-empt them and file first."

"I'm not sacrificing my family for my own hide, and the school didn't do anything wrong."

"Of course they did. The blond teacher at the door let Amanda—"

"Enough." Rose wanted to get real, finally. "It was an emergency, and that teacher did her best in the circumstances, just like I did. Do you think she wanted Amanda to get trapped in the fire? Did anybody really want *this*?"

"They left the doors propped open."

"It was *hot,* Oliver. People make mistakes, and they don't have to get sued for them." Rose was thinking of Thomas Pelal. "Don't you think that teacher feels bad enough? For the rest of her life?"

"Fine," Oliver snapped. "Then we won't sue, but you need good press for the public and the jury pools. We need to spin the story our way."

"No, it's not about the spin, it's about the truth. I'm not suing anybody, or threatening to. That's just being a bully. I hate bullies, and I'll be damned before I'll turn into one." Rose came finally to the point. "Oliver, I'm sorry, but you're fired."

"You can't be serious."

"I am. Bill me for the time we spent, and I'll send you a check."

"Rose, I'm the best criminal lawyer in the state. What are you going to do?"

"I'll figure it out. Good-bye, Oliver." Rose hung up and was about to start the engine when she caught sight of the dashboard clock.

And got a better idea.

Chapter Fifty-one

Rose pressed L for Leo and waited for the call to connect. It was 5:15, and court would be adjourned for the day. She knew the trial schedule because she'd helped him once in court, and he usually got a break before dinner and the night's witness prep began.

"Hey," Leo said coolly, taking the call.

"Hi. Did I catch you at a bad time or a good time?"

"I only have a minute. We're about to go eat."

"I figured, so I'll get to the point." Rose could hear the distance in his tone, but she hadn't expected more. "I just got off the phone with Oliver. He said you told him that it was okay to say we were considering suing. Is that true?"

"Yes."

"Why did you say that? They're angry at me in the office, and I don't blame them."

"I sent you to Oliver because he's one of the smartest lawyers I know, and he came up with a brilliant defense. Let him do his job."

"He won't be doing his job for me anymore, I just fired him. Litigation isn't always the answer, Leo. You're thinking too much like a lawyer."

"Can you blame me?"

Suddenly Rose realized what Leo had meant the other day. "Honey, listen. I'm sorry for not telling you about Thomas Pelal, and for how I've been acting. You were right. I haven't been thinking of us as a family, and now I know how it feels. Lousy. Because you weren't thinking of us as a family, either, by telling Oliver to go ahead."

"I *was* thinking of us. That's why I said that. The best way to protect our family is to sue the school."

"No, it's not. Do you know what they'll do to Melly? Her life will be hell." Rose didn't get it. "If we're really partners, it's fifty-fifty, and nobody has veto power over the other. So I won't do it to you, but you can't do it to me."

"I don't have time to deal with this now." Leo sighed, tense again.

"I'm not expecting you to. Also, I don't want to keep things from you anymore, so I'm telling you that I'm about to visit Kristen and ask her why she left school. I think she might have known about the fire, or maybe have been involved."

"*Really?*"

"Yes. The kids are with Gabriella and Mo."

"What are you going to do?" Leo asked, his tone changing to concern.

"Talk to her. Find out the truth."

"Is that wise?"

"I think so, and I have to do it."

"That's what law firm investigators do. Whichever lawyer we hire next can deal with it."

"Going to see Kristen is something I have to do, for myself, by myself. You may not understand it or agree, but I'm not asking your permission. I'll let you know what happens. I gotta go."

Leo paused. "Babe, what's come over you?"

"Adulthood," Rose answered, with a smile.

Chapter Fifty-two

It was sundown by the time Rose found Virginia Avenue, parked across the street from Kristen's house, and cut the ignition. Lavallette turned out to be a small, sleepy beach town on an island off the Jersey shore. The street was wide, criss-crossed with sagging telephone wires and lined with two- and three-story homes interspersed with bungalows. The Cantons' address was a newer three-story that looked like it contained several apartments. The apartment was 2-F, and Kristen was probably home, because a light was on in the second floor, front.

Rose grabbed her purse and got out of the car, then walked across the street and up the steps to the house, scanning the names by the buzzers. There were six, and Canton was next to 2-F. She buzzed 1-F, next to William and Mary Friedl. In a minute, an older woman answered. "Yes?"

"Mrs. Friedl, I'm sorry, can you buzz me in? My husband has my key and he's still at the beach."

The door buzzed, and Rose went inside, climbed the stairs, and knocked on 2-F, standing in full view of the peephole. "Kristen, let me in. I have to see you."

"Rose?" Kristen opened the door, her eyes an astonished blue. "What are you doing here?"

"I might ask you the same question." Rose entered the apartment and pushed the door closed behind her. "You told me you were in Maryland."

"You can't stay." Kristen edged backwards, a book in her hand. Her russet hair was in a ponytail, and she had on a gray sweatshirt with black gym shorts. "Please, leave now."

"Why don't you call the police?"

"Why are you here? How did you find me?"

"That's an odd question. Are you alone?" Rose glanced around the small living room, but it seemed empty and still, with a tan couch, matching chairs, and a big TV. Pictures of seashells covered the wall above a white entertainment center. "What are you up to, Kristen? You lied to me this morning about where you were, and I want to know why."

"Go, please." Kristen tried to walk to the door, but Rose stood in the way, sliding her phone from her purse.

"Let's call the police. You can explain to them that you just happened to be out of school the day it exploded, saving your own life but killing three other people, including your sub, Marylou Battle."

Kristen's eyes flared. "What are you saying?"

"I think someone rigged the explosion that caused the fire, either you or someone from the general contractor, Campanile, working with you."

Kristen gasped. "That's crazy! Why would I do that?"

"I don't know, but you're running away from something, and believe me, I know running away when I see it. It's my MO."

"You're wrong." Kristen sank into a wicker chair, placing the book next to the cushion in her seat. "I had nothing to do with the fire. It was an accident."

"Then why were you out that day?"

"I was sick."

"You didn't seem sick when I saw you. You don't seem sick now. And why did you lie to me on the phone today?"

"That's none of your business."

"It is so my business. You used to have lunch with Melly in that lounge. I have a right to know what's going on, because I trusted you with my *child*."

"You're wrong." Kristen flushed behind her pretty freckles. "I'm here because I wanted privacy, like I told you. I'm worried about those crazy parents, and the reporters, too."

"You could have told me or the school where you were."

"I did tell the school."

"That's another lie, Kristen." Rose felt anger flare in her chest. "They're forwarding your mail to your parents' house. That's where you told them you were."

"I don't have to tell everybody everything." Kristen squirmed in her chair, and Rose noticed the book she'd been reading, tucked by her side. Its cover wasn't visible, but she'd know that spine anywhere. Before Kristen could stop her, she reached over and snatched the book from the chair.

"I thought so. I read this book twice. *What to Expect When You're Expecting.*"

"This isn't your business," Kristen said, stricken, and Rose dialed back her tone, sitting down opposite her on the couch.

"You're right. But if you ask me, it's time to tell the truth."

"No."

"Try it. It works, and maybe I can help."

"I don't need help."

"Kristen." Rose lowered her voice. "You're pregnant and hiding it from everybody. That sounds like a girl who needs help."

"Okay, so I'm pregnant." Kristen's eyes brimmed, but she blinked her tears back. "My boyfriend Erik's in Reesburgh, in the insurance business. He broke up with me, and I don't know what to do. I don't want to tell my parents, and they're away anyway, so I came here to get back on my feet. That's why I was out of school the day of the fire. I had morning sickness."

"So you didn't know the fire was going to happen?"

"No."

"And you had nothing to do with it?"

"Of course not." Kristen laughed, sadly, and Rose felt relieved and puzzled, both at once.

"So your boyfriend doesn't want the baby?"

"It's not that. He doesn't know I'm pregnant. He broke up with me before I found out, and I'm not about to tell him, now."

"He does have a right to know. I bet he's the one trying to find you. Somebody called your parents' house for you, the housesitter told me."

"It was him. He calls my cell all the time, but he doesn't want me back." Kristen wiped her eyes with the back of her hand. "He wants his stupid truck keys, which I threw in the ocean."

"Aw, I'm sorry."

"Me, too, but not about the truck."

Rose smiled. "Why don't you tell your parents? I'm sure they'll help, and they'd want to know."

"You don't know my dad." Kristen shuddered.

"What are you going to do about the baby, if you don't mind my asking?"

"I think I'm keeping him, or her," Kristen answered, confident. "I think I can do it on my own."

Rose's heart went out to her. "What are you living on?"

"Savings, and I have money I inherited from an aunt. I'm fine, thanks." Kristen's lower lip buckled with regret. "I'm sorry I left Melly in the lurch, I really am. That's why I called you this morning."

"I know." Rose got up, went over, and gave her a hug. "Eat crackers every morning, first thing. Old-school Saltines. You won't feel so sick."

"Thanks."

"I'd better be going. It's a long drive." Rose went to the door, then stopped. "Let me just ask you something. Do you remember seeing cans of polyurethane in the teachers' lounge, recently?"

"Yes. They were varnishing the cabinets. I remember there were WET PAINT signs everywhere, and it reeked."

"When?"

"Thursday, the day before the fire. Why?"

"Somebody told me that the polyurethane is partly the reason for the explosion. It was left there, and it blew up."

"So?"

"So I don't get it." Rose shrugged. "Why does anybody varnish cabinets in October, a month after school opens? Especially if it smells and is going to ruin peoples' lunch. It doesn't make sense."

"I don't know. Maybe a second coat?" Kristen got up, walked to the door, and held it open. "You won't tell anyone I'm here, will you?"

"No, but you should." Rose went into her purse. "Here, take this." She found her wallet, pulled out a hundred bucks, and handed the money to Kristen, who put up her hand like a stop sign.

"No, I couldn't."

"Yes, you have to. Please." Rose put the money in Kristen's hands. "Good luck, sweetie."

"Thanks. This is so nice of you."

"Oh, wait. Take this, too." Rose pulled a folded paper from her purse, opened it, and showed it to Kristen. "This is Melly's drawing of the two of you. That's Albus Dumbledore in the hat."

"I knew that," Kristen said, with a newly teary smile, and Rose gave her a good-bye hug.

"Call me if you need me. And Melly wants you to know we eat Kristenburgers."

"They're yummy, right?"

"Not in bulk."

Kristen laughed. "Can I keep the picture?"

"Sure." Rose went to the door. "I told Melly I mailed it to you, and that's the last lie I'll ever tell my daughter, except for Santa Claus."

It was dark when Rose hit the street, but before she went back to the car, she walked to the beach and took off her shoes, enjoying the sensation of the cool sand as she went down to the shoreline and stood at the edge of the very continent. She still had a blister on her ankle, and the chilly wavelets rolled over her feet, healing and good. The gray foam made pale, shifting lines, one after the other all the way to the black horizon, where sea blended with sky. The stars shone bright white, encrusting heaven, and the full moon was a perfect circle, like a paper hole left by a hole-puncher in school. She breathed in the salty smells and the cool wetness of the air, standing at the intersection of summer and autumn, and at a crossroads in her life, too.

She thought of Leo, hoping she hadn't left him behind, because she wasn't sure where she was going. And she didn't know what to do or think about the school fire, either. She stared into the blackness at the horizon, looking for answers, knowing a line was surely out there, but she couldn't see it. Still, she looked hard and tried to find it, and she found herself thinking of Kurt Rehgard. He was gone, and she didn't know where he was going, either. Or where her mother had gone, or her father.

She thought about death, and life starting anew, in Kristen. And she thought about the place between life and death, where Amanda slept, waiting to wake up, or not. She said a silent prayer for her, and realized that Thomas Pelal had been there, too, in her mind. She had kept him alive, in death, for so long, and it was time to let him go. She realized that letting someone go was setting them free. So she set him free, letting his spirit soar over the great churning sea and up, up, up into the heavens.

The wind blew her hair back from her face, and she breathed in deeply, inhaling one lungful after another, letting it energize and renew her. She kept an eye on the horizon, or where she thought it was, and understood that not everything that existed could be seen. Not every border was clear. She kept thinking of Kurt and the fire, sensing that something still seemed out of whack. She didn't know the answers, and she didn't even know the questions, but they were out there.

As surely as earth met heaven.

Chapter Fifty-three

Back at the cabin, Rose sat over her laptop at the farm table, watching videotapes of the school fire. She'd done it before in her darkest moments, but now she had a new purpose. She was looking for something that could give her a clue about what had happened last Friday at school. She took a sip of fresh coffee, but didn't need the caffeine to keep going, though it was after midnight. Melly and John were sleeping over at the Vaughns', which was their babysitting routine when she and Leo were out past ten o'clock.

She hit PLAY on the most recent link, which was the thirty-fourth new viewer video. She was amazed at how many more there were, from cell phones, flip cams, iPods, and videocameras, made in a world where everybody filmed everything that happened around them, even as it happened, becoming observers in their own lives.

She was having a similar sensation as she watched the video, visualizing herself out of her own body, hunched over the laptop. The only light fixture was the lamp over her head, casting a cone of brightness onto her crown, like Dumbledore's peaked hat. She couldn't help projecting outward into the dim cabin and through its walls to the dark night, its blackness obliterating the outlines of the cabin roofs and the jagged tops of the tall evergreens, cutting into a blanket of dense clouds like so many hunters' knives. The full moon lurked behind, leaving the night opaque and inscrutable.

She hit another video, which showed the same terrified children running from the school, only from a different vantage point. She scanned the video titles backwards in time, reversing the chronology until she was a hero mom. Next to that video was a TV report that she hadn't seen: **More on Moms: Tanya Robertson Speaks with Eileen Gigot.** She clicked the link, and after a web commercial, the anchorwoman came onto the screen:

"I'm Tanya Robertson, and tonight I begin my 'More on Moms' report, which goes behind the scenes in the life of the single mom whose daughter was trapped in the fire at Reesburgh Elementary. Tonight I'd like to answer the question we all have about single moms—how do they do it?"

Rose watched, intrigued.

"By way of background, Eileen Gigot's life changed seven years ago, on August 11, in the world-famous Homestead factory, which started in 1948 with a 6200-foot plant that made only potato chips. Today, Homestead employs almost four thousand people and has grown to a plant totaling fifty-six thousand square feet. It makes potato chips, popcorn, and tons of other snack foods, shipping all over the world from right here in Reesburgh, Pennsylvania."

Rose thought Tanya was angling for a new commercial sponsor until the screen turned to a stop-time photo of the Homestead factory, then morphed into the present-day plant, with her voiceover: "Eileen's husband, William Gigot, loved his job at Homestead, but he was killed in a forklift accident at the plant."

Rose eyed the photo they showed next, of William Gigot and three other men wearing yellow Homestead shirts, with nameplates that read WIJEWSKI, MODJESKA, and FIGGS. Bill Gigot was a tall, handsome man with bright blue eyes that would find their way onto Amanda's pretty face. The screen switched to Tanya, sitting with a teary Eileen, near her breakfront.

Tanya asked, "How did you think you would get along, raising three children on your own?" The camera turned to Eileen, her eyes glistening in a face that looked prematurely lined, and she answered,

"I believe that the Lord gives all of us the burdens we can carry, and no more. Of course, I wish it turned out differently. I miss Bill, every day."

Rose felt a pang, but her thoughts kept coming back to the fire, the polyurethane, and Kurt. She navigated back to the home page, found the story about his crash, and clicked the video. Onto the screen popped the aerial footage, and she watched the coverage again, wondering about what he'd told her.

It's the GC's fault, the general contractor, Campanile.

She stopped the video, logged onto Google, plugged in Campanile, and found its website. It had a slick home page with a picture of a huge hotel, and the copy read:

> The Campanile Group is a cutting-edge construction corporation, a new way of doing things in an age-old business. The Campanile family gave us our beginnings over a century ago, and though we value our Pennsylvania origins, we have expanded and grown nationally. . . .

Rose got the gist. Her gaze fell on the About Us link, and she clicked it. There was a photo of another building, but no listing or bios of corporate officers, only a PR person. She remembered that Kurt had said a "buddy" told him Campanile was at fault, and she wondered if the buddy was somebody working with him at the school. Kurt had worked for Bethany Run Construction, so she plugged their name into Google.

A website popped up, much lower-budget than Campanile. The Bethany Run home page showed three men in brown Carhartt overalls in front of a cinderblock foundation. The caption read, **Vince Palumbo, Frank Reed, and Hank Powell, our famous founders.** The only pages on the sidebar were Current Jobs, Past Jobs, and Contact Us.

Rose clicked on Current Jobs, which turned out to be blank except for a banner that read, **Sorry, Our Current Construction Page Is Under Construction!** Reesburgh Elementary wasn't mentioned, and she clicked to Past Jobs, which showed three small new houses.

There was no About Us. She felt stumped, then thought back to the coverage of Kurt's crash. He'd been killed with a friend, and she had forgotten his name. She clicked back and read the online article until she found the name—Hank Powell. It sounded familiar. She clicked back to the Bethany Run website and double-checked; Hank Powell was one of the "famous founders."

She felt a twinge of sadness, and wondered if Powell was the buddy. A line under the articles had a link for obituaries, and she clicked the one for Kurt. It was brief and ended with **View and Sign the Guest Book.** She clicked, and the screen opened to a webpage designed to look like an open book, with entries for Kurt and Hank Powell:

Uncle Hank, We love you and miss you. We wish we could go to the beach with you again. Your niece and nephew, Mike and Sandy

Dear Kurt, A light has gone out of our lives. We pray for you, and say hi to Pop when you see him, for us. Love, Carline and Joani

Rose read each one, feeling her heart getting heavy.

Kurt, You were a great friend and a great carpenter. Signed, Vince

Rose remembered the name, Vince. She clicked back to the Bethany Run site, and Vince Palumbo was another of the founders; maybe he was the buddy. She mulled it over. Vince hadn't been out drinking with Kurt that night, and Hank Powell had been the one with Kurt, so Hank seemed more likely to be the buddy. It meant that the two men who knew something about how Campanile was at fault were both dead.

She got up, stretched, and walked around the room, ending at the window, looking out into the blackness. She kept thinking about Kurt, Campanile and the car crash, and she started to wonder if they were related. Another series of what-ifs popped into her mind. What if the crash hadn't been an accident? What if Kurt and Hank had been killed because they knew something about Campanile? What if Kurt was killed because he had been asking about the fire?

Rose didn't know if she was seeing connections that weren't there, or making connections that needed to be made. Kurt had been drinking, but maybe his drinking hadn't been what had caused the accident. He'd said something about new buddies, and she didn't know what he meant. Maybe someone had driven him off the road, or into a tree, or whatever had happened. She looked into the blackness, and all she could see was her own silhouette reflected in the window, an indistinct outline.

She eyed her dark reflection. If Kurt had been killed because he was asking about the fire, she was responsible for his murder. She owed it to him to find out the truth.

She wouldn't settle for anything less.

She couldn't, anymore.

Chapter Fifty-four

"Are you sure you don't mind, sitting again, Gabriella?" Rose asked, holding John. He reached up for her nose with splayed fingers, wet from being in his mouth, and she gave his cheek a kiss. "It's one thing to sit for a day, and another to sit for two more, maybe three."

"Not at all." Gabriella dismissed her with a wave. The sun hadn't risen over the trees yet, but the Vaughns' lovely kitchen was already flooded with light. "You know we adore the kids, and Mo loves spending time with Melly."

"Thanks. I hate to go without saying good-bye to her."

"Let her sleep in. We were up late, watching a Harry Potter movie. Call Melly later. She'll be fine."

"And the dog, you can deal?"

"The dog is great, too. I want a Cavalier, I already told Mo. She sleeps on Melly's pillow. It's charming."

"But what if I'm gone until the weekend?"

"Please, take your time."

"I will, thanks." Rose gave John a final kiss and handed him to Gabriella with a wrench in her chest, then walked to the door. "You have my cell number, right?"

"Yes, thanks. And you have mine." Gabriella opened the screen door onto an already warm day, alive with the sound of birds chirping. The Vaughns' front lawn spread out like a dew-laden carpet, and a tall butterfly bush near the door hosted yellow swallowtails and orange monarchs. "What a morning! Why do you have to go back again, anyway?"

"I have a few more appointments, lawyers and such." Rose stepped outside. She hated to lie to them, but they'd worry if they knew the truth. Living without lying was going to be harder than she'd thought, like counting carbs.

"Okay, good luck." Gabriella stepped on the front step. "Stay well."

"I will, thanks again." Rose kissed John's warm head one last time, but as she went down the steps, he started to cry, a choked little sob. She turned around at the heartbreaking sound, guilt-stricken when she saw his adorable face pink and contorted. "Aww, see you soon, Johnnie."

"Go on, he'll be fine, I promise." Gabriella waved her on, sympathetic, and Rose turned away with a sigh, vowing to make this trip count.

She hurried to the car, pulling out her phone on the fly, hit the speed-dial for Leo, and listened to the phone ring, then it went to voicemail and she left a message. She put her phone back, got in the car, and started the engine. She took one last look back, and Gabriella was comforting John on the top step.

Rose stifled another sigh, then hit the gas. She felt torn about leaving them again, but she had to figure out what was going on, for herself. She couldn't be right for them if she wasn't right for herself, and she hadn't been right for herself for a long time.

And that time was over, for good.

Chapter Fifty-five

Rose parked on a street south of the school, so the press wouldn't see her car, then got out and chirped it locked. She had on a white man-tailored shirt, jeans, and sneakers, and with sunglasses and her hair under a Phillies cap, no one would recognize her. She walked to the school and made a beeline for the cafeteria, noticing that the plywood wall was being painted by the students. The mural showed a smiling sun overlooking a grassy lawn covered with oversized sunflowers, undersized trees, and polka-dotted butterflies, a kiddie version of paradise that hid an adult version of hell.

Rose walked to the break in the plywood fence, where there was a makeshift entrance that had a clear plastic sheet as a door, then she stopped. It was quiet, for a construction site. No workmen were going in and out, like there had been before. She checked the street, and only one dusty pickup sat parked at the curb, where there had previously been a lineup.

She slid off her sunglasses, turned back to the entrance, and stepped around the plastic sheet. It was dark inside, and the cafeteria was a man-made cave with an eerie azure cast, from the tarp on the roof. It still smelled, though much of the debris had been cleared. Rose felt grit under her sneakers, and realized that she was at the end of the cafeteria, close to the handicapped bathroom. She didn't see anyone around, so she walked ahead, passing a construction lamp with high-intensity bulbs on a metal stalk. Toward the far side of the room, she spotted the broad back of a construction worker, dressed in a white hard hat, dirty white T-shirt, and painter's paints.

"Excuse me," she called out, and the workman turned. He was pushing a wheelbarrow, and his soft belly hung between its handles. Safety goggles dug into his fleshy cheeks, and he was plugged into an iPod.

"Sorry, I didn't see you," he said, with a slight twang. "Do I know you?" He popped out an earbud and squinted through his goggles, then set down the wheelbarrow and walked toward her. "Wait. Yes, I do. You're that chick Kurt liked, aren't you? That mom on TV."

"Uh, yes," Rose said, rethinking her disguise. "I wanted to talk to someone about Kurt."

"Fine." The workman slipped off a worn cotton glove and reached out his hand. "I'm Warren Minuti. I'm with Bethany Run, too. Nice to meet you."

"Rose McKenna." She extended a hand, which was swallowed up by Warren's huge, rough palm.

"My wife and her friends are all talking about you. She's glued to that TV." Warren unstuck his goggles and slipped them onto his hard-hat. "I tell her, you must be a good person because Kurt liked you."

"Thanks. I felt terrible to hear the news that he had been killed. I'm so sorry. He was a sweet guy."

"He was." Warren sighed heavily, his large shoulders sloping down. "We're a small crew at Bethany, only nine of us. We do a job at a time, maybe two, so to lose Kurt and Hank, it's the worst. And Hank, he has a wife and a new baby. *Had* a wife and a new baby." Warren shook his head. "Well, anyway. What is it you want to talk about?"

"Kurt called me Monday night, before the accident, and he mentioned something about a 'buddy of mine,' who told him that some guys from Campanile had left some polyurethane in the teachers' lounge. He said that that helped cause the fire. I was wondering who that buddy might be. Do you know?"

"Well, Kurt's best buddy was Hank."

"Hank Powell, who was killed with him?"

"Yeah. Both wakes are tonight, and the burials are tomorrow."

"Is that where everybody is?"

"Yeah, but I can't go, that's why I'm here. They all just left to go get ready, but I sent my wife. I go to Drexel at night, for law."

"That can't be easy. My husband's a lawyer." Rose paused, thinking. "Kurt said something about new buddies. You know anything about that?"

"No."

"Would Hank have known about Campanile or cans of polyurethane?"

"I don't know."

"Did anybody at Bethany Run used to work for Campanile?"

Warren snorted. "You wouldn't go from Campanile to us, not if you could help it. Campanile, they're a whole 'nother league from us. The bigs."

"Do *you* know anything about Campanile or cans of polyurethane?"

"No."

Rose thought a minute. "Do you think any of the other Bethany Run guys knew somebody at Campanile?"

"Possible, but I don't know. I never met any of the Campanile crew. We only came after the fire."

"What if I wanted to find out who from Campanile worked on the school? Would any of your guys know that?"

"No."

"Then I guess the only way to find out which Campanile guys worked on this job is to ask Campanile."

"Good luck." Warren chuckled. "They're not gonna give out that kind of information, especially if they think a lawsuit's coming down the pike, like they said on the news."

"You're right." Rose took a flyer. "Do you know what happened with Kurt's accident? I mean, how it happened exactly?"

"All I know is Kurt was driving, it was his truck, and it went off the side of the road and hit a tree. There was no shoulder on that stretch of the expressway."

Rose had to tell him what she was worrying about, or she wouldn't get anywhere. "Does it seem strange to you that alcohol was a factor?"

"Yes, I was a little surprised."

"Why?" Rose asked, intrigued.

"I figured that the newspapers played up the alcohol angle, but that wasn't like Kurt. Kurt woulda had a beer or two, at most. He must've been tired, dozed off, and the combination is what did them in."

"What about Hank? Did he drink?"

"Never, not anymore. He was three years sober. Marie woulda drop-kicked his ass."

Rose felt her heartbeat quicken. "When Kurt called me before the crash, he sounded a little drunk, slurring his words, a little."

Warren frowned. "That wouldn't be like him. He was a responsible guy. He took care of his sister and niece."

"I know. I could play you the voice message. I saved it, if you want to hear it." Rose hesitated. "It might be upsetting, now."

"No, play it."

Rose slid her phone from her purse, then thumbed to voicemail and played the message on speaker. Kurt's amplified words echoed eerily through the burned-out cafeteria, then the message clicked off. She eyed Warren for a reaction in the twilight-blue haze.

"Can't say I can explain that," he said, rubbing his chin.

"He sounds kinda drunk, right?"

"Kinda."

"If he was, why would Hank let him drive? Doesn't that seem weird to you? That a guy with a wife and a new baby would let his buzzed friend drive him home?"

"So what are you saying?"

"I'm wondering if someone killed Kurt because he was asking questions about the fire. Or because he knew about the polyurethane."

"*What?*" Warren's small eyes flew open. "You're talking about *murder.*"

"I know. I'm just trying to figure it out, and I can't explain why Hank would let Kurt drive drunk. Unless Hank didn't know." Rose thought about it, brainstorming. "Unless Hank saw Kurt have his usual one or two beers, but maybe someone slipped something into his drink. One of these new buddies he mentioned. It's plausible, isn't it? It could have happened."

"Maybe, but murder?"

"I'm just saying it smells, don't you agree? That guy on the tape doesn't sound like Kurt after only two beers, does he?"

"It doesn't but I still don't get why Hank got into the car with him."

"Maybe Hank couldn't tell. What if Kurt wasn't that talkative? What if Hank saw Kurt drink only two beers and figured he was fine to drive, even if he did slur a little?" Rose put her phone away. "Something's wrong with this picture, and two men are dead. And I think it's connected with the fire."

Warren frowned. "We should go to the police."

"With what? What do we say? A buzzed guy got in a truck, drove, and had an accident? That's not suspicious."

"True."

"And they think that the fire was accidental. Besides, I'm the last person who they'd believe, since I'm involved."

"That's true, too." Warren sighed, a huge exhale from his barrel chest. "But if someone murdered Kurt and Hank, I want to be the first to know about it."

"Then maybe you can help," Rose said, with hope.

Chapter Fifty-six

Rose hit the gas, with Warren in the passenger seat. He'd changed into slacks and a fresh polo shirt, which he'd had with him for night school, and he'd shaved in the school's men's room. She could see, in the light, that he was older than she'd thought, maybe thirty-five. Or maybe it was the grim set to his jaw, as if he were gearing up for the task ahead. They were in rush-hour traffic on the bucolic back roads out of Reesburgh, heading to Campanile's headquarters, near West Chester.

"Okay, so what's the plan?" Warren asked, looking over.

"Let's review, okay?" Rose wasn't sure what to do next. "We can't know where we're going if we don't know where we've been."

"That's deep."

"You're telling me. I just learned it." Rose smiled. "Now, Kurt thought that polyurethane left in the teachers' lounge contributed to the explosion, but he was killed before I could ask him how. So far I've heard a few different reasons for the explosion, like faulty wiring, a gas leak, and a punch list not done. What have you heard?"

"The same thing, except for the punch list. Punch lists never get done, and nothing explodes."

"So what caused the explosion?"

Warren shrugged. "The fire marshals' report won't come out for weeks, and that's what the lawsuits will be about, and all that."

"So let's try to figure it out, ourselves. You're an expert, and I'm a . . . mom."

Warren smiled crookedly. "You're kinda nutty, lady."

Rose smiled back. She slowed, passing an Amish man driving a buggy, his head tilted down and only his beard visible under the brim of his straw hat. "We have an advantage. They think it's accidental, and we don't."

"Okay."

"So how exactly do you make an explosion with gas, loose wires, and cans of polyurethane?"

Warren looked over. "Where did you say the poly was?"

"The polyurethane? In the teachers' lounge." Rose thought back to her conversation with Kristen. "Somebody shellacked the cabinets on Thursday, the day before the explosion, and left it there. That seems odd to me."

"Why?"

"Shellacking cabinets is the kind of thing they do before you move in, that's what we did at my new house, and it was already done in the lounge, I saw a photo. Why do the cabinets need a second coat, all of a sudden? It was a month after school opened."

Warren nodded slowly. "The teachers eat in there?"

"Some, yes."

Warren wrinkled his nose. "That would stink."

"It did, and that's what I thought." Rose thought again of Kristen. They whizzed by horse pastures with run-in sheds, and hand-painted signs advertising Halloween hay rides and corn mazes. "The lounge reeked of it, and there were WET PAINT signs everywhere."

"That's interesting."

"Why?"

"The poly would have hidden any gas smell."

Rose looked over, her ears pricking up. "So if a bad guy knew he was going to make a gas leak, he might shellac some cabinets to mask the odor."

"Right."

"How do you make a gas leak? Is that hard?"

"No, easy. The gas leaked in the wall between the kitchen and the lounge, and there was a big three-quarter-inch pipe there. I know, I cleaned up the debris. If somebody got into the building on Thursday or Thursday night, they could give the gas valve in the wall a quarter turn."

"Wouldn't that show, a hole in the wall?" Rose asked, as the country scenery gave way to a concrete ramp, heading to Route 202, going north.

"Not if it was behind a cabinet or an appliance. Gas would leak out, but nobody would smell it because of the poly, and they'd also get desensitized to it."

Rose remembered Kurt telling her the same thing, about being desensitized. "So let's say the bad guy shellacked the cabinets to hide the gas smell. How does the wall explode?"

"He needs a spark to make an explosion." Warren frowned, in thought.

"Wouldn't the loose wiring provide a spark?"

"It could, but not for sure." Warren shook his head. "It's not necessarily a live spark."

"So what causes a live spark in a wall?"

"The spark didn't have to be in the wall. The poly was in the teachers' lounge, so the spark could have been in the teachers' lounge. An appliance could do it, or the oven."

Rose thought a minute. The Kristenburgers. "How about a microwave?"

"Yes. They could have rigged the micro to spark."

"How?"

Warren looked over. "Ever put tinfoil in a microwave? You get live sparks, blue flashes, the whole nine."

"No, tinfoil wouldn't have worked. The teacher would have seen it."

"Not if it was hidden inside the micro, like in the plastic part on top." Warren's brown eyes came to life. "Here we go, I got it. On Thursday, you shellac the cabinets and leave the poly out. It stinks. Then on Thursday night, when nobody's around, you hide tinfoil in the microwave, turn a valve in the gas pipe, and loosen the wiring in the wall. An electrician could do all those things in fifteen minutes."

"Okay."

"Then, you leave the caps on the poly open a little, so the fumes leak into the micro. Nobody can tell because it stinks anyway, and you put up the signs."

Rose was confused. "But how do fumes leak *into* a microwave?"

"They drift in."

"I thought microwaves were closed, sealed."

"No, they're not. A spark in the micro, with poly fumes inside, would cause an explosion, and if the gas had been leaking in the wall, from a big, three-quarter-inch pipe, it would go *boom*!" Warren made an explosion with his thick fingers.

"What's the loose wiring have to do with it? Isn't that overkill?" Rose thought a minute, answering her own question. "Wait, maybe not."

"Why not?"

"Because that would show up later, when the fire marshals come in. In other words, if you want to make it look like an accident, you need an innocent cause, like faulty wiring." Rose felt astounded. It all made sense. "Like you said, a wire could spark, but you're not sure enough. So it's an explanation, but not a reliable-enough cause."

"True." Warren nodded, shifting forward. "An electrician could do all of this, easy. If he worked the job, he could have a key. Or somebody else would, like one of the higher-ups. Hell, Campanile is the GC, and they hire the guy who installs the damn locks."

"Right." Rose hadn't thought of that. "So we need to know the electrical sub and the electrical crew that Campanile used on the job, and we take it from there."

"How are you gonna get that?"

"I'm not, you are."

"Me?" Warren looked at her like she was nuts. "How?"

"You're a carpenter, right?"

"All my life. My dad was one."

"Okay, so let's say you could be looking for a job, at Campanile." Rose accelerated. She booked it because it was already 4:15 and they had to get to Campanile before closing time. "You go in, apply for a job, and get the info in an informal way. In conversation."

"How?"

"You can do it." Rose looked over. "You look the part because you *are* the part, and you're not from here, so you can ask a lot of questions without seeming suspicious. Where are you from, with your accent?"

"Arlington, Texas."

"Can you ham it up a little?"

"Sure thang, ma'am," Warren answered, slyly. "What're my lines?"

"Say you're from Texas and you think big. You need a new job and you want to start at the top, with the best. You heard Campanile was the best, stuff like that."

"Kiss some ass."

Rose nodded. "Say you need a new job, you want to move up. You want to work for Campanile and become—what's it called, what you would be?"

"I'd love to be project manager."

"Great. Does Campanile have project managers?"

"Sure. But I bet they promote from within."

"Well, let them say that. Tell them you're new to the area, so you don't know any of the subcontractors, but you can work with anybody."

"Should I mention Reesburgh?"

"No, I'd leave that out. I don't want them connecting you with the fire at all."

"But I have to get them to talk about subs on the Reesburgh job."

"You can't go about it directly." Rose glanced over as the car whizzed along. "Wait. Listen. Subcontractors are important, right?"

"Sure." Warren cocked his head, listening. "The finished job is only as good as the subs."

"Exactly. Say that, and say you're good at managing subs and getting them to do their best work. Tell some dumb story of a sub you managed in Texas."

"I didn't."

"Make it up." Rose didn't know if this plan broke her lie diet, but she wasn't the one lying. "Drop the names of some subs in Arlington, ask if they work with good subs, then bring the conversation around to electrical subs, then maybe you can get a name of an electrician or two on the job. How many could there have been? Not that many. Think you can do it?"

"Yes." Warren straightened up.

"They're big, so they might have a human resources person. If they don't know who the subs are, you might have to get through that interview to somebody who does, like somebody not in administration."

"I thought of that already. I'll say I want to talk to somebody who's been in the field. I'll say I flew up here and don't want to leave until I see somebody tonight."

"Okay, good." Rose felt a wave of worry for him. "If you can't get them to say it, then just leave. Don't do anything to arouse their suspicion. If they came after Kurt, they could come after you."

"Let 'em try." Warren lifted an eyebrow. "I'm from Texas."

Chapter Fifty-seven

Rose slouched down in the driver's seat, pretending to read her BlackBerry, though she could barely see the screen through her sunglasses. Warren had gone into Campanile headquarters at 4:50, and it was 5:45. It meant he had probably gotten to the second interviewer, but she was beginning to worry. She prayed she hadn't gotten him into anything dangerous.

She'd parked the car in the last row of the lot, where it couldn't be seen from the entrance, and kept an eye on the entrance in the rearview mirror, waiting for him to appear. The Campanile offices were in a typical corporate center: low-profile buildings with fieldstone façades and smoked-glass windows. Each company had its own signed parking lot, and there were dried cornstalks tied to the CAMPANILE sign, next to a hay bale and a gigantic pumpkin.

Rose watched as Campanile employees filed in a steady stream from the front doors, wearing white ID tags around their necks, talking, laughing, and lighting up cigarettes. Everybody went to their cars, chirping them unlocked on the way, like so many corporate crickets. It was mostly women in the beginning, then a mixed group later, many of the men in navy-blue Campanile polo shirts, carrying clipboards with navy covers or navy messenger bags that read THE CAMPANILE GROUP.

Rose had the driver's side window open because it was hot and she didn't want to keep the engine running, drawing attention to herself. The breeze carried some of the employees' conversations, and she caught snippets of some: "I told you not to email him, just call, Sue. He owes you an explanation." And, "We need to move the staircase, relocate it on the south side. Problem solved." And, "Run the numbers, Don. Do the math!"

Rose checked the rearview again, and two men in suits came out, one short and bald, and the other with dark hair and a massive build, maybe six-two and two hundred and fifty pounds. The big one struck her as familiar, but she didn't know where she knew him. He walked down the steps, bending to talk with the man, their conversation too low to hear.

She tried to place the big man as he walked toward a car. His suit jacket blew open in the breeze, showing a major paunch and something else. A gun, in a shoulder holster. She blinked, startled. She had seen him before, but she couldn't place him at all. The big man raised his key fob and unlocked a navy-blue SUV that read THE CAMPANILE GROUP on the side door.

Rose stayed low, racking her brain. She hadn't seen the big man at school. She would remember somebody that tall because she was tall. Where had she met him? At a party? She wasn't invited to parties. On the street? She didn't live here. She didn't know anybody at Campanile. She'd never heard of the company until the fire.

Suddenly, the bald man stopped by his car and turned back, calling to the big man. "Hey, Mojo!" he yelled, and the big man turned.

"What?"

"I take it back. Thursday's better!"

The big man waved, acknowledging him, then got into his SUV.

Mojo?

Rose didn't know any Mojo. It was obviously a nickname. She grabbed her phone and thumbed to the photo function as the man reversed in the SUV, then put it in drive and drove past her. As he went by, she snapped his photo, saved it, then hit ZOOM to enlarge it and studied the man's face. He looked so familiar. Long nose, dark hair, huge build.

Rose remembered how she'd recognized him. She'd seen him last night, on one of the videos she'd watched, from Tanya's TV station. She thumbed to the Internet on her phone, plugged in the website for the TV station, and pressed until she got to stories about the fire. She found the link for Tanya's "More on Moms" interview of Eileen Gigot, then pressed PLAY. She sat through the opening about single moms, then the story segued to the boilerplate about the Homestead factory. The photo of some men came onto the screen, and one of them stood much taller than the others.

She pressed STOP. The man in the photo looked like Mojo, but the screen was too small to read his full name. She didn't know if it mattered, but she didn't have time to think about it now.

Warren was walking toward her car.

Chapter Fifty-eight

"You made it, thank God." Rose unlocked the door, and Warren eased his large frame into the passenger seat and sat down.

"Here's the deal. I gotta tell you, I think we were wrong."

"What do you mean?" Rose could hear a change in his tone, and his blue eyes had cooled. She started the engine. "What happened? What'd they do?"

"Nothing. I went in, talked to the HR lady, and filed out an ap. She told me Campanile has no jobs right now. They promote PMs from within."

"PMs? Project managers?" Rose reversed out of the space, then cruised to the exit behind the other cars.

"Yes. I said I wanted to talk to somebody in the field, and they were all hanging out in the hallway, all nice guys, so she pulled one of 'em in. Chip McGlynn. I sat down with him, one-on-one. Take a left up here." Warren pointed. "If you'll drop me off at the train, I can still make my class. They told me the train station is on Lancaster Avenue. They even offered to drop me off."

"Did he tell you who the electrical sub was, on the school?"

"No, he didn't know the job, and I didn't press it."

"He didn't know?" Rose left the parking lot after the other cars.

"He's a guy in the field, and he didn't know about a job in the news?"

"To tell the truth, I think he did know, but he didn't want to say. I get that. Lots of big-time GCs keep quiet about which subs they use. It's like a trade secret."

"You didn't say that before." Rose frowned, driving.

"No, but once I sat down with him, and saw the operation, and how sweet the offices are, and met Chip and the guys, it's ridiculous to think they could murder anybody."

"You can't tell that from—"

"They even told me they'd give me the first job that came up, then move me up to PM if I make the grade. And if they call, I'll take it."

"You'd *work* for them?" Rose asked, surprised. "But they could be—"

"They got this thing they call the Wall of Fame, with tons of awards from every building association you can name, and some from the state, too. They get the big jobs."

"But what about Kurt and Hank? The driving?"

"I can't explain it, but there's a lot of things that people do I can't explain. I can tell you for sure, Chip and those guys didn't kill them, or blow up an elementary school." Warren shrugged his heavy shoulders. "They got photos of their kids everywhere. They sponsor a softball team, and for Make a Wish, they gave a little boy from Allentown a ride on a cherry picker."

"But Kurt said they left the polyurethane."

"Not exactly. He said, *somebody* left poly in the lounge, and I tell you, that's not on purpose. It happens all the time. The average laborer, he's a pig."

Rose flashed on Mojo. "One of their guys carries a gun. I saw it."

"He's probably in security, or carries payroll or petty cash. People have guns, and it doesn't mean they're bad guys. Hell, my dad has two rifles in his truck, and he's honest as they come."

"This guy doesn't look like he carries petty cash. He was an executive, with a tie. His name's Mojo."

"Mojo?" Warren's eyes lit up. "I just met him. He's a *great* guy. He's their security guy. Joe Modjeska."

Rose made a mental note of the name. "What do you mean, security guy?"

"Mojo's the Director of Security. That's why he carries. He shoots a sixty-three."

Rose recoiled. "He shoots who?"

"No, in golf. He shoots a sixty-three. He won the celebrity golf tournament. Cole Hamel was in it, and Werth, too. Mojo told me he'd get me tickets, next year." Warren looked as excited as a little boy. "I love the Phils!"

"Me, too, but Mojo isn't with the Phils." Rose turned onto Lancaster Avenue. "So they won you over."

"No, I got a reality check." Warren's tone stiffened. "You should just forget the whole thing."

"Do you think they manipulated you, intentionally?"

"Why would they? They don't know who I am. I didn't mention Reesburgh."

Rose fell silent, cruising up the street, congested in front of the Dunkin' Donuts, a bank, and a Starbucks. "Why does a construction firm need a Director of Security? Isn't that strange?"

"Not at all. You know how much theft goes on at job sites? People steal everything they can carry. Materials like copper piping, generators, drills, any tools at all. We're not big enough at Bethany Run to have a guy like that, but Campanile is."

Rose tried to imagine it. "So Mojo would travel around and visit the Campanile sites, to check on security?"

"Yes, sure."

"That means he would have access to all the sites, at any time. He'd even have keys."

Warren put up his hands. "Stop, wait, don't get carried away again."

"He could have rigged the microwave or put the poly in the lounge."

"That's crazy." Warren scoffed. "He'd never do that, and he's not an electrician; he's a guy at the top. I loved Kurt and Hank like they were my brothers, but I don't think anybody murdered them."

"I do." Rose felt a shudder run up her spine, saying it out loud.

"Wrong. Kurt made a bad choice, and Hank wasn't thinking, and they're both gone now. Nothing can bring them back, and no sense can be made of their deaths." Warren pointed to the left side of the street. "There's the station."

"Well, thanks for the assist." Rose turned into the parking lot.

"You're welcome." Warren got out of the car, took out his duffel bag, and looked at her. "You're not gonna let it go, are you?"

Rose thought of Leo, saying the same thing. "I can never let it go."

"Suit yourself. Stay well."

"You, too." Rose watched him go, wondering what to do next. She was thinking about Mojo and his gun, and she needed to know more. She slid out her phone, logged onto the Internet, and plugged Joseph Modjeska into Google. There was a page of entries, and she clicked on the first link:

> **Break-In at Corporate Center**
> **" . . . Director of Security Joe Modjeska said that he was pleased that the Campanile's offices weren't burglarized, and all of their laptops were . . ."**

She clicked and read a few more mentions, but they were all press releases, followed by photos of Mojo at the celebrity golf tournament, with Justin Timberlake and Charles Barkley. She scrolled backwards in time and came upon the press release that announced Mojo's hiring:

> **Campanile CEO Ralph Wenziger is pleased to announce the hiring of Joe Modjeska as the company's new Director of Security. Wenziger stated, "Joe comes to us with enormous expertise, having spent the past four years at the Maryland Occupational Safety & Health Administration in Baltimore, Maryland . . ."**

She looked at the date on the press release. It was less than six months ago, which meant that Mojo was new to Campanile. It seemed odd. She hadn't gotten the idea from Warren that Mojo was a new hire. She navigated to whitepages.com, typed in his name, and found his address.

837 Hummingbird Lane Malvern, PA

Rose plugged it into her GPS system and hit START.

Chapter Fifty-nine

Rose parked outside of Mojo's house, surprised. It was a fieldstone mansion, with a grand front door and a huge stone wing on either side. Tall trees surrounded the property in back, forming a screen of autumn color, and the house sat atop a steep hill, so far off the street she didn't have to worry about being spotted. She guessed she was looking at a $1.5 million house and she was practically an expert. She'd done the shopping for the house in Reesburgh and reading the MLS listings was her idea of online porn.

She didn't get it. Mojo had spent the last four years working for the state of Maryland and only six months at Campanile. Even if he was making a fortune now, how could he afford this house? What kind of security director had a multi-million-dollar house? What kind of state employee? Her phone interrupted her reverie, signaling she was getting a text. She picked it up and pressed to the text function. It was Leo:

Sorry, I'm too busy to call back. You okay?

Rose sighed. It wasn't warm and fuzzy, but at least she was still married. She hit REPLY.

Yes. Take care. Love, Me.

She checked the dashboard clock: 7:15 P.M. The sky was darkening, and she could feel the air cooling through the open window. Her thoughts turned to Melly and John, and she called Gabriella, who picked up after one ring.

"Rose, how are you, my dear? Getting things done?"

"Yes, thanks. How are you holding up?"

"We're all wonderful. Melly is out with Mo again, and John is fine, too. He discovered my bracelet, which amused him endlessly. He has expensive tastes."

Rose eyed Mojo's house. "I'm not finished just yet. Can you hang in another day or two, and I'll keep you posted?"

"I hope you let us keep them until the weekend. Melly is making a garden with Mo. Wait'll you see it."

"Thanks so much," Rose said, grateful. "I really appreciate this."

"We know, now let me go. I have a baby to teach to say Grandma. Love you, bye."

"You, too." Rose pressed END, watching darkness fall. She felt at a loss, eyeing the house. She was so used to bouncing ideas off Leo, and it was hard to do all the thinking a cappella. Her gaze fell on the next-to-last text, which she hadn't heard when it came in. It was from Annie.

What's this about Thomas Pelal? Please call. You need me now.

Rose went to her phone log, found Annie's number, and pressed CALL.

Chapter Sixty

Rose sat opposite Annie in a chair, next to a room-service table covered with the remains of roasted chicken. The aroma of rosemary filled the small hotel room, and its window overlooked the lights of Philadelphia and the Delaware River, black and thick as a python. She'd told Annie all about Thomas Pelal, bringing them both to tears, then caught her up on everything else, including Mojo's mansion.

"Well, well, well." Annie scratched her head, her blunt fingernails disappearing in her little corkscrews. "This Mojo guy is wack. He needs a gun, for what? To protect copper piping?"

"I know." Rose hugged her knees to her chest, finally feeling validated. "So I'm not nuts?"

"No, I think he's fishy, too, and it worries me, for your safety." Annie shifted in the patterned chair, tugging the hem of a white sundress over her sleek legs. Her feet were bare, her toenails bright red. "I get that you don't have enough evidence to go to the State Police with, but why don't you hire a private detective? That would be safer."

"I'd have to find one, and right now, I feel like I know what I'm doing and I want to do it myself. I want to get to the bottom of it, and somehow I think I'm the only one who can."

"What if something else is going on, with you?" Annie pursed her lips. "What if you're feeling so guilty about Amanda that you're trying to find some nefarious cause of the fire, so nobody thinks it's your fault?"

"No, I wish the town didn't hate me, but that's not it. It's not about me, Amanda, or even Melly."

"Are you trying to make up for what happened that night, with Thomas Pelal?"

"I don't think so."

"Why didn't you tell me about him, Rose?" Annie cocked her head, her tone gentle. "I wouldn't have judged you. It could have happened to anybody."

"I was ashamed, embarrassed. It's horrifying." Rose ran her fingers through her hair. "But I finally let him go. I'll always mourn him, but that's something different."

"I get that." Annie tilted her heard backwards, appraising Rose with calm, dark eyes. "You know, I see a change in you. You're digging in. Trying to get to what's really going on."

"Instead of running away?"

"Yes." Annie smiled softly. "I'm proud of you."

"Thanks," Rose said, touched.

"The only problem is, I'm also worried." Annie pursed her lips. "These dudes don't play. I don't like you spying on them, and they won't either."

"I know." Rose had been starting to worry, too. She was a mother, and the sight of Mojo's gun stuck in her mind.

Annie brightened. "I have an idea. You're staying the night here, aren't you? I have the extra bed."

"I'd like to, if you don't mind. I don't want to go home to Reesburgh. I'm kind of betwixt and between." Rose knew what the real problem was. "I hate when Leo and I are in a fight."

"I feel you." Annie shook her head, with a smile. "Look at us. Wild girls turned wives."

"I know, right?" Rose thought ahead to seeing Leo, not knowing how that would work, then getting Melly back to school, and not knowing how that would work, either. "All of a sudden, I don't fit into my old life."

"You never did, girl. Now, you finally have a chance. Make a life that fits you. Leo will come around. It's a rough patch, is all. That's marriage."

"We'll see." Rose knew it was more complicated than that. "We have to change a few things, both of us."

"That's just what I was thinking." Annie stood up, newly energized. "I can help you with that."

"How?"

"Get up. You're staying the night, and we need to get started." Annie was already in motion, heading toward her black bags, stacked up like blocks near the luggage carrier.

"What's going on?"

"You'll see."

Chapter Sixty-one

Rose kept her eyes closed, while Annie worked her magic. The built-in vanity was covered with powders, blushes, mascara wands, used Q-tips, and little wedges of white sponges, like tiny pieces of wedding cakes. They'd done the major stuff last night and were putting on the final touches this morning. The hotel room was sunny and bright, and *The Today Show* played in the background, with Meredith Viera interviewing a French chef.

"You almost finished?" Rose sipped her cooling coffee, her eyes shut. They'd had another room-service meal, and she was ready to get going. She had already figured out her next move.

"Now lift your eyebrows, but don't open your eyes. Two minutes until reveal."

Rose felt the pencil filling in her brows. "It doesn't have to be perfect."

"Be still, or I'll make you wear the fake nose."

"I don't need a fake nose."

"So what? I make the best noses in the business. It's a shame you don't need one. It's like ordering the salmon, in a steak house."

"No nose. Hurry."

"Okay, you're a masterpiece. Open your eyes."

"Amazing!" Rose looked at her reflection and almost didn't recognize herself. Her long dark hair was gone, dyed a warm red and cut into feathered layers that skimmed her ears. Annie had reshaped her eyebrows, changing their color to a red-brown, and darkening her skin with foundation. Nobody would recognize her from the TV or newspaper, and that was exactly what she needed for her plans to-day. She set down her coffee. "Thank you so much!"

"One more thing. Wear these." Annie handed her a pair of large eyeglasses, in pink plastic. "Heinous, right?"

"Yikes." Rose put the glasses on. "Where did you get these?"

"A vintage store in the Village. They're circa 1982. Now you're ready for Main Street, Anywhere, USA. Your distinctive natural beauty is gone, and you're completely forgettable."

"This is great."

"You're welcome." Annie put the eye pencil back. "Are your Band-Aids okay?"

"Yes, thanks." Rose checked her hand and ankle. The burns were healing nicely, and they'd gotten rid of her bandages.

"Now, please be careful and stay in touch. And don't wear your sunglasses anymore. People look longer at people in sunglasses. Love your hair."

"Me, too." Rose shook her head, like Googie drying off. "I feel so free!"

"Every woman does." Annie gathered up her compacts. "Only women equate a haircut with freedom. We're free, ladies. We can vote now."

Rose gave her a good-bye hug. "Mind if I leave you to clean up?"

"No worries. Go get 'em, tiger."

"I'm off." Rose went for her purse, but stopped short when she saw the TV. A local newsbreak had come on, and Tanya Robertson's face filled the screen. On the screen behind Tanya was a school photo of Amanda Gigot. Annie came up from behind, and they both stood watching the news, neither saying anything.

Oh no. Please be alive.

Tanya said, "Young Amanda Gigot remains in a coma, fighting for her life this morning, while the town of Reesburgh reacts this morn-ing to the official report of the county Fire Chief, who has ruled that the school fire was accidental. Students went back for their first full day on Tuesday, and plans are in place to rebuild the cafeteria, as life returns to normal in this lovely community, torn by tragedy and discord."

Rose shook her head. "They're not even looking for anything intentional."

On the TV, Tanya continued, "The District Attorney's Office reports that they are continuing their investigation, and indictments in connection with the school fire and Amanda Gigot's injuries will follow as soon as they are complete."

"That means me," Rose said, newly worried, and Annie clapped her on the back.

"Get going, and prove 'em all wrong."

"On it!" Rose grabbed her bag, rallying, and fifteen minutes later, she was back in the car, driving south on I-95. The sun was rising, the sky clear, and the road lay open ahead of her. Her short hair fluttered in the wind, and her resolve was stronger than ever.

She'd be there in two hours.

Chapter Sixty-two

Rose pushed up her fake glasses and walked up to the counter, holding a steno pad she'd bought at a drugstore down the street. The office of the Maryland Occupational Safety & Health Administration was small and cluttered, with an old-fashioned coat rack, a fake ficus plant, and an umbrella stand. Mismatched government-issue chairs were grouped in the waiting area around a rickety coffee table covered with stacks of Maryland Department of Labor forms, a multi-colored brochure entitled *Workplace Safety and YOU,* and a beat-up copy of *People* magazine.

"May I help you?" asked an older African-American woman behind the counter, smiling in a sweet way.

"Hi, I'm Annie Adler." Rose was sure this was going to be her last lie, but it was hard to quit cold turkey. Maybe if they had a patch, or something. "Joe Modjeska sent me. You know, Mojo? He worked here, until about six months ago."

"Mojo! Of course, how is he? I love that man."

"He's doing great, working for Campanile, just over the border, in Pennsylvania."

"I know. He always said he was meant for better things. A big man with a personality to match."

"Tell me about it. He shoots a sixty-three now, and it's all he talks about."

"Golf, golf, golf! That man *lived* for golf!"

"Don't they all? Me, I live for shoes."

"Ha!" The woman extended a hand over the counter. "I'm Julie Port. How can I help you?"

"I'm a writer for *Hunt Country Life,* a magazine in southern Pennsylvania, where Mojo lives." Rose brandished her steno pad. "We're doing a short profile on him, and I wonder if I can ask you a question or two. He said you might not mind, and the good press would help him out."

"Sure enough." Julie checked the waiting room, which was empty. "We're not busy today, and I can take a couple minutes. If it helps Mojo, I'm in." She moved to the side, opened a swinging door in the counter, and gestured. "Come with me. We'll go in the break room."

"Thanks." Rose followed her past a few workers talking on the phone and typing on computer keyboards, then they went down a hall to a lunchroom with round Formica tables, hard plastic chairs, and a bank of vending machines.

"Please, make yourself comfortable." Julie waved her into a chair, sitting down.

"Thanks." Rose took a seat, put her steno pad on the table, flipped it open to the first page, and slid a pen from her purse. "Now, he began working here about five years ago. He was at Homestead before that, wasn't he? In Reesburgh?"

"Yes, he was. He was their Director of Safety." Julie's face fell into lines, her jowls draping her lipsticked mouth. "He took it very hard."

"What did he take hard?" Rose didn't know what she meant.

"He blamed himself, but it wasn't his fault, any of it." Julie clucked. "Forklift accidents are among the most common, and it wasn't his fault that that man died."

Whoa. Rose realized she meant Bill Gigot. "Mojo has such a big heart."

"He surely does, and he was an excellent safety manager, I'm positive of that. He's very diligent."

"That sounds like him."

"Yes, and from what he told me, the lighting was insufficient in the loading area where the man worked, and he wasn't real experienced with the forklift. In fact, Mojo got him a job in the peanut building."

Rose made rapid notes, for real. "Peanut building?"

"Where they made the peanut butter crackers. They had to use dedicated equipment and such, to protect people with peanut allergies. It's FDA and state regs."

"So you were saying."

"Anyway, to get back to the story, the man didn't have enough experience operating a forklift. Also, they require forklift travel lanes and the like. You can't play fast and loose with a forklift."

"Of course not." Rose kept making notes.

"Mojo didn't like to talk about what happened, but I could tell how sad he was, inside. The man went over the side of the loading dock, killed when his head hit the floor. Mojo found him, on his rounds." Julie clucked. "He made sure the man's widow got herself a nice check without even having to file or sue."

"So that's the kind of man he is, huh?" Rose made another note, and Julie shook her head.

"No good deed goes unpunished, though. Before you know it, Mojo's tossed out."

"Oh no." Rose lowered her voice. "They fired him?"

"I think they asked for his resignation, you know how they do. But he was too proud to let on, with me." Julie frowned. "Don't put that in your story, okay?"

"None of this will be in, I promise." Rose suppressed a guilty pang.

"Thanks." Julie nodded. "Tell you somethin' else about him. He came in as a director after his training, but he never lorded it over anybody."

"What did he do here?"

"Oh, right. You might not know, because the compliance offices in Pennsylvania are run by the feds." Julie cleared her throat. "Well, OSHA, the Occupational Safety and Health Administration, administers workforce safety out of D.C. But some states, like Maryland, have their own compliance agencies, too."

"I see." Rose took notes, and Julie warmed to her topic.

"We cooperate with the feds, and we work hard to ensure that every man and woman in the state has safe and healthful working conditions."

"So Mojo came here after his training. Where did he train?"

"Baltimore, with everybody else."

"Why did he need training, if he'd been a safety manager at Homestead?"

"That's what *he* said!" Julie laughed. "We train anyway, and he didn't know the way we do things down here."

Rose thought a minute. "I didn't ask him, but was he a Maryland resident then?"

"No, he had to move here."

Rose hesitated, and Julie leaned over.

"Next, you're gonna ask me how he got the job, and that I don't know. He moved to Harford County, just over the state line. I knew he wouldn't stay forever. He wanted to go back to Pennsylvania, and they were building the house. You've seen that place of his?"

"Yes, that's where I interviewed him."

"His wife's family, they got money. That, he told me." Julie leaned over again. "How else you think he could afford to build custom, especially from that fancy company? He liked it so much, that's who he went to work for."

"Campanile." Rose made a fake note, and suddenly a fluorescent light began to flicker overhead.

"Uh-oh!" Julie looked up, curled her lip in annoyance. "Here we go again. Building Maintenance's gotta come change that bulb. I don't know how to do fluorescents, you know, those long, skinny ones."

"Me, neither."

"Mojo wouldn't have any of that, of course. If he was here, he'd get on a ladder, grab a screwdriver, take off that panel, and change that bulb himself, no waiting." Julie nodded. "Mojo can fix anything."

"Even lights?"

"Sure enough. That's something else you probably don't know about Mojo. You can put it in your article."

"What?"

"He's a master electrician."

Chapter Sixty-three

Rose hit the road on fire, flying up I-95, heading north. Traffic had picked up, and she kept her foot on the gas, passing slowpokes, full of nervous energy. Mojo was looking more and more like a killer; he had access to the school at any time, so he could have planted the polyurethane in the teachers' lounge, and he knew enough about electrical wiring to rig the microwave, loosen the wiring, and create a gas leak.

Rose sensed that Mojo had done it, but she didn't know why. Campanile had just built the school, so why would he want to blow it up, especially when lawsuits were likely to follow, against his own employer? She raced down the highway, and the questions kept coming. Why would he want to murder children? Even if he had known that they'd be at recess, it would be an awful chance to take, and he'd killed three staff members.

She steered smoothly around a Honda, thinking back. In a matter of days, there had been two deaths that looked like accidents that weren't, and after her trip to Baltimore, she felt even more paranoid. She hadn't realized that Mojo had any connection with Bill Gigot; wherever Mojo went, death seemed to follow, and she was beginning to wonder if Bill Gigot's death had been an accident, too.

Rose sped home, toward Reesburgh, but she wasn't sure of her next move. She still didn't have any evidence that Mojo had committed a murder, much less three of them, so she still couldn't go to the police. She had called Annie and Leo to tell them what was going on, but neither had answered, and this time, she didn't leave a message. She was on her own.

She took the exit ramp, and in time, the terrain grew familiar. White clapboard farms and tall blue silos. Sun-drenched stretches of corn and soybeans, their round, dark-green leaves shuddering in unseen winds. She whizzed past the scenery, thinking about Bill Gigot and Homestead. She had never been inside the plant; she and Melly had missed the school's field trip there, in second grade. Homestead staged the town's Halloween and Christmas parades, and sponsored a team in its softball and basketball leagues. Other than that, Rose knew very little about the company.

Maybe it was time to learn.

After all, she was a reporter.

Chapter Sixty-four

Rose got out of her car in the visitors' lot, breathed in the tantalizing aroma of frying potatoes, and eyed the Homestead factory, which was on the other side of the access road. It wasn't a single building, but a series of five buildings—immense corrugated metal boxes, painted a sparkling white, with a broad yellow stripe. Clouds of steam billowed from metal smokestacks and drifted from square metal vents near the flat rooflines, dissipating into the clear blue sky. Rose had known Homestead was a big company, but she hadn't realized it was this vast.

She turned around, pushed her fake glasses onto her nose, hoisted her purse to her shoulder, and walked to a sidewalk mobbed with kids on field trips, being shepherded by teachers, aides, and moms into lines for factory tours. She waded through the kids to the entrance of the Homestead corporate offices, a large, three-story office building of a sleek modern design, with a façade of dark brick and smoked-glass windows.

HOMESTEAD SNACK FOODS, read a discreet sign in yellow letters, and she reached the office doors, went inside, and found herself in a two-story waiting area dominated by a modern chandelier of frosted glass. A gleaming reception desk was at the back of the room, but the receptionist was talking on the phone, her head down.

Rose looked around. To her left was a waiting area, where two men in suits sat talking in front of a glass coffee table, and on the right was a display case of Homestead products, next to a bigger one of awards, made of engraved glass and Lucite. A set of crystal spikes were annual safety awards, and Rose could guess which year they hadn't won: seven years ago, when Bill Gigot was killed.

"May I help you?" the receptionist called out, and Rose turned, then froze. The receptionist was one of the moms from school, though not in Melly's class. Rose had no choice but to rely on her master disguise.

"Hi." Rose approached the desk. "I'm Annie Adler."

"Hello," the receptionist said, seeming not to recognize her.

"I'm with *Home Baking,* a new magazine. We're doing a story on how home cooks can make their own potato chips, and I was wondering if I could talk to someone about baking in the big leagues, like at Homestead. I'd love to know more about your operation here, including workplace safety practices."

"Of course." The receptionist smiled politely. "Would you like to make an appointment for next week? Our public relations manager, Tricia Hightower, is busy this week. The Harvest Conference, our annual corporate gathering, is held here at headquarters, with all the executives and top sales reps from all our branches."

"Thanks, but I've driven a long way. Does she have an assistant, or someone else I can talk to?"

"No, Trish handles all press relations personally."

Rose tried another tack. "Can I speak with someone in production, perhaps a supervisor on the line? I'd love to speak with someone who'd give me the inside track."

"Sorry, that's not our policy, and it's Group Day today, so there's no admittance to the plant if you're not with a group. Now, would you like to make an appointment for next week? May I take your phone number and she'll get back to you?"

"No thanks, that's past my deadline." Rose wanted to get out while the getting was good. "I'll call again. Thank you for your time."

"Thank you," the receptionist said, and Rose turned and headed for the door. She hit the sidewalk, breathed in the cooked potato aromas, and walked to the car, preoccupied. She wasn't sure what to do next, but she still wanted to know about Mojo and Bill Gigot's accident. The company would probably have had to file all sorts of accident reports, but she didn't know how to get them. Being a fake reporter could only take her so far.

"Line up, Jake!" one of the teachers shouted to the mob of kids. "Guys, come on! Behave, here we go!"

Rose threaded her way through the excited children as the teachers and moms wrangled them like runaway calves. A team of Homestead employees helped corral them for the factory tour.

"Excuse me," one of the employees called to Rose. "Aren't you with Holy Redeemer? You're all signed in and your group is leaving now!"

"Me?" Rose answered, then caught herself. She couldn't get into the factory otherwise, and she wanted to learn more about the loading dock area, where Bill Gigot had been killed. "Hold on, I'm coming!"

Chapter Sixty-five

Rose was herded through a crowded gift shop that contained Homestead snacks, T-shirts, baseball caps, key chains, cookbooks, and stuffed-toy potato chips. The store narrowed like a funnel at the back, into a hallway that reverberated with the noise of excited kids.

"The theater is this way!" called out a ponytailed Homestead employee. "We're gonna see a movie!"

Rose had no choice but to go with the flow, though the last thing she needed was to watch a corporate video with talking potato chips. Luckily, it lasted only twelve minutes, which was the average attention span of a six-year-old and a mom trying to solve a murder.

"Follow me, I'm Linda!" the ponytailed employee called out, and the group was herded down one hallway and another. The kids giggled, pointed, and pushed each other, and Rose decided there was a special place in heaven reserved for teachers and moms who chaperoned on field trips.

"First, the pretzel factory, then the potato chip factory!" Linda called out, taking them into a wide hallway that had floor-to-ceiling plastic windows, providing a complete view onto the factory floor, two stories below. The Holy Redeemer group merged with two other school groups already there, and Rose breathed easier, since all the moms would think she was with one of the other groups.

Linda started her spiel. "So, Homestead Snacks started with the Allen family and today it's a multi-national food producer, which owns seventy-five hundred acres of land in Reesburgh, including the Reesburgh Motor Inn, Reesburgh Visitor Center, the Potato Museum, and other things."

Seventy-five hundred acres? Rose looked over at Linda, amazed. That was practically the whole county.

"Homestead employs almost four thousand people in its Reesburgh headquarters, and many more in its thirty-five branches throughout the Mid-Atlantic states." Linda gestured to the window. "Here you see the first step of our pretzel baking, which is when the dough goes into the kneader, gets mixed up, and is extruded, which means pushed through . . ."

Rose tuned her out, eyeing the factory floor, below. It was a large, well-lit space, filled with huge lines of stainless steel equipment. The walls were white cinderblock, and the floor a dull red industrial tile. Oddly, there were only six employees, performing various tasks in their yellow jumpsuits, earplugs, and hairnets.

Linda asked, "Any questions before we move on?"

Rose caught her eye. "You have so many employees, but there are only six for this whole pretzel operation. Is that typical?"

"Good question!" Linda answered, officially perky. "Most of our employees are route drivers, and we have a fleet of one thousand trucks and vans on the road. And the machinery does all the baking, so our employees don't have to slave away in those hot temperatures. Also, you're seeing only a third of our plant employees at any one time, because we work around the clock, on three shifts; 6–2, 2–10, and the night shift, 10-6."

Rose wondered how many people would have seen what happened the night Bill Gigot was killed. "Do the same number of employees work on each shift?"

"No, many fewer work the night shift. Now, let's go!" Linda shuttled them to another window that showed superwide belts of uncooked pretzels moving slowly into a large oven.

"What are *those* things?" asked a little boy with glasses, pointing to red hoses that came from the production machines.

"Those are wires. Now, before we see the potato chips, we have a few offices to pass and we'll go by them quickly. Here's the office of our Quality Assurance Manager." Linda pointed through the window at an older woman in a hairnet and labcoat. "That lady eats potato chips *five* times a day. Who wants her job?" The kids hollered, and Linda hustled them ahead. "This is the office of our Director of Safety. As you see, all of our employees wear hairnets and earplugs, and there's even hairnets for beards!"

The kids erupted into laughter, but Rose was thinking that it was Mojo's former office, a small box of white cinderblock with a cluttered desk. No one was inside. She asked, "Does the Director of Safety make rounds at night, to check on things?"

"I'm sure he does." Linda smiled in a pat way that let Rose know her welcome was wearing thin. "Now, let's move along to our packing operation and warehouse." She ushered them past the office that read DIRECTOR OF SECURITY and onto a second-floor deck, which overlooked an expanse of floor-to-ceiling Homestead boxes.

"See all these boxes?" Linda took her place at the window. "They go for blocks and blocks! All these boxes will get shipped out tomorrow, not only all over the United States, but to Latin America, Mexico, Jamaica, and the Caribbean, too. You see that number on the side of the box? We know where every ingredient in the pretzels came from, where we bought the yeast, flour, salt, and malt, following strict FDA regulations."

"I have a question." Rose raised a hand. Julie had said that Bill Gigot worked in the peanut building, whatever that meant. "Is there a peanut building here, that's separate? My older son has mild peanut allergies, and I understand you make peanut butter crackers."

Another mother nodded. "My son has a peanut allergy, too. Very severe. We have to watch everything, or he goes into anaphylactic shock. He and another child have to eat alone at school, in the classroom. If they even breathe peanut butter, they could die."

A third mother added, "My daughter has a gluten allergy. It's a lot of trouble, but at least it's not lethal." The rest of the mothers started talking about their kids with soy and other allergies, and Linda raised her hand to get a word in edgewise.

"To answer your question, we do not use any peanuts in the preparation of our products, and they're all peanut-safe. We provide an extensive list of which of our products are allergen-free, soy-free, and gluten-free, and we also make kosher products, which are certified under kosher laws."

The other mom frowned. "But you *do* make peanut butter crackers. I saw them for sale, in the Acme."

"We don't make them, but we sell them under the Homestead name. They're made by another company, out of state."

Rose was thinking about Bill Gigot. "But you used to make peanut butter crackers here, didn't you? I heard there was a peanut building here."

"Yes, and we also made peanut-filled pretzel nuggets, but not in this building." Linda gestured behind her. "We used to make peanut-butter crackers and peanut-filled pretzel nuggets on the other side of the access road, behind the train tracks. That was called the peanut building, but it's been repurposed to make chocolate-filled pretzel nuggets. Now, time for the potato chips!"

"What's *that*?" asked the little boy with glasses, pointing at a long hook on a metal rod, hanging on the factory wall.

"That's what we use if something gets stuck in the machine." Linda led the group down the hall. "It's like a big, long toothpick."

Rose followed the group, lost in thought. It was entirely possible that Mojo had killed Gigot. It had happened on the night shift, in a smaller operation and a separate building. There would have been only one or two other employees there, and as Director of Safety, Mojo would have had free rein. It wasn't impossible to make a forklift injury look accidental. Mojo could have hit Gigot on the head, killing him, then sat him on a forklift and sent it over the side of the loading dock. And Mojo would have known how to disable any surveillance cameras, with his electrical expertise.

The tour ended, and Rose walked to her car, getting out her keys and chirping it unlocked. She couldn't stop wondering about Bill Gigot and if he'd been murdered. She wasn't sure what to do to find out more, and she still didn't know what his death had to do with the school fire, if anything.

She crossed the visitors parking lot, which was less full now, with the kids lining up to board their buses. It had to be after one o'clock, for them to get back to school in time for dismissal. She checked her watch, and it was almost two o'clock. She was about to get into her car but looked across the access road, where employees were leaving their cars in the parking lot and heading inside the factory. The second shift was starting at two, and she eyed the employees, wishing she could get inside the factory, to learn more about how Bill Gigot had been killed and see the loading dock in the peanut building.

Rose stowed her purse in the car, chirped it locked again, and slipped her car keys into her pocket, then walked toward the access road. She didn't know how she'd get inside the peanut building, but she'd play it by ear.

It was a potato chip factory, not the C.I.A.

Chapter Sixty-six

Rose followed the walkway to the other side of the corporate campus, across the access road. The land sloped down, and the walkway forked, with the right leading to the main plant and the left leading to a smaller building, also of corrugated metal, painted white with a yellow stripe. Next to it lay a single train track with round black tank cars, so it had to be the peanut building, where it was almost time for the second shift.

A small parking lot sat to the left of the peanut building, and employees were getting out of their cars, greeting each other, and heading together in a steady stream toward an entrance on its left side. There weren't many of them, maybe twenty or so, which meant she would stand out, unfortunately.

She developed a plan on the fly and took the left fork, noticing yet another building, large and sprawling, with several satellite buildings attached to it by walkways. When she got closer, she was able to read the HOMESTEAD CONFERENCE CENTER sign, decorated with pumpkins and a spooky scarecrow. A parking lot to its right was filling up, and she guessed it was the people arriving for the Harvest Conference.

She reached the steps down to the peanut building, crossed into the employee parking lot and approached the entrance, two yellow doors. Employees swiped in with the laminated ID cards they wore on their yellow lanyards, and Rose fell into step behind two women, one older white woman and one younger black woman, chatting away. The young one swiped her ID card and started through the door, then her friend followed, then Rose.

She found herself standing in a hallway with the two women, who each took a card from a yellow tray on the wall and swiped it into a time clock. Next to that was a sign: NOTICE: HEARING PROTECTION REQUIRED IN ALL PRODUCTION AREAS, and a less official, SAFETY IS EVERYONE'S JOB!

The older woman turned to Rose, smiling politely. She had a halo of curly gray hair and bifocals. "Can I help you?"

"Yes, thanks." Rose pushed up her glasses. "Is this where you make the chocolate-filled pretzel nuggets?"

"Yes, but you can't come in here. It's not open to the public."

"I'm not the public. I'm Annie Hightower. I'm new."

"A new hire?"

"Yes." Rose smiled in a way she hoped was convincing. "I'm supposed to start working here next week, near the loading dock. I'm Tricia Hightower's cousin, in PR. Do you know her?"

"Sure, I've met Trish, but there's no job opening that I know of." The older woman turned to her young friend. "Right, Sue?"

Sue looked nonplussed. She had clear green eyes, dark skin, and a pretty smile. "Not that I know of. We should call Trish."

"We can't." Rose hid her case of nerves. "She's busy with the Harvest Conference. She told me she'd meet me here and show me around, but she must have forgotten. Oh no, maybe I spilled the beans. It's a job that's *going* to be open. I was supposed to come and look around before I start."

"Uh-oh, I understand." Sue grimaced. "Somebody's going to get fired. Who? Do you drive a lift?"

Jeez! "No, wait." Rose wasn't about to fake-drive a forklift. "Did I say *this* shift? Sorry, I meant the *night* shift. That's why I'm here now. Trish wouldn't send me to look at a job that somebody was working, right now. She said I'd be doing the same job, but I'd replace somebody on the night shift."

"Oh, good." Sue grinned with relief. "If you don't drive a lift, I'd bet you'd be a screener. That's right next to the loading dock."

"I knew it!" Her older friend looked over. "Francine's gonna get the boot, and she deserves it, for sure."

"It's about damn time." Sue nodded in agreement, and the older woman turned to Rose, smiling and extending a hand.

"Annie, I'm June Hooster, and welcome to Homestead. You'll love it here, it's a great company. Juanita screens on this shift, and I'll introduce you to her."

"Great, thanks."

"Wonder what Trish was going to do with you? Put you in a uniform?" Sue eyed Rose's loafers. "And you got the wrong shoes on. You need 'shoes for crews,' that's what we call 'em."

"Sorry, she didn't say." Rose stepped aside as another employee walked in the door, punched in, then headed toward a room at the end of the hall. "I hate to go home after I drove all this way. I even got a sitter."

"Now that's a different story." Sue laughed, patting her shoulder. "Don't waste a sitter, I never do. I take the long way home if I have a sitter, just because I can."

June smiled at Rose. "Come with us, and we'll get you a uniform and show you the ropes. We're not allowed to have cell phones or purses on the floor, so you can stow your valuables in a locker."

"Thanks, but I left my purse in the car." Rose followed them down the hall and through the door that read WOMEN'S LOCKER ROOM. She felt bad lying to them, but it was hard to stick to a diet.

Especially in a potato chip factory.

Chapter Sixty-seven

Rose stood on the factory floor next to Juanita, feeling like her twin in an identical yellow jumpsuit, earplugs, and hairnet. Only ten employees worked in the immense room, which contained four huge lines of machinery that almost fully automated the production process, making chocolate-filled crackers and pretzel nuggets, then dropping them counted into bags which were sealed and packed into cardboard boxes. The boxes then traveled via a waist-high track of stainless steel rollers to Juanita and Rose, who X-rayed them.

"This job is easy, and don't let it intimidate you." Juanita kept her eyes trained on the X-ray machine. Its screen glowed an odd green hue, showing twelve ghostly circles. Juanita pointed to the image, her nail polish bright red under her clear plastic gloves. "Look. All you gotta do is make sure there's twelve bags in each box. Like right here, see?"

"Yes." Rose nodded. "Do you count them?"

"Yes, you got to, starting out. When you're experienced, you can eyeball it and tell. But in the beginning, you gotta count 'em."

"Okay."

"Watch." Juanita was already closing the box and sending it along the roller track. "If it's okay, you close the box. If it's not, you take it off the line and put it back here." She gestured to a wheeled table behind them, just as another box rolled in front of her and she had to feed it through the X-ray machine. The green screen came to life. "See, this one's okay, too."

"It's tough to keep up the pace," Rose said, meaning it.

"It is. You gotta be quick. The main thing here is production. We got to keep the lines moving. No stopping."

"It's like Lucy and the chocolate factory, huh?"

"Sometimes it is." Juanita smiled.

Rose hadn't realized how stressful a factory job could be. The boxes came at a relentless clip, and the room felt overly warm despite large industrial fans mounted on the ceiling. A low-level hum filled the air, challenging her earplugs, and the floor vibrated from the heavy production machinery.

"The other day, one of the lines broke down, and the engineers fixed it so fast it could make your head spin. Like they say, time is money. If a single line is down a day, it costs us a hundred thousand dollars." Another box appeared, and Juanita fed it into the X-ray machine, checked the green screen, then closed the flaps. "You can't let a box go through with less than twelve bags. Then an account paid for twelve, but only got eleven."

"That's bad."

"Sure is. Bad for me." Juanita pointed to a black number code on the side of the box. "This number tells which lot it was, and they can trace it back to which shift the mistake happened on, and then Scotty comes to me and says, 'Juanita, you're the screener, you screwed up.' You get a few warnings, then you're out, like Francine."

"Who's Scotty?"

"Our boss. Frank Scotty. He's the shift super."

"Is he around?" Rose hadn't counted on a supervisor.

"He stops by usually, but he's crazy with the Harvest Conference. They have their prom with all the muckety-mucks." Juanita rolled her eyes. "You can meet Scotty when he stops by. We've been working together ten years."

"That's a long time." Rose realized that Juanita had been here when Bill Gigot was killed and could still have information about his death, even though they hadn't been on the same shift. "You know,

Trish told me this used to be called the peanut building, back then, right?"

"Yep. We made peanut butter crackers and peanut-filled pretzel nuggets here. Had to keep 'em separate from the other products, because there's no peanuts in the big plant. You know, for the allergies. We're not peanut-free, there's a lot of real complicated rules, so we just go with there's no peanuts, like lots of companies. But that's now." Juanita sent the box on its way, then X-rayed the next one. "Then, we had all sorts of procedures, everything had to be separate. We were so careful, it was a pain. Look." Juniata pointed to the X-ray screen, and in the corner, there was empty space where a bag should have been. "Missing one. No good, right? Deal with it."

Rose grabbed the box and set it on the table behind them.

"Good job." Juanita smiled. "Anyway, back then, the peanut allergy thing was getting bigger. The orders went way down. Schools stopped buying anything with peanuts. Moms didn't want to take a chance and bring in a snack that could get the other kids sick. A kid can die from a peanut allergy, you know." Juanita shuddered. "I'd never want to be responsible for a child's death. I couldn't live with myself."

Rose flashed on Thomas Pelal, but suppressed the thought. She had to bring the conversation around to Bill Gigot.

"The peanut business went bust, especially the peanut-filled pretzel nuggets." Juanita positioned a box in the X-ray machine, then screened it, and sent it on its way. "We had four lines dedicated to peanut products, and we didn't get the orders, and they'd be sitting still for *days*. Meanwhile, the chocolate-filled nuggets were selling like crazy, especially in Latin America and the Caribbean, I think because it's so hot there. With the chocolate inside the pretzel, it doesn't mess up your hand, like M&Ms." Juanita turned with a wink. "We didn't have enough machines in the big plant to fill the orders for the chocolate-filled nuggets, and these machines here, in the peanut building, sat doing nothing, because they could only be used for peanut." Juanita screened another box. "We were losing money, hand over fist."

Rose had to get Juanita off the subject, but she was so chatty. "If you were here ten years ago, did you know—"

"Those were the bad old days. The bosses wanted to switch from peanuts to chocolate, make crackers with chocolate and fill the nuggets with chocolate, but it took time, switching over. We couldn't use the peanut machines right away for the chocolate." Juanita closed another box. "We had to get them completely cleaned, then we had to get them inspected and whatnot. The machines sat still, like they were broken. We had no work, we worked in the big plant. We ran the tours. We filled in. We swept. But the pay wasn't the same, and the managers were going nuts and so were the supers. We were down almost six months, this was seven years ago, I remember because my youngest was three, and he just turned ten."

Rose saw her opening to talk about Bill Gigot. "I heard from Trish that there was even a guy who got killed here, around that time."

"Yep. Bill." Juanita's mouth made a grim line. "He was on the night shift, where you'll be. I remember, because I was worried sick about Christmas. We didn't know what we could afford to get the kids or how long I'd have to take less pay." Juanita eyed the X-ray screen. "Finally, we started back with the chocolate-filled, and even though we don't make the peanut-filled nuggets or crackers anymore, we still don't put peanut-free on the bags. We can't take a chance, on account of the FDA and the lawsuits."

"I heard he had a forklift accident."

"He did." Juanita pointed to the left. "Right over there. You can see the loading dock."

"Creepy." Rose turned around, but she couldn't see around the corner. "Do accidents like that happen a lot, here?"

"A fatality, at Homestead? No way." Juanita eyed the X-ray screen. "Forklifts can be dangerous. Bill came over here from the big plant, wait, lemme think, I don't know exactly when he started"—Juanita positioned the next box—"but I know he was here by July. I remember because of the holiday. We had a company picnic, and he was the new guy, over from the big plant. The peanut people always stuck together. That was our joke." Juanita chuckled. "Bill was a nice guy, and he'd been with the company a long time. Then all of a sudden, I come in, I hear he died."

"I wonder how that happened. I guess he wasn't experienced on the forklift."

"No, he was. Very. Drove a forklift at the big plant, too."

Rose didn't get it. Mojo told Julie that Bill wasn't experienced. "So isn't that strange that he could have an accident, even though he's so experienced?"

"No, accidents happen to experienced people. I think they happen more, because the experienced guys don't watch as much. My neighbor is a roofer thirty years, and last week he fell off a ladder and broke his leg." Juanita shook her head, closing the flaps on the next box. "Still, I was so sad when Bill died."

"I'm sure. Did anybody see what happened, that night?"

"No, there weren't any other employees around. We were down to a skeleton crew at night because of what I told you." Juanita closed another box. "They didn't find him until it was too late. He bled to death."

"Yikes. Who found him?" Rose was verifying her facts.

"The Director of Safety. Joe Modjeska. Mojo." Juanita sent another box on its way. "Great guy."

Right. "Did you have a lot of interaction with him?"

"Mojo was here all the time. He was in our building so much, we called him Mr. Peanut." Juanita smiled, moving the next box along. "He resigned but I heard they asked for it. The captain goes down with the ship."

"Why was Mojo here so much? Did you have more safety problems than the big plant?" Rose didn't want to sound too inquisitive. "I don't want to work in a place with a lot of safety problems."

"Don't worry, the new guy hardly ever comes by." Juanita eyed the screen again. "Mojo just liked us, that's what he said. He thought we were more fun, and we are." Juanita smiled, and Rose joined her, but she was dying to get a look at the loading dock, to check the rest of Mojo's account.

"Can I take a bathroom break, boss?" she asked.

Chapter Sixty-eight

Rose went to the loading dock, slowing her pace as if she were just walking through. Two men in phosphorescent lime green uniforms, maybe for greater visibility, drove scuffed orange forklifts, whipping them around the concrete floor. The loading dock was a long, wide area, with flattened cardboard boxes piled on the floor, next to pallets stacked with boxes, shrink-wrapped with plastic sheets, to make a block. On the left was a line of white garage-type doors, with rectangular windows, and two of the doors were closed. The others opened into the containers of tractor-trailers, and at a glance, it looked as if the containers were a series of long, dark rooms.

Rose remembered Mojo had told Julie it was dark in the loading dock, but it was as light here as the factory floor, with panels of exposed fluorescent fixtures attached to a metal support overhead. She wondered if the lighting had been improved after Bill Gigot's death and made a mental note to ask Juanita. Even if his death was a murder, she was curious if they'd changed the lighting, for show.

Rose stepped aside as one of the men steered a forklift into one of the containers, carrying a pallet of shrink-wrapped boxes. Two large lamps on the cab, like the eyes on a hardshell crab, lit his way, and even if the loading dock had been dark, the lamps would have corrected for that problem. One of the garage doors was wide open, with no truck, and sunlight beamed through it in a slanted shaft. Rose could imagine how a forklift operator could drive too close to the edge of the dock and fall off, but she still didn't think that was what had happened to Bill Gigot.

Rose headed back to the factory floor to ask Juanita about the lighting, but stopped when she noticed a man approaching her at the screening station. It could have been the supervisor, Scotty, and Rose didn't want to take any chances of his calling Trish. She did an about-face, walked back toward the locker room, and hurried out of the building.

Five minutes later, she was in her car and driving away from the plant, in the late-day sun. She whipped off her hairnet, glasses, ear-plugs, and gloves, but she didn't pull over to take off her uniform. She couldn't risk getting caught, and her brain was buzzing. So Mojo had lied about Bill Gigot's death, trying to make it look more like an accident, which only made it more likely to be murder.

She hit the gas, heading into Reesburgh, where traffic was picking up. She didn't understand why Mojo would have killed Bill Gigot and she wished she could bounce it off of Leo. She glanced at the dashboard clock—5:15. He'd just be getting out of court, so maybe she could reach him. She fished her phone out of her purse, slowed her speed, and when she came to a traffic light, hit L. She waited for it to ring, but the voicemail came on, and she left a message. "Call me when you can. Love you."

She pressed END, then dialed Annie while the traffic light was still red, but there was no answer there, either. The traffic light turned green, and she cruised forward, trying to decide what to do next. She still didn't have any evidence to take to the state police, and she wasn't sure how the murder of Bill Gigot was connected to the school fire, except by Mojo. It was a puzzle with pieces missing, but she felt oddly closer than ever.

She drove ahead, looking through the windshield at the narrow strip of highway, barely seeing the trees with their turning leaves, and her phone rang. She didn't recognize the number on the screen, but didn't want to miss a return call if Leo or Annie were calling from a different phone, so she picked up. "Hello?"

"Rose?" a woman said, between sobs. "It's . . . Kristen."

"Kristen, what's the matter?" Rose asked, alarmed. The teacher sounded like she was crying hard.

"I need . . . help. Please . . . help me."

"My God, is it the baby? Are you okay? Kristen, call 911. I can't get to Lavallette in time."

"No, it's not . . . the baby. I'm so scared. Please, I need to talk to you. There's nobody else."

"What is it? I'm here. I can listen." Rose was already looking for a break in the traffic, to pull over on the shoulder. "What are you afraid of? What's going on?"

"I can't tell you over the phone." Kristen's crying slowed. "Where are you?"

"In Reesburgh. Where are you? Are you in New Jersey?"

"I can't say, but . . . I need to see you. I'll text you when and where to meet me, after we hang up."

"Why? What's going on?"

"Rose, everything I told you was a lie."

Chapter Sixty-nine

"What's going on?" Rose was sitting in her car with Kristen, having convinced the teacher that her appearance was a master disguise. It was after dark, and they were parked at the edge of a cornfield, in the middle of the farm country outside of Reesburgh. The air was cool and fresh, and the only light came from the full moon, her car's high beams, and the dashboard, which shone upward on Kristen's young face, showing the wetness to her eyes. Her gray T-shirt and sweats looked thrown on.

"Rose, I lied to you, about everything. Well, not one thing. I am pregnant."

"Okay." Rose tried to slow her heart, which was hammering. She'd taken off her Homestead uniform, which she'd had on over her clothes.

"But it's not my boyfriend's baby, like I told you."

"Whose is it?"

"Um . . ." Kristen hesitated, sighing. "Let me just say, I wish it was his baby, because he's a great guy. And he didn't break up with me, I broke up with him."

"Who is the baby's father?"

"Paul Martin. Senator Martin."

Rose felt her mouth drop open. "Are you kidding?"

"No. It's true."

"But he's married, older, and a United States Senator."

"I know. I used to think I loved him, but I must've been out of my mind." Kristen shook her head, sadly. "We've been seeing each other on the side since early summer. I met him when I was at school picking up some papers, and he was being shown around the construction site, by people from the school district. One of them introduced us, and I invited him to talk to my class. He called me, and we started up."

Rose remembered that Senator Martin had talked to Melly's class, at Kristen's behest. "Okay, so tell me what's going on."

"That explosion in the school, it was meant for me. I think he tried to kill me."

"*Senator Martin?*" Rose couldn't wrap her mind around it. She had thought that Kristen was involved in the explosion, but it turned out she hadn't been a villain, but a victim. "Senator Martin tried to *kill you?*"

"Well, he didn't do it himself, but I think he ordered it done. If I hadn't been out running this afternoon, they would have killed me."

"How do you know? What the hell's going on?"

"Paul knows my schedule. He knows that every Friday, I eat alone and microwave a veggieburger."

"How does he know that?"

"Because that's when we'd talk. That's the only time we talk during the work day. It's our secret." Kristen bit her lip, her eyes glistening. "You were right. Marylou Battle was where I would have been, at exactly the same time, and I think they did something to make the microwave blow up when I used it. She was killed, instead of me. And Melly could have been there, too. I'm so sorry, really sorry."

Rose didn't want to go there, not now. "Didn't the senator know you'd be out of school that day, sick?"

"No. I got morning sick, that much was true, and decided not to go, at the last minute. I didn't tell him. I figured I'd call him from home, at the same time, the way we always did."

"So why would he kill you? Is it because he doesn't want the baby? The scandal?"

"Of course, he doesn't want the baby. He's worried about the scandal and a divorce, and there's more than that. It's because of what I know, or what he *thinks* I know." Kristen sighed. "It happened this one time, when we were supposed to meet at our country place."

"What country place?"

"A house, about an hour from here, closer to D.C. It belongs to a friend of his, who keeps his mouth shut. We used to meet there when Paul had time. He called it our love shack."

Adorable.

"We were supposed to meet, but Mrs. Nuru wanted to go over a lesson plan. So I called and told him, but then she canceled, and I wanted to see him. I left a message on his cell, telling him I'd meet him there. He didn't call back, but he didn't always, if there were people around. I went, but he wasn't alone."

"Another woman?"

"No. He was with a man."

"He's *gay?*"

"No, it was a man I didn't know, and they were sitting in the living room. I had my key, so I let myself in, and when I came in, I could tell it was tense. You know how you can feel it in the air, when you come into a room after a fight?"

"Yes."

"Paul didn't expect me. Neither did the man."

"Wait. Didn't Paul, uh, the senator, get your voicemail message?"

"He must not have checked it. Or sometimes they get delayed, you know? Does that ever happen to you?"

"Yes." Rose nodded.

"Paul got the man out in a hurry, then we had a huge fight."

"What about?"

"Paul worried I heard what they were talking about, but I only heard one thing, and it made no sense. He was freaked that I saw him with this guy."

"Who was the guy?"

"I didn't know. But then, I saw his picture in the paper, at a celebrity golf tournament."

Rose gasped. "Joe Modjeska."

Kristen blinked. "Yes. Do you know him?"

"No. He works for Campanile, the general contractor at the school." Rose shifted up in the driver's seat. "When did you see them together?"

"The Wednesday before the explosion."

"And the explosion was on Friday." Rose put it together. "Modjeska is the guy who put the polyurethane in the lounge, which was supposed to kill you."

"How do you know all this?" Kristen asked, bewildered.

"Doesn't matter. What did you hear them say, that didn't make sense to you?"

"Something about peanuts and foreign countries."

"What do you mean?" Rose asked, her senses on alert.

"They were saying something about peanuts and Jamaica, Latin America, Chile, like a bunch of foreign countries. I asked him what they were talking about, and he freaked." Kristen threw up her hands, upset. "That's why it's so crazy. I had no idea what they even meant."

"I do. Modjeska killed Bill Gigot."

"Amanda's father?" Kristen's eyes widened. "But I thought he died years ago."

"He did. He worked at Homestead and was killed in a forklift accident, but I think it was murder. Joe Modjeska was Director of Safety at the time. Only one thing, I don't know why. I just can't put my finger on it." Rose looked through the windshield into the darkness. She flashed on the beach, when she'd looked into the darkness for answers, and she'd let her mind run free. Then suddenly, it came. "Oh my God. I think I know."

"What?"

"I found out tonight that during this time, Bill Gigot was transferred to the peanut plant, but the peanut business went bust. They wanted to convert the machinery to chocolate products, but it took time because the machinery had been used for peanuts and—"

"People are allergic to peanuts, like Jason."

Rose blinked. "Jason who?"

"Jason Gigot. Amanda's older brother. He has a severe peanut allergy, and Eileen told me this incredible story about how they found out."

"How?"

"They didn't know he was allergic, but their dad worked at Homestead and they switched him to making peanut-butter crackers or something like that. He came home one night, picked up Jason, and the little boy went into shock."

Rose listened, spellbound. It was the last piece of the puzzle, and she could feel it falling into place.

"Jason's throat swelled up, he couldn't breathe, and they had to rush him to the hospital. He almost died, and they didn't even know he had the allergy. He was, like, six years old. Amanda was a baby at the time."

Rose remembered what Juanita had said, and spun out a scenario. "If a production line isn't working at Homestead, it costs the company a hundred thousand dollars a day. During that time, the peanut machines weren't working for almost six months. That's millions, and Homestead had lots of orders for chocolate-filled nuggets. So they must have used the peanut machines to fill the chocolate orders, at night."

"That's terrible!" Kristen shook her head, incredulous. "Children would die. Would they really do that?"

"For that much money, yes." Rose thought about it, and it made sense. "They ran the machines in secret, making chocolate crackers and chocolate-filled nuggets on the peanut machines. Nobody would know the difference, only the skeleton crew at night and the Director of Safety."

"Modjeska?"

"They called him Mr. Peanut because he was around so often, and now we know why. The night shift knew, but that was only a few people, and they kept the secret. They were probably paid off, too." Rose could visualize how it all went down, having seen the plant and the peanut building herself. "I bet Bill Gigot was with them until his son Jason almost died, then he wanted to put a stop to it."

"What about Eileen? You don't think she knew, do you?"

"I doubt it. She would have known that he'd gotten transferred to the peanut plant, but not that they were running chocolate on the machines. He wouldn't risk telling her that." Rose thought of something else Juanita had said. "Homestead got a lot of orders for the chocolate products from Latin America and the Caribbean, so I'm thinking they filled the orders for export, only. Maybe that's what you heard when you interrupted that meeting."

"I see." Kristen nodded, grimly. "They were talking about countries where they sent the contaminated snacks."

"Right." Rose felt breathless at the depravity of the scheme. "It's sick, but brilliant. If they make the contaminated snacks for export only, there's much less risk. Then the kids who die would be from places that don't have the money to sue Homestead, or the FDA to watch out for them. Modjeska didn't care they were killing kids, as long as it wasn't American kids."

"But Bill Gigot did."

"Bill didn't want them to run the peanut machines anymore, and they killed him for it."

They both fell silent a minute. Rose felt Bill was owed that. A moment of silence for a loving father.

"One thing I don't understand." Kristen cocked her head. "What were Paul and Modjeska fighting about, then? The Gigot murder happened way too long ago."

Rose thought of Modjeska's magnificent house. "I bet Modjeska was blackmailing him, about the Gigot murder."

"But if Modjeska told, they'd both lose."

"The senator had more to lose than Modjeska, and more money to spend. I bet Modjeska's been blackmailing him since the murder. He has too much money to explain, otherwise." Rose thought about Julie. "He tells people it's his wife's money, but I bet that's a lie. The only thing I don't get is why Senator Martin got involved."

"He was at Homestead then."

"Right, he was at Homestead, I forgot!" Rose remembered Senator Martin's speech at the assembly. "He mentioned being at Homestead. When was he there, exactly? What did he do?"

"He was CEO until about seven years ago, when he got elected."

"Bill Gigot was killed seven years ago."

Kristen gasped. "You think that Paul—"

"If he was the CEO, I bet he made the plan."

"No!" Kristen's hand flew to her mouth. "God, this makes me sick. I'm *sick*."

"My God," Rose said, hushed. She felt the realization land like a blow. "He killed people to take care of company profits, and his career. Our U.S. Senator is a murderer."

"You really think?"

"Yes." Rose thought aloud. "When Bill Gigot stopped playing ball, Modjeska killed him, and Senator Martin covered it up. It went down as an accident, and the senator pulled the strings to protect himself and Homestead. I learned on the factory tour that the company owns most of the land in the county. That means it's a powerful contributor to the tax base. Plus I wonder how much it contributed to Martin's campaign. I bet that went up after the Gigot murder, too." Rose thought of something else. "Modjeska went from Homestead to a job in state government in Maryland. I bet the soon-to-be Senator got him the job."

"This is a nightmare." Kristen wiped away a tear. "So what do we do now?"

"We go to the state police, and lay it out. Now, we have proof. You, and your story."

"No, you can't go to them. He knows people there."

"Then we go to the FBI."

Kristen bit her lip. "But they're trying to kill me. Maybe I should get out of the country—"

"Think this through, honey." Rose put a hand on her shoulder. "You can't keep running away. It doesn't work, not for long. Modjeska is dangerous. I think he killed Kurt Rehgard and Hank Powell, carpenters who started asking questions about the fire."

Kristen quieted, her eyes widening with fear.

"That's six people they've killed so far, to protect their secret. They're ruthless, and you're not alone, anymore. You have a child to think of now."

"I know." Kristen's eyes welled up. "What kind of man is he? He'd kill his own child."

"The FBI can protect you, and you can't do it on your own." Rose took her phone from the console and pressed 411 for information. "I'm calling them."

"Think it's open?"

"It has to be. It's the FBI, right? Not a frozen yogurt shop." Rose waited for the mechanical operator to come on and ask for the listing. "In Philadelphia, Pennsylvania, may I have the offices of the Federal Bureau of Investigation? I need to report a crime."

Suddenly, a cell phone started ringing in Kristen's pocket, and she leaned over and retrieved it while Rose waited for her call to connect.

Kristen got the phone, checked the display, and said, "It's Eileen. Should I answer?"

"Eileen Gigot is calling you?" Rose asked, surprised. "Why?" There was a click on her phone line, but no ringing yet.

"I don't know, but she did earlier, when I was driving here. I checked my voicemail, and her message said to call as soon as possible." Kristen's phone kept ringing in her hand, insistent.

Oh no. "It could be about Amanda. Quick, hurry, take it!"

"Yes, hello?" Kristen said into her phone.

"What, hello?" Rose said into her phone. She opened the door and got out of the car, sending up a silent prayer.

Please let her live.

Chapter Seventy

Rose stood talking on her phone at the edge of the cornfield, trying to understand the federal bureaucracy and watching moths fly into her car headlights. There was an analogy there, but she couldn't put her finger on it and she had solved enough mysteries for one night.

"Let me get this straight, sir," she said. "You're with the FBI, aren't you?"

"Yes, I'm a Complaint Agent."

"But you can't take complaints?"

"Not after 4:45 P.M. or on weekends."

"So you're a Complaint Agent who can't take complaints?"

"Not at 8:36 at night, I can't."

Rose had told him that she had information regarding a murder, because six murders would have sounded crazy. For the same reason, she'd left out the Senator Martin part. "But the FBI switchboard operator transferred me to you."

"I know, but we don't take complaints over the phone after business hours."

"Then why did she transfer me?"

"So I could tell you that."

Rose was dumbfounded. "You took the call to tell me you can't take the call?"

The Complaint Agent hesitated. "It's important to the Bureau that the public be able to reach a human being rather than an answering machine, to speak to them as we are, now."

"I don't know if I feel better that I'm talking to a human being, when I tell him that I have information regarding a murder, and he tells me he can't hear it right now. That sounds like a machine, to me." Rose looked over at the car, where Kristen was still on the phone with Eileen, her head down. "Sir, I'm sorry. My friend's life is at stake, and I don't know what to do."

"If your friend is in danger, then he or she should call 911 or the local police."

"But she can't. She's worried they may be in on it, like a conspiracy." Rose heard herself, and even she thought she sounded crazy.

"Then I encourage you and your friend to come down to our offices and make a complaint, or call back tomorrow and we'll take it over the phone."

"Okay, thank you." Rose hung up just as Kristen was getting out of the car and walking toward her, her smooth cheeks stained with new tears. In her outstretched hand was an open cell phone. Rose went weak in the knees, and she flashed on the explosion in the cafeteria. The fireball. Amanda screaming. Blood in her blond hair. The missing sandal.

Kristen held out the phone. "Eileen wants to talk to you."

Rose stared at the phone, but she couldn't take it. She didn't want to know. She couldn't hear it, not now. And not from a grief-stricken mother.

"Take it," Kristen said, softly. "Please."

Rose shook her head, no. The only sound was the crickets chirping and the moths hitting the car headlamps.

"No, it's not that," Kristen said, reading Rose's expression. "Amanda's alive, still in Intensive Care, but I messed up, I'm so sorry. I told Eileen about Bill's being murdered, and she's freaking out. Please, take the phone. Calm her down."

"*What?*" Rose felt stunned. "You *told* her? Why would you do that?"

"It just came out." Kristen covered the phone with her palm, stricken. "She called to tell me that a man came by the hospital look-ing for me, saying he was my father. It had to be someone sent by Modjeska or even Modjeska himself. I said, 'Watch out, he's a mur-derer,' and she said, 'What are you talking about,' so I told her."

Rose kicked herself. She should have warned Kristen not to blab.

"Rose, talk to her. Explain it to her. She has a right to know, doesn't she?"

"Of course she does, but not now. Not this way. She's at her daugh-ter's bedside, for God's sake."

"Please talk to her. I told her we're calling the FBI, but she's going to the plant to confront them."

"To *Homestead*? When?"

"Now. Tonight. She says it's the Harvest Conference, and all the bosses will be there. She's going to confront them about what really happened to Bill and the peanut machines and—"

"No, she can't." Rose grabbed the phone. "Eileen, don't go to Homestead! It's dangerous for you—"

The phone line went dead.

"No!" Rose thumbed to the log, then pressed CALL to call Eileen back. The phone rang and rang, then went to voicemail, and she left a message. "Eileen, please stop! Don't go to the plant. They'll kill—"

"End of message," interrupted a mechanical voice.

Chapter Seventy-one

Rose took Kristen by the shoulders and looked her in the eye. "Listen to me. You have to go to the FBI. Right now, by yourself. There's no time to lose."

"I have to go without you?" Kristen's eyes rounded, panicky.

"Yes, I have to stop Eileen. If they think she knows what happened to Bill, they'll kill her before she can breathe a word."

"But what about you? They'll try to kill you—"

"No, they don't know me, and even if they did, I look different than I used to. You hardly knew me, remember? Let's go, hurry." Rose hustled to her car with Kristen behind her, tugging at her elbow.

"But I'm afraid."

"I know, honey." Rose opened the car door. "But there's no other way. You can't go to Reesburgh with me, that's walking into the lion's den."

"Can't I stay here?"

"In a cornfield?" Rose touched her arm. "The sooner you get to the FBI, the safer you are. Isn't there anybody you trust, who could go with you?"

"My boyfriend, I guess. Erik. He's the greatest guy ever, and I dumped him for the senator. He wanted to get married. He'd do anything in the world for me."

"Then call him, right now. Have him come get you. Go to the FBI in Philly, in his car. Do not stop." Rose got into her car, twisted the key in the ignition, and looked out the open window. "Call Eileen back, too. If she doesn't pick up, keep trying. Tell her not to go to Homestead."

"Okay."

"You'll be fine. You can do it. *Alohomora*."

Kristen smiled, shakily. "That unlocks things."

"Whatever. Be safe."

Kristen straightened up. "Okay. You, too."

Rose hit the gas, steered the car onto the road, and took off. She flew down the country lane, heading for the turnpike toward Reesburgh, keeping an eye out for cops. She passed one car, then another, barreling ahead in the cool, dark night, the gold stripe at the median glowing in her high beams.

Her heart was pounding, her teeth grinding. She hoped she could get to the plant in time. She'd left from farther away, and Eileen would have a forty-minute head start, unless one of her family members at the hospital had talked her out of going or delayed her.

Rose knew she wasn't as safe as she'd let Kristen believe. She'd left a major loose end at the plant today. The supervisor would wonder why the new hire had left and he'd probably call Trish, to check up on her alleged cousin. And when Trish told him she hadn't sent her cousin to the plant, they'd notify security, who'd be on the lookout, especially tonight, with the corporate prom.

Her left hand kept a death grip on the wheel while her right hand fumbled on the seat for her phone. She pressed L, and the phone rang and rang, then went to Leo's voicemail. She didn't want to scare him but she couldn't keep the emotion from her voice. "Babe, call me! I'm on my way to Homestead. Please, hurry—"

BEEP. Suddenly the phone went black. The battery had lost power.

"Damn it!" Rose tossed the phone aside and hit the gas.

Chapter Seventy-two

Rose tore down the turnpike and reached the Reesburgh exit in record time, but she still had the sinking sensation that it wouldn't be good enough. She squinted at the dashboard clock, its red digits aglow. 9:17.

She had failed. She'd be a full fifteen minutes behind Eileen. The realization brought tears to her eyes. There couldn't be one more death, not one. Not while she drew breath.

She blinked the wetness away and kept her foot on the gas, zipping down the fast lane. She flashed her high beams at a white VW to move out of her way, but all the cars were braking, their red taillights on at a curve in the road. She fed more gas, hoping the bottleneck would break up or she could pass on the right.

She zoomed around the curve, but the white VW was slowing even more, below the speed limit. The state cops had pulled somebody over on the right shoulder, and a police cruiser sat idling behind a blue van, its bar lights flashing red, white, and blue. Traffic slowed as it passed the scene, on temporary good behavior or gawking. The VW slowed to a crawl.

"Come on!" Rose slammed her palm on the wheel. She glanced over at the shoulder, then looked again. The driver of the stopped van looked like Eileen.

Rose switched into the slow lane, double-checking. A woman driver. Short blond hair. It *was* Eileen, and she was driving the same car she'd showed up in at the hospital, that awful night.

Well, are you happy now?

Rose passed Eileen and the state police car, her thoughts racing. What if the cop hadn't stopped Eileen for speeding? What if they'd found out that Eileen was on her way to the Harvest Conference? Would they alert someone at the plant? Homestead security? Mojo, too?

Rose's gut churned as the traffic picked up speed. She wasn't following Eileen anymore, she was leading her, and it put her in a better position. She steered off the exit and down the ramp, then took a left onto Allen Road, keeping an eye on the rearview for Eileen's blue van.

She sped up. She had to get to Homestead before Eileen, and now she had a fighting chance. There was no traffic, and Reesburgh was dark and empty, the town gone to sleep. She sped past the CVS, the line of box stores, and finally the elementary school, where it had all begun.

And now, finally, it would end.

Tonight.

Chapter Seventy-three

WELCOME TO HOMESTEAD SNACK FOODS, read the sign, and Rose saw it with new eyes. The campus was quiet without the hubbub of school groups and visitors, but the streetlamps and the windows in the corporate offices blazed with light, like a plastic town in a model train set-up. Bright, false, and lifeless.

She cruised down the access road, passing the exits signed for VISITORS, BUSES, and MAIN PLANT. The main plant had no windows to show the lights inside, but she could hear the faint noise of the production machinery. Clouds of steam spewed from the smokestacks, hissing when they hit the cool night air. The employee parking lot was only partly full, and Rose remembered from the tour that a third of the employees worked the night shift.

She kept an eye out for Eileen's van but it wasn't anywhere in sight. She hadn't seen it in the rearview mirror on the way over, but she hadn't gone slow enough to let Eileen catch up with her. She had a different plan in mind.

She took a left at the Conference Center sign, peeling off onto a long road that wound through the trees and fed into its large parking lot, almost full to capacity. Lamps illuminated the lot at regular intervals, casting cool light on the still cars. She parked at the back near the entrance, as far away from a lamp as possible, then cut the ignition, scanning the scene.

The lot was quiet, because everybody was already at the huge party at the Conference Center. The building had floor-to-ceiling glass windows, and inside, hundreds of dressed-up couples danced on the wooden floor or ate at round banquet tables, lit with candles. A large band played, and the *thumpa-thumpa* of bad seventies rock carried on the night air, then the horn section segued into some sort of fanfare. Men in tuxes ascended a decorated dais, presumably the Homestead CEO and other corporate officers. The last tuxedoed man in line was Senator Martin, who climbed the steps waving his hands, and the crowd broke into applause loud enough to be heard in the parking lot.

Rose checked the building entrance, on the side of the building facing the corporate offices. Smokers stood outside the main doors, the red tips of their cigarettes glowing, and two security guards were talking, visible only because of their bright white shirts and caps. Parked off to the side was a white sedan that read PLANT SECURITY, and she guessed that Senator Martin would have his own security detail inside.

Rose cracked her driver's side door, slipped outside, and stole across the access road to the other side, then ducked behind the shrubs. The ground was cool and the shrubs scratchy, but she stayed low, and waited. It didn't take long.

Eileen's blue van cruised slowly down the access road to the conference center, approaching the parking lot.

Rose got up into a crouching position, but stayed behind the bush.

Eileen glided into the lot and parked in a space far from the entrance to the conference center, near Rose's car. The window on the driver's side was closed, but Rose could see Eileen because of her light hair.

Eileen had faced the van so that she'd be away from the conference center, just as Rose had thought she would.

It was time to go.

Rose counted.

One, two, three.

Chapter Seventy-four

"Eileen, let me in, quick!" Rose whispered, trying the van door, which was locked. She showed her face, plastering her hands to the window. "It's me, Rose!"

Eileen turned in shock, her eyes wild with fear. She scrambled away from the window, toward the passenger seat.

"Let me in! It's okay, it's me, Rose."

Eileen's expression relaxed, then she leaned over and unlocked the door. "What are you doing here? You're a redhead now?"

"Shh, they'll hear us." Rose jumped into the driver's seat and closed the door behind her. "They'll come running. Is that what you want? Shhh."

"What do you want? What's the matter with you?"

"Eileen, we have to get out of here and go to the FBI—"

"Are you crazy?" Eileen's face was an anguished mask in the light from the streetlamps. "Didn't you do enough to my family? You're haunting me?"

"Eileen, it must have been awful to hear, about Bill, but—"

"Don't say his first name, like you know him. You didn't know him. You don't know me. Leave me alone."

"I'm on your side."

"No, you're not. You left Amanda in that fire."

"No, I didn't, but this isn't the time or the place to talk about that. You can hate me all you want, but let's leave now and convict these guys. One is Senator Martin!"

"This is none of your business. This is my business. Why are you in it at all?"

"I was looking into the cause of the fire and it led to Homestead, that's all. I'm sorry if you think I meddled, but this isn't the way to do—"

"Don't tell me what to do," Eileen interrupted, her eyes wild. "This is *my* husband we're talking about. You still have yours!"

"Eileen, listen. They could be watching us right now. I saw you get pulled over on the turnpike. What if they did it to stop you?"

"How do you know I got pulled over? Are you following me? Are you a stalker?"

"They'll kill you, Eileen. They don't want to go to prison and they'll have to, if the truth comes out." Rose gestured at the conference center. "Look at the entrance. They have security guards. What are you going to do? They won't let you in—"

"I know those guys. I've had them over for barbeques. They can't do a thing to me, not in front of the whole company." Eileen turned away, yanked on the door handle, and started to get out of the van, but Rose grabbed her arm.

"Please, don't go—"

"Get off!"

The last thing Rose saw was a manicured fist.

Heading for her face.

Chapter Seventy-five

Rose regained consciousness, groggy. She opened her eyes. She lay slumped in the driver's seat of the van. Her left cheek was killing her. She was alone. She came alive with one thought.

Eileen.

She boosted herself up in the seat and spotted a commotion at the entrance of the conference center. Two Homestead security guards were struggling to put Eileen into the security sedan. One clapped a hand over Eileen's mouth, and the other held her flailing arms, and they succeeded in getting her into the backseat and slamming the door closed.

Oh my God.

Rose looked to the right. Inside the conference center, the party continued as if nothing had happened. Oblivious, the guests filled the banquet tables, all of their attention on the dais, where Senator Martin was talking at the podium in front of the Homestead executives.

Rose looked back, aghast, as one security guard bolted to the driver's seat and the other hustled back to the entrance. The sedan emitted a plume of exhaust and steered smoothly to the left, then turned around and drove toward the access road.

Rose ducked down in the seat as it slid past, her heart hammering. If she got out of the van and screamed, they'd come and take her away, like Eileen. She didn't have a phone to call anybody. Her only advantage was that the security guards didn't know she was here, though they'd come looking for Eileen's van, later. If they killed Eileen, they wouldn't leave her van behind. They wouldn't leave any evidence. They hadn't, before.

Rose checked the ignition, and the keys were still there, hanging. She'd be ready to follow the sedan if it left the campus; but it drove up the access road, took the exit to the main plant, and vanished inside. It was as if the building had swallowed the sedan whole, with Eileen inside.

Rose cracked the door, crept out of the van, left the door open, and walked to the bumper in a crouch. She reached the end of the van and checked the entrance. The security guard remained out front, and a smoker had returned, lighting up. Neither was looking her way.

She took a deep breath and darted across the aisle to the next block of parked cars, still in a crouch. Then waited, catching her breath. The main plant was on the hill, and behind it, on the left side, where the sedan had gone in, was a loading dock, a paved area with huge tractor-trailers parked all around. One of the bays was open, making a rectangle of bright light, but there didn't appear to be any activity there.

She bolted ahead to the next block of cars, and ducked behind them, catching her breath. Her heart started to hammer from exertion and fear. She was a mom, not an action hero. Then she realized something:

Every mom is an action hero.

She ran ahead to the next block, then the next, with only one last set of parked cars between her and edge of the lot. She glanced around the sleek bumper of a Jaguar and checked the entrance. The guard and the smoker were still at the entrance. She ran to the next block of cars, then sized up the hillside ahead. Her knees were killing her, her heart was pumping. She'd be exposed while she ran up the grass to the plant, but she had no choice.

Go, go, go.

She tore up the incline, trying to stay low, but then gave up and ran as hard as she could up the hill. Her breath came in ragged bursts. Her heart thundered in her chest.

She dropped behind the first tractor-trailer she saw, then darted between two other trucks parked together. Bright security lights were mounted along the top of the plant, but there was nobody around outside. Still, she'd have to stay out of sight. She didn't hear any sirens or sounds, and it made her stronger, emboldening her.

She peeked around the front of the truck, trying to figure out her next move. The trucks were parked at the loading docks, cab fronts facing out, and there were four trucks in all; the lighted bay was to the far right, and she had to go left.

She ran from one cab to the next, just as she had with the parked cars, until she raced to the end of the plant, then flattened herself against the building. She could hear the noise of the machinery and feel its vibration against her back. She heard no other sound, so she peeked around the corner.

No one was around. Ahead lay more paved area, and lights mounted on the roofline shone ellipses onto the dry asphalt. It was the back of the plant, and there were no trucks or other vehicles. The building was a stretch of rough, white-painted cinderblock, with no window or door. A third of the way up, there was a break in the wall where she thought the white security sedan had gone.

Go!

She tore along the side of the plant until she got to the break in the wall, then stopped. There was no sound of people talking or cars running, so she peered around the side. The white security sedan sat parked inside a small U-shaped bay lined with blue recycling bins, galvanized cans, and flattened cardboard boxes. No one was inside the car or in sight. The bay had three doors, all painted yellow, none signed. One had to lead to the security office, where Eileen must have been taken, but Rose didn't know which one.

She felt stumped, momentarily. She couldn't remember enough from the factory tour to orient herself. She'd gotten turned around because she'd approached the plant from the back. All she could remember was that the security office was along a hall with the other offices, in the middle of the building.

"You have to be kidding me," said a man, from behind.

Chapter Seventy-six

Rose turned in fear. She was thrown against the building. Her head exploded in pain. A hand clamped over her mouth. She knew who it was before she opened her eyes.

Mojo.

"You're out of your depth, Mom." He snorted, standing so close she could smell the cigar on his breath.

She pushed her terror away. She hadn't come this far to be denied. Mojo thought she was only a mom. He didn't know she was an action hero. She kneed him in the groin with all of her might.

"Ooof!" He staggered backwards, and she took off down the side of the plant, running for her life.

"Help! Help!" Rose veered around the corner toward the lighted bay on the loading dock. It was time for Plan B. There had to be employees driving forklifts there. "Help!"

Suddenly a recorded announcement blared through speakers mounted at the roof of the building: "All Homestead employees, please exit the building immediately, using the main entrance. Please exit the building immediately. This is not a drill."

Oh no. Rose could hear the commotion inside the plant, alarmed voices and chatter, but she kept running.

"I'll kill you!" Mojo panted, almost at her heels. He couldn't use his gun or he would alarm everybody. He was big, but she was faster, scooting ahead.

"Help!" she screamed, but it was drowned out by the recorded announcement, on a continuous loop.

She tore past the tractor-trailers, aiming for the lighted bay. She could barely catch her breath. Terror and adrenaline powered her. Only four trucks to go. Then three, then two, then one. The loading dock was high, up close. Four feet off the ground.

Jump, jump, jump!

She leapt onto the dock, but it caught her in the waist. Pain arced through her stomach. She clawed the concrete for purchase, her legs flailing.

"Goddamn you!" Mojo growled, but Rose scrambled up just ahead of him, got to her feet, and darted through the open bay into the loading area inside the plant.

"Help!" she screamed, but the employees had evacuated. Forklifts stood where they'd been left, their headlights still on. The production machinery chugged away, like a ghost factory.

She raced through the loading area past the X-ray machines, deserted now. Boxes were piling up at the scanner.

She tore past the packing area, her thoughts racing. If she could find the main entrance, she could get help. She couldn't die here. Neither could Eileen.

"You bitch!" Mojo shouted, out of breath, but he kept coming.

Rose blew through two swinging doors, her legs churning. She tore down a long hallway, burst through another set of doors, and found herself surrounded by lines of huge stainless steel machines that read PPM TECHNOLOGIES, with a myriad of red tubes.

She spun around, looking for a place to get out. A line of whirring knives sliced the potatoes. A line of sorters dropped them into a funnel. Conveyor belts fed them into cooking oil in covered tanks. The oil boiled, the air felt hot. She panted, her heart thundered.

There! Go!

She bolted for a set of rubber-tipped metal stairs, praying she could take them easier than the heavyset Mojo. If she ran him hard enough, she could keep the advantage. She bounded up the stairs just ahead of him. At the top was a rickety metal catwalk. She took off, running, setting the catwalk swinging.

"You're dead!" Mojo shouted, charging after her. The catwalk jumped with his extra weight.

The next set of stairs lay ahead, and she ran down them, almost falling, then sprinted along the tile floor. She glanced over her shoulder.

Mojo was right behind her, almost falling, so she sprinted ahead and raced up the next set of stairs up to the catwalk, to tire him out.

"Damn you!" he shouted, but she ran along the catwalk, almost out of breath, clutching the metal rails not to fall.

Mojo ran behind her, keeping pace. She ran above the packing room, where the air got cooler, then got hot again over the next room, where the kettle-cooked chips were made. Stainless steel ovens with red tubes cooked the chips in open trays of boiling oil.

Rose tore down the next set of stairs. The room ended ten feet ahead. She had blown it. She whirled around on her heels, in terror. There was nowhere else to go.

She was trapped.

Chapter Seventy-seven

Mojo jumped from the stairs to the floor, grabbed a long metal hook from the wall, and whipped it at her face.

Rose raised her hands, leaping backwards. The hook sliced her forearm. She screamed in pain. On the downswing, the hook caught one of the red hoses on the machines, severing it. It was a bundle of live wires and it sprang free of the machine as if it were alive, sparking through the air like an electrified anaconda.

"You're dead!" Mojo grimaced. The live wire whipped and crackled in the air. He advanced with grim purpose, his dark eyes glittering.

Rose ran terrified to the back wall. There was nowhere else to go. She was too far from the stair. The only door was on the opposite diagonal.

Mojo stood in her path, swinging the hooked stick with the power of a drive off the fairway. His loafer slipped on the tile floor, and the hook hit the stainless steel oven with so much force that it embedded itself in the side.

Rose fled to the far corner. Above, the live wire lashed through the air, showering sparks.

Mojo yanked the hook from the machine. Boiling oil leaked from the hole onto the tile floor, bubbling hot. He sidestepped it, raising the hook high over his head. He was about to bring it down on Rose, but when he whipped it back, it connected with the live wire.

Mojo spasmed as electricity coursed through his body. His eyes popped. His mouth flew open. His throat emitted an inhuman cry. The skin on his face blistered. A disgusting stench filled the air. He collapsed, electrocuted. The hook fell from his hand, breaking the circuit. The live wire snapped away, showering sparks that ignited the oil, engulfing his body in flames.

Rose flattened herself into the corner, horrified. Oil poured from the hole in the oven, spreading all over the floor. Fire raced along its stream back to the huge oven, which exploded in flames.

Whoomp! went the sound. The fire jumped from one open tray to the next, the oil as flammable as jet fuel. *Whoomp! Whoomp! Whoomp!* In a minute, the ovens were beds of lethal flames.

Alarms blared, deafening. Hoods over the ovens sprayed a chemical mist. Overhead sprinklers showered water. The oil on the floor exploded when the water hit it, raging higher. Any speck of residual oil burst into flame; oil lining the ducts, oil coating the machinery, and oil covering the steps and the catwalk. The room became a blazing inferno.

Rose screamed in terror. A wall of flame stood between her and the exit doors. Sprinklers sprayed water, making the grease fire worse. Smoke billowed everywhere. She couldn't breathe for the heat. She flashed on the school fire. She never thought she'd find herself here again. She couldn't fail this time. She couldn't lose Eileen.

Think, think, think.

Rose knew there had to be fire extinguishers. She ran through the smoke along the wall, where the flames were lowest. She found a round metal fire extinguisher big enough for commercial kitchens, mounted on the wall. It looked like her red one at home, except gigantic. She wrenched the extinguisher off its mount, almost dropping it because it was heavy and hot.

She yanked out its pin, squeezed the handle, and grabbed the nozzle. She sprayed a chemical mist on the fire, smothering a path so she could get through the flames. She reached the doors and banged through them. She dropped the heavy extinguisher, which fell with a *clang* and rolled noisily away.

Thick smoke filled the hallway. Sprinklers drenched her. Fire alarms blared. She heard sirens in the distance, too far away. She coughed and coughed. Her eyes teared. Her lungs burned.

"Eileen!" Rose screamed through the sirens and the water.

Chapter Seventy-eight

Rose looked right, then left. Both hallways were identical cinder-block corridors, filling with smoke. She didn't know which way to go. Her eyes stung. Her lungs burned. She coughed and coughed. She tried to remember the plant layout from the tour. The offices had been in the hallway connecting the pretzel to the potato chip production. She had to find that junction.

She sensed it was to the right. She ran down the hall that way, burst through the double doors, and found herself in another hallway. The window onto the factory floor showed a horrific conflagration that burned cardboard boxes, wooden pallets, cellophane shrink-wrapping, and anything else in its path. Then she realized. If it was boxes, it had to be the warehouse. She flashed on what the tour guide had said:

See all these boxes? They go for blocks and blocks!

Rose remembered that the warehouse was between the chips and pretzel production. She was on the right track. She ran down the hall. Smoke filtered the air but it smelled of something else, too. Pretzels.

Go, go, go.

She flew through another set of double doors, her lungs burning and tears spilling from her eyes. The smell of burned pretzels got stronger and stronger, and each window showed a factory on fire. The hallways twisted left, then right. She pounded through another set of doors, and she was finally there, at the hallway of offices. QUALITY AS-SURANCE read the first sign, and she bolted to the next office. DIREC-TOR OF SECURITY.

"Eileen!" Rose tried the door. It was locked. She looked through the window beside the door. The anteroom was filling with smoke, slipping underneath the door. No one was inside. The door beyond it was closed. If Eileen was here, she was behind that door. Rose had to get inside.

She looked around for something, anything. On the floor down the hall was a large metal trashcan. She bolted to it, picked it up, and struggled back down the hall with it, trailing garbage. She reached the office and slammed the trashcan at the window.

Bam! The trashcan shattered the window but didn't break it all the way. *Bam!* Rose slammed it again, heaving it as hard as she could, straining with exertion. She couldn't breathe for the smoke. Her eyes teared uncontrollably.

Bam! Bam! She hit it twice more, widening the hole, breathing hard. She couldn't lift the trashcan another minute. She let it fall, and it dropped loudly to the floor.

She broke off pieces of the jagged plastic with her hand, then reached through and twisted the lock on the knob. It turned. She yanked her hand out of the jagged hole, opened the door, and ran inside.

"Eileen!" she screamed. Smoke made it almost impossible to breathe in the small room. She prayed she'd gotten to Eileen in time and that the security guys hadn't taken her away. She went to the door, and it was unlocked.

She twisted the knob and burst through the door.

Chapter Seventy-nine

"Eileen!" Rose cried out in relief. The office was smoky but Eileen was alive, struggling against rope that bound her to a metal chair. Her eyes were wide above duct tape covering her mouth. A bruise on her forehead showed fresh blood. She made guttural noises, trying to talk.

"Don't worry, I got you." Rose rushed to Eileen's side. Duct tape bound her ankles, and her arms were wrenched behind her back.

"Hang on, this'll hurt." Rose yanked the duct tape from her mouth. It came off with a *zzzp,* leaving a wide red welt.

"Oh, God." Eileen took a huge gulp of smoky air and started coughing.

"Wait, we need oxygen." Rose looked around. There was a windowless metal door between metal bookshelves on the back wall, and she hustled to it. "They brought you in through this door, right?"

"Yeah." Eileen coughed, her face turning red.

"Hold on." Rose turned the knob and pushed the door open. The bay was empty. The white security sedan was gone. Sirens sounded louder, closer. Fresh air *whoosh*ed in the office, making a whirlwind of the smoke that set Eileen coughing harder, and Rose went back to her side, kneeling. "You okay?" she asked, touching her back.

"Get your hands off me!" Eileen coughed. "Don't think we're friends now. You should have saved Amanda, instead of me."

Rose didn't have time to discuss it. She grabbed a scissors from the desk and wedged the blade between the rope around Eileen's hands. They had turned bright red, her circulation cut off.

"You left my daughter." Eileen kept coughing. "I'd give my life for hers any day."

Rose sawed through the rope, thinning it. She yanked, and it broke, then she started to cut and unravel the rest.

"Bastards." Eileen squirmed and shimmied, struggling to free herself. "They killed Bill. They were gonna kill me when Mojo got back. I bet he took off."

"No, he didn't." Rose snipped the last rope, flashing on that awful sight. "He's dead."

"How?" Eileen bent over and undid the tape on her left ankle. "In the fire?"

"More or less." Rose bent down and ripped the tape off of her right ankle.

"Sorry I hit you, but you deserved it." Eileen jumped up and shook off the pieces of rope.

"I've had better apologies, but let's get out of here. I'll show you the way, once we get outside."

"Gimme a break. I know this plant like the back of my hand." Eileen scooted out the door, with Rose on her heels.

Chapter Eighty

Rose and Eileen raced around the corner of the plant toward the lights and activity in front. The campus was in a state of emergency, abuzz with motion, shouting, and sirens. The air reeked of burned rubber, plastic, and oil. Black smoke leaked from the exhaust vents and stacks on the plant's roof, sending sparks and cinders into the night sky. Thirty-some firetrucks were already fighting the fire, raging at the opposite side of the plant. Firefighters in heavy coats with reflective stripes ran this way and that, hauling thick hoses that lay on the asphalt like a snakes' nest.

Rose and Eileen ran toward the access road, parked up with state police cruisers, ambulances, black sedans, and boxy white newsvans, forming an improvised cordon between the burning plant and the Homestead corporate offices. A massive crowd filled the corporate parking lot, and Rose and Eileen hurried toward it, out of harm's way.

Tears filled Rose's eyes when she realized that they were finally safe, and all she could think about was Leo and the kids. She felt a surge of deep emotion, a profound and unreasoning yearning to see them all, to be together again, whole and happy. She didn't know if Leo had gotten her message before the battery died, or if he could make it here in time. She looked for him in the crowd, but they were shapeless silhouettes, backlit by the emergency vehicles and illuminated windows of the offices.

Someone started shouting, and Assistant District Attorney Howard Kermisez, his young assistant Rick Artiss, and a cadre of state policemen, FBI agents in navy blue windbreakers, and black-uniformed EMTs came running toward Rose and Eileen.

"Help!" Eileen shouted, with Rose behind, and the first to reach them were the EMTs.

"We need to get you away from this building." An EMT eyed Eileen's forehead on the fly. "Is that bruise impairing your vision? Can you see?"

"I'm fine." Eileen hurried toward Howard, Rick, the state policemen, and the FBI agents, as a second EMT hustled to Rose.

"Let's get you to the hospital," the second EMT said, taking Rose's arm and hustling her forward. "We need to get you treated."

"Thanks." Rose kept looking for Leo, but the crowd was still too far away.

"Thank God you're here!" Eileen met the state police, the Assistant District Attorney, and the FBI on asphalt wet from the firehoses. "I'm Eileen Gigot and I was almost murdered tonight. Three men, security guards at Homestead, tried to kill me. I have their names and descriptions. They killed my husband, seven years ago."

"Mrs. Gigot, come with us," said one of the state policemen, his eyes alarmed under the wide brim of his hat. "You can give us a statement later. Please come away from this area. It's too dangerous."

Howard Kermisez took Eileen's arm, falling into step beside her. "Mrs. Gigot, we're fully briefed at my office—"

"No way, Howard." The FBI agent grabbed Eileen's other arm, flashing a brown billfold with a shiny badge at Eileen. "I'm Special Agent Jacob Morrisette, from the Wilmington office of the FBI. This is a matter of federal jurisdiction, and we'll handle this." He turned to Rose. "I know you're Rose McKenna, and we have Kristen Canton at our office in Philadelphia. Come with us, please."

Howard hurried along. "Jake, this is our case. It's a matter of state law, and the criminal acts took place in Reesburgh County—"

"Not now, gentlemen," the first EMT said firmly, on the fly. "These women need medical attention, first thing."

"No, I said, I'm fine." Eileen waved him away. "We have to catch those men. They left about twenty minutes ago."

"Here's the plan, people." Special Agent Morrisette hustled them along, followed by the authorities and EMTs. "The staties will put out an APB, and we'll get you ladies some medical attention, then we'll sort this all out at our offices. Hurry, come with us."

Rose let herself be hustled toward the crowd, scanning it for Leo. She didn't see him among the state policemen, Homestead employees in yellow jumpsuits, Harvest Conference executives in glittery gowns and tuxes, and Reesburgh residents, of all ages. Everyone's gazes were riveted to the fire, and every face showed shock, pain, and heartbreak. Some Homestead employees cried freely.

Rose thought of Juanita, June, and Sue, who'd been so kind to her, and she wondered if they'd be out of jobs now. She passed the crest-fallen executives and sales reps, thinking of the enormous loss to the employees, the residents, and the town itself. She realized with a shock that somewhere along the line, Reesburgh had become her home.

"Eileen, Rose, over here!" someone shouted. Tanya Robertson and her TV crew hurried toward them, their videocameras whirring and klieglights blinding. Tanya held out her microphone, but the state police rushed to prevent her from crossing the cordon.

"Eileen, why were you in the fire?" Tanya shouted. "What's going on? How did you and Rose get together?"

"Tanya, here's the scoop," Eileen answered, facing the camera. "My husband, Bill, was murdered seven years ago, and tonight they tried to kill me, too."

"*What?*" Tanya said, shocked. "Who?" The crowd burst into excited chatter. People in the back craned their necks, trying to see and hear. The FBI agents tried to pull Eileen away, but she didn't budge, grabbing the microphone.

"We need to find the men who killed my husband. The ones who tried to kill me are Roger Foster, Paul Jensen, and Deke Rainwater. They were in a conspiracy with Joseph Modjeska, who was killed in the fire. I want them arrested for murder and attempted murder."

"Do you have evidence to support these allegations?" Tanya asked, barely containing her excitement.

"I sure do. So does Rose, who saved my life." Eileen jerked a thumb at Rose, and Tanya turned to her, with the microphone.

"Did you really save her life, Ms. McKenna?" Tanya held out the microphone. "Don't you have any comment for me, this time?"

Suddenly, Rose spotted a motorcade of black sedans, behind the crowd. The cars were gliding away from the campus, heading out the access road and toward the highway. It had to be Senator Martin and his entourage.

"Yes, I do have something to say." Rose pointed to the motorcade. "There goes Senator Martin. He's the mastermind behind the conspiracy. He's responsible for the murders of Bill Gigot and also Kurt Rehgard and Hank Powell, of Bethany Run Construction." The crowd gasped, but Rose didn't stop, her voice ringing clear and strong, like truth itself. "He's even behind the fire last week at Reesburgh Elementary School, which killed three people and put my daughter and Amanda Gigot in the hospital. The fire wasn't an accident, it was premeditated murder, by Senator Martin and his coconspirators."

Tanya's mouth dropped open, Eileen cheered, and the crowd erupted into gasps, chatter, and shouting. The FBI agents looked at the state police, the state police looked at the Assistant District Attorneys, and all hell broke loose.

"That's enough of that, ladies," said Special Agent Morrisette, clamping a strong hand on Rose's arm and trying to tug her from the microphone.

"Hey, wait a minute," she said, tugging back, until she saw Leo fighting his way to the front of the roiling crowd, his tie flying.

"Let her speak!" he shouted, struggling past a state policeman, and Special Agent Morrisette turned on him.

"Sir! Get behind that cordon! Who do you think you are?"

"I'm her husband. And if she has something to say, then let her say it. Honey?" Leo turned to Rose, his eyes shining. "Like your new hair, by the way."

"I do have something to say." Rose felt tears come to her eyes and reached for him. "I love you."

Chapter Eighty-one

Rose and Leo left the FBI offices at dawn, holding hands as they walked along Market Street, in Philadelphia. The city was just waking up, and the sun was rising behind the buildings, painting the sky with swaths of yellow, like fresh latex from a roller. Only a few people were on the street, and two uniformed cops stood talking in front of the federal building. A street-cleaning truck with a rotary brush whirred water at the curb, and a SEPTA bus hissed past, half-empty. The only store open was the Dunkin' Donuts across the street.

Rose breathed in fresh air, carrying the scent of glazed doughnuts and the first chill of autumn. "Smells good."

"For a city, yes." Leo looked around. "But I spent all week here. I've had enough."

"Congratulations on your settlement."

"Thanks." Leo looked over with an easy smile. His eyes were tired, and his chin sported stubble, but he looked happy and relaxed, his tie loose and his khaki jacket catching the breeze. "I'd tell you how it went, but it doesn't compare with chasing murderous senators and exposing corporate conspiracies."

Rose smiled. "Not bad for a week's work."

Leo squeezed her hand. "Has it only been a week?"

"Yes." Rose couldn't believe it herself. "It's Friday morning. One week ago today, the cafeteria caught fire."

"Jeez." Leo shook his head, and Rose sent up a silent prayer that Amanda would be okay. Last night, she and Eileen had been questioned by the FBI and the Assistant District Attorneys, but they'd been in two separate interview rooms, and Eileen had left for the hospital before Rose was finished. "Too bad we didn't get to say good-bye to Eileen."

"What?" Leo looked at her like she was nuts. "She punched you in the face, babe."

"I would have done the same thing, if someone left Melly in a fire." Rose was oddly fine with it, maybe because her face didn't hurt that much. She'd iced the bump last night with a gel pack and felt like herself again, having washed off her makeup disguise. Although she was thinking about keeping the red hair, which suited the new her.

"Still, please, don't do anything like this again." Leo shuddered. "You could have been killed."

"It's all over now." Rose squeezed his hand, and she could feel his love in the warmth of his palm. "I'm fine."

"Never again, promise?"

"Promise."

"Nothing can happen to you. I'll never get another wife as good-lookin'."

"Stop."

Leo smiled. "One thing I don't understand. Why would Campanile let Mojo do all the stuff he did?"

"I don't think they knew." Rose had a worry, too. "It really bothers me that they might not be able to prove that Kurt and Hank Powell were murdered. Howard said they don't have the blood to do a toxicology screen, but I bet it would show that his new friends slipped him a drug."

"Maybe they can check out his car, see if it shows evidence that he was hit, like a paint scrape." Leo looked over, brightening. "I have an idea. When this all dies down, why don't we offer to take his niece out, with Melly? Baseball's over but I can get some Eagles tickets."

"That's a nice thought." Rose squeezed his hand. "I wonder when it will die down. I can't wait to see Senator Martin indicted. He played it smart, didn't he? Kept the conspiracy to just a few guys on the night shift and Mojo, who did the dirty work." Rose felt disgusted. "What is it with corporations? Aren't they just made of people? Don't they have kids?"

"They don't think that way when it comes to money. And it's somebody else's kids, not their own." Leo shook his head. "They'll get Martin. He'll be going away for life. Not only for his role in the murders, but for the corruption that was involved in the blackmail. It's just a matter of time."

Rose thought he was right. Late last night, the FBI had arrested the three Homestead security guards, in Virginia. "Maybe one of the security guards will flip."

"Flip?" Leo looked over, eyes narrowing.

"I heard it on *Law & Order*."

"Don't mess with a lunch mom."

"Exactly." Rose smiled. "I hope they can rebuild the plant. It was awful to see it burn. Would they be insured for that?"

"Sure. The bad guys will go to jail, the board will replace them, and the company will rebuild. It's too successful not to." Leo squeezed her hand again. "And by the way, we're in the clear, eh?"

"Thank God." Rose breathed a relieved sigh. The D.A. wouldn't hold her responsible for Mojo's death or for what had happened to Amanda. "And I really doubt Eileen will sue me now, on her own."

"It better go without saying. You saved her life." Leo smiled. "All's well that ends well."

"Except for one thing." Rose's thoughts kept circling back to the same place. "I hope to God that Amanda comes out of this."

"Me, too." They both lapsed into silence as they reached the corner and turned right toward the parking lot.

The wind disappeared, and they approached the grim gray column of the Federal Detention Center, with its slitted windows. Ahead lay the Police Administration Building and the expressway, where rush hour was starting. Rose felt the pulse of the city beginning to beat, but she didn't miss the excitement. She felt as if her life was starting over, in Reesburgh. She hoped that Melly would have it easier now, but that could be too much to ask.

"Wow." Leo shook his head, musing. "I still don't get how you figured all this out. A school fire that's intentional, set to kill a teacher who's having a senator's baby, and a forklift accident that's no accident, to cover up a scheme that would kill children."

"So many people are gone now." Rose sighed, sadly, thinking of them all. Marylou Battle, Serena Perez, Ellen Conze. Kurt Rehgard, Hank Powell, and Bill Gigot. Even Mojo. All that death, all so tragic and pointless.

"But still, you figured it out. I'm proud of you, and more importantly, I'm sorry." Leo stopped and turned to face her, eyeing her directly. His expression grew serious, and his entire body seemed to still. "I was wrong. I shouldn't have vetoed you with Oliver. We'll get him to make a statement that we won't be suing the school."

"Good."

"And from now on, you and I will talk about everything, until we're sick to death of talking, and we'll make no moves without agreeing. Forgive me, partner?"

"I do."

"You said that already, at the altar. And I do, too." Leo smiled, and Rose smiled back.

"Does this mean we're getting married, all over again?"

"Yes. So now I can kiss the bride, for keeps." Leo leaned over and gave her a soft kiss, then more deeply, and Rose kissed him back fully, feeling them reconnect as a couple, renewing their vows, on the fly.

"I love you," Rose said, when Leo released her.

"I love you, too. And I miss the kids."

"Me, too."

"Let's go get our family." Leo looped an arm around her shoulder, and Rose slid her hand around his waist.

And they walked to the car, together.

Chapter Eighty-two

Rose and Leo pulled into the driveway at the cabin and got out of the car, and Melly came tearing across the Vaughns' lawn toward them, her hair flying. Princess Google scampered behind, her plumed tail wagging furiously.

"Mom, Leo!" Melly called out, and Rose threw open her arms.

"Sweetie!" Rose hugged her close, breathing her in. "I missed you so much!"

"Ready for your surprise?"

"Sure." Rose kissed her and set her down. They'd called on the way, and Melly had told her she'd had a surprise for them. "Let's see."

"It's not here. We have to go somewhere else."

"Okay, you're the boss." Rose smiled, petting Princess Google, who had climbed up on her leg, resting feathery paws on her knee. "Hi, Googie girl!"

"Leo!" Melly ran to Leo, who lifted her up and gave her a bear hug and a little grunt.

"Melly Belly! Where you been all my life?" Leo kissed her on the cheek, and Rose turned to see Mo coming out of the house, in his navy polo and jeans, followed by Gabriella, dressed the same, holding John.

"How's my baby boy?" she said, hurrying toward him, and John burst into a smile, looking so natty in his white T-shirt, Mom jeans, and two whole teeth. "I missed you, buddy boy! I missed my baby!" She scooped him up, hugged him close, and kissed his head, then grinned at Gabriella. "Girl, do we owe you! How can I thank you? Dinner? A night on the town? A car?"

"Nonsense, we loved it." Gabriella beamed. "You're a celebrity. You're all over the news."

"Yes!" Mo came up from behind, grinning. "Why didn't you tell us you were a crimefighter?"

"Ha!" Leo smiled. "She didn't tell me, why would she tell you?"

"Let's go, Mo!" Melly started jumping up and down, and Rose noticed she had on new brown shoes with her jeans and Harry Potter T-shirt.

"Where'd you get those shoes?"

"They're boots! Come on, Mr. V.!" Melly ran to Mo, who checked his watch.

"You're right. Can't be late. Gotta go."

"Where?" Rose smiled, mystified.

"Not far," Gabriella answered. "You all go ahead. I'll stay here with the dog and get lunch ready. Come here, Googie!"

Mo nodded. "Let's hit the road. Rose, why don't you and Leo follow us in your car?"

Melly bounded after Mo. "I'll go with Mr. V."

Rose blinked. She couldn't remember Melly ever choosing not to ride with her. Mischief was afoot. She looked at Leo.

"Don't ask me," he said, with a happy shrug.

Chapter Eighty-three

Rose and Leo stood together in the back pasture of a small horse farm, down the road from the cabin. The trees blazed with orange, red, and gold, and dry, grassy hills rolled on and on. Post-and-rail fences separated the pastures, and in the middle sat a white barn with a tin roof, faded red. Mo and Melly had gone inside, asking Rose and Leo to stay here and wait for the surprise.

"I'm trying not to worry." Rose cuddled John, who hooked his little arm around her neck. "Mo's not putting her on a horse, is he?"

"Relax." Leo smiled easily, slipping an arm around her shoulder. "He wouldn't do anything unsafe with her."

Rose turned, and Melly was sitting atop a furry black horse, grinning as if she'd ridden all her life. She had on a black helmet and buckskin jodhpurs, and even though Mo stood beside her, Rose felt her heart jump into her throat. "Leo, you see this?"

"She'll be fine."

"Bsbsb!" John squealed, pumping his arm when he spotted Melly.

"How do you know she'll be fine?"

"Shh. He's coming over."

"Mo!" Rose managed not to freak as he strode over. "Is this safe? She's not that great in sports. She's double-jointed. She trips a lot."

"Don't worry." Mo put a hand on Rose's shoulder, smiling. "She's in total control."

"Mo, she's *eight*."

"Just the same, and double-jointed is good, for riding. Look at the flex in those ankles. Her heels drop very low. It increases her stability." Mo waved at Melly. "Walk on, Mel!"

Rose held her breath as Melly gave the horse a kick, and it walked quickly around in a circle. "Can't it go slower?"

"Any slower, she'll be in reverse."

Leo smiled, looking away.

Rose asked, "So, Mo, how did this come about?"

"Well, she got tired of mucking, so we went for a hack. She's become quite the barn rat. She has a perfect seat." Mo cupped his hand to his mouth. "Melly, eyes up, heels down! Good girl!"

Melly steered around the circle, and when she came around their side, she waved happily.

Leo waved back. "Lookin' good, cowgirl!"

Rose gasped. "Two hands, honey!"

Mo scoffed. "She can ride with no hands, her balance is that good. Want to see?"

"No," Rose shot back. "I mean, no thanks."

Mo and Leo laughed. Melly walked past them, and the horse swished his thick black tail. Mo cupped his mouth, calling out, "Mel, trot on!"

Melly kicked the horse, and it trotted around the circle, faster. She went up and down in the saddle, keeping the rhythm, even at speed.

Mo nodded. "Churchill said, 'The outside of a horse is good for the inside of a man.'"

"Churchill wasn't a mother." Rose bit her lip. "Why is she going up and down?"

"She's posting. Many people take a few lessons to pick it up, but she got it right away." Mo gestured at Melly. "She's happy as a clam. On a horse, you have to meet the world with your eyes front and your chin up. A girl who directs a thousand-pound animal learns confidence."

Rose watched Melly, who did look happy.

"Horses have a way of going, which means the way they move and relate to the world. People have a way of going, too. Melly's way of going is to keep her head down, to run and hide behind books and computers."

Rose winced. "These aren't the worst things, Mo."

"Don't mistake me. I think she needs all the things already in her life, but she loves horses and she's not afraid of them, even the biggest jumpers here."

"I know she's good with animals. The thing she needs to work on is people. She needs a friend in school, and riding isn't even a school sport."

"Ah, but riding is where it starts." Mo kept an eye on Melly. "She's making a friend, before your eyes."

"She's making friends with a horse."

"Not at all. She's making friends with *herself*."

Rose hadn't thought of it that way. She watched Melly.

"We all see Melly's problem, but she's got to find confidence in herself. Face the world as she is, on her own, with her eyes front and her chin up. The more she does it here, the more she'll do it at school. Look. She's moving that pony on her own. She's *succeeding*."

Rose watched Melly riding smoothly in the bright sun, with the lovely pastures and the gorgeous autumn backdrop, and felt her heart fill with emotion. Something had changed, and she was looking at it, and maybe things could turn around for Melly, someday. Maybe someday was starting right now.

"It's worth a try, babe," Leo said softly, his hand on her back.

"It surely is," Mo added. "I can give her a lesson when you come up, and there are plenty of schooling barns in Reesburgh. I looked into it online and found you a list."

Rose felt tears in her eyes, cuddling John close. It was hope, at long last. "Does she want lessons?"

Leo answered, "Ask her."

Chapter Eighty-four

"Hit the sack, kid!" Rose tucked Melly into bed, feeling like herself again, having showered and changed into clean clothes. It was twilight, her favorite time at the cabin, when the day was over and they'd go to bed early, in harmony with the rhythms of nature rather than TV or homework.

"It's cold tonight." Melly tugged up the comforter, next to Princess Google, already asleep. "Isn't Ebony so cute, Mom?"

"Very cute." Rose sat down on the edge of the single bed. The room was bare-bones, containing only a small bookshelf and bureau. A metal reading lamp was clamped to the headboard, and Rose turned it off, leaving them in the dim light from the window.

"Do you really like him?"

"Ebony? Of course. I think he's adorable and furry. You looked great up there."

"Harry rides brooms, and I ride horses." Melly smiled, and Rose gave her a kiss on the cheek.

"Do you like riding horses?"

"I love it. It's so fun, and Ebony is soft, really soft."

"I remember." Rose had petted the horse before they'd left, and he'd looked insanely tall, up close. "You know, I was wondering if you want to take riding lessons. Mo says there's barns around us, at home. Want to give it a try?"

"What do you think?"

Rose fell silent a moment, and through the screen came the scent of horse manure, but that could have been her imagination. She knew if she said the word, it would put a kibosh on this whole crazy venture. Every mother had moments like this, when she could sway things toward what she wanted, and not what her child wanted. Instead, she said, "I think it's a great idea, Mel. You're really good at it, and it's fun and really special."

"But I don't know any kids who ride. Nobody in my class does."

"Kids do it everywhere, like those girls at the barn. You'd have a great time."

"What if the kids make fun of me, at school?"

"If they do, you can deal with it. If they tease you, try not to let it bother you." Rose thought of what Mo had said. "Keep your head up and go forward. Tell yourself, trot on. So what do you say? Wanna give it a try?"

"Think I can do it?"

"I know you can, honey," Rose answered, without hesitation. She heard Leo's footsteps on the staircase, and turned. "Hey, honey. You up here for another good-night kiss?"

"Leo!" Melly called out. "I'm going to take riding lessons!"

"That's great!" Leo entered holding John, then leaned close to Rose's ear. "Phone for you, babe. It's Eileen, about Amanda."

Chapter Eighty-five

Rose walked down the glistening hospital corridor, holding Melly's hand. Amanda had come out of her coma and been moved from Intensive Care, though she'd developed motor problems in her left arm and was recovering her memory only slowly. Eileen had asked them to stop by on Sunday afternoon, and Rose was hoping it was a good idea.

"You okay, Mel?"

"Fine." Melly held their gift under her arm. "Are you giving her the present or am I?"

"You decide. You picked it out, but I'm happy to give it to her and say that."

"I'll give it to her."

"Good." Rose squeezed her hand. "She doesn't remember everything and she might not look very good, but she's going to get better, very slowly. She won't be back at school until the end of the year."

"Does she remember putting the jelly on her cheek?"

Rose flinched. "I don't know."

"Who's going to be there, visiting her? Any kids from my class? Danielle and Emily?"

"I don't think so, but I'm not sure."

Melly fell silent.

"You worried, Mel?"

"I'm trotting on."

Rose burst into laughter, and Melly giggled, releasing the tension. The hallway was empty, and the air smelled vaguely antiseptic. People talked in low tones in one room, and a football game played on a TV in another. They reached Amanda's room, where the door was propped open. Rose knocked on the jamb and peeked inside. "Any Gigots around?"

"Rose!" Eileen got up from her chair by the bed, and Amanda was awake under the covers, her head still bandaged and her face pale. She was hooked up to an IV, and her blue eyes were sleepy.

"Hi, Ms. McKenna." Amanda's voice sounded weak. "Hi, Melly."

"So good to see you both." Eileen came around the foot of the bed, looking relaxed in a sweatshirt and jeans, with light makeup and her hair in fluffy curls.

"I'm so glad Amanda is better."

"Thanks." Eileen nodded, her eyes shining, and she looked down at Melly. "Thanks for coming this afternoon. Amanda really wanted to see you."

"Why?" Melly asked, and Rose tried not to laugh.

"Good question." Eileen turned to Amanda. "Amanda, why don't you tell Melly why you wanted to see her?"

"I'm going home in two or three weeks and we're going to have a big Halloween party. Do you want to come?"

"Okay," Melly answered, her tone wary. She stepped to the bed and held out the present. "We got this for you."

"Thanks." Amanda took the gift with her right hand, though her left arm didn't move, apparently limp. "My arm and hand don't work right anymore. My brain didn't get enough oxygen, and I have to do rehab."

Rose felt a stab of sympathy, and Eileen moved to help her, but Melly beat her to it, and the two girls began to unwrap the package with much fussing, ripping, and eventually, giggling. Behind them, Eileen and Rose exchanged relieved and happy smiles. Never before had such significance been projected onto the unwrapping of a gift, as if it could lead to world peace.

"Cool!" Amanda became animated, holding up the present, an American Girl book. "Look, Mom. It's Lanie, my favorite!" She turned to Melly. "Who's your favorite?"

"Harry Potter."

Rose hid her smile.

Amanda said, "I like Harry Potter movies. Do you?"

"Yes," Melly answered. "If you want, I can bring your homework to the hospital. But I can't do it on Wednesdays because I'm starting my riding lessons."

Amanda's eyes widened. "You ride horses?"

"Yes. I ride Ebony."

"Felicity rides horses. I *love* Felicity. She's my old favorite. Lanie is only my new favorite."

"Who's Felicity?" Melly asked, puzzled.

"She's an American Girl, too. She lives in Virginia. I have the DVD at home. You can come over and watch it when I get home, okay?"

"Okay," Melly answered, cheering. "I never read American Girl but I have one of the books, too. Nicki."

"Nicki is the one who likes dogs."

Behind them, Eileen smiled at Rose. "Amanda knows everything about those American Girl books. She knows all the characters. She's *obsessed*. You can't imagine."

"Uh, yes, I can." Rose laughed, and Eileen motioned to her.

"Let's go outside and let them talk, huh?"

"Good idea." Rose followed her into the hallway, eavesdropping to make sure Melly was okay. The girls began to yammer about Felicity and Hermione, and Rose smiled. "Isn't that great?"

"Great." Eileen's expression grew serious. "But I have to say, in person, I'm really sorry, for everything."

"Forget it." Rose waved her off, but Eileen held up her hand.

"No, listen. I told you on the phone that Amanda's memory is in bad shape. It is. She doesn't remember much, and what she does comes in dribs and drabs."

"Okay."

"So yesterday, we were talking about you and Melly, and, well, she remembered something." Eileen frowned deeply, her regret plain.

"She remembered that when the fire broke out, you took her out to the hallway with Emily. That you told them to go to the playground, but she went back in for Jason's iPod, then got lost in the smoke. It wasn't your fault, at all." Tears brimmed in Eileen's blue eyes. "I'm so sorry, for everything I accused you of."

"Shh, it's okay, don't cry, the kids'll hear." Rose gave her a hug, and Eileen's chest heaved with a sob, then a soft cry escaped her lips.

"I'm so sorry. I thought you abandoned Amanda for Melly, and that you didn't even try."

"Hush a minute. Listen to those kids. They're laughing."

Eileen settled down, her tears subsiding, and the mothers eavesdropped while the daughters yammered about Lanie missing her best friend Dakota, and Harry missing his best friend Ron, then they segued into what costume they would wear for Halloween, which, as any mother knows, is a conversation that lasts several weeks.

And by the end of the visit, the daughters had gotten to know one another better, and so had the mothers.

And as far as Rose was concerned, that was world peace.

Chapter Eighty-six

The morning was clear and cold, finally October in earnest, and Rose walked toward the school, holding Melly's hand. John snoozed happily, cocooned in his Snugli, and Melly was bundled up, her red puffy coat making her backpack fit too tightly.

Rose tugged at her backpack strap, on the fly. "We have to adjust these when you get home."

"It's the coat, Mom. It's too heavy."

"It's cold today."

"Not *that* cold."

Rose smiled, delighted to be talking about normal things again. Meanwhile, mothers were turning their way, smiling and waving as they approached the entrance ramp. The news had been full of stories about her, the Homestead CFO had been indicted, and its board had announced that it was going to rebuild the plant and compensate any victims of its crimes. And the company had already reached a voluntary settlement with Eileen, in connection with Bill's murder.

"Way to go!" one mom called out, and a dad in a suit flashed her a thumbs-up. Another mom shouted, "Hi, Rose. Hi, Melly!"

"Hiya!" Rose called back, and Melly looked up, squinting against the bright sky.

"Who's that, Mom?"

"I have no idea."

Melly giggled, bewildered. "Mom, what's going on?"

"It's what I told you." Rose and Leo had tried to explain what had happened, but it wasn't something any eight-year-old should know in detail. "I helped catch some bad guys, and everybody's happy."

"It's so different." Melly looked around, in wonderment. Heads were turning everywhere, as they approached the ramp. "It's like a birthday party."

Mr. Rodriguez emerged from the front door and headed down the ramp and strode toward them with a big grin, buttoning his jacket. "Rose! Melly!"

"Hi, Mr. Rodriguez." Rose met him on the sidewalk. "Good to see you."

"Rose, I can't thank you enough. We're all so grateful to you. You risked your—" Mr. Rodriguez stopped, catching himself in front of Melly. "Well, we're grateful, leave it at that."

"Thanks, and I have to tell you that Leo and I never had any intention of filing any lawsuit."

"I know. I got a phone call this morning, from Oliver Charriere." Mr. Rodriguez looked down at Melly and touched her shoulder. "And I heard you volunteered to take Amanda her homework."

"Yes." Melly nodded.

"Thanks for helping out. That's the way all of our students should act, at Reesburgh. That's what community is all about." Mr. Rodriguez looked up at Rose. "Would you like to stop by the office? I know the staff wants to thank you in person."

Rose smiled, surprised. "I'd love to, thanks."

"Great. Mind if I escort Melly inside?"

"Not at all."

"Melly, come with me." Mr. Rodriguez smiled, taking Melly's hand. "Let's go to class together. I think there's someone you might want to see."

"Who?" Melly asked, as they went up the walkway.

The front door opened, and standing in the threshold was Kristen Canton, dressed and ready for work.

"Melly!" Kristen called out, and they ran into each other's arms.

Rose hung back, tears filming her eyes, finally letting go.

And setting free.

Chapter Eighty-seven

Halloween at the Gigots' was a houseful of witches, Iron Men, and vampires. Tables were stocked with sandwiches, ginger snaps, and candy bars that kept the boys chasing each other on a sugar high, while the girls bobbed for apples. Rose was dressed as a lawyer in a three-piece suit and a striped tie, Leo was her prisoner in an orange jumpsuit, and John had on a black onesie, as their resident baby judge.

She raised her plastic glass of cider and clicked it to Leo's. "You know what we're toasting, right?"

Leo smiled, his glass raised. "Senator Martin's indictment?"

"No. Guess again."

"That you look so hot as a redhead. Put me in jail and have your way with me. Got handcuffs?"

Rose leaned over. "This is the first Halloween that Melly hasn't worn a mask."

"Whoa, I didn't realize that." Leo looked around for Melly, who had dressed as a horseback rider in fringed chaps, paddock boots, and a sweatshirt that read THE BUCK STOPS HERE. At the moment, however, she was with Amanda, Emily, Danielle, and the other girls, her face stuck in a galvanized washtub of apples. They hadn't become best friends, but the worst of the bullying had stopped, and Amanda had shown a new empathy, after her injury.

"Now drink, felon." Rose raised her glass, Leo clicked it, and they sipped, then kissed over John's head.

"Get a room, you two." Eileen waltzed over, a beaming princess in a rhinestone tiara.

"Hey, girl." Rose smiled. They'd grown closer, with Melly bringing Amanda her homework in the hospital. "Love the costume. Every mom deserves a tiara."

"True, except I'm Paris Hilton." Eileen laughed, then Wanda came over dressed as a witch, followed by some other class parents, Rachel and Jacob Witmer as Barack and Michelle Obama, Susan and Abe Kramer as Bill and Hillary Clinton, and Elida and Ross Kahari as Sarah and Todd Palin. Rose regarded them all as new friends, regardless of political affiliation.

Wanda looked at Rose. "Honey, you know, I have to say it again, I'm so sorry for the way I treated you."

"That's okay," Rose said, meaning it. Lots of people had apologized, and her new email and Facebook page were flooded with virtual love.

"The new CEO at Homestead even mentioned you in his speech. He said the new broom's gonna sweep clean."

Jacob added, "I'm so happy that Martin got his."

"Nobody's happier than I am!" said a voice behind them, and they all turned around.

"Kristen!" Rose gave her a hug, and the young teacher looked pretty, even dressed as Humpty Dumpty.

"Rose, Leo, everybody, let me introduce you." Kristen gestured at the white knight beside her, dressed in tinfoil armor. "This is Erik, my boyfriend. Or should I say, my fiancé."

"Woohoo!" Rose hooted, and all the women clustered around Kristen, who showed off her engagement ring to the sound of much clucking.

"Mom!" a child shouted, and the women looked up, because they all answered to the same name.

"Yes, honey?" Eileen asked. It was Amanda standing there, her face wet from bobbing for apples.

"Can you fix my lightning bolt? It's coming off, from the water."

Rose smiled at the sight.

Amanda was dressed as Harry Potter.

Chapter Eighty-eight

Rose parked at the end of the street, twisted off the ignition, and sat in her rental car for a moment. She broke into a light sweat, and her heart pumped a little faster. She checked the dashboard clock—10:49. She was ten minutes early. She inhaled, trying to calm her nerves. She'd felt something come over her the moment she turned onto the street, a shudder that seemed to emanate from her marrow and reverberate out to her skin, like shockwaves from her soul.

She looked around, taking it all in. This end of the street looked different than it had twenty years ago, but she could see the way it had been, the same way she could look into Melly's face and see the baby she'd been. The past lived in the present, and nobody knew it better than a mother.

Mommy!

The houses were still close together, though the paint colors had changed, and the trees grew in the same places, though they were taller and fuller, their roots breaking up the concrete sidewalk, like so many tiny neighborhood earthquakes. Drying leaves littered the sidewalk, and big brown paper bags of them, stamped with the township's name, sat at the curb like a row of tombstones, just like then.

Rose closed her eyes, and it all came back to her. Halloween, and she was eighteen years old. She'd just turned onto the street when she saw the white blur and heard the horrible *thud*. Tears came to her eyes, just as they had then, instantly. That night, her heart knew what had happened before her brain did. It just didn't know how to tell her. Then she'd heard agonized scream of Thomas's mother.

Thomas!

Rose found a Kleenex in her purse and wiped her eyes. She eyed the house, which hadn't changed at all: a three-bedroom colonial, with a front porch, and wooden steps. The Pelals still lived here, and their phone number had been easy to find online. She'd called them yesterday, and they'd recognized her name. She'd asked if she could visit, and they'd suggested the very next day, today, but hadn't asked any questions.

Rose put the Kleenex away and slid the keys from the ignition. She knew that what happened here had set her in a pattern she hadn't recognized, and so couldn't stop. Then, when she was young, she'd been told not to talk to the Pelals, and she didn't want to, anyway. She could only run and hide. But it wasn't about law, any longer. It was about right and wrong, and she had become an adult. Jim and Janine Pelal were parents like her, and she had killed their child. She couldn't let another day pass until she said what needed to be said.

She got out of the car, closed the door, and made her way up the sidewalk to the house. She composed herself, then pressed the doorbell.

Chapter Eighty-nine

"Thanks for seeing me." Rose sat in a wing chair, the nicest seat in the living room, which had a worn brown sofa and a plain wooden coffee table, covered with a folded newspaper and an ashtray with a pipe and a pile of black ash. The air smelled like burned cherry-wood from its smoke.

"Of course." Jim sat down next to Janine, on the sofa. Both of them had short hair, his gray and hers a dark brown, with steel-rimmed bi-focals, plain polo shirts, wide-leg jeans, and newish white sneakers, so they looked paired but not identical, like salt-and-pepper shakers. They had a benevolent way about them, down to their smiles, which were polite, even kind.

"Well," Rose began, her mouth dry. "It was lucky for me that you still live here. It made you easy to find."

"Oh, we'd never move." Jim shook his head, once. "We love it here. It's our hometown, both of us. We're semi-retired, but all our friends are here, and our church. Our daughter lives in Seattle. Her husband's an engineer at Boeing."

Rose flashed on Thomas's sister running from the porch, then put it out of her mind.

"We have two grandchildren now, both boys. We love to visit 'em, but we love to come home, too." Jim chuckled. "I read in the newspaper, online, that you have children."

"Yes, a boy and a girl." Rose felt awkward making small talk, especially since Janine was so quiet, her small hands folded in her lap. Her nails were polished, and she wore a fair amount of makeup, with thick eyeliner. "My call must have come as a surprise."

"We thought we might hear from you someday. You were so young when Thomas died. Just a kid yourself."

"Not that young. I should have come before."

"As I say, we've been reading about you, but that's new. We didn't know where you lived until the fire. Some of our friends up north saw it on TV and called us."

"I hope that didn't cause you further . . . pain." Rose had to grope for the right word.

"Not at all. A TV reporter called us about it, too. Tanya." Jim rubbed his forehead. "What's her name?"

"Robertson?" Rose felt a pang. "She found you?"

"My wife, she didn't want us to talk to her. Seems like you did a bang-up job up there, in Pennsylvania. That crooked senator going to court, and all." Jim glanced at Janine, who remained quiet, so Rose got back on track.

"Thanks, but to come to the reason for my visit, I'm grateful that you agreed to see me. I want to apologize to you both, as inadequate as words may be, and to tell you how sorry I am about Thomas." Her throat caught, but she was determined to keep her emotions in check. "I think of him every day, and I replay that scene. I try to make it end differently. I wish I'd taken another way home, or gone slower, or seen him sooner. I think of how one little thing could have changed everything, and he'd be alive now, with you. I mourn him, but he was your son, and I'm so deeply sorry for what I did that night. Please accept my apology, if you can."

Jim met her eye, behind his bifocals. Janine lowered her head, a small gesture that broke Rose's heart.

"Thank you. Thank you for saying that. We do accept, but you don't have to apologize. We know it wasn't your fault. We saw what happened. We weren't that far up the street."

Rose blinked. She hadn't known. The lawyers had assumed that the Pelals hadn't seen it, and even if they had, that they'd sue her anyway.

"Thomas, he ran out in front of the car." Jim's lower lip trembled, then he seemed to recover. "It was horrible, seeing how it happened and knowing we couldn't get there, in time. But Thomas, he liked to run everywhere. He always had ants in his pants. Janine always thought he mighta had, you know, attention deficit. But in those days, well, we didn't get him to a doctor." Jim shook his head. "So he ran into the street. We used to tell him, don't do it, you'll get hurt. It wasn't the first time he did it, it was just the first time you were there, and this time, well, the Lord works in mysterious ways, that much is true."

Rose felt her throat thicken, but didn't cry. And she didn't feel better either. "Regardless, I wish it hadn't happened."

"We have our faith, and we rely on it, always." Jim nodded, his skinny shoulders suddenly slanting down. They both looked so sad for a minute, sagging together in the middle of the sagging couch. Janine said nothing, hanging her silvery head, with a whorl of gray at her crown, like a hurricane.

Jim sighed. "I just wish, well, I guess Janine, she wishes she was there. That she was there with him, for him, at the end. That's what wakes her up at night, almost tortures her, really. Any mother would want that for her child, I suppose."

Rose remembered holding Thomas in the street, then him looking up at her, seeing her in the Cleopatra makeup. Now that she'd gotten a good look at Janine, with her dark hair and eyeliner, Rose understood why he'd mistaken her for his mother, on that dark night.

"You can understand that," Jim continued, more softly. "She wishes that she'd been there, to hold him. Not for her, but for him. That he wouldn't think he was alone in this world. That he knew we loved him, that she loved him, right until the very end. He was our youngest, you know. Our baby. *Her* baby."

Rose swallowed hard. She would never forget what she'd said to Thomas, right before he passed. Maybe there was something she could do for the Pelals, after all. Maybe the words that had been haunting her all these years would be the words that eased Janine's heart.

"You can see that, can't you? Being a mother yourself."

"Yes, I do understand, and I'd feel exactly the same way." Rose took a deep breath. "Janine, I have something I think you should know."

Acknowledgments

I've written seventeen novels in almost as many years, and while I've always had emotionality in my books, more recently I've turned to writing about the most emotional of all relationships, mother and child. There may be some irony to this, now that I'm an empty-nester, but perhaps I finally have the perspective and the distance (and the time!) to examine the relationship and plumb it for my fiction. This is a long way of saying thank you very much to my amazing daughter, Francesca, and to my mother, Mary, both of whom have taught me everything I know about the richness and complexity of the bond between mother and child, not to mention, simply put, about love.

In this regard, thanks, too, to my gal pals, all of whom are terrific mothers: Nan Daley, Jennifer Enderlin, Molly Friedrich, Rachel Kull, Laura Leonard, Paula Menghetti, and Franca Palumbo. They're my kitchen cabinet, and if we're not talking about our daughters, we're talking about our mothers. All of our everyday conversations inform *Save Me*, so thanks, ladies, for being yourselves, and for helping me, every day.

This novel raises a number of legal, ethical, and moral questions, and for those I needed research and help. This is where I get to thank the experts, but also where I have to make clear that any and all mistakes are mine. Thanks to my ace detective, Arthur Mee, criminal lawyer Glenn Gilman, Esq., and special thanks to Nicolas Casenta, of the Chester County District Attorney's Office. I also want to thank Professor Marin Scordato, of the Catholic University of America, Columbus School of Law, for his excellent advice, expertise, and seminal article, *Understanding the Absence of a Duty to Reasonably Rescue in American Tort Law.*

Thanks so much to Principal Christopher Pickell, teacher Ed Jameson, and staff members June Regan, Kathy Kolb, and Brett Willson, and all the rest of the wonderful staff at Charlestown Elementary School. Principal Pickell took his valuable time to answer all of my questions to make *Save Me* as realistic as possible, and we should repeat that Reesburgh Elementary herein is not Charlestown Elementary, but is completely fictional. Still, I could not be more grateful to them all for their time and guidance, and more importantly, for all they do for children. There is no more important job than educating the generations to come. I've always admired teachers, and still do. I wouldn't be a writer but for the great public education I received, and I never realized how exhausting, albeit rewarding, teaching can be until I started teaching a course I developed titled "Justice & Fiction" at the University of Pennsylvania Law School. So thanks so much to all of my teachers, past and present, including my students—who are teachers, too, in their own way.

Thanks so much, too, to the team of genius firefighters who not only keep all of us safe, but even took time out of their day to help me imagine a fictional fire. Thank you so much to Mike Risell, Karen and Duke Griffin, Dave Hicks, and Mark Hughes of Kimberton Fire Company. And thanks for expert EMT advice and counsel to Rebecca Buonavolonta and Sergey Bortsov. And thanks to Robin Lynn Katz.

A special hug of thanks for their time and expertise to everybody at Herr Foods of Nottingham, Pennsylvania. It's important to reiterate here that everything in the book is fictional, but I was helped to create Homestead by the great people at Herr Foods, starting with ace Public Relations Manager Jennifer Arrigo, and most especially the Herr Family: J. M. Herr, Ed Herr, Gene Herr, and Daryl Thomas. A special thanks for the consultation to Fran Dolan, Jim Rock, Bill Beddow, and all the hard-working staff who showed me the ropes.

Thank you to the gang at St. Martin's Press, starting with my great editor and super-supportive coach, Jennifer Enderlin, who inspires me and guided this book, and to John Sargent, Sally Richardson, Matthew Shear, Matt Baldacci, Jeff Capshew, Nancy Trypuc, Monica Katz, John Murphy, John Karle, Sara Goodman, and all the wonderful sales reps. Big thanks to Michael Storrings, for an astounding cover design. Also hugs and kisses to Mary Beth Roche, Laura Wilson, and the great people in audio books. I love and appreciate all of you.

Thanks and big love to my wonderful agent and friend, Molly Friedrich, as well as the Amazing Paul Cirone, and the brilliant Lucy Carson. My dedicated and amazing assistant and best friend is Laura Leonard, and she's invaluable in every way, and has been for twenty years. And she's a great mom! Thanks, too, to Annette Earling, my Web diva, who runs scottoline.com, where I exist only in Photoshopped form.

Thanks to my family and friends, for everything. They know I love them and they usually get the last word, if not the dedication, in my books. But this book is different, because the last word, and the dedication, goes to my dear friend Joseph Drabyak, who recently passed away, much too soon. I dedicated this book to Joe because he was dedicated to books.

I met Joe almost twenty years ago as the bookseller at my local independent bookstore, Chester County Books & Music Company, and I grew to be great friends with him and his wife, Reggie. He was an early champion of my books and advocated for books he loved as well as for independent bookstores, and eventually he became the hardworking president of the New Atlantic Independent Booksellers Association. Joe understood that books bring people together, and that reading empowers, enriches, nurtures, and fuses us, one to the other. Before Joe passed, I sat with him and told him I'd dedicate my next book to him, which made him happy. And though he'd read every one of my books in manuscript form, he didn't get to read this one.

It is, now and forever, my loss.

SAVE ME
by Lisa Scottoline

About the Author

- A Conversation with Lisa Scottoline

Behind the Novel

- "Write What You Feel"
  An Original Essay by the Author

Keep on Reading

- Ideas for Book Groups

- Reading Group Questions

A Conversation with Lisa Scottoline

Like *Look Again*, *Save Me* is an emotional thriller that examines motherhood and the relationship between mother and child. Why did you return to this theme, and is this a new direction for you?

Although I love being a writer, my most important and cherished role in this life is being a mother. It always came naturally to me, even though it wasn't always easy, especially in the early days, when I was a broke, single mother. (I'm still single but not broke.) Still, I felt I was born to be a mother, and my daughter, Francesca Serritella, and I are best friends and, now, writing partners in our nonfiction books!

Being a mother is all about love, and I'm a love monster. Bottom line, if I meet you, I'm hugging you, case closed. Come to a signing and see.

And now that I'm an empty nester, I've had a lot of time to think about what it means to be a mother. I've learned that motherhood has no expiration date. You never stop being a mother, and you'll do everything you can for your child. I'm fascinated by the lengths to which a mother will go to protect her child, and that's something I really wanted to explore. And also to turn that on its head and see where sometimes protection can hinder, or even smother. I don't think it's all that new for me because relationships have always been the keystone of all my books, and I've written about motherhood before, in *Look Again* and in *Final Appeal*, which won the Edgar Award for excellence in suspense writing. The most special relationship in life is that between a mother and her child, so it's something I plan or continuing to write about, in books to come.

What sparked the idea for *Save Me*?

Everyone asks, "Where do you get your ideas? And you know what? I LOVE that question! It's one of the few I

> "Relationships have always been the keystone of all my books."

lways have an answer to. Yay!

he idea for this book came from a conversation I was
aving with my best friend, Laura. She's a mom of two sons
nd somehow we got to talking about if she had one car seat
nd she had to pick up a friend's child, which child would
et the car seat—her own child or her friend's? We yapped
bout that on the phone for an hour. It was something we
eally had to think about and would struggle with.

nd I knew I had my next novel.

1y goal always is to write an entertaining book, but I love
he idea of creating a realistic story that will spark conversa-
ion, and make people think about what they would do in
 given situation. Having a child is such an extraordinary
esponsibility, and it made me think about what would
appen if you were forced, maybe in an emergency, to
hoose between saving your own child or someone else's.

n *Save Me*, Rose was faced with making an instant
ecision of whether to save her daughter or her daughter's
ully, in a life-threatening situation. It could change her
fe forever, just like many situations we could face in our
wn lives. We really never know where life will lead us, do
e? You tackle the hot-button issue of bullying from a very
ifferent angle in *Save Me*. Why was that important
 you?

1any of us have been bullied as children, me included.
 was called "rat" since there weren't many Italian-
.mericans kids in my neighborhood, and the other kids
t school teased me that Italians lived in sewers, like rats.

Iot funny.

I never forgot it, and still feel that sting. But it's gotten worse, in our society. Bullying is a national epidemic that has been exacerbated by the Internet and social networks. Bullying is so damaging to children, and shapes so much of who they become and how they face life. The only thing equal to the pain of a bullied child is the pain of a parent watching it happen to their child. Parents are often in the very difficult position of trying to save their child from a bully. The more I thought about it, I realized that bullying not only affects children. Many adults are the victims of bullying as well, and the impact can be equally damaging. That was another angle of bullying that I wanted to explore. So in *Save Me*, the community of Reesburgh bullies Rose, and her lawyer encourages her to bully others, using litigation as a weapon.

All of your books have women as the star or main protagonists, even your nonfiction column books. Why is that?

When I first started writing, I noticed that in popular books and movies, women didn't get to be the star of the book. We were always the expendable girlfriend or sidekick.

And I missed Nancy Drew!

I wanted my books to feature ordinary, extraordinary women, like those in my life, such as my mother, daughter, and friends, and let them be the main protagonists. And a few years ago, I noticed that there weren't enough female voices in the newspapers, and I began writing "Chick Wit" with my daughter, Francesca. It's a funny, witty look at life as a woman in today's society.

And I missed Erma Bombeck!

The columns have given voice to women everywhere, and have been collected in *Why My Third Husband Will Be a Dog; My Nest Isn't Empty, It Just Has More Closet Space;* and *Best Friends, Occasional Enemies.*

What is your favorite part of being a writer?

My favorite part of being a writer is connecting with people. While this may sound ironic, as writing is such a solitary profession, I see it completely differently. Books connect us, heart to heart, and that's why they're so important. I always say that a book isn't completed until it's read, and that's because a book means something different to each reader, depending on who they are and what they've experienced. So, in effect, we write each book together, author and reader!

Cool, huh?

Nothing is more rewarding to me than getting out from behind the desk, and meeting, talking with, and hugging readers. I write for them, and they definitely help inform my writing. And I love feeling that I am tied to all of them, and everyone is tied one to the other. That's what being fully human is all about, and my heart is full, with gratitude, to all of my readers, every day.

So thanks.

And love.

oxoxoxo

An Original Essay by the Author

"Write What You Feel"

People say you should write what you know, and while I agree, I think that doesn't go far enough.

I think you should write what you feel.

Don't feel bad if you didn't know this, because it's taken me almost twenty years and twenty books to figure it out.

Call me slow on the uptake.

Let me explain what I mean by write what you feel. I'm what's known as a people person. I love people, and so it's no surprise that characterization and relationships between people are the strongest part of my novels. That's where my heart is.

That's what I feel.

> *"Characterization and plot are the same thing."*

Relationships between girlfriends, women and men, and family members populate every page of mine, and I like it that way. I try to write an entertaining story with a fast-moving plot, but what I want you to remember, when you close the book, is the people between the covers. Not to get too English major-y on you, but the fact is that characterization and plot are the same thing.

We are what we do, after all.

So to stay on point, it occurred to me that when I look at my life, the most important relationship to me, and the one that abides time and even space, is my relationship to my daughter, Francesca.

In other words, it's all about the mother-child relationship.

love her more than I can say, and I'm in the words business, so I should be fired. And as she's grown up and
moved out, I've gained a new perspective on her that makes
me want to write more and more about that relationship.
Paradoxically, now that she's moved out, I think about her
more. I see us with new eyes. And as our relationship has
changed and grown to one between two adults, I still remain
her parent, no matter how old she gets.

Motherhood has no expiration date.

I used to think that I felt our relationship so intensely
because I'm a single mother and she's an only child. In fact,
I remember that she came home from grade school one day
and asked this priceless question:

"Mom, if I'm an only child, does that mean you're an only
mom?"

Uh, yes.

But now that I'm a new empty nester, and comparing notes
with all of my girlfriends, I've come to the conclusion that
the intensity of the mother-child bond doesn't turn on how
many children you have, or if you have a hubby or not. It's
inborn, and cultivated, both, and it powers most of my
thoughts and hopes, worries and fears.

Feel me?

(As the kids say.)

So it makes sense that later in my life, which is now, I'd turn
to writing more and more about the mother-child relationship. I'd written about it in *Final Appeal,* which won an
Edgar, but hadn't returned to it often in the past, for one
very practical reason—in a suspense novel, you need a mom

getting herself in trouble, and if she did that with a kid, you wouldn't like her much.

Neither would I.

I needed a fictional sitter, and you know how hard those are to come by.

I returned to moms and children in *Look Again,* and I think the strength of the bond between a mother and her child gave the story an enormous force and emotional power.

If I don't say so myself.

And I think the same is true of *Save Me*.

It's intense, the story of a woman who tries to save her child, tries to save another, and finally, ends up saving herself. I think all mothers will find themselves in this book, and wonder what they'd do if they were in its heroine's shoes. And if you're a mother, you could be in her shoes. Tomorrow, or the next day. We never know where life will lead us, but we mothers know we can cope, and lead, and nurture, and love. Because that's our job, to me. Sometimes I feel as if I were put on earth to be a mother.

I feel it.

Reading
Group
Gold

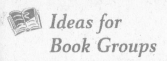

Ideas for Book Groups

I am a huge fan of book clubs because it means people are reading and discussing books. Mix that with wine and carbs, and you can't keep me away. I'm deeply grateful to all who read me, and especially honored when my book is chosen by a book club. I wanted an opportunity to say thank you to those who read me, which gave me the idea of a contest. Every year I hold a book-club contest and the winning book club gets a visit from me and a night of fabulous food and good wine. To enter is easy: All you have to do is take a picture of your entire book club with each member holding a copy of my newest hardcover and send it to me by mail or e-mail. No book club is too small or too big. Don't belong to a book club? Start one. Just grab a loved one, a neighbor, or friend, and send in your picture of you each holding my newest book. I look forward to coming to your town and wining and dining your group. For more details, just go to www.scottoline.com.

Keep on Reading

Tour time is my favorite time of year because I get to break out my fancy clothes and meet with interesting and fun readers around the country. The rest of the year I am a homebody, writing every day, but thrilled to be able to connect with readers through e-mail. I read all my e-mail, and answer as much as I can. So, drop me a line about books, families, pets, love, or whatever is on your mind at lisa@scottoline.com. For my latest book and tour information, special promotions, and updates you can sign up at www.scottoline.com for my newsletter.

The Wednesday Evening Ladies' Literary Guild of Mineola, New York, submit their photo for Lisa's book-club contest.

Reading Group Questions

1. *Save Me* explores the mother and child relationship, at its heart. What do you think defines a mother? How is a mother and child relationship different than any other relationship? Look at other forms of culture, like art, for example. How many depictions are there of mother and child? And how many of father and child? Are we discriminating against fathers, or diminishing them, by all this talk of the mother-child bond? And by doing so, do we create a self-fulfilling prophecy?

2. In *Save Me*, Melly is the victim of bullying because of a birthmark on her face. Do you think bullying is different today than years ago? Do you think that the bullying is getting worse, or are we just hearing more about it because of the Internet? What do you think parents and schools should do to help curb bullying? What kind of punishment do you think is appropriate for the child who is doing the bullying? What about those who watch and say nothing? Are they, or aren't they, equally as culpable? Do you think that school programs and curricula that build up self-esteem and a sense of community will really make a difference?

Keep on Reading

3. Rose experienced her own bullying at the hands of the angry parents, which gave her a new perspective on what Melly was going through. Do you have any experience with bullying between adults? In what ways are adults better equipped to deal with bullying than children? What impact can bullying have on adults, and what can adults do if they are faced with a bully? What impact does adult bullying have on children?

4. Rose steps in to defend Melly against her bully. Do you think it was a good idea? Why or why not? How do you think a parent's involvement hurts or helps the situation? At what point do you think parents need to involve themselves in the situation? What steps would *you* take to help your child if he or she was being bullied, and how far would you be willing to go?

5. What impact do you think a physical blemish has on a child, and how do you think it affects his or her identity, family relationships, and contact with the outside world? Take it a step further: What about physical disabilty, like a child in a wheel-chair? Or learning challenges, that aren't so visible? Or how about discriminations based on race, religion, or sexual orientation? Melly's father reacted very badly to Melly's birthmark. What did his reaction make you feel about him?

6. Many of Lisa's books center on single mothers or blended families. Do you think the love of one great parent is enough to sustain a child through life? Does it take a husband, too? Or a village?

7. As Rose found out, volunteering comes with risks. The book makes clear that this is a problem in the law of many states, maybe even where you live. What do you think of the laws in terms of protecting those who volunteer their time? What changes, if any, would you make to the Good Samaritan laws to protect volunteers?

8. How did you feel about Rose keeping her secret past from Leo? Did you understand her reasoning? Did you agree or disagree with it? What impact do you think Rose's past will have on her marriage as she moves forward? Do you think she will ever really be able to escape what happened? Will he forgive her for not telling him? How do secrets impact intimacy in our lives?

9. Rose was called a "helicopter"parent, a term often used in today's society with a negative connotation. What separates helicopter parenting from good parenting? What kind of parent do you think Rose was? What mistakes do you think she made? Do you think she was a good mother? Do you think she favors Melly or the baby? Or treats them equally?

10. How did you feel about Amanda in the beginning of the book? Did your opinion of her change by the end of the book? What do you think causes children to be bullies? Under what circumstances would you ever feel bad for the bully? In punishing a bully, do you think his or her personal circumstances should be taken into account?

11. What did you think of Rose's lawyers' strategy? Did you agree or disagree with it? Why or why not? Do you think they were just passing the blame, or do you think the school had a responsibility in what happened? Do you think that litigation is another form of bullying? Do you know anybody who is sue-happy?

Turn the page for a sneak peek at
Lisa Scottoline's next novel

ONE PERFECT LIE

Available April 2017

Chapter One

Chris Brennan was applying for a teaching job at Central Valley High School, but he was a fraud. His résumé was fake, and his identity completely phony. So far he'd fooled the personnel director, the assistant principal, and the chairperson of the social studies department. This morning was his final interview, with the principal, Dr. Wendy McElroy. It was make-or-break.

Chris waited in her office, shifting in his chair, though he wasn't nervous. He'd already passed the state and federal criminal background checks and filed a clear Sexual Misconduct/Abuse Disclosure form, Child Abuse History Clearance form, and Arrest/Conviction Report & Certification form. He knew what he was doing. He'd done it many times before. He knew he was perfect, on paper.

He'd scoped out the school and observed the male teachers, so he knew what to wear for the interview—a white oxford shirt, no tie, khaki Dockers, and Bass loafers, bought from the outlets in town. He was six-foot-two, 206 pounds, and his wide-set blue eyes, straight nose, broad cheekbones, and friendly smile were generic enough to blend in here, or mostly anywhere. His hair was sandy brown and he'd just gotten it cut at the local Supercuts. Everyone liked a clean-cut guy, and they tended to forget that appearances were deceiving.

His gaze took in Dr. McElroy's office. Sunlight spilled from a panel of windows behind the desk, which was shaped like an L of dark wood, its return stacked with forms, files, and binders labeled **Keystone Exams, Lit & Alg 1**. Stuffed bookshelves and black file cabinets lined the near wall, and on the far one hung framed diplomas from Penn State and West Chester University, a grease-board calendar, and a poster that read DREAM MORE, COMPLAIN LESS. The desk held family photographs, pump bottles of Jergens and Purell, and unopened correspondence next to a letter opener.

Chris's gaze lingered on the letter opener, an old-fashioned one. Its pointed blade gleamed in the sunlight, and out of nowhere, he flashed to a memory. *No!* the man had cried, which had been his last word. After that had come agonized guttural noises, barely human. Chris had stabbed the man in the throat, then yanked out the knife. Instantly a gruesome fan of blood had sprayed onto him, from residual pressure in the carotid. The knife must have served as a tamponade until Chris had pulled it out, breaking the seal. It had been a rookie mistake, but he was so young, back then.

"Sorry I'm late," said a voice at the doorway, and Chris rose as Dr. McElroy entered the office on a knee scooter, which held up one of her legs bent at the knee, with a black orthopedic boot on her right foot. It was an odd entrance, but otherwise she looked like what he'd expected: a middle-aged professional with hooded blue eyes behind wire-rimmed bifocals, and a lean face framed by clipped gray hair and dangling silver earrings. She even had on a dress with a gray and pink print. Chris got why women with gray hair dressed in gray things. It looked cool.

"Hello, Dr. McElroy, I'm Chris Brennan. Need a hand?" Chris rose to help her, but she scooted forward, waving him off.

"No, thanks. Call me Wendy. I know this looks ridiculous. I had bunion surgery, and this is the way I have to get around."

"Does it hurt?"

"Only my dignity. Please sit down." Dr. McElroy rolled the scooter toward her desk with difficulty. The basket in front of the scooter held a heavy tote bag stuffed with a laptop, files, and a quilted floral purse.

Chris sat back down, watching her struggle. He sensed she was proving a point, that she didn't need help, when she clearly did. People were funny. He had researched Dr. McElroy on social media and her faculty webpage, which had a bio and some photos. She'd taught French for twelve years at CVHS before being promoted to school administration. She lived in nearby Vandenberg with her husband, David, and their Pembroke Welsh corgi, Bobo. Her hobby was agility training with Bobo, who had earned MACH11 points from the American Kennel Club. Dr. McElroy's photo on her teacher webpage was from her younger days, like a permanent Throwback Thursday. Bobo's photo was current.

"Now you know why I'm late. It takes forever to get anywhere. I was home recuperating during your other interviews; that's why we're doing this now. Apologies about the inconvenience." Dr. McElroy parked the scooter next to her chair, picked her purse and tote bag from the basket, and set them noisily on her desk.

"That's okay, it's not a problem."

Dr. McElroy left the scooter, hopped to her chair on one foot, then flopped into the seat. "Well done, me!"

"Agree," Chris said pleasantly.

"Bear with me another moment, please." Dr. McElroy pulled a smartphone from her purse and put it on her desk, then reached inside her tote bag and slid out a manila folder. She looked up at him with a flustered smile. "So. Chris. Welcome back to Central Valley. I hear you wowed them at your interviews. You have fans here, already."

"Great, it's mutual." Chris flashed a grin. The other teachers liked him, though everything they knew about him was a lie. They didn't even know his real name, which was Constantine Rogolyi. In a week, when he had gone, they'd wonder how he'd duped them. There would be shock, anger, and resentment. Some would want closure; others would want blood.

"Chris, let's not be formal, let's just talk. Since we're running late, I have only a few questions for you." Dr. McElroy opened the manila folder, which contained a printout of Chris's job application, his fake résumé, and his other bogus papers.

"That's fine with me. Shoot."

"Chris, for starters, tell me about yourself. Where are you from?"

"Mostly the Midwest, Indiana, but we moved around a lot. My dad was a sales rep for a plumbing supply company, and his territory kept changing." Chris lied, excellently. In truth, he didn't remember his father or mother. He had grown up in Dayton, Ohio, in the foster-care system.

Dr. McElroy glanced at the fake résumé. "I see you went to the Northwest College in Wyoming."

"Yes."

"Got your certification there, too?"

"Yes."

"Hmmm." Dr. McElroy paused. "You know, most of us here went to local Pennsylvania schools. West Chester, Widener, Penn State."

"I understand." Chris had expected as much, which was why he'd picked the tiny Northwest College as his fraudulent alma mater. The odds of running into anyone here who had gone to college in Cody, Wyoming, were slim to none. People on the East Coast thought the West was flyover buffalo.

Dr. McElroy hesitated. "So, do you think you could fit in here?"

"Yes, of course. I fit in anywhere." Chris kept the irony from his tone. He'd already established his false identity online, with his neighbors, and in town at the local Dunkin' Donuts, Friendly's, and Wegmans, his persona as smoothly manufactured as the corporate brands with their bright logos, plastic key tags, and rewards programs.

"Where are you living?"

"I'm renting in a development nearby. Valley Oaks, do you know it?"

"Yes," Dr. McElroy answered, as he'd anticipated. Chris had picked Valley Oaks because there weren't many other decent choices. Central Valley was a small town in south-central Pennsylvania, known primarily for its outlet-shopping. The factory store of every American manufacturer filled strip mall after strip mall, and the bargain-priced sprawl was bisected by the main drag, Central Valley Road. Also on Central Valley Road were Central Valley Dry Cleaners, Central Valley Lockshop, and Central Valley High School, evidence that the town had no imagination, which Chris took as a good sign. Because nobody here could ever imagine what he was up to.

Dr. McElroy lifted a graying eyebrow. "What brings you to Central Valley?"

"I wanted a change of scenery. My parents passed away five years ago, in a crash. A drunk driver hit their car head-on." Chris kept self-pity from his tone. He had taught himself that the key to evoking the sympathy was to not act sorry for yourself.

"Oh no! How horrible." Dr. McElroy's expression softened. "My condolences. I'm so sorry for your loss."

"Thank you." Chris paused for dramatic effect.

"How about the rest of your family? Any brothers or sisters?"

"No, I was an only child. The silver lining is that I'm free to go anywhere I want. I came east because there are more teaching jobs and they're better-paying. Teachers here are rolling in dough, correct?"

Dr. McElroy chuckled, as Chris knew she would. His starting salary would be $55,282. Of course it was unfair that teachers earned less than crooks, but life wasn't fair. If it were, Chris wouldn't be here, pretending to be somebody else.

"Why did you become a teacher, Chris?"

"It know it sounds corny, but I love kids. You can really see the influence you have on them. My teachers shaped who I am, and I give them so much credit."

"I feel the same way." Dr. McElroy smiled briefly, then consulted the fake résumé again. "You've taught Government before?"

"Yes." Chris was applying to fill the opening in AP Government, as well as the non-AP course Government & Economics and an elective, Criminal Justice, which was ironic. He had fabricated his experience teaching AP Government, familiarized himself with an AP Government textbook, and copied a syllabus from one online, since the AP curriculum was nationally standardized. He wondered if the folks at Common Core ever imagined the use that people like Chris could make of that. But whatever, it worked for him if they wanted to turn the public schools into chain stores.

"I must warn you, you have big shoes to fill, in Mary Merriman.

She taught here for twenty-two years and was one of our most be-loved teachers. The students adore her."

"I'm sure, but I'm up to the task." Chris tried to sound gung-ho. Mary Merriman was the teacher he'd be replacing.

"Still it won't be easy for you, with the spring semester already in progress."

"Again, I can handle it. Don't worry."

"It couldn't be helped." Dr. McElroy sighed, frowning. "Of course, we all understood her need to take care of her father, after his fall. She's reachable by e-mail or phone and would be happy to help you in any way she can."

Whatever, Chris thought but didn't say. "That's great to know. How nice of her."

"Oh, she's a peach, Mary is. Even at her darkest hour, she's think-ing of her students." Dr. McElroy smiled. "You'd have to start right away. If I expedite your paperwork, I can get you in class for Thurs-day, April 16, when the sub leaves. So, you enjoy teaching at the secondary level. Why?"

"The kids are so able, so communicative, and you see their per-sonalities begin to form. Their identities, really, are shaping. They become adults." Chris heard the ring of truth in his own words, which helped his believability. He actually *was* interested in identity and the human psyche. Lately he'd been wondering who he was, when he wasn't impersonating someone.

"And why AP Government? What's interesting about AP Gov-ernment to you?"

"Politics is fascinating, especially these days. It's something that kids see on TV and media, and they want to talk about it. The real issues engage them." Chris knew that *engagement* was a teacher buzzword, like *grit*. He'd picked up terms online, where there were so many teacher blogs, Facebook groups, and Twitter accounts that it seemed like the Internet was what *engaged* teachers.

"You know, Chris, I grew up in Central Valley. Ten years ago, this county was dairyland, but then the outlets came in and took over. They brought jobs, but we still have a mix of old and new, and you see that in town. There's been an Agway and a John Deere dealership for decades, but they're being squeezed out by a Starbucks."

"I see." Chris acted sad, but that worked for him, too. He was relying on the fact that people here would be friendly, open-hearted, and above all, trusting.

"There's an unfortunate line between the haves and the have-nots, and it becomes obvious in junior year, which you would be teaching." Dr. McElroy paused. "The kids from the well-to-do families take the SATs and apply to college. The farm kids stay behind unless they get an athletic scholarship."

"Good to know," Chris said, trying to look interested.

"Tell me, how do you communicate with students best?"

"Oh, one-on-one, definitely. Eye-to-eye, there's no substitute. I'm a friendly guy. I want to be accessible to them on e-mail, social media, and such, but I believe in personal contact and mutual respect. That's why I coach, too." Chris was also applying to fill their opening for an assistant baseball coach. He'd never coached before, but he was a naturally gifted athlete. He'd been going to indoor batting cages to get back in shape. His right shoulder was killing him.

"Oh, my, I forgot." Dr. McElroy frowned, then shifted through his file. "You're applying for assistant baseball coach. Varsity."

"Yes. I feel strongly that coaching is teaching and vice versa. In other words, I'm always teaching, whether it's in the classroom or on the ball field. The setting doesn't matter, that's only about location."

"An insightful way to put it." Dr. McElroy pursed her lips. "As assistant baseball coach, you would report to Coach Hardwick. I must tell you, he doesn't keep assistants very long. His last one, well, moved on. You haven't met the coach yet, but he can be a man of few words."

"I look forward to meeting him." Chris had researched Coach Hardwick, evidently a well-known jerk.

"The assistant coaching position has remained vacant because Coach Hardwick uses Francie, a retired alum of the school, as his assistant. They're contemporaries."

"I'm sure I can assist Coach Hardwick. Whatever he's doing, he's doing it right. He's an institution in regional high-school baseball, and the Central Valley Musketeers have one of the finest programs in the state."

"That's true." Dr. McElroy nodded, brightening. "Last year, several players were recruited for Division I and II."

"Yes, I know." Chris had already scouted the team online for his own purposes. He hoped there would be a few boys from the baseball team in his Government classes, which would double his chances to evaluate them and choose one. He needed to befriend a quiet, insecure boy, most likely a kid with a troubled relationship to his father. Or better yet, a dead father. It was the same profile that a pedophile would use, but Chris was no pervert. His intent was to manipulate the boy, who was only the means to an end.

"So where do you see yourself in five years?"

"Oh, here, in Central Valley," Chris lied. In truth, he only had a week. It gave new meaning to the word deadline.

"Why here, though? Why us?" Dr. McElroy tilted her head skeptically, and Chris sensed he had to deliver on this answer.

"I love it here, and the rolling hills of Pennsylvania are a real thing. It's straight-up beautiful. I love the quiet setting and the small-town vibe." Chris leaned over in a way as if he were about to open his heart, when he wasn't even sure he had one. "But the truth is, I'm hoping to settle down and raise a family. Central Valley feels just feels like *home*."

"Well, that sounds wonderful! I must say, you lived up to my expectations." Dr. McElroy smiled warmly and closed the file. "Congratulations, Chris, you've got the job! Let me be the first to welcome you to Central Valley High School."

"Terrific!" Chris extended his hand over the desk, flashing his most sincere grin.

It was time to set his plan in motion, commencing with step one.